THE GIANT BOOK OF
NEW WORLD SF

ISAAC ASIMOV, one of America's great resources, has by now written more than 330 books. No other writer in history has published so much on such a wide variety of subjects, which range from science fiction and murder novels to books on history, the physical sciences, and Shakespeare. Born in the Soviet Union and raised in Brooklyn, he is married and lives in New York City.

MARTIN H. GREENBERG, who has been called 'the King of anthologists', now has some 130 to his credit. Greenberg is professor of regional analysis and political science at the University of Wisconsin, Green Bay, USA, where he also teaches a course in the history of science fiction.

CHARLES G. WAUGH is professor of psychology and mass communications at the University of Maine at Augusta, USA. He is a leading authority on science fiction and fantasy and has collaborated on more than 80 anthologies and single-author collections with Isaac Asimov, Martin H. Greenberg, and assorted colleagues.

THE GIANT BOOK OF
NEW WORLD SF

Short Novels of the 1960s

Edited by Isaac Asimov,
Charles G. Waugh and Martin H. Greenberg

This edition published and distributed by The Book Company.
Produced by Magpie Books, an imprint of Robinson Publishing Ltd,
London, 1997

The Book Company
9/9-13 Winbourne Road,
Brookvale 2100,
Sydney,
NSW, Australia

First published as
The Mammoth Book of New World Science Fiction
by Robinson Publishing 1991

A copy of the British Library Cataloguing in Publication Data
is available from the British Library

ISBN 1 85487 664 3

Printed and bound by Firmin-Didot (France),
Group Herissey. N° d'impression : 37147.

CONTENTS

ACKNOWLEDGEMENTS

The Highest Treason *by Randall Garrett—Copyright* © *1961 by Street & Smith Publications, Inc. Reprinted by permission of the Scott Meredith Literary Agency, Inc., 845 Third Avenue, New York, NY 10022.*

Mercenary *by Mack Reynolds—Copyright* © *1962 by Street & Smith Publications, Inc. Reprinted by permission of the Scott Meredith Literary Agency, Inc., 845 Third Avenue, New York, NY 10022.*

Code Three *by Rick Raphael—Copyright* © *1963 by Street & Smith Publications, Inc.; renewed* © *1991 by Rick Raphael. Reprinted by permission of the author and his agent, the Scott Meredith Literary Agency, Inc., 845 Third Avenue, New York, NY 10022.*

Night of the Trolls *by Keith Laumer—Copyright* © *1963 by Galaxy Publishing Corporation; renewed* © *1991 by Keith Laumer. Reprinted by permission of the author.*

Soldier Ask Not *by Gordon R. Dickson—Copyright* © *1964 by Galaxy Publishing Corporation. Reprinted by permission of the author.*

The Suicide Express *by Philip José Farmer—Copyright* © *1966 by Galaxy Publishing Corporation. Reprinted by permission of the author and his agent, the Scott Meredith Literary Agency, Inc., 845 Third Avenue, New York, NY 10022.*

Weyr Search *by Anne McCaffrey—Copyright* © *1967 by Anne McCaffrey. Reprinted by permission of the author and the author's agent, Virginia Kidd.*

The Eve of Rumoko *by Roger Zelazny—Copyright* © *1969, 1976 by Roger Zelazny. Reprinted by permission of the author.*

Hawk Among the Sparrows *by Dean McLaughlin—Copyright* © *1968 by Street & Smith Publications, Inc.;* © *1976 by Dean McLaughlin. Reprinted by permission of the author.*

How It Was When the Past Went Away—*Copyright* © *1969 by Agberg, Ltd. Reprinted by permission of the author and Agberg, Ltd.*

THE GIANT BOOK OF
NEW WORLD SF

THE EVE OF RUMOKO

Roger Zelazny

I was in the control room when the J-9 unit flaked out on us. I was there for purposes of doing some idiot maintenance work, among other things.

There were two men below in the capsule, inspecting the Highway to Hell, that shaft screwed into the ocean's bottom thousands of fathoms beneath us and soon to be opened for traffic. Ordinarily, I wouldn't have worried, as there were two J-9 technicians on the payroll. Only, one of them was on leave in Spitzbergen and the other had entered sick bay just that morning. As a sudden combination of wind and turbulent waters rocked the *Aquina* and I reflected that it was now the Eve of RUMOKO, I made my decision. I crossed the room and removed a side panel.

"Schweitzer! You're not authorized to fool around with that!" said Doctor Asquith.

I studied the circuits, and, "Do *you* want to work on it?" I asked him.

"Of course not. I wouldn't know how to begin. But—"

"Do you want to see Martin and Demmy die?"

"You know I don't. Only you're not—"

"Then tell me who is," I said. "That capsule down there is controlled from up here, and we've just blown something. If you know somebody better fit to work on it, then you'd better send for him. Otherwise, I'll try to repair the J-9 myself."

He shut up then, and I began to see where the trouble was. They had been somewhat obvious about things. They had even used solder. Four circuits had been rigged, and they had fed the whole mess back through one of the timers. . . .

So I began unscrewing the thing. Asquith was an oceanographer and so should know little about electronic circuits. I guessed that he couldn't tell that I was undoing sabotage. I worked for about ten minutes, and the drifting capsule hundreds of fathoms beneath us began to function once again.

As I worked, I had reflected upon the powers soon to be invoked, the forces that would traverse the Highway to Hell for a brief time, and then like the Devil's envoy—or the Devil himself, perhaps—be released, there in the mid-Atlantic. The bleak weather that prevails in these latitudes at this time of year did little to improve my mood. A deadly force was to be employed, atomic energy, to release an even more powerful phenomenon—live magma—which seethed and bubbled now miles beneath the sea itself. That anyone should play senseless games with something like this was beyond my comprehension. Once again, the ship was shaken by the waves.

"Okay," I said. "There were a few shorts and I straightened them out." I replaced the side panel. "There shouldn't be any more trouble."

He regarded the monitor. "It seems to be functioning all right now. Let me check. . . ."

He flipped the toggle and said, "*Aquina* to capsule. Do you read me?"

"Yes," came the reply. "What happened?"

"Short circuit in the J-9," he answered. "It has been repaired. What is your condition?"

"All systems returned to normal. Instructions?"

"Proceed with your mission," he said, then turned to me. "I'll recommend you for something or other," he said. "I'm sorry I snapped at you. I didn't know you could service the J-9."

"I'm an electrical engineer," I replied, "and I've studied this thing. I know it's restricted. If I hadn't been able to figure out what was wrong, I wouldn't have touched it."

"I take it you'd rather not be recommended for something or other?"

"That is correct."

"Then I will not do it."

Which was a very good thing, for the nonce, as I'd also disconnected a small bomb, which then resided in my left-hand jacket pocket and would soon be tossed overboard. It had had another five to eight minutes to go and would have blotted the record completely. As for me, I didn't even want a record; but if there had to be one, it would be mine, not the enemy's.

I excused myself and departed. I disposed of the evidence. I thought upon the day's doings.

Someone had tried to sabotage the project. So Don Walsh had been right. The assumed threat had been for real. Consume that and digest it. It meant that there was something big involved. The main question was, "What?" The second was, "What next?"

I lit a cigarette and leaned on the *Aquina*'s rail. I watched the cold north sea attack the hull. My hands shook. It was a decent, humanitarian project. Also, a highly dangerous one. Even forgetting the great risks, though, I could not come up with a good counterinterest. Obviously, however, there was one.

Would Asquith report me? Probably. Though he would not realize what he was doing. He would have to explain the discontinuance of function in the capsule in order to make his report jibe with the capsule's log. He would say that I had repaired a short circuit. That's all.

That would be enough.

I had already decided that the enemy had access to the main log. They would know about the disconnected bomb not being reported. They would also know who had stopped them; and they might be interested enough, at a critical time like this, to do something rash. Good. That was precisely what I wanted.

. . . Because I had already wasted an entire month waiting for this break. I hoped they would come after me soon and try to question me. I took a deep drag on the cigarette and watched a distant iceberg glisten in the sun. This was going to be a strange one—I had that feeling. The skies were gray and the oceans were dark. Somewhere, someone disapproved of what was going on here, but for the life of me I could not guess why.

Well, the hell with them all. I like cloudy days. I was born on one. I'd do my best to enjoy this one.

I went back to my cabin and mixed myself a drink, as I was then officially off duty.

After a time, there came a knocking on my door.

"Turn the handle and push," I said.

It opened and a young man named Rawlings entered.

"Mister Schweitzer," he said, "Carol Deith would like to speak with you."

"Tell her I'm on my way," I said.

"All right," and he departed.

I combed my sort of blond hair and changed my shirt, because she was pretty and young. She was the ship's Security Officer, though, so I had a good idea as to what she was really after.

I walked to her office and knocked twice on the door.

As I entered, I bore in mind the fact that it probably involved the J-9 and my doings of a half hour before. This would tend to indicate that she was right on top of everything.

"Hello," I said. "I believe you sent for me?"

"Schweitzer? Yes, I did. Have a seat, huh?" and she gestured at one on the other side of her expensive desk.

I took it.

"What do you want?"

"You repaired the J-9 this afternoon."

I shrugged. "Are you asking me or telling me?"

"You are not authorized to touch the thing."

"If you want, I can go back and screw it up and leave it the way I found it."

"Then you admit you worked on it?"

"Yes."

She sighed.

"Look, I don't care," she said. "You probably saved two lives today, so I'm not about to fault you for a security violation. What I want to know is something different."

"What?"

"Was it sabotage?"

And there it was. I had felt it coming.

"No," I said. "It was not. There were some short circuits—"

"Bull," she told me.

"I'm sorry. I don't understand—"

"You understand, all right. Somebody gimmicked that thing. You undid it, and it was trickier than a couple of short circuits. And there was a bomb. We monitored its explosion off the port bow about half an hour ago."

"You said it," I said. "I didn't."

"What's your game?" she asked me. "You cleaned up for us, and now you're covering up for somebody else. What do you want?"

"Nothing," I said.

I studied her. Her hair was sort of reddish and she had freckles, lots of them. Her eyes were green. They seemed to be set quite far apart beneath the ruddy line of her bangs. She was fairly tall—like five-ten—though she was not standing at the moment. I had danced with her once at a shipboard party.

"Well?"

"Quite well," I said. "And yourself?"

"I want an answer."

"To what?"

"Was it sabotage?"

"No," I said. "Whatever gave you that idea?"

"There have been other attempts, you know."

"No, I didn't know."

She blushed suddenly, highlighting her freckles. What had caused that?

"Well, there have been. We stopped all of them, obviously. But they were there."

"Who did it?"

"We don't know."

"Why not?"

"We never got hold of the people involved."

"How come?"

"They were clever."

I lit a cigarette.

"Well, you're wrong," I said. "There were some short circuits. I'm an electrical engineer and I spotted them. That was all, though."

She found one someplace, and I lit it for her.

"Okay," she said. "I guess I've got everything you want to tell me."

I stood then.

". . . By the way, I ran another check on you."

"Yes?"

"Nothing. You're clean as snow and swansdown."

"Glad to hear it."

"Don't be, Mister Schweitzer. I'm not finished with you yet."

"Try everything," I said. "You'll find nothing else."

. . . And I was sure of that.

So I left her, wondering when they would reach me.

I send one Christmas card each year, and it is unsigned. All it bears—in block print—is a list of four bars and the cities in which they exist. On Easter, May Day, the first day of summer, and Halloween, I sit in those bars and sip drinks from nine until midnight, local time. Then I go away. Each year, they're different bars.

Always, I pay cash, rather than using the Universal Credit Card which most people carry these days. The bars are generally dives, located in out-of-the-way places.

Sometimes Don Walsh shows up, sits down next to me and orders a beer. We strike up a conversation, then take a walk. Sometimes he doesn't show up. He never misses two in a

row, though. And the second time he always brings me some
cash.

A couple of months ago, on the day when summer came bustling
into the world, I was seated at a table in the back of the Inferno, in
San Miguel de Allende, Mexico. It was a cool evening, as they all
are in that place, and the air had been clean and the stars very bright
as I walked up the flagstone streets of that national monument.
After a time, I saw Don enter, wearing a dark, fake-wool suit
and yellow sport shirt, opened at the neck. He moved to the bar,
ordered something, turned and let his eyes wander about the tables.
I nodded when he grinned and waved. He moved toward me with a
glass in one hand and a Carta Blanca in the other.

"I know you," he said.

"Yeah, I think so. Have a seat?"

He pulled out a chair and seated himself across from me at
the small table. The ashtray was filled to overflowing, but not
because of me. The odor of tequila was on the breeze—make that
"draft"—from the opened front of the narrow barroom, and all
about us two-dimensional nudes fought with bullfight posters for
wall space.

"Your name is . . .?"

"Frank," I said, pulling it out of the air. "Wasn't it in New
Orleans . . .?"

"Yeah, at Mardi Gras—a couple years ago."

"That's right. And you're . . .?"

"George."

"Right. I remember now. We went drinking together. Played
poker all night long. Had a hell of a good time."

". . . And you took me for about two hundred bucks."

I grinned.

"So what've you been up to?" I asked him.

"Oh, the usual business. There are big sales and small sales. I've
got a big one going now."

"Congratulations. I'm glad to hear that. Hope it works out."

"Me, too."

So we made small talk while he finished his beer; then, "Have you
seen much of this town?" I asked.

"Not really. I hear it's quite a place."

"Oh, I think you'll like it. I was here for their Festival once.
Everybody takes bennies to stay awake for the whole three days.
Indios come down from the hills and put on dances. They still hold
paseos here, too, you know? And they have the only Gothic cathedral
in all of Mexico. It was designed by an illiterate Indian, who had seen

pictures of the things on postcards from Europe. They didn't think it would stay up when they took the scaffolding down, but it did and has done so for a long time."

"I wish I could stick around, but I'm only here for a day or so. I thought I'd buy some souvenirs to take home to the family."

"This is the place. Stuff is cheap here. Jewelry, especially."

"I wish I had more time to see some of the sights."

"There is a Toltec ruin atop a hill to the northeast, which you might have noticed because of the three crosses set at its summit. It is interesting because the government still refuses to admit it exists. The view from up there is great."

"I'd like to see it. How do you get in?"

"You just walk out there and climb it. It doesn't exist, so there are no restrictions."

"How long a hike?"

"Less than an hour, from here. Finish your beer, and we'll take a walk."

He did, and we did.

He was breathing heavily in a short time But then, he lived near sea level and this was like 6,500 feet, elevation.

We made it up to the top, though, and wandered amid cacti. We seated ourselves on some big stones.

"So, this place doesn't exist," he said, "the same as you."

"That's right."

"Then it's not bugged—no, it couldn't be—the way most bars are these days."

"It's still a bit of wilderness."

"I hope it stays this way."

"Me, too."

"Thanks for the Christmas card. You looking for a job?"

"You know it."

"All right. I've got one for you."

And that's how this one started.

"Do you know about the Leeward and Windward Islands?" he asked me. "Or Surtsey?"

"No. Tell me."

"Down in the West Indies—in the Lesser Antilles system—starting in an arc heading southeasterly from Puerto Rico and the Virgin Islands toward South America, are those islands north of Guadeloupe which represent the high points of a subterranean ridge ranging from forty to two hundred miles in width. These are oceanic islands, built up from volcanic materials. Every peak is a volcano—extinct or otherwise."

"So?"

"The Hawaiians grew up in the same fashion.—Surtsey, though, was a twentieth-century phenomenon: a volcanically created island which grew up in a very brief time, somewhat to the west of the Vestmanna Islands, near Iceland. That was in 1963. Capelinhos, in the Azores, was the same way, and had its origin undersea."

"So?" But I already knew, as I said it. I already knew about Project RUMOKO—after the Maori god of volcanoes and earthquakes. Back in the twentieth century, there had been an aborted Mohole Project and there had been natural-gas-mining deals which had involved deep drilling and the use of "shaped" atomic charges.

"RUMOKO," he said. "Do you know about it?"

"Somewhat. Mainly from the *Times* Science Section."

"That's enough. We're involved."

"How so?"

"Someone is attempting to sabotage the thing. I have been retained to find out who and how and why, and to stop him. I've tried, and have been eminently unsuccessful to date. In fact, I lost two of my men under rather strange circumstances. Then I received your Christmas card."

I turned toward him, and his green eyes seemed to glow in the dark. He was about four inches shorter than me and perhaps forty pounds lighter, which still made him a pretty big man. But he had straightened into a nearly military posture, so that he seemed bigger and stronger than the guy who had been wheezing beside me on the way up.

"You want me to move in?"

"Yes."

"What's in it for me?"

"Fifty thousand. Maybe a hundred fifty—depending on the results."

I lit a cigarette.

"What will I have to do?" I finally asked.

"Get yourself assigned as a crewman on the *Aquina*—better yet, a technician of some kind. Can you do that?"

"Yes."

"Well, do it. Then find out who is trying to screw the thing up. Then report back to me—or else take them out of the picture any way you see fit. *Then* report back to me."

I chuckled.

"It sounds like a big job. Who is your client?"

"A U.S. Senator," he said, "who shall remain nameless."

"With that I can guess," I said, "but I won't."

"You'll do it?"

"Yes. I could use the money."

"It will be dangerous."

"They all are."

We regarded the crosses, with the packs of cigarettes and other various goodies tied to them in the way of religious offerings.

"Good," he said. "When will you start?"

"Before the month is out."

"Okay. When will you report to me?"

I shrugged, under starlight.

"When I've got something to say."

'That's not good enough, this time. September 15 is the target date."

". . . If it goes off without a hitch?"

"Fifty grand."

"If it gets tricky, and I have to dispose of a *corpus* or three?"

"Like I said."

"Okay. You're on. Before September 15."

"No reports?"

". . . Unless I need help, or have something important to say."

"You may, this time."

I extended my hand.

"You've got yourself a deal, Don."

He bowed his head, nodding to the crosses.

"Give me this one," he finally said. "I want this one. The men I lost were very good men."

"I'll try. I'll give you as much as I can."

"I don't understand you, mister. I wish I knew how you—"

"Good. I'd be crushed if you ever knew how I."

And we walked back down the hill, and I left him off at the place where he was staying that night.

"Let me buy you a drink," said Martin, as I passed him on the foredeck on my way out of Carol Deith's cabin.

"All right," and we walked to the ship's lounge and had one.

"I've got to thank you for what you did while Demmy and I were down there. It—"

"It was nothing," I said. "You could have fixed it yourself in a minute if somebody else had been down and you'd been up here."

"It didn't work out that way, though, and we're happy you were handy."

"I consider myself thanked," I said, raising the plastic beer stein—they're all plastic these days. Damn it!

"What kind of shape was that shaft in?" I asked him.

"Excellent," he said, furrowing his wide, ruddy forehead and putting lots of wrinkles around his bluish eyes.

"You don't look as confident as you sound."

He chuckled, then took a small sip.

"Well, it's never been done before. Naturally, we're all a little scared. . . ."

I took that as a mild appraisal of the situation.

"But, top to bottom, the shaft was in good shape?" I asked.

He looked around him, probably wondering whether the place was bugged. It was, but he wasn't saying anything that could hurt him, or me. If he had been, I'd have shut him up.

"Yes," he agreed.

"Good," and I thought back on the sayings of the short man with the wide shoulders. "Very good."

"That's a strange attitude," he said. "You're just a paid technician."

"I take a certain pride in my work."

He gave me a look I did not understand, then, "That sounds strangely like a twentieth-century attitude."

I shrugged.

"I'm old-fashioned. Can't get away from it."

"I like that," he said. "I wish more people were that way, these days."

"What's Demmy up to, now?"

"He's sleeping."

"Good."

"They ought to promote you."

"I hope not."

"Why not?"

"I don't like responsibilities."

"But you take them on yourself, and you handle them well."

"I was lucky—once. Who knows what will happen, next time . . .?"

He gave me a furtive look.

"What do you mean, 'next time'?"

"I mean, if it happens again," I said. "I just happened to be in the control room. . . ."

I knew then that he was trying to find out what I knew—so neither of us knew much, though we both knew that something was wrong.

He stared at me, sipped his beer, kept staring at me, then nodded.

"You're trying to say that you're lazy?"

"That's right."

"Crap."

I shrugged and sipped mine.

Back around 1957—fifty years ago—there was a thing called AMSOC, and it was a joke. It was a takeoff on the funny names of alphabetized scientific organizations. It stood for the American Miscellaneous Society. It represented something other than a joke on the organization man, however. This was because Doctor Walter Munk of Scripps Institution of Oceanography and Doctor Harry Hess of Princeton were members, and they had come up with a strange proposal which later died for lack of funds. Like John Brown, however, while it lay moldering in its grave, its spirit kept shuffling its feet.

It is true that the Mohole Project died stillborn, but that which eventually came of the notion was even grander and more creative.

Most people know that the crust of the Earth is twenty-five or more miles thick under the continents, and that it would be rough drilling there. Many also know that under the oceans the crust is much thinner. It would be quite possible to drill there, into the top of the mantle, penetrating the Mohorovicic Discontinuity, however. They had talked about all kinds of data that could be picked up. Well, okay. But consider something else: sure, it's true that a sampling of the mantle would provide some answers to questions involving radioactivity and heat flow, geological structure and the age of the Earth. Working with natural materials, we would know boundaries, thicknesses of various layers within the crust; and we could check these against what we had learned from the seismic waves of earthquakes gone by. All that and more. A sample of the sediments would give us a complete record of the Earth's history, before man ever made the scene. But there is more involved than that, a lot more.

"Another one?" Martin asked me.

"Yeah. Thanks."

If you study the International Union of Geology and Geophysics publication, *Active Volcanoes of the World*, and if you map out all those which are no longer active, you will note certain volcanic and seismic belts. There is the "Ring of Fire" surrounding the Pacific Ocean. Start along the Pacific coast of South America, and you can follow it up north through Chile, Ecuador, Colombia, Central America, Mexico, the western United States, Canada, and Alaska, then around and down through Kamchatka, the Kuriles, Japan, the Philippines, Indonesia, and New Zealand. Forgetting about the Mediterranean, there is also an area in the Atlantic, near Iceland.

We sat there.

I raised mine and took a sip.

There are over six hundred volcanoes in the world which could be classified as *active*, though actually they don't do much most of the time.

We were going to add one more.

We were going to create a volcano in the Atlantic Ocean. More specifically, a volcanic island, like Surtsey. This was Project RUMOKO.

"I'm going down again," said Martin. "Sometime during the next few hours, I guess. I'd appreciate it if you would do me the favor of keeping an eye on that goddam machine next time around. I'd make it up to you, some way."

"Okay," I said. "Let me know when the next time is, as soon as you know it, and I'll try to hang around the control room. If something does go wrong, I'll try to do what I did earlier, if there's no one around who can do any better."

He slapped me on the shoulder.

"That's good enough for me. Thanks."

"You're scared."

"Yeah."

"Why?"

"This damned thing seems jinxed. You've been my good-luck charm. I'll buy you beers from here to hell and back again, just to hang around. I don't know what's wrong. Just bad luck, I guess."

"Maybe," I said.

I stared at him for a second, then turned my attention to my drink.

"The isothermic maps show that this is the right place, the right part of the Atlantic," I said. "The only thing I'm sacred about is none of my business."

"What's that?" he asked.

"There are various things about magma," I said, "and some of them frighten me."

"What do you mean?" he asked.

"You don't know what it's going to do, once it's released. It could be anything from a Krakatoa to an Etna. The magma itself may be of any composition. Its exposure to water and air could produce *any* results."

"I thought we had a guarantee it was safe?"

"A guess. An educated guess, but only a guess. That's all."

"You're scared?"

"You bet your ass."

"We're in danger . . .?"

"Not *us* so much, since we'll be the hell out of the way. But this thing could affect world temperatures, tides, weather. I'm a little leery, I'll admit it."

He shook his head. "I don't like it."

"You probably had all your bad luck already," I said. "I wouldn't lose any sleep. . . ."

"I guess you're right."

We finished our beers and I stood.

"I've got to be running."

"Can I buy you another?"

"No, thanks. I've got some work to do."

"Well, I'll be seeing you."

"Yes. Take it easy," and I left the lounge and moved back to the upper decks.

The moon spilled sufficient light to make shadows about me, and the evening was chilly enough for me to button my collar.

I watched the waves for a little while, then returned to my cabin.

I took a shower, listened to the late news, read for a time. Finally, I turned in and took the book to bed with me. After a while, I got drowsy, set the book on the bedside table, turned out the lamp, and let the ship rock me to sleep.

. . . Had to get a good night's sleep. After all, tomorrow was RUMOKO.

How long? A few hours, I guess. Then I was awakened by something.

My door was quietly unlocked, and I heard a light footfall.

I lay there, wide awake, with my eyes closed, waiting.

I heard the door close, lock.

Then the light came on, and there was a piece of steel near to my head, and a hand was upon my shoulder.

"Wake up, mister!" someone said.

I pretended to do so, slowly.

There were two of them, and I blinked and rubbed my eyes, regarding the gun about twenty inches away from my head.

"What the hell is this?" I said.

"No," said the man holding the metal. "We ask. You answer. It is not the other way around."

I sat up, leaned back against the headboard.

"Okay," I said. "What do you want?"

"Who are you?"

"Albert Schweitzer," I replied.

"We know the name you're using. Who are you—really?"

"That's it," I said.

"We don't think so."

"I'm sorry."

"So are we."

"So?"

"You will tell us about yourself and your mission."

"I don't know what you're talking about."

"Get up!"

"Then please give me my robe. It's hanging on the hook inside the bathroom door."

The gunsel leaned toward the other. "Get it, check it, give it to him," he said.

And I regarded him.

He had a handkerchief over the lower part of his face. So did the other guy. Which was kind of professional. Amateurs tend to wear masks. Upper type. Masks of this sort conceal very little. The lower part of the face is the most easily identifiable.

"Thanks," I said, when the one guy handed me my blue terry-cloth robe.

He nodded, and I threw it about my shoulders, put my arms into the sleeves, whipped it about me, and sat up on the edge of the bed.

"Okay," I said. "What do you want?"

"Who are you working for?" said the first.

"Project RUMOKO," I replied.

He slapped me, lightly, with his left hand, still holding the gun steady.

"No," he said. "The whole story, please."

"I don't know what you're talking about, but may I have a cigarette?"

"All right.—No. Wait. Take one of mine. I don't know what might be in your pack."

I took one, lit it, inhaled, breathed smoke.

"I don't understand you," I said. "Give me a better clue as to what you want to know and maybe I can help you. I'm not looking for trouble."

This seemed to relax them slightly, because they both sighed. The man asking the questions was about five foot eight in height, the other about five-ten. The taller man was heavy, though. Around two hundred pounds, I'd say.

They seated themselves in two nearby chairs. The gun was leveled at my breast.

"Relax, then, Mister Schweitzer. We don't want trouble, either," said the talkative one.

"Great," said I. "Ask me anything and I'll give you honest answers," prepared to lie my head off. "Ask away."

"You repaired the J-9 unit today."

"I guess everybody knows that."

"Why did you do it?"

"Because two men were going to die, and I knew how."

"How did you acquire this expertise?"

"For Chrissakes, I'm an electrical engineer!" I said. "I know how to figure circuits! Lots of people do!"

The taller guy looked at the shorter one. He nodded.

"Then why did you try to silence Asquith?" the taller one asked me.

"Because I broke a regulation by touching the unit," I said. "I'm not authorized to service it."

He nodded again. Both of them had very black and clean-looking hair and well-developed pectorals and biceps, as seen through their light shirts.

"You seem to be an ordinary, honest citizen," said the tall one, "who went to the school of his choice, graduated, remained unmarried, took this job. Perhaps everything is as you say, in which case we do you wrong. However, the circumstances are very suspicious. You repaired a complex machine which you had no right to repair. . . ."

I nodded.

"Why?" he asked.

"I've got a funny thing about death: I don't like to see people do it," I said. Then, "Who do *you* work for?" I asked. "Some sort of intelligence agency?"

The shorter one smiled. The other said, "We are not permitted to say. You obviously understand these things, however. Our interest is only a certain curiosity as to why you kept quiet with respect to what was obviously sabotage."

"So, I've told you."

"Yes, but you are lying. People do not disobey orders the way you did."

"Crap! There were lives at stake!"

He shook his head.

"I fear that we must question you further, and in a different manner."

Whenever I am awaiting the outcome of peril or reflecting upon the few lessons that can be learned in the course of a misspent life, a few bubbles of memory appear before me, are struck by all the color changes the skin of a bubble undergoes in the space of an instant, burst then, having endured no longer than a bubble, and persist as feelings for a long while after.

Bubbles . . . There is one down in the Caribbean called New Eden. Depth, approximately 175 fathoms. As of the most recent census, it was home to over 100,000 people. A huge, illuminated geodesic dome it is, providing an overhead view with which Euclid would have been pleased. For great distances about this dome, strung lights like street lamps line avenues among rocks, bridges over canyons, thoroughfares through mountains. The bottom-going seamobiles move like tanks along these ways; minisubs hover or pass at various altitudes; slick-seeming swimmers in tight and colorful garb come and go, entering and departing the bubble or working about it.

I vacationed there for a couple of weeks one time, and although I discovered claustrophobic tendencies of which I had previously been unaware, it was still quite pleasant. The people were different from surface dwellers. They were rather like what I fancy the old explorers and frontiersmen to have been. Somewhat more individualistic and independent than the average topside citizen, but with a certain sense of community and the feelings of responsibility attendant thereto. This is doubtless because they *are* frontiersmen, having volunteered for combinations of programs involving both the relief of minor population pressures and the exploitation of the ocean's resources. Whatever, they accept tourists. They accepted me, and I went there and swam with them, toured on their subs, viewed their mines and hydroponic gardens, their homes and their public buildings. I remember the beauty of it, I remember the people, I remember the way the sea hung overhead like the night sky as seen through the faceted eye of some insect. Or maybe like a giant insect on the other side, looking in. Yes, that seems more likely. Perhaps the personality of the place appealed to a certain rebellious tendency I occasionally felt stirring fathoms deep within my own psyche.

While it was not really an Eden Under Glass, and while those crazy and delightful little bubble cities are definitely not for me, there was something there that turned it into one of those funny, colorful things that sometimes come to me, bubblelike, whenever I am awaiting the outcome of peril or reflecting upon the few lessons that can be learned in the course of a misspent life.

I sighed, took a final drag on my cigarette and crushed it out, knowing that in a moment my bubble would burst.

What is it like to be the only man in the world who does not exist?
It is difficult to say. It is not easy to generalize when you are only sure
of the particulars in one case—your own. With me, it was a kind of
unusual deal, and I doubt there is a parallel one, anywhere. I used
to bitch and moan over progressive mechanization. No more.

It was strange, the way that it happened:

Once I wrote programs for computers. That is how the whole
thing got started.

One day, I learned an unusual and frightening piece of news . . .

I learned that the whole world was going to exist on tape.

How?

Well, it's tricky.

Everybody, nowadays, has a birth certificate, academic record,
credit rating, a history of all his travels and places of residence and,
ultimately, there is a death certificate somewhere on file. Once, all
things of this sort existed in separate places. Then, some people set
out to combine them. They called it a Central Data Bank. It resulted
in massive changes in the order of human existence. Not all of these
changes, I am now certain, were for the better.

I was one of those people, and it was not until things were well
along that I began to have second thoughts on the matter. By then,
it was too late to do anything about it, I supposed.

What the people in my project were doing was linking every
data bank in existence, so that public records, financial records,
medical records, specialized technical records all existed and
were available from one source—through key stations whose
personnel had access to this information at various levels of
confidentiality.

I have never considered anything to be wholly good or wholly
evil. But this time, I came close to the former feeling. I had thought
that it was going to be a very good thing indeed. I had thought that
in the wonderful, electrified *fin de siècle* of McLuhan in which we
lived, a thing like this was necessary: every home with closed-circuit
access to any book ever written, or any play ever recorded on tape
or in a crystal, or any college lecture in the past couple of decades,
or any bits of general statistical knowledge desired (you can't lie
with statistics, theoretically, if everybody has access to your source,
and can question it directly); every commercial and government
outfit with access to your assets, your income, and a list of every
expenditure you've ever made; every attorney with a court order
with access to a list of every place you've ever resided, and with
whom, and every commercial vehicle on which you've ever traveled,
and with whom. Your whole life, all your actions, laid out like a

chart of the nervous system in a neurology class—this impressed me as good.

For one thing, it seemed that it would eliminate crime. Only a crazy man, I thought, would care to err with all that to stand against him; and since medical records were all on file, even the psychopath could be stopped.

. . . And speaking of medicine, how fine if the computer and medical people diagnosing you for anything had instant access to all your past medical history! Think of all the cures which could be effected! Think of the deaths prevented!

Think of the status of the world economy, when it is known where every dime exists and where it is headed.

Think of the solving of traffic-control problems—land, sea, and air—when everything is regulated.

Think of . . . Oh, hell!

I foresaw the coming of a Golden Era.

Crap!

A friend of mine having peripheral connections with the Mafia, it was, laughed at me, all starry in my eyes and just up from the university and into the federal service.

"Do you seriously believe that every asset will be registered? Every transaction recorded?" he'd asked me.

"Eventually."

"They haven't pierced Switzerland yet; and if they do, other places will be found."

"There will be a certain allowance for residuals."

"Then don't forget mattresses, and holes in the backyard. Nobody knows how much money there really is in the world, and no one ever will."

So I stopped and thought and read up on economics. He was right. The things for which we were writing programs in this area were, basically, estimates and approximates, vis-à-vis that which got registered—a reconciliation factor included.

So I thought about travel. How many unregistered vessels? Nobody knew. You can't keep statistics on items for which you have no data. And if there is to be unregistered money, more vessels could be constructed. There is a lot of coastline in the world. So traffic control might not be as perfect as I had envisioned.

Medical? Doctors are as human and lazy as the rest of us. I suddenly realized that all medical reports might not get filed— especially if someone wanted to pocket the cash and not pay taxes on it, and was not asked for a receipt.

When it came to people, I had forgotten the human factor.

There were the shady ones, there were people who just liked their privacy, and there were those who would *honestly* foul up the reporting of necessary information. All of them people who would prove that the system was not perfect.

Which meant that the thing might not work in precisely the fashion anticipated. There might also be some resentment, some resistance, along with actual evasion. And perhaps these might even be warranted. . . .

But there was not much overt resistance, so the project proceeded. It occurred over a period of three years. I worked in the central office, starting out as a programmer. After I'd devised a system whereby key weather stations and meteorological observation satellites fed their reports directly into the central system, I was promoted to the position of senior programmer and given some supervisory responsibility.

By then, I had learned sufficient of the project so that my doubts had picked up a few small fears as companions. I found myself beginning to dislike the work, which made me study it all the more intensely. They kidded me about taking work home with me. No one seemed to realize that it was not dedication, but rather a desire, born of my fears, to learn all that I could about the project. Since my superiors misread my actions, they saw that I was promoted once more.

This was fine, because it gave me access to more information, at the policy level. Then, for a variety of reasons, there came a spate of deaths, promotions, resignations, retirements. This left things wide open for fair-haired boys, and I rose higher within the group.

I came to be an adviser to old John Colgate, who was in charge of the entire operation.

One day, when we had just about achieved our mission, I told him of my fears and my doubts. I told the gray-haired, sallow-faced, spaniel-eyed old man that I felt we might be creating a monster and committing the ultimate invasion of human privacy.

He stared at me for a long while, fingering the pink coral paperweight on his desk: then, "You may be right." he said. "What are you going to do about it?"

"I don't know," I replied. "I just wanted to tell you my feelings on the matter."

He sighed then and turned in his swivel chair and stared out the window.

After a time, I thought he had gone to sleep, as he sometimes did right after lunch.

Finally, though, he spoke: "Don't you think I've heard those arguments a thousand times before?"

"Probably," I replied "and I've always wondered how you might have answered them."

"I have no answers," he said abruptly. "I feel it is for the better, or I would not be associated with it. I could be wrong, though. I will admit that. But some means has to be found to record and regulate all the significant features of a society as complex as ours has become. If you think of a better way of running the show, tell me about it."

I was silent. I lit a cigarette and waited for his next words. I did not know at the time that he only had about six months of life remaining to him.

"Did you ever consider buying out?" he finally asked.

"What do you mean?"

"Resigning. Quitting the system."

"I'm not sure that I understand. . . ."

"We in the system will be the last to have our personal records programmed in."

"Why?"

"Because I wanted it that way, in case anyone came to me as you have today and asked me what you have asked me."

"Has anyone else done it?"

"I would not say if they had, to keep the intended purity of the thing complete."

"'Buying out.' By this, I take it that you mean destroying my personal data before someone enters it into the system?"

"That is correct," he said.

"But I would not be able to get another job, with no academic record, no past work history . . ."

"That would be your problem."

"I couldn't purchase anything with no credit rating."

"I suppose you would have to pay cash."

"It's all recorded."

He swiveled back and gave me a smile. "Is it?" he asked me. "Is it really?"

"Well, not all of it," I admitted.

"So?"

I thought about it while he lit his pipe, smoke invading wide, white sideburns. Was he just kidding me along, being sarcastic? Or was he serious?

As if in answer to my thought, he rose from his chair, crossed the room, opened a file cabinet. He rummaged around in it for a time, then returned holding a sheaf of punchcards like a poker hand. He dropped them onto the desk in front of me.

"That's you," he said. "Next week, you go into the system, like everybody else," and he puffed a smoke ring and reseated himself.

"Take them home with you and put them under your pillow," he said. "Sleep on them. Decide what you want to do with them."

"I don't understand."

"I am leaving it up to you."

"What if I tore them up? What would you do?"

"Nothing."

"Why not?"

"Because I do not care."

"That's not true. You're head of this thing."

He shrugged.

"Don't you believe in the value of the system yourself?"

He dropped his eyes and drew on his pipe.

"I am no longer so certain as once I was," he stated.

"If I did this thing I would cease to exist, officially," I said.

"Yes."

"What would become of me?"

"That would be your problem."

I thought about it for a moment; then, "Give me the cards," I said.

He did, with a gesture.

I picked them up, placed them in my inside coat pocket.

"What are you going to do now?"

"Sleep on them, as you suggested," I said.

"Just see that you have them back by next Tuesday morning."

"Of course."

And he smiled, nodded, and that was it.

I took them, went home with them. But I didn't sleep.

No, that's not it. I wouldn't sleep, couldn't sleep.

I thought about it for centuries—well, all night long—pacing and smoking. To exist outside the system. . . . How could I do anything if it did not recognize my existence?

Then, about four in the morning, I decided that I should have phrased that question the other way around.

How could the system recognize me, no matter what I did?

I sat down then and made some careful plans. In the morning, I tore my cards through the middle, burned them, and stirred the ashes.

"Sit in that chair," the taller one said, gesturing with his left hand. I did so.

They moved around and stood behind me.

I regulated my breathing and tried to relax.

Over a minute must have gone by; then, "All right, tell us the whole story." he said.

"I obtained this job through a placement bureau," I told him. "I accepted it, came to work, performed my duties, met you. That's it."

"It has been said for some time, and we believe it to be true, that the government can obtain permission—for security reasons—to create a fictitious individual in the central records. An agent is then fitted into that slot in life. If anyone is able to check on him, his credentials appear to be bona fide."

I didn't answer him.

"Is that true?" he asked.

"Yes," I said. "It has been said that this can be done. I don't know whether it's true or not, though."

"You do not admit to being such an agent?"

"No."

Then they whispered to one another for a time. Finally, I heard a metal case click open.

"You are lying."

"No, I'm not. I maybe save a couple guys' lives and you start calling me names. I don't know why, though I'd like to. What have I done that's wrong?"

"I'll ask the questions, Mister Schweitzer."

"I'm just curious. Perhaps if you would tell me—"

"Roll up your sleeve. Either one, it doesn't matter."

"Why?"

"Because I told you to."

"What are you going to do?"

"Administer an injection."

"Are you an M.D.?"

"That is none of your business."

"Well, I refuse it—for the record. After the cops get hold of you, for a variety of reasons, I'll even see to it that the Medical Association is on your back."

"Your sleeve, please."

"Under protest," I observed, and I rolled up the left one. "If you're to kill me when you've finished playing games," I added, "murder is kind of serious. If you are not, I'll be after you. I may find you one day. . . ."

I felt a sting behind my biceps.

"Mind telling me what you gave me?" I asked.

"It's called TC-6," he replied. "Perhaps you've read about it. You will retain consciousness, as I might need your full reasoning abilities. But you will answer me honestly."

I chuckled, which they doubtless attributed to the effects of the drug, and I continued practicing my yoga breathing techniques. These could not stop the drug, but they made me feel better. Maybe they gave me a few extra seconds, also, along with the detached feeling I had been building up.

I keep up on things like TC-6. This one, I knew, left you rational, unable to lie, and somewhat literal-minded. I figured on making the most of its weak points by flowing with the current. Also, I had a final trick remaining.

The thing that I disliked most about TC-6 was that it sometimes had a bad side effect, cardiac-wise.

I did not exactly feel myself going under. I was just suddenly there, and it did not feel that different from the way I always feel. I knew that to be an illusion. I wished I had had prior access to the antidote kit I kept within a standard-looking first-aid kit hidden in my dresser.

"You hear me, don't you?" he asked.

"Yes," I heard myself saying.

"What is your name?"

"Albert Schweitzer," I replied.

There were a couple of quick breaths taken behind me, and my questioner silenced the other fellow, who had started to say something.

Then, "What do you do?" he asked me.

"I'm a technician."

"I know that much. What else?"

"I do many things—"

"Do you work for the government—*any* government?"

"I pay taxes, which means I work for the government, part of the time. Yes."

"I did not mean it in that sense. Are you a secret agent in the employ of any government?"

"No."

"A *known* agent?"

"No."

"Then why are you here?"

"I am a technician. I service the machines."

"What else?"

"I do not—"

"What else? Who else do you work for, besides the Project?"

"Myself."

"What do you mean?"

"My activities are directed to maintaining my personal economic status and physical well-being."

"I am talking about other employers. Have you any?"

"No."

From the other man, I heard, "He sounds clean."

"Maybe." Then, to me, "What would you do if you met me somewhere and recognized me?"

"Bring you to law."

". . . And failing that?"

"If I were able, I would hurt you severely. Perhaps I would kill you, if I were able to give it the appearance of self-defense or make it seem to be an accident."

"Why?"

"Because I wish to preserve my own physical well-being. The fact that you had disturbed it once means that you might attempt it again. I will not permit this access to me."

"I doubt that I will attempt it again."

"Your doubts mean nothing to me."

"So you saved two lives today, yet you are willing to take one."

I did not reply.

"Answer me."

"You did not ask me a question."

"Could he have drug-consciousness?" asked the other.

"I never thought of that.—Do you?"

"I do not understand the question."

"This drug allows you to remain oriented in all three spheres. You know who you are, where you are, and when you are. It saps that thing called the will, however, which is why you must answer my questions. A person with a lot of experience with truth drugs can sometimes beat them, by rephrasing the questions to himself and giving a literally honest reply. Is this what you are doing?"

"That's the wrong question," said the other.

"What's right?"

"Have you had any prior experience with drugs?" that one asked me.

"Yes."

"What ones?"

"I've had aspirin, nicotine, caffeine, alcohol—"

"Truth serums," he said. "Things like this, things that make you talk. Have you had them before?"

"Yes."

"Where?"

"At Northwestern University."

"Why?"

"I volunteered for a series of experiments."

"What did they involve?"

"The effects of drugs on consciousness."

"Mental reservations," he said to the other. "It could take days. I think he has primed himself."

"Can you beat a truth drug?" the other one asked me.

"I do not understand."

"Can you lie to us—now?"

"No."

"Wrong question, again," said the shorter. "He is not lying. Anything he says is literally true."

"So how do we get an answer out of him?"

"I'm not sure."

So they continued to hit me with questions. After a time, things began to wane.

"He's got us," said the shorter one. "It would take days to beat him down."

"Should we . . .?"

"No. We've got the tape. We've got his answers. Let's let a computer worry about it."

But by then it was near morning, and I had the funny feeling, accompanied by cold flashes on the back of my neck, that I might be able to manage a fib or three once again. There was some light on the other side of my portholes. They had been going at me for what seemed to be many hours. I decided to try.

"I think this place is bugged," I said.

"What? What do you mean?"

"Ship's Security," I stated. "I believe all technicians are so monitored."

"Where is it?"

"I don't know."

"We've got to find it," said the one.

"What good will it do?" said the other, in a whisper, for which I respected him, as whispers do not often get recorded. "They'd have been here long before this, if it were."

"Unless they're waiting, letting us hang ourselves."

The first began looking, however, and I rose, met with no objections, and staggered across the room to collapse upon the bed.

My right hand slipped down around the headboard, as though by accident. It found the gun.

I flipped off the safety as I withdrew it. I sat upon the bed and pointed it at them.

"All right, morons," I said. "Now you answer *my* questions."

The big one made a move toward his belt and I shot him in the shoulder.

"Next?" I asked, tearing away the silencer, which had done its work, and replacing it with a pillow.

The other man raised his hands and looked at his buddy.

"Let him bleed," I said.

"He nodded and stepped back.

"Sit down," I told them both.

They did.

I moved over behind the two of them.

"Give me that arm," and I took it. I cleaned it and dressed it, as the bullet had gone on through. I had placed their weapons on the dresser. I tore off their hankies and studied their faces. I did not know them from anywhere.

"Okay, why are you here?" I asked. "And why do you want to know what you want to know?"

There were no replies.

"I don't have as much time as you did," I said. "So I'm about to tape you in place. I don't think I can afford to fool around with drugs."

I fetched the adhesive tape from the medicine chest and did it.

"These places are pretty soundproof," I remarked, putting the gun aside, "and I lied about them being bugged.—So you can do a bit of screaming if you want. I caution you against it, however. Each one earns you one broken bone.

"So who do *you* work for?" I repeated.

"I'm a maintenance man on the shuttler," said the shorter one. "My friend is a pilot."

He received a dirty look for this.

"Okay," I said. "I'll buy that, because I've never seen you around here before. Think carefully over your answer to the next one: who do you *really* work for?"

I asked this knowing that they did not have the advantages that I had had. I work for myself because I am self-employed—an independent contractor. My name is Albert Schweitzer right now, so that's what it is, period. I always become the person I must. Had they asked me who I had been before, they might have gotten a different answer. It's a matter of conditioning and mental attitudes.

"Who pulls the strings?" I asked.

No replies.

"All right," I said. "I guess I'll have to ask you in a different fashion."

Heads turned toward me.

"You were willing to violate my physiology for the sake of a few answers," I said. "Okay. I guess I'll return the favor upon your anatomy. I'll get an answer or three, I promise. Only I'll be a little more basic about it. I'll simply torture you until you talk."

"You wouldn't do that," said the taller man. "You have a low violence index."

I chuckled.

"Let's see," I said.

How do you go about ceasing to exist while continuing your existence? I found it quite easy. But then, I was in on the project from the first, was trusted, had been given an option . . .

After I tore up my cards, I returned to work as usual. There, I sought and located the necessary input point. That was my last day on the job.

It was Thule, way up where it's cold, a weather station. . . .

An old guy who liked rum ran the place. I can still remember the day when I took my ship, the *Proteus*, into his harbor and complained of rough seas.

"I'll put you up," he said to me.

The computer had not let me down.

"Thanks."

He led me in, fed me, talked to me about the seas, the weather. I brought in a case of Bacardi and turned him loose on it.

"Ain't things pretty much automatic here?" I asked.

"That's right."

"Then what do they need you for?"

He laughed a little and said, "My uncle was a Senator. I needed a place to go. He fixed me up.—Let's see your ship.—So what if it's raining?"

So we did.

It was a decent-sized cabin cruiser with powerful engines—and way out of its territory.

"It's a bet," I told him. "I wanted to hit the Arctic Circle and get proof that I did."

"Kid, you're nuts."

"I know, but I'll win."

"Prob'ly," he agreed. "I was like you once—all full of the necessary ingredients and ready to go.—Gettin' much action these days?" And he stroked his pepper-and-salt beard and gave me an evil grin from inside it.

"Enough," I said, and, "Have a drink," because he had made me think of Eva.

He did, and I left it at, "Enough," for a time. She was not like that, though. I mean, it was not something he would really want to hear about.

It had been about four months earlier that we had broken up. It was not religion or politics; it was much more basic.

So I lied to him about an imaginary girl and made him happy.

I had met her in New York, back when I was doing the same things she was—vacationing and seeing plays and pix.

She was a tall girl, with close-cropped blond hair. I helped her find a subway station, got on with her, got off with her, asked her to dinner, was told to go to hell.

Scene:

"I'm not like that."

"Neither am I. But I'm hungry.—So *will* you?"

"What are you looking for?"

"Someone to talk to," I said. "I'm lonesome."

"I think you're looking in the wrong place."

"Probably."

"I don't know you from anywhere."

"That makes two of us, but I could sure use some spaghetti with meat sauce and a glass of Chianti."

"Will you be hard to get rid of?"

"No. I go quietly."

"Okay. I'll eat spaghetti with you."

And we did.

That month we kept getting closer and closer until we were there. The fact that she lived in one of those crazy little bubble cities under the sea meant nothing. I was liberal enough to appreciate the fact that the Sierra Club had known what it was doing in pushing for their construction.

I probably should have gone along with her when she went back. She had asked me.

She had been on vacation—seeing the Big Place—and so had I. I didn't get into New York that often.

"Marry me," though, I'd said.

But she would not give up her bubble and I would not give up my dream. I wanted the big, above-the-waves world—all of it. I loved that blue-eyed bitch from five hundred fathoms, though, and I realize now that I probably should have taken her on her own terms. I'm too damned independent. If either of us had been normal . . . Well, we weren't, and that's that.

Eva, wherever you are, I hope you and Jim are happy.

"Yeah—with Coke," I said. "It's good that way," and I drank Cokes and he drank doubles with Cokes until he announced his weariness.

"It's starting to get to me, Mister Hemingway," he said.

"Well, let's sack out."

"Okay. You can have the couch there."

"Great."

"I showed you where the blankets are?"

"Yes."

"Then good night, Ernie. See you in the morning."

"You bet, Bill. I'll make breakfast for us."

"Thanks."

And he yawned and stretched and went away.

I gave him half an hour and went to work.

His weather station had a direct line into the central computer. I was able to provide for a nice little cut-in. Actuated by short wave. Little-used band. I concealed my tamperings well.

When I was finished, I knew that I had it made.

I could tell Central anything through that thing, from hundreds of miles away, and it would take it as fact.

I was damn near a god.

Eva, maybe I should have gone the other way. I'll never know.

I helped Bill Mellings over his hangover the following morning, and he didn't suspect a thing. He was a very decent old guy, and I was comforted by the fact that he would never get into trouble over what I had done. This was because nobody would ever catch me, I was sure. And even if they do, I don't think he'll get into trouble. After all, his uncle was a Senator.

I had the ability to make it as anybody I cared to. I'd have to whip up the entire past history—birth, name, academics, and *et cet*—and I could then fit myself in anywhere I wanted in modern society. All I had to do was tell Central via the weather station via short wave. The record would be created and I would have existence in any incarnation I desired. *Ab initio*, like.

But Eva, I wanted you. I—Well . . .

I think the government does occasionally play the same tricks. But I am positive they don't suspect the existence of an independent contractor.

I know most of that which is worth knowing—more than is necessary, in fact—with respect to lie detectors and truth serums.

I hold my name sacred. Nobody gets it. Do you know that the polygraph can be beaten in no fewer than seventeen different ways? It has not been much improved since the mid-twentieth century. A lower-chest strap plus some fingertip perspiration detectors could do it wonders. But things like this never get the appropriations. Maybe a few universities play around with it from this standpoint—but that's about it. I could design one today that damn near nobody could beat, but its record still wouldn't be worth much in court. Drugs, now, they're another matter.

A pathological liar can beat Amytal and Pentothal. So can a drug-conscious guy.

What is drug-consciousness?

Ever go looking for a job and get an intelligence test or an aptitude test or a personality inventory for your pains? Sure. Everybody has by now, and they're all on file in Central. You get used to taking them after a time. They start you in early, and throughout your life you learn about taking the goddamn things. You get to be what psychologists refer to as "test-conscious." What it means is that you get so damned used to them that you know what kind of asininity is right, according to the book.

So okay. You learn to give them the answers they're looking for. You learn all the little time-saving tricks. You feel secure, you know it is a game and you are game-conscious.

It's the same thing.

If you do not get scared, and if you have tried a few drugs before for this express purpose, you can beat them.

Drug-consciousness is nothing more than knowing how to handle yourself under that particular kind of fire.

"Go to hell. You answer my questions," I said.

I think that the old tried-and-true method of getting answers is the best: pain, threatened and actual.

I used it.

I got up early in the morning and made breakfast. I took him a glass of orange juice and shook him by the shoulder.

"What the goddam—!"

"Breakfast," I said. "Drink this."

He did, and then we went out to the kitchen and ate.

"The sea looks pretty good today," I said. "I guess I can be moving on."

He nodded above his eggs.

"You ever up this way, you stop in again. Hear?"

"I will," I said, and I have—several times since—because I came to like him. It was funny.

We talked all that morning, going through three pots of coffee. He was an M.D. who had once had a fairly large practice going for him. (At a later date, he dug a few bullets out of me and kept quiet about their having been there.) He had also been one of the early astronauts, briefly. I learned subsequently that his wife had died of cancer some six years earlier. He gave up his practice at that time, and he did not remarry. He had looked for a way to retire from the world, found one, done it.

Though we are very close friends now, I have never told him that he's harboring a bastard input unit. I may, one day, as I know he is one of the few guys I can trust. On the other hand, I do not want to make him a genuine accomplice to what I do. Why trouble your friends and make them morally liable for your strange doings?

So I became the man who did not exist. But I had acquired the potential for becoming anybody I chose. All I had to do was write the program and feed it to Central via that station. All I needed then was a means of living. This latter was a bit tricky.

I wanted an occupation where payment would always be made to me in cash. Also, I wanted one where payment would be large enough for me to live as I desired.

This narrowed the field considerably and threw out lots of legitimate things. I could provide myself with a conventional-seeming background in any area that amused me, and work as an employee there. Why should I, though?

I created a new personality and moved into it. Those little things you always toy with and dismiss as frivolous whims—I did them then. I lived aboard the *Proteus*, which at that time was anchored in the cove of a small island off the New Jersey coast.

I studied judo. There are three schools of it, you know: there is the Kodokon, or the pure Japanese style, and there are the Budo Kwai and the French Federation systems. The latter two have pretty much adopted the rules of the former, with this exception: while they use the same chokes, throws, bone-locks, and such, they're sloppier about it. They feel that the pure style was designed to accommodate the needs of a smaller race, with reliance upon speed, leverage, and agility, rather than strength. So they attempted to adapt the basic techniques to the needs of a larger race. They allowed for the use of strength and let the techniques be a little less than perfect. This was fine so far as I was concerned, because I'm a big, sloppy guy. Only, I may be haunted one day because of my laxity. If you learn it the Kodokon way, you can be

eighty years old and still carry off a *nage-no-kata* perfectly. This is
because there is very little effort involved; it's all technique. My
way, though, when you start pushing fifty, it gets rougher and
rougher because you're not as strong as you once were. Well, that
still gave me a couple of decades in which to refine my form. Maybe
I'll make it. I made *Nidan* with the French Federation, so I'm not a
complete slouch. And I try to stay in shape.

While I was going for all this physical activity I took a locksmith
course. It took me weeks to learn to pick even the simplest lock,
and I still think that the most efficient way, in a pinch, is to break
the door in, get what you want, and run like hell.

I was not cut out to be a criminal, I guess. Some guys have it and
some don't.

I studied every little thing I could think of that I thought would
help me get by. I still do. While I am probably not an expert in
anything, except perhaps for my own peculiar mode of existence,
I know a little bit about lots of esoteric things. And I have the
advantage of not existing going for me.

When I ran low on cash, I went to see Don Walsh. I knew who
he was, although he knew nothing about me, and I hoped that he
never would. I'd chosen him as my modus vivendi.

That was over ten years ago, and I still can't complain. Maybe I
am even a little better with the locks and *nages* these days, as a result
thereof—not to mention the drugs and bugs.

Anyhow, that is a part of it, and I send Don a card every
Christmas.

I couldn't tell whether they thought I was bluffing. They had
said I had a low violence index, which meant they had had access
to my personnel file or to Central. Which meant I had to try
keeping them off balance for the time I had remaining, there
on the Eve of RUMOKO. But my bedside alarm showed five
till six, and I went on duty at eight o'clock. If they knew as
much as they seemed to know, they probably had access to the
duty rosters also.

So here was the break I had spent the entire month seeking, right
in the palm of my hand on the Eve of RUMOKO's rumble. Only,
if they knew how much time I actually had in which to work them
over, they might—probably could—be able to hold out on me. I was
not about to leave them in my cabin all day; and the only alternative
was to turn them over to Ship's Security before I reported for duty. I
was loath to do this, as I did not know whether there were any others
aboard—whoever *they* were—or if they had anything more planned,

since the J-9 trouble had not come off as they had expected. Had it succeeded, it would surely have postponed the September 15 target date.

I had a fee to earn, which meant I had a package to deliver. The box was pretty empty, so far.

"Gentlemen," I said, my voice sounding strange to me and my reflexes seeming slow. I therefore attempted to restrict my movements as much as possible, and to speak slowly and carefully. "Gentlemen, you've had your turn. Now it is mine." I turned a chair backward and seated myself upon it, resting my gun hand on my forearm and my forearm on the back of the chair. "I will, however," I continued, "preface my actions with that which I have surmised concerning yourselves.

"You are *not* government agents," I said, glancing from one to the other. "No. You represent a private interest of some sort. If you are agents, you should doubtless have been able to ascertain that I am not one. You resorted to the extreme of questioning me in this fashion, however, so my guess is that you are civilians and perhaps somewhat desperate at this point. This leads me to link you with the attempted sabotage of the J-9 unit this previous afternoon.—Yes, let's call it sabotage. You know that it was, and you know that I know it—since I worked on the thing and it didn't come off as planned. This obviously prompted your actions of this evening. Therefore, I shan't even ask you the question.

"Next, and predicated upon my first assumption, I know that your credentials are genuine. I could fetch them from your pockets in a moment, if they are there, but your names would mean nothing to me. So I will not even go looking. There is really only one question that I want answered, and it probably won't even hurt your employer or employers, who will doubtless disavow any knowledge of you.

"I want to know who you represent," I said.

"Why?" asked the larger man, his frown revealing a lip-side scar which I had not noticed at his unmasking.

"I want to know who put you up to being so casual with my person," I said.

"To what end?"

I shrugged.

"Personal vengeance, perhaps."

He shook his head.

"You're working for somebody, too," he said. "If it is not the government, it is still somebody we wouldn't like."

"So you admit you are not independent operators. If you will not tell me who you work for, will you tell me why you want to stop the project?"

"No."

"All right. Drop that one.—I see you as associated with some large contractor who got cut out on something connected with this job. How does that sound? Maybe I can even make suggestions."

The other guy laughed, and the big one killed it with a quick glare.

"Well, that's out," I said. "Thanks. Now, let's consider another thing: I can simply turn you in for breaking and entering. I might even be willing to say you were drunk and indicated that you thought this cabin belonged to a friend of yours who didn't mind a little foolery and who you thought might stand you to a final round before you staggered off to bed. How does that sound?"

"*Is* this place bugged, or isn't it?" asked the shorter one, who seemed a bit younger than the other.

"Of course not," said his partner. "Just keep your mouth shut."

"Well, how does it sound?" I asked.

He shook his head again.

"Well, the alternative is my telling the whole story, drugs, questions, and all. How does *that* sound? How will you stand up under protracted questioning?"

The big one thought about it, shook his head again.

"*Will* you?" he finally asked me.

"Yes, I will."

He seemed to consider this.

". . . Then," I concluded, "I cannot save you the pain, as I wish to. Even if you possess drug-consciousness, you know that you will break within a couple of days if they use drugs as well as all the other tricks. It is simply a matter of talking now or talking later. Since you prefer to defer it, I can only assume that you have something else planned to stop RUMOKO—"

"He's too damned smart!"

"Tell him to shut up again," I said. "He's giving me my answers too fast and depriving me of my fun.—So what is it? Come on," I said. "I'll get it, one way or another, you know."

"He is right," said the man with the scar. "You *are* too damned smart. Your I.Q. and your Personality Profile show nothing like this. Would you be open to an offer?"

"Maybe," I said. "But it would have to be a big one. Give me the terms, and tell me who's offering."

"Terms: a quarter of a million dollars, cash," he said, "and that is the maximum I can offer. Turn us loose and go about your business. Forget about tonight."

I *did* think about it. Let's face it, it was tempting. But I go through a lot of money in a few years' time, and I hated to report failure to Walsh's Private Investigations, the third-largest detective agency in the world, with whom I wished to continue associating myself, as an independent contractor.

"So who foots the bill? How? And why?"

"I can get you half that amount tonight, in cash, and the other half in a week to ten days. You tell us how you want it, and that is the way it will be. 'Why?' though, do not ask that question. It will be one of the things we will be buying."

"Your boss obviously has a lot of money to throw around," I said, glancing at the clock and seeing that it was now six fifteen. "No, I must refuse your offer."

"Then you could not be a government man. One of them would take it, and then make an arrest."

"I already told you that. So what else is new?"

"We seem to have reached an impasse, Mister Schweitzer."

"Hardly," I replied. "We have simply reached the end of my preface. Since reasoning with you has failed, I must now take positive action. I apologize for this, but it is necessary."

"You are really going to resort to physical violence?"

"I'm afraid so," I said. "And don't worry. I expected a hangover this morning, so I signed for sick leave last night. I have all day. You already have a painful flesh wound, so I'll give *you* a break this time around."

Then I stood, cautiously, and the room swayed, but I did not let it show. I crossed to the smaller guy's chair and seized its arms and his together and raised them up from off the floor. Woozy, I was; but not weak.

I carried him off to the bathroom and set him, chair and all, in the shower stall, avoiding the while many forward thrustings of his head.

Then I returned to the other.

"Just to keep you abreast of what is going on," I said, "it all depends on the time of day. I have measured the temperature of the hot water in that stall at various times, and it can come out of there at anything from 140° to 180° Fahrenheit. Your buddy is about to get it, hot and full blast, as soon as I open his shirt and trousers and expose as much bare flesh as possible. You understand?"

"I understand."

I went back inside and opened him up and turned the shower on, using the hot water only. Then I went back to the main room. I studied the features of his buddy, who I then noted bore him something of a resemblance. It struck me that they might be relatives.

When the screaming began, he sought to compose his features. But I could see I was getting through to him. He tested his restraints once again, looked at my clock, looked at me.

"Turn it off, God damn you!" he cried.

"Your cousin?" I asked him.

"My half brother! Shut it down, you baboon!"

"Only if you've got something to say to me."

"Okay! But leave him in there and close the door!"

I dashed and did it. My head was beginning to clear, though I still felt like hell.

I burned my right hand shutting the thing down. I left my chosen victim slouched there in the steam, and I shut the door behind me as I returned to the main room.

"What do you have to say?"

"Could you give me one free hand and a cigarette?"

"No, but you can have a cigarette."

"How about the right one? I can hardly move it."

I considered, and said, "Okay," picking up my gun again.

I lit the stick, stuck it in his mouth, then cut the tape and tore it off his right forearm. He dropped the cigarette when I did it, and I picked it up and restored it to him.

"All right," I said, "take ten seconds and enjoy yourself. After that, we talk cases."

He nodded, looked around the room, took a deep drag, and exhaled.

"I guess you *do* know how to hurt," he said. "If you are not government, I guess your file is very much off."

"I am not government."

"Then I wish you were on our side, because it is a pretty bad thing. Whatever you are, or do," he stated, "I hope you are aware of the full implications."

. . . And he glanced at my clock, again.

Six twenty-five.

He had done it several times, and I had dismissed it. But now it seemed something more than a desire to know the time.

"When does it go off?" I asked, on chance.

Buying that, on chance, he replied, "Bring my brother back, where I can see him."

"When does it go off?" I repeated.

"Too soon," he replied, "and then it will not matter. You are too late."

"I don't think so," I said. "But now that I know, I'll have to move, fast. So . . . Don't lose any sleep over it. I think I am going to turn you in now."

"What if I could offer you more money?"

"Don't. You'd only embarrass me. And I'd still say, 'No.'"

"Okay. But bring him back, please—and take care of his burns." So I did.

"You guys will remain here for a brief while," I finally said, snuffing the older one's cigarette and retaping his wrist. Then I moved toward the door.

"You don't know, you really don't know!" I heard from behind me.

"Don't fool yourself," I said, over my shoulder.

I didn't know. I really didn't know.

But I could guess.

I stormed through the corridors until I reached Carol Deith's cabin. There I banged upon the door until I heard some muffled cursing and a "Wait a minute!" Then the door opened and she stared out at me, her eyes winking at the light, a slumber cap of sorts upon her head and a bulky robe about her.

"What do you want?" she asked me.

"Today is the day indeed," I said. "I've got to talk to you. May I come in?"

"No," she said. "I'm not accustomed to—"

"Sabotage," I said. "I know. That's what it's all about, and it isn't finished yet.—Please . . ."

"Come in." The door was suddenly wide open and she was standing to one side.

I entered.

She closed the door behind me, leaned back against it and said, "All right, what is it?"

There was a feeble light glowing, and a messed-up bed from which I had obviously aroused her.

"Look, maybe I didn't give you the whole story the other day," I told her. "Yes, it was sabotage—and there was a bomb, and I disposed of it. That's over and done with. Today is the big day, though, and the final attempt is in the offing. I know that for a fact. I think I know what it is and where it is. Can you help me? Can I help you? Help."

"Sit down," she said.

"There isn't much time."

"Sit down, please. I have to get dressed."

"Please hurry."

She stepped into the next room and left the door open. I was around the corner from it, though, so it should not have bothered her if she trusted me—and I guess she did, because she did.

"What is it?" she asked me, amidst the rustle of clothing.

"I believe that one or more of our three atomic charges has been booby-trapped, so that the bird will sing a bit prematurely within its cage."

"Why?" she said.

"Because there are two men back in my cabin, both of them taped to chairs, who tried to make me talk earlier this evening, with respect to my servicing of the J-9."

"What does that prove?"

"They were kind of rough on me."

"So?"

"When I got the upper hand, I got the same way with them. I made them talk."

"How?"

"None of your business. But they talked. I think RUMOKO's ignitors need another check."

"I can pick them up in your cabin?"

"Yes."

"How did you apprehend them?"

"They didn't know I had a gun."

"I see. Neither did I.—We'll get them, don't worry. But you are telling me that you took both of them and beat some answers out of them?"

"More or less," I said, "and yes and no, and off the record—in case this place is bugged. Is it?"

She came in, nodded her head and put a finger to her lips.

"Well, let's go do something," I said. "We'd better act quickly, I don't want these guys fouling the project all up."

"They won't. Okay. I'll give it to you that you know what you are doing. I will take you at face value as a strange creature. You did something which nobody expected of you. This does happen occasionally. We sometimes meet up with a guy who knows his job thoroughly and can see when something is going wrong—and who cares enough about it to proceed from there and damn the torpedoes. You say an atomic bomb will soon be going off aboard this ship. Right?"

"Yes."

"You think one of the charges has been attached, and has a timer cued in?"

"Right," and I looked at my wristwatch and saw that it was going on seven.

"I'd bet less than an hour from now."

"They're going down in a few minutes," she told me.

"What are you going to do about it?"

She picked up the telephone on the little table next to her bed.

"Operations," she said. "Stop the countdown." Then, "Give me the barracks. "Sergeant," she then said, "I want you to make some arrests." She looked at me. "What is your room number?" she asked.

"Six-forty," I replied.

"Six-forty," she said. "Two men.—Right.—Yes.—Thank you." And she hung up.

"They're taken care of," she told me. "So, you think a charge might go off prematurely?"

"That's what I said—twice."

"Could you stop it?"

"With the proper equipment—though I'd rather you send in a service—"

"Get it," she said to me.

"Okay," and I went and did that thing.

I came back to her cabin around five minutes later, with a heavy pack slung over my shoulder.

"I had to sign my name in blood," I told her. "But I've got what I need.—Why don't you get yourself a good physicist?"

"I want you," she said. "You were in from the beginning. You know what you're doing. Let's keep the group small and tight."

"Tell me where to go to do it," I said, and she led the way.

It was pushing seven by then.

It took me ten minutes to find out which one they had done it to.

It was child's play. They had used the motor from an advanced kid's erector set—with self-contained power unit. It was to be actuated by a standard clock-type timer, which would cause it to pull the lead shielding. The damned thing would go off while it was on the way down.

It took me less than ten minutes to disarm it.

We stood near the railing, and I leaned upon it.

"Good," I said.

"Very good," she said.

"While you're at it," she continued, "get on your guard. You are about to be the subject of the biggest security investigation I have ever set off."

"Go ahead. I'm pure as snow and swansdown."

"You aren't real," she told me. "They don't make people like that."

"So touch me," I said. "I am sorry if you don't like the way I go about existing."

"If you don't turn into a frog come midnight, a girl could learn to like a guy like you."

"That would require a very stupid girl," I said.

And she gave me a strange look which I did not really care to try interpreting.

Then she stared me straight in the eyes.

"You've got some kind of secret I do not quite understand yet." she said. "You seem like a leftover from the Old Days."

"Maybe I am. Look, you've already said that I've been of help. Why not leave it at that? I haven't done anything wrong."

"I've got a job to do. But, on the other hand, you're right. You have helped, and you haven't really broken any regs.—Except with reference to the J-9, for which I'm sure nobody is going to cause you trouble. On the opposite hand, I've got a report to write. Of necessity, your actions will figure in it prominently. I can't very well leave you out."

"I wasn't asking that," I said.

"What do you want me to do?"

Once it got into Central, I knew, I could kill it. But prior to that, it would be filtered through a mess of humans. They could cause trouble. "You kept the group small and tight," I said. "You could drop one."

"No."

"Okay. I could be a draftee, from the beginning."

"That's better."

"Then maybe we could let it be that way."

"I see no great problems."

"You'll do it?"

"I will see what I can do."

"That's enough. Thanks."

"What will you do when your job here is finished?"

"I don't know. Take a vacation, maybe."

"All alone?"

"Maybe."

"Look, I like you. I'll do things to keep you out of trouble."

"I'd appreciate that."

"You seem to have answers for everything."

"Thank you."

"What about a girl?"

"What do you mean?"

"Could you use one, in whatever you do?"

"I thought you had a pretty good job here."

"I do. That's not what I'm talking about.—Do you have one?"

"One what?"

"Stop playing the stupid role.—A girl, is what I mean."

"No."

"Well?"

"You're nuts," I said. "What the hell could I do with an Intelligence-type girl? Do you mean that you would actually take the chance of teaming up with a stranger?"

"I've watched you in action, and I'm not afraid of you. Yes, I would take the chance."

"This is the strangest proposal I've ever received."

"Think quick," she said.

"You don't know what you're asking," I told her.

"What if I like you—an awful lot?"

"Well, I disarmed your bomb. . . ."

"I'm not talking about being grateful.—But thanks, anyway.—The answer, I take it, is, 'No.'"

"Stop that! Can't you give a man a chance to think?"

"Okay," she said, and turned away.

"Wait. Don't be that way. You can't hurt me, so I can talk honestly. I *do* have a crush on you. I have been a confirmed bachelor for many years, though. You are a complication."

"Let's look at it this way," she told me. "You're different, I know that. I wish *I* could do different things."

"Like what?"

"Lie to computers and get away with it."

"What makes you say that?"

"It's the only answer, if you're real."

"I'm real."

"Then you know how to beat the system."

"I doubt it."

"Take me along," she said. "I'd like to do the same thing."

And I looked at her. A little wisp of hair was touching her cheek, and she looked as if she wanted to cry.

"I'm your last chance, aren't I? You met me at a strange moment in your life, and you want to gamble."

"Yes."

"You're nuts, and I can't promise you security unless you want to quit the game—and *I* can't. I play it by my own rules, though—and they're kind of strange. If you and I got together, you would probably be a young widow. —So you would have *that* going for you."

"You're tough enough to disarm bombs."

"I will meet an early grave. I do lots of stupid things when I have to."

"I think I might be in love with you."

"Then, for gods' sakes, let me talk to you later. I have lots of things to think about, now."

"All right."

"You're a dumb broad."

"I don't think so."

"Well, we'll see."

After I woke up from one of the deepest sleeps in my life, I went and signed for duty.

"You're late," said Morrey.

"So have them dock me."

I went then and watched the thing itself begin to occur.

RUMOKO was in the works.

They went down, Martin and Demmy, and planted the charge. They did the necessary things, and we got out of there. Everything was set, and waiting for our radio signal. My cabin had been emptied of intruders, and I was grateful.

We got far enough away, and the signal was given.

All was silent for a time. Then the bomb went off.

Over the port bow, I saw the man stand up. He was old and gray and wore a wide-brimmed hat. He stood, slouched, fell on his face.

"We've just polluted the atmosphere some more," said Martin.

"Hell," said Demmy.

The oceans rose and assailed us. The ship held anchor.

For a time, there was nothing. Then, it began.

The ship shook, like a wet dog. I clung to the rail and watched. Next came a mess of waves, and they were bastards, but we rode them out.

"We've got the first reading," said Carol. "It's beginning to build."

I nodded and did not say anything. There wasn't much to say.

"It's getting bigger," she said, after a minute, and I nodded again.

Finally, later on that morning, the whole thing that had come loose made its scene upon the surface.

The waters had been bubbling for a long while by then. The bubbles grew larger. The temperature readings rose. There came a glow.

Then there was one fantastic spout. It was blasted into the air to a great height, golden in the morning sunshine, like Zeus when he had visited one of his girlfriends or other. It was accompanied by a loud roar. It hung there for a few brief moments, then descended in a shower of sparks.

Immediately thereafter, there was greater turbulence.

It increased and I watched, the regular way and by means of the instruments.

The waters frothed and glistened. The roaring came and went. There came another spout, and another. The waters burned beneath the waves. Four more spouts, each larger than its predecessor. . . .

Then an ocean-riving blast caught the *Aquina* in something close to a tidal wave. . . .

We were ready, though—built that way—and faced into it.

We rode with it, and there was no letup.

We were miles away, and it seemed as if but an arm's distance separated us.

The next spout just kept going up, until it became a topless pillar. It pierced the sky, and a certain darkness began at that point. It began to swell, and there were fires all about its base.

After a time, the entire sky was fading over into a false twilight, and a fine dust filled the air, the eyes, the lungs. Occasionally, a crowd of ashes passed in the distance, like a covey of dark birds. I lit a cigarette to protect my lungs against pollution, and watched the fires rise.

With our early evening, the seas darkened. The kraken himself, disturbed, might have been licking our hull. The glow continued, and a dark form appeared.

RUMOKO.

It was the cone. An artificially created island. A piece of long-sunk Atlantis itself, perhaps, was rising in the distance. Man had succeeded in creating a landmass. One day it would be habitable. Now, if we made a chain of them . . .

Yes. Perhaps another Japan. More room for the expanding human race. More space. More places in which to live.

Why had I been questioned? Who had opposed this? It was a good thing, as I saw it.

I went away. I went and had dinner.

Carol came into the commissary and joined me, as if by accident. I nodded, and she seated herself across from me and ordered.

"Hi."

"Hi."

"Maybe you've done some of your thinking by now?" she said, between the salad and the ersatz beef.

"Yes," I replied.

"What are the results?"

"I still don't know. It was awfully quick and, frankly, I'd like the opportunity to get to know you a little better."

"Signifying what?"

"There is an ancient custom known as 'dating.' Let's do it for a little while."

"You don't like me? I've checked our compatibility indices. They show that we would be okay together—buying you at face value, that is—but I think I know more of you than that."

"Outside of the fact that I'm not for sale, what does that mean?"

"I've made lots of guesses and I think I could also get along with an individualist who knows how to play the right games with machines."

I knew that the commissary was bugged, and I guessed that she didn't know that I did. Therefore, she had a reason for saying what she had said—and she didn't think I knew about it.

"Sorry. Too quick," I told her. "Give a man a chance, will you?"

"Why don't we go someplace and discuss it?"

We were ready for dessert at that point.

"Where?"

"Spitzbergen."

I thought about it, then, "Okay," I said.

"I'll be ready in about an hour and a half."

"Whoa!" I said. "I thought you meant, like—perhaps this weekend. There are still tests to run, and I'm scheduled for duty."

"But your job here is finished, isn't it?"

I started in on my dessert—apple pie, and pretty good, too, with a chunk of cheddar—and I sipped coffee along with it. Over the rim of the cup, I cocked my head at her and shook it, slowly, from one side to the other.

"I can get you off duty for a day," she told me. "There will be no harm done."

"Sorry. I'm interested in the results of the tests. Let's make it this weekend."

She seemed to think about this for a while.

"All right," she said finally, and I nodded and continued with my dessert.

The "all right" instead of a "yes" or an "okay" or a "sure" must have been a key word of some sort. Or perhaps it was something else that she did or said. I don't know. I don't care any more.

When we left the commissary, she was slightly ahead of me—as I had opened the door for her—and a man moved in from either side.

She stopped and turned.

"Don't bother saying it," I said. "I wasn't quick enough, so I'm under arrest. Please don't recite my rights. I know what they are," and I raised my hands when I saw the steel in one man's hand. "Merry Christmas," I added.

But she recited my rights anyway, and I stared at her all the while. She didn't meet my eyes.

Hell, the whole proposition had been too good to be true. I didn't think she was very used to the role she had played, though—and I wondered, idly, whether she would have gone through with it, if circumstances dictated. She had been right about my job aboard the *Aquina* being ended, however. I would have to be moving along, and seeing that Albert Schweitzer died within the next twenty-four hours.

"You *are* going to Spitzbergen tonight," she said, "where there are better facilities for questioning you."

How was I going to manage it? Well—

As if reading my thoughts, she said, "Since you seem to be somewhat dangerous, I wish to advise you that your escorts are highly trained men."

"Then you won't be coming with me, after all?"

"I'm afraid not."

"Too bad. Then this is going to have to be 'Good-bye.' I'd like to have gotten to know you somewhat better."

"That meant nothing!" she said. "It was just to get you there."

"Maybe. But you will always wonder, and now you will never know."

"I am afraid we are going to have to handcuff you," said one of the men.

"Of course."

I held my hands out and he said, almost apologetically, "No, sir. Behind your back, please."

So I did, but I watched the men move in and I got a look at the cuffs. They were kind of old-fashioned. Government budgets generally produce such handy savings. If I bent over backward, I

could step over them, and then they would be in front of me. Give
me, say, twenty seconds . . .

"One thing," I asked. "Just for the sake of curiosity and because
I told it to you straight. Did you ever find out why those two guys
broke into my room to question me, and what they really wanted?
If you're allowed to tell me, I would like to know, because it made
for some rough sleeping."

She bit her lip, thought a moment, I guess, then said, "They
were from New Salem—a bubble city off the North American
continental shelf. They were afraid that RUMOKO would crack
their dome."

"Did it?" I asked.

She paused.

"We don't know yet," she said. "The place has been silent for a
while. We have tried to get through to them, but there seems to be
some interference."

"What do you mean by that?"

"We have not yet succeeded in reestablishing contact."

"You mean to say that we might have killed a city?"

"No. The chances were minimal, according to the scientists."

"*Your* scientists," I said. "Theirs must have felt differently about
it."

"Of course," she told me. "There are always obstructionists.
They sent saboteurs because they did not trust our scientists. The
inference—"

"I'm sorry," I said.

"For what?"

"That I put a guy into a shower.—Okay. Thanks. I can read all
about it in the papers. Send me to Spitzbergen now."

"Please," she said. "I do what I must. I think it's right. You may
be as clean as snow and swansdown. If that is the case, they will
know in a very short time, Al. Then—then I'd like you to bear in
mind that what I said before may still be good."

I chuckled.

"Sure, and I've already said, 'Good-bye.' Thanks for answering
my question, though."

"Don't hate me."

"I don't. But I could never trust you."

She turned away.

"Good night," I said.

And they escorted me to the helicopter. They helped me aboard.
There were just the two of them and the pilot.

"She liked you," said the man with the gun.

"No." I said.

"If she's right and you're clean, will you see her again?"

"I'll never see her again," I said.

He seated me, to the rear of the craft. Then he and his buddy took window seats and gave a signal.

The engines throbbed, and suddenly we rose.

In the distance, RUMOKO rumbled, burned, and spat.

Eva, I am sorry. I didn't know. I'd never guessed it might have done what it did.

"You're supposed to be dangerous," said the man on my right. "Please don't try anything."

Ave, atque, avatque, I said, in my heart of hearts, like.

Twenty-four hours, I told Schweitzer.

After I collected my money from Walsh, I returned to the *Proteus* and practiced meditation for a few days. Since it did not produce the desired results, I went up and got drunk with Bill Mellings. After all, I had used his equipment to kill Schweitzer. I didn't tell him anything, except for a made-up story about a *ni-hi* girl with large mammaries.

Then we went fishing, two weeks' worth.

I did not exist any longer. I had erased Albert Schweitzer from the world. I kept telling myself that I did not want to exist any longer.

If you have to murder a man—*have to*, I mean, like no choice in the matter—I feel that it should be a bloody and horrible thing, so that it burns itself into your soul and gives you a better appreciation of the value of human existence.

It had not been that way, however.

It had been quiet and viral. It was a thing to which I have immunized myself, but of which very few other persons have even heard. I had opened my ring and released the spores. That was all. I had never known the names of my escorts or the pilot. I had not even had a good look at their faces.

It had killed them within thirty seconds, and I had the cuffs off in less than the twenty seconds I'd guessed.

I crashed the 'copter on the beach, sprained my right wrist doing it, got the hell out of the vehicle, and started walking.

They'd look like myocardial infarcts or arteriosclerotic brain syndromes—depending on how it hit them.

Which meant I should lay low for a while. I value my own existence slightly more than that of anyone who wishes to disturb it. This does not mean that I didn't feel like hell, though.

Carol will suspect, I think, but Central only buys facts. And I saw that there was enough sea water in the plane to take care of the spores. No test known to man could prove that I had murdered them.

The body of Albert Schweitzer had doubtless been washed out to sea through the sprung door.

If I ever met with anybody who had known Al, so briefly, I'd be somebody else by then—with appropriate identification—and that person would be mistaken.

Very neat. But maybe I'm in the wrong line of work. I *still* feel like hell.

RUMOKO From All Those Fathoms fumed and grew like those Hollywood monsters that used to get blamed on science fiction. In a few months, it was predicted, its fires would desist. A layer of soil would then be imported, spread, and migrating birds would be encouraged to stop and rest, maybe nest, and to use the place as a lavatory. Mutant red mangroves would be rooted there, linking the sea and the land. Insects would even be brought aboard. One day, according to theory, it would be a habitable island. One other day, it would be one of a chain of habitable islands.

A double-pronged answer to the population problem, you might say: create a new place for men to live, and in doing so kill off a crowd of them living elsewhere.

Yes, the seismic shocks had cracked New Salem's dome. Many people had died.

And Project RUMOKO's *second* son is nevertheless scheduled for next summer.

The people in Baltimore II are worried, but the Congressional investigation showed that the fault lay with the constructors of New Salem, who should have provided against the vicissitudes. The courts held several of the contractors liable, and two of them went into receivership despite the connections that had gotten them the contracts in the first place.

It ain't pretty, and it's big, and I sort of wish I had never put that guy into the shower. He is all alive and well, I understand—a New Salem man—but I know that he will never be the same.

More precautions are supposed to be taken with the next one—whatever that means. I do not trust these precautions worth a damn. But then, I do not trust anything anymore.

If another bubble city goes, as yours did, Eva, I think it will slow things down. But I do not believe it will stop the RUMOKO Project. I think they will find another excuse then. I think they will try for a third one after that.

While it has been proved that we can create such things, I do not believe that the answer to our population problem lies in the manufacturing of new lands. No.

Offhand, I would say that since everything else is controlled these days, we might as well do it with the population, too. I will even get myself an identity—many identities, in fact—and vote for it, if it ever comes to a referendum. And I submit that there should be more bubble cities, and increased appropriations with respect to the exploration of outer space. But no more RUMOKO's. No.

Despite past reservations, I am taking on a free one. Walsh will never know. Hopefully, no one will. I am no altruist, but I guess I owe something to the race that I leech off of. After all, I was once a member. . . .

Taking advantage of my nonexistence, I am going to sabotage that bastard so well that it will be the last.

How?

I will see that it is a Krakatoa, at least. As a result of the last one, Central knows a lot more about magma—and as a result of this, so do I.

I will manipulate the charge, probably even make it a multiple. When that baby goes off, I will have arranged for it to be the worst seismic disturbance in the memory of man. It should not be too difficult to do.

I could possibly murder thousands of people by this action—and certainly I will kill some. However, RUMOKO in its shattering of New Salem scared the hell out of so many folks that I think RUMOKO II will scare even more. I am hoping that there will be a lot of topside vacations about that time. Add to this the fact that I know how rumors get started, and I can do it myself. I will.

I am at least going to clear the decks as much as I can.

They will get results, all right—the planners—like a Mount Everest in the middle of the Atlantic and some fractured domes. Laugh that off, and you are a good man.

I baited the line and threw it overboard. Bill took a drink of orange juice and I took a drag on my cigarette.

"You're a consulting engineer these days?" he asked.

"Yeah."

"What are you up to now?"

"I've got a job in mind. Kind of tricky."

"Will you take it?"

"Yes."

"I sometimes wish I had something going for me now—the way you do."

"Don't. It's not worth it."

I looked out over the dark waters, able to bear prodigies. The morning sun was just licking the waves, and my decision was, like, solid. The wind was chilly and pleasant. The sky was going to be beautiful. I could tell from the breaks in the cloud cover.

"It sounds interesting. This is demolition work, you say?"

And I, Judas Iscariot, turned a glance his way and said, "Pass me the bait can, please. I think I've got something on the line."

"Me, too. Wait a minute."

The day, like a mess of silver dollars, fell upon the deck.

I landed mine and hit it on the back of the head with the stick, to be merciful.

I kept telling myself that I did not exist. I hope it is true, even though I feel that it is not. I seem to see old Colgate's face beneath an occasional whitecap.

Eva, Eva . . .

Forgive me, my Eva. I would welcome your hand on my brow.

It is pretty, the silver. The waves are blue and green this morning, and God! how lovely the light!

"Here's the bait."

"Thanks."

I took it and we drifted.

Eventually, everybody dies, I noted. But it did not make me feel any better.

But nothing, really, could.

The next card will be for Christmas, as usual, Don, one year late this time around.

Never ask me why.

THE NIGHT OF THE TROLLS

Keith Laumer

It was different this time. There was a dry pain in my lungs, and a deep ache in my bones, and a fire in my stomach that made me want to curl into a ball and mew like a kitten. My mouth tasted as though mice had nested in it, and when I took a deep breath wooden knives twisted in my chest.

I made a mental note to tell Mackenzie a few things about his pet controlled-environment tank—just as soon as I got out of it. I squinted at the overface panel: air pressure, temperature, humidity, O-level, blood sugar, pulse, and respiration—all okay. That was something. I flipped the intercom key and said, "Okay, Mackenzie, let's have the story. You've got problems . . ."

I had to stop to cough. The exertion made my temples pound.

"How long have you birds run this damned exercise?" I called. "I feel lousy. What's going on around here?"

No answer.

This was supposed to be the terminal test series. They couldn't all be out having coffee. The equipment had more bugs than a two-dollar hotel room. I slapped the emergency release lever. Mackenzie wouldn't like it, but to hell with it! From the way I felt, I'd been in the tank for a good long stretch this time—maybe a week or two. And I'd told Ginny it would be a three-dayer at the most. Mackenzie was a great technician, but he had no more human emotions than a used-car salesman. This time I'd tell him.

Relays were clicking, equipment was reacting, the tank cover sliding back. I sat up and swung my legs aside, shivering suddenly.

It was cold in the test chamber. I looked around at the dull gray walls, the data recording cabinets, the wooden desk where Mac sat by the hour rerunning test profiles—

That was funny. The tape reels were empty and the red equipment light was off. I stood, feeling dizzy. Where was Mac? Where were Bonner and Day and Mallon?

"Hey!" I called. I didn't even get a good echo.

Someone must have pushed the button to start my recovery cycle; where were they hiding now? I took a step, tripped over the cables trailing behind me. I unstrapped and pulled the harness off. The effort left me breathing hard. I opened one of the wall lockers; Banner's pressure suit hung limply from the rack beside a rag-festooned coat hanger. I looked in three more lockers. My clothes were missing—even my bathrobe. I also missed the usual bowl of hot soup, the happy faces of the techs, even Mac's sour puss. It was cold and silent and empty here—more like a morgue than a top-priority research center.

I didn't like it. What the hell was going on?

There was a weather suit in the last locker. I put it on, set the temperature control, palmed the door open, and stepped out into the corridor. There were no lights, except for the dim glow of the emergency route indicators. There was a faint, foul odor in the air.

I heard a dry scuttling, saw a flick of movement. A rat the size of a red squirrel sat up on his haunches and looked at me as if I were something to eat. I made a kicking motion and he ran off, but not very far.

My heart was starting to thump a little harder now. The way it does when you begin to realize that something's wrong—bad wrong.

Upstairs in the Admin Section I called again. The echo was a little better here. I went along the corridor strewn with papers, past the open doors of silent rooms. In the Director's office a blackened wastebasket stood in the center of the rug. The air-conditioner intake above the desk was felted over with matted dust nearly an inch thick. There was no use shouting again.

The place was as empty as a robbed grave—except for the rats.

At the end of the corridor, the inner security door stood open. I went through it and stumbled over something. In the faint light, it took me a moment to realize what it was.

He had been an MP, in steel helmet and boots. There was nothing left but crumbled bone and a few scraps of leather and metal. A .38 revolver lay nearby. I picked it up, checked the cylinder, and tucked ed it in the thigh pocket of the weather suit. For some reason it made me feel a little better.

I went on along B corridor and found the lift door sealed. The emergency stairs were nearby. I went to them and started the two-hundred-foot climb to the surface.

The heavy steel doors at the tunnel had been blown clear.

I stepped past the charred opening, looked out at a low gray sky burning red in the west. Fifty yards away, the five-thousand-gallon water tank lay in a tangle of rusty steel. What had it been? Sabotage, war, revolution—an accident? And where was everybody?

I rested for a while, then went across the innocent-looking fields to the west, dotted with the dummy buildings that were supposed to make the site look from the air like another stretch of farmland complete with barns, sheds and fences. Beyond the site the town seemed intact: there were lights twinkling here and there, a few smudges of smoke rising. I climbed a heap of rubble for a better view.

Whatever had happened at the site, at least Ginny would be all right—Ginny and Tim. Ginny would be worried sick, after—how long? A month?

Maybe more. There hadn't been much left of that soldier . . .

I twisted to get a view to the south, and felt a hollow sensation in my chest. Four silo doors stood open; the Colossus missiles had hit back—at something. I pulled myself up a foot or two higher for a look at the Primary Site. In the twilight the ground rolled smooth and unbroken across the spot where *Prometheus* lay ready in her underground berth. Down below she'd be safe and sound, maybe. She had been built to stand up to the stresses of a direct extra-solar orbital launch; with any luck, a few near misses wouldn't have damaged her.

My arms were aching from the strain of holding on. I climbed down and sat on the ground to get my breath, watching the cold wind worry the dry stalks of dead brush around the fallen tank.

At home, Ginny would be alone, scared, maybe even in serious difficulty. There was no telling how far municipal services had broken down. But before I headed that way, I had to make a quick check on the ship. *Prometheus* was a dream that I—and a lot of others—had lived with for three years. I had to be sure.

I headed toward the pillbox that housed the tunnel head on the off chance that the car might be there.

It was almost dark and the going was tough; the concrete slabs under the sod were tilted and dislocated. Something had sent a ripple across the ground like a stone tossed into a pond.

I heard a sound and stopped dead. There was a clank and rumble from beyond the discolored walls of the blockhouse a hundred yards away. Rusted metal howled; then something as big as a beached freighter moved into view.

Two dull red beams glowing near the top of the high silhouette swung, flashed crimson, and held on me. A siren went off—an ear-splitting whoop! *whoop!* WHOOP!

It was an unmanned Bolo Mark II Combat Unit on automated sentry duty—and its intruder-sensing circuits were tracking me.

The Bolo pivoted heavily; the *whoop! whoop!* sounded again; the robot watchdog was bellowing the alarm.

I felt sweat pop out on my forehead. Standing up to a Mark II Bolo without an electropass was the rough equivalent of being penned in with an ill-tempered dinosaur. I looked toward the Primary blockhouse: too far. The same went for the perimeter fence. My best bet was back to the tunnel mouth. I turned to sprint for it, hooked a foot on a slab and went down hard . . .

I got up, my head ringing, tasting blood in my mouth. The chipped pavement seemed to rock under me. The Bolo was coming up fast. Running was no good. I had to have a better idea.

I dropped flat and switched my suit control to maximum insulation.

The silvery surface faded to dull black. A two-foot square of tattered paper fluttered against a projecting edge of concrete; I reached for it, peeled it free, then fumbled with a pocket flap, brought out a permatch, flicked it alight. When the paper was burning well, I tossed it clear. It whirled away a few feet, then caught in a clump of grass.

"Keep moving, damn you!" I whispered. The swearing worked. The gusty wind pushed the paper on. I crawled a few feet and pressed myself into a shallow depression behind the slab. The Bolo churned closer; a loose treadplate was slapping the earth with a rhythmic thud. The burning paper was fifty feet away now, a twinkle of orange light in the deep twilight.

At twenty yards, looming up like a pagoda, the Bolo halted, sat rumbling and swiveling its rust-streaked turret, looking for the radiating source its I-R had first picked up. The flare of the paper caught its electronic attention. The turret swung, then back. It was puzzled. It whooped again, then reached a decision.

Ports snapped open. A volley of antipersonnel slugs whoofed into the target; the scrap of paper disappeared in a gout of tossed dirt.

I hugged the ground like gold lamé hugs a torch singer's hip, and waited; nothing happened. The Bolo sat, rumbling softly to itself. Then I heard another sound over the murmur of the idling engine, a distant roaring, like a flight of low-level bombers. I raised my head half an inch and took a look. There were lights moving beyond the field—the paired beams of a convoy approaching from the town.

The Bolo stirred, moved heavily forward until it towered over me no more than twenty feet away. I saw gun ports open high on the armored facade—the ones that housed the heavy infinite repeaters. Slim black muzzles slid into view, hunted for an instant, then depressed and locked.

They were bearing on the oncoming vehicles that were spreading out now in a loose skirmish line under a roiling layer of dust. The watchdog was getting ready to defend its territory—and I was caught in the middle. A blue-white floodlight lanced out from across the field, glared against the scaled plating of the Bolo. I heard relays click inside the monster fighting machine, and braced myself for the thunder of her battery . . .

There was a dry rattle.

The guns traversed, clattering emptily. Beyond the fence the floodlight played for a moment longer against the Bolo, then moved on across the ramp, back, across and back, searching . . .

Once more the Bolo fired its empty guns. Its red I-R beams swept the scene again; then relays snicked, the impotent guns retracted, the port covers closed.

Satisfied, the Bolo heaved itself around and moved off, trailing a stink of ozone and ether, the broken tread thumping like a cripple on a stair.

I waited until it disappeared in the gloom two hundred yards away, then cautiously turned my suit control to vent off the heat. Full insulation could boil a man in his own gravy in less than half an hour.

The floodlight had blinked off now. I got to my hands and knees and started toward the perimeter fence. The Bolo's circuits weren't tuned as fine as they should have been; it let me go.

There were men moving in the glare and dust, beyond the rusty lacework that had once been a chain-link fence. They carried guns and stood in tight little groups, staring across toward the block-house.

I moved closer, keeping flat and avoiding the avenues of yellowish light thrown by the headlamps of the parked vehicles—halftracks, armored cars, a few light manned tanks.

There was nothing about the look of this crowd that impelled me to leap up and be welcomed. They wore green uniforms, and half of them sported beards. What the hell: had Castro landed in force?

I angled off to the right, away from the big main gate that had been manned day and night by guards with tommyguns. It hung now by one hinge from a scarred concrete post, under a cluster of dead polyarcs in corroded brackets. The big sign that had read GLENN AEROSPACE CENTER—AUTHORIZED PERSONNEL ONLY lay face down in hip-high underbrush.

More cars were coming up. There was a lot of talk and shouting; a squad of men formed and headed my way, keeping to the outside of the fallen fence.

I was outside the glare of the lights now. I chanced a run for it, got over the sagged wire and across a potholed blacktop road before they reached me. I crouched in the ditch and watched as the detail dropped men in pairs at fifty-yard intervals.

Another five minutes and they would have intercepted me—along with whatever else they were after. I worked my way back across an empty lot and found a strip of lesser underbrush lined with shaggy trees, beneath which a patch of cracked sidewalk showed here and there.

Several things were beginning to be a little clearer now: The person who had pushed the button to bring me out of stasis hadn't been around to greet me, because no one pushed it. The automatics, triggered by some malfunction, had initiated the recovery cycle.

The system's self-contained power unit had been designed to maintain a starship crewman's minimal vital functions indefinitely, at reduced body temperature and metabolic rate. There was no way to tell exactly how long I had been in the tank. From the condition of the fence and the roads, it had been more than a matter of weeks—or even months.

Had it been a year . . . or more? I thought of Ginny and the boy, waiting at home—thinking the old man was dead, probably. I'd neglected them before for my work, but not like this . . .

Our house was six miles from the base, in the foothills on the other side of town. It was a long walk, the way I felt—but I had to get there.

2

Two hours later I was clear of the town, following the river bank west.

I kept having the idea that someone was following me. But when I stopped to listen, there was never anything there; just the still, cold night and the frogs, singing away patiently in the low ground to the south.

When the ground began to rise, I left the road and struck off across the open field. I reached a wide street, followed it in a curve that would bring me out at the foot of Ridge Avenue—my street. I could make out the shapes of low, rambling houses now.

It had been the kind of residential section the local Junior Chamber members had hoped to move into some day. Now the starlight that filtered through the cloud cover showed me broken windows, doors that sagged open, automobiles that squatted on flat, dead tires under collapsing car shelters—and here and there a blackened, weed-grown foundation, like a gap in a row of rotting teeth.

The neighborhood wasn't what it had been. How long had I been away? How long . . .?

I fell down again, hard this time. It wasn't easy getting up. I seemed to weigh a hell of a lot for a guy who hadn't been eating regularly. My breathing was very fast and shallow now, and my skull was getting ready to split and give birth to a live alligator—the ill-tempered kind. It was only a few hundred yards more; but why the hell had I picked a place halfway up a hill?

I heard the sound again—a crackle of dry grass. I got the pistol out and stood flatfooted in the middle of the street, listening hard.

All I heard was my stomach growling. I took the pistol off cock and started off again, stopped suddenly a couple of times to catch him off guard; nothing. I reached the corner of Ridge Avenue, started up the slope. Behind me a stick popped loudly.

I picked that moment to fall down again. Heaped leaves saved me from another skinned knee. I rolled over against a low fieldstone wall and propped myself against it. I had to use both hands to cock the pistol. I stared into the dark, but all I could see were the little lights whirling again. The pistol got heavy; I put it down, concentrated on taking deep breaths and blinking away the fireflies.

I heard footsteps plainly, close by. I shook my head, accidentally banged it against the stone behind me. That helped. I saw him, not over twenty feet away, coming up the hill toward me, a black-haired man with a full beard, dressed in odds and ends of rags and furs, gripping a polished club with a leather thong.

I reached for the pistol, found only leaves, tried again, touched the gun and knocked it away. I was still groping when I heard a scuffle of feet. I swung around, saw a tall, wide figure with a mane of untrimmed hair.

He hit the bearded man like a pro tackle taking out the practice dummy. They went down together hard and rolled over in a flurry of dry leaves. The cats were fighting over the mouse; that was my signal to leave quietly.

I made one last grab for the gun, found it, got to my feet and staggered off up the grade that seemed as steep now as penthouse rent. And from down slope, I heard an engine gunned, the clash of a heavy transmission that needed adjustment. A spotlight flickered, made shadows dance.

I recognized a fancy wrought-iron fence fronting a vacant lot; that had been the Adams house. Only half a block to go—but I was losing my grip fast. I went down twice more, then gave up and started crawling. The lights were all around now, brighter than ever. My head split open, dropped off, and rolled downhill.

A few more yards and I could let it all go. Ginny would put me in a warm bed, patch up my scratches, and feed me soup. Ginny would . . . Ginny . . .

I was lying with my mouth full of dead leaves. I heard running feet, yells. An engine idled noisily down the block.

I got my head up and found myself looking at chipped brickwork and the heavy brass hinges from which my front gate had hung. The gate was gone and there was a large chunk of brick missing. Some delivery truck had missed his approach.

I got to my feet, took a couple of steps into deep shadow with feet that felt as though they'd been amputated and welded back on at the ankle. I stumbled, fetched up against something scaled over with rust. I held on, blinked and made out the seeping flank of my brand new '79 Pontiac. There was a crumbled crust of whitish glass lining the brightwork strip that had framed the rear window.

A fire . . .?

A footstep sounded behind me, and I suddenly remembered several things, none of them pleasant. I felt for my gun; it was gone. I moved back along the side of the car, tried to hold on.

No use. My arms were like unsuccessful pie crust. I slid down among dead leaves, sat listening to the steps coming closer. They stopped, and through a dense fog that had sprung up suddenly

I caught a glimpse of a tall white-haired figure standing over me.

Then the fog closed in and swept everything away.

I lay on my back this time, looking across at the smoky yellow light of a thick brown candle guttering in the draft from a glassless window. In the center of the room a few sticks of damp-looking wood heaped on the cracked asphalt tiles burned with a grayish flame. A thin curl of acrid smoke rose up to stir cobwebs festooned under ceiling beams from which wood veneer had peeled away. Light alloy trusswork showed beneath.

It was a strange scene, but not so strange that I didn't recognize it: it was my own living room—looking a little different than when I had seen it last. The odors were different, too; I picked out mildew, badly cured leather, damp wool, tobacco . . .

I turned my head. A yard from the rags I lay on, the white-haired man, looking older than pharaoh, sat sleeping with his back against the wall.

The shotgun was gripped in one big, gnarled hand. His head was tilted back, blue-veined eyelids shut. I sat up, and at my movement his eyes opened.

He lay relaxed for a moment, as though life had to return from some place far away. Then he raised his head. His face was hollow and lined. His white hair was thin. A coarse-woven shirt hung loose across wide shoulders that had been Herculean once. But now Hercules was old, old. He looked at me expectantly.

"Who are you?" I said. "Why did you follow me? What happened to the house? Where's my family? Who owns the bully-boys in green?" My jaw hurt when I spoke. I put my hand up and felt it gingerly.

"You fell," the old man said, in a voice that rumbled like a subterranean volcano.

"The understatement of the year, pop." I tried to get up. Nausea knotted my stomach.

"You have to rest," the old man said, looking concerned. "Before the Baron's men come . . ." He paused, looking at me as though he expected me to say something profound.

"I want to know where the people are that live here!" My yell came out as weak as church-social punch. "A woman and a boy . . ."

He was shaking his head. "You have to do something quick. The soldiers will come back, search every house—"

I sat up, ignoring the little men driving spikes into my skull. "I don't give a damn about soldiers! Where's my family? What's

happened?" I reached out and gripped his arm. "How long was I
down there? What year is this?"

He only shook his head. "Come eat some food. Then I can help
you with your plan."

It was no use talking to the old man; he was senile.

I got off the cot. Except for the dizziness and a feeling that my
knees were made of papier-mâché, I was all right. I picked up the
hand-formed candle, stumbled into the hall.

It was a jumble of rubbish. I climbed through, pushed open the
door to my study. There was my desk, the tall bookcase with the
glass doors, the gray rug, the easy chair. Aside from a layer of dust
and some peeling wallpaper, it looked normal. I flipped the switch.
Nothing happened.

"What is that charm?" the old man said behind me. He pointed
to the light switch.

"The power's off," I said. "Just habit."

He reached out and flipped the switch up, then down again. "It
makes a pleasing sound."

"Yeah." I picked up a book from the desk; it fell apart in my
hands.

I went back into the hall, tried the bedroom door, looked in at
heaped leaves, the remains of broken furniture, an empty window
frame. I went on to the end of the hall and opened the door to the
bedroom.

Cold night wind blew through a barricade of broken timbers. The
roof had fallen in, and a sixteen-inch tree trunk slanted through the
wreckage. The old man stood behind me, watching.

"Where is she, damn you?" I leaned against the door frame to
swear and fight off the faintness. "Where's my wife?"

The old man looked troubled. "Come, eat now . . ."

"Where is she? Where's the woman who lived here?"

He frowned, shook his head dumbly. I picked my way through
the wreckage, stepped out into knee-high brush. A gust blew my
candle out. In the dark I stared at my back yard, the crumbled
pit that had been the barbecue grill, the tangled thickets that had
been rose beds—and a weathered length of boards upended in the
earth.

"What the hell's this . . .?" I fumbled out a permatch, lit my
candle, leaned close, and read the crude letters cut into the
crumbling wood: VIRGINIA ANNE JACKSON. BORN JAN.
8 1957. KILL BY THE DOGS WINTER 1992.

3

The Baron's men came twice in the next three days. Each time the old man carried me, swearing but too weak to argue, out to a lean-to of branches and canvas in the woods behind the house. Then he disappeared, to come back an hour or two later and haul me back to my rag bed by the fire.

Three times a day he gave me a tin pan of stew, and I ate it mechanically. My mind went over and over the picture of Ginny, living on for twelve years in the slowly decaying house, and then—

It was too much. There are some shocks the mind refuses.

I thought of the tree that had fallen and crushed the east wing. An elm that size was at least fifty to sixty years old—maybe older. And the only elm on the place had been a two-year sapling. I knew it well; I had planted it.

The date carved on the headboard was 1992. As nearly as I could judge another thirty-five years had passed since then at least. My shipmates—Banner, Day, Mallon—they were all dead, long ago. How had they died? The old man was too far gone to tell me anything useful. Most of my questions produced a shake of the head and a few rumbled words about charms, demons, spells, and the Baron.

"I don't believe in spells," I said. "And I'm not too sure I believe in this Baron. Who is he?"

"The Baron Trollmaster of Filly. He holds all this country—" the old man made a sweeping gesture with his arm—"all the way to Jersey."

"Why was he looking for me? What makes me important?"

"You came from the Forbidden Place. Everyone heard the cries of the Lesser Troll that stands guard over the treasure there. If the Baron can learn your secrets of power—"

"Troll, hell! That's nothing but a Bolo on automatic!"

"By any name every man dreads the monster. A man who walks in its shadow has much *mana*. But the others—the ones that run in a pack like dogs—would tear you to pieces for a demon if they could lay hands on you."

"You saw me back there. Why didn't you give me away? And why are you taking care of me now?"

He shook his head—the all-purpose answer to any question.

I tried another tack: "Who was the rag man you tackled just outside? Why was he laying for me?"

The old man snorted. "Tonight the dogs will eat him. But forget that. Now we have to talk about your plan—"

"I've got about as many plans as the senior boarder in death row. I don't know if you know it, old timer, but somebody slid the world out from under me while I wasn't looking."

The old man frowned. I had the thought that I wouldn't like to have him mad at me, for all his white hair . . .

He shook his head. "You must understand what I tell you. The soldiers of the Baron will find you someday. If you are to break the spell—"

"Break the spell, eh?" I snorted. "I think I get the idea, pop. You've got it in your head that I'm valuable property of some kind. You figure I can use my supernatural powers to take over this menagerie—and you'll be in on the ground floor. Well, listen, you old idiot! I spent sixty years—maybe more—in a stasis tank two hundred feet underground. My world died while I was down there. This Baron of yours seems to own everything now. If you think I'm going to get myself shot bucking him, forget it!"

The old man didn't say anything.

"Things don't seem to be broken up much," I went on. "It must have been gas, or germ warfare—or fallout. Damn few people around. You're still able to live on what you can loot from stores; automobiles are still sitting where they were the day the world ended. How old were you when it happened, pop? The war, I mean. Do you remember it?"

He shook his head. "The world has always been as it is now."

"What year were you born?"

He scratched at his white hair. "I knew the number once. But I've forgotten."

"I guess the only way I'll find out how long I was gone is to saw that damned elm in two and count the rings—but even that wouldn't help much; I don't know when it blew over. Never mind. The important thing now is to talk to this Baron of yours. Where does he stay?"

The old man shook his head violently. "If the Baron lays his hands on you, he'll wring the secrets from you on the rack! I know his ways. For five years I was a slave in the palace stables."

"If you think I'm going to spend the rest of my days in this rat nest, you get another guess on the house! This Baron has tanks, an army. He's kept a little technology alive. That's the outfit for me—not this garbage detail! Now, where's this place of his located?"

"The guards will shoot you on sight like a pack-dog!"

"There has to be a way to get to him, old man! Think!"

The old head was shaking again. "He fears assassination. You can never approach him . . ." He brightened. "Unless you know a spell of power?"

I chewed my lip. "Maybe I do at that. You wanted me to have a plan. I think I feel one coming on. Have you got a map?"

He pointed to the desk beside me. I tried the drawers, found mice, roaches, moldy money—and a stack of folded maps. I opened one carefully; faded ink on yellowed paper falling apart at the creases. The legend in the corner read: "PENNSYLVANIA 40M:1. Copyright 1970 by ESSO Corporation."

"This will do, pop," I said. "Now, tell me all you can about this Baron of yours."

"You'll destroy him?"

"I haven't even met the man."

"He is evil."

"I don't know; he owns an army. That makes up for a lot . . ."

After three more days of rest and the old man's stew I was back to normal—or near enough. I had the old man boil me a tub of water for a bath and a shave. I found a serviceable pair of synthetic-fiber long-johns in a chest of drawers, pulled them on and zipped the weather suit over them, then buckled on the holster I had made from a tough plastic.

"That completes my preparations, pop," I said. "It'll be dark in another half hour. Thanks for everything."

He got to his feet, a worried look on his lined face, like a father the first time Junior asks for the car.

"The Baron's men are everywhere."

"If you want to help, come along and back me up with that shotgun of yours." I picked it up. "Have you got any shells for this thing?"

He smiled, pleased now. "There are shells—but the magic is gone from many."

"That's the way magic is, pop. It goes out of things before you notice."

"Will you destroy the Great Troll now?"

"My motto is let sleeping trolls lie. I'm just paying a social call on the Baron."

The joy ran out of his face like booze from a dropped jug.

"Don't take it so hard, old timer. I'm not the fairy prince you were expecting. But I'll take care of you—if I make it."

I waited while he pulled on a moth-eaten mackinaw. He took the shotgun and checked the breech, then looked at me.

"I'm ready," he said.

"Yeah," I said. "Let's go . . ."

The Baronial palace was a forty-story slab of concrete and glass that had been known in my days as the Hilton Garden East. We made it in three hours of groping across country in the dark, at the end of which I was puffing but still on my feet. We moved out from the cover of the trees and looked across a dip in the ground at the lights, incongruously cheerful in the ravaged valley.

"The gates are there—" the old man pointed—"guarded by the Great Troll."

"Wait a minute. I thought the Troll was the Bolo back at the Site."

"That's the Lesser Troll. This is the Great One."

I selected a few choice words and muttered them to myself. "It would have saved us some effort if you'd mentioned this troll a little sooner, old timer. I'm afraid I don't have any spells that will knock out a Mark II, once it's got its dander up."

He shook his head. "It lies under enchantment. I remember the day when it came, throwing thunder-bolts. Many men were killed. Then the Baron commanded it to stand at his gates to guard him."

"How long ago was this, old timer?"

He worked his lips over the question. "Long ago," he said finally. "Many winters."

"Let's go take a look."

We picked our way down the slope, came up along a rutted dirt road to the dark line of trees that rimmed the palace grounds. The old man touched my arm.

"Softly here. Maybe the Troll sleeps lightly . . ."

I went the last few yards, eased around a brick column with a dead lantern on top, stared across fifty yards of waist-high brush at a dark silhouette outlined against the palace lights.

Cables, stretched from trees outside the circle of weeds, supported a weathered tarp which drooped over the Bolo. The wreckage of a helicopter lay like a crumpled dragonfly at the far side of the ring. Nearer, fragments of a heavy car chassis lay scattered. The old man hovered at my shoulder.

"It looks as though the gate is off limits," I hissed. "Let's try farther along."

He nodded. "No one passes here. There is a second gate, there." He pointed. "But there are guards."

"Let's climb the wall between gates."

"There are sharp spikes on top of the wall. But I know a place, farther on, where the spikes have been blunted."

"Lead on, pop."

Half an hour of creeping through wet brush brought us to the spot we were looking for. It looked to me like any other stretch of eight-foot masonry wall overhung with wet poplar trees.

"I'll go first," the old man said, "to draw the attention of the guard."

"Then who's going to boost me up? I'll go first."

He nodded, cupped his hands and lifted me as easily as a sailor lifting a beer glass. Pop was old—but he was nobody's softie.

I looked around, then crawled up, worked my way over the corroded spikes, dropped down on the lawn.

Immediately I heard a crackle of brush. A man stood up not ten feet away. I lay flat in the dark trying to look like something that had been there a long time . . .

I heard another sound, a thump and a crashing of brush. The man before me turned, disappeared in the darkness. I heard him beating his way through shrubbery; then he called out, got an answering shout from the distance.

I didn't loiter. I got to my feet and made a sprint for the cover of the trees along the drive.

4

Flat on the wet ground, under the wind-whipped branches of an ornamental cedar, I blinked the fine misty rain from my eyes, waiting for the halfhearted alarm behind me to die down.

There were a few shouts, some sounds of searching among the shrubbery. It was a bad night to be chasing imaginary intruders in the Baronial grounds. In five minutes all was quiet again.

I studied the view before me. The tree under which I lay was one of a row lining a drive. It swung in a graceful curve, across a smooth half-mile of dark lawn, to the tower of light that was the palace of the Baron of Filly. The silhouetted figures of guards and late-arriving guests moved against the gleam from the collonaded entrance. On a terrace high above, dancers twirled under colored lights. The faint glow of the repellor field kept the cold rain at a distance. In a lull in the wind, I heard music, faintly. The Baron's weekly grand ball was in full swing.

I saw shadows move across the wet gravel before me, then heard the purr of an engine. I hugged the ground and watched a long svelte Mercedes—about an '88 model, I estimated—barrel past.

The mob in the city ran in packs like dogs, but the Baron's friends did a little better for themselves.

I got to my feet and moved off toward the palace, keeping well in the shadows. When the drive swung to the right to curve across in front of the building, I left it, went to hands and knees, and followed a trimmed privet hedge past dark rectangles of formal garden to the edge of a secondary pond of light from the garages. I let myself down on my belly and watched the shadows that moved on the graveled drive.

There seemed to be two men on duty—no more. Waiting around wouldn't improve my chances. I got to my feet, stepped out into the drive, and walked openly around the corner of the gray fieldstone building into the light.

A short, thickset man in greasy Baronial green looked at me incuriously. My weather suit looked enough like ordinary coveralls to get me by—at least for a few minutes. A second man, titled back against the wall in a wooden chair, didn't even turn his head.

"Hey!" I called. "You birds got a three-ton jack I can borrow?"

Shorty looked me over sourly. "Who you drive for, Mac?"

"The High Duke of Jersey. Flat. Left rear. On a night like this. Some luck."

"The Jersey can't afford a jack?"

I stepped over to the short man, prodded him with a forefinger. "He could buy you and gut you on the altar any Saturday night of the week, low-pockets. And he'd get a kick out of doing it. He's like that."

"Can't a guy crack a harmless joke without somebody talks about altar-bait? You wanna jack, take a jack."

The man in the chair opened one eye and looked me over. "How long you on the Jersey payroll?" he growled.

"Long enough to know who handles the rank between Jersey and Filly." I yawned, looked around the wide, cement-floored garage, glanced over the four heavy cars with the Filly crest on their sides.

"Where's the kitchen? I'm putting a couple of hot coffees under my belt before I go back out into that."

"Over there. A flight up and to your left. Tell the cook Pintsy invited you."

"I tell him Jersey sent me, low-pockets." I moved off in a dead silence, opened the door and stepped up into spicy-scented warmth.

A deep carpet—even here—muffled my footsteps. I could hear the clash of pots and crockery from the kitchen a hundred feet distant along the hallway. I went along to a deep-set doorway ten feet from the kitchen, tried the knob, and looked into a dark room. I pushed the door shut and leaned against it, watching the kitchen. Through the woodwork I could feel the thump of the bass notes from the orchestra blasting away three flights up. The odors of food—roast fowl, baked ham, grilled horsemeat—curled under the kitchen door and wafted under my nose. I pulled my belt up a notch and tried to swallow the dryness in my throat. The old man had fed me a half a gallon of stew before we left home, but I was already working up a fresh appetite.

Five slow minutes passed. Then the kitchen door swung open and a tall round-shouldered fellow with a shiny bald scalp stepped into view, a tray balanced on the spread fingers of one hand. He turned, the black tails of his cutaway swirling, called something behind him, and started past me. I stepped out, clearing my throat. He shied, whirled to face me. He was good at his job: the two dozen tiny glasses on the tray stood fast. He blinked, got an indignant remark ready—

I showed him the knife the old man had lent me—a bonehandled job with a six-inch switchblade. "Make a sound and I'll cut your throat," I said softly. "Put the tray on the floor."

He started to back. I brought the knife up. He took a good look, licked his lips, crouched quickly, and put the tray down.

"Turn around."

I stepped in and chopped him at the base of the neck with the edge of my hand. He folded like a two-dollar umbrella.

I wrestled the door open and dumped him inside, paused a moment to listen. All quiet. I worked his black coat and trousers off, unhooked the stiff white dickey and tie. He snored softly. I pulled the clothes on over the weather suit. They were a fair fit. By the light of my pencil-flash I cut down a heavy braided cord hanging by a high window, used it to truss the waiter's hands and feet together behind him. There was a small closet opening off the room. I put him in it, closed the door, and stepped back into the hall. Still quiet. I tried one of the drinks. It wasn't bad.

I took another, then picked up the tray and followed the sounds of music.

The grand ballroom was a hundred yards long, fifty wide, with walls of rose, gold and white, banks of high windows hung with crimson velvet, a vaulted ceiling decorated with cherubs, and a polished acre of floor on which gaudily gowned and uniformed couples moved in time to the heavy beat of the traditional foxtrot. I moved slowly along the edge of the crowd, looking for the Baron.

A hand caught my arm and hauled me around. A glass fell off my tray, smashed on the floor.

A dapper little man in black and white headwaiter's uniform glared up at me.

"What do you think you're doing, cretin?" he hissed. "That's the genuine ancient stock you're slopping on the floor." I looked around quickly; no one else seemed to be paying any attention.

"Where are you from?" he snapped. I opened my mouth—

"Never mind, you're all the same." He waggled his hands disgustedly. "The field hands they send me—a disgrace to the Black. Now, you! Stand up! Hold your tray proudly, gracefully! Step along daintily, not like a knight taking the field! and pause occasionally—just on the chance that some noble guest might wish to drink."

"You bet, pal," I said. I moved on, paying a little more attention to my waiting. I saw plenty of green uniforms; pea green, forest green, emerald green—but they were all hung with braid and medals. According to pop, the Baron affected a spartan simplicity. The diffidence of absolute power.

There were high white and gold doors every few yards along the side of the ballroom. I spotted one standing open and sidled toward it. It wouldn't hurt to reconnoiter the area.

Just beyond the door, a very large sentry in a bottle-green uniform almost buried under gold braid moved in front of me. He was dressed like a toy soldier, but there was nothing playful about the way he snapped his power gun to the ready. I winked at him.

"Thought you boys might want a drink," I hissed. "Good stuff."

He looked at the tray, licked his lips. "Get back in there, you fool," he growled. "You'll get us both hanged."

"Suit yourself, pal." I backed out. Just before the door closed between us, he lifted a glass off the tray.

I turned, almost collided with a long lean cookie in a powder-blue outfit complete with dress sabre, gold frogs, leopard-skin facings, a pair of knee-length white gloves looped under an epaulette, a pistol in a fancy holster, and an eighteen-inch swagger stick. He gave me the kind of look old maids give sin.

"Look where you're going, swine," he said in a voice like a pine board splitting.

"Have a drink, admiral," I suggested.

He lifted his upper lip to show me a row of teeth that hadn't had their annual trip to the dentist lately. The ridges along each side of his mouth turned greenish white. He snatched for the gloves on his shoulder, fumbled them; they slapped the floor beside me.

"I'd pick those up for you, boss," I said, "but I've got my tray . . ."

He drew a breath between his teeth, chewed it into strips, and snorted it back at me, then snapped his fingers and pointed with his stick toward the door behind me.

"Through there, instantly!" It didn't seem like the time to argue; I pulled it open and stepped through.

The guard in green ducked his glass and snapped to attention when he saw the baby-blue outfit. My new friend ignored him, made a curt gesture to me. I got the idea, trailed along the wide, high, gloomy corridor to a small door, pushed through it into a well-lit tile-walled latrine. A big-eyed slave in white ducks stared.

Blue-boy jerked his head. "Get out!" The slave scuttled away. Blue-boy turned to me.

"Strip off your jacket, slave! Your owner has neglected to teach you discipline."

I looked around quickly, saw that we were alone.

"Wait a minute while I put the tray down, corporal," I said. "We don't want to waste any of the good stuff." I turned to put the tray on a soiled linen bin, caught a glimpse of motion in the mirror.

I ducked, and the nasty-looking little leather quirt whistled past my ear, slammed against the edge of a marble-topped lavatory with a crack like a pistol shot. I dropped the tray, stepped in fast and threw a left to Blue-boy's jaw that bounced his head against the tiled wall. I followed up with a right to the belt buckle, then held him up as he bent over, gagging, and hit him hard under the ear.

I hauled him into a booth, propped him up and started shedding the waiter's blacks.

5

I left him on the floor wearing my old suit, and stepped out into the hall.

I liked the feel of his pistol at my hip. It was an old-fashioned .38, the same model I favored. The blue uniform was a good fit, what with the weight I'd lost. Blue-boy and I had something in common after all.

The latrine attendant goggled at me. I grimaced like a quadruple amputee trying to scratch his nose and jerked my head toward the door I had come out of. I hoped the gesture would look familiar.

"Truss that mad dog and throw him outside the gates," I snarled. I stamped off down the corridor, trying to look mad enough to discourage curiosity.

Apparently it worked. Nobody yelled for the cops.

I reentered the ballroom by another door, snagged a drink off a passing tray, checked over the crowd. I saw two more powder-blue getups, so I wasn't unique enough to draw special attention. I made a mental note to stay well away from my comrades in blue. I blended with the landscape, chatting and nodding and not neglecting my drinking, working my way toward a big arched doorway on the other side of the room that looked like the kind of entrance the head man might use. I didn't want to meet him. Not yet. I just wanted to get him located before I went any further.

A passing wine slave poured a full inch of genuine ancient stock into my glass, ducked his head, and moved on. I gulped it like sour bar whiskey. My attention was elsewhere.

A flurry of activity near the big door indicated that maybe my guess had been accurate. Potbellied officials were forming up in a sort of reception line near the big double door. I started to drift back into the rear rank, bumped against a fat man in medals and a sash who glared, fingered a monocle with a plump ring-studded hand, and said, "Suggest you take your place, colonel," in a suety voice.

I must have looked doubtful, because he bumped me with his paunch, and growled, "Foot of the line! Next to the Equerry, you idiot." He elbowed me aside and waddled past.

I took a step after him, reached out with my left foot, and hooked his shiny black boot. He leaped forward, off balance, medals jangling. I did a fast fade while he was still groping for his monocle, eased into a spot at the end of the line.

The conversation died away to a nervous murmur. The doors swung back and a pair of guards with more trimmings than a phony stock certificate stamped into view, wheeled to face each other, and presented arms—chrome-plated automatic rifles, in this case. A dark-faced man with thinning gray hair, a pug nose, and a trimmed gray Vandyke came into view, limping slightly from a stiffish knee.

His unornamented gray outfit made him as conspicuous in this gathering as a crane among peacocks. He nodded perfunctorily to left and right, coming along between the waiting rows of flunkeys, who snapped-to as he came abreast, wilted and let out sighs behind him. I studied him closely. He was fifty, give or take the age of a bottle of second-rate bourbon, with the weather-beaten complexion of a former outdoor man and the same look of alertness grown bored that a rattlesnake farmer develops—just before the fatal bite.

He looked up and caught my eye on him, and for a moment I thought he was about to speak. Then he went on past.

At the end of the line he turned abruptly and spoke to a man who hurried away. Then he engaged in conversation with a cluster of head-bobbing guests.

I spent the next fifteen minutes casually getting closer to the door nearest the one the Baron had entered by. I looked around; nobody was paying any attention to me. I stepped past a guard who presented arms. The door closed softly, cutting off the buzz of talk and the worst of the music.

I went along to the end of the corridor. From the transverse hall, a grand staircase rose in a sweep of bright chrome and pale wood. I didn't know where it led, but it looked right. I headed for it, moving along briskly like a man with important business in mind and no time for light chitchat.

Two flights up, in a wide corridor of muted lights, deep carpets, brocaded wall hangings, mirrors, urns, and an odor of expensive tobacco and *cuir russe*, a small man in black bustled from a side corridor. He saw me. He opened his mouth, closed it, half turned away, then swung back to face me. I recognized him; he was the headwaiter who had pointed out the flaws in my waiting style half an hour earlier.

"Here—" he started.

I chopped him short with a roar of what I hoped was authentic upper-crust rage.

"Direct me to his Excellency's apartments, scum! And thank your guardian imp I'm in too great haste to cane you for the insolent look about you!"

He went pale, gulped hard, and pointed. I snorted and stamped past him down the turning he had indicated.

This was Baronial country, all right. A pair of guards stood at the far end of the corridor.

I'd passed half a dozen with no more than a click of heels to indicate they saw me. These two shouldn't be any different—and it wouldn't look good if I turned and started back at sight of them. The first rule of the gate-crasher is to look as if you belong where you are.

I headed in their direction.

When I was fifty feet from them they both shifted rifles—not to present-arms position, but at the ready. The nickle-plated bayonets were aimed right at me. It was no time for me to look doubtful; I kept on coming. At twenty feet, I heard their rifle bolts snick home. I could see the expressions on their faces now; they looked as nervous as a couple of teenage sailors on their first visit to a joyhouse.

"Point those butter knives into the corner, you banana-fingered cotton choppers!" I said, looking bored, and didn't waver. I unlimbered my swagger stick and slapped my gloved hand with it, letting them think it over. The gun muzzles dropped—just slightly. I followed up fast.

"Which is the anteroom to the Baron's apartments?" I demanded.

"Uh . . . this here is his Excellency's apartments, sir, but—"

"Never mind the lecture, you milk-faced fool," I cut in. "Which is the anteroom, damn you!"

"We got orders, sir. Nobody's to come closer than that last door back there."

"We got orders to shoot," the other interrupted. He was a little older—maybe twenty-two. I turned on him.

"I'm waiting for an answer to a question!"

"Sir, the Articles—"

I narrowed my eyes. "I think you'll find paragraph Two B covers Special Cosmic Top Secret Couriers. When you go off duty, report yourselves on punishment. Now, the anteroom! And be quick about it!"

The bayonets were sagging now. The younger of the two licked his lips. "Sir, we never been inside. We don't know how it's laid out in there. If the colonel wants to just take a look . . ."

The other guard opened his mouth to say something. I didn't wait to find out what it was. I stepped between them, muttering something about bloody recruits and important messages, and worked the fancy handle on the big gold and white door. I paused to give the two sentries a hard look.

"I hope I don't have to remind you that any mention of the movements of a Cosmic Courier is punishable by slow death. Just forget you ever saw me." I went on in and closed the door without waiting to catch the reaction to that one.

The Baron had done well by himself in the matter of decor. The room I was in—a sort of lounge-cum-bar—was paved in two-inch-deep nylon fuzz, the color of a fog at sea, that foamed up at the edges against walls of pale blue brocade with tiny yellow flowers. The bar was a teak log split down the middle and polished. The glasses sitting on it were like tissue paper engraved with patterns of nymphs and satyrs. Subdued light came from somewhere, along with a faint melody that seemed to speak of youth, long ago.

I went on into the room. I found more soft light, the glow of hand-rubbed rare woods, rich fabrics, and wide windows with a view of dark night sky. The music was coming from a long, low, built-in speaker with a lamp, a heavy crystal ashtray, and a display of hothouse roses. There was a scent in the air. Not the *cuir russe* and Havana leaf I'd smelled in the hall, but a subtler perfume.

I turned and looked into the eyes of a girl with long black lashes. Smooth black hair came down to bare shoulders. An arm as smooth and white as whipped cream was draped over a chair back, the hand holding an eight-inch cigarette holder and sporting a diamond as inconspicuous as a chrome-plated hubcap.

"You must want something pretty badly," she murmured, batting her eyelashes at me. I could feel the breeze at ten feet. I nodded. Under the circumstances that was about the best I could do.

"What could it be," she mused, "that's worth being shot for?" Her voice was like the rest of her: smooth, polished and relaxed—and with plenty of moxie held in reserve. She smiled casually, drew on her cigarette, tapped ashes onto the rug.

"Something bothering you, colonel?" she inquired. "You don't seem talkative."

"I'll do my talking when the Baron arrives," I said.

"In that case, Jackson," said a husky voice behind me, "you can start any time you like."

I held my hands clear of my body and turned around slowly—just in case there was a nervous gun aimed at my spine. The Baron was standing near the door, unarmed, relaxed. There were no guards in sight. The girl looked mildly amused. I put my hand on the pistol butt.

"How do you know my name?" I asked.

The Baron waved toward a chair. "Sit down, Jackson," he said, almost gently. "You've had a tough time of it—but you're all right now." He walked past me to the bar, poured out two glasses, turned, and offered me one. I felt a little silly standing there fingering the gun; I went over and took the drink.

"To the old days." The Baron raised his glass.

I drank. It was the genuine ancient stock, all right. "I asked you how you knew my name," I said.

"That's easy. I used to know you."

He smiled faintly. There was something about his face . . .

"You look well in the uniform of the Penn dragoons," he said. "Better than you ever did in Aerospace blue."

"Good God!" I said. "Toby Mallon!"

He ran a hand over his bald head. "A little less hair on top, plus a beard as compensation, a few wrinkles, a slight pot. Oh, I've changed, Jackson."

"I had it figured as close to eighty years," I said. "The trees, the condition of the buildings—"

"Not far off the mark. Seventy-eight years this spring."

"You're a well-preserved hundred and ten, Toby."

He nodded. "I know how you feel. Rip Van Winkle had nothing on us."

"Just one question, Toby. The men you sent out to pick me up seemed more interested in shooting than talking. I'm wondering why."

Mallon threw out his hands. "A little misunderstanding, Jackson. You made it; that's all that counts. Now that you're here, we've got some planning to do together. I've had it tough these last twenty years. I started off with nothing: a few hundred scavengers living in the ruins, hiding out every time Jersey or Dee-Cee raided for supplies. I built an organization, started a systematic salvage operation. I saved everything the rats and the weather hadn't gotten to, spruced up my palace here, and stocked it. It's a rich province, Jackson—"

"And now you own it all. Not bad, Toby."

"They say knowledge is power. I had the knowledge."

I finished my drink and put the glass on the bar.

"What's this planning you say we have to do?"

Mallon leaned back on one elbow.

"Jackson, it's been a long haul—alone. It's good to see an old shipmate. But we'll dine first."

"I might manage to nibble a little something. Say a horse, roasted whole. Don't bother to remove the saddle."

He laughed. "First we eat," he said. "Then we conquer the world."

6

I squeezed the last drop from the Beaujolais bottle and watched the girl, whose name was Renada, hold a light for the cigar Mallon had taken from a silver box. My blue mess jacket and holster hung over the back of the chair. Everything was cosy now.

"Time for business, Jackson," Mallon said. He blew out smoke and looked at me through it. "How did things look—inside?"

"Dusty. But intact, below ground level. Upstairs, there's blast damage and weathering. I don't suppose it's changed much since you came out twenty years ago. As far as I could tell, the Primary Site is okay."

Mallon leaned forward. "Now, you made it out past the Bolo. How did it handle itself? Still fully functional?"

I sipped my wine, thinking over my answer, remembering the Bolo's empty guns . . .

"It damn near gunned me down. It's getting a little old and it can't see as well as it used to, but it's still a tough baby."

Mallon swore suddenly. "It was Mackenzie's idea. A last-minute move when the tech crews had to evacuate. It was a dusting job, you know."

"I hadn't heard. How did you find out all this?"

Mallon shot me a sharp look. "There were still a few people around who'd been in it. But never mind that. What about the Supply Site? That's what we're interested in. Fuel, guns, even some nuclear stuff. Heavy equipment; there's a couple more Bolos, mothballed, I understand. Maybe we'll even find one or two of the Colossus missiles still in their silos. I made an air recon a few years back before my chopper broke down—"

"I think two silo doors are still in place. But why the interest in armament?"

Mallon snorted. "You've got a few things to learn about the setup, Jackson. I need that stuff. If I hadn't lucked into a stock of weapons and ammo in the armory cellar, Jersey would be wearing the spurs in my palace right now!"

I drew on my cigar and let the silence stretch out.

"You said something about conquering the world, Toby. I don't suppose by any chance you meant that literally?"

Mallon stood up, his closed fists working like a man crumpling unpaid bills. "They all want what I've got! They're all waiting." He walked across the room, back. "I'm ready to move against them now! I can put four thousand trained men in the field—"

"Let's get a couple of things straight, Mallon," I cut in. "You've got the natives fooled with this Baron routine. But don't try it on me. Maybe it was even necessary once; maybe there's an excuse for some of the stories I've heard. That's over now. I'm not interested in tribal warfare or gang rumbles. I need—"

"Better remember who's running things here, Jackson!" Mallon snapped. "It's not what you need that counts." He took another turn up and down the room, then stopped, facing me.

"Look, Jackson. I know how to get around in this jungle; you don't. If I hadn't spotted you and given some orders, you'd have been gunned down before you'd gone ten feet past the ballroom door."

"Why'd you let me in? I might've been gunning for you."

"You wanted to see the Baron alone. That suited me, too. If word got out—" He broke off, cleared his throat. "Let's stop wrangling, Jackson. We can't move until the Bolo guarding the site has been neutralized. There's only one way to do that: knock it out! And the only thing that can knock out a Bolo is another Bolo."

"So?"

"I've got another Bolo, Jackson. It's been covered, maintained. It can go up against the Troll—" He broke off, laughed shortly. "That's what the mob called it."

"You could have done that years ago. Where do I come in?"

"You're checked out on a Bolo, Jackson. You know something about this kind of equipment."

"Sure. So do you."

"I never learned," he said shortly.

"Who's kidding who, Mallon? We all took the same orientation course less than a month ago—"

"For me it's been a long month. Let's say I've forgotten."

"You parked that Bolo at your front gate and then forgot how you did it, eh?"

"Nonsense. It's always been there."

I shook my head. "I know different."

Mallon looked wary. "Where'd you get that idea?"

"Somebody told me."

Mallon ground his cigar out savagely on the damask cloth. "You'll point the scum out to me!"

"I don't give a damn whether you moved it or not. Anybody with your training can figure out the controls of a Bolo in half an hour—"

"Not well enough to take on the Tr—another Bolo."

I took a cigar from the silver box, picked up the lighter from the table, turned the cigar in the flame. Suddenly it was very quiet in the room.

I looked across at Mallon. He held out his hand.

"I'll take that," he said shortly.

I blew out smoke, squinted through it at Mallon. He sat with his hand out, waiting. I looked down at the lighter.

It was a heavy windproof model with embossed Aerospace wings. I turned it over. Engraved letters read: *Lieut. Commander Don G. Banner, USAF*. I looked up. Renada sat quietly, holding my pistol trained dead on my belt buckle.

"I'm sorry you saw that," Mallon said. "It could cause misunderstandings."

"Where's Banner?"

"He . . . died. I told you—"

"You told me a lot of things, Toby. Some of them might even be true. Did you make him the same offer you've made me?"

Mallon darted a look at Renada. She sat holding the pistol, looking at me distantly, without expression.

"You've got the wrong idea, Jackson—" Mallon started.

"You and he came out about the same time," I said. "Or maybe you got the jump on him by a few days. It must have been close; otherwise you'd never have taken him. Don was a sharp boy."

"You're out of your mind!" Mallon snapped. "Why, Banner was my friend!"

"Then why do you get nervous when I find his lighter on your table? There could be ten perfectly harmless explanations."

"I don't make explanations," Mallon said flatly.

"That attitude is hardly the basis for a lasting partnership, Toby. I have an unhappy feeling there's something you're not telling me."

Mallon pulled himself up in the chair. "Look here, Jackson. We've no reason to fall out. There's plenty for both of us—and one day I'll be needing a successor. It was too bad about Banner, but that's ancient history now. Forget it. I want you with me, Jackson! Together we can rule the Atlantic seaboard—or even more!"

I drew on my cigar, looking at the gun in Renada's hand. "You hold the aces, Toby. Shooting me would be no trick at all."

"There's no trick involved, Jackson!" Mallon snapped. "After all," he went on, almost wheedling now, "we're old friends. I want to give you a break, share with you—"

"I don't think I'd trust him if I were you, Mr. Jackson," Renada's quiet voice cut in. I looked at her. She looked back calmly. "You're more important to him than you think."

"That's enough, Renada," Mallon barked. "Go to your room at once."

"Not just yet, Toby," she said. "I'm also curious about how Commander Banner died." I looked at the gun in her hand.

It wasn't pointed at me now. It was aimed at Mallon's chest.

Mallon sat sunk deep in his chair, looking at me with eyes like a python with a bellyache. "You're fools, both of you," he grated. "I gave you everything, Renada. I raised you like my own daughter. And you, Jackson. You could have shared with me—all of it."

"I don't need a share of your delusions, Toby. I've got a set of my own. But before we go any farther, let's clear up a few points. Why haven't you been getting any mileage out of your tame Bolo? And what makes me important in the picture?"

"He's afraid of the Bolo machine," Renada said. "There's a spell on it which prevents men from approaching—even the Baron."

"Shut your mouth, you fool!" Mallon choked on his fury. I tossed the lighter in my hand and felt a smile twitching at my mouth.

"So Don was too smart for you after all. He must have been the one who had control of the Bolo. I suppose you called for a truce, and then shot him out from under the white flag. But he fooled you. He plugged a command into the Bolo's circuits to fire on anyone who came close—unless he was Banner."

"You're crazy!"

"It's close enough. You can't get near the Bolo. Right? And after twenty years, the bluff you've been running on the other Barons with your private troll must be getting a little thin. Any day now one of them may decide to try you."

Mallon twisted his face in what may have been an attempt at a placating smile. "I won't argue with you, Jackson. You're right about the command circuit. Banner set it up to fire an antipersonnel blast at anyone coming within fifty yards. He did it to keep the mob from tampering with the machine. But there's a loophole. It wasn't only Banner who could get close. He set it up to accept any of the *Prometheus* crew—except me. He hated me. It was a trick to try to get me killed."

"So you're figuring I'll step in and de-fuse her for you, eh, Toby? Well, I'm sorry as hell to disappoint you, but somehow in the confusion I left my electropass behind."

Mallon leaned toward me. "I told you we need each other, Jackson: I've got your pass. Yours and all the others. Renada, hand me my black box." She rose and moved across to the desk, holding the gun on Mallon—and on me, too, for that matter.

"Where'd you get my pass, Mallon?"

"Where do you think? They're the duplicates from the vault in the old command block. I knew one day one of you would come out. I'll tell you, Jackson, it's been hell, waiting all these years—and hoping. I gave orders that any time the Great Troll bellowed, the mob was to form up and stop anybody who came out. I don't know how you got through them . . ."

"I was too slippery for them. Besides," I added, "I met a friend."

"A friend? Who's that?"

"An old man who thought I was Prince Charming, come to wake everybody up. He was nuts. But he got me through."

Renada came back, handed me a square steel box. "Let's have the key, Mallon," I said. He handed it over. I opened the box, sorted through half a dozen silver-dollar-sized ovals of clear plastic, lifted one out.

"Is it a magical charm?" Renada asked, sounding awed. She didn't seem so sophisticated now—but I liked her better human.

"Just a synthetic crystalline plastic, designed to resonate to a pattern peculiar to my EEG," I said. "It amplifies the signal and gives off a characteristic emission that the psychotronic circuit in the Bolo picks up."

"That's what I thought. Magic."

"Call it magic, then, kid." I dropped the electropass in my pocket, stood and looked at Renada. "I don't doubt that you know how to use that gun, honey, but I'm leaving now. Try not to shoot me."

"You're a fool if you try it," Mallon barked. "If Renada doesn't shoot you, my guards will. And even if you made it, you'd still need me!"

"I'm touched by your concern, Toby. Just why do I need you?"

"You wouldn't get past the first sentry post without help, Jackson. These people know me as the Trollmaster. They're in awe of me—of my *mana*. But together—we can get to the controls of the Bolo, then use it to knock out the sentry machine at the Site—"

"Then what? With an operating Bolo I don't need anything else. Better improve the picture, Toby. I'm not impressed."

He wet his lips.

"It's *Prometheus*, do you understand? She's stocked with every-thing from Browning needlers to Norge stunners. Tools, weapons, instruments. And the power plants alone."

"I don't need needlers if I own a Bolo, Toby."

Mallon used some profanity. "You'll leave your liver and lights on the palace altar, Jackson. I promise you that!"

"Tell him what he wants to know, Toby," Renada said. Mallon narrowed his eyes at her. "You'll live to regret this, Renada."

"Maybe I will, Toby. But you taught me how to handle a gun—and to play cards for keeps."

The flush faded out of his face and left it pale. "All right, Jackson," he said, almost in a whisper. "It's not only the equipment. It's . . . the men."

I heard a clock ticking somewhere.

"What men, Toby?" I said softly.

"The crew. Day, Macy, the others. They're still in there, Jackson—aboard the ship, in stasis. We were trying to get the ship off when the attack came. There was forty minutes' warning. Everything was ready to go. You were on a test run; there wasn't time to cycle you out . . . ."

"Keep talking," I rapped.

"You know how the system was set up; it was to be a ten-year run out, with an automatic turnaround at the end of that time if Alpha Centauri wasn't within a milliparsec." He snorted. "It wasn't. After twenty years, the instruments checked. They were satisfied. There was a planetary mass within the acceptable range. So they brought me out." He snorted again. "The longest dry run in history. I unstrapped and came out to see what was going on. It took me a little while to realize what had happened. I went back in and cycled Banner and Mackenzie out. We went into the town; you know what we found. I saw what we had to do, but Banner and Mac argued. The fools wanted to reseal *Prometheus* and proceed with the launch. For what? So we could spend the rest of our lives squatting in the ruins, when by stripping the ship we could make ourselves kings?"

"So there was an argument?" I prompted.

"I had a gun. I hit Mackenzie in the leg, I think—but they got clear, found a car and beat me to the Site. There were two Bolos. What chance did I have against them?" Mallon grinned craftily. "But Banner was a fool. He died for it." The grin dropped like a stripper's bra. "But when I went to claim my spoils, I discovered how the jackals had set the trap for me."

"That was downright unfriendly of them, Mallon. Oddly enough, it doesn't make me want to stay and hold your hand."

"Don't you understand yet!" Mallon's voice was a dry screech. "Even if you got clear of the palace, used the Bolo to set yourself up as Baron—you'd never be safe! Not as long as one man was still alive aboard the ship. You'd never have a night's rest, wondering when one of them would walk out to challenge your rule . . ."

"Uneasy lies the head, eh, Toby? You remind me of a queen bee. The first one out of the chrysalis dismembers all her rivals."

"I don't mean to kill them. That would be a waste; I mean to give them useful work to do."

"I don't think they'd like being your slaves, Toby. And neither would I." I looked at Renada. "I'll be leaving you now," I said. "Whichever way you decide, good luck."

"Wait." She stood. "I'm going with you."

I looked at her. "I'll be traveling fast, honey. And that gun in my back may throw off my timing."

She stepped to me, reversed the pistol, and laid it in my hand.

"Don't kill him, Mr. Jackson. He was always kind to me."

"Why change sides now? According to Toby, my chances look not too good."

"I never knew before how Commander Banner died," she said. "He was my great-grandfather."

7

Renada came back bundled in a gray fur as I finished buckling on my holster.

"So long, Toby," I said. "I ought to shoot you in the belly just for Don, but—"

I saw Renada's eyes widen at the same instant that I heard the click.

I dropped flat and rolled behind Mallon's chair—and a gout of blue flame yammered into the spot where I'd been standing. I whipped the gun up and fired a round into the peach-colored upholstery an inch from Toby's ear.

"The next one nails you to the chair," I yelled. "Call 'em off!" There was a moment of dead silence. Toby sat frozen. I couldn't see who'd been doing the shooting. Then I heard a moan. Renada.

"Let the girl alone or I'll kill him," I called.

Toby sat rigid, his eyes rolled toward me.

"You can't kill me, Jackson! I'm all that's keeping you alive."

"You can't kill me either, Toby. You need my magic touch, remember? Maybe you'd better give me a safe-conduct out of here. I'll take the freeze off your Bolo—after I've seen to my business."

Toby licked his lips. I heard Renada again. She was trying not to moan—but moaning anyway.

"You tried, Jackson. It didn't work out," Toby said through gritted teeth. "Throw out your gun and stand up. I won't kill you—you know that. You do as you're told and you may still live to a ripe old age—and the girl, too."

She screamed then—a mindless ululation of pure agony.

"Hurry up, you fool, before they tear her arm off," Mallon grated. "Or shoot. You'll get to watch her for twenty-four hours under the knife. Then you'll have your turn."

I fired again—closer this time. Mallon jerked his head and cursed.

"If they touch her again, you get it, Toby," I said. "Send her over here. Move!"

"Let her go!" Mallon snarled. Renada stumbled into sight, moved around the chair, then crumpled suddenly to the rug beside me.

"Stand up, Toby," I ordered. He rose slowly. Sweat glistened on his face now. "Stand over here." He moved like a sleepwalker. I got to my feet. There were two men standing across the room beside a small open door. A sliding panel. Both of them held power rifles leveled—but aimed offside, away from the Baron.

"Drop 'em!" I said. They looked at me, then lowered the guns, tossed them aside.

I opened my mouth to tell Mallon to move ahead, but my tongue felt thick and heavy. The room was suddenly full of smoke. In front of me, Mallon was wavering like a mirage. I started to tell him to stand still, but with my thick tongue, it was too much trouble. I raised the gun, but somehow it was falling to the floor—slowly, like a leaf—and then I was floating, too, on waves that broke on a dark sea . . .

"Do you think you're the first idiot who thought he could kill me?" Mallon raised a contemptuous lip. "This room's rigged ten different ways."

I shook my head, trying to ignore the film before my eyes and the nausea in my body. "No, I imagine lots of people would like a crack at you, Toby. One day one of them's going to make it."

"Get him on his feet," Mallon snapped. Hard hands clamped on my arms, hauled me off the cot. I worked my legs, but they were like yesterday's celery; I sagged against somebody who smelled like uncured hides.

"You seem drowsy," Mallon said. "We'll see if we can't wake you up."

A thumb dug into my neck. I jerked away, and a jab under the ribs doubled me over.

"I have to keep you alive—for the moment," Mallon said. "But you won't get a lot of pleasure out of it."

I blinked hard. It was dark in the room. One of my handlers had a ring of beard around his mouth—I could see that much. Mallon was standing before me, hands on hips. I aimed a kick at him, just for fun. It didn't work out; my foot seemed to be wearing a lead boat. The unshaven man hit me in the mouth and Toby chuckled.

"Have your fun, Dunger," he said, "but I'll want him alive and on his feet for the night's work. Take him out and walk him in the fresh air. Report to me at the Pavilion of the Troll in an hour." He turned to something and gave orders about lights and gun emplacements, and I heard Renada's name mentioned.

Then he was gone and I was being dragged through the door and along the corridor.

The exercise helped. By the time the hour had passed, I was feeling weak but normal—except for an aching head and a feeling that there was a strand of spiderweb interfering with my vision.

Toby had given me a good meal. Maybe before the night was over he'd regret that mistake . . .

Across the dark grounds, an engine started up, spluttered, then settled down to a steady hum.

"It's time," the one with the whiskers said. He had a voice like soft cheese to match his smell. He took another half-twist in the arm he was holding.

"Don't break it," I grunted. "It belongs to the Baron, remember?"

Whiskers stopped dead. "You talk too much—and too smart." He let my arm go and stepped back. "Hold him, Pig Eye." The other man whipped a forearm across my throat and levered my head back; then Whiskers unlimbered the two-foot club from his belt and hit me hard in the side, just under the ribs. Pig Eye let go and I folded over and waited while the pain swelled up and burst inside me.

Then they hauled me back to my feet. I couldn't feel any bone ends grating, so there probably weren't any broken ribs—if that was any consolation.

There were lights glaring now across the lawn. Moving figures cast long shadows against the trees lining the drive—and on the side of the Bolo Combat Unit parked under its canopy by the sealed gate.

A crude breastwork had been thrown up just over fifty yards from it. A wheel-mounted generator putted noisily in the background, laying a layer of bluish exhaust in the air.

Mallon was waiting with a 9-mm power rifle in his hands as we came up, my two guards gripping me with both hands to demonstrate their zeal, and me staggering a little more than was necessary. I saw Renada standing by, wrapped in a gray fur. Her face looked white in the harsh light. She made a move toward me and a greenback caught her arm.

"You know what to do, Jackson," Mallon said speaking loudly against the clatter of the generator. He made a curt gesture and a man stepped up and buckled a stout chain to my left ankle. Mallon held out my electropass. "I want you to walk straight to the Bolo. Go in by the side port. You've got one minute to cancel the instructions punched into the command circuit and climb back outside. If you don't show, I close a switch there—" He pointed to a wooden box mounting an open circuit-breaker, with a tangle of heavy cable leading toward the Bolo—"and you cook in your shoes. The same thing happens if I see the guns start to traverse or the antipersonnel ports open." I followed the coils of armored wire from the chain on my ankle back to the wooden box—and on to the generator.

"Crude, maybe, but it will work. And if you get any idea of letting fly a round or two at random—remember the girl will be right beside me."

I looked across at the giant machine. "Suppose it doesn't recognize me? It's been a while. Or what if Don didn't plug my identity pattern in to the recognition circuit?"

"In that case, you're no good to me anyway," Mallon said flatly.

I caught Renada's eye, gave her a wink and a smile I didn't feel, and climbed up on top of the revetment.

I looked back at Mallon. He was old and shrunken in the garish light, his smooth gray suit rumpled, his thin hair mussed, the gun held in a white-knuckled grip. He looked more like a harassed shopkeeper than a would-be world-beater.

"You must want the Bolo pretty bad to take the chance, Toby," I said. "I'll think about taking that wild shot. You sweat me out."

I flipped slack into the wire trailing my ankle, jumped down, and started across the smooth-trimmed grass, a long black shadow stalking before me. The Bolo sat silent, as big as a bank in the circle of the spotlight. I could see the flecks of rust now around the port covers, the small vines that twined up her sides from the ragged stands of weeds that marked no-man's-land.

There was something white in the brush ahead. Broken human bones.

I felt my stomach go rigid again. The last man had gotten this far; I wasn't in the clear yet . . .

I passed two more scattered skeletons in the next twenty feet. They must have come in on the run, guinea pigs to test the alertness of the Bolo. Or maybe they'd tried creeping up, dead slow, an inch a day; it hadn't worked . . .

Tiny night creatures scuttled ahead. They would be safe here in the shadow of the troll where no predator bigger than a mouse could move. I stumbled, diverted my course around a ten-foot hollow, the eroded crater of a near miss.

Now I could see the great moss-coated treads sunk a foot into the earth, the nests of field mice tucked in the spokes of the yard-high bogies. The entry hatch was above, a hairline against the great curved flank. There were rungs set in the flaring tread shield. I reached up, got a grip and hauled myself up. My chain clanked against the metal. I found the door lever, held on and pulled.

It resisted, then turned. There was the hum of a servo motor, a crackling of dead gaskets. The hairline widened and showed me a narrow companionway, green-anodized dural with black polymer treads, a bulkhead with a fire extinguisher, an embossed steel data plate that said BOLO DIVISION OF GENERAL MOTORS CORPORATION and below, in smaller type, UNIT, COMBAT, BOLO MARK III.

I pulled myself inside and went up into the Christmas-tree glow of instrument lights.

The control cockpit was small, utilitarian, with two deep-padded seats set among screens, dials, levers. I sniffed the odors of oil, paint, the characteristic ether and ozone of a nuclear generator. There was a faint hum in the air from idling relay servos. The clock showed ten past four. Either it was later than I thought, or the chronometer had lost time in the last eighty years. But I had no time to lose . . .

I slid into the seat, flipped back the cover of the command control console. The Cancel key was the big white one. I pulled it down and let it snap back, like a clerk ringing up a sale.

A pattern of dots on the status display screen flicked out of existence. Mallon was safe from his pet troll now.

It hadn't taken me long to carry out my orders. I knew what to do next; I'd planned it all during my walk out. Now I had thirty seconds to stack the deck in my favor.

I reached down, hauled the festoon of quarter-inch armored cable up in front of me. I hit a switch, and the inner conning cover—a disk of inch-thick-armor—slid back. I shoved a loop of the flexible cable up through the aperture, reversed the switch. The cover slid back—slicing the armored cable like macaroni.

I took a deep breath, and my hands went to the combat alert switch, hovered over it.

It was the smart thing to do—the easy thing. All I had to do was punch a key, and the 9-mm's would open up, scythe Mallon and his crew down like cornstalks.

But the scything would mow Renada down, along with the rest. And if I went—even without firing a shot—Mallon would keep his promise to cut that white throat . . .

My head was out of the noose now, but I would have to put it back—for a while.

I leaned sideways, reached back under the panel, groped for a small fuse box. My fingers were clumsy. I took a breath, tried again. The fuse dropped out in my hand. The Bolo's I-R circuit was dead now. With a few more seconds to work, I could have knocked out other circuits—but the time had run out.

I grabbed the cut ends of my lead wire, knotted them around the chain and got out fast.

8

Mallon waited, crouched behind the revetment.

"It's safe now, is it?" he grated. I nodded. He stood, gripping his gun.

"Now we'll try it together."

I went over the parapet, Mallon following with his gun ready. The lights followed us to the Bolo. Mallon clambered up to the open port, looked around inside, then dropped back down beside me. He looked excited now.

"That does it, Jackson! I've waited a long time for this. Now I've got all the *mana* there is!"

"Take a look at the cable on my ankle," I said softly. He narrowed his eyes, stepped back, gun aimed, darted a glance at the cable looped to the chain.

"I cut it, Toby. I was alone in the Bolo with the cable cut—and I didn't fire. I could have taken your toy and set up in business for myself, but I didn't."

"What's that supposed to buy you?" Mallon rasped.

"As you said—we need each other. That cut cable proves you can trust me."

Mallon smiled. It wasn't a nice smile. "Safe, were you? Come here." I walked along with him to the back of the Bolo. A heavy copper wire hung across the rear of the machine, trailing off into the grass in both directions.

"I'd have burned you at the first move. Even with the cable cut, the armored cover would have carried the full load right into the cockpit with you. But don't be nervous. I've got other jobs for you." He jabbed the gun muzzle hard into my chest, pushing me back. "Now get moving," he snarled. "And don't ever threaten the Baron again."

"The years have done more than shrivel your face, Toby," I said. "They've cracked your brain."

He laughed, a short bark. "You could be right. What's sane and what isn't? I've got a vision in my mind—and I'll make it come true. If that's insanity, it's better than what the mob has."

Back at the parapet, Mallon turned to me. "I've had this campaign planned in detail for years, Jackson. Everything's ready. We move out in half an hour—before any traitors have time to take word to my enemies. Pig Eye and Dunger will keep you from being lonely while I'm away. When I get back—Well, maybe you're right about working together." He gestured and my whiskery friend and his sidekick loomed up. "Watch him," he said.

"Genghis Khan is on the march, eh?" I said, "With nothing between you and the goodies but a five-hundred-ton Bolo . . ."

"The Lesser Troll . . ." He raised his hands and made crushing motions, like a man crumbling dry earth. "I'll trample it under my treads."

"You're confused, Toby. The Bolo has treads. You just have a couple of fallen arches."

"It's the same. I am the Great Troll." He showed me his teeth and walked away.

I moved along between Dunger and Pig Eye, toward the lights of the garage.

"The back entrance again," I said. "Anyone would think you were ashamed of me."

"You need more training, hah?" Dunger rasped. "Hold him, Pig Eye." He unhooked his club and swung it loosely in his hand, glancing around. We were near the trees by the drive. There was no one in sight except the crews near the Bolo and a group by the front of the palace. Pig Eye gave my arm a twist and shifted his grip to his old favorite strangle hold. I was hoping he would.

Dunger whipped the club up, and I grabbed Pig Eye's arm with both hands and leaned forward like a Japanese admiral reporting to the Emperor. Pig Eye went up and over just in time to catch Dunger's club across the back. They went down together. I went for the club, but Whiskers was faster than he looked. He rolled clear, got to his knees, and laid it across my left arm, just below the shoulder.

I heard the bone go . . .

I was back on my feet, somehow. Pig Eye lay sprawled before me. I heard him whining as though from a great distance. Dunger stood six feet away, the ring of black beard spread in a grin like a hyena smelling dead meat.

"His back's broke," he said. "Hell of a sound he's making. I been waiting for you; I wanted you to hear it."

"I've heard it," I managed. My voice seemed to be coming off a worn sound track. "Surprised . . . you didn't work me over . . . while I was busy with the arm."

"Uh-uh. I like a man to know what's going on when I work him over." He stepped in, rapped the broken arm lightly with the club. Fiery agony choked a groan off in my throat. I backed a step; he stalked me.

"Pig Eye wasn't much, but he was my pal. When I'm through with you, I'll have to kill him. A man with a broken back's no use to nobody. His'll be finished pretty soon now, but not with you. You'll be around a long time yet; but I'll get a lot of fun out of you before the Baron gets back."

I was under the trees now. I had some wild thoughts about grabbing up a club of my own, but they were just thoughts. Dunger set himself and his eyes dropped to my belly. I didn't wait for it; I lunged at him. He laughed and stepped back, and the club cracked my head. Not hard; just enough to send me down. I got my legs under me and started to get up—

There was a hint of motion from the shadows behind Dunger. I shook my head to cover any expression that might have showed, let myself drop back.

"Get up," Dunger said. The smile was gone now. He aimed a kick. "Get up—"

He froze suddenly, then whirled. His hearing must have been as keen as a jungle cat's; I hadn't heard a sound.

The old man stepped into view, his white hair plastered wet to his skull, his big hands spread. Dunger snarled, jumped in and whipped the club down; I heard it hit. There was a flurry of struggle, then Dunger stumbled back, empty-handed.

I was on my feet again now. I made a lunge for Dunger as he roared and charged. The club in the old man's hand rose and fell. Dunger crashed past and into the brush. The old man sat down suddenly, still holding the club. Then he let it fall and lay back. I went toward him and Dunger rushed me from the side. I went down again.

I was dazed, but not feeling any pain now. Dunger was standing over the old man. I could see the big lean figure lying limply, arms outspread—and a white bone handle, incongruously new and neat against the shabby mackinaw. The club lay on the ground a few feet away. I started crawling for it. It seemed a long way, and it was hard for me to move my legs, but I kept at it. The light rain was falling again now, hardly more than a mist. Far away there were shouts and the sound of engines starting up. Mallon's convoy moving out. He had won. Dunger had won, too. The old man had tried, but it hadn't been enough. But if I could reach the club, and swing it just once . . .

Dunger was looking down at the old man. He leaned, withdrew the knife, wiped it on his trouser leg, hitching up his pants to tuck it away in its sheath. The club was smooth and heavy under my hand. I got a good grip on it, got to my feet. I waited until Dunger turned,

and then I hit him across the top of the skull with everything I had
left . . .

I thought the old man was dead until he blinked suddenly. His
features looked relaxed now, peaceful, the skin like parchment
stretched over bone. I took his gnarled old hand and rubbed it.
It was as cold as a drowned sailor.

"You waited for me, old timer?" I said inanely. He moved his
head minutely, and looked at me. Then his mouth moved. I leaned
close to catch what he was saying. His voice was fainter than lost
hope.

"Mom . . . told . . . me . . . wait for you . . . She said . . . you'd
. . . come back some day . . ."

I felt my jaw muscles knotting.

Inside me something broke and flowed away like molten metal.
Suddenly my eyes were blurred—and not only with rain. I looked at
the old face before me, and for a moment, I seemed to see a ghostly
glimpse of another face, a small round face that looked up.

He was speaking again. I put my head down:

"Was I . . . good . . . boy . . . Dad?" Then the eyes closed.

I sat for a long time, looking at the still face. Then I folded the
hands on the chest and stood.

"You were more than a good boy, Timmy," I said. "You were a
good man."

9

My blue suit was soaking wet and splattered with mud, plus a few
flecks of what Dunger had used for brains, but it still carried the
gold eagles on the shoulders.

The attendant in the garage didn't look at my face. The eagles
were enough for him. I stalked to a vast black Bentley—a '90 model,
I guessed, from the conservative eighteen-inch tail fins—and jerked
the door open. The gauge showed three-quarters full. I opened
the glove compartment, rummaged, found nothing. But then it
wouldn't be up front with the chauffeur . . .

I pulled open the back door. There was a crude black leather
holster riveted against the smooth pale-gray leather, with the butt
of a 4-mm showing. There was another one on the opposite door,
and a power rifle slung from straps on the back of the driver's seat.

Whoever owned the Bentley was overcompensating his insecu-
rity. I took a pistol, tossed it onto the front seat, and slid in beside

it. The attendant gaped at me as I eased my left arm into my lap and twisted to close the door. I started up. There was a bad knock, but she ran all right. I flipped a switch and cold lances of light speared out into the rain.

At the last instant, the attendant started forward with his mouth open to say something, but I didn't wait to hear it. I gunned out into the night, swung into the graveled drive, and headed for the gate. Mallon had had it all his way so far, but maybe it still wasn't too late . . .

Two sentries, looking miserable in shiny black ponchos, stepped out of the guard hut at I pulled up. One peered in at me, then came to a sloppy position of attention and presented arms. I reached for the gas pedal and the second sentry called something. The first man looked startled, then swung the gun down to cover me. I eased a hand toward my pistol, brought it up fast, and fired through the glass. Then the Bentley was roaring off into the dark along the potholed road that led into town. I thought I heard a shot behind me, but I wasn't sure.

I took the river road south of town, pounding at reckless speed over the ruined blacktop, gaining on the lights of Mallon's horde paralleling me a mile to the north. A quarter mile from the perimeter fence, the Bentley broke a spring and skidded into a ditch.

I sat for a moment taking deep breaths to drive back the compulsive drowsiness that was sliding down over my eyes like a visor. My arm throbbed like a cauterized stump. I needed a few minutes' rest . . .

A sound brought me awake like an old maid smelling cigar smoke in the bedroom: the rise and fall of heavy engines in convoy. Mallon was coming up at flank speed.

I got out of the car and headed off along the road at a trot, holding my broken arm with my good one to ease the jarring pain. My chances had been as slim as a gambler's wallet all along, but if Mallon beat me to the objective, they dropped to nothing.

The eastern sky had taken on a faint gray tinge, against which I could make out the silhouetted gateposts and the dead floodlights a hundred yards ahead.

The roar of engines was getting louder. There were other sounds, too: a few shouts, the chatter of a 9-mm, the *boom*! of something heavier, and once a long-drawn *whoosh*! of falling masonry. With his new toy, Mallon was dozing his way through the men and buildings that got in his way.

I reached the gate, picked my way over fallen wire mesh, then headed for the Primary Site.

I couldn't run now. The broken slabs tilted crazily, in no pattern. I slipped, stumbled, but kept my feet. Behind me, headlights threw shadows across the slabs. It wouldn't be long now before someone in Mallon's task force spotted me and opened up with the guns—

The whoop! *whoop!* WHOOP! of the guardian Bolo cut across the field.

Across the broken concrete I saw the two red eyes flash, sweeping my way. I looked toward the gate. A massed rank of vehicles stood in a battalion front just beyond the old perimeter fence, engines idling, ranged for a hundred yards on either side of a wide gap at the gate. I looked for the high silhouette of Mallon's Bolo, and saw it far off down the avenue, picked out in red, white, and green navigation lights, a jeweled dreadnaught. A glaring cyclopean eye at the top darted a blue-white cone of light ahead, swept over the waiting escort, outlined me like a set-shifter caught onstage by the rising curtain.

The *whoop! whoop!* sounded again; the automated sentry Bolo was bearing down on me along the dancing lane of light.

I grabbed at the plastic disk in my pocket as though holding it in my hand would somehow heighten its potency. I didn't know if the Lesser Troll was programmed to exempt me from destruction or not; and there was only one way to find out.

It wasn't too late to turn around and run for it. Mallon might shoot—or he might not. I could convince him that he needed me, that together we could grab twice as much loot. And then, when he died—

I wasn't really considering it; it was the kind of thought that flashes through a man's mind like heat lightning when time slows in the instant of crisis. It was hard to be brave with broken bone ends grating, but what I had to do didn't take courage. I was a small, soft, human grub, stepped on but still moving, caught on the harsh plain of broken concrete between the clash of chrome-steel titans. But I knew which direction to take.

The Lesser Troll rushed toward me in a roll of thunder and I went to meet it.

It stopped twenty yards from me, loomed massive as a cliff. Its heavy guns were dead, I knew. Without them it was no more dangerous than a farmer with a shotgun—

But against me a shotgun was enough.

The slab under me trembled as if in anticipation. I squinted against the dull red I-R beams that pivoted to hold me, waiting while the Troll considered. Then the guns elevated, pointed over my head like a benediction. The Bolo knew me.

The guns traversed fractionally. I looked back toward the enemy line, saw the Great Troll coming up now, closing the gap, towering over its waiting escort like a planet among moons. And the guns of the Lesser Troll tracked it as it came—the empty guns that for twenty years had held Mallon's scavengers at bay.

The noise of engines was deafening now. The waiting line moved restlessly, pulverizing old concrete under churning treads. I didn't realize I was being fired on until I saw chips fly to my left and heard the howl of ricochets.

It was time to move. I scrambled for the Bolo, snorted at the stink of hot oil and ozone, found the rusted handholds, and pulled myself up—

Bullets spanged off metal above me. Someone was trying for me with a power rifle.

The broken arm hung at my side like a fence post nailed to my shoulder, but I wasn't aware of the pain now. The hatch stood open half an inch. I grabbed the lever, strained; it swung wide. No lights came up to meet me. With the port cracked, they'd burned out long ago. I dropped down inside, wriggled through the narrow crawl space into the cockpit. It was smaller than the Mark III—and it was occupied.

In the faint green light from the panel, the dead man crouched over the controls, one desiccated hand in a shriveled black glove clutching the control bar. He wore a GI weather suit and a white crash helmet, and one foot was twisted nearly backward, caught behind a jack lever.

The leg had been broken before he died. He must have jammed the foot and twisted it so that the pain would hold off the sleep that had come at last. I leaned forward to see the face. The blackened and mummified features showed only the familiar anonymity of death, but the bushy reddish mustache was enough.

"Hello, Mac," I said. "Sorry to keep you waiting; I got held up."

I wedged myself into the copilot's seat, flipped the I-R screen switch. The eight-inch panel glowed, showed me the enemy Bolo trampling through the fence three hundred yards away, then moving onto the ramp, dragging a length of rusty chain-link like a bridal train behind it.

I put my hand on the control bar. "I'll take it now, Mac." I moved the bar, and the dead man's hand moved with it.

"Okay, Mac," I said. "We'll do it together."

I hit the switches, canceling the preset response pattern. It had done its job for eighty years, but now it was time to crank in a little human strategy.

My Bolo rocked slightly under a hit and I heard the tread shields drop down. The chair bucked under me as Mallon moved in, pouring in the fire.

Beside me Mac nodded patiently. It was old stuff to him. I watched the tracers on the screen. Hosing me down with contact exploders probably gave Mallon a lot of satisfaction, but it couldn't hurt me. It would be a different story when he tired of the game and tried the heavy stuff.

I threw in the drive, backed rapidly. Mallon's tracers followed for a few yards, then cut off abruptly. I pivoted, flipped on my polyarcs, raced for the position I had selected across the field, then swung to face Mallon as he moved toward me. It had been a long time since he had handled the controls of a Bolo; he was rusty, relying on his automatics. I had no heavy rifles, but my popguns were okay. I homed my 4-mm solid-slug cannon on Mallon's polyarc, pressed the FIRE button.

There was a scream from the high-velocity-feed magazine. The blue-white light flared and went out. The Bolo's defense could handle anything short of an H-bomb, pick a missile out of the stratosphere fifty miles away, devastate a county with one round from its mortars—but my BB gun at point-blank range had poked out its eye.

I switched everything off and sat silent, waiting. Mallon had come to a dead stop. I could picture him staring at the dark screens, slapping levers, and cursing. He would be confused, wondering what had happened. With his lights gone, he'd be on radar now—not very sensitive at this range, not too conscious of detail . . .

I watched my panel. An amber warning light winked. Mallon's radar was locked on me.

He moved forward again, then stopped; he was having trouble making up his mind. I flipped a key to drop a padded shock frame in place and braced myself. Mallon would be getting mad now.

Crimson danger lights flared on the board and I rocked under the recoil as my interceptors flashed out to meet Mallon's C-S C's and detonate them in incandescent rendezvous over the scarred concrete between us. My screens went white, then dropped back to secondary brilliance, flashing stark black-and-white. My ears hummed like trapped hornets.

The sudden silence was like a vault door closing.

I sagged back, feeling like Quasimodo after a wild ride on the
bells. The screens blinked bright again, and I watched Mallon,
sitting motionless now in his near blindness. On his radar screen I
would show as a blurred hill; he would be wondering why I hadn't
returned his fire, why I hadn't turned and run, why . . . why . . .

He lurched and started toward me. I waited, then eased back,
slowly. He accelerated, closing in to come to grips at a range where
even the split microsecond response of my defenses would be too
slow to hold off his fire. And I backed, letting him gain, but not
too fast . . .

Mallon couldn't wait.

He opened up, throwing a mixed bombardment from his 9-mm's,
his infinite repeaters, and his C-S C's. I held on, fighting the
battering frame, watching the screens. The gap closed; a hundred
yards, ninety, eighty.

The open silo yawned in Mallon's path now, but he didn't see it.
The mighty Bolo came on, guns bellowing in the night, closing for
the kill. On the brink of the fifty-foot-wide, hundred-yard-deep pit,
it hesitated as though sensing danger. Then it moved forward.

I saw it rock, dropping its titanic prow, showing its broad back,
gouging the blasted pavement as its guns bore on the ground.
Great sheets of sparks flew as the treads reversed, too late. The
Bolo hung for a moment longer, then slid down majestically as a
sinking liner, its guns still firing into the pit like a challenge to
Hell. And then it was gone. A dust cloud boiled for a moment, then
whipped away as displaced air tornadoed from the open mouth of
the silo.

And the earth trembled under the impact far below.

10

The doors of the Primary Site blockhouse were nine-foot-high,
eight-inch-thick panels of solid chromalloy that even a Bolo would
have slowed down for, but they slid aside for my electropass like a
shower curtain at the YW. I went into a shadowy room where eighty
years of silence hung like black crepe on a coffin. The tiled floor was
still immaculate, the air fresh. Here at the heart of the Aerospace
Center, all systems were still go.

In the Central Control bunker, nine rows of green lights glowed
on the high panel over red letters that spelled out STAND BY
TO FIRE. A foot to the left, the big white lever stood in the

unlocked position, six inches from the outstretched fingertips of the mummified corpse strapped into the controller's chair. To the right, a red glow on the monitor panel indicated the lock doors open.

I rode the lift down to K level, stepped out onto the steel-railed platform that hugged the sweep of the starship's hull and stepped through into the narrow COC.

On my right, three empty stasis tanks stood open, festooned cabling draped in disorder. To the left were the four sealed covers under which Day, Macy, Cruciani, and Black waited. I went close, read dials. Slender needles trembled minutely to the beating of sluggish hearts.

They were alive.

I left the ship, sealed the inner and outer ports. Back in the control bunker, the monitor panel showed ALL CLEAR FOR LAUNCH now. I studied the timer, set it, turned back to the master panel. The white lever was smooth and cool under my hand. It seated with a click. The red hand of the launch clock moved off jerkily, the ticking harsh in the silence.

Outside, the Bolo waited. I climbed to a perch in the open conning tower twenty feet above the broken pavement, moved off toward the west where sunrise colors picked out the high towers of the palace.

I rested the weight of my splinted and wrapped arm on the balcony rail, looking out across the valley and the town to the misty plain under which *Prometheus* waited.

"There's something happening now," Renada said. I took the binoculars, watched as the silo doors rolled back.

"There's smoke," Renada said.

"Don't worry, just cooling gases being vented off." I looked at my watch. "Another minute or two and man makes the biggest jump since the first lungfish crawled out on a mud flat."

"What will they find out there?"

I shook my head. "*Homo terra firma* can't even conceive of what *Homo astra* has ahead of him."

"Twenty years they'll be gone. It's a long time to wait."

"We'll be busy trying to put together a world for them to come back to. I don't think we'll be bored."

"Look!" Renada gripped my good arm. A long silvery shape, huge even at the distance of miles, rose slowly out of the earth, poised on a brilliant ball of white fire. Then the sound came, a thunder that penetrated my bones, shook the railing under my hand. The fireball lengthened into a silver-white column with the ship balanced at its tip. Then the column broke free, rose up, up . . .

I felt Renada's hand touch mine. I gripped it hard. Together we watched as *Prometheus* took man's gift of fire back to the heavens.

MERCENARY

Mack Reynolds

Joseph Mauser spotted the recruiting line-up from two or three
blocks down the street, shortly after driving into Kingston. The local
offices of Vacuum Tube Transport, undoubtedly. Baron Haer would
be doing his recruiting for the fracas with Continental Hovercraft
there if for no other reason than to save on rents. The Baron was
watching pennies on this one and that was bad.

In fact, it was so bad that even as Joe Mauser let his sport
hovercar sink to a parking level and vaulted over its side he was
still questioning his decision to sign up with the Vacuum Tube outfit
rather than with their opponents. Joe was an old pro and old pros do
not get to be old pros in the Category Military without developing an
instinct to stay away from losing sides.

Fine enough for Low-Lowers and Mid-Lowers to sign up with
this outfit as opposed to that, motivated by no other reasoning
than the snappiness of the uniform and the stock shares offered,
but an old pro considered carefully such matters as budget. Baron
Haer was watching every expense, was, it was rumored, figuring on
commanding himself and calling upon relatives and friends for his
staff. Continental Hovercraft, on the other hand, was heavy with
variable capital and was in a position to hire Stonewall Cogswell
himself for their tactician.

However, the die was cast. You didn't run up a caste level, not to
speak of two at once, by playing it careful. Joe had planned this out;
for once, old pro or not, he was taking risks.

Recruiting line-ups were not for such as he. Not for many a year,
many a fracas. He strode rapidly along this one, heading for the
offices ahead, noting only in passing the quality of the men who

were taking service with Vacuum Tube Transport. These were
the soldiers he'd be commanding in the immediate future, and the
prospects looked grim. There were few veterans among them. Their
stance, their demeanor, their . . . well, you could tell a veteran even
though he be Rank Private. You could tell a veteran of even one
fracas. It showed.

He knew the situation. The word had gone out. Baron Malcolm
Haer was due for a defeat. You weren't going to pick up any lush
bonuses signing up with him, and you definitely weren't going to
jump a caste. In short, no matter what Haer's past record, choose
what was going to be the winning side—Continental Hovercraft.
Continental Hovercraft and old Stonewall Cogswell who had lost
so few fracases that many a Telly buff couldn't remember a single
one.

Individuals among these men showed promise, Joe Mauser
estimated even as he walked, but promise means little if you don't
live long enough to cash in on it.

Take that small man up ahead. He'd obviously got himself into
a hassle maintaining his place in line against two or three heftier
would-be soldiers. The little fellow wasn't backing down a step in
spite of the attempts of the other Lowers to usurp his place. Joe
Mauser liked to see such spirit. You could use it when you were in
the dill.

As he drew abreast of the altercation, he snapped from the side of
his mouth, "Easy, lads. You'll get all the scrapping you want with
Hovercraft. Wait until then."

He'd expected his tone of authority to be enough, even though
he was in mufti. He wasn't particularly interested in the situation,
beyond giving the little man a hand. A veteran would have
recognized him as an old timer and probable officer, and heeded,
automatically.

These evidently weren't veterans.

"Says who?" one of the Lowers growled back at him. "You one
of Baron Haer's kids, or something?"

Joe Mauser came to a halt and faced the other. He was irritated,
largely with himself. He didn't want to be bothered. Nevertheless,
there was no alternative now.

The line of men, all Lowers so far as Joe could see, had fallen
silent in an expectant hush. They were bored with their long wait.
Now something would break the monotony.

By tomorrow, Joe Mauser would be in command of some of these
men. In as little as a week he would go into a full fledged fracas with
them. He couldn't afford to lose face. Not even at this point when all,

including himself, were still civilian garbed. When matters pickled, in a fracas, you wanted men with complete confidence in you.

The man who had grumbled the surly response was a near physical twin of Joe Mauser, which put him in his early thirties, gave him five foot eleven of altitude and about one hundred and eighty pounds. His clothes casted him Low-Lower—nothing to lose. As with many who have nothing to lose, he was willing to risk all for principle. His face now registered that ideal. Joe Mauser had no authority over him, nor his friends.

Joe's eyes flicked to the other two who had been pestering the little fellow. They weren't quite so aggressive and as yet had come to no conclusion about their stand. Probably the three had been unacquainted before their bullying alliance to deprive the smaller man of his place. However, a moment of hesitation and Joe would have a trio on his hands.

He went through no further verbal preliminaries. Joe Mauser stepped closer. His right hand lanced forward, not doubled in a fist but fingers close together and pointed, spearlike. He sank it into the other's abdomen, immediately below the rib cage—the solar plexus.

He had misestimated the other two. Even as his opponent crumpled, they were upon him, coming in from each side. And at least one of them, he could see now, had been in hand-to-hand combat before. In short, another pro, like Joe himself.

He took one blow, rolling with it, and his feet automatically went into the shuffle of the trained fighter. He retreated slightly to erect defenses, plan attack. They pressed him strongly, sensing victory in his retreat.

The one mattered little to him. Joe Mauser could have polished off the oaf in a matter of seconds, had he been allotted seconds to devote. But the second, the experienced one, was the problem. He and Joe were well matched, and with the oaf as an ally really he had all the best of it.

Support came from a forgotten source, the little chap who had been the reason for the whole hassle. He waded in now as big as the next man so far as spirit was concerned, but a sorry fate gave him to attack the wrong man, the veteran rather than the tyro. He took a crashing blow to the side of his head which sent him sailing back into the recruiting line, now composed of excited, shouting verbal participants of the fray.

However, the extinction of Joe Mauser's small ally had taken a moment or two, and time was what Joe needed most. For a double second he had the oaf alone on his hands, and that was sufficient. He caught a flailing arm, turned his back and automatically went into the movements which result in that spectacular hold of the wrestler, the Flying Mare. Just in time he recalled that his opponent was a future comrade-in-arms and twisted the arm so that it bent at the elbow, rather than breaking. He hurled the other over his shoulder and as far as possible, to take the scrap out of him, and twirled quickly to meet the further attack of his sole remaining foe.

That phase of the combat failed to materialize.

A voice of command bit out, "Hold it, you lads!"

The original situation which had precipitated the fight was being duplicated. But while the three Lowers had failed to respond to Joe Mauser's tone of authority, there was no similar failure now.

The owner of the voice, beautifully done up in the uniform of Vacuum Tube Transport, complete to kilts and the swagger stick of the officer of Rank Colonel or above, stood glaring at them. Age, Joe estimated even as he came to attention, somewhere in the late twenties—an Upper in caste. Born to command. His face holding that arrogant, contemptuous expression once common to the patricians of Rome, the Prussian Junkers, the British ruling class of the Nineteenth Century. Joe knew the expression well. How well he knew it. On more than one occasion, he had dreamt of it.

Joe said, "Yes, sir."

"What in Zen goes on here? Are you lads overtranked?"

"No, sir," Joe's veteran opponent grumbled, his eyes on the ground, a schoolboy before the principal.

Joe said, evenly, "A private disagreement, sir."

"Disagreement!" the Upper snorted. His eyes went to the three fallen combatants, who were in various stages of reviving. "I'd hate to see you lads in a real scrap."

That brought a response from the noncombatants in the recruiting line. The *bon mot* wasn't that good but caste has its privileges and the laughter was just short of uproarious.

Which seemed to placate the kilted officer. He tapped his swagger stick against the side of his leg while he ran his eyes up and down Joe Mauser and the others, as though memorizing them for future reference.

"All right," he said. "Get back into the line, and you trouble-makers quiet down. We're processing as quickly as we can." And at that point he added insult to injury with an almost word-for-word repetition of what Joe had said a few moments earlier. "You'll get all the fighting you want from Hovercraft, if you can wait until then."

The four original participants of the rumpus resumed their places in various stages of sheepishness. The little fellow, nursing an obviously aching jaw, made a point of taking up his original position even while darting a look of thanks to Joe Mauser, who still stood where he had when the fight was interrupted.

The Upper looked at Joe. "Well, lad, are you interested in signing up with Vacuum Tube Transport or not?"

"Yes, sir," Joe said evenly. Then, "Joseph Mauser, sir. Category Military, Rank Captain."

"Indeed." The officer looked him up and down all over again, his nostrils high. "A Middle, I assume. And brawling with recruits." He held a long silence. "Very well, come with me." He turned and marched off.

Joe inwardly shrugged. This was a fine start for his pitch—fine start. He had half a mind to give it all up, here and now and head on up to Catskill to enlist with Continental Hovercraft. His big scheme would wait for another day. Nevertheless, he fell in behind the aristocrat and followed him to the offices which had been his original destination.

Two Rank Privates with 45–70 Springfields and wearing the Haer kilts in such wise as to indicate permanent status in Vacuum Tube Transport came to the salute as they approached. The Upper preceding Joe Mauser flicked his swagger stick in an easy nonchalance. Joe felt envious amusement. How long did it take to learn how to answer a salute with that degree of arrogant ease?

There were desks in here, and typers humming, as Vacuum Tube Transport office workers, mobilized for this special service, processed volunteers for the company forces. Harried noncoms and junior-grade officers buzzed everywhere, failing miserably to bring order to the chaos. To the right was a door with a medical cross newly painted on it. When it occasionally popped open to admit or emit a recruit, white-robed doctors, male nurses and half-nude men could be glimpsed beyond.

Joe followed the other through the press and to an inner office at which door he didn't bother to knock. He pushed his way through, waved in greeting with his swagger stick to the single occupant who looked up from the paper– and tape-strewn desk at which he sat.

Joe Mauser had seen the face before on Telly, though never so tired as this and never with the element of defeat to be read in the expression. Bullet-headed, barrel-figured Baron Malcolm

Haer of Vacuum Tube Transport. Category Transportation, Mid-Upper, and strong candidate for Upper-Upper upon retirement. However, there would be few who expected retirement in the immediate future. Hardly. Malcolm Haer found too obvious a lusty enjoyment in the competition between Vacuum Tube Transport and its stronger rivals.

Joe came to attention, bore the sharp scrutiny of his chosen commander-to-be. The older man's eyes went to the kilted Upper officer who had brought Joe along. "What is it, Balt?"

The other gestured with his stick at Joe. "Claims to be Rank Captain. Looking for a commission with us, Dad. I wouldn't know why." The last sentence was added lazily.

The older Haer shot an irritated glance at his son. "Possibly for the same reason mercenaries usually enlist for a fracas, Balt." His eyes came back to Joe.

Joe Mauser, still at attention even though in mufti, opened his mouth to give his name, category and rank, but the older man waved a hand negatively. "Captain Mauser, isn't it? I caught the fracas between Carbonaceous Fuel and United Miners, down on the Panhandle Reservation. Seems to me I've spotted you once or twice before, too."

"Yes, sir," Joe said. This was some improvement in the way things were going.

The older Haer was scowling at him. "Confound it, what are you doing with no more rank than captain? On the face of it, you're an old hand, a highly experienced veteran."

An old pro, we call ourselves, Joe said to himself. *Old pros, we call ourselves, among ourselves.*

Aloud, he said, "I was born a Mid-Lower, sir."

There was understanding in the old man's face, but Balt Haer said loftily, "What's that got to do with it? Promotion is quick and based on merit in Category Military."

At a certain point, if you are good combat officer material, you speak your mind no matter the rank of the man you are addressing. On this occasion, Joe Mauser needed few words. He let his eyes go up and down Balt Haer's immaculate uniform, taking in the swagger stick of the Rank Colonel or above. Joe said evenly, "Yes, sir."

Balt Haer flushed quick temper. "What do you mean by—"

But his father was chuckling. "You have spirit, captain. I need spirit now. You are quite correct. My son, though a capable officer, I assure you, has probably not participated in a fraction of the fracases you have to your credit. However, there is something to be said for the training available to we Uppers in the academies. For instance, captain, have you ever commanded a body of lads larger than, well, a *company?*"

Joe said flatly, "In the Douglas-Boeing versus Lockheed-Cessna fracas we took a high loss of officers when the Douglas-Boeing outfit rang in some fast-firing French *mitrailleuse* we didn't know they had. As my superiors took casualties I was field promoted to acting battalion commander, to acting regimental commander, to acting brigadier. For three days I held the rank of acting commander of brigade. We won."

Balt Haer snapped his fingers. "I remember that. Read quite a paper on it." He eyed Joe Mauser, almost respectfully. "Stonewall Cogswell got the credit for the victory and received his marshal's baton as a result."

"He was one of the few other officers that survived," Joe said dryly.

"But, Zen! You mean you got no promotion at all?"

Joe said, "I was upped to Low-Middle from High-Lower, sir. At my age, at the time, quite a promotion."

Baron Haer was remembering, too. "That was the fracas that brought on the howl from the Sovs. They claimed those *mitrailleuse* were post-1900 and violated the Universal Disarmament Pact. Yes, I recall that. Douglas-Boeing was able to prove that the weapon was used by the French as far back as the Franco-Prussian War." He eyed Joe with new interest now. "Sit down, captain. You too, Balt. Do you realize that Captain Mauser is the only recruit of officer rank we've had today?"

"Yes," the younger Haer said dryly. "However, it's too late to call the fracas off now. Hovercraft wouldn't stand for it, and the Category Military Department would back them. Our only alternative is unconditional surrender, and you know what that means."

"It means our family would probably be forced from control of the firm," the older man growled. "But nobody has suggested surrender on any terms. Nobody, thus far." He glared at his officer son, who took it with an easy shrug and swung a leg over the edge of his father's desk in the way of a seat.

Joe Mauser found a chair and lowered himself into it. Evidently, the foppish Balt Haer had no illusions about the spot his father had got the family corporation into. And the younger man was right, of course.

But the Baron wasn't blind to reality any more than he was a coward. He dismissed Balt Haer's defeatism from his mind and came back to Joe Mauser. "As I say, you're the only officer recruit today. Why?"

Joe said evenly, "I wouldn't know, sir. Perhaps free-lance Category Military men are occupied elsewhere. There's always a shortage of trained officers."

Baron Haer was waggling a finger negatively. "That's not what I mean, captain. You are an old hand. This is your category and you must know it well. Then why are *you* signing up with Vacuum Tube Transport rather than Hovercraft?"

Joe Mauser looked at him for a moment without speaking.

"Come, come, captain. I am an old hand too, in my category, and not a fool. I realize there is scarcely a soul in the West-world that expects anything but disaster for my colors. Pay rates have been widely posted. I can offer only five common shares of Vacuum Tube for a Rank Captain, win or lose. Hovercraft is doubling that, and can pick and choose among the best officers in the hemisphere."

Joe said softly, "I have all the shares I need."

Balt Haer had been looking back and forth between his father and the newcomer and becoming obviously more puzzled. He put in, "Well, what in Zen motivates you if it isn't the stock we offer?"

Joe glanced at the younger Haer to acknowledge the question but he spoke to the Baron. "Sir, as you said, you're no fool. However, you've been sucked in, this time. When you took on Hovercraft, you were thinking in terms of a regional dispute. You wanted to run one of your vacuum tube deals up to Fairbanks from Edmonton. You were expecting a minor fracas, involving possibly five thousand men. You never expected Hovercraft to parlay it up, through their connections in the Category Military Department, to a divisional magnitude fracas which you simply aren't large enough to afford. But Hovercraft was getting sick of your corporation. You've been nicking away at them too long. So they decided to do you in. They've hired Marshal Cogswell and the best combat officers in North America, and they're hiring the most competent veterans they can find. Every fracas buff who watches Telly figures you've had it. They've been watching you come up the aggressive way, the hard way, for a long time, but now they're all going to be sitting on the edges of their sofas waiting for you to get it."

Baron Haer's heavy face had hardened as Joe Mauser went on relentlessly. He growled, "Is this what everyone thinks?"

"Yes. Everyone intelligent enough to have an opinion." Joe made a motion of his head to the outer offices where the recruiting was proceeding. "Those men out there are rejects from Catskill, where old Baron Zwerdling is recruiting. Either that or they're inexperienced Low-Lowers, too stupid to realize they're sticking their necks out. Not one man in ten is a veteran. And when things begin to pickle, you want veterans."

Baron Malcolm Haer sat back in his chair and stared coldly at Captain Joe Mauser. He said, "At first I was moderately surprised that an old-time mercenary like yourself should chose my uniform, rather than Zwerdling's. Now I am increasingly mystified about motivation. So all over again I ask you captain: why are you requesting a commission in my force which you seem convinced will meet disaster?"

Joe wet his lips carefully. "I think I know a way you can win."

2

His permanent military rank the Haers had no way to alter, but they were short enough of competent officers that they gave him an acting rating and pay scale of major and command of a squadron of cavalry. Joe Mauser wasn't interested in a cavalry command this fracas, but he said nothing. Immediately, he had to size up the situation; it wasn't time as yet to reveal the big scheme. And, meanwhile, they could use him to whip the Rank Privates into shape.

He had left the offices of Baron Haer to go through the red tape involved in being signed up on a temporary basis in the Vacuum Tube Transport forces and reentered the confusion of the outer offices where the Lowers were being processed and given medicals. He reentered in time to run into a Telly team which was doing a live broadcast.

Joe Mauser remembered the news reporter who headed the team. He'd run into him two or three times in fracases. As a matter of fact, although Joe held the standard Military Category prejudices against Telly, he had a basic respect for this particular newsman. On the occasions he'd seen him before, the fellow was hot in the midst of the action even when things were in the dill. He took as many chances as did the average combatant, and you can't ask for more than that.

The other knew him, too, of course. It was part of his job to be able to spot the celebrities and near celebrities. He zeroed in on Joe now, making flicks of his hand to direct the cameras. Joe, of course, was fully aware of the value of Telly and was glad to co-operate.

"Captain! Captain Mauser, isn't it? Joe Mauser who held out for four days in the swamps of Louisiana with a single company while his ranking officers reformed behind him."

That was one way of putting it, but both Joe and the newscaster who had covered the debacle knew the reality of the situation. When the front had collapsed, his commanders—of Upper caste, of course—had hauled out, leaving him to fight a delaying action while they mended their fences with the enemy, coming to the best terms possible. Yes, that had been the United Oil versus Allied Petroleum fracas, and Joe had emerged with little either in glory or pelf.

The average fracas fan wasn't on an intellectual level to appreciate anything other than victory. The good guys win, the bad guys lose—that's obvious, isn't it? Not one out of ten Telly followers of the fracases was interested in a well-conducted retreat or holding action. They wanted blood, lots of it, and they identified with the winning side.

Joe Mauser wasn't particularly bitter about this aspect. It was part of his way of life. In fact, his pet peeve was the *real* buff. The type, man or woman, who could remember every fracas you'd ever been in, every time you'd copped one, and how long you'd been in the hospital. Fans who could remember, even better than you could, every time the situation had pickled on you and you'd had to fight your way out as best you could. They'd tell you about it, their eyes gleaming, sometimes a slightest trickle of spittle at the sides of their mouths. They usually wanted an autograph, or a souvenir such as a uniform button.

Now Joe said to the Telly reporter, "That's right, Captain Mauser. Acting major, in this fracas, ah—"

"Freddy. Freddy Soligen. You remember me, captain—"

"Of course I do, Freddy. We've been in the dill, side by side, more than once, and even when I was too scared to use my side arm, you'd be scanning away with your camera."

"Ha ha, listen to the captain, folks. I hope my boss is tuned in. But seriously, Captain Mauser, what do you think the chances of Vacuum Tube Transport are in this fracas?"

Joe looked into the camera lens, earnestly. "The best, of course, or I wouldn't have signed up with Baron Haer, Freddy. Justice triumphs, and anybody who is familiar with the issues in this fracas knows that Baron Haer is on the side of true right."

Freddy said, holding any sarcasm he must have felt, "What would you say the issues were, captain?"

"The basic North American free enterprise right to compete. Hovercraft has held a near monopoly in transport to Fairbanks. Vacuum Tube Transport wishes to lower costs and bring the consumers of Fairbanks better service through running a vacuum tube to that area. What could be more in the traditions of the West-world? Continental Hovercraft stands in the way and it is they who have demanded of the Category Military Department a trial by arms. On the face of it, justice is on the side of Baron Haer."

Freddy Soligen said into the camera, "Well, all you good people of the Telly world, that's an able summation the captain has made, but it certainly doesn't jibe with the word of Baron Zwerdling we heard this morning, does it? However justice triumphs and we'll see what the field of combat will have to offer. Thank you, thank you very much, Captain Mauser. All of us, all of us tuned in today, hope that you personally will run into no dill in this fracas."

"Thanks, Freddy. Thanks all," Joe said into the camera before turning away. He wasn't particularly keen about this part of the job, but you couldn't underrate the importance of pleasing the buffs. In the long run it was your career, your chances for promotion both in military rank and ultimately in caste. It was the way the fans took you up, boosted you, idolized you, worshipped you if you really made it. He, Joe Mauser, was only a minor celebrity; he appreciated every chance he had to be interviewed by such a popular reporter as Freddy Soligen.

Even as he turned, he spotted the four men with whom he'd had his spat earlier. The little fellow was still to the fore. Evidently, the others had decided the one place extra that he represented wasn't worth the trouble he'd put in their way defending it.

On an impulse he stepped up to the small man, who began a grin of recognition, a grin that transformed his feisty face. A revelation of an inner warmth beyond average in a world which had lost much of its human warmth.

Joe said, "Like a job, soldier?"

"Name's Max. Max Mainz. Sure I want a job. That's why I'm in this everlasting line."

Joe said, "First fracas for you, isn't it?"

"Yeah, but I had basic training in school."

"What do you weigh, Max?"

Max's face soured. "About one twenty."

"Did you check out on semaphore in school?"

"Well, sure. I'm Category Food, Sub-division Cooking, Branch Chef, but, like I say, I took basic military training, like most everybody else."

"I'm Captain Joe Mauser. How'd you like to be my batman?"

Max screwed up his already not overly handsome face. "Gee, I don't know. I kinda joined up to see some action. Get into the dill. You know what I mean."

Joe said dryly, "See here, Mainz, you'll probably find more pickled situations next to me than you'll want—and you'll come out alive."

The recruiting sergeant looked up from the desk. It was Max Mainz's turn to be processed. The sergeant said, "Lad, take a good opportunity when it drops in your lap. The captain is one of the best in the field. You'll learn more, get better chances for promotion, if you stick with him."

Joe couldn't remember ever having run into the sergeant before, but he said, "Thanks, sergeant."

The other said, evidently realizing Joe didn't recognize him, "We were together on the Chihuahua Reservation, on the jurisdictional fracas between the United Miners and the Teamsters, sir."

It had been almost fifteen years ago. About all that Joe Mauser remembered of that fracas was the abnormal number of casualties they'd taken. His side had lost, but from this distance in time Joe couldn't even remember what force he'd been with. But now he said, "That's right. I thought I recognized you, sergeant."

"It was my first fracas, sir." The sergeant went business-like. "If you want I should hustle this lad though, captain—"

"Please do, sergeant." Joe added to Max, "I'm not sure where my billet will be. When you're through all this, locate the officer's mess and wait there for me."

"Well, O.K.," Max said doubtfully, still scowling but evidently a servant of an officer, if he wanted to be or not.

"Sir," the sergeant added ominously. "If you've had basic, you know enough how to address an officer."

"Well, yes sir," Max said hurriedly.

Joe began to turn away, but then spotted the man immediately behind Max Mainz. He was one of the three with whom Joe had tangled earlier, the one who'd obviously had previous combat experience. He pointed the man out to the sergeant. "You'd better give this lad at least temporary rank of corporal. He's a veteran and we're short of veterans."

The sergeant said, "Yes, sir. We sure are." Joe's former foe looked properly thankful.

Joe Mauser finished off his own red tape and headed for the street to locate a military tailor who could do him up a set of the Haer kilts and fill his other dress requirements. As he went, he wondered vaguely just how many different uniforms he had worn in his time.

In a career as long as his own from time to time you took semi-permanent positions in bodyguards, company police, or possibly the permanent combat troops of this corporation or that. But largely, if you were ambitious, you signed up for the fracases, and that meant into a uniform and out of it again in as short a period as a couple of weeks.

At the door he tried to move aside but was too slow for the quick-moving young woman who caromed off him. He caught her arm to prevent her from stumbling. She looked at him with less than thanks.

Joe took the blame for the collision. "Sorry," he said. "I'm afraid I didn't see you, Miss."

"Obviously," she said coldly. Her eyes went up and down him, and for a moment he wondered where he had seen her before. Somewhere, he was sure.

She was dressed as they dress who have never considered cost and she had an elusive beauty which would have been even the more hadn't her face projected quite such a serious outlook. Her features were more delicate than those to which he was usually attracted. Her lips were less full, but still—he was reminded of the classic ideal of the British Romantic Period, the women sung of by Byron and Keats, Shelley and Moore.

She said, "Is there any particular reason why you should be staring at me, Mr.—"

"Captain Mauser," Joe said hurriedly. "I'm afraid I've been rude, Miss—well, I thought I recognized you."

She took in his civilian dress, typed it automatically, and came to an erroneous conclusion. She said, "Captain? You mean that with everyone else I know drawing down ranks from Lieutenant Colonel to Brigadier General, you can't make anything better than Captain?"

Joe winced. He said carefully, "I came up from the ranks, Miss. Captain is quite an achievement, believe me."

"Up from the ranks!" She took in his clothes again. "You mean you're a Middle? You neither talk nor look like a Middle, captain." She used the caste rating as though it was not *quite* a derogatory term.

Not that she meant to be deliberately insulting, Joe knew, wearily. How well he knew. It was simply born in her. As once a well-educated aristocracy had, not necessarily unkindly, named their status inferiors *niggers*: or other aristocrats, in another area of the country, had named theirs *greasers*. Yes, how well he knew.

He said very evenly, "Mid-Middle now, Miss. However, I was born in the Lower castes."

An eyebrow went up. "Zen! You must have put in many an hour studying. You talk like an Upper, captain." She dropped all interest in him and turned to resume her journey.

"Just a moment," Joe said. "You can't go in there, Miss—"

Her eyebrows went up again. "The name is Haer," she said. "Why can't I go in here, captain?"

Now it came to him why he had thought he recognized her. She had basic features similar to those of that overbred poppycock Balt Haer.

"Sorry," Joe said. "I suppose under the circumstances, you can. I was about to tell you that they're recruiting with lads running around half clothed. Medical inspections, that sort of thing."

She made a noise through her nose and said over her shoulder, even as she sailed on. "Besides being a Haer, I'm an M.D., captain. At the ludicrous sight of a man shuffling about in his shorts, I seldom blush."

She was gone.

Joe Mauser looked after her. "I'll bet you don't," he muttered.

Had she waited a few minutes he could have explained his Upper accent and his unlikely education. When you'd copped one you had plenty of opportunity in hospital beds to read, to study, to contemplate—and to fester away in your own schemes of rebellion against fate. And Joe had copped many in his time.

3

By the time Joe Mauser called it a day and retired to his quarters he was exhausted to the point where his basic dissatisfaction with the trade he followed was heavily upon him.

He had met his immediate senior officers, largely dilettante Uppers with precious little field experience, and was unimpressed. And he'd met his own junior officers and was shocked. By the looks of things at this stage, Captain Mauser's squadron would be going into this fracas both undermanned with Rank Privates and with junior officers composed largely of temporarily promoted noncoms. If this was typical of Baron Haer's total force, then Balt Haer had been correct, unconditional surrender was to be considered, no matter how disastrous to Haer family fortunes.

Joe had been able to take immediate delivery of one kilted uniform. Now, inside his quarters, he began stripping out of his jacket. Somewhat to his surprise, the small man he had selected earlier in the day to be his batman entered from an inner room, also resplendent in the Haer uniform and obviously happily so.

He helped his superior out of the jacket with an ease that held no subservience but at the same time was correctly respectful. You'd have thought him a batman specially trained.

Joe grunted, "Max, isn't it? I'd forgotten about you. Glad you found our billet all right."

Max said, "Yes, sir. Would the captain like a drink? I picked up a bottle of applejack. Applejack's the drink around here, sir. Makes a topnotch highball with gingerale and a twist of lemon."

Joe Mauser looked at him. Evidently his tapping this man for orderly had been sheer fortune. Well, Joe Mauser could use some good luck on this job. He hoped it didn't end with selecting a batman.

Joe said, "An applejack highball sounds wonderful, Max. Got ice?"

"Of course, sir." Max left the small room.

Joe Mauser and his officers were billeted in what had once been a motel on the old road between Kingston and Woodstock. There was a shower and a tiny kitchenette in each cottage. That was one advantage in a fracas held in an area where there were plenty of facilities. Such military reservations as that of the Little Big Horn in Montana and particularly some of those in the Southwest and Mexico were another thing.

Joe lowered himself into the room's easy chair and bent down to untie his laces. He kicked his shoes off. He could use that drink. He began wondering all over again if his scheme for winning this Vacuum Tube Transport versus Continental Hovercraft fracas would come off. The more he saw of Baron Haer's inadequate forces, the more he wondered. He hadn't expected Vacuum Tube to be in *this* bad a shape. Baron Haer had been riding high for so long that one would have thought his reputation for victory would have lured many a veteran to his colors. Evidently they hadn't bitten. The word was out all right.

Max Mainz returned with the drink.

Joe said, "You had one yourself?"

"No, sir."

Joe said, "Well, Zen, go get yourself one and come on back and sit down. Let's get acquainted."

"Well, yessir." Max disappeared back into the kitchenette to return almost immediately. The little man slid into a chair, drink awkwardly in hand.

His superior sized him up, all over again. Not much more than a kid, really. Surprisingly aggressive for a Lower who must have been raised from childhood in a trank-bemused, Telly-entertained household. The fact that he'd broken away from that environment at all was to his credit; it was considerably easier to conform. But then it is always easier to conform, to run with the herd, as Joe well knew. His own break hadn't been an easy one. "Relax," he said now.

Max said, "Well, this is my first day."

"I know. And you've been seeing Telly shows all your life showing how an orderly conducts himself in the presence of his superior." Joe took another pull and yawned. "Well, forget about it. With any man who goes into a fracas with me, I like to be on close terms. When things pickle, I want him to be on my side, not nursing some peeve brought on by his officer trying to give him an inferiority complex."

The little man was eying him in surprise.

Joe finished his highball and came to his feet to get another one. He said, "On two occasions I've had an orderly save my life. I'm not taking any chances but that there might be a third opportunity."

"Well, yessir. Does the captain want me to get him—"

"I'll get it," Joe said.

When he'd returned to his chair, he said, "Why did you join up with Baron Haer, Max?"

The other shrugged it off. "The usual. The excitement. The idea of all those fans watching me on Telly. The share of common stock I'll get. And, you never know, maybe a promotion in caste. I wouldn't mind making Upper-Lower."

Joe said sourly, "One fracas and you'll be over that desire to have the buffs watching you on Telly while they sit around in their front rooms sucking on tranks. And you'll probably be over the desire for the excitement, too. Of course, the share of stock is another thing."

"You aren't just countin' down, captain," Max said, an almost surly overtone in his voice. "You don't know what it's like being born with no more common stock shares than a Mid-Lower."

Joe held his peace, sipping at his drink, taking this one more slowly. He let his eyebrows rise to encourage the other to go on.

Max said doggedly, "Sure, they call it People's Capitalism and everybody gets issued enough shares to insure him a basic living all the way from the cradle to the grave, like they say. But let me tell you, you're a Middle, and you don't realize how basic the basic living of a Lower can be."

Joe yawned. If he hadn't been so tired, there would have been more amusement in the situation.

Max was still dogged. "Unless you can add to those shares of stock, it's pretty drab, captain. You wouldn't know."

Joe said, "Why don't you work? A Lower can always add to his stock by working."

Max stirred in indignity. "Work? Listen, sir, that's just one more field that's been automated right out of existence. Category Food Preparation, Sub-division Cooking, Branch Chef. Cooking isn't left in the hands of slobs who might drop a cake of soap into the soup. It's done automatic. The only new changes made in cooking are by real top experts, almost scientists like. And most of them are Uppers, mind you."

Joe Mauser sighed inwardly. So his find in batmen wasn't going to be as wonderful as all that, after all. The man might have been born into the food preparation category from a long line of chefs, but evidently he knew precious little about his field. Joe might have suspected. He himself had been born into Clothing Category, Sub-division Shoes, Branch Repair—Cobbler—a meaningless trade since shoes were no longer repaired but discarded upon showing signs of wear. In an economy of complete abundance, there is little reason for repair of basic commodities. It was high time the government investigated category assignment and reshuffled and reassigned half the nation's population. But then, of course, was the question of what to do with the technologically unemployed.

Max was saying, "The only way I could figure on a promotion to a higher caste, or the only way to earn stock shares, was by crossing categories. And you know what that means. Either Category Military or Category Religion, and I sure as Zen don't know nothing about religion."

Joe said mildly, "Theoretically, you can cross categories into any field you want, Max."

Max snorted. "Theoretically is right . . . sir. You ever heard about anybody born a Lower, or even a Middle like yourself, cross categories to, say, some Upper category like banking?"

Joe chuckled. He liked this peppery little fellow. If Max worked out as well as Joe thought he might, there was a possibility of taking him along to the next fracas.

Max was saying, "I'm not saying anything against the old-time way of doing things or talking against the government, but I'll tell you, captain, every year goes by it gets harder and harder for a man to raise his caste or to earn some additional stock shares."

The applejack had worked enough on Joe for him to rise against one of his pet peeves. He said, "That term, the old-time way, is strictly Telly talk, Max. We don't do things *the old-time way*. No nation in history ever has—with the possible exception of Egypt. Socioeconomics are in a continual flux, and here in this country we no more do things in the way they did fifty years ago than fifty years ago they did them the way the American Revolutionists outlined back in the Eighteenth Century."

Max was staring at him. "I don't get that, sir."

Joe said impatiently, "Max, the politico-economic system we have today is an outgrowth of what went earlier. The welfare state, the freezing of the status quo, the Frigid Fracas between the West-world and the Sov-world, industrial automation until useful employment is all but needless—all these things were to be found in embryo more than fifty years ago."

"Well, maybe the captain's right, but you gotta admit, sir, that mostly we do things the old way. We still got the Constitution and the two-party system and—"

Joe was wearying of the conversation now. You seldom ran into anyone, even in Middle caste, the traditionally professional class, interested enough in such subjects to be worth arguing with. He said, "The Constitution, Max, has got to the point of the Bible. Interpret it the way you wish, and you can find anything. If not, you can always make a new amendment. So far as the two-party system is concerned, what effect does it have when there are no differences between the two parties? That phase of pseudo-democracy was beginning as far back as the 1930s when they began passing State laws hindering the emerging of new political parties. By the time they were insured against a third party working its way through the maze of election laws, the two parties had become so similar that elections became almost as big a farce as over in the Sov-world."

"A farce?" Max ejaculated indignantly, forgetting his servant status. "That means not so good, doesn't it? Far as I'm concerned, election day is tops. The one day a Lower is just as good as an Upper. The one day how many shares you got makes no difference. Everybody has everything."

"Sure, sure, sure," Joe sighed. "The modern equivalent of the Roman Bacchanalia. Election day in the West-world when no one, for just that one day, is freer than anyone else."

"Well, what's wrong with that?" The other was all but belligerent. "That's the trouble with you Middles and Uppers, you don't know how it is to be a Lower and—"

Joe snapped suddenly, "I was born a Mid-Lower myself, Max. Don't give me that nonsense."

Max gaped at him, utterly unbelieving.

Joe's irritation fell away. He held out his glass. "Get us a couple of more drinks, Max, and I'll tell you a story."

By the time the fresh drink came, Joe Mauser was sorry he'd made the offer. He thought back. He hadn't told anyone the Joe Mauser story in many a year. And, as he recalled, the last time had been when he was well into his cups, on an election day at that, and his listener had been a Low-Upper, a hereditary aristocrat, one of the one per cent of the upper strata of the nation. Zen! How the man had laughed. He'd roared his amusement till the tears ran.

However, Joe said, "Max, I was born in the same caste you were—average father, mother, sisters and brothers. They subsisted on the basic income guaranteed from birth, sat and watched Telly for an unbelievable number of hours each day, took trank to keep themselves happy. And thought I was crazy because I didn't. Dad was the sort of man who'd take his belt off to a child of his who questioned such school-taught slogans as *What was good enough for Daddy is good enough for me.*

"They were all fracas fans, of course. As far back as I can remember the picture is there of them gathered around the Telly, screaming excitement." Joe Mauser sneered, uncharacteristically.

"You don't sound much like you're in favor of your trade, captain," Max said.

Joe came to his feet, putting down his still half-full glass. "I'll make this epic story short, Max. As you said, the two actually valid methods of rising above the level in which you were born are in the Military and Religious Categories. Like you, even I couldn't stomach the latter."

Joe Mauser hesitated, then finished it off. "Max, there have been few societies that man has evolved that didn't allow in some manner for the competent or sly, the intelligent or the opportunist, the brave or the strong, to work his way to the top. I don't know which of these I personally fit into, but I rebel against remaining in the lower categories of a stratified society. Do I make myself clear?"

"Well, no sir, not exactly."

Joe said flatly, "I'm going to fight my way to the top and nothing is going to stand in the way. Is that clearer?"

"Yessir," Max said, taken aback.

4

After routine morning duties, Joe Mauser returned to his billet and mystified Max Mainz by not only changing into mufti himself but having Max do the same.

In fact, the new batman protested faintly. He hadn't nearly, as yet, got over the glory of wearing his kilts and was looking forward to parading around town in them. He had a point, of course. The appointed time for the fracas was getting closer and buffs were beginning to stream into town to bask in the atmosphere of threatened death. Everybody knew what a military center, on the outskirts of a fracas reservation such as the Catskills, was like immediately preceding a clash between rival corporations. The high-strung gaiety, the drinking, the overtranking, the relaxation of mores. Even a Rank Private had it made. Admiring civilians to buy drinks and hang on your every word, and more important still, sensuous-eyed women, their faces slack in thinly suppressed passion. It was a recognized phenomenon, even Max Mainz knew—this desire on the part of women Telly fans to date a man, and then watch him later, killing or being killed.

"Time enough to wear your fancy uniform," Joe Mauser growled at him. "In fact, tomorrow's a local election day. Parlay that up on top of all the fracas fans gravitating into town and you'll have a wingding the likes of nothing you've seen before."

"Well, yessir," Max begrudged. "Where're we going now, captain?"

"To the airport. Come along."

Joe Mauser led the way to his sports hovercar and as soon as the two were settled into the bucket seats, hit the lift lever with the butt of his left hand. Aircushion-borne, he tread down on the accelerator.

Max Mainz was impressed. "You know," he said. "I never been in one of these swanky sports jobs before. The kinda car you can afford on the income of a Mid-Lower's stock aren't—"

"Knock it off," Joe said wearily. "Carping we'll always have with us evidently, but in spite of all the beefing in every strata from Low-Lower to Upper-Middle, I've yet to see any signs of organized protest against our present politico-economic system."

"Hey," Max said. "Don't get me wrong. What was good enough for Dad is good enough for me. You won't catch me talking against the government."

"Hm-m-m," Joe murmured. "And all the other clichés taught to us to preserve the status quo, our People's Capitalism." They were reaching the outskirts of town, crossing the Esopus. The airport lay only a mile or so beyond.

It was obviously too deep for Max, and since he didn't understand, he assumed his superior didn't know what he was talking about. He said, tolerantly, "Well, what's wrong with People's Capitalism? Everybody owns the corporations. Damnsight better than the Sovs have."

Joe said sourly, "We've got one optical illusion, they've got another, Max. Over there they claim the proletariat owns the means of production. Great. But the Party members are the ones who control it, and, as a result they manage to do all right for themselves. The Party hierarchy over there are like our Uppers over here."

"Yeah." Max was being particularly dense. "I've seen a lot about it on Telly. You know, when there isn't a good fracas on, you tune to one of them educational shows, like—"

Joe winced at the term *educational*, but held his peace.

"It's pretty rugged over there. But in the West-world, the people own a corporation's stock and they run it and get the benefit."

"At least it makes a beautiful story," Joe said dryly. "Look, Max. Suppose you have a corporation that has two hundred thousand shares out and they're distributed among one hundred thousand and one persons. One hundred thousand of these own one share apiece, but the remaining stockholder owns the other hundred thousand."

"I don't know what you're getting at," Max said.

Joe Mauser was tired of the discussion. "Briefly," he said, "we have the illusion that this is a People's Capitalism, with all stock in the hands of the People. Actually, as ever before, the stock is in the hands of the Uppers, all except a mere dribble. They own the country and they run it for their own benefit."

Max shot a less than military glance at him. "Hey, you're not one of these Sovs yourself, are you?"

They were coming into the parking area near the Administration Building of the airport. "No," Joe said so softly that Max could hardly hear his words. "Only a Mid-Middle on the make."

Followed by Max, he strode quickly to the Administration Building, presented his credit identification at the desk and requested a light aircraft for a period of three hours. The clerk, hardly looking up, began going through motions, speaking into telescreens.

The clerk said finally, "You might have a small wait, sir. Quite a few of the officers involved in this fracas have been renting out taxi-planes almost as fast as they're available."

That didn't surprise Joe Mauser. Any competent officer made a point of an aerial survey of the battle reservation before going into a fracas. Aircraft, of course, couldn't be used *during* the fray, since they postdated the turn of the century, and hence were relegated to the cemetery of military devices along with such items as nuclear weapons, tanks, and even gasoline-propelled vehicles of size to be useful.

Use an aircraft in a fracas, or even *build* an aircraft for military usage, and you'd have a howl go up from the military attachés from the Sov-world that would be heard all the way to Budapest. Not a fracas went by but there were scores, if not hundreds, of military observers, keen-eyed-to check whether or not any really modern tools of war were being illegally utilized. Joe Mauser sometimes wondered if the West-world observers, over in the Sov-world, were as hair-fine in their living up to the rules of the Universal Disarmament Pact. Probably. But, for that matter, they didn't have the same system of fighting fracases over there as in the West.

Max took a chair while he waited and thumbed through a fan magazine. From time to time he found his own face in such publications. He was a third-rate celebrity, really. Luck hadn't been with him so far as the buffs were concerned. They wanted spectacular victories, murderous situations in which they could lose themselves in vicarious sadistic thrills. Joe had reached most of his peaks while in retreat, or commanding a holding action. His officers appreciated him and so did the ultra-knowledgable fracas buffs—but he was all but an unknown to the average dimwit who spent most of his life glued to the Telly set, watching men butcher each other.

On the various occasions when matters had pickled and Joe had to fight his way out against difficult odds, using spectacular tactics in desperation, he was almost always off camera. Purely luck. On top of skill, determination, experience and courage, you had to have luck in the Military Category to get anywhere.

This time Joe was going to manufacture his own.

A voice said, "Ah, Captain Mauser."

Joe looked up, then came to his feet quickly. In automatic reflex, he began to come to the salute but then caught himself. He said stiffly, "My compliments, Marshal Cogswell."

The other was a smallish man, but strikingly strong of face and strongly built. His voice was clipped, clear and had the air of command as though born with it. He, like Joe, wore mufti and now extended his hand to be shaken.

"I hear you've signed up with Baron Haer, captain. I was rather expecting you to come in with me. Had a place for a good aide de camp. Liked your work in that last fracas we went through together."

"Thank you, sir," Joe said. Stonewall Cogswell was as good a tactician as freelanced, and he was more than that. He was a judge of men and a stickler for detail. And right now, if Joe Mauser knew Marshal Stonewall Cogswell as well as he thought, Cogswell was smelling a rat. There was no reason why old pro Joe Mauser should sign up with a sure loser like Vacuum Tube when he could have earned more shares taking a commission with Hovercraft.

He was looking at Joe brightly, the question in his eyes. Three or four of his staff were behind a few paces, looking polite, but Cogswell didn't bring them into the conversation. Joe knew most by sight. Good men all. Old pros all. He felt another twinge of doubt.

Joe had to cover. He said, "I was offered a particularly good contract, sir. Too good to resist."

The other nodded, as though inwardly coming to a satisfactory conclusion. "Baron Haer's connections, eh? He's probably offered to back you for a bounce in caste. Is that it, Joe?"

Joe Mauser flushed. Stonewall Cogswell knew what he was talking about. He'd been born into Middle status himself and had become an Upper the hard way. His path wasn't as long as Joe's was going to be, but long enough, and he knew how rocky the climb was. How very rocky.

Joe said stiffly, "I'm afraid I'm in no position to discuss my commander's military contracts, marshal. We're in mufti, but after all—"

Cogswell's lean face registered one of his infrequent grimaces of humor. "I understand, Joe. Well, good luck and I hope things don't pickle for you in the coming fracas. Possibly we'll find ourselves aligned together again at some future time."

"Thank you, sir," Joe said, once more having to catch himself to prevent an automatic salute.

Cogswell and his staff went off, leaving Joe looking after them. Even the marshal's staff members were top men any of whom could have conducted a divisional magnitude fracas. Joe felt the coldness in his stomach again. Although it must have looked like a cinch, the enemy wasn't taking any chances whatsoever. Cogswell and his officers were undoubtedly here at the airport for the same reason as Joe. They wanted a thorough aerial reconnaissance of the battlefield-to-be, before the issue was joined.

Max was standing at his elbow. "Who was that, sir? Looks like a real tough one."

"He is a real tough one," Joe said sourly. "That's Stonewall Cogswell, the best field commander in North America."

Max pursed his lips. "I never seen him out of uniform before. Lots of times on Telly, but never out of uniform. I thought he was taller than that."

"He fights with his brains," Joe said, still looking after the craggy field marshal. "He doesn't have to be any taller."

Max scowled. "Where'd he ever get that nickname, sir?"

"Stonewall?" Joe was turning to resume his chair and magazine. "He's supposed to be a student of a top general back in the American Civil War. Uses some of the original Stonewall's tactics."

Max was out of his depth. "American Civil War? Was that much of a fracas, captain? It musta been before my time."

"It was quite a fracas," Joe said dryly. "Lot of good lads died. A hundred years after it was fought, the *reasons* it was fought seemed about as valid as those we fight fracases for today. Personally I—"

He had to cut it short. They were calling him on the address system. His aircraft was ready. Joe made his way to the hangars, followed by Max Mainz. He was going to pilot the airplane himself and old Stonewall Cogswell would have been surprised at what Joe Mauser was looking for.

5

By the time they had returned to quarters, there was a message waiting for Captain Mauser. He was to report to the officer commanding reconnaissance.

Joe redressed in the Haer kilts and proceeded to headquarters.

The officer commanding reconnaissance turned out to be none other than Balt Haer, natty as ever, and, as ever, arrogantly tapping his swagger stick against his leg.

"Zen! Captain," he complained. "Where have you been? Off on a trank kick? We've got to get organized."

Joe Mauser snapped him a salute. "No, sir. I rented an aircraft to scout out the terrain over which we'll be fighting."

"Indeed. And what were your impressions, captain?" There was an overtone which suggested that it made little difference what impressions a captain of cavalry might have gained.

Joe shrugged. "Largely mountains, hills, woods. Good reconnaissance is going to make the difference in this one. And in the fracas itself cavalry is going to be more important than either artillery or infantry. A Nathan Forrest fracas, sir. A matter of getting there fastest with the mostest."

Balt Haer said amusedly, "Thanks for your opinion, captain. Fortunately, our staff has already come largely to the same conclusions. Undoubtedly, they'll be glad to hear your wide experience bears them out."

Joe said evenly, "It's a rather obvious conclusion, of course." He took this as it came, having been through it before. The dilettante amateur's dislike of the old pro. The amateur in command who knew full well he was less capable than many of those below him in rank.

"Of course, captain," Balt Haer flicked his swagger stick against his leg. "But to the point. Your squadron is to be deployed as scouts under my overall command. You've had cavalry experience, I assume."

"Yes, sir. In various fracases over the past fifteen years."

"Very well. Now then, to get to the reason I have summoned you. Yesterday in my father's office you intimated that you had some grandiose scheme which would bring victory to the Haer colors. But then, on some thin excuse, refused to divulge just what the scheme might be."

Joe Mauser looked at him unblinkingly.

Balt Haer said: "Now I'd like to have your opinion on just how Vacuum Tube Transport can extract itself from what would seem a poor position at best."

In all there were four others in the office, two women clerks fluttering away at typers, and two of Balt Haer's junior officers. They seemed only mildly interested in the conversation between Balt and Joe.

Joe wet his lips carefully. The Haer scion was his commanding officer. He said, "Sir, what I had in mind is a new gimmick. At this stage, if I told anybody and it leaked, it'd never be effective, not even this first time."

Haer observed him coldly. "And you think me incapable of keeping your secret, ah, *gimmick*, I believe is the idiomatic term you used."

Joe Mauser's eyes shifted around the room, taking in the other four, who were now looking at him.

Balt Haer rapped, "These members of my staff are all trusted Haer employees, Captain Mauser. They are not fly-by-night freelancers hired for a week or two."

Joe said, "Yes, sir. But it's been my experience that one person can hold a secret. It's twice as hard for two, and from there on it's a decreasing probability in a geometric ratio."

The younger Haer's stick rapped the side of his leg, impatiently. "Suppose I inform you that this is a command, captain? I have little confidence in a supposed gimmick that will rescue our forces from disaster and I rather dislike the idea of a captain of one of my squadrons dashing about with such a bee in his bonnet when he should be obeying my commands."

Joe kept his voice respectful. "Then, sir, I'd request that we take the matter to the Commander in Chief, your father."

"Indeed!"

Joe said, "Sir, I've been working on this a long time. I can't afford to risk throwing the idea away."

Balt Haer glared at him. "Very well, captain. I'll call your bluff. Come along." He turned on his heel and headed from the room.

Joe Mauser shrugged in resignation and followed him.

The old Baron wasn't much happier about Joe Mauser's secrets than was his son. It had only been the day before that he had taken Joe on, but already he had seemed to have aged in appearance. Evidently, each hour that went by made it increasingly clear just how perilous a position he had assumed. Vacuum Tube Transport had elbowed, buffaloed, bluffed and edged itself up to the outskirts of the really big time. The Baron's ability, his aggressiveness, his flair, his political pull, had all helped, but now the chips were down. He was up against one of the biggies, and this particular biggy was tired of ambitious little Vacuum Tube Transport.

He listened to his son's words, listened to Joe's defense.

He said, looking at Joe, "If I understand this, you have some scheme which you think will bring victory in spite of what seems a disastrous situation."

"Yes, sir."

The two Haers looked at him, one impatiently, the other in weariness.

Joe said, "I'm gambling everything on this, sir. I'm no Rank Private in his first fracas. I deserve to be given some leeway."

Balt Haer snorted. "Gambling everything! What in Zen would *you* have to gamble, captain? The whole Haer family fortunes are tied up. Hovercraft is out for blood. They won't be satisfied with a token victory and a negotiated compromise. They'll devastate us. Thousands of mercenaries killed, with all that means in indemnities; millions upon millions in expensive military equipment, most of which we've had to hire and will have to recompensate for. Can you imagine the value of our stock after Stonewall Cogswell has finished with us? Why, every two-by-four trucking outfit in North

America will be challenging us, and we won't have the forces to meet a minor skirmish."

Joe reached into an inner pocket and laid a sheaf of documents on the desk of Baron Malcolm Haer. The Baron scowled down at them.

Joe said simply, "I've been accumulating stock since before I was eighteen and I've taken good care of my portfolio in spite of taxes and the various other pitfalls which make the accumulation of capital practically impossible. Yesterday, I sold all of my portfolio I was legally allowed to sell and converted to Vacuum Tube Transport." He added, dryly, "Getting it at an excellent rate, by the way."

Balt Haer mulled through the papers, unbelievingly. "Zen!" he ejaculated. "The fool really did it. He's sunk a small fortune into our stock."

Baron Haer growled at his son, "You seem considerably more convinced of our defeat than the captain, here. Perhaps I should reverse your positions of command."

His son grunted, but said nothing.

Old Malcolm Haer's eyes came back to Joe. "Admittedly, I thought you on the romantic side yesterday, with your hints of some scheme which would lead us out of the wilderness, so to speak. Now I wonder if you might not really have something. Very well, I respect your claimed need for secrecy. Espionage is not exactly an antiquated military field."

"Thank you, sir."

But the Baron was still staring at him. "However, there's more to it than that. Why not take this great scheme to Marshal Cogswell? And yesterday you mentioned that the Telly sets of the nation would be tuned in on this fracas, and obviously you are correct. The question becomes, what of it?"

The fat was in the fire now. Joe Mauser avoided the haughty stare of young Balt Haer and addressed himself to the older man. "You have political pull, sir. Oh, I know you don't make and break presidents. You couldn't even pull enough wires to keep Hovercraft from making this a divisional magnitude fracas—but you have pull enough for my needs."

Baron Haer leaned back in his chair, his barrellike body causing that article of furniture to creak. He crossed his hands over his stomach. "And what are your needs, Captain Mauser?"

Joe said evenly, "If I can bring this off, I'll be a fracas buff celebrity. I don't have any illusions about the fickleness of the Telly fans, but for a day or two I'll be on top. If at the same time I had your all-out support, pulling what strings you could reach—"

"Why then, you'd be promoted to Upper, wouldn't you, captain?" Balt Haer finished for him, amusement in his voice.

"That's what I'm gambling on," Joe said evenly.

The younger Haer grinned at his father superciliously. "So our captain says he will defeat Stonewall Cogswell in return for your sponsoring his becoming a member of the nation's elite."

"Good Heavens, is the supposed cream of the nation now selected on no higher a level than this?" There was sarcasm in the words.

The three men turned. It was the girl Joe had bumped into the day before. The Haers didn't seem surprised at her entrance.

"Nadine," the older man growled. "Captain Joseph Mauser, who has been given a commission in our forces."

Joe went through the routine of a Middle of officer's rank being introduced to a lady of Upper caste. She smiled at him, somewhat mockingly, and failed to make standard response.

Nadine Haer said, "I repeat, what is this service the captain can render the house of Haer so important that pressure should be brought to raise him to Upper caste? It would seem unlikely that he is a noted scientist, an outstanding artist, a great teacher—"

Joe said, uncomfortably, "They say the military is a science, too."

Her expression was almost as haughty as that of her brother. "Do they? I have never thought so."

"Really, Nadine," her father grumbled. "This is hardly your affair."

"No? In a few days I shall be repairing the damage you have allowed, indeed sponsored, to be committed upon the bodies of possibly thousands of now healthy human beings."

Balt said nastily, "Nobody asked you to join the medical staff, Nadine. You could have stayed in your laboratory, figuring out new methods of preventing the human race from replenishing itself."

The girl was obviously not the type to redden, but her anger was manifest. She spun on her brother. "If the race continues its present maniac course, possibly more effective methods of birth control *are* the most important development we could make. Even to the ultimate discovery of preventing all future conception."

Joe caught himself in mid-chuckle.

But not in time. She spun on him in his turn. "Look at yourself in that silly skirt. A professional soldier! A killer! In my opinion the most useless occupation ever devised by man. Parasite on the best and useful members of society. Destroyer by trade!"

Joe began to open his mouth, but she overrode him. "Yes, yes. I know. I've read all the nonsense that has accumulated down through the ages about the need for, the glory of, the sacrifice of the professional soldier. How they defend their country. How they give all for the common good. Zen! What nonsense."

Balt Haer was smirking sourly at her. "The theory today is, Nadine, old thing, that professionals such as the captain are gathering experience in case a serious fracas with the Sovs ever develops. Meanwhile his training is kept at a fine edge fighting in our inter-corporation, inter-union, or union-corporation fracases that develop in our private enterprise society."

She laughed her scorn. "And what a theory! Limited to the weapons which prevailed before 1900. If there was ever real conflict between the Sov-world and our own, does anyone really believe either would stick to such arms? Why, aircraft, armored vehicles, yes, and nuclear weapons and rockets, would be in overnight use."

Joe was fascinated by her furious attack. He said, "Then, what would you say was the purpose of the fracases, Miss—"

"Circuses," she snorted. "The old Roman games, all over again, and a hundred times worse. Blood-and-guts sadism. The quest of a frustrated person for satisfaction in another's pain. Our Lowers of today are as useless and frustrated as the Roman proletariat, and potentially they're just as dangerous as the mob that once dominated Rome. Automation, the second industrial revolution, has eliminated for all practical purposes the need for their labor. So we give them bread and circuses. And every year that goes by the circuses must be increasingly sadistic, death on an increasing scale, or they aren't satisfied. Once it was enough to have fictional mayhem, cowboys and Indians, gangsters, or G.I.s versus the Nazis, Japs or Commies, but that's passed. Now we need *real* blood and guts."

Baron Haer snapped finally, "All right, Nadine. We've heard this lecture before. I doubt if the captain is interested, particularly since you don't seem to be able to get beyond the protesting stage and have yet to come up with an answer."

"I have an answer!"

"Ah?" Balt Haer raised his eyebrows, mockingly.

"Yes! Overthrow this silly status society. Resume the road to progress. Put our people to useful endeavor, instead of sitting in front of their Telly sets, taking trank pills to put them in a happy daze and watching sadistic fracases to keep them in thrills, and their minds from their condition."

Joe had figured on keeping out of the controversy with this firebrand, but now, really interested, he said, "Progress to where?"

She must have caught in his tone that he wasn't needling. She frowned at him. "I don't know man's goal, if there is one. I'm not even sure it's important. It's the road that counts. The endeavor. The dream. The effort expended to make a world a better place than it was at the time of your birth."

Balt Haer said mockingly, "That's the trouble with you, Sis. Here we've reached Utopia and you don't admit it."

"Utopia!"

"Certainly. Take a poll. You'll find nineteen people out of twenty happy with things just the way they are. They have full tummies and security, lots of leisure and trank pills to make matters seem even rosier than they are—and they're rather rosy already."

"Then what's the necessity of this endless succession of bloody fracases, covered to the most minute bloody detail on the Telly?"

Baron Haer cut things short. 'We've hashed and rehashed this before, Nadine, and now we're too busy to debate further." He turned to Joe Mauser. "Very well, captain, you have my pledge. I wish I felt as optimistic as you seem to be about your prospects. That will be all for now, captain."

Joe saluted and executed an about face.

In the outer offices, when he had closed the door behind him, he rolled his eyes upward in mute thanks to whatever powers might be. He had somehow gained the enmity of Balt, his immediate superior, but he'd also gained the support of Baron Haer himself, which counted considerably more.

He considered, for a moment, Nadine Haer's words. She was obviously a malcontent, but, on the other hand, her opinions of his chosen profession weren't too different than his own. However, given this victory, this upgrading in caste, and Joe Mauser would be in a position to retire.

The door opened and shut behind him, and he half turned.

Nadine Haer, evidently still caught up in the hot words between herself and her relatives, glared at him. All of which stressed the beauty he had noticed the day before. She was an almost unbelievably pretty girl, particularly when flushed with anger.

It occurred to him with a blowlike suddenness that, if his caste was raised to Upper, he would be in a position to woo such as Nadine Haer.

He looked into her furious face and said, "I was intrigued, Miss Haer, with what you had to say, and I'd like to discuss some of your points. I wonder if I could have the pleasure of your company at some nearby refreshment—"

"My, how formal an invitation, captain. I suppose you had in mind sitting and flipping back a few trank pills."

Joe looked at her. "I don't believe I've had a trank in the past twenty years, Miss Haer. Even as a boy, I didn't particularly take to having my senses dulled with drug-induced pleasure."

Some of her fury was abating, but she was still critical of the professional mercenary. Her eyes went up and down his uniform in scorn. "You seem to make pretenses of being cultivated, captain. Then why your chosen profession?"

He'd had the answer to that for long years. He said now, simply, "I told you I was born a Lower. Given that, little counts until I fight my way out of it. Had I been born in a feudal society, I would have attempted to batter myself into the nobility. Under classical capitalism, I would have done my utmost to accumulate a fortune, enough to reach an effective position in society. Now, under People's Capitalism . . ."

She snorted. "Industrial Feudalism would be the better term."

". . . I realize I can't even start to fulfill myself until I am a member of the Upper caste."

Her eyes had narrowed, and the anger was largely gone. "But you chose the military field in which to better yourself?"

"Government propaganda to the contrary, it is practically impossible to raise yourself in other fields. I didn't build this world, possibly I don't even approve of it, but since I'm in it I have no recourse but to follow its rules."

Her eyebrows arched. "Why not try to change the rules?"

Joe blinked at her.

Nadine Haer said, "Let's look up that refreshment you were talking about. In fact, there's a small coffee bar around the corner where it'd be possible for one of Baron Haer's brood to have a cup with one of her father's officers of Middle caste."

6

The following morning, hands on the pillow beneath his head, Joe Mauser stared up at the ceiling of his room and rehashed his session with Nadine Haer. It hadn't taken him five minutes to come to the conclusion that he was in love with the girl, but it had taken him the rest of the evening to keep himself under rein and not let the fact get through to her.

He wanted to talk about the way her mouth tucked in at the corners, but she was hot on the evolution of society. He would have liked to have kissed that impossibly perfectly shaped ear of hers, but she was all for exploring the reasons why man had reached his present impasse. Joe was for holding hands, and staring into each other's eyes, she was for delving into the differences between the West-world and the Sov-world and the possibility of resolving them.

Of course, to keep her company at all it had been necessary to suppress his own desires and to go along. It obviously had never occurred to her that a Middle might have romantic ideas involving Nadine Haer. It had simply not occurred to her, no matter the radical teachings she advocated.

Most of their world was predictable from what had gone before. In spite of popular fable to the contrary, the division between classes had become increasingly clear. Among other things, tax systems were such that it became all but impossible for a citizen born poor to accumulate a fortune. Through ability he might rise to the point of earning fabulous sums—and wind up in debt to the tax collector. A great inventor, a great artist, had little chance of breaking into the domain of what finally became the small percentage of the population now known as Uppers. Then, too, the rising cost of a really good education became such that few other than those born into the Middle or Upper castes could afford the best of schools. Castes tended to perpetuate themselves.

Politically, the nation had fallen increasingly deeper into the two-party system, both parties of which were tightly controlled by the same group of Uppers. Elections had become a farce, a great national holiday in which stereotyped patriotic speeches, pretenses of unity between all castes, picnics, beer busts and trank binges predominated for one day.

Economically, too, the augurs had been there. Production of the basics had become so profuse that poverty in the old sense of the word had become nonsensical. There was an abundance of the necessities of life for all. Social security, socialized medicine, unending unemployment insurance, old age pensions, pensions for veterans, for widows and children, for the unfit, pensions and doles for this, that and the other, had doubled, and doubled again, until everyone had security for life. The Uppers, true enough, had opulence far beyond that known by the Middles and lived like gods compared to the Lowers. But all had security.

They had agreed, thus far, Joe and Nadine. But then had come debate.

"Then why," Joe had asked her, "haven't we achieved what your brother called it? Why isn't this Utopia? Isn't it what man has been yearning for, down through the ages? Where did the wheel come off? What happened to the dream?"

Nadine had frowned at him—beautifully, he thought. "It's not the first time man has found abundance in a society, though never to this degree. The Incas had it, for instance."

"I don't know much about them," Joe admitted. "An early form of communism with a sort of military-priesthood at the top."

She had nodded, her face serious, as always. "And for themselves, the Romans more or less had it—at the expense of the nations they conquered, of course."

"And—" Joe prodded.

"And in these examples the same thing developed. Society ossified. Joe," she said, using his first name for the first time, and in a manner that set off a new count down in his blood, "a ruling caste and a socioeconomic system perpetuates itself, just so long as it ever can. No matter what damage it may do to society as a whole, it perpetuates itself even to the point of complete destruction of everything.

"Remember Hitler? Adolf the Aryan and his Thousand Year Reich? When it became obvious he had failed, and the only thing that could result from continued resistance would be destruction of Germany's cities and millions of her people, did he and his clique resign or surrender? Certainly not. They attempted to bring down the whole German structure in a Götterdämmerung."

Nadine Haer was deep into her theme, her eyes flashing her conviction. "A socioeconomic system reacts like a living organism. It attempts to live on, indefinitely, agonizingly, no matter how antiquated it might have become. The Roman politico-economic system continued for centuries after it should have been replaced. Such reformers as the Gracchus brothers were assassinated or thrust aside so that the entrenched elements could perpetuate themselves, and when Rome finally fell, darkness descended for a thousand years on Western progress."

Joe had never gone this far in his thoughts. He said now, somewhat uncomfortably, "Well, what would replace what we have now? If you took power from you Uppers, who could direct the country? The Lowers? That's not even funny. Take away their fracases and their trank pills and they'd go berserk. They don't *want* anything else."

Her mouth worked. "Admittedly, we've already allowed things to deteriorate much too far. We should have done something long ago. I'm not sure I know the answer. All I know is that in order to maintain the status quo, we're not utilizing the efforts of more than a fraction of our people. Nine out of ten of us spend our lives sitting before the Telly, sucking tranks. Meanwhile, the motivation for continued progress seems to have withered away. Our Upper political circles are afraid some seemingly minor change might avalanche, so more and more we lean upon the old way of doing things."

Joe had put up mild argument. "I've heard the case made that the Lowers are fools and the reason our present socio-economic system makes it so difficult to rise from Lower to Upper is that you cannot make a fool understand he is one. You can only make him angry. If some, who are not fools, are allowed to advance from Lower to Upper, the vast mass who are fools will be angry because they are not allowed to. That's why the Military Category is made a channel of advance. To take that road, a man gives up his security, and he'll die if he's a fool."

Nadine had been scornful. "That reminds me of the old contention by racial segregationalists that the Negroes *smelled* bad. First they put them in a position where they had insufficient bathing facilities, their diet inadequate, and their teeth uncared for, and then protested that they couldn't be associated with because of their odor. Today, we are born within our castes. If an Upper is inadequate, he nevertheless remains an Upper. An accident of birth makes him an aristocrat; environment, family, training, education, friends, traditions and laws maintain him in that position. But a Lower who potentially has the greatest of value to society, is born handicapped and he's hard put not to wind up before a Telly, in a mental daze from trank. Sure he's a fool, he's never been *allowed* to develop himself."

Yes, Joe reflected now, it had been quite an evening. In a life of more than thirty years devoted to rebellion, he had never met anyone so outspoken as Nadine Haer, nor one who had thought it through as far as she had.

He grunted. His own revolt was against the level at which he had found himself in society, not the structure of society itself. His whole *raison d'être* was to lift himself to Upper status. It came as a shock to him to find a person he admired who had been born into Upper caste, desirous of tearing the whole system down.

His thoughts were interrupted by the door opening and the face of Max Mainz grinning in at him. Joe was mildly surprised at his orderly's not knocking before opening the door. Max evidently had a lot to learn.

The little man blurted, "Come on, Joe. Let's go out on the town!"

"*Joe?*" Joe Mauser raised himself to one elbow and stared at the other. "Leaving aside the merits of your suggestion for the moment, do you think you should address an officer by his first name?"

Max Mainz came fully into the bedroom, his grin still wider. "You forgot! It's election day!"

"Oh." Joe Mauser relaxed into his pillow. "So it is. No duty for today, eh?"

"No duty for anybody," Max crowed. "What'd you say we go into town and have a few drinks in one of the Upper bars?"

Joe grunted, but began to arise. "What'll that accomplish? On election day, most of the Uppers get done up in their oldest clothes and go slumming down in the Lower quarters."

Max wasn't to be put off so easily. "Well, wherever we go, let's get going. Zen! I'll bet this town is full of fracas buffs from as far as Philly. And on election day, to boot. Wouldn't it be something if I found me a real fracas fan, some Upper-Upper dame?"

Joe laughed at him, even as he headed for the bathroom. As a matter of fact, he rather liked the idea of going into town for the show. "Max," he said over his shoulder, "you're in for a big disappointment. They're all the same. Upper, Lower, or Middle."

"Yeah?" Max grinned back at him. "Well, I'd like the pleasure of finding out if that's true by personal experience."

7

In a faraway past, Kingston had once been the capital of the United States. For a short time, when Washington's men were in flight after the debacle of their defeat in New York City, the government of the United Colonies had held session in this Hudson River town. It had been its one moment of historic glory, and afterward Kingston had slipped back into being a minor city on the edge of the Catskills, approximately halfway between New York and Albany.

Of most recent years, it had become one of the two recruiting centers which bordered the Catskill Military Reservation, which in turn was one of the score or so population-cleared areas throughout the continent where rival corporations or unions could meet and settle their differences in combat—given permission of the Military Category Department of the government. And permission was becoming ever easier to acquire.

It had slowly evolved, the resorting to trial by combat to settle disputes between competing corporations, disputes between corporations and unions, disputes between unions over jurisdiction. Slowly, but predictably. Since the earliest days of the first industrial revolution, conflict between these elements had often broken into violence, sometimes on a scale comparable to minor warfare. An early example was the union organizing in Colorado when armed elements of the Western Federation of Miners shot it out with similarly armed "detectives" hired by the mine owners, and later with the troops of an unsympathetic State government.

By the middle of the Twentieth Century, unions had become one of the biggest businesses in the country, and by this time a considerable amount of the industrial conflict had shifted to fights between them for jurisdiction over dues-paying members. Battles on the waterfront, assassination and counter-assassination by gun-toting goon squads dominated by gangsters, industrial sabotage, frays between pickets and scabs—all were common occurrences.

But it was the coming of Telly which increasingly brought such conflicts literally before the public eye. Zealous reporters made ever greater effort to bring the actual mayhem before the eyes of their viewers, and never were their efforts more highly rewarded.

A society based upon private endeavor is as jealous of a vacuum as is mother nature. Give a desire that can be filled profitably, and the means can somehow be found to realize it.

At one point in the nation's history, the railroad lords had dominated the economy, later it became the petroleum princes of Texas and elsewhere, but toward the end of the Twentieth Century the communications industries slowly gained prominence. Nothing was more greatly in demand than feeding the insatiable maw of the Telly fan; nothing, ultimately, became more profitable.

And increasingly, the Telly buff endorsed the more sadistic of the fictional and nonfictional programs presented him. Even in the earliest years of the industry, producers had found that murder and mayhem, war and frontier gunfights, took precedence over less gruesome subjects. Music was drowned out by gunfire, the dance replaced by the shuffle of cowboy and rustler advancing down a dusty street toward each other, their fingertips brushing the grips of their six-shooters, the comedian's banter fell away before the chatter of the gangster's tommy gun.

And increasing realism was demanded. The Telly reporter on the scene of a police arrest, preferably a murder, a rumble between rival gangs of juvenile delinquents, a longshore-man's fray in which scores of workers were hospitalized. When attempts were made to suppress such broadcasts, the howl of freedom of speech and the press went up, financed by tycoons clever enough to realize the value of the subjects they covered so adequately.

The vacuum was there, the desire, the *need*. Bread the populace had. Trank was available to all. But the need was for the circus, the vicious, sadistic circus, and bit by bit, over the years and decades, the way was found to circumvent the country's laws and traditions to supply the need.

Aye, a way is always found. The final Universal Disarmament Pact which had totally banned all weapons invented since the year 1900 and provided for complete inspection, had not ended the fear of war. And thus there was excuse to give the would-be soldier, the potential defender of the country in some future internation conflict, practical experience.

Slowly tolerance grew to allow union and corporation to fight it out, hiring the services of mercenaries. Slowly rules grew up to govern such fracases. Slowly a department of government evolved. The Military Category became as acceptable as the next, and the mercenary a valued, even idolized, member of society. And the field became practically the only one in which a status-quo-orientated socioeconomic system allowed for advancement in caste.

Joe Mauser and Max Mainz strolled the streets of Kingston in an extreme of atmosphere seldom to be enjoyed. Not only was the advent of a divisional magnitude fracas only a short period away, but the freedom of an election day as well. The carnival, the Mardi Gras, the fete, the fiesta, of an election. Election day, when each aristocrat became only a man, and each man an aristocrat, free of all society's artificially conceived, caste perpetuating rituals and taboos.

Carnival! The day was young, but already the streets were thick with revelers, with dancers, with drunks. A score of bands played, youngsters in particular ran about attired in costume, there were barbecues and flowing beer kegs. On the outskirts of town were roller coasters and ferris wheels, fun houses and drive-it-yourself miniature cars. Carnival!

Max said happily, "You drink, Joe? Or maybe you like trank, better." Obviously, he loved to roll the other's first name over his tongue.

Joe wondered in amusement how often the little man had found occasion to call a Mid-Middle by his first name. "No trank," he said. "Alcohol for me. Mankind's old faithful."

"Well," Max debated, "get high on alcohol and bingo, a hangover in the morning. But trank? You wake up with a smile."

"And a desire for more trank to keep the mood going," Joe said wryly. "Get smashed on alcohol and you suffer for it eventually."

"Well, that's one way of looking at it," Max argued happily. "So let's start off with a couple of quick ones in this here Upper joint."

Joe looked the place over. He didn't know Kingston overly well, but by the appearance of the building and by the entry, it was probably the swankiest hotel in town. He shrugged. So far as he was concerned, he appreciated the greater comfort and the better service of his Middle caste bars, restaurants and hotels over the ones he had patronized when a Lower. However, his wasn't an immediate desire to push into the preserves of the Uppers; not until he had won rightfully to their status.

But on this occasion the little fellow wanted to drink at an Upper bar. Very well, it was election day. "Let's go," he said to Max.

In the uniform of a Rank Captain of the Military Category, there was little to indicate caste level, and ordinarily given the correct air of nonchalance, Joe Mauser, in uniform, would have been able to go anywhere, without so much as a raised eyebrow—until he had presented his credit card, which indicated his caste. But Max was another thing. He was obviously a Lower, and probably a Low-Lower at that.

But space was made for them at a bar packed with election day celebrants, politicians involved in the day's speeches and voting, higher ranking officers of the Haer forces, having a day off, and various Uppers of both sexes in town for the excitement of the fracas to come.

"Beer," Joe said to the bartender.

"Not me," Max crowed. "Champagne. Only the best for Max Mainz. Give me some of that champagne liquor I always been hearing about."

Joe had the bill credited to his card, and they took their bottles and glasses to a newly abandoned table. The place was too packed to have awaited the services of a waiter, although poor Max probably would have loved such attention. Lower and even Middle bars and restaurants were universally automated, and the waiter or waitress a thing of yesteryear.

Max looked about the room in awe. "This is living," he announced. "I wonder what they'd say if I went to the desk and ordered a room."

Joe Mauser wasn't as highly impressed as his batman. In fact, he'd often stayed in the larger cities in hostelries as sumptuous as this, though only of Middle status. Kingston's best was on the mediocre side. He said, "They'd probably tell you they were filled up."

Max was indignant. "Because I'm a Lower? It's *election* day."

Joe said mildly, "Because they probably are filled up. But for that matter, they might brush you off. It's not as though an Upper went to a Middle or Lower hotel and asked for accommodations. But what do you want, justice?"

Max dropped it. He looked down into his glass. "Hey," he complained, "what'd they give me? This stuff tastes like weak hard cider."

Joe laughed. "What did you think it was going to taste like?"

Max took another unhappy sip. "I thought it was supposed to be the best drink you could buy. You know, really strong. It's just bubbly wine."

A voice said, dryly, "Your companion doesn't seem to be a connoisseur of the French vintages, captain."

Joe turned. Balt Haer and two others occupied the table next to them.

Joe chuckled amiably and said, "Truthfully, it was my own reaction, the first time I drank sparkling wine, sir."

"Indeed," Haer said. "I can imagine." He fluttered a hand. "Lieutenant Colonel Paul Warren of Marshal Cogswell's staff, and Colonel Lajos Arpàd, of Budapest—Captain Joseph Mauser."

Joe Mauser came to his feet and clicked his heels, bowing from the waist in approved military protocol. The other two didn't bother to come to their feet, but did condescend to shake hands.

The Sov officer said, disinterestedly, "Ah yes, this is one of your fabulous customs, isn't it? On an election day, everyone is quite entitled to go anywhere. Anywhere at all. And, ah"—he made a sound somewhat like a giggle—"associate with anyone at all."

Joe Mauser resumed his seat, then looked at him. "That is correct. A custom going back to the early history of the country when all men were considered equal in such matters as law and civil rights. Gentlemen, may I present Rank Private Max Mainz, my orderly."

Balt Haer, who had obviously already had a few, looked at him dourly. "You can carry these things to the point of the ludicrous, captain. For a man with your ambitions, I'm surprised."

The infantry officer the younger Haer had introduced as Lieutenant Colonel Warren, of Stonewall Cogswell's staff, said idly, "Ambitions? Does the captain have ambitions? How in Zen can a Middle have ambitions, Balt?" He stared at Joe Mauser superciliously, but then scowled. "Haven't I seen you somewhere before?"

Joe said evenly, "Yes, sir. Five years ago we were both with the marshal in a fracas on the Little Big Horn reservation. Your company was pinned down on a knoll by a battery of field artillery. The marshal sent me to your relief. We sneaked in, up an arroyo, and were able to get most of you out."

"I was wounded," the colonel said, the superciliousness gone and a strange element in his voice above the alcohol there earlier.

Joe Mauser said nothing to that. Max Mainz was stirring unhappily now. These officers were talking above his head, even as they ignored him. He had a vague feeling that he was being defended by Captain Mauser, but he didn't know how, or why.

Balt Haer had been occupied in shouting fresh drinks. Now he turned back to the table. "Well, colonel, it's all very secret, these ambitions of Captain Mauser. I understand he's been an aide de camp to Marshal Cogswell in the past, but the marshal will be distressed to learn that on this occasion Captain Mauser has a secret by which he expects to rout your forces. Indeed, yes, the captain is quite the strategist." Balt Haer laughed abruptly. "And what good will this do the captain? Why on my father's word, if he succeeds, all efforts will be made to make the captain a caste equal of ours. Not just on election day, mind you, but all three hundred sixty-five days of the year."

Joe Mauser was on his feet, his face expressionless. He said, "Shall we go, Max? Gentlemen, it's been a pleasure. Colonel Arpàd, a privilege to meet you. Colonel Warren, a pleasure to renew acquaintance." Joe Mauser turned and, trailed by his orderly, left.

Lieutenant Colonel Warren, pale, was on his feet too.

Balt Haer was chuckling. "Sit down, Paul. Sit down. Not important enough to be angry about. The man's a clod."

Warren looked at him bleakly. "I wasn't angry, Balt. The last time I saw Captain Mauser I was slung over his shoulder. He carried, tugged and dragged me some two miles through enemy fire."

Balt Haer carried it off with a shrug. "Well, that's his profession. Category Military. A mercenary for hire. I assume he received his pay."

"He could have left me. Common sense dictated that he leave me."

Balt Haer was annoyed. "Well, then we see what I've contended all along. The ambitious captain doesn't have common sense."

Colonel Paul Warren shook his head. "You're wrong there. Common sense Joseph Mauser has. Considerable ability, he has. He's one of the best combat men in the field. But I'd hate to serve under him."

The Hungarian was interested. "But why?"

"Because he doesn't have luck, and in the dill you need luck." Warren grunted in sour memory. "Had the Telly cameras been focused on Joe Mauser, there at the Little Big Horn, he would have been a month-long sensation to the Telly buffs, with all that means."

He grunted again. "There wasn't a Telly team within a mile."

"The captain probably didn't realize that," Balt Haer snorted. "Otherwise his heroics would have been modified."

Warren flushed his displeasure and sat down. He said, "Possibly we should discuss the business before us. If your father is in agreement, the fracas can begin in three days." He turned to the representative of the Sov-world. "You have satisfied yourselves that neither force is violating the Disarmament Pact?"

Lajos Arpàd nodded. "We will wish to have observers on the field, itself, of course. But preliminary observation has been satisfactory." He had been interested in the play between these two and the lower caste officer. He said now, "Pardon me. As you know, this is my first visit to the, uh, *West*. I am fascinated. If I understand what just transpired, our Captain Mauser is a capable junior officer ambitious to rise in rank and status in your society." He looked at Balt Haer. "Why are you opposed to his so rising?"

Young Haer was testy about the whole matter. "Of what purpose is an Upper caste if every Tom, Dick and Harry enters it at will?"

Warren looked at the door through which Joe and Max had exited from the cocktail lounge. He opened his mouth to say something, closed it again, and held his peace.

The Hungarian said, looking from one of them to the other, "In the Sov-world we seek out such ambitious persons and utilize their abilities."

Lieutenant Colonel Warren laughed abruptly. "So do we here, *theoretically*. We are *free*, whatever that means. However," he added sarcastically, "it does help to have good schooling, good connections, relatives in positions of prominence, abundant shares of good stocks, that sort of thing. And these one is born with, in this free world of ours, Colonel Arpàd."

The Sov military observer clucked his tongue. "An indication of a declining society."

Balt Haer turned on him. "And is it any different in your world?" he said sneeringly. "Is it merely coincidence that the best positions in the Sov-world are held by Party members, and that it is all but impossible for anyone not born of Party member parents to become one? Are not the best schools filled with the children of Party members? Are not only Party members allowed to keep servants? And isn't it so that—"

Lieutenant Colonel Warren said, "Gentlemen, let us not start World War Three at this spot, at this late occasion."

8

Baron Malcolm Haer's field headquarters were in the ruins of a farmhouse in a town once known as Bearsville. His forces, and those of Marshal Stonewall Cogswell, were on the march but as yet their main bodies had not come in contact. Save for skirmishes between cavalry units, there had been no action. The ruined farmhouse had been a victim of an earlier fracas in this reservation, which had seen in its comparatively brief time more combat than Belgium, that cockpit of Europe.

There was a sheen of oily moisture on the Baron's bulletlike head, and his officers weren't particularly happy about it. Malcolm Haer characteristically went into a fracas with confidence, an aggressive confidence so strong that it often carried the day. In battles past, it had become a tradition that Haer's morale was worth a thousand men; the energy he expended was the despair of his doctors, who had been warning him for a decade. But now, something was missing.

A forefinger traced over the military chart before them. "So far as we know, Marshal Cogswell has established his command here in Saugerties. Anybody have any suggestions as to why?"

A major grumbled, "It doesn't make much sense, sir. You know the marshal. It's probably a fake. If we have any superiority at all, it's our artillery."

"And the old fox wouldn't want to join the issue on the plains, down near the river," a colonel added. "It's his game to keep up into the mountains with his cavalry and light infantry. He's got Jack Alshuler's cavalry. Most experienced veterans in the field."

"I know who he's got," Haer growled in irritation. "Stop reminding me. Where in the devil is Balt?"

"Coming up, sir," Balt Haer said. He had entered only moments ago, a sheaf of signals in his hand. "Why didn't they make that date 1910, instead of 1900? With radio, we could speed up communications—"

His father interrupted testily. "Better still, why not make it 1945? Then we could speed up to the point where we could polish ourselves off. What have you got?"

Balt Haer said, his face in sulk, "Some of my lads based in West Hurley report concentrations of Cogswell's infantry and artillery near Ashokan reservoir."

"Nonsense," somebody snapped. "We'd have him."

The younger Haer slapped his swagger stick against his bare leg and kilt. "Possibly it's a feint," he admitted.

"How much were they able to observe?" his father demanded.

"Not much. They were driven off by a superior squadron. The Hovercraft forces are screening everything they do with heavy cavalry units. I told you we needed more—"

"I don't need your advice at this point," his father snapped. The older Haer went back to the map, scowling still. "I don't see what he expects to do, working out of Saugerties."

A voice behind them said, "Sir, may I have your permission—"

Half of the assembled officers turned to look at the newcomer.

Balt Haer snapped, "Captain Mauser. Why aren't you with your lads?"

"Turned them over to my second in command, sir," Joe Mauser said. He was standing to attention, looking at Baron Haer.

The Baron glowered at him. "What is the meaning of this cavalier intrusion, captain? Certainly you must have your orders. Are you under the illusion that you are part of my staff?"

"No, sir," Joe Mauser clipped. "I came to report that I am ready to put into execution—"

"The great plan!" Balt Haer ejaculated. He laughed brittlely. "The second day of the fracas, and nobody really knows where old Cogswell is, or what he plans to do. And here comes the captain with his secret plan."

Joe looked at him. He said evenly, "Yes, sir."

The Baron's face had gone dark, as much in anger at his son as with the upstart cavalry captain. He began to growl ominously, "Captain Mauser, rejoin your command and obey your orders."

Joe Mauser's facial expression indicated that he had expected this. He kept his voice level, however, even under the chuckling scorn of his immediate superior, Balt Haer.

He said, "Sir, I will be able to tell you where Marshal Cogswell is, and every troop at his command."

For a moment there was silence, all but a stunned silence. Then the major who had suggested the Saugerties field command headquarters were a fake blurted a curt laugh.

"This is no time for levity, captain," Balt Haer clipped. "Get to your command."

A colonel said, "Just a moment, sir. I've fought with Joe Mauser before. He's a good man."

"Not that good," someone else huffed. "Does he claim to be clairvoyant?"

Joe Mauser said flatly, "Have a semaphore man posted here this afternoon. I'll be back at that time." He spun on his heel and left them.

Balt Haer rushed to the door after him, shouting, "Captain! That's an order! Return—"

But the other was obviously gone. Enraged, the younger Haer began to shrill commands to a noncom in the way of organizing a pursuit.

His father called wearily, "That's enough, Balt. Mauser has evidently taken leave of his senses. We made the initial mistake of encouraging this idea he had, or thought he had."

"*We?*" his son snapped in return. "I had nothing to do with it."

"All right, all right. Let's tighten up, here. Now, what other information have your scouts come up with?"

9

At the Kingston airport, Joe Mauser rejoined Max Mainz, his face drawn now.

"Everything go all right?" the little man said anxiously.

"I don't know," Joe said. "I still couldn't tell them the story. Old Cogswell is as quick as a coyote. We pull this little caper today, and he'll be ready to meet it tomorrow."

He looked at the two-place sailplane which sat on the tarmac. "Everything all set?"

"Far as I know," Max said. He looked at the motorless aircraft. "You sure you been checked out on these things, captain?"

"Yes," Joe said. "I bought this particular soaring glider more than a year ago, and I've put almost a thousand hours in it. Now, where's the pilot of that light plane?"

A single-engined sports plane was attached to the glider by a fifty-foot nylon rope. Even as Joe spoke, a youngster poked his head from the plane's window and grinned back at them. "Ready?" he yelled.

"Come on, Max," Joe said. "Let's pull the canopy off this thing. We don't want it in the way while you're semaphoring."

A figure was approaching them from the Administration Building. A uniformed man, and somehow familiar.

"A moment, Captain Mauser!"

Joe placed him now. The Sov-world representative he'd met at Balt Haer's table in the Upper bar a couple of days ago. What was his name? Colonel Arpàd. Lajos Arpàd.

The Hungarian approached and looked at the sailplane in interest. "As a representative of my government, a military attaché checking upon possible violations of the Universal Disarmament Pact, may I request what you are about to do, captain?"

Joe Mauser looked at him emptily. "How did you know I was here and what I was doing?"

The Sov colonel smiled gently. "It was by suggestion of Marshal Cogswell. He is a great man for detail. It disturbed him that an . . . what did he call it? . . . an *old pro* like yourself should join with Vacuum Tube Transport, rather than Continental Hovercraft. He didn't think it made sense and suggested that possibly you had in mind some scheme that would utilize weapons of a post-1900 period in your efforts to bring success to Baron Haer's forces. So I have investigated, Captain Mauser."

"And the marshal knows about this sailplane?" Joe Mauser's face was blank.

"I didn't say that. So far as I know, he doesn't."

"Then, Colonel Arpàd, with your permission, I'll be taking off."

The Hungarian said, "With what end in mind, captain?"

"Using this glider as a reconnaissance aircraft."

"Captain, I warn you! Aircraft were not in use in warfare until—"

But Joe Mauser cut him off, equally briskly. "Aircraft were first used in combat by Pancho Villa's forces a few years previous to World War I. They were also used in the Balkan Wars of about the same period. But those were powered craft. This is a glider, invented and in use before the year 1900 and hence open to utilization."

The Hungarian clipped, "But the Wright brothers didn't fly even gliders until—"

Joe looked him full in the face. "But you of the Sov-world do not admit that the Wrights were the first to fly, do you?"

The Hungarian closed his mouth, abruptly.

Joe said evenly, "But even if Ivan Ivanovitch, or whatever you claim his name was, didn't invent flight of heavier-than-air craft, the glider was flown variously before 1900, including by Otto Lilienthal in the 1890s, and was designed as far back as Leonardo da Vinci."

The Sov-world colonel stared at him for a long moment, then gave an inane giggle. He stepped back and flicked Joe Mauser a salute. "Very well, captain. As a matter of routine, I shall report this use of an aircraft for reconnaissance purposes, and undoubtedly a commission will meet to investigate the propriety of the departure. Meanwhile, good luck!"

Joe returned the salute and swung a leg over the cockpit's side. Max was already in the front seat, his semaphore flags, maps and binoculars on his lap. He had been staring in dismay at the Sov officer, now was relieved that Joe had evidently pulled it off.

Joe waved to the plane ahead. Two mechanics had come up to steady the wings for the initial ten or fifteen feet of the motorless craft's passage over the ground behind the towing craft.

Joe said to Max, "did you explain to the pilot that under no circumstances was he to pass over the line of the military reservation, that we'd cut before we reached that point?"

"Yes, sir," Max said nervously. He'd flown before, on the commercial lines, but he'd never been in a glider.

They began lurching across the field, slowly, then gathering speed. And as the sailplane took speed, it took grace. After it had been pulled a hundred feet or so, Joe eased back the stick and it slipped gently into the air, four or five feet off the ground. The towing airplane was still taxiing, but with its tow airborne it picked up speed quickly. Another two hundred feet and it, too, was in the air and beginning to climb. The glider behind held it to a speed of sixty miles or so.

At ten thousand feet, the plane leveled off and the pilot's head swiveled to look back at them. Joe Mauser waved to him and dropped the release lever which ejected the nylon rope from the glider's nose. The plane dove away, trailing the rope behind it. Joe knew that the plane pilot would later drop it over the airport where it could easily be retrieved.

In the direction of Mount Overlook he could see cumulus clouds and the dark turbulence which meant strong updraft. He headed in that direction.

Except for the whistling of wind, there is complete silence in a soaring glider. Max Mainz began to call back to his superior, was taken back by the volume, and dropped his voice. He said, "Look, captain. What keeps it up?"

Joe grinned. He liked the buoyance of glider flying, the nearest approach of man to the bird, and thus far everything was going well. He told Mac, "An airplane plows through the air currents, a glider rides on top of them."

"Yeah, but suppose the current is going down?"

"Then we avoid it. This sailplane only has a gliding angle ratio of one to twenty-five, but it's a workhorse with a payload of some four hundred pounds. A really high-performance glider can have a ratio of as much as one to forty."

Joe had found a strong updraft where a wind ran up the side of a mountain. He banked, went into a circling turn. The gauge indicated they were climbing at the rate of eight meters per second, nearly fifteen hundred feet a minute.

Max hadn't got the rundown on the theory of the glider. That was obvious in his expression.

Joe Mauser, even while searching the ground below keenly, went into it further. "A wind up against a mountain will give an updraft, or storm clouds will, even a newly plowed field in a bright sun. So you go from one of these to the next."

"Yeah, great, but when you're between," Max protested.

"Then, when you have a one to twenty-five ratio, you go twenty-five feet forward for each one you drop. If you started a mile high, you could go twenty-five miles before you touched ground." He cut himself off quickly. "Look, what's that, down there? Get your glasses on it."

Max caught his excitement. His binoculars were tight to his eyes. "Sojers. Cavalry. They sure ain't ours. They must be Hovercraft lads. And look, field artillery."

Joe Mauser was piloting with his left hand, his right smoothing out a chart on his lap. He growled, "What are they doing there? That's at least a full brigade of cavalry. Here, let me have those glasses.

With his knees gripping the stick, he went into a slow circle, as he stared down at the column of men. "Jack Alshuler," he whistled in surprise. "The marshal's crack heavy cavalry. And several batteries of artillery." He swung the glasses in a wider scope and the whistle turned into a hiss of comprehension. "They're doing a complete circle of the reservation. They're going to hit the Baron from the direction of Phoenecia."

10

Marshal Stonewall Cogswell directed his old-fashioned telescope in the direction his chief of staff indicated.

"What is it?" he grunted.

"It's an airplane, sir."

"Over a military reservation with a fracas in progress?"

"Yes, sir." The other put his glasses back on the circling object.

"Then what is it, sir? Certainly not a free balloon."

"Balloons," the marshal snorted, as though to himself. "Legal to use. The Union forces had them toward the end of the Civil War. But practically useless in a fracas of movement."

They were standing before the former resort hotel which housed the marshal's headquarters. Other staff members were streaming from the building, and one of the ever-present Telly reporting crews were hurriedly setting up cameras.

The marshal turned and barked, "Does anybody know what in Zen that confounded thing, circling up there, is?"

Baron Zwerdling, the aging Category Transport magnate, head of Continental Hovercraft, hobbled onto the wooden veranda and stared with the others. "An airplane," he croaked. "Haer's gone too far this time. Too far, too far. This will strip him. Strip him, understand." Then he added, "Why doesn't it make any noise?"

Lieutenant Colonel Paul Warren stood next to his commanding officer. "It looks like a glider, sir."

Cogswell glowered at him. "A what?"

"A glider, sir. It's a sport not particularly popular these days."

"What keeps it up, confound it?"

Paul Warren looked at him. "The same thing that keeps a hawk up, an albatross, a gull—"

"A vulture, you mean," Cogswell snarled. He watched it for another long moment, his face working. He whirled on his chief of artillery. "Jed, can you bring that thing down?"

The other had been viewing the craft through field binoculars, his face as shocked as the rest of them. Now he faced his chief, and lowered the glasses, shaking his head. "Not with the artillery of pre-1900. No, sir."

"What can you do?" Cogswell barked.

The artillery man was shaking his head. "We could mount some Maxim guns on wagon wheels, or something. Keep him from coming low."

"He doesn't have to come low," Cogswell growled unhappily. He spun on Lieutenant Colonel Warren again. "When were they invented?" He jerked his thumb upward. "Those things."

Warren was twisting his face in memory. "Some time about the turn of the century."

"How long can the things stay up?"

Warren took in the surrounding mountainous countryside. "Indefinitely, sir. A single pilot, as long as he is physically able to operate. If there are two pilots up there to relieve each other, they could stay until food and water ran out."

"How much weight do they carry?"

"I'm not sure. One that size, certainly enough for two men and any equipment they'd need. Say, five hundred pounds."

Cogswell had his telescope glued to his eyes again; he muttered under his breath, "Five hundred pounds! They could even unload dynamite over our horses. Stampede them all over the reservation."

"What's going on?" Baron Zwerdling shrilled. "What's going on, Marshal Cogswell?"

Cogswell ignored him. He watched the circling, circling craft for a full five minutes, breathing deeply. Then he lowered his glass and swept the assembled officers of his staff with an indignant glare. "Ten Eyck!" he grunted.

An infantry colonel came to attention. "Yes, sir."

Cogswell said heavily, deliberately. "Under a white flag. A dispatch to Baron Haer. My compliments and request for his terms. While you're at it, my compliments also to Captain Joseph Mauser."

Zwerdling was bug-eyeing him. "Terms!" he rasped.

The marshal turned to him. "Yes, sir. Face reality. We're in the dill. I suggest you sue for terms as short of complete capitulation as you can make them."

"You call yourself a soldier—!" the transport tycoon began to shrill.

"Yes, sir," Cogswell snapped. "A soldier, not a butcher of the lads under me." He called to the Telly reporter who was getting as much of this as he could. "Mr. Soligen, isn't it?"

The reporter scurried forward, flicking signals to his cameramen for proper coverage. "Yes, sir. Freddy Soligen, marshal. Could you tell the Telly fans what this is all about, Marshal Cogswell? Folks, you all know the famous marshal. Marshal Stonewall Cogswell, who hasn't lost a fracas in nearly ten years, now commanding the forces of Continental Hovercraft."

"I'm losing one now," Cogswell said grimly. "Vacuum Tube Transport has pulled a gimmick out of the hat and things have pickled for us. It will be debated before the Military Category Department, of course, and undoubtedly the Sov-world military attachés will have things to say. But as it appears now, the fracas, as we have known it, has been revolutionized."

"Revolutionized?" Even the Telly reporter was flabbergasted. "You mean by that thing?" He pointed upward, and the lenses of the cameras followed his finger.

"Yes," Cogswell growled unhappily. "Do all of you need a blueprint? Do you think I can fight a fracas with that thing dangling above me, throughout the day hours? Do you understand the importance of reconnaissance in warfare?" His eyes glowered. "Do you think Napoleon would have lost Waterloo if he'd had the advantage of perfect reconnaissance such as that thing can deliver? Do you think Lee would have lost Gettysburg? Don't be ridiculous." He spun on Baron Zwerdling, who was stuttering his complete confusion.

"As it stands, Baron Haer knows every troop dispensation I make. All I know of his movements are from my cavalry scouts. I repeat, I am no butcher, sir. I will gladly cross swords with Baron Haer another day, when I, too, have . . . what did you call the confounded things, Paul?"

"Gliders," Lieutenant Colonel Warren said.

11

Major Joseph Mauser, now attired in his best off-duty Category Military uniform, spoke his credentials to the receptionist. "I have no definite appointment, but I am sure the Baron will see me," he said.

"Yes, sir." The receptionist did the things that receptionists do, then looked up at him again. "Right through that door, major."

Joe Mauser gave the door a quick double rap and then entered before waiting an answer.

Balt Haer, in mufti, was standing at a far window, a drink in his hand, rather than his customary swagger stick. Nadine Haer sat in an easychair. The girl Joe Mauser loved had been crying.

Joe Mauser, suppressing his frown, made with the usual amenities.

Balt Haer, without answering them, finished his drink in a gulp and stared at the newcomer. The old stare, the aloof stare, an aristocrat looking at an underling as though wondering what made the fellow tick. He said, finally, "I see you have been raised to Rank Major."

"Yes, sir," Joe said.

"We are obviously occupied, major. What can either my sister or I possibly do for you?"

Joe kept his voice even. He said, "I wanted to see the Baron."

Nadine Haer looked up, a twinge of pain crossing her face.

"Indeed," Balt Haer said flatly. "You are talking to the Baron, Major Mauser."

Joe Mauser looked at him, then at his sister, who had taken to her handkerchief again. Consternation ebbed up and over him in a flood. He wanted to say something such as, "Oh *no*," but not even that could he utter.

Haer was bitter. "I assume I know why you are here, major. You have come for your pound of flesh, undoubtedly. Even in these hours of our grief—"

"I . . . I didn't know. Please believe . . ."

". . . You are so constituted that your ambition has no decency. Well, Major Mauser, I can only say that your arrangement was with my father. Even if I thought it a reasonable one, I doubt if I would sponsor your ambitions myself."

Nadine Haer looked up wearily. "Oh, Balt, come off it," she said. "The fact is, the Haer fortunes contracted a debt to you, major.

Unfortunately, it is a debt we cannot pay." She looked into his face. "First, my father's governmental connections do not apply to us. Second, six months ago, my father, worried about his health and attempting to avoid certain death taxes, transferred the family stocks into Balt's name. And Balt saw fit, immediately before the fracas, to sell all Vacuum Tube Transport stocks, and invest in Hovercraft."

"That's enough, Nadine," her brother snapped nastily.

"I see," Joe said. He came to attention. "Dr. Haer, my apologies for intruding upon you in your time of bereavement." He turned to the new Baron. "Baron Haer, my apologies for *your* bereavement."

Balt Haer glowered at him.

Joe Mauser turned and marched for the door, which he opened then closed behind him.

On the street, before the New York offices of Vacuum Tube Transport, he turned and for a moment looked up at the splendor of the building.

Well, at least the common shares of the concern had skyrocketed following the victory. His rank had been upped to Major, and old Stonewall Cogswell had offered him a permanent position on his staff in command of aerial operations, no small matter of prestige. The difficulty was, he wasn't interested in the added money that would accrue to him, nor the higher rank—nor the prestige, for that matter.

He turned to go to his hotel.

An unbelievably beautiful girl came down the steps of the building. She said, "Joe."

He looked at her. "Yes?"

She put a hand on his sleeve. "Let's go somewhere and talk, Joe."

"About what?" He was infinitely weary now.

"About goals," she said. "As long as they exist, whether for individuals, or nations, or a whole species, life is still worth the living. Things are a bit bogged down right now, but at the risk of sounding very trite, there's tomorrow."

SOLDIER ASK NOT

Gordon R. Dickson

Soldier, ask not—now or ever—
Where to war your banners go . . .

As I got off the spaceliner on St. Marie, the little breeze from the higher pressure of the ship's atmosphere at my back was like a hand from the darkness behind me, shoving me into the dark day and the rain. My Newsman's cloak covered me. The wet chill of the day wrapped around me but did not enter me. I was like the naked claymore of my own early ancestors, wrapped and hidden in the plaid—sharpened on a stone—and carried now at last to the meeting for which it had been guarded over three years of waiting.

A meeting in the cold rain of spring. I felt it, cold as old blood on my hands and tasteless on my lips. Above, the sky was low and clouds flowing to the east. The rain fell steadily.

The sound of it was like a rolling of drums as I went down the outside landing stairs, the multitude of raindrops sounding their own end against the unyielding concrete all around. The concrete stretched far from the ship in every direction, hiding the earth, as bare and clean as the last page of an account book before the final entry. At its far edge, the spaceport terminal stood like a single gravestone. The curtains of falling water between it and me thinned and thickened like the smoke of battle, but could not hide it entirely from my sight.

It was the same rain that falls in all places and on all worlds. It had fallen like this on Athens of Old Earth, when I was only a boy, on the dark, unhappy house of the uncle who brought me up after

148

my parents' death, on the ruins of the Parthenon as I saw it from my bedroom window.

I listened to it now as I went down the landing stairs, drumming on the great ship behind me which had shifted me free between the stars—from Old Earth to this second smallest of the worlds, this small terraformed planet under the Procyon suns—and drumming hollowly upon the Credentials case sliding down the conveyor belt beside me. That case now meant nothing to me—neither my papers nor the Credentials of Impartiality I had carried six years and worked so long to earn. Now I thought less of these than of the name of the man I should find dispatching groundcars at the edge of the field. If, that was, he was actually the man my Earth informants had named to me. And if they had not lied . . .

". . . Your luggage, sir?"

I woke from my thoughts and the rain. I had reached the concrete. The debarking officer smiled at me. He was older than I, though he looked younger. As he smiled some beads of moisture broke and spilled like tears from the brown visor-edge of his cap onto the tally sheet he held.

"Send it to the Friendly compound," I said. "I'll take the Credentials case."

I took it up from the conveyor belt and turned to walk off. The man standing in a dispatcher's uniform by the first groundcar in line did fit the description.

"Name, sir?" he said. "Business on St. Marie?"

If he had been described to me, I must have been described to him. But I was prepared to humor him.

"Tam Olyn," I said. "Old Earth resident and Interworld News Network representative. I'm here to cover the Friendly-Exotic conflict." I opened my case and gave him my papers.

"Fine, Mr. Olyn." He handed them back to me, damp from the rain. He turned away to open the door of the car beside him and set the automatic pilot. "Follow the highway straight to Joseph's Town. Put it on automatic at the city limits and the car'll take you to the Friendly compound."

"All right," I said. "Just a minute."

He turned back. He had a young, good-looking face with a little mustache and he looked at me with a bright blankness. "Sir?"

"Help me get in the car."

"Oh, I'm sorry, sir." He came quickly over to me. "I didn't realize your leg—"

"Damp stiffens it," I said. He adjusted the seat and I got my left leg in behind the steering column. He started to turn away.

"Wait a minute," I said again. I was out of patience. "You're Walter Imera, aren't you?"

"Yes, sir," he said softly.

"Look at me," I said. "You've got some information for me, haven't you?"

He turned slowly back to face me. His face was still blank.

"No, sir."

I waited a long moment, looking at him.

"All right," I said then, reaching for the car door. "I guess you know I'll get the information anyway. And they'll believe you told me."

His little mustache began to look like it was painted on.

"Wait—" he said.

"What for?"

"Look," he said, "you've got to understand. Information like that's not part of your news, is it? I've got a family—"

"And I haven't," I said. I felt nothing for him.

"But you don't understand. They'd kill me. That's the sort of organization the Blue Front is now, here on St. Marie. What d'you want to know about them for? I didn't understand you meant—"

"All right," I said. I reached for the car door.

"Wait—" He held out a hand to me in the rain. "How do I know you can make them leave me alone if I tell you?"

"They may be back in power here some day," I said. "Not even outlawed political groups want to antagonize the Interplanetary News Network." I started to close the door once more.

"All right—" he said quickly. "All right. You go to New San Marcos. The Wallace Street Jewelers there. It's just beyond Joseph's Town, where the Friendly compound is you're going to." He licked his lips. "You'll tell them about me?"

"I'll tell them." I looked at him. Above the edge of the blue uniform collar on the right side of his neck I could see an inch or two of fine silver chain, bright against winter-pale skin. The crucifix attached to it would be down under his shirt. "The Friendly soldiers have been here two years now. How do people like them?"

He grinned a little. His color was coming back.

"Oh, like anybody," he said. "You just have to understand them. They've got their own ways."

I felt the ache in my stiff leg where the doctors on New Earth had taken the needle from the spring rifle out of it three years before.

"Yes, they have," I said. "Shut the door."

He shut it. I drove off.

There was a St. Christopher's medal on the car's instrument panel. One of the Friendly soldiers would have ripped it off and thrown it away, or refused the car. And so it gave me a particular pleasure to leave it where it was, though it meant no more to me than it would to him. It was not just because of Dave, my brother-in-law, and the other prisoners they had shot down on New Earth. It was simply because there are some duties that have a small element of pleasure. After the illusions of childhood are gone and there is nothing left but duties, such pleasures are welcome. Fanatics, when all is said and done, are no worse than mad dogs.

But mad dogs have to be destroyed; it is a simple common sense.

And you return to common sense after a while in life, inevitably. When the wild dreams of justice and progress are all dead and buried, when the painful beatings of feeling inside you are finally stilled, then it becomes best to be still, unliving, and unyielding as—the blade of a sword sharpened on a stone. The rain through which such a blade is carried to its using does not stain it, any more than the blood in which it is bathed at last. Rain and blood are alike to sharpened iron.

I drove for half an hour past wooded hills and plowed meadows. The furrows of the fields were black in the rain. I thought it a kinder black than some other shades I had seen; and at last I reached the outskirts of Joseph's Town.

The autopilot of the car threaded me through a small, neat, typical St. Marie City of about a hundred thousand people. We came out on the far side into a cleared area, beyond which lifted the massive, sloping concrete walls of a military compound.

A Friendly non-com stopped my car at the gate with his black spring rifle, and opened the car door at my left.

"Thee have business here?"

His voice was harsh and high in his nose. The cloth tabs of a groupman edged his collar. Above them his forty-year-old face was lean and graven with lines. Both face and hands, the only uncovered parts of him, looked unnaturally white against the black cloth and rifle.

I opened the case beside me and handed him my papers.

"My Credentials," I said. "I'm here to see your acting Commander of Expeditionary Forces, Commandant Jamethon Black."

"Move over, then," he said nasally. "I must drive thee."

I moved.

He got in and took the stick. We drove through the gate and turned down an approach alley. I could see an interior square at the alley's far end. The close concrete walls on either side of us echoed the sound of our passage as we went. I heard drill commands growing louder as we approached the square. When we rolled out into it, soldiers were drawn up in ranks for their midday service, in the rain.

The groupman left me and went in the entrance of what seemed to be an office inset in the wall on one side of the square. I looked over the soldiers standing in formation. They stood at present-arms, their position of worship under field conditions; and as I watched, the officer standing facing them, with his back to a wall, led them into the words of their Battle Hymn.

> Soldier, ask not—now or ever,
> Where to war your banners go.
> Anarch's legions, all surround us.
> Strike! And do not count the blow!

I sat trying not to listen. There was no musical accompaniment, no religious furniture or symbols except the thin shape of the cross whitewashed on the gray wall behind the officer. The massed male voices rose and fell slowly in the dark, sad hymn that promised them only pain, and suffering, and sorrow. At last, the final line mourned its harsh prayer for a battle death, and they ordered arms.

A groupman dismissed the ranks as the officer walked back past my car without looking at me, and passed in through the entrance where my non-commissioned guide had disappeared. As he passed I saw the officer was young.

A moment later the guide came for me. Limping a little on my stiffened leg, I followed him to an inner room with the lights on above a single desk. The young officer rose and nodded as the door closed behind me. He wore the faded tabs of a commandant on his uniform lapels.

As I handed my credentials across the desk to him, the glare of the light over the desk came full in my eyes, blinding me. I stepped back and blinked at his blurred face. As it came back into focus I saw it for a moment as if it was older, harsher, twisted and engraved with the lines of years of fanaticism.

Then my eyes refocused completely, and I saw him as he actually was. Dark-faced, but thin with the thinness of youth rather than that of self-starvation. He was not the face burned in my memory.

His features were regular to the point of being handsome, his eyes tired and shadowed; and I saw the straight, weary line of his mouth above the still, self-controlled stiffness of his body, smaller and slighter than mine.

He held the credentials without looking at them. His mouth quirked a little, dryly and wearily, at the corners. "And no doubt, Mr. Olyn," he said, "you've got another pocket filled with authorities from the Exotic Worlds to interview the mercenary soldiers and officers they've hired from the Dorsai and a dozen other worlds to oppose God's Chosen in War?"

I smiled. Because it was good to find him as strong as that, to add to my pleasure of breaking him.

2

I looked across the ten feet or so of distance that separated us. The Friendly non-com who had killed the prisoners on New Earth had also spoken of God's Chosen.

"If you'll look under the papers directed to you," I said, "you'll find them. The News Network and its people are impartial. We don't take sides."

"Right," said the dark young face opposing me, "takes sides."

"Yes, Commandant," I said. "That's right. Only sometimes it's a matter of debate where Right is. You and your troops here now are invaders on the world of a planetary system your ancestors never colonized. And opposing you are mercenary troops hired by two worlds that not only belong under the Procyon suns but have a commitment to defend the smaller worlds of their system—of which St. Marie is one. I'm not sure right *is* on your side."

He shook his head slightly and said, "We expect small understanding from those not Chosen." He transferred his gaze from me to the papers in his hand.

"Mind if I sit down?" I said. "I've got a bad leg."

"By all means." He nodded to a chair beside his desk and, as I sat down, seated himself. I looked across the papers on the desk before him and saw, standing to one side, the solidograph of one of the windowless high-peaked churches the Friendlies build. It was a legitimate token for him to own—but there just happened to be three people, an older man and woman and a young girl of about fourteen, in the foreground of the image. All three of them bore a family resemblance to Jamethon Black. Glancing up from my credentials he saw me looking at them; and his gaze shifted

momentarily to the graph and away again, as if he would protect
it.

"I'm required, I see," he said, drawing my eyes back to him, "to
provide you with cooperation and facilities. We'll find quarters for
you here. Do you need a car and driver?"

"Thanks," I said. "That commercial car outside will do. And I'll
manage my own driving."

"As you like." He detached the papers directed to him, passed
the rest back to me and leaned toward a grill in his desktop.
"Groupman."

"Sir," the grill answered promptly.

"Quarters for a single male civilian. Parking assignment for a
civilian vehicle, personnel."

"Sir."

The voice from the grill clicked off. Jamethon Black looked
across his desk at me. I got the idea he was waiting for my departure.

"Commandant," I said, putting my credentials back in their case,
"two years ago your Elders of the United Churches on Harmony
and Association found the planetary government of St. Marie
in default of certain disputed balances of credit, so they sent
an expedition in here to occupy and enforce payment. Of that
expedition, how much in the way of men and equipment do you
have left?"

"That, Mr. Olyn," he said, "is restricted military information."

"However—" and I closed the case "—you, with the regular rank
of commandant, are acting Commander of Forces for the remnants
of your expedition. That position calls for someone about five ranks
higher than you. Do you expect such an officer to arrive and take
charge?"

"I'm afraid you'd have to ask that question of Headquarters on
Harmony, Mr. Olyn."

"Do you expect reinforcements of personnel and more supplies?"

"If I did—" his voice was level "—I would have to consider that
restricted information, too."

"You know that it's been pretty widely mentioned that your
General Staff on Harmony has decided that this expedition to
St. Marie is a lost cause? But that to avoid loss of face they
prefer you here to be cut up, instead of withdrawing you and
your men."

"I see," he said.

"You wouldn't care to comment?"

His dark, young, expressionless face did not change. "Not in the
case of rumors, Mr. Olyn."

"One last question then. Do you plan to retreat west-ward, or surrender when the spring offensive of the Exotic mercenary forces begins to move against you?"

"The Chosen in War never retreat," he said. "Neither do they abandon, or suffer abandonment by, their Brothers in the Lord." He stood up. "I have work I must get back to, Mr. Olyn."

I stood up, too. I was taller than he was, older, and heavier-boned. It was only his almost unnatural composure that enabled him to maintain his appearance of being my equal or better.

"I'll talk to you later, perhaps, when you've got more time," I said.

"Certainly." I heard the office door open behind me. "Groupman," he said, speaking past me, "take care of Mr. Olyn."

The groupman he had turned me over to found me a small concrete cubicle with a single high window, a camp bed and a uniform cabinet. He left me for a moment and returned with a signed pass.

"Thanks," I said as I took it. "Where do I find the Headquarters of the Exotic Forces?"

"Our latest advice, sir," he said, "is that they're ninety kilometers east of here. New San Marcos." He was my height, but, like most of them, half a dozen years younger than I, with an innocence that contrasted with the strange air of control they all had.

"San Marcos." I looked at him. "I suppose you enlisted men know your General Headquarters on Harmony has decided against wasting replacements for you?"

"No, sir," he said. I might have commented on the rain for all the reaction he showed. Even these boys were still strong and unbroken. "Is there something else?"

"No," I said. "Thanks."

He went out. And I went out, to get in my car and head ninety kilometers east through the same sort of country to New San Marcos. I reached it in about three-quarters of an hour. But I did not go directly to find the Exotic Field Headquarters. I had other fish to fry.

These took me to the Wallace Street Jewelers. There, three shallow steps down from street level and an opaqued door let me in to a long, dim-lighted room filled with glass cases. There was a small elderly man at the back of the store behind the final case and I saw him eyeing my correspondent's cloak and badge as I got closer.

"Sir?" he said, as I stopped across the case from him. He raised gray, narrow old eyes in a strangely smooth face to look at me.

"I think you know what I represent," I said. "All worlds know the News Services. We're not concerned with local politics."

"Sir?"

"You'll find out how I learned your address anyway," I kept on smiling at him. "So I'll tell you it was from a spaceport autodispatcher named Imera. I promised him protection for telling me. We'd appreciate it if he remains well and whole."

"I'm afraid—" He put his hands on the glass top of the case. They were veined with the years. "You wanted to buy something?"

"I'm willing to pay in good will," I said, "for information."

His hands slid off the countertop.

"Sir." He sighed a little. "I'm afraid you're in the wrong store."

"I'm sure I am," I said. "But your store'll have to do. We'll pretend it's the right store and I'm talking to someone who's a member of the Blue Front."

He shook his head slowly and stepped back from the case.

"The Blue Front is illegal," he said. "Good-by, sir."

"In a moment. I've got a few things to say first."

"Then I'm sorry." He retreated toward some drapes covering a doorway. "I can't listen. No one will come into this room with you, sir, as long as you talk like that."

He slipped through the drapes and was gone. I looked around the long, empty room.

"Well," I said, a little more loudly, "I guess I'll have to speak to the walls. I'm sure the walls can hear me."

I paused. There was no sound.

"All right," I said. "I'm a correspondent. All I'm interested in is information. Our assessment of the military situation here on St. Marie—" and here I told the truth—"shows the Friendly Expeditionary Forces abandoned by their home headquarters and certain to be overrun by the Exotic Forces as soon as the ground dries enough for heavy equipment to move."

There was still no answer, but the back of my neck knew they were listening, and watching me.

"As a result," I went on—and here I lied, though they would have no way of knowing—"we consider it inevitable that the Friendly Command here will have got in contact with the Blue Front. Assassination of enemy commanders is expressly in violation of the Mercenaries' Code and the Articles of Civilized Warfare—but civilians could do what soldiers could not."

Still there was no sound or movement beyond the drapes.

"A news representative," I said, "carries Credentials of Impartiality. You know how highly these are held. I only want to ask a few questions. And the answers will be kept confidential . . ."

For a last time I waited, and there was still no answer. I turned and went up the long room and out. It was not until I was well out on to the street that I let the feeling of triumph within spread out and warm me.

They would take the bait. People of their sort always did. I found my car and drove to Exotic Headquarters.

These were outside the town. There a mercenary commandant named Janol Marat took me in charge. He conducted me to the bubble structure of their HQ building. There was a feel of purpose, there, a sure and cheerful air of activity. They were well armed, well trained. After the Friendlies it jumped at me. I said so to Janol.

"We've got a Dorsai Commander and we outnumber the opposition." He grinned at me. He had a deeply tanned, long face that went into deep creases as his lips curved up. "That makes everybody pretty optimistic. Besides, our commander gets promoted if he wins. Back to the Exotics and staff rank—out of field combat for good. It's good business for us to win."

I laughed and he laughed.

"Tell me more, though," I said. "I want reasons I can use in the stories I send back to News Network."

"Well—" he answered the snappy salute of a passing groupman, a Cassidan, by the look of him—"I guess you might mention the usual—the fact our Exotic employers don't permit themselves to use violence and consequently they're always rather generous than otherwise when it comes to paying for men and equipment. And the OutBond—that's the Exotic Ambassador to St. Marie, you know—"

"I know."

"He replaced the former OutBond here three years ago. Anyway, he's something special, even for someone from Mara or Kultis. He's an expert in ontogenic calculations. If that means much to you. It's all over my head." Janol pointed. "Here's the Field Commander's office. He's Kensie Graeme."

"Graeme?" I said, frowning. I had spent a day at the Hague looking up Kensie Graeme before I came, but I wanted Janol's reactions to him. "Sounds familiar." We approached the office building. "Graeme . . ."

"You're probably thinking of another member of the same family." Janol took the bait. "Donal Graeme. A nephew. The one who pulled that wild stunt not long ago, attacking Newton with just a handful of Freiland ships. Kensie is Donal's uncle. Not as spectacular as the young Graeme, but I'll bet you'll like him better than you would the nephew. Kensie's got two men's likeableness." He looked at me, grinning slightly again.

"That supposed to mean something special?" I said.

"That's right," said Janol. "His own likeableness and his twin brother's, too. Meet Ian Graeme sometime when you're in Blauvain. That's where the Exotic embassy is, east of here. Ian's a dark man."

We walked into the office.

"I can't get used," I said, "to how so many Dorsai seem related."

"Neither can I. Actually, I guess it's because there really aren't so many of them. The Dorsai's a small world, and those that live more than a few years—" Janol stopped by a commandant sitting at a desk. "Can we see the Old Man, Hari? This is a News Network man."

"Why, I guess so." The other looked at his desk signal board. "The OutBond's with him, but he's just leaving now. Go on in."

Janol led me between the desks. A door at the back of the room opened before we reached it and a calm-faced man of middle age wearing a blue robe and close-cropped white hair came out. He looked strange but not ridiculous—particularly after you met his odd, hazel-colored eyes.

He was an Exotic.

I knew of Padma, as I knew the Exotics. I had seen them on their own home worlds of Mara and Kultis. A people committed to non-violence, mystics but very practical mystics, masters of what were known as the "strange sciences"—a dozen wizardic step-children of early psychology, sociology and the humanistic fields of research.

"Sir," said Janol to Padma, "this is—"

"Tam Olyn. I know," said Padma softly. He smiled up at me, and those eyes of his seemed to catch light for a moment and blind me. "I was sorry to learn about your brother-in-law, Tam."

I went quite cool all over. I had been ready to walk on, but now I stood stock still and looked at him.

"My brother-in-law?" I said.

"The young man who died near Castlemain, on New Earth."

"Oh, yes," I said, between stiff lips. "I'm surprised that you'd know."

"I know because of you, Tam." Once more the hazel eyes of Padma seemed to catch light. "We have a science called ontogenics, by which we calculate the probabilities of human actions in present and future situations. You've been an important factor in those calculations for some time." He smiled. "That's why I was expecting to meet you here, and now. We've calculated you into our present situation here on St. Marie, Tam."

"Have you?" I said. "Have you? That's interesting."

"I thought it would be," said Padma softly. "To you, especially. Someone like a newsman, like yourself, would find it interesting."

"It is," I said. "It sounds like you know more than I do about what I'm going to be doing here."

"We've got calculations," said Padma in his soft voice, "to that effect. Come see me in Blauvain, Tam; and I'll show you."

"I'll do that," I said.

"You'll be very welcome." Padma inclined his head. His blue robe whispered on the floor as he turned, and went out of the room.

"This way," said Janol, touching my elbow. I started as if I had just wakened from a deep sleep. "The commander's in here."

I followed him automatically into a further office. The individual I had come to see stood up as we came through the door. He was a great, lean man in field uniform, with a heavy-boned, but open, smiling face under black, slightly curly hair. A sort of golden warmth of personality—a strange thing in a Dorsai—seemed to flow out from him as he rose to meet me and his long-fingered, powerful hand swallowed mine in a handshake.

"Come on in," he said. "Let me fix you up with a drink. Janol," he added to my mercenary commandant from New Earth, "no need for you to stick around. Go on to chow. And tell the rest of them in the outer office to knock off."

Janol saluted and went. I sat down as Graeme turned to a small bar cabinet behind his desk. And for the first time in three years, under the magic of the unusual fighting man opposite me, a little peace came into my soul. With someone like this on my side, I could not lose.

3

"Credentials?" asked Graeme, as soon as we were settled with drinks of Dorsai whisky—which is a fine whisky—in our hands.

I passed my papers over. He glanced through them, picking out the letters from Sayona, the Bond of Kultis, to "*Commander—St. Marie Field Forces.*" He looked these over and put them aside. He handed me back the credentials folder.

"You stopped at Joseph's Town first?" he said.

I nodded. I saw him looking at my face, and his own sobered.

"You don't like the Friendlies," he said.

His words took my breath away. I had come prepared to fence for an opening to tell him. It was too sudden. I looked away.

I did not dare answer right away. I could not. There was either too much or too little to say if I let it come out without thinking. Then I got a grip on myself.

"If I do anything at all with the rest of my life," I said, slowly, "it'll be to do everything in my power to remove the Friendlies and all they stand for from the community of civilized human beings."

I looked back up at him. He was sitting with one massive elbow on his desktop, watching me.

"That's a pretty harsh point of view, isn't it?"

"No harsher than theirs."

"Do you think so?" he said seriously. "I wouldn't say so."

"I thought," I said, "you were the one who was fighting them."

"Why, yes." He smiled a little. "But we're soldiers on both sides."

"I don't think they think that way."

He shook his head a little.

"What makes you say that?" he said.

"I've seen them," I answered. "I got caught up front in the lines on Castlemain on New Earth, three years ago." I tapped my stiff knee. "I got shot and I couldn't navigate. The Cassidans around me began to retreat—they were mercenaries, and the troops opposing them were Friendlies hired out as mercenaries."

I stopped and took a drink of the whisky. When I took the glass away, Graeme had not moved. He sat as if waiting.

"There was young Cassidan, a buck soldier," I said. "I was doing a series on the campaign from an individual point of view. I'd picked him for my individual. It was a natural choice. You see—" I drank again, and emptied the glass—"my younger sister went out on contract as an accountant to Cassida two years before that, and she'd married him. He was my brother-in-law."

Graeme took the glass from my hand and silently replenished it.

"He wasn't actually a military man," I said. "He was studying shift mechanics and he had about three years to go. But he stood low on one of the competitive examinations at a time when Cassida owed a contractual balance of troops to New Earth." I took a deep breath. "Well, to make a long story short, he ended up on New

Earth in this same campaign I was covering. Because of the series I was writing, he was assigned to me. We both thought it was a good deal for him, that he'd be safer that way."

I drank some more of the whisky.

"But," I said, "you know, there's always a better story a little deeper in the combat zone. We got caught up front one day when the New Earth troops were retreating. I picked up a needle through the kneecap. The Friendly armor was moving up and things were getting hot. The soldiers around us took off toward the rear in a hurry, but Dave tried to carry me, because he thought the Friendly armor would fry me before they had time to notice I was a non-combatant. Well," I took another deep breath, "the Friendly ground troops caught us. They took us to a sort of clearing where they had a lot of prisoners and kept us there for a while. Then a Groupman—one of their fanatic types, a tall, starved-looking soldier about my age—came up with orders they were to reform for a fresh attack."

I stopped and took another drink. But I could not taste it.

"That meant they couldn't spare men to guard the prisoners. They'd have to turn them loose back of the Friendly lines. The Groupman said that wouldn't work. They'd have to make sure the prisoners couldn't endanger them."

Graeme was still watching me.

"I didn't understand. I didn't even catch on when the other Friendlies—none of them were non-coms like the Groupman—objected." I put my glass on the desk beside me and stared at the wall of the office, seeing it all over again, as plainly as if I looked through a window at it. "I remember how the Groupman pulled himself up straight. I saw his eyes. As if he'd been insulted by the others, objecting.

"'*Are they Chosen of God?*' he shouted at them. '*Are they of the Chosen?*'"

I looked across at Kensie Graeme and saw him still motionless, still watching me, his own glass small in one big hand.

"You understand?" I said to him. "As if because the prisoners weren't Friendlies, they weren't quite human. As if they were some lower order it was all right to kill." I shook, suddenly. "And he did it! I sat there against a tree, safe because of my News Correspondent's uniform and watched him shoot them down. All of them. I sat there and looked at Dave, and he looked at me, sitting there, as the Groupman shot him!"

I quit all at once. I hadn't meant to have it all come out like that. It was just that I'd been able to tell no one who would understand how helpless I had been. But something about Graeme had given me the idea he would understand.

"Yes," he said after a moment, and took and filled my glass again. "That sort of thing's very bad. Was the Groupman found and tried under the Mercenaries' Code?"

"After it was too late, yes."

He nodded and looked past me at the wall. "They aren't all like that, of course."

"There's enough to give them a reputation for it."

"Unfortunately, yes. Well"—he smiled slightly at me—"we'll try and keep that sort of thing out of this campaign."

"Tell me something," I said, putting my glass down. "Does that sort of thing—as you put it—ever happen to the Friendlies, themselves?"

Something took place then in the atmosphere of the room. There was a little pause before he answered. I felt my heart beat slowly, three times, as I waited for him to speak.

He said at last, "No, it doesn't."

"Why not?" I said.

The feeling in the room became stronger. And I realized I had gone too fast. I had been sitting talking to him as a man and forgetting what else he was. Now I began to forget that he was a man and become conscious of him as a Dorsai—an individual as human as I was, but trained all his life, and bred down the generations to a difference. He did not move or change the tone of his voice, or any such thing; but somehow he seemed to move off some distance from me, up into a higher, colder, stonier land into which I could venture only at my peril.

I remembered what was said about his people from that small, cold stony-mountained world: that if the Dorsai chose to withdraw their fighting men from the services of all the other worlds, and challenge those other worlds, not the combined might of the rest of civilization could stand against them. I had never really believed that before. I had never even really thought much about it. But sitting there just then, because of what was happening in the room, suddenly it became real to me. I could feel the knowledge, cold as a wind blowing on me off a glacier, that it was true; and then he answered my question.

"Because," said Kensie Graeme, "anything like that is specifically prohibited by Article Two of the Mercenaries' Code."

Then he broke out abruptly into a smile and what I had just felt in the room withdrew. I breathed again.

"Well," he said, putting his glass down empty on the desk, "how about joining us in the Officers' Mess for something to eat?"

I had dinner with them and the meal was very pleasant. They wanted to put me up for the night—but I could feel myself being pulled back to that cold, joyless compound near Joseph's Town, where all that waited for me was a sort of cold and bitter satisfaction at being among my enemies.

I went back.

It was about 11 PM when I drove through the gate of the compound and parked, just as a figure came out of the entrance to Jamethon's headquarters. The square was dim-lighted with only a few spotlights about the walls, their light lost in the rain-wet pavement. For a moment I did not recognize the figure—and then I saw it was Jamethon.

He would have passed by me at some little distance, but I got out of my car and went to meet him. He stopped when I stepped in front of him.

"Mr. Olyn," he said evenly. In the darkness I could not make out the expression of his face.

"I've got a question to ask," I said, smiling in the darkness.

"It's late for questions."

"This won't take long." I strained to catch the look on his face, but it was all in shadow. "I've been visiting the Exotic camp. Their commander's a Dorsai. I suppose you know that?"

"Yes." I could barely see the movement of his lips.

"We got to talking. A question came up and I thought I'd ask you, Commandant. Do you ever order your men to kill prisoners?"

An odd, short silence came between us. Then he answered.

"The killing or abuse of prisoners of war," he said without emotion, "is forbidden by Article Two of the Mercenaries' Code."

"But you aren't Mercenaries here, are you? You're native troops in service to your own True Church and Elders."

"Mr. Olyn," he said, while I still strained without success to make out the expression of his shadowed face—and it seemed that the words came slowly, though the tone of the voice that spoke them remained as calm as ever. "My Lord has set me to be His servant and a leader among men of war. In neither of those tasks will I fail Him."

And with that he turned, his face still shadowed and hidden from me, and passed around me and went on.

Alone, I went back inside to my quarters, undressed and lay down on the hard and narrow bed they had given me. The rain outside had stopped at last. Through my open, unglazed window I could see a few stars showing.

I lay there getting ready to sleep and making mental notes on what I would need to do tomorrow. The meeting with Padma the OutBond had jolted me sharply. I took his so-called calculations of human actions with reservation—but I had been shaken to learn of them. I would have to find out more about how much his science of ontogenics knew and could predict. If necessary, from Padma himself. But I would start first with ordinary reference sources.

No one, I thought, would ordinarily entertain the fantastic thought that one man like myself could destroy a culture involving the populations of two worlds. No one, except perhaps a Padma. What I knew, he with his calculations might have discovered. And that was that the Friendly worlds of Harmony and Association were facing a decision that would mean life or death to their way of living. A very small thing could tip the scales they weighed on.

For there was a new wind blowing between the stars.

Four hundred years before we had all been men of Earth—Old Earth, the mother planet which was my native soil. One people.

Then, with the movement out to new worlds, the human race had "splintered," to use an Exotic term. Every small social fragment and psychological type had drawn apart by itself, and joined others like it and progressed toward specialized types. Until we had half a dozen fragments of human types—the warrior on the Dorsai, the philosopher on the Exotic worlds, the hard scientist on Newton, Cassida and Venus, and so forth . . .

Isolation had bred specific types. Then a growing intercommunication between the younger worlds, now established, and an ever-increasing rate of technological advance had forced specialization. The trade between the worlds was the trade of skilled minds. Generals from the Dorsai were worth their exchange rate in psychiatrists from the Exotics. Communications men like myself from Old Earth bought spaceship designers from Cassida. And so it had been for the last hundred years.

But now the worlds were drifting together. Economics was fusing the race into one whole, again. And the struggle on each world was to gain the advantages of that fusion while holding on to as much as possible of their own ways.

Compromise was necessary—and the harsh, stiff-necked Friendly religion forbade compromise and had made many enemies. Already public opinion moved against the Friendlies on other worlds. Discredit them, smear them publicly here in this campaign, and they would not be able to hire out their soldiers. They would lose the balance of trade they needed to hire the skilled specialists trained by the special facilities of other worlds, and which they needed to keep their own two poor-in-natural-resources worlds alive. They would die.

As young Dave had died. Slowly. In the dark.

. . . In the darkness now, as I thought of it, it rose up before me once again. It had been only noon when we were taken prisoner, but by the time the Groupman came with his orders for our guards to move up, the sun was almost down.

After they left, after it was all over and I was left alone, I crawled to the bodies in the clearing. And I found Dave among them; and he was not quite gone.

He was wounded in the body and I could not stop the bleeding. It would not have helped if I had, they told me afterwards. But then it seemed that it would have. So I tried. But finally I gave up and by that time it was quite dark. I only held him and did not know he was dead until he began to grow cold. And then was when I had begun to change into what my uncle had always tried to make me. I felt myself die inside. Dave and my sister were to have been my family, the only family I had ever had hopes of keeping. Instead, I could only sit there in the darkness, holding him and hearing the blood from his red-soaked clothing, falling drop by drop, slowly on the dead variform oak leaves beneath us.

I lay there now in the Friendly compound, not able to sleep and remembering. And after a while I heard the soldiers marching, forming in the square for midnight service.

I lay on my back, listening to them. Their marching feet stopped at last. The single window of my room was over my bed—high in the wall against which the left side of my cot was set. It was unglazed and the night air with its sounds came freely through it along with the dim light from the square which painted a pale rectangle on the opposite wall of my room. I lay watching that rectangle and listening to the service outside; and I heard the duty officer lead them in a prayer for worthiness. After that they sang their battle hymn again, and I lay hearing it, this time, all the way through.

> *Soldier, ask not—now, or ever,*
> *Where to war your banners go.*
> *Anarch's legions all surround us.*
> *Strike—and do not count the blow.*

> *Glory, honor—praise and profit,*
> *Are but toys of tinsel worth.*
> *Render up your work, unasking,*
> *Leave the human clay to earth.*
>
> *Blood and sorrow—pain unending,*
> *Are the portion of us all.*
> *Grasp the naked sword, opposing,*
> *Gladly in the battle fall.*
>
> *So shall we, anointed soldiers,*
> *Stand at last before the Throne.*
> *Baptized in our wounds, red-flowing,*
> *Sealed unto our Lord—alone!*

After that they dispersed to cots no different from mine.

I lay there listening to the silence in the square and the measured dripping of a rain-spout outside by my window, its slow drops falling after the rain, one by one, uncounted in the darkness.

4

After the day I landed, there was no more rain. Day by day the fields dried. Soon they would be firm underneath the weight of heavy surface-war equipment, and everyone knew that then the Exotic spring offensive would get under way. Meanwhile both Exotic and Friendly troops were in training.

During the next few weeks, I was busy about my newswork. Mostly feature and small stories on the soldiers and the native people. I had dispatches to send and I sent them faithfully. A correspondent is only as good as his contacts; I made contacts everywhere but among the Friendly troops. These remained aloof, though I talked to many of them. They refused to show fear or doubt.

I had heard these Friendly soldiers were generally undertrained because the suicidal tactics of their officers kept their ranks always filled with green replacements. But the ones here were the remnants of an Expeditionary Force six times their present numbers. They were all veterans, though most of them were in their teens. Only here and there, among the non-coms, and more often among the commissioned officers, I saw the prototype of the non-com who had ordered the prisoners shot on New Earth. Here, the men of this type looked like rabid, gray wolves mixed among polite, well-schooled young dogs just out of puppyhood.

It was a temptation to think that they alone were what I had set out to destroy.

To fight that temptation I told myself that Alexander the Great had led expeditions against the hill tribes and ruled in Pella, capital of Macedonia, and ordered men put to death when he was sixteen. But still the Friendly soldiers looked young to me. I could not help contrasting them with the adult, experienced mercenaries in Kensie Graeme's forces. For the Exotics, in obedience to their principles, would hire no drafted troops or soldiers who were not in uniform of their own free will.

Meanwhile I had heard no word from the Blue Front. But by the time two weeks had gone, I had my own connections in New San Marcos, and at the beginning of the third week one of these brought me word that the jewelers shop in Wallace Street there had closed its door—had pulled its blinds and emptied the long room of stock and fixtures, and moved or gone out of business. That was all I needed to know.

For the next few days, I stayed in the vicinity of Jamethon Black himself, and by the end of the week my watching him paid off.

At ten o'clock that Friday night I was up on a catwalk just above my quarters and under the sentry-walk of the walls, watching as three civilians with Blue Front written all over them drove into the square, got out and went into Jamethon's office.

They stayed a little over an hour. When they left, I went back down to bed. That night I slept soundly.

The next morning I got up early, and there was mail for me. A message had come by spaceliner from the director of News Network back on Earth, personally congratulating me on my dispatches. Once, three years before, this would have meant a great deal to me. Now, I only worried that they would decide I had made the situation here newsworthy enough to require extra people being sent out to help me. I could not risk having other news personnel here now to see what I was doing.

I got in my car and headed east along the highway to New San Marcos and the Exotic Headquarters. The Friendly troops were already out in the field; eighteen kilometers east of Joseph's Town, I was stopped by a squad of five young soldiers with no non-com over them. They recognized me.

"In God's name, Mr. Olyn," said the first one to reach my car, bending down to speak to me through the open window at my left shoulder. "You cannot go through."

"Mind if I ask why?" I said.

He turned and pointed out and down into a little valley between two wooded hills at our left.

"Tactical survey in progress."

I looked. The little valley or meadow was perhaps a hundred yards wide between the wooded slopes, and it wound away from me and curved to disappear to my right. At the edge of the wooded slopes where they met open meadow, there were lilac bushes with blossoms several days old. The meadow itself was green and fair with the young chartreuse grass of early summer and the white and purple of the lilacs, and the variform oaks behind the lilacs were fuzzy in outline, with small, new leaves.

In the middle of all this, in the center of the meadow, were black-clad figures moving about with computing devices, measuring and figuring the possibilities of death from every angle. In the very center of the meadow for some reason they had set up marking stakes—a single stake, then a stake in front of that with two stakes on either side of it, and one more stake in line before these. Farther on was another single stake, down, as if fallen on the grass and discarded.

I looked back up into the lean young face of the soldier.

"Getting ready to defeat the Exotics?" I said.

He took it as if it had been a straightforward question, with no irony in my voice at all.

"Yes sir," he said seriously. I looked at him and at the taut skin and clear eyes of the rest.

"Ever think you might lose?"

"No, Mr. Olyn." He shook his head solemnly. "No man loses who goes to battle for the Lord." He saw that I needed to be convinced, and he went about it earnestly. "He hath set His hand upon His soldiers. And all that is possible to them is victory—or sometimes death. And what is death?"

He looked to his fellow soldiers and they all nodded.

"What is death?" they echoed.

I looked at them. They stood there asking me and each other what was death as if they were talking about some hard but necessary job.

I had an answer for them, but I did not say it. Death was a Groupman, one of their own kind, giving orders to soldiers just like themselves to assassinate prisoners. That was death.

"Call an officer," I said. "My pass lets me through here."

"I regret, sir," said the one who had been talking to me. "We cannot leave our posts to summon an officer. One will come soon."

I had a hunch what "soon" meant, and I was right. It was high noon before a Force Leader came by to order them to chow and let me through.

As I pulled into Kensie Graeme's Headquarters, the sun was low, patterning the ground with the long shadows of trees. Yet it was as if the camp was just waking up. I did not need experience to see the Exotics were beginning to move at last against Jamethon.

I found Janol Marat, the New Earth commandant.

"I've got to see Field Commander Graeme," I said.

He shook his head, for all that we now knew each other well.

"Not now, Tam. I'm sorry."

"Janol," I said, "this isn't for an interview. It's a matter of life and death. I mean that. I've got to see Kensie."

He stared at me. I stared back.

"Wait here," he said. We were standing just inside the headquarters office. He went out and was gone for perhaps five minutes. I stood, listening to the wall clock ticking away. Then he came back.

"This way," he said.

He led me outside and back between the bubble roundness of the plastic buildings to a small structure half-hidden in some trees. When we stepped through its front entrance, I realized it was Kensie's personal quarters. We passed through a small sitting room into a combination bedroom and bath. Kensie had just stepped out of the shower and was getting into battle clothes. He looked at me curiously, then turned his gaze back on Janol.

"All right, Commandant," he said, "you can get back to your duties, now."

"Sir," said Janol, without looking at me.

He saluted and left.

"All right, Tam," Kensie said, pulling on a pair of uniform slacks. "What is it?"

"I know you're ready to move out," I said.

He looked at me a little humorously as he locked the waistband of his slacks. He had not yet put on his shirt, and in that relatively small room he loomed like a giant, like some irresistible natural force. His body was tanned like dark wood and the muscles lay in flat bands across his chest and shoulders. His belly was hollow and the cords in his arms came and went as he moved them. Once more I felt the particular, special element of the Dorsai in him. It was not just his physical size and strength. It was not even the fact that he was someone trained from birth to war, someone bred for battle. No, it was something living but

untouchable—the same quality of difference to be found in the
pure Exotic like Padma the OutBond, or in some Newtonian
or Cassidan researchist. Something so much above and beyond
the common form of man that it was like a serenity, a sense of
conviction where his own type of thing was concerned that was
so complete it made him beyond all weaknesses, untouchable,
unconquerable.

I saw the slight, dark shadow of Jamethon Black in my mind's
eye, standing opposed to such a man as this; and the thought of any
victory for Jamethon was unthinkable, an impossibility.

But there was always danger.

"All right, I'll tell you what I came about," I said to Kensie. "I've
just found out Black's been in touch with the Blue Front, a native
terrorist political group with its headquarters in Blauvain. Three of
them visited him last night. I saw them."

Kensie picked up his shirt and slid a long arm into one sleeve.

"I know," he said.

I stared at him.

"Don't you understand?" I said. "They're assassins. It's their
stock in trade. And the one man they and Jamethon Black both
could use out of the way is you."

He put his other arm in a sleeve.

"I know that," he said. "They want the present government
here on St. Marie out of the way and themselves in power—which
isn't possible with Exotic money hiring us to keep the peace
here."

"They haven't had Jamethon Black's help."

"Have they got it now?" he asked, sealing the shirt closure
between thumb and forefinger.

"The Friendlies are desperate," I said. "Even if reinforcements
arrived tomorrow, Jamethon knows what his chances are with you
ready to move. Assassins may be outlawed by the Conventions
of War and the Mercenaries' Code, but you and I know the
Friendlies."

Kensie looked at me oddly and picked up his jacket.

"Do we?" he said.

I met his eyes. "Don't we?"

"Tam." He put on the jacket and closed it. "I know the men I
have to fight. It's my business to know. But what makes you think
you know them?"

"They're my business too," I said. "Maybe you'd forgotten. I'm
a newsman. People are my business, first, last and always."

"But you've got no use for the Friendlies."

"Should I?" I said. "I've been on all the worlds. I've seen the Cetan entrepreneur—and he wants his margin, but he's a human being. I've seen the Newtonian and the Cassidan with their heads in the clouds, but if you yanked on their sleeves hard enough, you could pull them back to reality. I've seen Exotics like Padma at their mental parlor tricks, and the Freilander up to his ears in his own red tape. I've seen them from my own world of Old Earth, and Coby, and Venus and even from the Dorsai, like you. And I tell you they've all got one thing in common. Underneath it all they're human. Every one of them's human—they've just specialized in some one, valuable way."

"And the Friendlies haven't?"

"Fanaticism," I said. "Is that valuable? It's just the opposite. What's good—what's even permissible about blind, deaf, dumb, unthinking faith that doesn't let a man reason for himself?"

"How do you know they don't reason?" Kensie asked. He was standing facing me now.

"Maybe some of them do," I said. "Maybe the young ones, before the poison's had time to work in. What good does that do, as long as the culture exists?"

A sudden silence came into the room.

"What are you talking about?" said Kensie.

"I mean you want the assassins," I said. "You don't want the Friendly troops. Prove that Jamethon Black has broken the Conventions of War by arranging with them to kill you; and you can win St. Marie for the Exotics without firing a shot."

"And how would I do that?"

"Use me," I said. "I've got a pipeline to the political group the assassins represent. Let me go to them as your representative and outbid Jamethon. You can offer them recognition by the present government, now. Padma and the present St. Marie government heads would have to back you up if you could clean the planet of Friendlies that easily."

He looked at me with no expression at all.

"And what would I be supposed to buy with this?" he said.

"Sworn testimony they'd been hired to assassinate you. As many of them as needed could testify."

"No Court of Interplanetary Inquiry would believe people like that," Kensie said.

"Ah," I said, and I could not help smiling. "But they'd believe me as a News Network Representative when I backed up every word that was said."

There was a new silence. His face had no expression at all.

"I see," he said.

He walked past me into the salon. I followed him. He went to his phone, put his finger on a stud and spoke into an imageless, gray screen.

"Janol," he said.

He turned away from the screen, crossed the room to an arms cabinet and began putting on his battle harness. He moved deliberately and neither looked nor spoke in my direction. After a few long minutes, the building entrance slid aside and Janol stepped in.

"Sir?" said the Freilander officer.

"Mr. Olyn stays here until further orders."

"Yes sir," said Janol.

Graeme went out.

I stood numb, staring at the entrance through which he had left. I could not believe that he would violate the Conventions so far himself as not only to disregard me, but to put me essentially under arrest to keep me from doing anything further about the situation.

I turned to Janol. He was looking at me with a sort of wry sympathy on his long, brown face.

"Is the OutBond here in camp?" I asked him.

"No." He came up to me. "He's back in the Exotic Embassy in Blauvain. Be a good fella now and sit down, why don't you? We might as well kill the next few hours pleasantly."

We were standing face to face; I hit him in the stomach.

I had done a little boxing as an undergraduate on the college level. I mention this not to make myself out a sort of muscular hero, but to explain why I had sense enough not to try for his jaw. Graeme could probably have found the knockout point there without even thinking, but I was no Dorsai. The area below a man's breastbone is relatively large, soft, handy and generally just fine for amateurs. And I did know something about how to punch.

For all that, Janol was not knocked out. He went over on the floor and lay there doubled up with his eyes still open. But he was not ready to get up right away. I turned and went quickly out of the building.

The camp was busy. Nobody stopped me. I got back into my car, and five minutes later I was free on the darkening road for Blauvain.

5

From New San Marcos to Blauvain and Padma's Embassy was fourteen hundred kilometers. I should have made it in six hours, but a bridge was washed out and I took fourteen.

It was after eight the following morning when I burst into the half-park, half-building that was the embassy.

"Padma—" I said. "Is he still—"

"Yes, Mr. Olyn," said the girl receptionist. "He's expecting you."

She smiled above her purple robe. I did not mind. I was too busy being glad Padma had not already taken off for the fringe areas of the conflict.

She took me down and around a corner and turned me over to a young male Exotic, who introduced himself as one of Padma's secretaries. He took me a short distance and introduced me to another secretary, a middle-aged man this time, who led me through several rooms and then directed me down a long corridor and around a corner, beyond which he said was the entrance to the office area where Padma worked at the moment. Then he left me.

I followed his direction. But when I stepped through that entrance it was not into a room, but into a further short corridor. And I checked, stopping myself dead. For what I suddenly thought I saw coming at me was Kensie Graeme—Kensie with murder on his mind.

But the man who looked like Kensie merely glanced at me and dismissed me, continuing to come on. Then I knew.

Of course, he was not Kensie. He was Kensie's twin brother, Ian, commander of Garrison Forces for the Exotics, here in Blauvain. He strode on toward me; and I began once more to walk toward him, but the shock stayed with me until we had passed one another.

I do not think anyone could have come on him like that, in my position and not been hit the same way. From Janol, at different times, I had gathered how Ian was the converse of Kensie. Not in a military sense—they were both magnificent specimens of Dorsai officers—but in the matter of their individual natures.

Kensie had had a profound effect on me from the first moment, with his cheerful nature and the warmth of being that at times obscured the very fact that he was a Dorsai. When the pressure of military affairs was not directly on him he seemed all sunshine; you could warm yourself in his presence as you might in the sun. Ian, his physical duplicate, striding toward me like some two-eyed Odin, was all shadow.

Here at last was the Dorsai legend come to life. Here was the grim man with the iron heart and the dark and solitary soul. In the powerful fortress of his body, what was essentially Ian dwelt as isolated as a hermit on a mountain. He was the fierce and lonely Highlandman of his distant ancestry, come to life again.

Not law, not ethics, but the trust of the given word, clan-loyalty and the duty of the blood feud held sway in Ian. He was a man who would cross hell to pay a debt for good or ill; and in that moment when I saw him coming toward me and recognized him at last, I suddenly thanked whatever gods were left, that he had no debt with me.

Then we had passed each other, and he was gone around a corner.

Rumour had it, I remembered then, that the blackness around him never lightened except in Kensie's presence. That he was truly his twin brother's other half. And that if he should ever lose the light that Kensie's bright presence shed on him, he would be doomed to his own lightlessness forever.

It was a statement I was to remember at a later time, as I was to remember seeing him come toward me in that moment.

But now I forgot him as I went forward through another entrance into what looked like a small conservatory and saw the gentle face and short-cropped white hair of Padma, the OutBond, wearing a pale yellow robe.

"Come in, Mr. Olyn," he said, getting up. "And come along with me."

He turned and walked out through an archway of purple clematis blooms. I followed him, and found a small courtyard, all but filled with the elliptical shape of a sedan aircar. Padma was already climbing into one of the seats facing the controls. He held the door for me.

"Where are we going?" I asked as I got in.

He touched the autopilot panel; the ship rose in the air. He left it to its own navigation, and pivoted his chair about to face me.

"To Commander Graeme's headquarters in the field," he answered.

His eyes were a light hazel color, but they seemed to catch and swim with the sunlight striking through the transparent top of the aircar, as we reached altitude and began to move horizontally. I could not read them, or the expression on his face.

"I see," I said. "Of course, I know a call from Graeme's HQ could get to you much faster than I could by groundcar from the same spot. But I hope you aren't thinking of having him kidnap me or something like that. I have Credentials of Impartiality protecting me as a Newsman, as well as authorizations from both the Friendly and the Exotic worlds. And I don't intend to be held responsible for any conclusions drawn by Graeme after the conversation the two of us had earlier this morning—*alone*."

Padma sat still in his aircar seat, facing me. His hands were folded in his lap together, pale against the yellow robe, but with strong sinews showing under the skin of their backs.

"You're coming with me now by my decision, not Kensie Graeme's."

"I want to know why," I said tensely.

"Because," he said slowly, "you are very dangerous." And he sat still, looking at me with unwavering eyes.

I waited for him to go on, but he did not. "Dangerous?" I said. "Dangerous to who?"

"To the future of all of us."

I stared at him, then I laughed. I was angry.

"Cut it out!" I said.

He shook his head slowly, his eyes never leaving my face. I was baffled by those eyes. Innocent and open as a child's, but I could not see through them into the man himself.

"All right," I said. "Tell me, why am I dangerous?"

"Because you want to destroy a race of people. And you know how."

There was a short silence. The aircar fled on through the skies without a sound.

"Now that's an odd notion," I said slowly and calmly. "I wonder where you got it?"

"From our ontogenic calculations," said Padma, as calmly as I had spoken. "And it's not a notion, Tam. As you know yourself."

"Oh, yes," I said. "Ontogenics. I was going to look that up."

"You did look it up, didn't you, Tam?"

"Did I?" I said. "I guess I did, at that. It didn't seem very clear to me, though, as I remember. Something about evolution."

"Ontogenics," said Padma, "is the study of the effect of evolution upon the interacting forces of human society."

"Am I an interacting force?"

"At the moment and for the past several years, yes," said Padma. "And possibly for some years into the future. But possibly not."

"That sounds almost like a threat."

"In a sense it is." Padma's eyes caught the light as I watched them. "You're capable of destroying yourself as well as others."

"I'd hate to do that."

"Then," said Padma, "you'd better listen to me."

"Why, of course," I said. "That's my business, listening. Tell me all about ontogenics—and myself."

He made an adjustment in the controls, then swung his seat back to face mine once more.

"The human race," said Padma, "broke up in an evolutionary explosion at the moment in history when interstellar colonization became practical." He sat watching me. I kept my face attentive. "This happened for reasons stemming from racial instinct which we haven't completely charted yet, but which was essentially self-protective in nature."

I reached into my jacket pocket.

"Perhaps I'd better take a few notes," I said.

"If you want to," said Padma, unperturbed. "Out of that explosion came cultures individually devoted to single facets of the human personality. The fighting, combative facet became the Dorsai. The facet which surrendered the individual wholly to some faith or other became the Friendly. The philosophical facet created the Exotic culture to which I belong. We call these Splinter Cultures."

"Oh, yes," I said. "I know about Splinter Cultures."

"You know about them, Tam, but you don't know them."

"I don't?"

"No," said Padma, "because you, like all our ancestors, are from Earth. You're old, full-spectrum man. The Splinter peoples are evolutionarily advanced over you."

I felt a little twist of bitter anger knot suddenly inside me.

"Oh? I'm afraid I don't see that."

"Because you don't want to," said Padma. "If you did, you'd have to admit that they were different from you, and had to be judged by different standards."

"Different? How?"

"Different in a sense that all Splinter people, including myself, understand instinctively, but full-spectrum man has to extrapolate to imagine." Padma shifted a little in his seat. "You'll get some idea, Tam, if you imagine a member of a Splinter culture to be a man like yourself, only with a monomania that shoves him wholly toward being one type of person. But with this difference: Instead of all parts of his mental and physical self outside the limits of that monomania being ignored and atrophied as, they would be with you—"

I interrupted, "Why specifically with me?"

"With any full-spectrum man, then," said Padma calmly. "These parts, instead of being atrophied, are altered to agree with and support the monomania, so that we don't have a sick man—but a healthy, different one."

"Healthy?" I said, seeing the Friendly non-com on New Earth again in my mind's eye.

"Healthy as a culture. Not as occasional crippled individuals of that culture. But as a culture."

"Sorry," I said. "I don't believe it."

"But you do, Tam," said Padma, softly. "Unconsciously you do. Because you're planning to take advantage of the weakness such a culture must have to destroy it."

"And what weakness is that?"

"The obvious weakness that's the converse of any strength," said Padma. "The Splinter Cultures are not viable."

I must have blinked. I was honestly bewildered.

"Not viable? You mean they can't live on their own?"

"Of course not," said Padma. "Faced with an expansion into space, the human race reacted to the challenge of a different environment by trying to adapt to it. It adapted by trying out separately all the elements of its personality, to see which could survive best. Now that all elements—the Splinter Cultures—have survived and adapted, it's time for them to breed back into each other again, to produce a more hardy, universe-oriented human.

The aircar began to descend. We were nearing our destination.

"What's that got to do with me?" I said, at last.

"If you frustrate one of the Splinter Cultures, it can't adapt on its own as full-spectrum man would do. It will die. And when the race breeds back to a whole, that valuable element will be lost to the race."

"Maybe it'll be no loss," I said, softly in my turn.

"A vital loss," said Padma. "And I can prove it. You, a full-spectrum man, have in you an element from every Splinter Culture. If you admit this you can identify even with those you want to destroy. I have evidence to show you. Will you look at it?"

The ship touched ground; the door beside me opened. I got out with Padma and found Kensie waiting.

I looked from Padma to Kensie, who stood with us and a head taller than I—two heads taller than OutBond. Kensie looked back down at me with no particular expression. His eyes were not the eyes of his twin brother—but just then, for some reason, I could not meet them.

"I'm a newsman," I said. "Of course my mind is open."

Padma turned and began walking toward the headquarters building. Kensie fell in with us and I think Janol and some of the others came along behind, though I didn't look back to make sure. We went to the inner office where I first met Graeme—just Kensie, Padma and myself. There was a file folder on Graeme's desk. He picked it up, extracted a photocopy of something and handed it to me as I came up to him.

I took it. There was no doubting its authenticity.

It was a memo from Eldest Bright, ranking elder of the joint government of Harmony and Association, to the Friendly War Chief at the Defense X Center, on Harmony. It was dated two months previously. It was on the single-molecule sheet, where the legend cannot be tampered with, or removed once it is on.

Be Informed, in God's Name—

—That since it does seem the Lord's Will that our Brothers on St. Marie make no success, it is ordered that henceforth no more replacements or personnel or supplies be sent them. For if our Captain does intend us the victory, surely we shall conquer without further expenditure. And if it be His will that we conquer not, then surely it would be an impiety to throw away the substance of God's Churches in an attempt to frustrate that Will.

Be it further ordered that our Brothers on St. Marie be spared the knowledge that no further assistance is forthcoming, that they may bear witness to their faith in battle as ever, and God's Churches be undismayed.

Heed this Command, in the Name of the Lord:

By order of he who is called . . .
Bright
Eldest Among the Chosen

I looked up from the memo. Both Graeme and Padma were watching me.

"How'd you get hold of this?" I said. "No, of course you won't tell me." The palms of my hands were suddenly sweating so that the slick material of the sheet in my fingers was slippery. I held it tightly, and talked fast to keep their eyes on my face. "But what about it? We already knew this, everybody knew Bright had abandoned them. This just proves it. Why even bother showing it to me?"

"I thought," said Padma, "it might move you just a little. Perhaps enough to make you take a different view of things."

I said, "I didn't say that wasn't possible. I tell you a Newsman keeps an open mind at all times. Of course," I picked my words carefully, "if I could study it—"

"I'd hoped you'd take it with you," said Padma.

"Hoped?"

"If you dig into it and really understand what Bright means there, you might understand all the Friendlies differently. You might change your mind about them."

"I don't think so," I said. "But—"

"Let me ask you to do that much," said Padma. "Take the memo with you."

I stood for a moment, with Padma facing me and Kensie looming behind him, then shrugged and put the memo in my pocket.

"All right," I said. "I'll take it back to my quarters and think about it. —I've got a groundcar here somewhere, haven't I?" And I looked at Kensie.

"Ten kilometers back," said Kensie. "You wouldn't get through anyway. We're moving up for the assault and the Friendlies are maneuvering to meet us."

"Take my aircar," said Padma. "The Embassy flags on it will help."

"All right," I said.

We went out together toward the aircar. I passed Janol in the outer office and he met my eyes coldly. I did not blame him. We walked to the aircar and I got in.

"You can send the aircar back whenever you're through with it," said Padma, as I stepped in through the entrance section of its top. "It's an Embassy loan to you, Tam. I won't worry about it."

"No," I said. "You needn't worry."

I closed the section and touched the controls.

It was a dream of an aircar. It went up into the air as lightly as thought, and in a second I was two thousand feet up and well away from the spot. I made myself calm down, though, before I reached into my pocket and took the memo out.

I looked at it. My hand still trembled a little as I held it.

Here it was in my grasp at last. What I had been after from the start. And Padma himself had insisted I carry it away with me.

It was the lever, the Archimedes pry-bar which would move not one world but fourteen. And push the Friendly Peoples over the edge to extinction.

6

They were waiting for me. They converged on the aircar as I landed it in the interior square of the Friendlies compound, all four of them with black rifles at the ready.

They were apparently the only ones left. Black seemed to have turned out every other man of his remnant of a battle unit. And these were all men I recognized, case-hardened veterans. One was the Groupman who had been in the office that first night when I had come back from the Exotic camp and stepped in to speak to Black, asking him if he ever ordered his men to kill prisoners. Another was a forty-year-old Force Leader, the lowest commissioned rank, but acting Major—just as Black, a Commandant, was acting as Expeditionary Field Commander—a position equivalent to Kensie Graeme's. The other two soldiers were non-commissioned, but similar. I knew them all. Ultra-fanatics. And they knew me.

We understood each other.

"I have to see the commandant," I said, as I got out, before they could begin to question me.

"On what business?" said the Force-Leader. "This aircar hath no business here. Nor thyself."

I said, "I must see Commandant Black immediately. I wouldn't be here in a car flying the flags of the Exotic Embassy if it wasn't necessary."

They could not take the chance that my reason for seeing Black wasn't important, and I knew it. They argued a little, but I kept insisting I had to see the Commandant. Finally, the Force-Leader took me across into the same outer office where I had always waited to see Black.

I faced Jamethon Black alone in the office.

He was putting on his battle harness, as I had seen Graeme putting on his earlier. On Graeme, the harness and the weapons it carried had looked like toys. On Jamethon's slight frame they looked almost too heavy to bear.

"Mr. Olyn," he said.

I walked across the room toward him, drawing the memo from my pocket as I came. He turned a little to face me, his fingers sealing the locks on his harness, jingling slightly with his weapons and his harness as he turned.

"You're taking the field against the Exotics," I said.

He nodded. I had never been this close to him before. From across the room I would have believed he was holding his usual stony expression, but standing just a few feet from him now I saw the tired wraith of a smile touch the corners of his straight mouth in that dark, young face, for a second.

"That is my duty, Mr. Olyn."

"Some duty," I said. "When your superiors back on Harmony have already written you off their books."

"I've already told you," he said, calmly. "The Chosen are not betrayed in the Lord, one by another."

"You're sure of that?" I said.

Once more I saw that little ghost of a weary smile.

"It's a subject, Mr. Olyn, on which I am more expert than you."

I looked into his eyes. They were exhausted but calm. I glanced aside at the desk where the picture of the church, the older man and woman and the young girl stood still.

"Your family?" I asked.

"Yes," he said.

"It seems to me you'd think of them in a time like this."

"I think of them quite often."

"But you're going to go out and get yourself killed just the same."

"Just the same," he said.

"Sure!" I said. "You would!" I had come in calm and in control of myself. But now it was as if a cork had been pulled on all that had been inside me since Dave's death. I began to shake. "Because that's the kind of hypocrites you are—all of you Friendlies. You're so lying, so rotten clear through with your own lies, if someone took them away from you there'd be nothing left. Would there? So you'd rather die now than admit committing suicide like this isn't the most glorious thing in the universe. You'd rather die than admit you're just as full of doubts as anyone else, just as afraid."

I stepped right up to him. He did not move.

"Who're you trying to fool?" I said. "Who? I see through you just like the people on all the other worlds do! I know you know what a mumbo-jumbo your United Churches are. I know you know the way of life you sing of through your nose so much isn't what you claim it is. I know your Eldest Bright and his gang of narrow-minded old men are just a gang of world-hungry tyrants that don't give a damn for religion or anything as long as they get what they want. I know you know it—and I'm going to make you admit it!"

And I shoved the memo under his nose.

"Read it!"

He took it from me. I stepped back from him, shaking badly as I watched him.

He studied it for a long minute, while I held my breath. His face did not change. Then he handed it back to me.

"Can I give you a ride to meet Graeme?" I said. "We can get across the lines in the OutBond's aircar. You can get the surrender over with before any shooting breaks out."

He shook his head. He was looking at me in a particularly level way, with an expression I could not understand.

"What do you mean—no?"

"You'd better stay here," he said. "Even with ambassadorial flags, that aircar may be shot at over the lines." And he turned as if he would walk away from me, out the door.

"Where're you going?" I shouted at him. I got in front of him and pushed the memo before his eyes again. "That's real. You can't close your eyes to that!"

He stopped and looked at me. Then he reached out and took my wrist and put my arm and hand with the memo aside. His fingers were thin, but much stronger than I thought, so that I let the arm go down in front of him when I hadn't intended to do so.

"I know it's real. I'll have to warn you not to interfere with me any more, Mr. Olyn. I've got to go now." He stepped past me and walked toward the door.

"You're a liar!" I shouted after him. He kept on going. I had to stop him. I grabbed the solidograph from his desk and smashed it on the floor.

He turned like a cat and looked at the broken pieces at my feet.

"That's what you're doing!" I shouted, pointing at them.

He came back without a word and squatted down and carefully gathered up the pieces, one by one. He put them into his pocket and got back to his feet, and raised his face at last to mine. And when I saw his eyes I stopped breathing.

"If my duty," he said, in a low, controlled voice, "were not in this minute to—"

His voice stopped. I saw his eyes staring into me; and slowly I saw them change and the murder that was in them soften into something like wonder.

"Thou—" he said, softly—"Thou hast *no* faith?"

I had opened my mouth to speak. But what he said stopped me. I stood as if punched in the stomach, without the breath for words. He stared at me.

"What made you think," he said, "that that memo would change my mind?"

"You read it!" I said. "Bright wrote you were a losing proposition here, so you weren't to get any more help. And no one was to tell you for fear you might surrender if you knew."

"Is that how you read it?" he said. "Like that?"

"How else? How else can you read it?"

"As it is written." He stood straight facing me now and his eyes never moved from mine. "You have read it without faith, leaving out the Name and the will of the Lord. Eldest Bright wrote not that we were to be abandoned here—but that since our cause was sore tried, we be put in the hands of our Captain and our God. And further he wrote that we should not be told of this, that none here should be tempted to a vain and special seeking of the martyr's crown. Look, Mr. Olyn. It's down there in black and white."

"But that's not what he meant! *That's not what he meant!*"

He shook his head. "Mr. Olyn, I can't leave you in such delusion."

I stared at him, for it was sympathy I saw in his face. For me.

"It's your own blindness that deludes you," he said. "You see nothing, and so believe no man can see. Our Lord is not just a name, but all things. That's why we have no ornament in our churches, scorning any painted screen between us and our God. Listen to me, Mr. Olyn. Those churches themselves are but tabernacles of the earth. Our Elders and Leaders, though they are Chosen and Anointed, are still but mortal men. To none of these things or people do we hearken in our faith, but to the very voice of God within us."

He paused. Somehow I could not speak.

"Suppose it was even as you think," he went on, even more gently. "Suppose that all you say was a fact; and that our Elders were but greedy tyrants, ourselves abandoned here by their selfish will and set to fulfill a false and prideful purpose. No." Jamethon's voice rose. "Let me attest as if it were only for myself. Suppose that you could give me proof that all our Elders lied, that our very Covenant was false. Suppose that you could prove to me—" his face lifted to mine and his voice drove at me— "that all was perversion and falsehood, and nowhere among the Chosen, not even in the house of my father, was there faith or hope! If you could prove to me that no miracle could save me, that no soul stood with me—and that opposed were all the legions of the universe—still I, I *alone*, Mr. Olyn, would go forward as I have been commanded, to the end of the universe, to the culmination of eternity. For without my faith I am but common earth. But with my faith, there is no power can stay me!"

He stopped speaking and turned about. I watched him walk across the room and out the door.

Still I stood there, as if I had been fastened in place—until I heard from outside, in the square of the compound, the sound of a military aircar starting up.

I broke out of my stasis then and ran out of the building.

As I burst into the square, the military aircar was just taking off. I could see Black and his four hard-shell subordinates in it. And I yelled up into the air after them.

"That's all right for you, but what about your men?"

They could not hear me. I knew that. Uncontrollable tears were running down my face, but I screamed up into the air after him anyway—

"You're killing your men to prove your point! Can't you listen? You're murdering helpless men!"

Unheeding, the military aircar dwindled rapidly to the west and south, where the converging battle forces waited. And the heavy concrete walls and buildings about the empty compound threw back my words with a hollow, wild and mocking echo.

7

I should have gone to the spaceport. Instead, I got back into the aircar and flew back across the lines looking for Graeme's Battle Command Center.

I was as little concerned about my own life just then as a Friendly. I think I was shot at once or twice, in spite of the ambassadorial flags on the aircar, but I don't remember exactly. Eventually I found the Command Center and descended.

Enlisted men surrounded me as I stepped out of the aircar. I showed my credentials and went up to the battle screen, which had been set up in open air at the edge of shadow from some tall variform oaks. Graeme, Padma and his whole staff were grouped around it, watching the movements of their own and the Friendly troops reported on it. A continual low-voiced discussion of the movements went on, and a steady stream of information came from the communications center fifteen feet off.

The sun slanted steeply through the trees. It was almost noon and the day was bright and warm. No one looked at me for a long time; and then Janol, turning away from the screen, caught sight of me standing off at one side by the flat-topped shape of a tactics computer. His face went cold. He went on about what he was doing. But I must have been looking pretty bad, because after a while he came by with a canteen cup and set it down on the computer top.

"Drink that," he said shortly, and went off. I picked it up, found it was Dorsai whisky and swallowed it down. I could not taste it; but evidently it did me some good, because in a few minutes the world began to sort itself out around me and I began to think again.

I went up to Janol. "Thanks."

"All right." He did not look at me, but went on with the papers on the field desk before him.

"Janol," I said. "Tell me what's going on."

"See for yourself," he said, still bent over his papers.

"I can't see for myself. You know that. Look—I'm sorry about what I did. But this is my job, too. Can't you tell me what's going on now and fight with me afterwards?"

"You know I can't brawl with civilians." Then his face relaxed. "All right," he said, straightening up. "Come on."

He led me over to the battle screen, where Padma and Kensie were standing, and pointed to a sort of small triangle of darkness between two snakelike lines of light. Other spots and shapes of light ringed it about.

"These—" he pointed to the two snakelike lines—"are the Macintok and Sarah Rivers, where they come together—just about ten miles this side of Joseph's Town. It's fairly high ground, hills thick with cover, fairly open between them. Good territory for setting up a stubborn defense, bad area to get trapped in."

"Why?"

He pointed to the two river lines.

"Get backed up in here and you find yourself hung up on high bluffs over the river. There is no easy way across, no cover for retreating troops. It's nearly all open farmland the rest of the way, from the other sides of the rivers to Joseph's Town."

His finger moved back out from the point where the river lines came together, past the small area of darkness and into the surrounding shapes and rings of light.

"On the other hand, the approach to this territory from our position is through open country, too—narrow strips of farmland interspersed with a lot of swamp and marsh. It's a tight situation for either command, if we commit to a battle here. The first one who has to backpedal will find himself in trouble in a hurry."

"Are you going to commit?"

"It depends. Black sent his light armor forward. Now he's pulling back into the high ground, between the rivers. We're far superior in strength and equipment. There's no reason for us not to go in after him, as long as he's trapped himself—" Janol broke off.

"No reason?" I asked.

"Not from a tactical standpoint." Janol frowned at the screen. "We couldn't get into trouble unless we suddenly had to retreat. And we wouldn't do that unless he suddenly acquired some great tactical advantage that'd make it impossible for us to stay there."

I looked at his profile.

"Such as losing Graeme?" I said.

He transferred his frown to me. "There's no danger of that."

There was a certain change in the movement and the voices of the people around us. We both turned and looked.

Everybody was clustering around a screen. We moved in with the crowd and, looking between the soldiers of two of the officers of Graeme's staff, I saw on the screen the image of a small grassy meadow enclosed by wooded hills. In the centre of the meadow, the Friendly flag floated its thin black cross on white background beside a long table on the grass. There were folding chairs on each side of the table, but only one person—a Friendly officer, standing on the table's far side as if waiting. There were the lilac bushes along the edge of the wooded hills where they came down in variform oak and ash to the meadow's edge; and the lavender blossoms were beginning to brown and darken for their season was almost at an end. So much difference had twenty-four hours made. Off to the left of the screen I could see the gray concrete of a highway.

"I know that place—" I started to say, turning to Janol.

"Quiet!" he said, holding up a finger. Around us, everybody else had fallen still. Up near the front of our group a single voice was talking.

"—it's a truce table."

"Have they called?" said the voice of Kensie.

"No, sir."

"Well, let's go see." There was a stir up front. The group began to break up and I saw Kensie and Padma walking off toward the area where the aircars were parked. I shoved myself through the thinning crowd like a process server, running after them.

I heard Janol shout behind me, but I paid no attention. Then I was up to Kensie and Padma, who turned.

"I want to go with you," I said.

"It's all right, Janol," Kensie said, looking past me. "You can leave him with us."

"Yes, sir." I could hear Janol turn and leave.

"So you want to come with me, Mr. Olyn?" Kensie said.

"I know that spot," I told him. "I drove by it just earlier today.

The Friendlies were taking tactical measurements all over that meadow and the hills on both sides. They weren't setting up truce talks."

Kensie looked at me for a long moment, as if he was taking some tactical measurements himself.

"Come on, then," he said. He turned to Padma. "You'll be staying here?"

"It's a combat zone. I'd better not." Padma turned his unwrinkled face to me. "Good luck, Mr. Olyn," he said, and walked away. I watched his yellow-robed figure glide over the turf for a second, then turned to see Graeme halfway to the nearest military aircar. I hurried after him.

It was a battle car, not luxurious like the OutBond's, and Kensie did not cruise at two thousand feet, but snaked it between the trees just a few feet above ground. The seats were cramped. His big frame overfilled his, crowding me where I sat. I felt the butt-plate of his spring pistol grinding into my side with every movement he made on the controls.

We came at last to the edge of the wooded and hilly triangle occupied by the Friendlies and mounted a slope under the cover of the new-leaved variform oaks.

They were massive enough to have killed off most ground cover. Between their pillar-like trunks the ground was shaded, and padded with the brown shapes of dead leaves. Near the crest of the hill, we came upon a unit of Exotic troops resting and waiting the orders to advance. Kensie got out of the car and returned the Force-Leader's salute.

"You've seen these tables the Friendlies set up?" Kensie asked.

"Yes, Commander. That officer they've got is still standing there. If you go just up over the crest of the slope here, you can see him—and the furniture."

"Good," said Kensie. "Keep your men here, Force. The Newsman and I'll go take a look."

He led the way up among the oak trees. At the top of the hill we looked down through about fifty yards more of trees and out into the meadow. It was two hundred yards across, the table right in the middle, the unmoving black figure of the Friendly officer standing on its far side.

"What do you think of it, Mr. Olyn?" asked Kensie, looking down through the trees.

"Why hasn't somebody shot him?" I asked.

He glanced sideways at me.

"There's plenty of time to shoot him," he said, "before he can get back to cover on the far side. If we have to shoot him at all. That wasn't what I wanted to know. You've seen the Friendly commander recently. Did he give you the impression he was ready to surrender?"

"No!" I said.

"I see," said Kensie.

"You don't really think he means to surrender? What makes you think something like that?"

"Truce tables are generally set up for the discussion of terms between opposing forces," he said.

"But he hasn't asked you to meet him?"

"No," Kensie watched the figure of the Friendly officer, motionless in the sunlight. "It might be against his principles to call for a discussion, but not to discuss—if we just happened to find ourselves across a table from one another."

He turned and signaled with his hand. The Force-Leader, who had been waiting down the slope behind us, came up.

"Sir?" he said to Kensie.

"Any Friendly strength in those trees across the way?"

"Four men, that's all, sir. Our scopes pick out their body heats clear and sharp. They aren't attempting to hide."

"I see." He paused. "Force."

"Sir?"

"Be good enough to go down there in the meadow and ask that Friendly officer what this is all about."

"Yes, sir."

We stood and watched as the Force-Leader went stiff-legging it down the steep slope between the trees. He crossed the grass—it seemed very slowly—and came up to the Friendly officer.

They stood facing each other. They were talking but there was no way to hear their voices. The flag with its thin black cross whipped in the little breeze that was blowing there. Then the Force-Leader turned and climbed back toward us.

He stopped in front of Kensie, and saluted. "Commander," he said, "the Commander of the Chosen Troops of God will meet with you in the field to discuss a surrender." He stopped to draw a fresh breath. "If you'll show yourself at the edge of the opposite woods at the same time; and you can approach the table together."

"Thank you, Force-Leader," said Kensie. He looked past his officer at the field and the table. "I think I'll go down."

"He doesn't mean it." I said.

"Force-Leader," said Kensie. "Form your men ready, just under the crown of the slope on the back side, here. If he surrenders, I'm going to insist he come back with me to this side immediately."

"Yes, sir."

"All this business without a regular call for parley may be because he wants to surrender first and break the news of it to his troops afterwards. So get your men ready. If Black intends to present his officers with an accomplished fact, we don't want to let him down."

"He's not going to surrender," I said.

"Mr. Olyn," said Kensie, turning to me. "I suggest you go back behind the crest of the hill. The Force-Leader will see you're taken care of."

"No," I said. "I'm going down. If it's a truce parley to discuss surrender terms, there's no combat situation involved and I've got a perfect right to be there. If it isn't, what're you doing going down yourself?"

Kensie looked at me strangely for a moment.

"All right," he said. "Come with me."

Kensie and I turned and went down the sharply pitched slope between the trees. Our bootsoles slipped until our heels dug in, with every step downward. Coming through the lilacs I smelled the faint, sweet scent—almost gone now—of the decaying blossoms.

Across the meadow, directly in line with the table, four figures in black came forward as we came forward. One of them was Jamethon Black.

Kensie and Jamethon saluted each other.

"Commandant Black," said Kensie.

"Yes, Commander Graeme. I am indebted to you for meeting me here," said Jamethon.

"My duty and a pleasure, Commandant."

"I wished to discuss the terms of a surrender."

"I can offer you," said Kensie, "the customary terms extended to troops in your position under the Mercenaries' Code."

"You misunderstand me, sir," said Jamethon. "It was your surrender I came here to discuss."

The flag snapped.

Suddenly I saw the men in black measuring the field here, as I had seen them the day before. They had been right where we were now.

"I'm afraid the misunderstanding is mutual, Commandant," said Kensie. "I am in a superior tactical position and your defeat is normally certain. I have no need to surrender."

"You will not surrender?"

"No," said Kensie strongly.

All at once I saw the five stakes, in the position the Friendly non-coms, officers and Jamethon were now, and the stake up in front of them fallen down.

"Look out!" I shouted at Kensie—but I was far too late.

Things had already begun to happen. The Force-Leader had jerked back in front of Jamethon and all five of them were drawing their sidearms. I heard the flag snap again, and the sound of its rolling seemed to go on for a long time.

For the first time then I saw a man of the Dorsai in action. So swift was Kensie's reaction that it was eerily as if he had read Jamethon's mind in the instant before the Friendlies began to reach of their weapons. As their hands touched their sidearms, he was already in movement forward over the table and his spring pistol was in his hand. He seemed to fly directly into the Force-Leader and the two of them went down together, but Kensie kept travelling. He rolled on off the Force-Leader who now lay still in the grass. He came to his knees, fired, and dived forward, rolling again.

The Groupman on Jamethon's right went down. Jamethon and the remaining two were turned nearly full about now, trying to keep Kensie before them. The two that were left shoved themselves in front of Jamethon, their weapons not yet aimed. Kensie stopped moving as if he had run into a stone wall, came to his feet in a crouch, and fired twice more. The two Friendlies fell apart, one to each side.

Jamethon was facing Kensie now, and Jamethon's pistol was in his hand and aimed. Jamethon fired, and a light blue streak leaped through the air, but Kensie had dropped again. Lying on his side on the grass, propped on one elbow, he pressed the firing button on his spring pistol twice.

Jamethon's sidearm sagged in his hand. He was backed up against the table now, and he put out his free hand to steady himself against the table top. He made another effort to lift his sidearm but he could not. It dropped from his hand. He bore more of his weight on the table, half-turning around, and his face came about to look in my direction. His face was as controlled as it had ever been, but there was something different about his eyes as he looked into mine and recognized me—something oddly like the look a man gives a competitor whom he had just beaten, and who was no real threat to begin with. A little smile touched the corners of his thin lips. Like a smile of inner triumph.

"Mr. Olyn . . ." he whispered. And then the life went out of his face and he fell beside the table.

Nearby explosions shook the ground under my feet. From the crest of the hill behind us the Force-Leader whom Kensie had left there was firing smoke bombs between us and the Friendly side of the meadow. A gray wall of smoke was rising between us and the far hillside, to screen us from the enemy. It towered up the blue sky like some impassable barrier, and under the looming height of it, only Kensie and I were standing.

On Jamethon's dead face there was a faint smile.

8

In a daze I watched the Friendly troops surrender that same day. It was the one situation in which their officers felt justified in doing so.

Not even their Elders expected subordinates to fight a situation set up by a dead Field Commander for tactical reasons unexplained to his officers. And the live troops remaining were worth more than the indemnity charges for them that the Exotics would make.

I did not wait for the settlements. I had nothing to wait for. One moment the situation on this battlefield had been poised like some great, irresistable wave above all our heads, cresting, curling over and about to break downward with an impact that would reverberate through all the worlds of Man. Now, suddenly, it was no longer above us. There was nothing but a far-flooding silence, already draining away into the records of the past.

There was nothing for me. Nothing.

If Jamethon had succeeded in killing Kensie—even if as a result he had won a practically bloodless surrender of the Exotic troops—I might have done something damaging with the incident of the truce table. But he had only tried; and died, failing. Who could work up emotion against the Friendlies for that?

I took ship back to Earth like a man walking in a dream, asking myself why.

Back on Earth, I told my editors I was not in good shape physically; and they took one look at me and believed me. I took an indefinite leave from my job and sat around the News Network Center Library, at the Hague, searching blindly through piles of writings and reference material on the Friendlies, the Dorsai and the Exotic worlds. For what? I did not know. I also watched the news dispatches from St. Marie concerning the settlement, and drank too much while I watched.

I had the numb feeling of a soldier sentenced to death for failure on duty. Then in the news dispatches came the information that

Jamethon's body would be returned to Harmony for burial; and I realized suddenly it was this I had been waiting for: the unnatural honoring by fanatics of the fanatic who with four henchmen had tried to assassinate the lone enemy commander under a truce flag. Things could still be written.

I shaved, showered, pulled myself together after a fashion and went to see my superiors about being sent to Harmony to cover the burial of Jamethon, as a wrap-up.

The congratulations of the Director of News Network, that had reached me on St. Marie earlier, stood me in good stead. It was still fresh in the minds of the men just over me. I was sent.

Five days later I was on Harmony, in a little town called Remembered-of-the-Lord. The buildings in the town were of concrete and bubble plastic, though evidently they had been up for many years. The thin, stony soil about the town had been tilled as the fields on St. Marie had been tilled when I got to that other world—for Harmony now was just entering the spring of its northern hemisphere. And it was raining as I drove from the spaceport of the town, as it had on St. Marie that first day. But the Friendly fields I saw did not show the rich darkness of the fields of St. Marie. Only a thin, hard blackness in the wet that was like the color of Friendly uniforms.

I got to the church just as people were beginning to arrive. Under the dark, draining skies, the interior of the church was almost too dim to let me see my way about—for the Friendlies permit themselves no windows and no artificial lighting in their houses of worship. Gray light, cold wind and rain entered the doorless portal at the back of the church. Through the single rectangular opening in the roof watery sunlight filtered over Jamethon's body, on a platform set up on trestles. A transparent cover had been set up to protect the body from the rain, which was channeled off the open space and ran down a drain in the back wall. But the elder conducting the Death Service and anyone coming up to view the body was expected to stand exposed to sky and weather.

I got in line with the people moving slowly down the central aisle and past the body. To right and left of me the barriers at which the congregation would stand during the service were lost in gloom. The rafters of the steeply pitched roof were hidden in darkness. There was no music, but the low sound of voices individually praying to either side of me in the ranks of barriers and in the line blended into a sort of rhythmic undertone of sadness. Like Jamethon, the people were all very dark here, being of North

African extraction. Dark into dark, they blended, and were lost about me in the gloom.

I came up and passed at last by Jamethon. He looked as I remembered him. Death had had no power to change him. He lay on his back, his hands at his sides, and his lips were as firm and straight as ever. Only his eyes were closed.

I was limping noticeably because of the dampness, and as I turned away from the body, I felt my elbow touched. I turned back sharply. I was not wearing my correspondent's uniform. I was in civilian clothes, so as to be inconspicuous.

I looked down into the face of the young girl in Jamethon's solidograph. In the gray rainy light her unlined face was like something from the stained glass window of an ancient cathedral back on Old Earth.

"You've been wounded," she said in a soft voice to me. "You must be one of the mercenaries who knew him on Newton, before he was ordered to Harmony. His parents, who are mine as well, would find solace in the Lord by meeting you."

The wind blew rain down through the overhead opening all about me, and its icy feel sent a chill suddenly shooting through me, freezing me to my very bones.

"No!" I said. "I'm not. I didn't know him." And I turned sharply away from her and pushed my way into the crowd, back up the aisle.

After about fifteen feet, I realized what I was doing and slowed down. The girl was already lost in the darkness of the bodies behind me. I made my way more slowly toward the back of the church, where there was a little place to stand before the first ranks of the barriers began. I stood watching the people come in. They came and came, walking in in their black clothing with their heads down and talking or praying in low voices.

I stood where I was, a little back from the entrance, half numbed and dull-minded with the chill about me and the exhaustion I had brought with me from Earth. The voices droned about me. I almost dozed, standing there. I could not remember why I had come.

Then a girl's voice emerged from the jumble, bringing me back to full consciousness again.

"—he did deny it, but I am sure he is one of those mercenaries who was with Jamethon on Newton. He limps and can only be a soldier who hath been wounded."

It was the voice of Jamethon's sister, speaking with more of the Friendly cant on her tongue than she had used speaking to me, a stranger. I woke fully and saw her standing by the entrance only a few feet from me, half-facing two elder people who I recognized as the older couple in Jamethon's solidograph. A bolt of pure, freezing horror shot through me.

"No!" I nearly shouted at them. "I don't know him. I never knew him—I don't understand what you're talking about!" And I turned and bolted out through the entrance of the church into the concealing rain.

I all but ran for about thirty or forty feet. Then I heard no footsteps behind me; I stopped.

I was alone in the open. The day was even darker now and the rain suddenly came down harder. It obscured everything around me with a drumming, shimmering curtain. I could not even see the groundcars in the parking lot toward which I was facing; and for sure they could not see me from the church. I lifted my face up to the downpour and let it beat upon my cheeks and my closed eyelids.

"So," said a voice from behind me. "You did not know him?"

The words seemed to cut me down the middle, and I felt as a cornered wolf must feel. Like a wolf I turned.

"Yes, I knew him!" I said.

Facing me was Padma, in a blue robe the rain did not seem to dampen. His empty hands that had never held a weapon in their life were clasped together before him. But the wolf part of me knew that as far as I was concerned, he was armed and a hunter.

"You?" I said. "What are you doing here?"

"It was calculated you would be here," said Padma, softly. "So I am here, too. But why *are* you here, Tam? Among those people in there, there's sure to be at least a few fanatics who've heard the camp rumors of your responsibility in the matter of Jamethon's death and the Friendlies' surrender."

"Rumors!" I said. "Who started them?"

"You did," Padma said. "By your actions on St. Marie." He gazed at me. "Didn't you know you were risking your life, coming here today?"

I opened my mouth to deny it. Then I realized I had known.

"What if someone should call out to them," said Padma, "that Tam Olyn, the St. Marie campaign Newsman, is here incognito?"

I looked at him with my wolf-feeling, grimly.

"Can you square it with your Exotic principles if you do?"

"We are misunderstood," answered Padma calmly. "We hire soldiers to fight for us not because of some moral commandment, but because our emotional perspective is lost if we become involved."

There was no fear left in me. Only a hard, empty feeling.

"Then call them," I said.

Padma's strange, hazel eyes watched me through the rain.

"If that was all that was needed," he said. "I could have sent word to them. I wouldn't have needed to come myself."

"Why did you come?" My voice tore at my throat. "What do you care about me, or the Exotics?"

"We care for every individual," said Padma. "But we care more for the race. And you remain dangerous to it. You're an idealist, Tam, warped to destructive purpose. There is a law of conservation of energy in the pattern of cause-and-effect as in other sciences. Your destructiveness was frustrated on St. Marie. Now it may turn inward to destroy you, or outward against the whole race of man."

I laughed, and heard the harshness of my laughter.

"What're you going to do about it?" I said.

"Show you how the knife you hold cuts the hand that holds it as well as what you turn it against. I have news for you, Tam. Kensie Graeme is dead."

'Dead?' The rain seemed to roar around me suddenly and the parking lot shifted unsubstantially under my feet.

"He was assassinated by three men of the Blue Front in Blauvain five days ago."

"Assassinated . . ." I whispered. "Why?"

"Because the war was over," said Padma. "Because Jamethon's death and the surrender of the Friendly troops without the preliminary of a war that would tear up the countryside left the civilian population favorably disposed toward our troops. Because the Blue Front found themselves farther from power than ever, as a result of this favorable feeling. They hoped by killing Graeme to provoke his troops into retaliation against the civilian population, so that the St. Marie government would have to order them home to our Exotics, and stand unprotected to face a Blue Front revolt."

I stared at him.

"All things are interrelated," said Padma. "Kensie was slated for a final promotion to a desk command back on Mara or Kultis. He and his brother Ian would have been out of the wars for the rest of their professional lives. Because of Jamethon's death, that allowed the surrender of his troops without fighting, a situation was set up which led the Blue Front to assassinate Kensie. If you and Jamethon had not come together on St. Marie, and Jamethon had won, Kensie would still be alive. So our calculations show."

"Jamethon and I?" The breath went dry in my throat without warning, and the rain came down harder.

"You were the factor," said Padma, "that helped Jamethon to his solution."

"I helped him!" I said. "*I* did?"

"He saw through you," said Padma. "He saw through the revenge-bitter, twisted surface you thought was yourself, to the idealistic core that was so deep in the bone of you that even your uncle hadn't been able to eradicate it."

The rain thundered between us. But Padma's every word came clearly through it to me.

"I don't believe you!" I shouted. "I don't believe he did anything like that!"

"I told you," said Padma, "you didn't fully appreciate the evolutionary advances of our Splinter Cultures. Jamethon's faith was not the kind that can be shaken by outer things. If you had been in fact like your uncle, he would not even have listened to you. He would have dismissed you as a soulless man. As it was, he thought of you instead as a man possessed. A man speaking with what he would have called Satan's voice."

"I don't believe it!" I yelled.

"You do believe it," said Padma. "You've got no choice except to believe it. Because only because of it could Jamethon find his solution."

"Solution!"

"He was a man ready to die for his faith. But as a commander he found it hard his men should go out to die for no other reasonable cause." Padma watched me, and the rain thinned for a moment. "But you offered him what he recognized as the devil's choice—his life in this world, if he would surrender his faith and his men, to avoid the conflict that would end in his death and theirs."

"What crazy thinking was that?" I said. Inside the church, the praying had stopped, and a single strong, deep voice was beginning the burial service.

"Not crazy," said Padma. "The moment he realized this, his answer became simple. All he had to do was begin by denying whatever the Satan offered. He must start with the absolute necessity of his own death."

"And that was a solution?" I tried to laugh but my throat hurt.

"It was the only solution," said Padma. "Once he decided that, he saw immediately that the one situation in which his men would permit themselves to surrender was if he was dead and they were in an untenable position for reasons only he had known."

I felt the words go through me with a soundless shock.

"But he didn't mean to die!" I said.

"He left it to his God," said Padma. "He arranged it so only a miracle could save him."

"What're you talking about?" I stared at him. "He set up a table with a flag of truce. He took four men—"

"There was no flag. The men were overage, martyrdom-seekers."

"He took four!" I shouted. "Four and one made five. The five of them against one man. I stood there by that table and saw. Five against—"

"Tam."

The single word stopped me. Suddenly I began to be afraid. I did not want to hear what he was about to say. I was afraid I knew what he was going to tell me. That I had known it for some time. And I did not want to hear it, I did not want to hear him say it. The rain grew even stronger, driving upon us both and mercilessly on the concrete, but I heard every word relentlessly through all its sound and noise.

Padma's voice began to roar in my ears like the rain, and a feeling came over me like the helpless floating sensation that comes in high fever. "Did you think that Jamethon for a minute fooled himself? He was a product of a Splinter Culture. He recognized another in Kensie. Did you think that for a minute he thought that barring a miracle he and four overage fanatics could kill an armed, alert and ready man of the Dorsai—*a man like Kensie Graeme?* Before they were gunned down and killed themselves?"

Themselves . . . themselves . . . themselves . . .

I rode off a long way on that word from the dark day and the rain. Like the rain and the wind behind the clouds it lifted me and carried me away at last to that high, hard and stony land I had glimpsed when I had asked Kensie Graeme that question about his ever allowing Friendly prisoners to be killed. It was this land I had always avoided, but to it I was come at last.

And I remembered . . .

From the beginning I had known inside myself that the fanatic who had killed Dave and the others was not the image of all Friendlies. Jamethon was no casual killer. I had tried to make him into one in order to hide my own shame, my own self-destruction. For three years I had lied to myself. It had not been with me as I claimed, at Dave's death.

I had sat there under that tree watching Dave and the others die, watching the black-clad Groupman killing them with his machine rifle. And, in that moment, the thought in my mind had not been the one with which I justified three years of hunting for an opportunity to ruin someone like Jamethon and destroy the Friendly peoples.

It had not been me, thinking, *what is he doing there, what is he doing
to those helpless, innocent men!* I had thought nothing so noble. Only
one thought had filled all my mind and body in that instant. It had
been simply—*after he's done, is he going to turn that gun on me?*

I came back to the day and to the rain. The rain was slackening
and Padma was holding me upright. As with Jamethon, I was
amazed at the strength of his hands.

"Let me go," I mumbled.

"Where would you go, Tam?" said Padma.

"Any place," I muttered. "I'll get out of it. I'll go hole up
somewhere and get out of it. I'll give up."

"An action," said Padma, letting me go, "goes on reverberating
for ever. Cause never ceases its effects. You can't let go now, Tam.
You can only change sides."

"Sides!" I said. The rain was dwindling fast. "What sides?" I
stared at him drunkenly.

"Your uncle's side which is one," said Padma. "And the opposing
side, which is yours—which is ours as well." The rain was falling
only lightly now, and the day was lightening. A little pale sunlight
worked through thin clouds and illuminated the space between us.
"In addition there are two strong influences besides we Exotics
concerned with the attempt of man to evolve. We can't calculate
or understand them yet, beyond the fact they act almost as
single powerful individual wills. One seems to try to aid, one
to frustrate, the evolutionary process; and their influences can be
traced back at least as far as man's first venture into space from
Earth."

I shook my head.

"I don't understand it," I muttered. "It's not my business."

"It is. It has been all your life." Padma eyes caught light for a
moment. "A force intruded on the pattern on St. Marie, in the shape
of a unit warped by personal loss and oriented toward violence. That
was you, Tam."

I tried to shake my head again, but I knew he was right.

"You are blocked in your effort," said Padma. "But the law of
conservation of energies could not be denied. When you were
frustrated by Jamethon, your force, transmuted, left the pattern in
the unit of another individual, warped by personal loss and oriented
toward violent effect on the fabric."

I stared at him and wet my lips. "What other individual?"

"Ian Graeme."

I stared at him.

"Ian found his brother's three assassins hiding in a hotel room in Blauvain. He killed them with his hands—and in doing that he calmed the mercenaries and frustrated the Blue Front. But then he resigned and went home to the Dorsai. He's charged now with the sense of loss and bitterness you were charged with when you came to St. Marie." Padma paused and added softly. "Now he has great causal potential for some purpose we can't yet calculate."

"But—" I looked at Padma. "You mean I'm free!"

Padma shook his head.

"You're only charged with a different force instead," he said. "You received the full impact and charge of Jamethon's self-sacrifice."

He looked at me almost with sympathy, and in spite of the sunlight I began to shiver.

It was so. I could not deny it. Jamethon, in giving his life up for a belief, when I had thrown away all belief before the face of death, had melted and changed me as lightning melts and changes the uplifted sword-blade that it strikes. I could not deny what had happened to me.

"No," I said, shivering, "I can't do anything about it."

"You can," said Padma, calmly. "You will."

He unclasped his hands that he had held together earlier.

"The purpose for which we calculated I should meet you here is accomplished now," he said. "The idealism which was basic in you remains. Even your uncle couldn't take it from you. He could only attack it so that the threat of death on New Earth could twist it for a while against itself. Now you've been hammered straight in the forge of events on St. Marie."

I laughed, and the laugh hurt my throat still.

"I don't feel straight," I said.

"Give yourself time," said Padma. "Healing takes time. New growth has to harden, like muscle, before it becomes useful. Now you understand much more about the faith of the Friendlies, the courage of the Dorsai—and something of the philosophical strength for man we work toward on the Exotics."

He stopped and smiled at me. Almost an impish smile.

"It should have been clear to you a long while ago, Tam," he said. "Your job's the job of translator—between the old and the new. Your work will prepare the minds of the people on all the worlds—full-spectrum and Splinter Culture alike—for the day when the talents of the race will combine into the new breed." The smile softened, his face saddened. "You'll live to see more of it than I. Good-by, Tam."

He turned. Through the still misty, but brightening air, I saw him walking alone toward the church, from which came the voice of the speaker within, now announcing the number of the final hymn.

Dazedly, I turned away myself, went to my car and got in. Now the rain was almost over and the sky was brightening fast. The faint moisture fell, it seemed, more kindly; and the air was fresh and new.

I put the car windows open as I pulled out of the lot onto the long road back to the spaceport. And through the open window beside me I heard them beginning to sing the final hymn inside the church.

It was the Battle Hymn of the Friendly Soldiers that they sang. As I drove away down the road the voices seemed to follow me strongly. Not sounding slowly and mournfully as if in sadness and farewell, but strongly and triumphantly, as in a marching song on the lips of those taking up a route at the beginning of a new day.

> Soldier, ask not—now or ever!—
> Where to war your banners go!

The singing followed me as I drove away. And as I got farther into the distance, the voices seemed to blend until they sounded like one voice alone, powerfully singing. Ahead, the clouds were breaking. With the sun shining through, the patches of blue sky were like bright flags waving—like the banners of an army, marching forever forward into lands unknown.

I watched them, as I drove forward toward where they blended into open sky; and for a long time I heard the singing behind me, as I drove to the spaceport and the ship for Earth that waited in the sunlight.

WEYR SEARCH

Anne McCaffrey

When is a legend legend? Why is a myth a myth? How old and disused must a fact be for it to be relegated to the category: Fairy tale? And why do certain facts remain incontrovertible, while others lose their validity to assume a shabby, unstable character?

Rukbat, in the Sagittarian sector, was a golden G-type star. It had five planets, plus one stray it had attracted and held in recent millennia. Its third planet was enveloped by air man could breathe, boasted water he could drink, and possessed a gravity which permitted man to walk confidently erect. Men discovered it, and promptly colonized it, as they did every habitable planet they came to and then—whether callously or through collapse of empire, the colonists never discovered, and eventually forgot to ask—left the colonies to fend for themselves.

When men first settled on Rukbat's third world, and named it Pern, they had taken little notice of the stranger-planet, swinging around its primary in a wildly erratic elliptical orbit. Within a few generations they had forgotten its existence. The desperate path the wanderer pursued brought it close to is stepsister every two hundred [Terran] years at perihelion.

When the aspects were harmonious and the conjunction with its sister-planet close enough, as it often was, the indigenous life of the wanderer sought to bridge the space gap to the more temperate and hospitable planet.

It was during the frantic struggle to combat this menace dropping through Pern's skies like silver threads, that Pern's contact with the mother-planet weakened and broke. Recollections of Earth receded further from Pernese history with each successive generation until memory of their origins degenerated past legend or myth, into oblivion.

To forestall the incursions of the dreaded Threads, the Pernese, with the ingenuity of their forgotten Yankee forebears and between first onslaught and return, developed a highly specialized variety of a life form indigenous to their adopted planet—the winged, tailed, and firebreathing dragons, named for the Earth legend they resembled. Such humans as had a high empathy rating and some innate telepathic ability were trained to make use of and preserve this unusual animal, whose ability to teleport was of immense value in the fierce struggle to keep Pern bare of Threads.

The dragons and their dragonmen, a breed apart, and the shortly renewed menace they battled, created a whole new group of legends and myths.

As the menace was conquered the populace in the Holds of Pern settled into a more comfortable way of life. Most of the dragon Weyrs eventually were abandoned, and the descendants of heroes fell into disfavor, as the legends fell into disrepute.

This, then, is a tale of legends disbelieved and their restoration. Yet—how goes a legend? When is myth?

> Drummer, beat, and piper, blow,
> Harper, strike, and soldier, go.
> Free the flame and sear the grasses
> Till the dawning Red Star passes.

Lessa woke, cold. Cold with more than the chill of the everlastingly clammy stone walls. Cold with the prescience of a danger greater than when, ten full Turns ago, she had run, whimpering, to hide in the watch-wher's odorous lair.

Rigid with concentration, Lessa lay in the straw of the redolent cheese room, sleeping quarters shared with the other kitchen drudges. There was an urgency in the ominous portent unlike any other forewarning. She touched the awareness of the watch-wher, slithering on its rounds in the courtyard. It circled at the choke-limit of its chain. It was restless, but oblivious to anything unusual in the pre-dawn darkness.

The danger was definitely not within the walls of Hold Ruath. Nor approaching the paved perimeter without the Hold where relentless grass had forced new growth through the ancient mortar, green witness to the deterioration of the once stone-clean Hold. The danger was not advancing up the now little-used causeway from the valley, nor lurking in the craftsmen's stony holdings at the foot of the Hold's cliff. It did not scent the wind that blew from Tillek's cold shores. But still it twanged sharply through her senses, vibrating every nerve in Lessa's slender frame. Fully roused, she sought to identify it before the prescient mood dissolved. She cast outward, toward the Pass, farther than she had ever pressed. Whatever threatened was not in Ruatha . . . yet. Nor did it have a familiar flavor. It was not, then, Fax.

Lessa had been cautiously pleased that Fax had not shown himself at Hold Ruath in three full Turns. The apathy of the craftsmen, the decaying farmholds, even the green-etched stones of the Hold infuriated Fax, self-styled Lord of the High Reaches, to the point where he preferred to forget the reason why he had subjugated the once proud and profitable Hold.

Lessa picked her way among the sleeping drudges, huddled together for warmth, and glided up the worn steps to the kitchen-proper. She slipped across the cavernous kitchen to the stable-yard door. The cobbles of the yard were icy through the thin soles of her sandals and she shivered as the pre-dawn air penetrated her patched garment.

The watch-wher slithered across the yard to greet her, pleading, as it always did, for release. Glancing fondly down at the awesome head, she promised it a good rub presently. It crouched, groaning, at the end of its chain as she continued to the grooved steps that led to the rampart over the Hold's massive gate. Atop the tower, Lessa stared towards the east where the stony breasts of the Pass rose in black relief against the gathering day.

Indecisively she swung to her left, for the sense of danger issued from that direction as well. She glanced upward, her eyes drawn to the red star which had recently begun to dominate the dawn sky. As she stared, the star radiated a final ruby pulsation before its magnificence was lost in the brightness of Pern's rising sun.

For the first time in many Turns, Lessa gave thought to matters beyond Pern, beyond her dedication to vengeance on the murderer Fax for the annihilation of her family. Let him but come within Ruath Hold now and he would never leave.

But the brilliant ruby sparkle of the Red Star recalled the Disaster Ballads—grim narratives of the heroism of the dragonriders as they braved the dangers of *between* to breathe fiery death on the silver Threads that dropped through Pern's skies. Not one Thread must fall to the rich soil, to burrow deep and multiply, leaching the earth of minerals and fertility. Straining her eyes as if vision would bridge the gap between peril and person, she stared intently eastward. The watch-wher's thin, whistled question reached her just as the prescience waned.

Dawnlight illumined the tumbled landscape, the unplowed fields in the valley below. Dawnlight fell on twisted orchards, where the

sparse herds of milchbeasts hunted stray blades of spring grass.
Grass in Ruatha grew where it should not, died where it should
flourish. An odd brooding smile curved Lessa's lips. Fax realized
no profit from his conquest of Ruatha . . . nor would he, while she,
Lessa, lived. And he had not the slightest suspicion of the source of
this undoing.

Or had he? Lessa wondered, her mind still reverberating from
the savage prescience of danger. East lay Fax's ancestral and only
legitimate Hold. Northeast lay little but bare and stony mountains
and Benden, the remaining Weyr, which protected Pern.

Lessa stretched, arching her back, inhaling the sweet, untainted
wind of morning.

A cock crowed in the stableyard. Lessa whirled, her face alert,
eyes darting around the outer Hold lest she be observed in such
an uncharacteristic pose. She unbound her hair, letting it fall about
her face concealingly. Her body drooped into the sloppy posture
she affected. Quickly she thudded down the the stairs, crossing to
the watch-wher. It lurred piteously, its great eyes blinking against
the growing daylight. Oblivious to the stench of its rank breath,
she hugged the scaly head to her, scratching its ears and eye
ridges. The watch-wher was ecstatic with pleasure, its long body
trembling, its clipped wings rustling. It alone knew who she was
or cared. And it was the only creature in all Pern she trusted since
the day she had blindly sought refuge in its dark stinking lair to
escape Fax's thirsty swords that had drunk so deeply of Ruathan
blood.

Slowly she rose, cautioning it to remember to be as vicious to her
as to all, should anyone be near. It promised to obey her, swaying
back and forth to emphasize its reluctance.

The first rays of the sun glanced over the Hold's outer wall.
Crying out, the watch-wher darted into its dark nest. Lessa crept
back to the kitchen and into the cheese room.

> From the Weyr and from the Bowl
> Bronze and brown and blue and green
> Rise the dragonmen of Pern,
> Aloft, on wing, seen, then unseen.

F'lar on bronze Mnementh's great neck appeared first in the skies
above the chief Hold of Fax, so-called Lord of the High Reaches.
Behind him, in proper wedge formation, the wingmen came into
sight. F'lar checked the formation automatically; as precise as at
the moment of entry to *between*.

As Mnementh curved in an arc that would bring them to the perimeter of the Hold, consonant with the friendly nature of this visitation. F'lar surveyed with mounting aversion the disrepair of the ridge defenses. The firestone pits were empty and the rock-cut gutters radiating from the pits were greentinged with a mossy growth.

Was there even one lord in Pern who maintained his Hold rocky in observance of the ancient Laws? F'lar's lips tightened to a thinner line. When this Search was over and the Impression made, there would have to be a solemn, punitive Council held at the Weyr. And by the golden shell of the queen, he, F'lar, meant to be its moderator. He would replace lethargy with industry. He would scour the green and dangerous scum from the heights of Pern, the grass blades from its stoneworks. No verdant skirt would be condoned in any farmhold. And the tithings which had been so miserly, so grudgingly presented would, under pain of firestoning, flow with decent generosity into the Dragonweyr.

Mnementh rumbled approvingly as he vaned his pinions to land lightly on the grass-etched flagstones of Fax's Hold. The bronze dragon furled his great wings, and F'lar heard the warning klaxon in the Hold's Great Tower. Mnementh dropped to his knees as F'lar indicated he wished to dismount. The bronze rider stood by Mnementh's huge wedge-shaped head, politely awaiting the arrival of the Hold lord. F'lar idly gazed down the valley, hazy with warm spring sunlight. He ignored the furtive heads that peered at the dragonman from the parapet slits and the cliff windows.

F'lar did not turn as a rush of air announced the arrival of the rest of the wing. He knew, however, when F'nor, the brown rider, his halfbrother, took the customary position on his left, a dragon-length to the rear. F'lar caught a glimpse of F'nor's boot-heel twisting to death the grass crowding up between the stones.

An order, muffled to an intense whisper, issued from within the great court, beyond the open gates. Almost immediately a group of men marched into sight, led by a heavyset man of medium height.

Mnementh arched his neck, angling his head so that his chin rested on the ground. Mnementh's many-faceted eyes, on a level with F'lar's head, fastened with disconcerting interest on the approaching party. The dragons could never understand why they generated such abject fear in common folk. At only one point in his lifespan would a dragon attack a human and that could be excused on the grounds of simple ignorance. F'lar could not explain to the dragon the politics behind the necessity of inspiring awe in the holders, lord and craftsman alike. He could only observe that the fear and apprehension showing in the faces of the advancing squad which troubled Mnementh was oddly pleasing to him, F'lar.

"Welcome, Bronze Rider, to the Hold of Fax, Lord of the High Reaches. He is at your service," and the man made an adequately respectful salute.

The use of the third person pronoun could be construed, by the meticulous, to be a veiled insult. This fit in with the information F'lar had on Fax, so he ignored it. His information was also correct in describing Fax as a greedy man. It showed in the restless eyes which flicked at every detail of F'lar's clothing, at the slight frown when the intricately etched swordhilt was noticed.

F'lar noticed, in his own turn, the several rich rings which flashed on Fax's left hand. The overlord's right hand remained slightly cocked after the habit of the professional swordsman. His tunic, of rich fabric, was stained and none too fresh. The man's feet, in heavy wher-hide boots, were solidly planted, weight balanced forward on his toes. A man to be treated cautiously, F'lar decided, as one should the conqueror of five neighboring Holds. Such greedy audacity was in itself a revelation. Fax had married into a sixth . . . and had legally inherited, however unusual the circumstances, the seventh. He was a lecherous man by reputation.

Within these seven Holds, F'lar anticipated a profitable Search. Let R'gul go southerly to pursue Search among the indolent, if lovely, women there. The Weyr needed a strong woman this time; Jora had been worse than useless with Nemorth. Adversity, uncertainty: those were the conditions that bred the qualities F'lar wanted in a weyrwoman.

"We ride in Search," F'lar drawled softly, "and request the hospitality of your Hold, Lord Fax."

Fax's eyes widened imperceptibly at mention of Search.

"I had heard Jora was dead," Fax replied, dropping the third person abruptly as if F'lar had passed some sort of test by ignoring it. "So Nemorth has a new queen, hm-m-m?" he continued, his eyes darting across the rank of the ring, noting the disciplined stance of the riders, the healthy color of the dragons.

F'lar did not dignify the obvious with an answer.

"And, my Lord—?" Fax hesitated, expectantly inclining his head slightly toward the dragonman.

For a pulse beat, F'lar wondered if the man were deliberately provoking him with such subtle insults. The name of bronze riders should be as well known throughout Pern as the name of the

Dragonqueen and her Weyrwoman. F'lar kept his face composed, his eyes on Fax's.

Leisurely, with the proper touch of arrogance, F'nor stepped forward, stopping slightly behind Mnementh's head, one hand negligently touching the jaw hinge of the huge beast.

"The Bronze Rider of Mnementh, Lord F'lar, will require quarters for himself. I, F'nor, brown rider, prefer to be lodged with the wingmen. We are, in number, twelve."

F'lar liked that touch of F'nor's, totting up the wing strength, as if Fax were incapable of counting. F'nor had phrased it so adroitly as to make it impossible for Fax to protest the insult.

"Lord F'lar," Fax said through teeth fixed in a smile, "the High Reaches are honored with your Search."

"It will be to the credit of the High Reaches," F'lar replied smoothly, "if one of its own supplies the Weyr."

"To our everlasting credit," Fax replied as suavely. "In the old days, many notable weyrwomen came from my Holds."

"Your Holds?" asked F'lar, politely smiling as he emphasized the plural. "Ah, yes, you are now overlord of Ruatha, are you not? There have been many from that Hold."

A strange tense look crossed Fax's face. "Nothing good comes from Ruath Hold." Then he stepped aside, gesturing F'lar to enter the Hold.

Fax's troop leader barked a hasty order and the men formed two lines, their metal-edged boots flicking sparks from the stones.

At unspoken orders, all the dragons rose with a great churning of air and dust. F'lar strode nonchalantly past the welcoming files. The men were rolling their eyes in alarm as the beasts glided above to the inner courts. Someone on the high tower uttered a frightened yelp as Mnementh took his position on that vantage point. His great wings drove phosphoric-scented air across the inner court as he maneuvered his great frame onto the inadequate landing space.

Outwardly oblivious to the consternation, fear, and awe the dragons inspired, F'lar was secretly amused and rather pleased by the effect. Lords of the Holds needed this reminder that they must deal with dragons, not just with riders, who were men, mortal and murderable. The ancient respect for dragonmen as well as dragonkind must be reinstilled in modern breasts.

"The Hold has just risen from table, F'lar, if . . ." Fax suggested. His voice trailed off at F'lar's smiling refusal.

"Convey my duty to your lady, Lord Fax," F'lar rejoined, noticing with inward satisfaction the tightening of Fax's jaw muscles at the ceremonial request.

"You would prefer to see your quarters first?" Fax countered.

F'lar flicked an imaginary speck from his soft wher-hide sleeve and shook his head. Was the man buying time to sequester his ladies as the old-time lords had?

"Duty first," he said with a rueful shrug.

"Of course," Fax all but snapped and strode smartly ahead, his heels pounding out the anger he could not express otherwise. F'lar decided he had guessed correctly.

'F'lar and F'nor followed at a slower pace through the double-doored entry with its massive metal panels, into the great hall, carved into the cliffside.

"They eat not badly," F'nor remarked casually to F'lar, appraising the remnants still on the table.

"Better than the Weyr, it would seem," F'lar replied dryly.

"Young roasts and tender," F'nor said in a bitter undertone, "While the stringy, barren beasts are delivered up to us."

"The change is overdue," F'lar murmured, then raised his voice to conversational level. "A well-favored hall," he was saying amiably as they reached Fax. Their reluctant host stood in the portal to the inner Hold, which, like all such Holds, burrowed deep into stone, traditional refuge of all in time of peril.

Deliberately, F'lar turned back to the banner-hung Hall. "Tell me, Lord Fax, do you adhere to the old practices and mount a dawn guard?"

Fax frowned, trying to grasp F'lar's meaning.

"There is always a guard at the Tower."

"An easterly guard?"

Fax's eyes jerked towards F'lar, then to F'nor.

"There are always guards," he answered sharply, "on all the approaches."

"Oh, just the approaches," and F'lar nodded wisely to F'nor.

"Where else?' demanded Fax, concerned, glancing from one dragonman to the other.

"I must ask that of your harper. You do keep a trained harper in your Hold?"

"Of course. I have several trained harpers," and Fax jerked his shoulders straighter.

F'lar affected not to understand.

"Lord Fax is the overlord of six other Holds," F'nor reminded his wingleader.

"Of course," F'lar assented, with exactly the same inflection Fax had used a moment before.

The mimicry did not go unnoticed by Fax, but as he was unable to construe deliberate insult out of an innocent affirmative, he stalked into the glow-lit corridors. The dragonmen followed.

The women's quarters in Fax's Hold had been moved from the traditional innermost corridors to those at cliff-face. Sunlight poured down from three double-shuttered, deep-casement windows in the outside wall. F'lar noted that the bronze hinges were well oiled, and the sills regulation spear-length. Fax had not, at least, diminished the protective wall.

The chamber was richly hung with appropriately gentle scenes of women occupied in all manner of feminine tasks. Doors gave off the main chamber on both sides into smaller sleeping alcoves and from these, at Fax's bidding, his women hesitantly emerged. Fax sternly gestured to a blue-gowned woman, her hair white-streaked, her face lined with disappointments and bitterness, her body swollen with pregnancy. She advanced awkwardly, stopping several feet from her lord. From her attitude, F'lar deduced that she came no closer to Fax than was absolutely necessary.

"The Lady of Crom, mother of my heirs," Fax said without pride or cordiality.

"My Lady—" F'lar hesitated, waiting for her name to be supplied.

She glanced warily at her lord. "Gemma," Fax snapped curtly.

F'lar bowed deeply. "My Lady Gemma, the Weyr is on Search and requests the Hold's hospitality."

"My Lord F'lar," the Lady Gemma replied in a low voice, "you are most welcome."

F'lar did not miss the slight slur on the adverb nor the fact that Gemma had no trouble naming him. His smile was warmer than courtesy demanded, warm with gratitude and sympathy. Looking at the number of women in these quarters, F'lar thought there might be one or two Lady Gemma could bid farewell without regret.

Fax preferred his women plump and small. There wasn't a saucy one in the lot. If there once had been, the spirit had been beaten out of her. Fax, no doubt, was stud, not lover. Some of the covey had not all winter long made much use of water, judging by the amount of sweet oil gone rancid in their hair. Of them all, if these were all, the Lady Gemma was the only willful one; and she, too old.

The amenities over, Fax ushered his unwelcome guests outside, and led the way to the quarters he had assigned the bronze rider.

"A pleasant room," F'lar acknowledged, stripping off gloves and wher-hide tunic, throwing them carelessly to the table. "I shall see to my men and the beasts. They have been fed recently," he commented, pointing up Fax's omission in inquiring. "I request liberty to wander through the crafthold."

Fax sourly granted what was a dragonman's traditional privilege.

"I shall not further disrupt your routine, Lord Fax, for you must have many demands on you, with seven Holds to supervise." F'lar inclined his body slightly to the overlord, turning away as a gesture of dismissal. He could imagine the infuriated expression on Fax's face from the stamping retreat.

F'nor and the men had settled themselves in a hastily vacated barrackroom. The dragons were perched comfortably on the rocky ridges above the Hold. Each rider kept his dragon in light, but alert, charge. There were to be no incidents on a Search.

As a group, the dragonmen rose at F'lar's entrance.

"No tricks, no troubles, but look around closely," he said laconically. "Return by sundown with the names of any likely prospects." He caught F'nor's grin, remembering how Fax had slurred over some names. "Descriptions are in order and craft affiliation."

The men nodded, their eyes glinting with understanding. They were flatteringly confident of a successful Search even as F'lar's doubts grew now that he had seen Fax's women. By all logic, the pick of the High Reaches should be in Fax's chief Hold—but they were not. Still, there were many large craftholds, not to mention the six other High Holds to visit. All the same . . .

In unspoken accord F'lar and F'nor left the barracks. The men would follow, unobtrusively, in pairs or singly, to reconnoiter the crafthold and the nearer farmholds. The men were as overtly eager to be abroad as F'lar was privately. There had been a time when dragonmen were frequent and favored guests in all the great Holds throughout Pern, from southern Fort to high north Igen. This pleasant custom, too, had died along with other observances, evidence of the low regard in which the Weyr was presently held. F'lar vowed to correct this.

He forced himself to trace in memory the insidious changes. The Records, which each Weyrwoman kept, were proof of the gradual, but perceptible, decline, traceable through the past two hundred full Turns. Knowing the facts did not alleviate the condition. And F'lar was of that scant handful in the Weyr itself who did credit Records and Ballad alike. The situation might shortly reverse itself radically if the old tales were to be believed.

There was a reason, an explanation, a purpose, F'lar felt, for every one of the Weyr laws from First Impression to the Firestones: from the grass-free heights to ridge-running gutters. For elements as minor as controlling the appetite of a dragon to limiting the inhabitants of the Weyr. Although why the other five Weyrs had been abandoned, F'lar did not know. Idly he wondered if there were records, dusty and crumbling, lodged in the disused Weyrs. He must contrive to check when next his wings flew patrol. Certainly there was no explanation in Benden Weyr.

"There is industry but no enthusiasm," F'nor was saying, drawing F'lar's attention back to their tour of the crafthold.

They had descended the guttered ramp from the Hold into the crafthold proper, the broad roadway lined with cottages up to the imposing stone crafthalls. Silently F'lar noted moss-clogged gutters on the roofs, the vines clasping the walls. It was painful for one of his calling to witness the flagrant disregard of simple safety precautions. Growing things were forbidden near the habitations of mankind.

"News travels fast," F'nor chuckled, nodding at a hurrying craftsman, in the smock of a baker, who gave them a mumbled good day. "Not a female in sight."

His observation was accurate. Women should be abroad at this hour, bringing in supplies from the storehouses, washing in the river on such a bright warm day, or going out to the farmholds to help with planting. Not a gowned figure in sight.

"We used to be preferred mates," F'nor remarked caustically.

"We'll visit the Clothmen's Hall first. If my memory serves me right . . ."

"As it always does . . ." F'nor interjected wryly. He took no advantage of their blood relationship but he was more at ease with the bronze rider than most of the dragonmen, the other bronze riders included. F'lar was reserved in a closeknit society of easy equality. He flew a tightly disciplined wing but men maneuvered to serve under him. His wing always excelled in the Games. None ever floundered in *between* to disappear forever and no beast in his wing sickened, leaving a man in dragonless exile from the Weyr, a part of him numb forever.

"L'tol came this way and settled in one of the High Reaches," F'lar continued.

"L'tol?"

"Yes, a green rider from S'lel's wing. You remember."

An ill-timed swerve during the Spring Games had brought L'tol and his beast into the full blast of a phosphene emission from S'lel's bronze Tuenth. L'tol had been thrown from his beast's neck as the dragon tried to evade the blast. Another wingmate had swooped to catch the rider but the green dragon, his left wing crisped, his body scorched, had died of shock and phosphene poisoning.

"L'tol would aid our Search," F'nor agreed as the two dragonmen walked up to the bronze doors of the Clothmen's Hall. They paused on the threshold, adjusting their eyes to the dimmer light within. Glows punctuated the wall recesses and hung in clusters above the larger looms where the finer tapestries and fabrics were woven by master craftsmen. The pervading mood was one of quiet, purposeful industry.

Before their eyes had adapted, however, a figure glided to them, with a polite, if curt, request for them to follow him.

They were led to the right of the entrance, to a small office, curtained from the main hall. Their guide turned to them, his face visible in the wallglows. There was that air about him that marked him indefinably as a dragonman. But his face was lined deeply, one side seamed with old burnmarks. His eyes, sick with a hungry yearning, dominated his face. He blinked constantly.

"I am now Lytol," he said in a harsh voice.

F'lar nodded acknowledgement.

"You would be F'lar," Lytol said, "and you, F'nor. You've both the look of your sire."

F'lar nodded again.

Lytol swallowed convulsively, the muscles in his face twitching as the presence of dragonmen revived his awareness of exile. He essayed a smile.

"Dragons in the sky! The news spread faster than Threads."

"Nemorth has a new queen."

"Jora dead?' Lytol asked concernedly, his face cleared of its nervous movement for a second.

F'lar nodded.

Lytol grimaced bitterly. "R'gul again, huh." He stared off in the middle distance, his eyelids quiet but the muscles along his jaw took up the constant movement.

"You've the High Reaches? All of them?" Lytol asked, turning back to the dragonman, a slight emphasis on "all."

F'lar gave an affirmative nod again.

"You've seen the women." Lytol's disgust showed through the words. It was a statement, not a question, for he hurried on. "Well, there are no better in all the High Reaches," and his tone expressed utmost disdain.

"Fax likes his women comfortably fleshed and docile," Lytol rattled on. "Even the Lady Gemma has learned. It'd be different if he didn't need her family's support. Oh, it would be different indeed. So he keeps her pregnant, hoping to kill her in childbed one day. And he will. He will."

Lytol drew himself up, squaring his shoulders, turning full to the two dragonmen. His expression was vindictive, his voice low and tense.

"Kill that tyrant, for the sake and safety of Pern. Of the Weyr. Of the queen. He only bides his time. He spreads discontent among the other lords. He"—Lytol's laughter had an hysterical edge to it now—"he fancies himself as good as dragonmen."

"There are no candidates then in this Hold?" F'lar said, his voice sharp enough to cut through the man's preoccupation with his curious theory.

Lytol stared at the bronze rider. "Did I not say it?"

"What of Ruath Hold?"

Lytol stopped shaking his head and looked sharply at F'lar, his lips curling in a cunning smile. He laughed mirthlessly.

"You think to find a Torene, or a Moreta, hidden at Ruath Hold in these times? Well, all of that Blood are dead. Fax's blade was thirsty that day. He knew the truth of those harpers' tales, that Ruathan lords gave full measure of hospitality to dragonmen and the Ruathan were a breed apart. There were, you know," Lytol's voice dropped to a confiding whisper, "exiled Weyrmen like myself in that Line."

F'lar nodded gravely, unable to contradict the man's pitiful attempt at self-esteem.

"No," and Lytol chuckled softly. "Fax gets nothing from that Hold but trouble. And the women Fax used to take . . ." his laugh turned nasty in tone. "It is rumored he was impotent for months afterwards.'

"Any families in the holdings with Weyr blood?"

Lytol frowned, glanced surprised at F'lar. He rubbed the scarred side of his face thoughtfully.

"There were," he admitted slowly. "There were. But I doubt if any live on." He thought a moment longer, then shook his head emphatically.

F'lar shrugged.

"I wish I had better news for you," Lytol murmured.

"No matter," F'lar reassured him, one hand poised to part the hanging in the doorway.

Lytol came up to him swiftly, his voice urgent.

"Heed what I say, Fax is ambitious. Force R'gul, or whoever is Weyrleader next, to keep watch on the High Reaches."

Lytol jabbed a finger in the direction of the Hold. "He scoffs openly at tales of the Threads. He taunts the harpers for the stupid nonsense of the old ballads and has banned from their repertoire all dragonlore. The new generation will grow up totally ignorant of duty, tradition, and precaution."

F'lar was not surprised to hear that on top of Lytol's other disclosures. Yet the Red Star pulsed in the sky and the time was drawing near when they would hysterically reavow the old allegiances in fear for their very lives.

"Have you been abroad in the early morning of late?" asked F'nor, grinning maliciously.

"I have," Lytol breathed out in a hushed, choked whisper. "I have . . ." A groan was wrenched from his guts and he whirled away from the dragonmen, his head bowed between hunched shoulders. "Go," he said, gritting his teeth. And, as they hesitated, he pleaded, "*Go!*"

F'lar walked quickly from the room, followed by F'nor. The bronze rider crossed the quiet dim Hall with long strides and exploded into the startling sunlight. His momentum took him into the center of the square. There he stopped so abruptly that F'nor, hard on his heels, nearly collided with him.

"We will spend exactly the same time within the other Halls," he announced in a tight voice, his face averted from F'nor's eyes. F'lar's throat was constricted. It was difficult, suddenly, for him to speak. He swallowed hard, several times.

"To be dragonless . . ." murmured F'nor, pityingly. The encounter with Lytol had roiled his depths in a mournful way to which he was unaccustomed. That F'lar appeared equally shaken went far to dispel F'nor's private opinion that his half-brother was incapable of emotion.

"There is no other way once First Impression has been made. You know that," F'lar roused himself to say curtly. He strode off to the Hall bearing the Leathermen's device.

> The Hold is barred
> The Hall is bare.
>> And men vanish.
> The soil is barren,
> The rock is bald.
>> All hope banish.

Lessa was shoveling ashes from the hearth when the agitated messenger staggered into the Great Hall. She made herself as inconspicuous as possible so the Warder would not dismiss her. She had contrived to be sent to the Great Hall that morning, knowing that the Warder intended to brutalize the Head Clothman for the shoddy quality of the goods readied for shipment to Fax.

"Fax is coming! With dragonmen!" the man gasped out as he plunged into the dim Great Hall.

The Warder, who had been about to lash the Head Clothman, turned, stunned, from his victim. The courier, a farmholder from the edge of Ruatha, stumbled up to the Warder, so excited with his message that he grabbed the Warder's arm.

"How dare you leave your Hold?" and the Warder aimed his lash at the astonished holder. The force of the first blow knocked the man from his feet. Yelping, he scrambled out of reach of a second lashing. "Dragonmen indeed! Fax? Ha! He shuns Ruatha. There!" The Warder punctuated each denial with another blow, kicking the helpless wretch for good measure, before he turned breathless to glare at the clothman and the two underwarders. "How did he get in here with such a threadbare lie?" The Warder stalked to the great door. It was flung open just as he reached out for the iron handle. The ashen-faced guard officer rushed in, nearly toppling the Warder.

"Dragonmen! Dragons! All over Ruatha!" the man gibbered, arms flailing wildly. He, too, pulled at the Warder's arm, dragging the stupefied official toward the outer courtyard, to bear out the truth of his statement.

Lessa scooped up the last pile of ashes. Picking up her equipment, she slipped out of the Great Hall. There was a very pleased smile on her face under the screen of matted hair.

A dragonman at Ruatha! She must somehow contrive to get Fax so humiliated, or so infuriated, that he would renounce his claim to the Hold, in the presence of a dragonman. Then she could claim her birthright.

But she would have to be extraordinarily wary. Dragonriders were men apart. Anger did not cloud their intelligence. Greed did not sully their judgment. Fear did not dull their reactions. Let the dense-witted believe human sacrifice, unnatural lusts, insane revel. She was not so gullible. And those stories went against her grain. Dragonmen were still human and there was Weyr blood in *her* veins. It was the same color as that of anyone else; enough of hers had been spilled to prove that.

She halted for a moment, catching a sudden shallow breath. Was this the danger she had sensed four days ago at dawn? The final encounter in her struggle to regain the Hold? No—there had been more to that portent than revenge.

The ash bucket banged against her shins as she shuffled down the low-ceilinged corridor to the stable door. Fax would find a cold welcome. She had laid no new fire on the hearth. Her laugh echoed back unpleasantly from the damp walls. She rested her bucket and propped her broom and shovel as she wrestled with the heavy bronze door that gave into the new stables.

They had been built outside the cliff of Ruatha by Fax's first Warder, a subtler man than all eight of his successors. He had achieved more than all the others and Lessa had honestly regretted the necessity of his death. But he would have made her revenge impossible. He would have caught her out before she had learned how to camouflage herself and her little interferences. What had his name been? She could not recall. Well, she regretted his death.

The second man had been properly greedy, and it had been easy to set up a pattern of misunderstanding between Warder and craftsmen. That one had been determined to squeeze all profit from Ruathan goods so that some of it would drop into his pocket before Fax suspected a shortage. The craftsmen who had begun to accept the skillful diplomacy of the first Warder bitterly resented the second's grasping, high-handed ways. They resented the passing of the Old Line and, even more so, the way of its passing. They were unforgiving of the insult to Ruatha, its now secondary position in the High Reaches; and they resented the individual indignities that holders, craftsmen and farmers alike, suffered under the second Warder. It took little manipulation to arrange for matters at Ruatha to go from bad to worse.

The second was replaced and his successor fared no better. He was caught diverting goods, the best of the goods at that. Fax had had him executed. His bony head still hung in the main firepit above the great Tower.

The present incumbent had not been able to maintain the Hold in even the sorry condition in which he had assumed its management. Seemingly simple matters developed rapidly into disasters. Like the production of cloth . . . Contrary to his boasts to Fax, the quality had not improved, and the quantity had fallen off.

Now Fax was here. And with dragonmen! Why dragonmen? The import of the question froze Lessa, and the heavy door closing behind her barked her heels painfully. Dragonmen used to be

frequent visitors at Ruatha, that she knew, and even vaguely
remembered. Those memories were like a harper's tale, told of
someone else, not something within her own experience. She had
limited her fierce attention to Ruatha only. She could not even
recall the name of Queen or Weyrwoman from the instructions of
her childhood, nor could she recall hearing mention of any queen
or weyrwoman by anyone in the Hold these past ten Turns.

Perhaps the dragonmen were finally going to call the lords of the
Holds to task for the disgraceful show of greenery about the Holds.
Well, Lessa was to blame for much of that in Ruatha, but she defied
even a dragonman to confront her with her guilt. Did all Ruatha fall
to the Threads it would be better than remaining dependent to Fax!
The heresy shocked Lessa even as she thought it.

Wishing she could as easily unburden her conscience of such
blasphemy, she ditched the ashes on the stable midden. There was
a sudden change in air pressure around her. Then a fleeting shadow
caused her to glance up.

From behind the cliff above glided a dragon, its enormous wings
spread to their fullest as he caught the morning updraft. Turning
effortlessly, he descended. A second, a third, a full wing of dragons
followed in soundless flight and patterned descent, graceful and
awesome. The klaxon rang belatedly from the Tower and from
within the kitchen there issued the screams and shrieks of the
terrified drudges.

Lessa took cover. She ducked into the kitchen, where she was
instantly seized by the assistant cook and thrust with a buffet and
a kick toward the sinks. There she was put to scrubbing grease-
encrusted serving bowls with cleansing sand.

The yelping canines were already lashed to the spitrun, turning a
scrawny herdbeast that had been set to roast. The cook was ladling
seasonings on the carcass, swearing at having to offer so poor a meal
to so many guests, and some of them high-rank. Winter-dried fruits
from the last scanty harvest had been set to soak and two of the oldest
drudges were scraping roots.

An apprentice cook was kneading bread; another, carefully
spicing a sauce. Looking fixedly at him, she diverted his hand
from one spice box to a less appropriate one as he gave a final
shake to the concoction. She added too much wood to the wall
oven, insuring ruin for the breads. She controlled the canines
deftly, slowing one and speeding the other so that the meat would
be underdone on one side, burned on the other. That the feast
should be a fast, the food presented found inedible, was her whole
intention.

Above in the Hold, she had no doubt that certain other measures, undertaken at different times for this exact contingency, were being discovered.

Her fingers bloodied from a beating, one of the Warder's women came shrieking into the kitchen, hopeful of refuge there.

"Insects have eaten the best blankets to shreds! And a canine who had littered on the best linens snarled at me as she gave suck! And the rushes are noxious, the best chambers full of debris driven in by the winter wind. Somebody left the shutters ajar. Just a tiny bit, but it was enough . . ." the woman wailed, clutching her hand to her breast and rocking back and forth.

Lessa bent with great industry to shine the plates.

> Watch-wher, watch-wher,
> In your lair,
> Watch well, watch-wher!
> Who goes there?

"The watch-wher is hiding something," F'lar told F'nor as they consulted in the hastily cleaned Great Hall. The room delighted to hold the wintry chill although a generous fire now burned on the hearth.

"It was but gibbering when Canth spoke to it," F'nor remarked. He was leaning against the mantel, turning slightly from side to side to gather some warmth. He watched his wingleader's impatient pacing.

"Mnementh is calming it down," F'lar replied. "He may be able to sort out the nightmare. The creature may be more senile than aware, but . . ."

"I doubt it," F'nor concurred helpfully. He glanced with apprehension up at the webhung ceiling. He was certain he'd found most of the crawlers, but he didn't fancy their sting. Not on top of the discomforts already experienced in this forsaken Hold. If the night stayed mild, he intended curling up with Canth on the heights. "That would be more reasonable than anything Fax or his Warder have suggested."

"Hm-m-m," F'lar muttered, frowning at the brown rider.

"Well, it's unbelievable that Ruatha could have fallen to such disrepair in ten short Turns. Every dragon caught the feeling of power and it's obvious the watch-wher has been tampered with. That takes a good deal of control."

"From someone of the Blood," F'lar reminded him.

F'nor shot his wingleader a quick look, wondering if he could possibly be serious in the light of all information to the contrary.

"I grant you there is power here, F'lar," F'nor conceded. "It could easily be a hidden male of the old Blood. But we need a female. And Fax made it plain, in his inimitable fashion, that he left none of the old Blood alive in the Hold the day he took it. No, no." The brown rider shook his head, as if he could dispel the lack of faith in his wingleader's curious insistence that the Search would end in Ruath with Ruathan blood.

"That watch-wher is hiding something and only someone of the Blood of its Hold can arrange that," F'lar said emphatically. He gestured around the Hall and toward the walls, bare of hangings. "Ruatha has been overcome. But she resists . . . subtly. I say it points to the old Blood, *and* power. Not power alone."

The obstinate expression in F'lar's eyes, the set of his jaw, suggested that F'nor seek another topic.

"The pattern was well-flown today," F'nor suggested tentatively. "Does a dragonman good to ride a flaming beast. Does the beast good, too. Keeps the digestive process in order."

F'lar nodded sober agreement. "Let R'gul temporize as he chooses. It is fitting and proper to ride a firespouting beast and these holders need to be reminded of Weyr power."

"Right now, anything would help our prestige," F'nor commented sourly. "What had Fax to say when he hailed you in the Pass?" F'nor knew his question was almost impertinent but if it were, F'lar would ignore it.

F'lar's slight smile was unpleasant and there was an ominous glint in his amber eyes.

"We talked of rule and resistance."

"Did he not also draw on you?" F'nor asked.

F'lar's smile deepened. "Until he remembered I was dragon-mounted."

"He's considered a vicious fighter," F'nor said.

"I am at some disadvantage?" F'lar asked, turning sharply on his brown rider, his face too controlled.

"To my knowledge, no," F'nor reassured his leader quickly. F'lar had tumbled every man in the Weyr, efficiently and easily. "But Fax kills often and without cause."

"And because we dragonmen do not seek blood, we are not to be feared as fighters?" snapped F'lar. "Are you ashamed of your heritage?"

"I? No!" F'nor sucked in his breath. "Nor any of our wing!" he added proudly. "But there is that in the attitude of the men in this progression of Fax's that . . . that makes me wish some excuse to fight."

"As you observed today, Fax seeks some excuse. And," F'lar added thoughtfully, "there is something here in Ruatha that unnerves our noble overlord."

He caught sight of Lady Tela, whom Fax had so courteously assigned him for comfort during the progression, waving to him from the inner Hold portal.

"A case in point. Fax's Lady Tela is some three months gone."

F'nor frowned at that insult to his leader.

"She giggles incessantly and appears so addlepated that one cannot decide whether she babbles out of ignorance or at Fax's suggestion. As she has apparently not bathed all winter, and is not, in any case, my ideal, I have"—F'lar grinned maliciously— "deprived myself of her kind offices."

F'nor hastily cleared his throat and his expression as Lady Tela approached them. He caught the unappealing odor from the scarf or handkerchief she waved constantly. Dragonmen endured a great deal for the Weyr. He moved away, with apparent courtesy, to join the rest of the dragonmen entering the Hall.

F'lar turned with equal courtesy to Lady Tela as she jabbered away about the terrible condition of the rooms which Lady Gemma and the other ladies had been assigned.

"The shutters, both sets, were ajar all winter long and you should have seen the trash on the floors. We finally got two of the drudges to sweep it all into the fireplace. And then that smoked something fearful 'til a man was sent up." Lady Tela giggled. "He found the access blocked by a chimney stone fallen aslant. The rest of the chimney, for a wonder, was in good repair."

She waved her handkerchief. F'lar held his breath as the gesture wafted an unappealing odor in his direction.

He glanced up the Hall toward the inner Hold door and saw Lady Gemma descending, her steps slow and awkward. Some subtle difference about her gait attracted him and he stared at her, trying to identify it.

"Oh, yes, poor Lady Gemma," Lady Tela babbled, sighing deeply. "We are so concerned. Why Lord Fax insisted on her coming, I do not know. She is not near her time and yet . . ." The lighthead's concern sounded sincere.

F'lar's incipient hatred for Fax and his brutality matured abruptly. He left his partner chattering to thin air and courteously extended his arm to Lady Gemma to support her down the steps and to the table. Only the brief tightening of her fingers on his forearm betrayed her gratitude. Her face was very white and drawn, the lines deeply etched around mouth and eyes, showing the effort she was expending.

"Some attempt has been made, I see, to restore order to the Hall," she remarked in a conversational tone.

"Some," F'lar admitted dryly, glancing around the grandly proportioned Hall, its rafter festooned with the webs of many Turns. The inhabitants of those gossamer nests dropped from time to time, with ripe splats, to the floor, onto the table and into the serving platters. Nothing replaced the old banners of the Ruathan Blood, which had been removed from the stark brown stone walls. Fresh rushes did obscure the greasy flagstones. The trestle tables appeared recently sanded and scraped, and the platters gleamed dully in the refreshed glows. Unfortunately, the brighter light was a mistake for it was much too unflattering.

"This was such a graceful Hall," Lady Gemma murmured for F'lar's ears alone.

"You were a friend?" he asked, politely.

"Yes, in my youth," her voice dropped expressively on the last word, evoking for F'lar a happier girlhood. "It was a noble line!"

"Think you *one* might have escaped the sword?"

Lady Gemma flashed him a startled look, then quickly composed her features, lest the exchange be noted. She gave a barely perceptible shake of her head and then shifted her awkward weight to take her place at the table. Graciously she inclined her head towards F'lar, both dismissing and thanking him.

F'lar returned to his own partner and placed her at the table on his left. As the only person of rank who would dine that night at Ruath Hold, Lady Gemma was seated on his right; Fax would be beyond her. The dragonmen and Fax's upper soldiery would sit at the lower tables. No guildmen had been invited to Ruatha. Fax arrived just then with his current lady and two underleaders, the Warder bowing then effusively into the Hall. The man, F'lar noticed, kept a good distance from his overlord—as well a Warder might whose responsibility was in this sorry condition. F'lar flicked a crawler away. Out of the corner of his eye, he saw Lady Gemma wince and shudder.

Fax stamped up to the raised table, his face black with suppressed rage. He pulled back his chair roughly, slamming it into Lady Gemma's before he seated himself. He pulled the chair to the table with a force that threatened to rock the none-too-stable trestle-top from its supporting legs. Scowling, he inspected his goblet and plate, fingering the surface, ready to throw them aside if they displeased him.

"A roast and fresh bread, Lord Fax, and such fruits and roots as are left. Had I but known of your arrival, I could have sent to Crom for . . ."

"Sent to Crom?" roared Fax, slamming the plate he was inspecting onto the table so forcefully the rim bent under his hands. The Warder winced again as if he himself had been maimed.

"The day one of my Holds cannot support itself *or* the visit of its rightful overlord, I shall renounce it."

Lady Gemma gasped. Simultaneously the dragons roared. F'lar felt the unmistakable surge of power. His eyes instinctively sought F'nor at the lower table. The brown rider—all the dragonmen—had experienced that inexplicable shaft of exultation.

"What's wrong, Dragonman?" snapped Fax.

F'lar, affecting unconcern, stretched his legs under the table and assumed an indolent posture in the heavy chair.

"Wrong?"

"The dragons!"

"Oh, nothing. They often roar . . . at the sunset, at a flock of passing wherries, at mealtimes," and F'lar smiled amiably at the Lord of the High Reaches. Beside him his tablemate gave a squeak.

"Mealtimes? Have they not been fed?"

"Oh, yes. Five days ago."

"Oh. Five . . . days ago? And are they hungry . . . now?" Her voice trailed into a whisper of fear, her eyes grew round.

"In a few days," F'lar assured her. Under cover of his detached amusement, F'lar scanned the Hall. That surge had come from nearby. Either in the Hall or just outside. It must have been from within. It came so soon upon Fax's speech that his words must have triggered it. And the power had had an indefinably feminine touch to it.

One of Fax's women? F'lar found that hard to credit. Mnementh had been close to all of them and none had shown a vestige of power. Much less, with the exception of Lady Gemma, any intelligence.

One of the Hall women? So far he had seen only the sorry drudges and the aging females the Warder had as housekeepers. The Warder's personal woman? He must discover if that man had one. One of the Hold guards' women? F'lar suppressed an intense desire to rise and search.

"You mount a guard?" he asked Fax casually.

"Double at Ruath Hold!" he was told in a tight, hard voice, ground out from somewhere deep in Fax's chest.

"Here?" F'lar all but laughed out loud, gesturing around the sadly appointed chamber.

"Here! Food!" Fax changed the subject with a roar.

Five drudges, two of them women in brown-gray rags such that F'lar hoped they had had nothing to do with the preparation of the meal, staggered in under the emplattered herdbeast. No one with so much as a trace of power would sink to such depths, unless . . .

The aroma that reached him as the platter was placed on the serving table distracted him. It reeked of singed bone and charred meat. The Warder frantically sharpened his tools as if a keen edge could somehow slice acceptable portions from this unlikely carcass.

Lady Gemma caught her breath again, and F'lar saw her hands curl tightly around the armrests. He saw the convulsive movement of her throat as she swallowed. He, too, did not look forward to this repast.

The drudges reappeared with wooden trays of bread. Burnt crusts had been scraped and cut, in some places, from the loaves before serving. As other trays were borne in, F'lar tried to catch sight of the faces of the servitors. Matted hair obscured the face of the one who presented a dish or legumes swimming in greasy liquid. Revolted, F'lar poked through the legumes to find properly cooked portions to offer Lady Gemma. She waved them aside, her face ill-concealing her discomfort.

As F'lar was about to turn and serve Lady Tela, he saw Lady Gemma's hand clutch convulsively at the chair arms. He realized that she was not merely nauseated by the unappetizing food. She was seized with labor contractions.

F'lar glanced in Fax's direction. The overlord was scowling blackly at the attempts of the Warder to find edible portions of meat to serve.

F'lar touched Lady Gemma's arm with light fingers. She turned just enough to look at F'lar from the corner of her eye. She managed a socially correct half-smile.

"I dare not leave just now, Lord F'lar. He is always dangerous at Ruatha. And it may only be false pangs."

F'lar was dubious as he saw another shudder pass through her frame. The woman would have been a fine weyrwoman, he thought ruefully, were she but younger.

The Warder, his hands shaking, presented Fax the sliced meats. There were slivers of overdone flesh and portions of almost edible meats, but not much of either.

One furious wave of Fax's broad fist and the Warder had the plate, meats and juice, square in the face. Despite himself, F'lar

sighed, for those undoubtedly constituted the only edible portions
of the entire beast.

"You call this food? *You call this food?*" Fax bellowed. His voice
boomed back from the bare vault of the ceiling, shaking crawlers
from their webs as the sound shattered the fragile strands. "Slop!
Slop!"

F'lar rapidly brushed crawlers from Lady Gemma, who was
helpless in the throes of a very strong contraction.

"It's all we had on such short notice," the Warder squealed, juices
streaking down his cheeks. Fax threw the goblet at him and the wine
went streaming down the man's chest. The steaming dish of roots
followed, and the man yelped as the hot liquid splashed over him.

"My lord, my lord, had I but known!"

"Obviously, Ruatha *cannot* support the visit of its Lord. You
must renounce it," F'lar heard himself saying.

His shock at such words issuing from his mouth was as great
as that of everyone else in the Hall. Silence fell, broken by the
splat of falling crawlers and the drip of root liquid from the
Warder's shoulders to the rushes. The grating of Fax's boot-heel
was clearly audible as he swung slowly around to face the bronze
rider.

As F'lar conquered his own amazement and rapidly tried to
predict what to do next to mend matters, he saw F'nor rise slowly
to his feet, hand on dagger hilt.

"I did not hear you correctly?" Fax asked, his face blank of all
expression, his eyes snapping.

Unable to comprehend how he could have uttered such an arrant
challenge, F'lar managed to assumed a languid pose.

"You did mention," he drawled, "that if any of your Holds could
not support itself and the visit of its rightful overlord, you would
renounce it."

Fax stared back at F'lar, his face a study of swiftly suppressed
emotions, the glint of triumph dominant. F'lar, his face stiff with
the forced expression of indifference, was casting swiftly about
in his mind. In the name of the Egg, had he lost all sense of
discretion?

Pretending utter unconcern, he stabbed some vegetables onto
his knife and began to munch on them. As he did so, he noticed
F'nor glancing slowly around the Hall, scrutinizing everyone.
Abruptly F'lar realized what had happened. Somehow, in making
that statement, he, a dragonman, had responded to a covert use of
the power. F'lar, the bronze rider, was being put into a position
where he would *have* to fight Fax. Why? For what end? To get

Fax to renounce the Hold? Incredible! But there could be only one possible reason for such a turn of events. An exultation as sharp as pain swelled within F'lar. It was all he could do to maintain his pose of bored indifference, all he could do to turn his attention to thwarting Fax, should he press for a duel. A duel would serve no purpose. He, F'lar, had no time to waste on it.

A groan escaped Lady Gemma and broke the eye-locked stance of the two antagonists. Irritated, Fax looked down at her, fist clenched and half-raised to strike her for her temerity in interrupting her lord and master. The contraction that contorted the swollen belly was as obvious as the woman's pain. F'lar dared not look toward her but he wondered if she had deliberately groaned aloud to break the tension.

Incredibly, Fax began to laugh. He threw back his head, showing big, stained teeth, and roared.

"Aye, renounce it, in favor of her issue, if it is male . . . and lives!" he crowed, laughing raucously.

"Heard and witnessed!" F'lar snapped, jumping to his feet and pointing to his riders. They were on their feet in the instant. "Heard and witnessed!" they averred in the traditional manner.

With that movement, everyone began to babble at once in nervous relief. The other women, each reaching in her way to the imminence of birth, called orders to the servants and advice to each other. They converged toward Lady Gemma, hovering undecidedly out of Fax's range, like silly wherries disturbed from their roosts. It was obvious they were torn between their fear of their lord and their desire to reach the laboring woman.

He gathered their intentions as well as their reluctance and, still stridently laughing, knocked back his chair. He stepped over it. strode down to the meatstand and stood hacking off pieces with his knife, stuffing them, juice dripping, into his mouth without ceasing his guffawing.

As F'lar bent toward Lady Gemma to assist her out of her chair, she grabbed his arm urgently. Their eyes met, hers clouded with pain. She pulled him closer.

"He means to kill you, Bronze Rider. He loves to kill," she whispered.

"Dragonmen are not easily killed, but I am grateful to you."

"I do not want you killed," she said, softly, biting at her lip. "We have so few bronze riders."

F'lar stared at her, startled. Did she, Fax's lady, actually believe in the Old Laws?

F'lar beckoned to two of the Warder's men to carry her up into the Hold. He caught Lady Tela by the arm as she fluttered past him.

"What do you need?"

"Oh, oh," she exclaimed, her face twisted with panic; she was distractedly wringing her hands, "water, hot. Clean cloths. And a birthing-woman. Oh, yes, we must have a birthing-woman."

F'lar looked about for one of the Hold women, his glance sliding over the first disreputable figure who had started to mop up the spilled food. He signalled instead for the Warder and peremptorily ordered him to send for the woman. The Warder kicked at the drudge on the floor.

"You . . . you! Whatever your name is, go get her from the crafthold. You must know who she is."

The drudge evaded the parting kick the Warder aimed in her direction with a nimbleness at odds with her appearance of extreme age and decrepitude. She scurried across the Hall and out the kitchen door.

Fax sliced and speared meat, occasionally bursting out with a louder bark of laughter as his inner thoughts amused him. F'lar sauntered down to the carcass and, without waiting for invitation from his host, began to carve neat slices also, beckoning his men over. Fax's soldiers, however, waited until their lord had eaten his fill.

> Lord of the Hold, your charge is sure
> In thick walls, metal doors and no verdure.

Lessa sped from the Hall to summon the birthing-woman, seething with frustration. So close! So close! How could she come so close and yet fail? Fax should have challenged the dragonman. And the dragonman was strong and young, his face that of a fighter, stern and controlled. He should not have temporized. Was all honor dead in Pern, smothered by green grass?

And why, oh why, had Lady Gemma chosen that precious moment to go into labor? If her groan hadn't distracted Fax, the fight would have begun and not even Fax, for all his vaunted prowess as a vicious fighter, would have prevailed against a dragonman who had her—Lessa's—support! The Hold must be secured to its rightful Blood again. Fax must not leave Ruatha, alive, again!

Above her, on the High Tower, the great bronze dragon gave forth a weird croon, his many-faceted eyes sparkling in the gathering darkness.

Unconsciously she silenced him as she would have done the watch-wher. Ah, that watch-wher. He had not come out of his den at her passing. She knew the dragons had been at him. She could hear him gibbering in panic.

The slant of the road toward the crafthold lent impetus to her flying feet and she had to brace herself to a sliding stop at the birthing-woman's stone threshold. She banged on the closed door and heard the frightened exclamation within.

"A birth. A birth at the Hold," Lessa cried.

"A birth?" came the muffled cry and the latches were thrown up on the door. "At the Hold?"

"Fax's lady and, as you love life, hurry! For if it is male, it will be Ruatha's own lord."

That ought to fetch her, thought Lessa, and in that instant, the door was flung open by the man of the house. Lessa could see the birthing-woman gathering up her things in haste, piling them into her shawl. Lessa hurried the woman out, up the steep road to the Hold, under the Tower gate, grabbing the woman as she tried to run at the sight of a dragon peering down at her. Lessa drew her into the Court and pushed her, resisting, into the Hall.

The woman clutched at the inner door, balking at the sight of the gathering there. Lord Fax, his feet up on the trestle table, was paring his fingernails with his knife blade, still chuckling. The dragonmen in their wher-hide tunics were eating quietly at one table while the soldiers were having their turn at the meat.

The bronze rider noticed their entrance and pointed urgently towards the inner Hold. The birthing-woman seemed frozen to the spot. Lessa tugged futilely at her arm, urging her to cross the Hall. To her surprise, the bronze rider strode to them.

"Go quickly, woman, Lady Gemma is before her time," he said, frowning with concern, gesturing imperatively towards the Hold entrance. He caught her by the shoulder and led her all unwilling, Lessa tugging away at her other arm.

When they reached the stairs, he relinquished his grip, nodding to Lessa to escort her the rest of the way. Just as they reached the massive inner door, Lessa noticed how sharply the dragonman was looking at them—at her hand, on the birthing-woman's arm. Warily, she glanced at her hand and saw it, as if it belonged to a stranger: the long fingers, shapely despite dirt and broken nails; her small hand, delicately boned, gracefully placed despite the urgency of the grip. She blurred it and hurried on.

Honor those the dragons heed,
In thought and favor, word and deed.
Worlds are lost or worlds are saved
By those dangers dragon-braved.

Dragonman, avoid excess;
Greed will bring the Weyr distress;
To the ancient Laws adhere,
Prospers thus the Dragonweyr.

An unintelligible ululation raised the waiting men to their feet, startled from private meditations and the diversion of Bonethrows. Only Fax remained unmoved at the alarm, save that the slight sneer, which had settled on his face hours past, deepened to smug satisfaction.

"Dead-ed-ed," the tidings reverberated down the rocky corridors of the Hold. The weeping lady seemed to erupt out of the passage from the Inner Hold, flying down the steps to sink into an hysterical heap at Fax's feet. "She's dead. Lady Gemma is dead. There was too much blood. It was too soon. She was too old to bear more children."

F'lar couldn't decide whether the woman was apologizing for, or exulting in, the woman's death. She certainly couldn't be criticizing her Lord for placing Lady Gemma in such peril. F'lar, however, was sincerely sorry at Gemma's passing. She had been a brave, fine woman.

And now, what would be Fax's next move? F'lar caught F'nor's identically quizzical glance and shrugged expressively.

"The child lives!" a curiously distorted voice announced, penetrating the rising noise in the Great Hall. The words electrified the atmosphere. Every head slewed round sharply toward the portal to the Inner Hold where the drudge, a totally unexpected messenger, stood poised on the top step.

"It is male!" This announcement rang triumphantly in the still Hall.

Fax jerked himself to his feet, kicking aside the wailer at his feet, scowling ominously at the drudge. "What did you say, woman?"

"The child lives. It is male," the creature repeated, descending the stairs.

Incredulity and rage suffused Fax's face. His body seemed to coil up.

"Ruatha has a new lord!" Staring intently at the overlord, she advanced, her mien purposeful, almost menacing.

The tentative cheers of the Warder's men were drowned by the roaring of the dragons.

Fax erupted into action. He leaped across the intervening space, bellowing. Before Lessa could dodge, his fist crashed down across her face. She fell heavily to the stone floor, where she lay motionless, a bundle of dirty rags.

"Hold, Fax!" F'lar's voice broke the silence as the Lord of the High Reaches flexed his leg to kick her.

Fax whirled, his hand automatically closing on his knife hilt.

"It was heard and witnessed, Fax," F'lar cautioned him, one hand outstretched in warning, "by dragonmen. Stand by your sworn and witnessed oath!"

"Witnessed? By dragonmen?" cried Fax with a derisive laugh. "Dragonwomen, you mean," he sneered, his eyes blazing with contempt, as he made one sweeping gesture of scorn.

He was momentarily taken aback by the speed with which the bronze rider's knife appeared in his hand.

"Dragonwomen?" F'lar queried, his lips curling back over his teeth, his voice dangerously soft. Glowlight flickered off his circling knife as he advanced on Fax.

"Women! Parasites on Pern. The Weyr power is over. Over!" Fax roared, leaping forward to land in a combat crouch.

The two antagonists were dimly aware of the scurry behind them, of tables pulled roughly aside to give the duelists space. F'lar could spare no glance at the crumpled form of the drudge. Yet he was sure, through and beyond instinct sure, that she was the source of power. He had felt it as she entered the room. The dragons' roaring confirmed it. If that fall had killed her . . . He advanced on Fax, leaping high to avoid the slashing blade as Fax unwound from the crouch with a powerful lunge.

F'lar evaded the attack easily, noticing his opponent's reach, deciding he had a slight advantage there. But not much. Fax had had much more actual hand-to-hand killing experience than had he whose duels had always ended at first blood on the practice floor. F'lar made due note to avoid closing with the burly lord. The man was heavy-chested, dangerous from sheer mass. F'lar must use agility as his weapon, not brute strength.

Fax feinted, testing F'lar for weakness or indiscretion. The two crouched, facing each other across six feet of space, knife hands weaving, their free hands, spread-fingered, ready to grab.

Again Fax pressed the attack. F'lar allowed him to close, just near enough to dodge away with a backhanded swipe. Fabric ripped under the tip of his knife. He heard Fax snarl. The overlord was faster on his feet than his bulk suggested and F'lar had to dodge a second time, feeling Fax's knife score his wherhide jerkin.

Grimly the two circled, each looking for an opening in the other's defense. Fax plowed in, trying to corner the lighter, faster man between raised platform and wall.

F'lar countered, ducking low under Fax's flailing arm, slashing obliquely across Fax's side. The overlord caught at him, yanking savagely, and F'lar was trapped against the other man's side, straining desperately with his left hand to keep the knife arm up. F'lar brought up his knee and ducked away as Fax gasped and buckled from the pain in his groin, but Fax struck in passing. Suddenly fire laced F'lar's left shoulder.

Fax's face was red with anger and he wheezed from pain and shock. But the infuriated lord straightened up and charged. F'lar was forced to sidestep quickly before Fax could close with him. F'lar put the meat table between them, circling warily, flexing his shoulder to assess the extent of the knife's slash. It was painful, but the arm could be used.

Suddenly Fax scooped up some fatty scraps from the meat tray and hurled them at F'lar. The dragonman ducked and Fax came around the table with a rush. F'lar leaped sideways. Fax's flashing blade came within inches of his abdomen, as his own knife sliced down the outside of Fax's arm. Instantly the two pivoted to face each other again, but Fax's left arm hung limply at his side.

F'lar darted in, pressing his luck as the Lord of the High Reaches staggered. But F'lar misjudged the man's condition and suffered a terrific kick in the side as he tried to dodge under the feinting knife. Doubled with pain, F'lar rolled frantically away from his charging adversary. Fax was lurching forward, trying to fall on him, to pin the lighter dragonman down for a final thrust. Somehow F'lar got to his feet, attempting to straighten to meet Fax's stumbling charge. His very position saved him. Fax overreached his mark and staggered off balance. F'lar brought his right hand over with as much strength as he could muster and his blade plunged through Fax's unprotected back until he felt the point stick in the chest plate.

The defeated lord fell flat to the flagstones. The force of his descent dislodged the dagger from his chestbone and an inch of bloody blade re-emerged.

F'lar stared down at the dead man. There was no pleasure in killing, he realized, only relief that he himself was still alive. He wiped his forehead on his sleeve and forced himself erect, his side throbbing with the pain of that last kick and his left

shoulder burning. He half-stumbled to the drudge, still sprawled
where she had fallen.

He gently turned her over, noting the terrible bruise spreading
across her cheek under the dirty skin. He heard F'nor take
command of the tumult in the Hall.

The dragonman laid a hand, trembling in spite of an effort to
control himself, on the woman's breast to feel for a heartbeat. . . .
It was there, slow but strong.

A deep sigh escaped him for either blow or fall could have proved
fatal. Fatal, perhaps, for Pern as well.

Relief was colored with disgust. There was no telling under the
filth how old this creature might be. He raised her in his arms, her
light body no burden even to his battleweary strength. Knowing
F'nor would handle any trouble efficiently, F'lar carried the drudge
to his own chamber.

Putting the body on the high bed, he stirred up the fire and
added more glows to the bedside bracket. His gorge rose at the
thought of touching the filthy mat of hair but nonetheless and
gently, he pushed it back from the face, turning the head this way
and that. The features were small, regular. One arm, clear of rags,
was reasonably clean above the elbow but marred by bruises and old
scars. The skin was firm and unwrinkled. The hands, when he took
them in his, were filthy but well-shaped and delicately boned.

F'lar began to smile. Yes, she had blurred that hand so skillfully
that he had actually doubted what he had first seen. And yes,
beneath grime and grease, she was young. Young enough for
the Weyr. And no born drab. There was no taint of common
blood here. It was pure, no matter whose the line, and he rather
thought was indeed Ruathan. One who had by some unknown
agency escaped the massacre ten Turns ago and bided her time
for revenge. Why else force Fax to renounce the Hold?

Delighted and fascinated by this unexpected luck, F'lar reached
out to tear the dress from the unconscious body and found himself
constrained not to. The girl had roused. Her great, hungry eyes
fastened on his, not fearful or expectant; wary.

A subtle change occurred in her face. F'lar watched, his smile
deepening, as she shifted her regular features into an illusion of
disagreeable ugliness and great age.

"Trying to confuse a dragonman, girl?" he chuckled. He made
no further move to touch her but settled against the great carved
post of the bed. He crossed his arms sternly on his chest, thought
better of it immediately, and eased his sore arm. "Your name, girl,
and rank, too."

She drew herself upright slowly against the headboard, her features no longer blurred. They faced each other across the high bed.

"Fax?"

"Dead. Your name!"

A look of exulting triumph flooded her face. She slipped from the bed, standing unexpectedly tall. "Then I reclaim my own. I am of the Ruathan Blood. I claim Ruath," she announced in a ringing voice.

F'lar stared at her a moment, delighted with her proud bearing. Then he threw back his head and laughed.

"This? This crumbling heap?" He could not help but mock the disparity between her manner and her dress. "Oh, no. Besides, Lady, we dragonmen heard and witnessed Fax's oath renouncing the Hold in favor of his heir. Shall I challenge the babe, too, for you? And choke him with his swaddling cloths?" Her eyes flashed, her lips parted in a terrible smile.

"There is no heir. Gemma died, the babe unborn. I lied."

"Lied?" F'lar demanded, angry.

"Yes," she taunted him with a toss of her chin, "I lied. There was no babe born. I merely wanted to be sure you challenged Fax."

He grabbed her wrist, stung that he had twice fallen to her prodding.

"You provoked a dragonman to fight? To kill? *When he is on Search?*"

"Search? Why should I care about a Search? I've Ruatha as my Hold again. For ten Turns, I have worked and waited, schemed and suffered for that. What could your Search mean to me?"

F'lar wanted to strike that look of haughty contempt from her face. He twisted her arm savagely, bringing her to his feet before he released his grip. She laughed at him, and scuttled to one side. She was on her feet and out the door before he could give chase.

Swearing to himself, he raced down the rocky corridors, knowing she would have to make for the Hall to get out of the Hold. However, when he reached the Hall, there was no sign of her fleeing figure among those still loitering.

"Has that creature come this way?" he called to F'nor who was, by chance, standing by the door to the Court.

"No. Is she the source of power after all?"

"Yes, she is," F'lar answered, galled all the more. "And Ruathan Blood at that!"

"Oh ho! Does she depose the babe, then?" F'nor asked, gesturing toward the birthing-woman, who occupied a seat close to the now-blazing hearth.

F'lar paused, about to return to search the Hold's myriad passages. He stared, momentarily confused, at the brown rider.

"Babe? What babe?"

"The male child Lady Gemma bore," F'nor replied, surprised by F'lar's uncomprehending look.

"It lives?"

"Yes. A strong babe, the woman says, for all that he was premature and taken forcibly from his dead dame's belly."

F'lar threw back his head with a shout of laughter. For all her scheming, she had been outdone by truth.

At that moment, he heard Mnementh roar in unmistakable elation and the curious warble of other dragons.

"Mnementh has caught her," F'lar cried, grinning with jubilation. He strode down the steps, past the body of the former Lord of the High Reaches and out into the main court.

He saw that the bronze dragon was gone from his Tower perch and called him. An agitation drew his eyes upward. He saw Mnementh spiraling down into the Court, his front paws clasping something. Mnementh informed F'lar that he had seen her climbing from one of the high windows and had simply plucked her from the ledge, knowing the dragonman sought her. The bronze dragon settled awkwardly onto his hind legs, his wings working to keep him balanced. Carefully he set the girl on her feet and formed a precise cage around her with his huge talons. She stood motionless within that circle, her face toward the wedge-shaped head that swayed above her.

The watch-wher, shrieking terror, anger, and hatred, was lunging violently to the end of its chain, trying to come to Lessa's aid. It grabbed at F'lar as he strode to the two.

"You've courage enough, girl," he admitted, resting one hand casually on Mnementh's upper claw. Mnementh was enormously pleased with himself and swiveled his head down for his eye ridges to be scratched.

"You did not lie, you know," F'lar said, unable to resist taunting the girl.

Slowly she turned toward him, her face impassive. She was not afraid of dragons, F'lar realized with approval.

"The babe lives. And it is male."

She could not control her dismay and her shoulders sagged briefly before she pulled herself erect.

"Ruatha is mine," she insisted in a tense low voice.

"Aye, and it would have been, had you approached me directly when the wing arrived here."

Her eyes widened. "What do you mean?"

"A dragonman may champion anyone whose grievance is just. By the time we reached Ruath Hold, I was quite ready to challenge Fax given any reasonable cause, despite the Search." This was not the whole truth but F'lar must teach this girl the folly of trying to control dragonmen. "Had you paid any attention to your harper's songs, you'd know your rights. And," F'lar's voice held a vindictive edge that surprised him, "Lady Gemma might not now lie dead. She suffered far more at that tyrant's hand than you."

Something in her manner told him that she regretted Lady Gemma's death, that it had affected her deeply.

"What good is Ruatha to you now?" he demanded, a broad sweep of his arm taking in the ruined courtyard and the Hold, the entire unproductive valley of Ruatha. "You have indeed accomplished your ends; a profitless conquest and its conqueror's death." F'lar snorted: "All seven Holds will revert to their legitimate Blood, and time they did. One Hold, one lord. Of course, you might have to fight others, infected with Fax's greed. Could you hold Ruatha against attack . . . now . . . in her decline?"

"Ruatha is mine!"

"Ruatha?" F'lar's laugh was derisive. "When you could be Weyrwoman?"

"Weyrwoman?" she breathed, staring at him.

"Yes, little fool. I said I rode in Search . . . it's about time you attended to more than Ruatha. And the object of my Search is . . . you!"

She stared at the finger he pointed at her as if it were dangerous.

"By the First Egg, girl, you've power in you to spare when you can turn a dragonman, all unwitting, to do your bidding. Ah, but never again, for now I am on guard against you."

Mnementh crooned approvingly, the sound a soft rumble in his throat. He arched his neck so that one eye was turned directly on the girl, gleaming in the darkness of the court.

F'lar noticed with detached pride that she neither flinched nor blanched at the proximity of an eye greater than her own head.

"He likes to have his eye ridges scratched," F'lar remarked in a friendly tone, changing tactics.

"I know," she said softly and reached out a hand to do that service.

"Nemorth's queen," F'lar continued, "is close to death. This time we must have a strong Weyrwoman."

"This time—the Red Star?" the girl gasped, turning frightened eyes to F'lar.

"You understand what it means?"

"There is danger . . ." she began in a bare whisper, glancing apprehensively eastward.

F'lar did not question by what miracle she appreciated the imminence of danger. He had every intention of taking her to the Weyr by sheer force if necessary. But something within him wanted very much for her to accept the challenge voluntarily. A rebellious Weyrwoman would be even more dangerous than a stupid one. This girl had too much power and was too used to guile and strategy. It would be a calamity to antagonize her with injudicious handling.

"There is danger for all Pern. Not just Ruatha," he said, allowing a note of entreaty to creep into his voice. "And *you* are needed. Not by Ruatha," a wave of his hand dismissed that consideration as a negligible one compared to the total picture. "We are doomed without a strong Weyrwoman. Without you."

"Gemma kept saying *all* the bronze riders were needed," she murmured in a dazed whisper.

What did she mean by that statement? F'lar frowned. Had she heard a word he had said? He pressed his argument, certain only that he had already struck one responsive chord.

"You've won here. Let the babe," he saw her startled rejection of that idea and ruthlessly qualified it, ". . . Gemma's babe . . . be reared at Ruatha. You have command of all the Holds as Weyrwoman, not ruined Ruatha alone. You've accomplished Fax's death. Leave off vengeance."

She stared at F'lar with wonder, absorbing his words.

"I never thought beyond Fax's death," she admitted slowly. "I never thought what should happen then."

Her confusion was almost childlike and struck F'lar forcibly. He had had no time, or desire, to consider her prodigious accomplishment. Now he realized some measure of her indomitable character. She could not have been much over ten Turns of age herself when Fax had murdered her family. Yet somehow, so young, she had set herself a goal and managed to survive both brutality and detection long enough to secure the usurper's death. What a Weyrwoman she would be! In the tradition of those of Ruathan blood. The light of the paler moon made her look young and vulnerable and almost pretty.

"You can be Weyrwoman," he insisted gently.

"Weyrwoman," she breathed, incredulous, and gazed round the inner court bathed in soft moonlight. He thought she wavered.

"Or perhaps you enjoy rags?' he said, making his voice harsh, mocking. "And matted hair, dirty feet, and cracked hands? Sleeping in straw, eating rinds? You are young . . . that is, I assume you are young," and his voice was frankly skeptical. She glared at him, her lips firmly pressed together. "Is this the be-all and end-all of your ambition? What are you that this little corner of the great world is *all* you want?" He paused and with utter contempt added, "The blood of Ruatha has thinned, I see. You're afraid!"

"I am Lessa, daughter of the Lord of Ruath," she countered, stung. She drew herself erect. Her eyes flashed. "I am afraid of nothing!"

F'lar contented himself with a slight smile.

Mnementh, however, threw up his head, and stretched out his sinuous neck to its whole length. His full-throated peal rang out down the valley. The bronze communicated his awareness to F'lar that Lessa had accepted the challenge. The other dragons answered back, their warbles shriller than Mnementh's bellow. The watch-wher which had cowered at the end of its chain lifted its voice in a thin, unnerving screech until the Hold emptied of its startled occupants.

"F'nor," the bronze rider called, waving his wingleader to him. "Leave half the flight to guard the Hold. Some nearby lord might think to emulate Fax's example. Send one rider to the High Reaches with the glad news. You go directly to the Cloth Hall and speak to L'to . . . Lytol." F'lar grinned. "I think he would make an exemplary Warder and Lord Surrogate for this Hold in the name of the Weyr and the babe."

The brown rider's face expressed enthusiasm for his mission as he began to comprehend his leader's intentions. With Fax dead and Ruatha under the protection of dragonmen, particularly that same one who had dispatched Fax, the Hold would have wise management.

"She caused Ruatha's deterioration?" he asked.

"And nearly ours with her machinations," F'lar replied, but having found the admirable object of his Search he could now be magnanimous. "Suppress your exultation, brother," he advised quickly as he took note of F'nor's expression. "The new queen must also be Impressed."

"I'll settle arrangements here. Lytol is an excellent choice," F'nor said.

"Who is this Lytol?" demanded Lessa pointedly. She had twisted the mass of filthy hair back from her face. In the moonlight the dirt was less noticeable. F'lar caught F'nor looking at her with an all-too-easily-read expression. He signaled F'nor, with a peremptory gesture, to carry out his orders without delay.

"Lytol is a dragonless man," F'lar told the girl, "no friend to Fax. He will ward the Hold well and it will prosper." He added persuasively with a quelling stare full on her, "Won't it?"

She regarded him somberly, without answering, until he chuckled softly at her discomfiture.

"We'll return to the Weyr," he announced, proffering a hand to guide her to Mnementh's side.

The bronze one had extended his head toward the watch-wher who now lay panting on the ground, its chain limp in the dust.

"Oh," Lessa sighed, and dropped beside the grotesque beast. It raised its head slowly, lurring piteously.

"Mnementh says it is very old and soon will sleep itself to death."

Lessa cradled the bestial head in her arms, scratching it behind the ears.

"Come, Lessa of Pern," F'lar said, impatient to be up and away.

She rose slowly but obediently. "It saved me. It knew me."

"It knows it did well," F'lar assured her, brusquely, wondering at such an uncharacteristic show of sentiment in her.

He took her hand again, to help her to her feet and lead her back to Mnementh. As they turned, he glimpsed the watch-wher, launching itself at a dead run after Lessa. The chain, however, held fast. The beast's neck broke, with a sickeningly audible snap.

Lessa was on her knees in an instant, cradling the repulsive head in her arms.

"Why, you foolish thing, why?" she asked in a stunned whisper as the light in the beast's green-gold eyes dimmed and died out.

Mnementh informed F'lar that the creature had lived this long only to preserve the Ruathan line. At Lessa's imminent departure, it had welcomed death.

A convulsive shudder went through Lessa's slim body. F'lar watched as she undid the heavy buckle that fastened the metal collar about the watch-wher's neck. She threw the tether away with a violent motion. Tenderly she laid the watch-wher on the cobbles. With one last caress to the clipped wings, she rose in a fluid movement and walked resolutely to Mnementh without a single backward glance. She stepped calmly to the dragon's raised leg and seated herself, as F'lar directed, on the great neck.

F'lar glanced around the courtyard at the remainder of his wing, which had reformed there. The Hold folk had retreated back into

the safety of the Great Hall. When his wingmen were all astride, he
vaulted to Mnementh's neck, behind the girl.

"Hold tightly to my arms," he ordered her as he took hold of the
smallest neck ridge and gave the command to fly.

Her fingers closed spasmodically around his forearm as the great
bronze dragon took off, the enormous wings working to achieve
height from the vertical takeoff. Mnementh preferred to fall into
flight from a cliff or tower. Like all dragons, he tended to indolence.
F'lar glanced behind him, saw the other dragonmen form the flight
line, spread out to cover those still on guard at Ruatha Hold.

When they had reached a sufficient altitude, he told Mnementh
to transfer, going *between* to the Weyr.

Only a gasp indicated the girl's astonishment as they hung
between. Accustomed as he was to the sting of the profound cold,
to the awesome utter lack of light and sound, F'lar still found the
sensations unnerving. Yet the uncommon transfer spanned no more
time than it took to cough thrice.

Mnementh rumbled approval of this candidate's calm reaction as
they flicked out of the eerie *between*.

And then they were above the Weyr, Mnementh setting his wings
to glide in the bright daylight, half a world away from night-time
Ruatha.

As they circled above the great stony trough of the Weyr, F'lar
peered at Lessa's face, pleased with the delight mirrored there; she
showed no trace of fear as they hung a thousand lengths above the
high Benden mountain range. Then, as the seven dragons roared
their incoming cry, an incredulous smile lit her face.

The other wingmen dropped into a wide spiral, down, down
while Mnementh elected to descend in lazy circles. The dragonmen
peeled off smartly and dropped, each to his own tier in the caves of
the Weyr. Mnementh finally completed his leisurely approach to
their quarters, whistling shrilly to himself as he braked his forward
speed with a twist of his wings, dropping lightly at last to the ledge.
He crouched as F'lar swung the girl to the rough rock, scored from
thousands of clawed landings.

"This leads only to our quarters," he told her as they entered
the corridor, vaulted and wide for the easy passage of great bronze
dragons.

As they reached the huge natural cavern that had been his since
Mnementh achieved maturity, F'lar looked about him with eyes
fresh from his first prolonged absence from the Weyr. The huge
chamber was unquestionably big, certainly larger than most of the
halls he had visited in Fax's procession. Those halls were intended

as gathering places for men, not the habitations of dragons. But suddenly he saw his own quarters were nearly as shabby as all Ruatha. Benden was, of a certainty, one of the oldest dragonweyrs, as Ruatha was one of the oldest Holds, but that excused nothing. How many dragons had bedded in that hollow to make solid rock conform to dragon proportions! How many feet had worn the path past the dragon's weyr into the sleeping chamber, to the bathing room beyond where the natural warm spring provided ever-fresh water! But the wall hangings were faded and unraveling and there were grease stains on lintel and floor that should be sanded away.

He noticed the wary expression on Lessa's face as he paused in the sleeping room.

"I must feed Mnementh immediately. So you may bathe first," he said, rummaging in a chest and finding clean clothes for her, discards of other previous occupants of his quarters, but far more presentable than her present covering. He carefully laid back in the chest the white wool robe that was traditional Impression garb. She would wear that later. He tossed several garments at her feet and a bag of sweetsand, gesturing to the hanging that obscured the way to the bath.

He left her, then, the clothes in a heap at her feet, for she made no effort to catch anything.

Mnementh informed him that F'nor was feeding Canth and that he, Mnementh, was hungry too. *She* didn't trust F'lar but she wasn't afraid of himself.

"Why should she be afraid of you?" F'lar asked. "You're cousin to the watch-wher who was her only friend."

Mnementh informed F'lar that he, a fully matured bronze dragon, was no relation to any scrawny, crawling, chained, and wing-clipped watch-wher.

F'lar, pleased at having been able to tease the bronze one, chuckled to himself. With great dignity, Mnementh curved down to the feeding ground.

> By the Golden Egg of Faranth
> By the Weyrwoman, wise and true,
> Breed a flight of bronze and brown wings,
> Breed a flight of green and blue.
> Breed riders, strong and daring,
> Dragon-loving, born as hatched,
> Flight of hundreds soaring skyward,
> Man and dragon fully matched.

Lessa waited until the sound of the dragonman's footsteps proved he had really gone away. She rushed quickly through the big cavern, heard the scrape of claw and the *whoosh* of the mighty wings. She raced down the short passageway, right to the edge of the yawning entrance. There was the bronze dragon circling down to the wider end of the mile-long barren oval that was Benden Weyr. She had heard of the Weyrs, as any Pernese had, but to be in one was quite a different matter.

She peered up, around, down that sheer rock face. There was no way off but by dragon wing. The nearest cave mouths were an unhandy distance above her, to one side, below her on the other. She was neatly secluded here.

Weyrwoman, he had told her. His woman? In his weyr? Was that what he had meant? No, that was not the impression she got from the dragon. It occurred to her, suddenly, that it was odd she had understood the dragon. Were common folk able to? Or was it the dragonman blood in her line? At all events, Mnementh had inferred something greater, some special rank. She remembered vaguely that, when dragonmen went on Search, they looked for certain women. Ah, certain women. She was one, then, of several contenders. Yet the bronze rider had offered her the position as if she and she, alone, qualified. He had his own generous portion of conceit, that one, Lessa decided. Arrogant he was, though not a bully like Fax.

She could see the bronze dragon swoop down to the running herdbeasts, saw the strike, saw the dragon wheel up to settle on a far ledge to feed. Instinctively she drew back from the opening, back into the dark and relative safety of the corridor.

The feeding dragon evoked scores of horrid tales. Tales at which she had scoffed but now . . . Was it true, then, that dragons did eat human flesh? Did . . . Lessa halted that trend of thought. Dragonkind was no less cruel than mankind. The dragon, at least, acted from bestial need rather than bestial greed.

Assured that the dragonman would be occupied a while, she crossed the larger cave into the sleeping room. She scooped up the clothing and the bag of cleansing sand and proceeded to the bathing room.

To be clean! To be completely clean and to be able to stay that way. With distaste, she stripped off the remains of the rags, kicking them to one side. She made a soft mud with the sweetsand and scrubbed her entire body until she drew blood from various half-healed cuts. Then she jumped into the pool, gasping as the warm water made the sweetsand foam in the lacerations.

It was a ritual cleansing of more than surface soil. The luxury of cleanliness was ecstasy.

Finally satisfied she was as clean as one long soaking could make her, she left the pool, reluctantly. Wringing out her hair she tucked it up on her head as she dried herself. She shook out the clothing and held one garment against her experimentally. The fabric, a soft green, felt smooth under her watershrunken fingers, although the nap caught on her roughened hands. She pulled it over her head. It was loose but the darker green overtunic had a sash which she pulled in tight at the waist. The unusual sensation of softness against her bare skin made her wriggle with voluptuous pleasure. The skirt, no longer a ragged hem of tatters, swirled heavily around her ankles. She smiled. She took up a fresh drying cloth and began to work on her hair.

A muted sound came to her ears and she stopped, hands poised, head bent to one side. Straining, she listened. Yes, there were sounds without. The dragonman and his beast must have returned. She grimaced to herself with annoyance at this untimely interruption and rubbed harder at her hair. She ran fingers through the half-dry tangles, the motions arrested as she encountered snarls. Vexed, she rummaged on the shelves until she found, as she had hoped to, a coarse-toothed metal comb.

Dry, her hair had a life of its own suddenly, crackling about her hands and clinging to face and comb and dress. It was difficult to get the silky stuff under control. And her hair was longer than she had thought, for clean and unmatted, it fell to her waist—when it did not cling to her hands.

She paused, listening, and heard no sound at all. Apprehensively, she stepped to the curtain and glanced warily to the sleeping room. It was empty. She listened and caught the perceptible thoughts of the sleepy dragon. Well, she would rather meet the man in the presence of a sleepy dragon than in a sleeping room. She started across the floor and, out of the corner of her eye, caught sight of a strange woman as she passed a polished piece of metal hanging on the wall.

Amazed, she stopped short, staring, incredulous, at the face the metal reflected. Only when she put her hands to her prominent cheekbones in a gesture of involuntary surprise and the reflection imitated the gesture, did she realize she looked at herself.

Why, that girl in the reflector was prettier than Lady Tela, than the clothman's daughter! But so thin. Her hands of their own volition dropped to her neck, to the protruding collarbones, to her breasts which did not entirely accord with the gauntness of the rest of her. The dress was too large for her frame, she noted with an unexpected emergence of conceit born in that instant of delighted appraisal. And her hair . . . it stood out around her head like an aureole. It wouldn't lie contained. She smoothed it down with impatient fingers, automatically bringing locks forward to hang around her face. As she irritably pushed them back, dismissing a need for disguise, the hair drifted up again. A slight sound, the scrape of a boot against stone, caught her back from her bemusement. She waited, momentarily expecting him to appear. She was suddenly timid. With her face bare to the world, her hair behind her ears, her body outlined by a clinging fabric, she was stripped of her accustomed anonymity and was, therefore, in her estimation, vulnerable.

She controlled the desire to run away—the irrational fear. Observing herself in the looking metal, she drew her shoulders back, tilted her head high, chin up; the movement caused her hair to crackle and cling and shift about her head. She was Lessa of Ruatha, of a fine old Blood. She no longer needed artifice to preserve herself; she must stand proudly bare-faced before the world . . . and that dragonman.

Resolutely she crossed the room, pushing aside the hanging on the doorway to the great cavern.

He was there, beside the head of the dragon, scratching its eye ridges, a curiously tender expression on his face. The tableau was at variance with all she had heard of dragonmen.

She had, of course, heard of the strange affinity between rider and dragon but this was the first time she realized that love was part of that bond. Or that this reserved, cold man was capable of such deep emotion.

He turned slowly, as if loath to leave the bronze beast. He caught sight of her and pivoted completely round, his eyes intense as he took note of her altered appearance. With quick, light steps, he closed the distance between them and ushered her back into the sleeping room, one strong hand holding her by the elbow.

"Mnementh has fed lightly and will need quiet to rest," he said in a low voice. He pulled the heavy hanging into place across the opening.

Then he held her away from him, turning her this way and that, scrutinizing her closely, curious and slightly surprised.

"You wash up . . . pretty, yes, almost pretty," he said, amused condescension in his voice. She pulled roughly away from him, piqued. His low laugh mocked her. "After all, how could one guess what was under the grime of . . . ten full Turns?"

At length he said, "No matter. We must eat and I shall require your services." At her startled exclamation, he turned, grinning maliciously now as his movement revealed the caked blood on his left sleeve. "The least you can do is bathe wounds honorably received fighting your battle."

He pushed aside a portion of the drape that curtained the inner wall. "Food for two!" he roared down a black gap in the sheer stone.

She heard a subterranean echo far below as his voice resounded down what must be a long shaft.

"Nemorth is nearly rigid," he was saying as he took supplies from another drape-hidden shelf, "and the Hatching will soon begin anyhow."

A coldness settled in Lessa's stomach at the mention of a Hatching. The mildest tales she had heard about that part of dragonlore were chilling, the worst dismayingly macabre. She took the things he handed her numbly.

"What? Frightened?" the dragonman taunted, pausing as he stripped off his torn and bloodied shirt.

With a shake of her head, Lessa turned her attention to the wide-shouldered, well-muscled back he presented her, the paler skin of his body decorated with random bloody streaks. Fresh blood welled from the point of his shoulder for the removal of his shirt had broken the tender scabs.

"I will need water," she said and saw she had a flat pan among the items he had given her. She went swiftly to the pool for water, wondering how she had come to agree to venture so far from Ruatha. Ruined though it was, it had been hers and was familiar to her from Tower to deep cellar. At the moment the idea had been proposed and insidiously prosecuted by the dragonman, she had felt capable of anything, having achieved, at last, Fax's death. Now, it was all she could do to keep the water from slopping out of the pan that shook unaccountably in her hands.

She forced herself to deal only with the wound. It was a nasty gash, deep where the point had entered and torn downward in a gradually shallower slice. His skin felt smooth under her fingers as she cleansed the wound. In spite of herself, she noticed the masculine odor of him, compounded not unpleasantly of sweat, leather, and an unusual muskiness which must be from close association with dragons.

She stood back when she had finished her ministration. He flexed his arm experimentally in the constricting bandage and the motion set the muscles rippling along side and back.

When he faced her, his eyes were dark and thoughtful.

"Gently done. My thanks." His smile was ironic.

She backed away as he rose but he only went to the chest to take out a clean, white shirt.

A muted rumble sounded, growing quickly louder.

Dragons roaring? Lessa wondered, trying to conquer the ridiculous fear that rose within her. Had the Hatching started? There was no watch-wher's lair to secrete herself in, here.

As if he understood her confusion, the dragonman laughed good-humoredly and, his eyes on hers, drew aside the wall covering just as some noisy mechanism inside the shaft propelled a tray of food into sight.

Ashamed of her unbased fright and furious that he had witnessed it, Lessa sat rebelliously down on the fur-covered wall seat, heartily wishing him a variety of serious and painful injuries which she could dress with inconsiderate hands. She would not waste future opportunities.

He placed the tray on the low table in front of her, throwing down a heap of furs for his own seat. There was meat, bread, a tempting yellow cheese, and even a few pieces of winter fruit. He made no move to eat nor did she, though the thought of a piece of fruit that was ripe, instead of rotten, set her mouth to watering. He glanced up at her, and frowned.

"Even in the Weyr, the lady breaks bread first," he said, and inclined his head politely to her.

Lessa flushed, unused to any courtesy and certainly unused to being first to eat. She broke off a chunk of bread. It was like nothing she remembered having tasted before. For one thing, it was fresh-baked. The flour had been finely sifted, without trace of sand or hull. She took the slice of cheese he proffered her and it, too, had an uncommonly delicious sharpness. Made bold by this indication of her changed status, Lessa reached for the plumpest piece of fruit.

"Now," the dragonman began, his hand touching hers to get her attention.

Guiltily she dropped the fruit, thinking she had erred. She stared at him, wondering at her fault. He retrieved the fruit and placed it back in her hand as he continued to speak. Wide-eyed, disarmed, she nibbled, and gave him her full attention.

"Listen to me. You must not show a moment's fear, whatever happens on the Hatching Ground. And you must not let her overeat." A wry expression crossed his face. "One of our main functions is to keep a dragon from excessive eating."

Lessa lost interest in the taste of the fruit. She placed it carefully back in the bowl and tried to sort out not what he had said, but what his tone of voice implied. She looked at the dragonman's face, seeing him as a person, not a symbol, for the first time.

There was a blackness about him that was not malevolent; it was a brooding sort of patience. Heavy black hair, heavy black brows; his eyes, a brown light enough to seem golden, were all too expressive of cynical emotions, or cold hauteur. His lips were thin but well-shaped and in repose almost gentle. Why must he always pull his mouth to one side in disapproval or in one of those sardonic smiles? At this moment, he was completely unaffected.

He meant what he was saying. He did not want her to be afraid. There was no reason for her, Lessa, *to* fear.

He very much wanted her to succeed. In keeping whom from overeating what? Herd animals? A newly hatched dragon certainly wasn't capable of eating a full beast. That seemed a simple enough task to Lessa . . . Main function? *Our* main function?

The dragonman was looking at her expectantly.

"Our main function?" she repeated, an unspoken request for more information inherent in her inflection.

"More of that later. First things first," he said, impatiently waving off other questions.

"But what happens?" she insisted.

"As I was told so I tell you. No more, no less. Remember these two points. No fear, and no overeating."

"But . . ."

"You, however, need to eat. Here." He speared a piece of meat on his knife and thrust it at her, frowning until she managed to choke it down. He was about to force more on her but she grabbed up her half-eaten fruit and bit down into the firm sweet sphere instead. She had already eaten more at this one meal than she was accustomed to having all day at the Hold.

"We shall soon eat better at the Weyr," he remarked, regarding the tray with a jaundiced eye.

Lessa was surprised. This was a feast, in her opinion.

"More than you're used to? Yes, I forgot you left Ruatha with bare bones indeed."

She stiffened.

"You did well at Ruatha. I mean no criticism," he added, smiling at her reaction. "But look at you," and he gestured at her body, that curious expression crossing his face, half-amused, half-contemplative. "I should not have guessed you'd clean up pretty," he remarked. "Nor with such hair." This time his expression was frankly admiring.

Involuntarily she put one hand to her head, the hair crackling over her fingers. But what reply she might have made him, indignant as she was, died aborning. An unearthly keening filled the chamber.

The sounds set up a vibration that ran down the bones behind her ear to her spine. She clapped both hands to her ears. The noise rang through her skull despite her defending hands. As abruptly as it started, it ceased.

Before she knew what he was about, the dragonman had grabbed her by the wrist and pulled her over to the chest.

"Take those off," he ordered, indicating dress and tunic. While she stared at him stupidly, he held up a loose white robe, sleeveless and beltless, a matter of two lengths of fine cloth fastened at shoulder and side seams. "Take it off, or do I assist you?" he asked, with no patience at all.

The wild sound was repeated and its unnerving tone made her fingers fly faster. She had no sooner loosened the garments she wore, letting them slide to her feet, than he had thrown the other over her head. She managed to get her arms in the proper places before he grabbed her wrist again and was speeding with her out of the room, her hair whipping out behind her, alive with static.

As they reached the outer chamber, the bronze dragon was standing in the center of the cavern, his head turned to watch the sleeping-room door. He seemed impatient to Lessa; his great eyes sparkled iridescently. His manner breathed an inner excitement of great proportions and from his throat a high-pitched croon issued, several octaves below the unnerving cry that had roused them all.

With a yank that rocked her head on her neck, the dragonman pulled her along the passage. The dragon padded beside them at such speed that Lessa fully expected they would all catapult off the ledge. Somehow, at the crucial stride, she was a-perch the bronze neck, the dragonman holding her firmly about the waist. In the same fluid movement, they were gliding across the great bowl of the Weyr to the higher wall opposite. The air was full of wings and dragon tails, rent with a chorus of sounds, echoing and re-echoing across the stony valley.

Mnementh set what Lessa was certain would be a collision course with other dragons, straight for a huge round blackness in the cliff face, high up. Magically, the beasts filed in, the greater wingspread of Mnementh just clearing the sides of the entrance.

The passageway reverberated with the thunder of wings. The air compressed around her thickly. Then they broke out into a gigantic cavern.

Why, the entire mountain must be hollow, thought Lessa, incredulous. Around the enormous cavern, dragons perched in serried ranks, blues, greens, browns, and only two great bronze beasts like Mnementh, on ledges meant to accommodate hundreds. Lessa gripped the bronze neck scales before her, instinctively aware of the imminence of a great event.

Mnementh wheeled downward, disregarding the ledge of the bronze ones. Then all Lessa could see was what lay on the sandy floor of the great cavern: dragon eggs. A clutch of ten monstrous, mottled eggs, their shells moving spasmodically as the fledglings within tapped their way out. To one side, on a raised portion of the floor, was a golden egg, larger by half again the size of the mottled ones. Just beyond the golden egg lay the motionless ochre hulk of the old queen.

Just as she realized Mnementh was hovering over the floor in the vicinity of that egg, Lessa felt the dragonman's hands on her, lifting her from Mnementh's neck.

Apprehensively, she grabbed at him. His hands tightened and inexorably swung her down. His eyes, fierce and gray, locked with hers.

"Remember, Lessa!"

Mnementh added an encouragement, one great compound eye turned on her. Then he rose from the floor. Lessa half-raised one hand in entreaty, bereft of all support, even that of the sure inner compulsion which had sustained her in her struggle for revenge on Fax. She saw the bronze dragon settle on the first ledge, at some distance from the other two bronze beasts. The dragonman dismounted and Mnementh curved his sinuous neck until his head was beside his rider. The man reached up absently, it seemed to Lessa, and caressed his mount.

Loud screams and wailings diverted Lessa and she saw more dragons descend to hover just above the cavern floor, each rider depositing a young woman until there were twelve girls, including Lessa. She remained a little apart from them as they clung to each other. She regarded them curiously. The girls were not injured in any way she could see, so why such weeping? She took a deep breath against the coldness within her. Let *them* be afraid. She was Lessa of Ruatha and did not need to be afraid.

Just then, the golden egg moved convulsively. Gasping as one, the girls edged away from it, back against the rocky wall. One, a lovely blonde, her heavy plait of golden hair swinging just above the ground, started to step off the raised floor and stopped, shrieking, backing fearfully toward the scant comfort of her peers.

Lessa wheeled to see what cause there might be for the look of horror on the girl's face. She stepped back involuntarily herself.

In the main section of the sandy arena, several of the handful of eggs had already cracked wide open. The fledglings, crowing weakly, were moving toward . . . and Lessa gulped . . . the young boys standing stolidly in a semi-circle. Some of them were no older than she had been when Fax's army had swooped down on Ruath Hold.

The shrieking of the women subsided to muffled gasps. A fledgling reached out with claw and beak to grab a boy.

Lessa forced herself to watch as the young dragon mauled the youth, throwing him roughly aside as if unsatisfied in some way. The boy did not move and Lessa could see blood seeping onto the sand from dragon-inflicted wounds.

A second fledgling lurched against another boy and halted, flapping its damp wings impotently, raising its scrawny neck and croaking a parody of the encouraging croon Mnementh often gave. The boy uncertainly lifted a hand and began to scratch the eye ridge. Incredulous, Lessa watched as the fledgling, its crooning increasingly more mellow, ducked its head, pushing at the boy. The child's face broke into an unbelieving smile of elation.

Tearing her eyes from this astounding sight, Lessa saw that another fledgling was beginning the same performance with another boy. Two more dragons had emerged in the interim. One had knocked a boy down and was walking over him, oblivious to the fact that its claws were raking great gashes. The fledgling who followed its hatch-mate stopped by the wounded child, ducking its head to the boy's face, crooning anxiously. As Lessa watched, the boy managed to struggle to his feet, tears of pain streaming down his cheeks. She could hear him pleading with the dragon not to worry, that he was only scratched a little.

It was over very soon. The young dragons paired off with boys. Green riders dropped down to carry off the unacceptable. Blue riders settled to the floor with their beasts and led the couples out of the cavern, the young dragons squealing, crooning, flapping wet wings as they staggered off, encouraged by their newly acquired weyrmates.

Lessa turned resolutely back to the rocking golden egg, knowing what to expect and trying to divine what the successful boys had, or had not done, that caused the baby dragons to single them out.

A crack appeared in the golden shell and was greeted by the terrified screams of the girls. Some had fallen into little heaps of white fabric, others embraced tightly in their mutual fear. The

crack widened and the wedge head broke through, followed quickly
by the neck, gleaming gold. Lessa wondered with unexpected
detachment how long it would take the beast to mature, considering
its by no means small size at birth. For the head was larger than that
of the male dragons and they had been large enough to overwhelm
sturdy boys of ten full Turns.

Lessa was aware of a loud hum within the Hall. Glancing up at
the audience, she realized it emanated from the watching bronze
dragons, for this was the birth of their mate, their queen. The hum
increased in volume as the shell shattered into fragments and the
golden, glistening body of the new female emerged. It staggered
out, dipping its sharp beak into the soft sand, momentarily trapped.
Flapping its wet wings, it righted itself, ludicrous in its weak
awkwardness. With sudden and unexpected swiftness, it dashed
toward the terror-stricken girls.

Before Lessa could blink, it shook the first girl with such
violence her head snapped audibly and she fell limply to the
sand. Disregarding her, the dragon leaped toward the second girl
but misjudged the distance and fell, grabbing out with one claw
for support and raking the girl's body from shoulder to thigh.
The screaming of the mortally injured girl distracted the dragon
and released the others from their horrified trance. They scattered
in panicky confusion, racing, running, tripping, stumbling, falling
across the sand toward the exit the boys had used.

As the golden beast, crying piteously, lurched down from the
raised arena toward the scattered women, Lessa moved. Why
hadn't that silly clunk-headed girl stepped aside, Lessa thought,
grabbing for the wedge-head, at birth not much larger than her own
torso. The dragon's so clumsy and weak she's her own worst enemy.

Lessa swung the head round so that the many-faceted eyes were
forced to look at her . . . and found herself lost in that rainbow
regard.   −

A feeling of joy suffused Lessa, a feeling of warmth; tenderness,
unalloyed affection and instant respect and admiration flooded
mind and heart and soul. Never again would Lessa lack an advocate,
a defender, an intimate, aware instantly of the temper of her
mind and heart, of her desires. How wonderful was Lessa, the
thought intruded into Lessa's reflections, how pretty, how kind,
how thoughtful, how brave and clever!

Mechanically, Lessa reached out to scratch the exact spot on the
soft eye ridge.

The dragon blinked at her wistfully, extremely sad that she had
distressed Lessa. Lessa reassuringly patted the slightly damp, soft

neck that curved trustingly toward her. The dragon reeled to one side and one wing fouled on the hind claw. It hurt. Carefully, Lessa lifted the erring foot, freed the wing, folding it back across the dorsal ridge with a pat.

The dragon began to croon in her throat, her eyes following Lessa's every move. She nudged at Lessa and Lessa obediently attended the other eye ridge.

The dragon let it be known she was hungry.

"We'll get you something to eat directly," Lessa assured her briskly and blinked back at the dragon in amazement. How could she be so callous? It was a fact that this little menace had just now seriously injured, if not killed, two women.

She wouldn't have believed her sympathies could swing so alarmingly toward the beast. Yet it was the most natural thing in the world for her to wish to protect this fledgling.

The dragon arched her neck to look Lessa squarely in the eyes. Ramoth repeated wistfully how exceedingly hungry she was, confined so long in that shell without nourishment.

Lessa wondered how she knew the golden dragon's name, and Ramoth replied: Why shouldn't she know her own name since it was hers and no one else's? And then Lessa was lost again in the wonder of those expressive eyes.

Oblivious to the descending bronze dragons, uncaring of the presence of their riders, Lessa stood caressing the head of the most wonderful creature on all Pern, fully prescient of troubles and glories, but most immediately aware that Lessa of Pern was Weyrwoman to Ramoth the Golden, for now and forever.

CODE THREE

Rick Raphael

The late afternoon sun hid behind gray banks of snow clouds and a cold wind whipped loose leaves across the drill field in front of the Philadelphia Barracks of the North American Continental Thruway Patrol. There was the feel of snow in the air but the thermometer hovered just at the freezing mark and the clouds could turn either into icy rain or snow.

Patrol Sergeant Ben Martin stepped out of the door of the barracks and shivered as a blast of wind hit him. He pulled up the zipper on his loose blue uniform coveralls and paused to gauge the storm clouds building up to the west.

The broad planes of his sunburned face turned into the driving cold wind for a moment and then he looked back down at the weather report secured to the top of a stack of papers on his clipboard.

Behind him, the door of the barracks was shouldered open by his junior partner, Patrol Trooper Clay Ferguson. The young, tall Canadian officer's arms were loaded with paper sacks and his patrol work helmet dangled by its strap from the crook of his arm.

Clay turned and moved from the doorway into the wind. A sudden gust swept around the corner of the building and a small sack perched atop one of the larger bags in his arms blew to the ground and began tumbling towards the drill field.

"Ben," he yelled, "grab the bag."

The sergeant lunged as the sack bounced by and made the retrieve. He walked back to Ferguson and eyed the load of bags in the blond-haired officer's arms.

"Just what is all this?" he inquired.

"Groceries," the youngster grinned. "Or to be more exact, little gourmet items for our moments of gracious living."

Ferguson turned into the walk leading to the motor pool and Martin swung into step beside him. "Want me to carry some of that junk?"

"Junk," Clay cried indignantly. "You keep your grimy paws off these delicacies, peasant. You'll get yours in due time and perhaps it will help Kelly and me to make a more polished product of you instead of the clodlike cop you are today."

Martin chuckled. This patrol would mark the start of the second year that he, Clay Ferguson and Medical-Surgical Officer Kelly Lightfoot had been teamed together. After twenty-two patrols, cooped up in a semiarmored vehicle with a man for ten days at a time, you got to know him pretty well. And you either liked him or you hated his guts.

As senior officer, Martin had the right to reject or keep his partner after their first eleven-month duty tour. Martin had elected to retain the lanky Canadian. As soon as they had pulled into New York Barracks at the end of their last patrol, he had made his decisions. After eleven months and twenty-two patrols on the Continental Thruways, each team had a thirty-day furlough coming.

Martin and Ferguson had headed for the city the minute they put their signatures on the last of the stack of reports needed at the end of a tour. Then, for five days and nights, they tied one on. MSO Kelly Lightfoot had made a beeline for a Columbia Medical School seminar on tissue regeneration. On the sixth day, Clay staggered out of bed, swigged down a handful of antireaction pills, showered, shaved and dressed and then waved good-by. Twenty minutes later he was aboard a jet, heading for his parents' home in Edmonton, Alberta. Martin soloed around the city for another week, then rented a car and raced up to his sister's home in Burlington, Vermont, to play Uncle Bountiful to Carol's three kids and to lap up as much as possible of his sister's real cooking.

While the troopers and their med officer relaxed, a service crew moved their car down to the Philadelphia motor pool for a full overhaul and refitting for the next torturous eleven-month-tour of duty.

The two patrol troopers had reported into the Philadelphia Barracks five days ago—Martin several pounds heavier courtesy of his sister's cooking; Ferguson several pounds lighter courtesy of three assorted, starry-eyed, uniform-struck Alberta maidens.

They turned into the gate of the motor pool and nodded to the sentry at the gate. To their left, the vast shop buildings echoed to the sound of body-banging equipment and roaring jet engines. The darkening sky made the brilliant lights of the shop seem even brighter and the hulls of a dozen patrol cars cast deep shadows around the work crews.

The troopers turned into the dispatcher's office and Clay carefully placed the bags on a table beside the counter. Martin peered into one of the bags. "Seriously, kid, what do you have in that grab bag?"

"Oh, just a few essentials," Clay replied. "*Pâté de foie gras*, sharp cheese, a smidgen of cooking wine, a handful of spices. You know, stuff like that. Like I said—essentials."

"Essentials," Martin snorted, "you give your brains to one of those Alberta chicks of yours for a souvenir?"

"Look, Ben," Ferguson said earnestly, "I suffered for eleven months in that tin mausoleum on tracks because of what you fondly like to think is edible food. You've got as much culinary imagination as Beulah. I take that back. Even Beulah turns out some better smells when she's riding on high jet than you'll ever get out of her galley in the next one hundred years. This tour, I intend to eat like a human being once again. And I'll teach you how to boil water without burning it."

"Why you ungrateful young—" Martin yelped.

The patrol dispatcher, who had been listening with amused tolerance, leaned across the counter.

"If Oscar Waldorf is through with his culinary lecture, gentlemen," he said, "perhaps you two could be persuaded to take a little pleasure ride. It's a lovely night for a drive and it's just twenty-six hundred miles to the next service station. If you two aren't cooking anything at the moment, I know that NorCon would simply adore having the services of two such distinguished Continental Commandos.

Ferguson flushed and Martin scowled at the dispatcher. "Very funny, clown. I'll recommend you for trooper status one of these days."

"Not me," the dispatcher protested. "I'm a married man. You'll never get me out on the road in one of those blood-and-gut factories."

"So quit sounding off to us heroes," Martin said, "and give us the clearances."

The dispatcher opened a loose-leaf reference book on the counter and then punched the first of a series of buttons on a panel. Behind him, the wall lighted with a map of the eastern United States to the

Mississippi River. Ferguson and Martin had pencils out and poised over their clipboards.

The dispatcher glanced at the order board across the room where patrol car numbers and team names were displayed on an illuminated board. "Car 56—Martin-Ferguson-Lightfoot," glowed with an amber light. In the column to the right was the number "26–W." The dispatcher punched another button. A broad belt of multi-colored lines representing the eastern segment of North American Thruway 26 flashed onto the map in a band extending from Philadelphia to St. Louis. The thruway went on to Los Angeles in its western segment, not shown on the map. Ten bands of color—each five separated by a narrow clear strip, detailed the thruway. Martin and Ferguson were concerned with the northern five bands; NAT 26-westbound. Other unlighted lines radiated out in tangital spokes to the north and south along the length of the multi-colored belt of NAT 26.

This was just one small segment of the Continental Thruway system that spanned North America from coast to coast and crisscrossed north and south under the Three Nation Road Compact from the southern tip of Mexico into Canada and Alaska.

Each arterial cut a five-mile-wide path across the continent and, from one end to the other, the only structures along the roadways were the turretlike NorCon Patrol check and relay stations—looming up at one-hundred-mile intervals like the fire control islands of earlier-day aircraft carriers.

Car 56 with Trooper Sergeant Ben Martin, Trooper Clay Ferguson and Medical-Surgical Officer Kelly Lightfoot, would take their first ten-day patrol on NAT 26-west. Barring major disaster, they would eat, sleep and work the entire time from their car; out of sight of any but distant cities until they had reached Los Angeles at the end of the patrol. Then a five-day resupply and briefing period and back onto another thruway.

During the coming patrol they would cross ten state lines as if they didn't exist. And as far as thruway traffic control and authority was concerned, state and national boundaries actually didn't exist. With the growth of the old interstate highway system and the Alcan Highway it became increasingly evident that variation in motor vehicle laws from state to state and country to country were creating impossible situations for any uniform safety control.

With the establishment of the Continental Thruway System two decades later, came the birth of the supra-cop—The North American Thruway Patrol, known as NorCon. Within the five-mile bands of the thruways—all federally-owned land by each of the three nations—the blue-coveralled "Continental Commandos" of NorCon were the sole law enforcement agency and authority. Violators of thruway law were cited into NorCon district traffic courts located in the nearest city to each access port along every thruway.

There was no challenge to the authority of NorCon. Public demand for faster and more powerful vehicles had forced the automotive industry to put more and more power under the touch of the ever-growing millions of drivers crowding the continent's roads. Piston drive gave way to turbojet; turbojet was boosted by a modification of ram jet and air-cushion drive was added. In the last two years, the first of the nuclear reaction mass engines had hit the roads. Even as the hot Ferraris and Jags of the mid-'60s would have been suicide vehicles on the T-model roads of the '20s so would today's vehicles be on the interstates of the '60s. But building roads capable of handling three hundred to four hundred miles an hour speeds was beyond the financial and engineering capabilities of individual states and nations. Thus grew the continental thruways with their four speed lanes in each direction, each a half-mile wide separated east and west and north and south by a half-mile-wide landscaped divider. Under the Three Nation Compact, the thruways now wove a net across the entire North American continent.

On the big wall map, NAT 26-west showed as four colored lines; blue and yellow as the two high and ultra-high speed lanes; green and white for the intermediate and slow lanes. Between the blue and yellow and the white and green was a red band. This was the police emergency lane, never used by other than official vehicles and crossed by the traveling public shifting from one speed lane to another only at sweeping cross-overs.

The dispatcher picked up an electric pointer and aimed the light beam at the map. Referring to his notes, he began to recite.

"Resurfacing crews working on 26-W blue at milestone Marker 185 to Marker 187, estimated clearance 0300 hours Tuesday—Let's see, that's tomorrow morning."

The two officers were writing the information down on their trip-analysis sheets.

"Ohio State is playing Cal under the lights at Columbus tonight so you can expect a traffic surge sometime shortly after 2300 hours but most of it will stay in the green and white. Watch out for the drunks though. They might filter out onto the blue or yellow.

"The crossover for NAT 163 has painting crews working. Might watch out for any crud on the roadway. And they've got the entrance blocked there so that all 163 exchange traffic is being re-routed to 164 west of Chillicothe."

The dispatcher thumbed through his reference sheets. "That seems to be about all. No, wait a minute. This is on your trick. The Army's got a priority missile convoy moving out of the Aberdeen Proving Grounds bound for the west coast tonight at 1800 hours. It will be moving at green lane speeds so you might watch out for it. They'll have thirty-four units in the convoy. And that is all. Oh, yes. Kelly's already aboard. I guess you know about the weather.

Martin nodded. "Yup. We should be hitting light snows by 2300 hours tonight in this area and it could be anything from snow to ice-rain after that." He grinned at his younger partner. "The vacation is over, sonny. Tonight we make a man out of you."

Ferguson grinned back. "Nuts to you, pop. I've got character witnesses back in Edmonton who'll give you glowing testimonials about my manhood."

"Testimonials aren't legal unless they're given by adults," Martin retorted. "Come on, lover boy. Duty calls."

Clay carefully embraced his armload of bundles and the two officers turned to leave. The dispatcher leaned across the counter.

"Oh, Ferguson, one thing I forgot. There's some light corrugations in red lane just east of St. Louis. You might be careful with your soufflés in that area. Wouldn't want them to fall, you know."

Clay paused and started to turn back. The grinning dispatcher ducked into the back office and slammed the door.

The wind had died down by the time the troopers entered the brilliantly lighted parking area. The temperature seemed warmer with the lessening winds but in actuality, the mercury was dropping. The snow clouds to the west were much nearer and the overcast was getting darker.

But under the great overhead light tubes, the parking area was brighter than day. A dozen huge patrol vehicles were parked on the front "hot" line. Scores more were lined out in ranks to the back of the parking zone. Martin and Ferguson walked down the line of military blue cars. Number 56 was fifth on the line. Service mechs were just re-housing fueling lines into a ground panel as the troopers walked up. The technician corporal was the first to speak. "All set, Sarge," he said. "We had to change an induction jet at the last minute and I had the port engine running up to reline the flow. Thought I'd better top 'er off for you, though, before you pull out. She sounds like a purring kitten."

He tossed the pair a waving salute and then moved out to his service dolly where three other mechs were waiting.

The officers paused and looked up at the bulk of the huge patrol car.

"Beulah looks like she's been to the beauty shop and had the works," Martin said. He reached out and slapped the maglurium plates. "Welcome home, sweetheart. I see you've kept a candle in the window for your wandering son." Ferguson looked up at the lighted cab, sixteen feet above the pavement.

Car 56—Beulah to her team—was a standard NorCon Patrol vehicle. She was sixty feet long, twelve feet wide and twelve feet high; topped by a four-foot-high bubble canopy over her cab. All the way across her nose was a three-foot-wide luminescent strip. This was the variable beam headlight that could cut a day-bright swath of light through night, fog, rain or snow and could be varied in intensity, width and elevation. Immediately above the headlight strip were two red-black plastic panels which when lighted, sent out a flashing red emergency signal that could be seen for miles. Similar emergency lights and back-up white light strips adorned Beulah's stern. Her bow rounded down like an old-time tank and blended into the track assembly of her dual propulsion system. With the exception of the cabin bubble and a two-foot stepdown on the last fifteen feet of her hull, Beulah was free of external protrusions. Racked into a flush-decked recess on one side of the hull was a crane arm with a two-hundred-ton lift capacity. Several round hatches covered other extensible gear and periscopes used in the scores of multiple operations the NorCon cars were called upon to accomplish on routine road patrols.

Beulah resembled a gigantic off-spring of a military tank, sans heavy armament. But even a small stinger was part of the patrol car equipment. As for armament, Beulah had weapons to meet every conceivable skirmish in the deadly battle to keep Continental Thruways fast-moving and safe. Her own two-hundred-fifty-ton bulk could reach speeds of close to six hundred miles an hour utilizing one or both of her two independent propulsion systems.

At ultra-high speeds, Beulah never touched the ground—floating on an impeller air cushion and driven forward by a pair of one hundred fifty thousand pound thrust jets and ram jets. At intermediate high speeds, both her air cushion and the four-foot-wide tracks on each side of the car pushed her along at two hundred-mile-an-hour-plus speeds. Synchro mechanisms reduced the air cushion as the speeds dropped to afford more surface traction

for the tracks. For slow speeds and heavy duty, the tracks carried the
burden.

Martin thumbed open the portside ground-level cabin door.

"I'll start the outside check," he told Clay. "You stow that garbage
of yours in the galley and start on the dispensary. I'll help you after
I finish out here."

As the younger officer entered the car and headed up the short
flight of steps to the working deck, the sergeant unclipped a check
list from the inside of the door and turned towards the stern of the
big vehicle.

Clay mounted to the work deck and turned back to the little galley
just aft of the cab. As compact as a spaceship kitchen—as a matter of
fact, designed almost identically from models on the Moon run—the
galley had but three feet of open counter space. Everything else,
sink, range, oven and freezer, were built-ins with pull-downs for
use as needed. He set his bags on the small counter to put away
after the pre-start check. Aft of the galley and on the same side of the
passageway were the double-decked bunks for the patrol troopers.
Across the passageway was a tiny latrine and shower. Clay tossed
his helmet on the lower bunk as he went down the passageway.
At the bulk-head to the rear, he pressed a wall panel and a thick,
insulated door slid back to admit him to the engine compartment.
The service crews had shut down the big power plants and turned
off the air exchangers and already the heat from the massive engines
made the compartment uncomfortably warm.

He hurried through into a small machine shop. In an emergency,
the troopers could turn out small parts for disabled vehicles or for
other uses. It also stocked a good supply of the most common failure
parts. Racked against the ceiling were banks of cutting torches, a
grim reminder that death or injury still rode the thruways with
increasing frequency.

In the tank storage space between the ceiling and top of the hull
were the chemical fire-fighting liquids and foam that could be
applied by nozzles, hoses and towers now telescoped into recesses
in the hull. Along both sides and beneath the galley, bunks, engine
and machine-shop compartments between the walls, deck and hull,
were Beulah's fuel storage tanks.

The last after compartment was a complete dispensary, one that
would have made the emergency room or even the light surgery
rooms of earlier-day hospitals proud.

Clay tapped on the door and went through. Medical-Surgical
Officer Kelly Lightfoot was sitting on the deck, stowing sterile

bandage packs into a lower locker. She looked up at Clay and smiled. "Well, well, you DID manage to tear yourself away from your adoring bevies," she said. She flicked back a wisp of golden-red hair from her forehead and stood up. The patrol-blue uniform coverall with its belted waist didn't do much to hide a lovely, properly curved figure. She walked over to the tall Canadian trooper and reached up and grabbed his ear. She pulled his head down, examined one side critically and then quickly snatched at his other ear and repeated the scrutiny. She let go of his ear and stepped back. "Damned if you didn't get all the lipstick marks off, too."

Clay flushed. "Cut it out, Kelly," he said. "Sometimes you act just like my mother."

The olive-complexioned redhead grinned at him and turned back to her stack of boxes on the deck. She bent over and lifted one of the boxes to the operating table. Clay eyed her trim figure. "You might act like ma sometimes," he said, "but you sure don't look like her."

It was the Irish-Cherokee Indian girl's turn to flush. She became very busy with the contents of the box. "Where's Ben?" she asked over her shoulder.

"Making outside check. You about finished in here?"

Kelly turned and slowly scanned the confines of the dispensary. With the exception of the boxes on the table and floor, everything was behind secured locker doors. In one corner, the compact diagnostican—capable of analyzing many known human bodily ailments and every possible violent injury to the body—was locked in its riding clamps. Surgical trays and instrument racks were all hidden behind locker doors along with medical and surgical supplies. On either side of the emergency ramp door at the stern of the vehicle, three collapsible auto-litters hung from clamps. Six hospital bunks in two tiers of three each, lined another wall. On patrol, Kelly utilized one of the hospital bunks for her own use except when they might all be occupied with accident or other kind of patients. And this would never be for more than a short period, just long enough to transfer them to a regular ambulance or hospital vehicle. Her meager supply of personal items needed for the ten-day patrol were stowed in a small locker and she shared the latrine with the male members of the team.

Kelly completed her scan, glanced down at the checklist in her hand. "I'll have these boxes stowed in five minutes. Everything else is secure." She raised her hand to her forehead in mock salute. "Medical-Surgical Officer Lightfoot reports dispensary ready for patrol, sir."

Clay smiled and made a checkmark on his clipboard. "How was the seminar, Kelly?" he asked.

Kelly hiked herself onto the edge of the operating table. "Wonderful, Clay, just wonderful. I never saw so many good-looking, young, rich and eligible doctors together in one place in all my life." She sighed and smiled vacantly into space.

Clay snorted. "I thought you were supposed to be learning something new about tissue regeneration," he said.

"Generation, regeneration, who cares," Kelly grinned.

Clay started to say something, got flustered and wheeled around to leave—and bounded right off Ben Martin's chest. Ferguson mumbled something and pushed past the older officer.

Ben looked after him and then turned back to Car 56's combination doctor, surgeon and nurse. "Glad to see the hostess aboard for this cruise. I hope you make the passengers more comfortable than you've just made the first mate. What did you do to Clay, Kelly?"

"Hi, Ben," Kelly said. "Oh, don't worry about junior. He just gets all fluttery when a girl takes away his masculine prerogative to make cleverly lewd witticisms. He'll be all right. Have a happy holiday, Ben? You look positively fat."

Ben patted his stomach. "Carol's good cooking. Had a nice restful time. And how about you. That couldn't have been all work. You've got a marvelous tan."

"Don't worry," Kelly laughed, "I had no intention of letting it be all study. I spent just about as much time under the sun dome at the pool as I did in class. I learned a lot though."

Ben grinned and headed back to the front of the car. "Tell me more after we're on the road," he said from the doorway. "We'll be rolling in ten minutes."

When he reached the cab, Clay was already in the right-hand control seat and was running down the instrument panel check. The sergeant lifted the hatch door between the two control seats and punched on a light to illuminate the stark compartment at the lower front end of the car. A steel grill with a dogged handle on the upper side covered the opening under the hatch cover. Two swing-down bunks were racked up against the walls on either side and the front hull door was without an inside handle. This was the patrol car brig, used for bringing in unwilling violators or other violent or criminal subjects who might crop up in the course of a patrol tour. Satisfied with the appearance of the brig, Ben closed the hatch cover and slid into his own control seat on the left of the cab. Both control seats were molded and plastiformed padded to the contours of the troopers and the armrests on both were studded with buttons an a series of small, finger-operated knobs. All drive, communication and fire fighting controls for the massive vehicle were centered in the knobs and buttons on the seat arms, while acceleration and braking controls were duplicated in two footrest pedals beneath their feet.

Ben settled into his seat and glanced down to make sure his work-helmet was racked beside him. He reached over and flipped a bank of switches on the instrument panel. "All communications to 'on'," he said. Clay made a checkmark on his list. "All pre-engine start check complete," Clay replied.

"In that case, the senior trooper said, "let's give Beulah some exercise. Start engines."

Clay's fingers danced across the array of buttons on his seat arms and flicked lightly at the throttle knobs. From deep within the engine compartment came the muted, shrill whine of the starter engines, followed a split-second later by the full-throated roar of the jets as they caught fire. Clay eased the throttles back and the engine noise softened to a muffled roar.

Martin fingered a press-panel on the right arm of his seat.

"Car 56 to Philly Control," Ben called.

The speakers mounted around the cab came to life. "Go ahead Five Six."

"Five Six fired up and ready to roll," Martin said.

"Affirmative Five Six," came the reply, "You're clear to roll. Philly Check estimates white density 300; green, 840; blue 400; yellow, 75."

Both troopers made mental note of the traffic densities in their first one-hundred-mile patrol segment; an estimated three hundred vehicles for each ten miles of thruway in the white or fifty to one hundred miles an hour low lane; eight hundred forty vehicles in the one hundred to one hundred fifty miles an hour green, and so on. More than sixteen thousand westbound vehicles on the thruway in the first one hundred miles; nearly five thousand of them traveling at speeds between one hundred fifty and three hundred miles an hour.

Over the always-hot intercom throughout the big car Ben called out. "All set, Kelly?"

"I'm making coffee," Kelly answered from the galley. "Let 'er roll."

Martin started to kick off the brakes, then stopped. "Ooops," he exclaimed, "almost forgot." His finger touched another button and a blaring horn reverberated through the vehicle.

In the galley, Kelly hurled herself into a corner. Her body activated a pressure plant and a pair of mummy-like plastifoam plates slid curvingly out the wall and locked her in a soft cocoon.

A dozen similar safety clamps were located throughout the car at
every working and relaxation station.

In the same instant, both Ben and Clay touched another plate
on their control seats. From kiosk-type columns behind each seat,
pairs of body-molded crash pads snapped into place to encase both
troopers in their seats, their bodies cushioned and locked into place.
Only their fingers were loose beneath the spongy substance to work
arm controls. The half-molds included headforms with a padded
band that locked across their foreheads to hold their heads rigidly
against the backs of their reinforced seats. The instant all three crew
members were locked into their safety gear, the bull horn ceased.

"All tight," Ben called out as he wiggled and tried to free himself
from the cocoon. Kelly and Clay tested their harnesses.

Satisfied that the safety cocoons were operating properly, Ben
released them and the molds slid back into their recesses. The
cocoons were triggered automatically in any emergency run or chase
at speeds in excess of two hundred miles an hour.

Again he kicked off the brakes, pressed down on the foot feed and
Car 56—Beulah—rolled out of the Philadelphia motor pool on the
start of its ten-day patrol.

The motor pool exit opened into a quarter-mile wide tunnel
sloping gently down into the bowels of the great city. Car 56 glided
down the slight incline at a steady fifty miles an hour. A mile from
the mouth of the tunnel the roadway leveled off and Ben kicked
Beulah up another twenty-five miles an hour. Ahead, the main
tunnel ended in a series of smaller portal ways, each emblazoned
with a huge illuminated number designating a continental thruway.

Ben throttled back and began edging to the left lanes. Other
patrol cars were heading down the main passageway, bound for
their assigned thruways. As Ben eased down to a slow thirty,
another patrol vehicle slid alongside. The two troopers in the cab
waved. Clay flicked on the "car-to-car" transmit.

The senior trooper in Car 104 looked over at Martin and
Ferguson. "If it isn't the gruesome twosome," he called. "Where
have you two been? We thought the front office had finally caught
up with you and found out that neither one of you could read or write
and that they had canned you."

"We can't read," Ben quipped back. "That's why we're still on
the job. The front office would never hire anyone who would
embarrass you two by being smarter than either of you. Where're
you headed, Eddie?"

"Got 154-north," the other officer said.

"Hey," Clay called out, "I've got a real hot doll in Toronto and I'll gladly sell her phone number for a proper price."

"Wouldn't want to hurt you, Clay," the other officer replied. "If I called her up and took her out, she'd throw rocks at you the next time you drew the run. It's all for your own good."

"Oh, go get lost in a cloverleaf," Clay retorted.

The other car broke the connection and with a wave, veered off to the right. The thruway entrances were just ahead. Martin aimed Beulah at the lighted orifice topped by the number 26-W. The patrol car slid into the narrower tunnel, glided along for another mile and then turned its bow upwards. Three minutes later, they emerged from the tunnel into the red patrol lane of Continental Thruway 26-West. The late afternoon sky was a covering of gray wool and a drop or two of moisture struck the front face of the cab canopy. For a mile on either side of the police lane, streams of cars sped westward. Ben eyed the sky, the traffic and then peered at the outer hull thermometer. It read thirty-two degrees. He made a mental bet with himself that the weather bureau was off on its snow estimates by six hours. His Vermont upbringing told him it would be flurrying within the hour.

He increased speed to a steady one hundred and the car sped silently and easily along the police lane. Across the cab, Clay peered pensively at the steady stream of cars and cargo carriers racing by in the green and blue lanes—all of them moving faster than the patrol car.

The young officer turned in his seat and looked at his partner.

"You know, Ben," he said gravely, "I sometimes wonder if those oldtime cowboys got as tired looking at the south end of northbound cows as I get looking at the vanishing tail pipes of cars."

The radio came to life.

"Philly Control to Car 56."

Clay touched his transmit plate. "This is Five Six. Go ahead."

"You've got a bad one at Marker 82," Control said. "A sideswipe in the white."

"Couldn't be too bad in the white," Ben broke in, thinking of the one-hundred mile-an-hour limit in the slow lane.

"That's not the problem," Control came back. "One of the sideswiped vehicles was flipped around and bounded into the green, and that's where the real mess is. Make it code three."

"Five Six acknowledge," Ben said. "On the way."

He slammed forward on the throttles. The bull horn blared and a second later, with MSO Kelly Lightfoot snugged in her dispensary cocoon and both troopers in body cushions, Car 56 lifted a foot from the road-way, and leaped forward on a turbulent pad of air. It accelerated from one hundred to two hundred fifty miles an hour.

The great red emergency lights on the bow and stern began to blink and from the special transmitter in the hull a radio siren wail raced ahead of the car to be picked up by the emergency receptor antennas required on all vehicles.

The working part of the patrol had begun.

Conversation died in the speeding car, partly because of the concentration required by the troopers, secondly because all transmissions whether intercom or radio, on a code two or three run, were taped and monitored by Control. In the center of the instrument panel, an oversized radio-dometer was clicking off the mileage marks as the car passed each milestone. The milestone posts beamed a coded signal across all five lanes and as each vehicle passed the marker, the radiodometer clicked up another number.

Car 56 had been at MM 23 when the call came. Now, at better than four miles a minute, Beulah whipped past MM 45 with ten minutes yet to go to reach the scene of the accident. Light flurries of wet snow bounced off the canopy, leaving thin, fast-drying trails of moisture. Although it was still a few minutes short of 1700 hours, the last of the winter afternoon light was being lost behind the heavy snow clouds overhead. Ben turned on the patrol car's dazzling headlight and to the left and right, Clay could see streaks of white lights from the traffic on the green and blue lanes on either side of the quarter-mile wide emergency lane.

The radio filled them in on the movement of other patrol emergency vehicles being routed to the accident site. Car 82, also assigned to NAT 26-West, was more than one hundred fifty miles ahead of Beulah. Pittsburgh Control ordered Eight Two to hold fast to cover anything else that might come up while Five Six was handling the current crisis. East-bound Car 119 was ordered to cut across to the scene to assist Beulah's crew, and another eastbound patrol vehicle was held in place to cover for One One Nine.

At mile marker 80, yellow caution lights were flashing on all westbound lanes, triggered by Philadelphia Control the instant the word of the crash had been received. Traffic was slowing down and piling up despite the half-mile wide lanes.

"Philly Control this is Car 56."

"Go ahead Five Six."

"It's piling up in the green and white," Ben said. "Let's divert to blue on slowdown and seal the yellow."

"Philly Control acknowledged," came the reply.

The flashing amber caution lights on all lanes switched to red. As Ben began de-acceleration, diagonal red flashing barriers rose out of the roadway on the green and white lanes at the 85 mile marker and lane crossing. This channelled all traffic from both lanes to the left and into the blue lane where the flashing reds now prohibited speeds in excess of fifty miles an hour around the emergency situation. At the same time, all crossovers on the ultra high yellow lane were sealed by barriers to prevent changing of lanes into the over-congested area.

As Car 56's speed dropped back below the two hundred mile an hour mark the cocoon automatically slid open. Freed from her safety restraints, Kelly jumped for the rear entrance of the dispensary and cleared the racking clamps from the six autolitters. That done, she opened another locker and reached for the mobile first-aid kit. She slid it to the door entrance on its retractable casters. She slipped on her work helmet with the built-in transmitter and then sat down on the seat by the rear door to wait until the car stopped.

Car 56 was now less than two miles from the scene of the crash and traffic in the green lane to the left was at a standstill. A half mile farther westward, lights were still moving slowly along the white lane. Ahead, the troopers could see a faint wisp of smoke rising from the heaviest congregation of headlights. Both officers had their work helmets on and Clay had left his seat and descended to the side door, ready to jump out the minute the car stopped.

Martin saw a clear area in the green lane and swung the car over the dividing curbing. The big tracks floated the patrol car over the two-foot high, rounded abutment that divided each speed lane. Snow was falling faster as the headlight picked out a tangled mass of wreckage smoldering a hundred feet inside the median separating the green and white lanes. A crumpled body lay on the pavement twenty feet from the biggest clump of smashed metal, and other fragments of vehicles were strung out down the roadway for fifty feet. There was no movement.

NorCon thruway laws were strict and none were more rigidly enforced than the regulation that no one other than a member of the patrol set foot outside of their vehicle while on any thruway traffic lane. This meant not giving any assistance whatsoever to accident victims. The ruling had been called inhuman, monstrous, unthinkable, and lawmakers in the three nations of the compact had forced NorCon to revoke the rule in the early days of the thruways. After speeding cars and cargo carriers had cut down twice as many do-gooders on foot at accident scenes than the accidents themselves caused, the law was reinstated. The lives of the many were more vital than the lives of a few.

Martin halted the patrol vehicle a few feet from the wreckage and Beulah was still rocking gently on her tracks by the time both Patrol Trooper Clay Ferguson and MSO Kelly Lightfoot hit the pavement on the run.

In the cab, Martin called in on the radio. "Car 56 is on scene. Release blue at Marker 95 and resume speeds all lanes at Marker 95 in—" he paused and looked back at the halted traffic piled up before the lane had been closed "—seven minutes." He jumped for the steps and sprinted out of the patrol car in the wake of Ferguson and Kelly.

The team's surgeon was kneeling beside the inert body on the road. After an ear to the chest, Kelly opened her field kit bag and slapped an electrode to the victim's temple. The needle on the encephalic meter in the lid of the kit never flickered. Kelly shut the bag and hurried with it over to the mass of wreckage. A thin column of black, oily smoke rose from somewhere near the bottom of the heap. It was almost impossible to identify at a glance whether the mangled metal was the remains of one or more cars. Only the absence of track equipment made it certain that they even had been passenger vehicles.

Clay was carefully climbing up the side of the piled up wrecks to a window that gaped near the top.

"Work fast, kid," Martin called up. "Something's burning down there and this whole thing may go up. I'll get this traffic moving."

He turned to face the halted mass of cars and cargo carriers east of the wreck. He flipped a switch that cut his helmet transmitter into the remote standard vehicular radio circuit aboard the patrol car.

"Attention, please, all cars in green lane. All cars in the left line move out now, the next line fall in behind. You are directed to clear the area immediately. Maintain fifty miles an hour for the next mile. You may resume desired speeds and change lanes at mile Marker 95. I repeat, all cars in green lane . . ." he went over the instructions once more, relayed through Beulah's transmitter to the standard receivers on all cars. He was still talking as the traffic began to move.

By the time he turned back to help his teammates, cars were moving in a steady stream past the huge, red-flashing bulk of the patrol car.

Both Clay and Kelly were lying flat across the smashed, upturned side of the uppermost car in the pile. Kelly had her field bag open on the ground and she was reaching down through the smashed window.

"What is it Clay?" Martin called.

The younger officer looked down over his shoulder. "We've got a woman alive down here but she's wedged in tight. She's hurt pretty badly and Kelly's trying to slip a hypo into her now. Get the arm out, Ben."

Martin ran back to the patrol car and flipped up a panel on the hull. He pulled back on one of the several levers recessed into the hull and the big wrecking crane swung smoothly out of its cradle and over the wreckage. The end of the crane arm was directly over Ferguson. "Lemme have the spreaders," Clay called. The arm dipped and from either side of the tip, a pair of flanges shot out like tusks on an elephant. "Put 'er in neutral," Clay directed. Martin pressed another lever and the crane now could be moved in any direction by fingertip pulls at its extremity. Ferguson carefully guided the crane with its projecting tusks into the smashed orifice of the car window. "O.K., Ben, spread it."

The crane locked into position and the entire arm split open in a "V" from its base. Martin pressed steadily on the two levers controlling each side of the divided arm and the tusks dug into the sides of the smashed window. There was a steady screeching of tearing and ripping metal as the crane tore window and frame apart. "Hold it," Ferguson yelled and then eased himself into the widened hole.

"Ben," Kelly called from her perch atop the wreckage, "litter."

Martin raced to the rear of the patrol car where the sloping ramp stood open to the lighted dispensary. He snatched at one of the autolitters and triggered its tiny drive motor. A homing beacon in his helmet guided the litter as it rolled down the ramp, turned by itself and rolled across the pavement a foot behind him. It stopped when he stopped and Ben touched another switch, cutting the homing beacon.

Clay's head appeared out of the hole. "Get it up here, Ben. I can get her out. And I think there's another one alive still further down."

Martin raised the crane and its ripper bars retracted. The split arms spewed a pair of cables terminating in magnalocks. The cables dangled over the ends of the autolitter, caught the lift plates on the litter and a second later, the cart was swinging beside the smashed window as Clay and Kelly eased the torn body of a woman out of the wreckage and onto the litter. As Ben brought the litter back to the pavement, the column of smoke had thickened. He disconnected the cables and homed the stretcher back to the patrol car. The hospital cart with its unconscious victim, rolled smoothly back to the car, up the ramp and into the dispensary to the surgical table.

Martin climbed up the wreckage beside Kelly. Inside the twisted interior of the car, the thick smoke all but obscured the bent back of the younger trooper and his powerful handlight barely penetrated the gloom. Blood was smeared over almost every surface and the stink of leaking jet fuel was virtually over-powering. From the depths of the nightmarish scene came a tortured scream. Kelly reached into a coverall pocket and produced another sedation hypo. She squirmed around and started to slip down into the wreckage with Ferguson. Martin grabbed her arm. "No, Kelly, this thing's ready to blow. Come on, Clay, get out of there. Now!"

Ferguson continued to pry at the twisted plates below him.

"I said 'get out of there' Ferguson," the senior officer roared. "And that's an order."

Clay straightened up and put his hands on the edge of the window to boost himself out. "Ben, there's a guy alive down there. We just can't leave him."

"Get down from there, Kelly," Martin ordered. "I know that man's down there just as well as you do, Clay. But we won't be helping him one damn bit if we get blown to hell and gone right along with him. Now get outta there and maybe we can pull this thing apart and get to him before it does blow."

The lanky Canadian eased out of the window and the two troopers moved back to the patrol car. Kelly was already in her dispensary, working on the injured woman.

Martin slid into his control seat. "Shut your ramp, Kelly," he called over the intercom, "I'm going to move around to the other side."

The radio broke in. "Car 119 to Car 56, we're just turning into the divider. Be there in a minute."

"Snap it up," Ben replied. "We need you in a hurry."

As he maneuvered Beulah around the wreckage he snapped orders to Ferguson.

"Get the foam nozzles up, just in case, and then stand by on the crane."

A mile away, they saw the flashing emergency lights of Car 119 as it raced diagonally across the yellow and blue lanes, whipping with ponderous ease through the moving traffic.

"Take the south side, 119," Martin called out. "We'll try and pull this mess apart."

"Affirmative," came the reply. Even before the other patrol vehicle came to a halt, its crane was swinging out from the side, and the ganged magnalocks were dangling from their cables.

"O.K., kid," Ben ordered, "hook it."

At the interior crane controls, Clay swung Beulah's crane and cable mags towards the wreckage. The magnalocks slammed into the metallic mess with a bang almost at the same instant the locks hit the other side from Car 119.

Clay eased up the cable slack. "Good," Ben called to both Clay and the operating trooper in the other car, "now let's pull it . . . LOOK OUT! FOAM . . . FOAM . . . FOAM," he yelled.

The ugly, deep red fireball from the exploding wreckage was still growing as Clay slammed down on the fire-control panel. A curtain of thick chemical foam burst from the poised nozzles atop Beulah's hull and a split-second later, another stream of foam erupted from the other patrol car. The dense, oxygen-absorbing retardant blanket snuffed the fire out in three seconds. The cranes were still secured to the foam-covered heap of metal. "Never mind the caution," Ben called out, "get it apart. Fast."

Both crane operators slammed their controls into reverse and with an ear-splitting screech, the twisted frames of the two vehicles ripped apart into tumbled heaps of broken metal and plastics. Martin and Ferguson jumped down the hatch steps and into ankle-deep foam and oil. They waded and slipped around the front of the car to join the troopers from the other car.

Ferguson was pawing at the scum-covered foam near the mangled section of one of the cars. "He should be right about," Clay paused and bent over, "here." He straightened up as the others gathered around the scorched and ripped body of a man, half-submerged in the thick foam. "Kelly," he called over the helmet transmitter, "open your door. We'll need a couple of sacks."

He trudged to the rear of the patrol car and met the girl standing in the door with a pair of folded plastic morgue bags in her hands. Behind her, Clay could see the body of the woman on the surgical table, an array of tubes and probes leading to plasma drip bottles and other equipment racked out over the table.

"How is she?"

"Not good," Kelly replied. "Skull fracture, ruptured spleen, broken ribs and double leg fractures. I've already called for an ambulance."

Ferguson nodded, took the bags from her and waded back through the foam.

The four troopers worked in the silence of the deserted traffic lane. A hundred yards away, traffic was moving steadily in the slow white lane. Three-quarters of a mile to the south, fast and ultra high traffic sped at its normal pace in the blue and yellow lanes. Westbound green was still being rerouted into the slower white lane, around the scene of the accident. It was now twenty-six minutes since Car 56 had received the accident call. The light snow flurries had turned to a steady fall of thick wet flakes, melting as they hit on the warm pavement but beginning to coat the pitiful flotsam of the accident.

The troopers finished the gruesome task of getting the bodies into the morgue sacks and laid beside the dispensary ramp for the ambulance to pick up with the surviving victim. Car 119's MSO had joined Kelly in Beulah's dispensary to give what help she might. The four patrol troopers began the grim task of probing the scattered wreckage for other possible victims, personal possessions and identification. They were stacking a small pile of hand luggage when the long, low bulk of the ambulance swung out of the police lane and rolled to a stop. Longer than the patrol cars but without the non-medical emergency facilities, the ambulance was in reality a mobile hospital. A full, scrubbed-up surgical team was waiting in the main operating room even as the ramps opened and the techs headed for Car 56. The team had been briefed by radio on the condition of the patient; had read the full recordings of the diagnostican; and were watching transmitted pulse and respiration graphs on their own screens while the transfer was being made.

The two women MSOs had unlocked the surgical table in Beulah's dispensary and a plastic tent covered not only the table and the patient, but also the plasma and Regen racks overhead. The entire table and rig slid down the ramp onto a motor-driven dolly from the ambulance. Without delay, it wheeled across the open few feet of pavement into the ambulance and to the surgery room. The techs locked the table into place in the other vehicle and left the surgery. From a storage compartment, they wheeled out a fresh patrol dispensary table and rack and placed it in Kelly's miniature surgery. The dead went into the morgue aboard the ambulance, the ramp closed and the ambulance swung around and headed across the traffic lanes to eastbound NAT-26 and Philadelphia.

Outside, the four troopers had completed the task of collecting what little information they could from the smashed vehicles.

They returned to their cars and One One Nine's medical-surgical officer headed back to her own cubby-hole.

The other patrol car swung into position almost touching Beulah's left flank. With Ben at the control seat, on command, both cars extended broad bulldozer blades from their bows. "Let's go," Ben ordered. The two patrol vehicles moved slowly down the roadway, pushing all of the scattered scraps and parts onto a single great heap. They backed off, shifted direction towards the center police lane and began shoving the debris, foam and snow out of the green lane. At the edge of the police lane, both cars unshipped cranes and magnalifted the junk over the divider barrier onto the one-hundred-foot-wide service strip bordering the police lane. A slow cargo wrecker was already on the way from Pittsburgh barracks to pick up the wreckage and haul it away. When the last of the metallic debris had been deposited off the traffic lane, Martin called Control.

"Car 56 is clear. NAT 26-west green is clear."

Philly Control acknowledged. Seven miles to the east, the amber warning lights went dark and the detour barrier at Crossover 85 sank back into the roadway. Three minutes later, traffic was again flashing by on green lane past the two halted patrol cars.

"Pitt Control, this is Car 119 clear of accident," the other car reported.

"Car 119 resume eastbound patrol," came the reply.

The other patrol car pulled away. The two troopers waved at Martin and Ferguson in Beulah. "See you later and thanks," Ben called out. He switched to intercom. "Kelly. Any ID on that woman?"

"Not a thing, Ben," she replied. "About forty years old, and she had a wedding band. She never was conscious, so I can't help you."

Ben nodded and looked over at his partner. "Go get into some dry clothes, kid," he said, "while I finish the report. Then you can take it for a while."

Clay nodded and headed back to the crew quarters.

Ben racked his helmet beside his seat and fished out a cigarette. He reached for an accident report form from the work rack behind his seat and began writing, glancing up from time to time to gaze thoughtfully at the scene of the accident. When he had finished, he thumbed the radio transmitter and called Philly Control. Somewhere in the bloody, oil and foam covered pile of wreckage were the registration plates for the two vehicles involved. When the wrecker collected the debris, it would be machine sifted in Pittsburgh and the plates fed to records and then relayed to Philadelphia where the identifications could be added to Ben's report. When he had finished reading his report he asked, "How's the woman?"

"Still alive, but just barely," Philly Control answered. "Ben, did you say there were just two vehicles involved?"

"That's all we found," Martin replied.

"And were they both in the green?"

"Yes, why?"

"That's funny," Philly controller replied, "we got the calls as a sideswipe in white that put one of the cars over into the green. There should have been a third vehicle."

"That's right," Ben exclaimed. "We were so busy trying to get that gal out and then making the try for the other man I never even thought to look for another car. You suppose that guy took off?"

"It's possible," the controller said. "I'm calling a gate filter until we know for sure. I've got the car number on the driver that reported the accident. I'll get hold of him and see if he can give us a lead on the third car. You go ahead with your patrol and I'll let you know what I find out."

"Affirmative," Ben replied. He eased the patrol car onto the police lane and turned west once again. Clay reappeared in the cab, dressed in fresh coveralls. "I'll take it, Ben. You go and clean up now. Kelly's got a pot of fresh coffee in the galley." Ferguson slid into his control seat.

A light skiff of snow covered the service strip and the dividers as Car 56 swung back westward in the red lane. Snow was falling steadily but melting as it touched the warm ferrophalt pavement in all lanes. The wet roadways glistened with the lights of hundreds of vehicles. The chronometer read 1840 hours. Clay pushed the car up to a steady 75, just about apace with the slowest traffic in the white lane. To the south, densities were much lighter in the blue and yellow lanes and even the green had thinned out. It would stay moderately light now for another hour until the dinner stops were over and the night travelers again rolled onto the thruways.

Kelly was putting frozen steaks into the infra-oven as Ben walked through to crew quarters. Her coverall sleeves were rolled to the elbows as she worked and a vagrant strand of copper hair curled over her forehead. As Martin passed by, he caught a faint whisper of perfume and he smiled appreciatively.

In the tiny crew quarters, he shut the door to the galley and stripped out of his wet coveralls and boots. He eyed the shower stall across the passageway.

"Hey, mother," he yelled to Kelly, "have I got time for a shower before dinner?"

"Yes, but make it a quickie," she called back.

Five minutes later he stepped into the galley, his dark, crew-cut hair still damp. Kelly was setting plastic, disposable dishes on the little swing-down table that doubled as a food bar and work desk. Ben peered into a simmering pot and sniffed. "Smells good. What's for dinner, Hiawatha?"

"Nothing fancy. Steak, potatoes, green beans, apple pie and coffee."

Ben's mouth watered. "You know, sometimes I wonder whether one of your ancestors didn't come out of New England. Your menus always seem to coincide with my ideas of a perfect meal." He noted the two places set at the table. Ben glanced out the galley port into the headlight-triped darkness. Traffic was still light. In the distance, the night sky glowed with the lights of Chambersburg, north of the thruway.

"We might as well pull up for dinner," he said. "It's pretty slow out there."

Kelly shoved dishes over and began laying out a third setting. About half the time on patrol, the crew ate in shifts on the go, with one of the patrol troopers in the cab at all times. When traffic permitted, they pulled off to the service strip and ate together. With the communications system always in service, control stations could reach them anywhere in the big vehicle.

The sergeant stepped into the cab and tapped Ferguson on the shoulder. "Dinnertime, Clay. Pull her over and we'll try some of your gracious living."

"Light the candles and pour the wine," Clay quipped, "I'll be with you in a second."

Car 56 swung out to the edge of the police lane and slowed down. Clay eased the car onto the strip and stopped. He checked the radiodometer and called in. "Pitt Control, this is Car 56 at Marker 158. Dinner is being served in the dining car to the rear. Please do not disturb."

"Affirmative, Car 56," Pittsburgh Control responded. "Eat heartily, it may be going out of style." Clay grinned and flipped the radio to remote and headed for the galley.

Seated around the little table, the trio cut into their steaks. Parked at the north edge of the police lane, the patrol car was just a few feet from the green lane divider strip and cars and cargo carriers flashed by as they ate.

Clay chewed on a sliver of steak and looked at Kelly. "I'd marry you, Pocahontas, if you'd ever learn to cook steaks like beef instead of curing them like your ancestral buffalo robes.

When are you going to learn that good beef has to be bloody to be edible?"

The girl glared at him. "If that's what it takes to make it edible, you're going to be an epicurean delight in just about one second if I hear another word about my cooking. And that's also the second crack about my noble ancestors in the past five minutes. I've always wondered about the surgical techniques my great-great-great grandpop used when he lifted a paleface's hair. One more word, Clay Ferguson, and I'll have your scalp flying from Beulah's antenna like a coontail on a kid's scooter."

Ben bellowed and nearly choked. "Hey, kid," he spluttered at Clay, "ever notice how the wrong one of her ancestors keeps coming to the surface? That was the Irish."

Clay polished off the last of his steak and reached for the individual frozen pies Kelly had put in the oven with the steaks. "Now that's another point," he said, waving his fork at Kelly. "The Irish lived so long on potatoes and prayers that when they get a piece of meat on their menu, they don't know how to do anything but boil it."

"That tears it," the girl exploded. She pushed back from the table and stood up. "I've cooked the last meal this big, dumb Canuck will ever get from me. I hope you get chronic indigestion and then come crawling to me for help. I've got something back there I've been wanting to dose you with for a long time."

She stormed out of the galley and slammed the door behind her. Ben grinned at the stunned look on Clay's face. "Now what got her on the warpath?" Clay asked. Before Ben could answer the radio speaker in the ceiling came to life.

"Car 56 this is Pitt Control."

Martin reached for the transmit switch beside the galley table. "This is Five Six, go ahead."

"Relay from Philly Control," the speaker blared. "Reference the accident at Marker 92 at 1648 hours this date; Philly Control reports a third vehicle definitely involved."

Ben pulled out a pencil and Clay shoved a message pad across the table.

"James J. Newhall, address 3409 Glen Cove Drive, New York City, license number BHT 4591 dash 747 dash 1609, was witness to the initial impact. He reports that a white over green, late model Travelaire, with two men in it, sideswiped one of the two vehicles involved in the fatal accident. The Travelaire did not stop but accelerated after the impact. Newhall was unable to get the full license number but the first six units were QABR dash 46 . . . rest of numerals unknown."

Ben cut in. "Have we got identification on our fatalities yet?"

"Affirmative, Five Six," the radio replied. "The driver of the car struck by the hit-and-run vehicle was a Herman Lawrence Hanover, age forty-two, of 13460 One Hundred Eighty-First Street South, Camden, New Jersey, license number LFM 4151 dash 603 dash 2738. With him was his wife, Clara, age forty-one, same address. Driver of the green lane car was George R. Hamilton, age thirty-five, address Box 493, Route 12, Tucumcari, New Mexico."

Ben broke in once more. "You indicate all three are fatalities. Is this correct, Pitt Control? The woman was alive when she was transferred to the ambulance."

"Stand by, Five Six, and I'll check."

A moment later Pitt Control was back. "That is affirmative, Five Six. The woman died at 1745 hours. Here is additional information. A vehicle answering to the general description of the hit-and-run vehicle is believed to have been involved in an armed robbery and multiple murder earlier this date at Wilmington, Delaware. Philly Control is now checking for additional details. Gate filters have been established on NAT 26-West from Marker-Exit 100 to Marker-Exit 700. Also, filters on all interchanges. Pitt Control out."

Kelly Lightfoot, her not-too-serious peeve forgotten, had come back into the galley to listen to the radio exchange. The men got up from the table and Clay gathered the disposable dishware and tossed them into the waste receiver.

"We'd better get rolling," Ben said, "those clowns could still be on the thruway, although they could have got off before the filters went up."

They moved to the cab and took their places. The big engines roared into action as Ben rolled Car 56 back onto the policeway. Kelly finished straightening up in the galley and then came forward to sit on the jump seat between the two troopers. The snow had stopped again but the roadways were still slick and glistening under the headlights. Beulah rolled steadily along on her broad tracks, now cruising at one hundred miles an hour. The steady whine of the cold night wind penetrated faintly into the sound-proofed and insulated cabin canopy. Clay cut out the cabin lights, leaving only the instrument panel glowing faintly along with the phosphorescent buttons and knobs on the arms of the control seats.

A heavy express cargo carrier flashed by a quarter of a mile away in the blue lane, its big bulk lit up like a Christmas tree with running and warning lights. To their right Clay caught the first glimpse of a set of flashing amber warning lights coming up from behind in the green lane. A minute later, a huge cargo carrier came abreast of the patrol car and then pulled ahead. On its side was a glowing star of the United States Army. A minute later, another Army carrier rolled by.

"That's the missile convoy out of Aberdeen," Clay told Kelly. "I wish our hit-runner had tackled one of those babies. We'd have scraped him up instead of those other people."

The convoy rolled on past at a steady one hundred twenty-five miles an hour. Car 56 flashed under a crossover and into a long, gentle curve. The chronometer clicked up to 2100 hours and the radio sang out. "Cars 207, 56 and 82, this is Pitt Control. 2100 hours density report follows . . ."

Pittsburgh Control read off the figures for the three cars. Car 82 was one hundred fifty miles ahead of Beulah, Car 207 about the same distance to the rear. The density report ended and a new voice came on the air.

"Attention all cars and all stations, this is Washington Criminal Control." The new voice paused, and across the continent, troopers on every thruway, control station, check-point and relay block, reached for clipboard and pen.

"Washington Criminal Control continuing, all cars and all stations, special attention to all units east of the Mississippi. At 1510 hours this date, two men held up the First National Bank of Wilmington, Delaware, and escaped with an estimated one hundred seventy-five thousand dollars. A bank guard and two tellers, together with five bank customers were killed by these subjects using automatic weapon fire to make good their escape. They were observed leaving the scene in a late model, white-over-green Travelaire sedan, license unknown. A car of the same make, model and color was stolen from Annapolis, Maryland, a short time prior to the holdup. The stolen vehicle, now believed to be the getaway car, bears USN license number QABR dash 468 dash 1113 . . ."

"That's our baby," Ben murmured as he and Clay scribbled on their message forms.

". . . Motor number ZB 1069432," Washington Criminal Control continued. "This car is also now believed to have been involved in a hit-and-run fatal accident on NAT 26-West at Marker 92 at approximately 1648 hours this date.

"Subject Number One is described as WMA, twenty to twenty-five years, five feet eleven inches tall, medium complexion, dark hair and eyes, wearing a dark-gray sports jacket and dark pants, and wearing a gray sports cap. He was wearing a ring with a large red stone on his left hand.

"Subject Number Two is described as WMA, twenty to twenty-five years, six feet, light, ruddy complexion and reddish brown hair, light colored eyes. Has scar on back left side of neck. Wearing light-brown suit, green shirt and dark tie, no hat.

"These subjects are believed to be armed and psychotically dangerous. If observed, approach with extreme caution and inform nearest control of contact. Both subjects now under multiple federal warrants charging bank robbery, murder and hit-and-run murder. All cars and stations acknowledge. Washington Criminal Control out."

The air chattered as the cars checked into their nearest controls with "acknowledged."

"This looks like it could be a long night," Kelly said, rising to her feet. "I'm going to sack out. Call me if you need me."

"Good night, princess," Ben called.

"Hey, Hiawatha," Clay called out as Kelly paused in the galley door. "I didn't mean what I said about your steaks. Your great-great-great grandpop would have gone around with his bare scalp hanging out if he had had to use a buffalo hide cured like that steak was cooked."

He reached back at the same instant and slammed the cabin door just as Kelly came charging back. She slammed into the door, screamed and then went storming back to the dispensary while Clay doubled over in laughter.

Ben smiled at his junior partner. "Boy, you're gonna regret that. Don't say I didn't warn you."

Martin turned control over to the younger trooper and relaxed in his seat to go over the APB from Washington. Car 56 bored steadily through the night. The thruway climbed easily up the slight grade cut through the hills north of Wheeling, West Virginia, and once more snow began falling.

Clay reached over and flipped on the video scanners. Four small screens, one for each of the westbound lanes, glowed with a soft red light. The monitors were synchronized with the radiometer and changed view at every ten-mile marker. Viewing cameras mounted on towers between each lane, lined the thruway, aimed eastward at the on-coming traffic back to the next bank of cameras ten miles away. Infra-red circuits took over from standard scan at dark. A selector system in the cars gave the troopers the option of viewing either the block they were currently patroling; the one ahead of the next ten-mile block; or, the one they had just passed. As a rule, the selection was based on the speed of the car. Beamed signals from

each block automatically switched the view as the patrol car went
past the towers. Clay put the slower lane screens on the block they
were in, turned the blue and yellow lanes to the block ahead.

They rolled past the interchange with NAT 114-South out of
Cleveland and the traffic densities picked up in all lanes as many
of the southbound vehicles turned west on to NAT 26. The screens
flicked and Clay came alert. Some fifteen miles ahead in the one-
hundred-fifty-to-two-hundred-mile an hour blue lane, a glowing dot
remained motionless in the middle of the lane and the other racing
lights of the blue lane traffic were sheering around it like a racing
river current parting around a boulder.

"Trouble," he said to Martin, as he shoved forward on the
throttle.

A stalled car in the middle of the highspeed lane was an invitation
to disaster. The bull horn blared as Beulah leaped past the two
hundred mile an hour mark and safety cocoons slid into place. Aft
in the dispensary, Kelly was sealed into her bunk by a cocoon rolling
out of the wall and encasing the hospital bed.

Car 5 slanted across the police lane with red lights flashing and
edged into the traffic flow in the blue lane. The great, red winking
lights and the emergency radio siren signal began clearing a path
for the troopers. Vehicles began edging to both sides of the lane
to shift to crossovers to the yellow or green lanes. Clay aimed
Beulah at the motionless dot on the screen and eased back from the
four-mile-a-minute speed. The patrol car slowed and the headlight
picked up the stalled vehicle a mile ahead. The cocoons opened and
Ben slipped on his work helmet and dropped down the steps to the
side hatch. Clay brought Beulah to a halt a dozen yards directly to
the rear of the stalled car, the great bulk of the patrol vehicle with its
warning lights serving as a shield against any possible fuzzy-headed
speeders that might not be oberving the road.

As Martin reached for the door, the Wanted bulletin flashed
through his head. "What make of car is that, Clay?"

"Old jalopy Tritan with some souped-up rigs. Probably kids," the
junior officer replied. "It looks O.K."

Ben nodded and swung down out of the patrol car. He walked
quickly to the other car, flashing his handlight on the side of the
vehicle as he went up to the driver. The interior lights were on and
inside, two obviously frightened young couples smiled with relief
at the sight of the uniform coveralls. A freckled-faced teenager in
a dinner jacket was in the driver's seat and had the blister window
open. He grinned up at Martin. "Boy, am I glad to see you, officer,"
he said.

"What's the problem?" Ben asked.

"I guess she blew an impeller," the youth answered. "We were heading for a school dance at Cincinnati and she was boiling along like she was in orbit when blooey she just quit."

Ben surveyed the old jet sedan. "What year is this clunker?" he asked. The kid told him. "You kids have been told not to use this lane for any vehicle that old." He waved his hand in protest as the youngster started to tell him how many modifications he had made on the car. "It doesn't make one bit of difference whether you've put a first-stage Moon booster on this wreck. It's not supposed to be in the blue or yellow. And this thing probably shouldn't have been allowed out of the white—or even on the thruway."

The youngster flushed and bit his lip in embarrassment at the giggles from the two evening-frocked girls in the car.

"Well, let's get you out of here." Ben touched his throat mike. "Drop a light, Clay and then let's haul this junk pile away."

In the patrol car, Ferguson reached down beside his seat and tugged at a lever. From a recess in Beulah's stern, a big portable red warning light dropped to the pavement. As it touched the surface, it automatically flashed to life, sending out a bright, flashing red warning signal into the face of any approaching traffic. Clay eased the patrol car around the stalled vehicle and then backed slow into position, guided by Martin's radioed instructions. A tow-bar extruded from the back of the police vehicle and a magnaclamp locked onto the front end of the teenager's car. The older officer walked back to the portable warning light and rolled it on its four wheels to the rear plate of the jalopy where another magnalock secured it to the car. Beulah's two big rear warning lights still shone above the low silhouette of the passenger car, along with the mobile lamp on the jalopy. Martin walked back to the patrol car and climbed in.

He slid into his seat and nodded at Clay. The patrol car, with the disabled vehicle in tow moved forward and slanted left towards the police lane. Martin noted the mileage marker on the radiodometer and fingered the transmitter. "Chillicothe Control this is Car 56."

"This Chillicothe. Go ahead Five Six."

"We picked up some kids in a stalled heap on the blue at Marker 382 and we've got them in tow now," Ben said. "Have a wrecker meet us and take them off our hands."

"Affirmative, Five Six. Wrecker will pick you up at Marker 412."

Clay headed the patrol car and its trailed load into an emergency entrance to the middle police lane and slowly rolled westward. The senior trooper reached into his records rack and pulled out a citation book.

"You going to nail these kids?" Clay asked.

"You're damn right I am," Martin replied, beginning to fill in the violation report. "I'd rather have this kid hurting in the pocketbook than dead. If we turn him loose, he'll think he got away with it this time and try it again. The next time he might not be so lucky."

"I suppose you're right," Clay said, "but it does seem a little rough."

Ben swung around in his seat and surveyed his junior officer. "Sometimes I think you spent four years in the patrol academy with your head up your jet pipes," he said. He fished out another cigarette and took a deep drag.

"You've had four solid years of law; three years of electronics and jet and air-drive engine mechanics and engineering; pre-med, psychology, math, English, Spanish and a smattering of Portuguese, to say nothing of dozens of other subjects. You graduated in the upper tenth of your class with a B.S. in both Transportation and Criminology which is why you're riding patrol and not punching a computer or tinkering with an engine. You'd think with all that education that somewhere along the line you'd have learned to think with your head instead of your emotions."

Clay kept a studied watch on the roadway. The minute Ben had turned and swung his legs over the side of the seat and pulled out a cigarette, Clay knew that it was school time in Car 56. Instructor Sergeant Ben Martin was in a lecturing mood. It was time for all good pupils to keep their big, fat mouths shut.

"Remember San Francisco de Borja?" Ben queried. Clay nodded. "And you still think I'm too rough on them?" Ben pressed.

Ferguson's memory went back to last year's fifth patrol. He and Ben with Kelly riding hospital, had been assigned to NAT 200-North, running out of Villahermosa on the Guatamalan border of Mexico to Edmonton Barracks in Canada. It was the second night of the patrol. Some seven hundred fifty miles north of Mexico City, near the town of San Francisco de Borja, a gang of teenage Mexican youngsters had gone roaring up the yellow at speeds touching on four hundred miles an hour. Their car, a beat-up, fifteen-year-old veteran of less speedy and much rockier local mountain roads, had been gimmicked by the kids so that it bore no resemblance to its original manufacture.

From a junkyard they had obtained a battered air lift, smashed almost beyond use in the crackup of a ten-thousand dollar sports cruiser. The kids pried, pounded and bent the twisted impeller lift blades back into some semblance of alignment. From another wreck of a cargo carrier came a pair of 4000-pound thrust engines. They had jury-rigged the entire mess so that it stuck together on the old heap. Then they hit the thruway—nine of them packed into the jalopy—the oldest one just seventeen years old. They were doing three hundred fifty when they flashed past the patrol car and Ben had roared off in pursuit. The senior officer whipped the big patrol car across the crowded high speed blue lane, jockeyed into the ultra-high yellow and then turned on the power.

By this time the kids realized they had been spotted and they cranked their makeshift power plant up to the last notch. The most they could get out of it was four hundred and it was doing just that as Car 56, clocking better than five hundred, pulled in behind them. The patrol car was still three hundred yards astern when one of the bent and re-bent impeller blades let go. The out-of-balance fan, turning at close to 35,000 rpm's, flew to pieces and the air cushion vanished. At four hundred miles an hour, the body of the old jalopy fell the twelve inches to the pavement and both front wheels caved under. There was a momentary shower of sparks, then the entire vehicle snapped cart-wheeling more than eighty feet into the air and exploded. Pieces of car and bodies were scattered for a mile down the thruway and the only whole, identifiable human bodies were those of the three youngsters thrown out and sent hurtling to their deaths more than two hundred feet away.

Clay's mind snapped back to the present.

"Write 'em up," he said quietly to Martin. The senior officer gave a satisfied nod and turned back to his citation pad.

At marker 412, which was also the Columbus turnoff, a big patrol wrecker was parked on the side strip, engines idling, service and warning lights blinking. Clay pulled the patrol car alongside and stopped. He disconnected the tow bar and the two officers climbed out into the cold night air. They walked back to the teenager's car. Clay went to the rear of the disabled car and unhooked the warning light while Martin went to the driver's window. He had his citation book in hand. The youngster in the driver's seat went white at the sight of the violation pad. "May I see your license, please," Ben asked. The boy fumbled in a back pocket and then produced a thin, metallic tab with his name, age, address and license number etched into the indestructible and unalterable metal.

"Also your car registration," Ben added. The youth unclipped a similar metal strip from the dashboard.

The trooper took the two tabs and walked to the rear of the patrol car. He slid back a panel to reveal two thin slots in the hull. Martin slid the driver's license into one of the slots, the registration tab into the other. He pressed a button below each slot. Inside the car, a magnetic reader and auto-transmitter "scanned" the magnetic symbols implanted in the tags. The information was fed instantly to Continental Headquarters Records division at Colorado Springs. In fractions of a second, the great computers at Records were comparing the information on the tags with all previous traffic citations issued anywhere in the North American continent in the past forty-five years since the birth of the Patrol. The information from the driver's license and registration tab had been relayed from Beulah via the nearest patrol relay point. The answer came back the same way.

Above the license recording slot were two small lights. The first flashed green, "license is in order and valid." The second flashed green as well, "no previous citations." Ben withdrew the tag from the slot. Had the first light come on red, he would have placed the driver under arrest immediately. Had the second light turned amber, it would have indicated a previous minor violation. This, Ben would have noted on the new citation. If the second light had been red, this would have meant either a major previous violation or more than one minor citation. Again, the driver would have been under immediate arrest. The law was mandatory. One big strike and you're out—two foul tips and the same story. And "out" meant just that. Fines, possibly jail or prison sentence and lifetime revocation of driving privileges.

Ben flipped the car registration slot to "stand-by" and went back to the teenager's car. Even though they were parked on the service strip of the police emergency lane, out of all traffic, the youngsters stayed in the car. This one point of the law they knew and knew well. Survival chances were dim anytime something went wrong on the highspeed thruways. That little margin of luck vanished once outside the not-too-much-better security of the vehicle body.

Martin finished writing and then slipped the driver's license into a pocket worked into the back of the metallic paper foil of the citation blank. He handed the pad into the window to the driver together with a carbon stylus.

The boy's lip trembled and he signed the citation with a shaky hand.

Ben ripped off the citation blank and license, fed them into the slot on the patrol car and pressed both the car registration and license "record" buttons. Ten seconds later the permanent record of the citation was on file in Colorado Springs and a duplicate recording of the action was in the Continental traffic court docket recorder nearest to the driver's home-town. Now, no power in three nations could "fix" that ticket. Ben withdrew the citation and registration tag and walked back to the car. He handed the boy the license and registration tab, together with a copy of the citation. Ben bent down to peer into the car.

"I made it as light on you as I could," he told the young driver. "You're charged with improper use of the thruway. That's a minor violation. By rights, I should have cited you for illegal usage." He looked around slowly at each of the young people. "You look like nice kids," he said. "I think you'll grow up to be nice people. I want you around long enough to be able to vote in a few years. Who knows, maybe I'll be running for president then and I'll need your votes. It's a cinch that falling apart in the middle of two-hundred-mile an hour traffic is no way to treat future voters.

"Good night, Kids." He smiled and walked away from the car. The three young passengers smiled back at Ben. The young driver just stared unhappily at the citation.

Clay stood talking with the wrecker crewmen. Ben nodded to him and mounted into the patrol car. The young Canadian crushed out his cigarette and swung up behind the sergeant. Clay went to the control seat when he saw Martin pause in the door to the galley.

"I'm going to get a cup of coffee," the older officer said, "and then take the first shift. You keep Beulah 'til I get back."

Clay nodded and pushed the throttles forward. Car 56 rolled back into the police lane while behind it, the wrecker hooked onto the disabled car and swung north into the crossover. Clay checked both the chronometer and radiodometer and then reported in. "Cinncy Control this is Car 56 back in service." Cincinnati Control acknowledged.

Ten minutes later, Ben reappeared in the cab, slid into the left-hand seat. "Hit the sack, kid," he told Ferguson. The chronometer read 2204. "I'll wake you at midnight—or sooner, if anything breaks."

Ferguson stood up and stretched, then went into the galley. He poured himself a cup of coffee and carrying it with him, went back to the crew quarters. He closed the door to the galley and sat down on the lower bunk to sip his coffee. When he had finished, he tossed the cup into the basket, reached and dimmed the cubby lights and kicked off his boots. Still in his coveralls, Clay stretched out on the bunk and sighed luxuriously. He reached up and pressed a switch on the bulkhead above his pillow and the muted sounds of music from a standard broadcast commercial station drifted into the bunk area. Clay closed his eyes and let the sounds of the music and the muted rumble of the engines lull him to sleep. It took almost fifteen seconds for him to be in deep slumber.

Ben pushed Beulah up to her steady seventy-five-mile-an-hour cruising speed, moved to the center of the quarter-mile-wide police lane and locked her tracks into autodrive. He relaxed back in his seat and divided his gaze between the video monitors and the actual scene on either side of him in the night. Once again the sky was lighted, this time much brighter on the horizon as the road ways swept to the south of Cincinnati.

Traffic was once again heavy and fast with the blue and green carrying almost equal loads while white was really crowded and even the yellow "zoom" lane was beginning to fill. The 2200 hour density reports from Cinncy had been given before the Ohio State-Cal football game traffic had hit the thruways and densities now were peaking near twenty thousand vehicles for the one-hundred-mile block of westbound NAT 26 out of Cincinnati.

Back to the east, near the eastern Ohio state line, Martin could hear Car 207 calling for a wrecker and meat wagon. Beulah rumbled on through the night. The video monitors flicked to the next ten-mile stretch as the patrol car rolled past another interchange. More vehicles streamed onto the westbound thruway, crossing over and dropping down into the same lanes they held coming out of the north-south road. Seven years on patrols had created automatic reflexes in the trooper sergeant. Out of the mass of cars and cargoes streaming along the rushing tide of traffic, his eye picked out the track of one vehicle slanting across the white lane just a shade faster than the flow of traffic. The vehicle was still four or five miles ahead. It wasn't enough out of the ordinary to cause more than a second, almost unconscious glance, on the part of the veteran officer. He kept his view shifting from screen to screen and out to the sides of the car.

But the reflexes took hold again as his eye caught the track of the same vehicle as it hit the crossover from white to green, squeezed into the faster lane and continued its sloping run towards the next faster cross-over. Now Martin followed the movement of the car almost constantly. The moving blip had made the cut-over across the half-mile wide green lane in the span of one crossover and was now whipping into the merger lane that would take it over the top of the police lane and drop down into the one hundred fifty to two hundred mile an hour blue. If the object of his scrutiny straightened out in the blue, he'd let it go. The driver had been bordered on violation in his fast crossover in the face of heavy traffic. If he kept it up in the now-crowded high-speed lane, he was asking for sudden death. The monitors flicked to the next block and Ben waited just long enough to see the speeding car make a move to the left, cutting in front of a speeding cargo carrier. Ben slammed Beulah into high. Once again the bull horn blared as the cocoons slammed shut, this time locking both Clay and Kelly into their bunks, sealing Ben into the control seat.

Beulah lifted on her air cushion and the twin jets roared as she accelerated down the police lane at three hundred miles an hour. Ben closed the gap on the speeder in less than a minute and then edged over to the south side of the police lane to make the jump into the blue lane. The red emergency lights and the radio siren had already cleared a hole for him in the traffic pattern and he eased back on the finger throttles as the patrol car sailed over the divider and into the blue traffic lane. Now he had eye-ball contact with the speeding car, still edging over towards the ultra-high lane. On either side of the patrol car traffic gave way, falling back or moving to the left and right. Car 56 was now directly behind the speeding passenger vehicle. Ben fingered the cut-in switch that put his voice signal onto the standard vehicular emergency frequency—the band that carried the automatic siren-warning to all vehicles.

The patrol car was still hitting above the two-hundred-mile-an-hour mark and was five hundred feet behind the speeder. The headlamp bathed the other car in a white glare, punctuated with angry red flashes from the emergency lights.

"You are directed to halt or be fired upon," Ben's voice roared out over the emergency frequency. Almost without warning, the speeding car began braking down with such deceleration that the gargantuan patrol car with its greater mass came close to smashing over it and crushing the small passenger vehicle like an insect. Ben cut all forward power, punched up full retrojet and at the instant he felt Beulah's tracks touch the pavement as the air cushion blew, he slammed on the brakes. Only the safety cocoon kept Martin from being hurled against the instrument panel and in their bunks, Kelly Lightfoot and Clay Ferguson felt their insides dragging down into their legs.

The safety cocoons snapped open and Clay jumped into his boots and leaped for the cab. "Speeder," Ben snapped as he jumped down the steps to the side hatch. Ferguson snatched up his helmet from the rack beside his seat and leaped down to join his partner. Ben ran up to the stopped car through a thick haze of smoke from the retrojets of the patrol car and the friction-burning braking of both vehicles. Ferguson circled to the other side of the car. As they flashed their handlights into the car, they saw the driver of the car kneeling on the floor beside the reclined passenger seat. A woman lay stretched out on the seat, twisting in pain. The man raised an agonized face to the officers. "My wife's going to have her baby right here!"

"Kelly," Ben yelled into his helmet transmitter. "Maternity!"

The dispensary ramp was halfway down before Ben had finished calling. Kelly jumped to the ground and sprinted around the corner of the patrol car, medical bag in hand.

She shoved Clay out of the way and opened the door on the passenger side. On the seat, the woman moaned and then muffled a scream. The patrol doctor laid her palm on the distended belly. "How fast are your pains coming?" she asked. Clay and Ben had moved away from the car a few feet.

"Litter," Kelly snapped over her shoulder. Clay raced for the patrol car while Ben unshipped a portable warning light and rolled it down the lane behind the patrol car. He flipped it to amber "caution" and "pass." Blinking amber arrows pointed to the left and right of the halted passenger vehicle and traffic in the blue lane began picking up speed and parting around the obstructions.

By the time he returned to the patrol car, Kelly had the expectant mother in the dispensary. She slammed the door in the faces of the three men and then she went to work.

The woman's husband slumped against the side of the patrol vehicle.

Ben dug out his pack of cigarettes and handed one to the shaking driver.

He waited until the man had taken a few drags before speaking.

"Mister, I don't know if you realize it or not but you came close to killing your wife, your baby and yourself," Ben said softly, "to say nothing of the possibility of killing several other families. Just what did you think you were doing?"

The driver's shoulders sagged and his hand shook as he took the cigarette from his mouth. "Honestly, officer, I don't know. I just got frightened to death," he said. He peered up at Martin. "This is our first baby, you see, and Ellen wasn't due for another week. We thought it would be all right to visit my folks in Cleveland and Ellen was feeling just fine. Well, anyway, we started home tonight—we live in Jefferson City—and just about the time I got on the thruway, Ellen started having pains. I was never so scared in my life. She screamed once and then tried to muffle them but I knew what was happening and all I could think of was to get her to a hospital. I guess I went out of my head, what with her moaning and the traffic and everything. The only place I could think of that had a hospital was Evansville, and I was going to get her there come hell or high water." The young man tossed away the half-smoked cigarette and looked up at the closed dispensary door. "Do you think she's all right?"

Ben sighed resignedly and put his hand on the man's shoulder. "Don't you worry a bit. She's got one of the best doctors in the continent in there with her. Come on." He took the husband by the arm and led him around to the patrol car cab hatch. "You climb up there and sit down. I'll be with you in a second."

The senior officer signaled to Ferguson. "Let's get his car out of the traffic, Clay," he directed. "You drive it."

Ben went back and retrieved the caution blinker and re-racked it in the side of the patrol car, then climbed up into the cab. He took his seat at the controls and indicated the jump seat next to him. "Sit down, son. We're going to get us and your car out of this mess before we all get clobbered."   He flicked the headlamp at Ferguson in the control seat of the passenger car and the two vehicles moved out. Ben kept the emergency lights on while they eased carefully cross-stream to the north and the safety of the police lane. Clay picked up speed at the outer edge of the blue lane and rolled along until he reached the first "patrol only" entrance through the divider to the service strip. Ben followed him in and then turned off the red blinkers and brought the patrol car to a halt behind the other vehicle.

The worried husband stood up and looked to the rear of the car. "What's making it so long?" he asked anxiously. "They've been in there a long time."

Ben smiled. "Sit down, son. These things take time. Don't you worry. If there were anything wrong, Kelly would let us know. She can talk to us on the intercom anytime she wants anything."

The man sat back down. "What's your name?" Ben inquired.

"Haverstraw," the husband replied distractedly, "George Haverstraw. I'm an accountant. That's my wife back there," he cried, pointing to the closed galley door. "That's Ellen."

"I know," Ben said gently. "You told us that."

Clay had come back to the patrol car and dropped into his seat across from the young husband. "Got a name picked out for the baby?" he asked.

Haverstraw's face lighted. "Oh, yes," he exclaimed. "If it's a boy, we're going to call him Harmon Pierce Haverstraw. That was my grandfather's name. And if she's a girl, it's going to be Caroline May after Ellen's mother and grandmother."

The intercom came to life. "Anyone up there?" Kelly's voice asked. Before they could answer, the wail of a baby sounded over the system. Haverstraw yelled.

"Congratulations, Mr. Haverstraw," Kelly said, "you've got a fine-looking son."

"Hey," the happy young father yelped, "hey, how about that? I've got a son." He pounded the two grinning troopers on the back. Suddenly he froze. "What about Ellen? How's Ellen?" he called out.

"She's just fine," Kelly replied. "We'll let you in here in a couple of minutes but we've got to get us gals and your new son looking pretty for papa. Just relax."

Haverstraw sank down onto the jump seat with a happy dazed look on his face.

Ben smiled and reached for the radio. "I guess our newest citizen deserves a ride in style," he said. "We're going to have to transfer Mrs. Haverstraw and er, oh yes, Master Harmon Pierce to an ambulance and then to a hospital now, George. You have any preference on where they go?"

"Gosh, no," the man replied. "I guess the closest one to wherever we are." He paused thoughtfully. "Just where are we? I've lost all sense of distance or time or anything else."

Ben looked at the radiodometer. "We're just about due south of Indianapolis. How would that be?"

"Oh, that's fine," Haverstraw replied.

"You can come back now, Mr. Haverstraw," Kelly called out. Haverstraw jumped up. Clay got up with him. "Come on, papa," he grinned, "I'll show you the way."

Ben smiled and then called into Indianapolis Control for an ambulance.

"Ambulance on the way," Control replied. "Don't you need a wrecker, too, Five Six?"

Ben grinned. "Not this time. We didn't lose one. We gained one."

He got up and went back to have a look at Harmon Pierce Haverstraw, age five minutes, temporary address, North American Continental Thruway 26-West, Mile Marker 632.

Fifteen minutes later, mother and baby were in the ambulance heading north to the hospital. Haverstraw, calmed down with a

sedative administered by Kelly, had nearly wrung their hands off
in gratitude as he said good-by.

"I'll mail you all cigars when I get home," he shouted as he waved
and climbed into his car.

Beulah's trio watched the new father ease carefully into the
traffic as the ambulance headed down the police-way. Haverstraw
would have to cut over to the next exchange and then go north to
Indianapolis. He'd arrive later than his family. This time, he was
the very picture of careful driving and caution as he threaded his
way across the green.

"I wonder if he knows what brand of cigars I smoke?" Kelly
mused.

The chrono clicked up to 2335 as Car 56 resumed patrol. Kelly
plumped down onto the jump seat beside Ben. Clay was fiddling in
the galley. "Why don't you go back to the sack?" Ben called.

"What, for a lousy twenty-five minutes," Clay replied. "I had a
good nap before you turned the burners up to high. Besides, I'm
hungry. Anyone else want a snack?"

Ben shook his head. "No, thanks," Kelly said. Ferguson finished
slapping together a sandwich. Munching on it, he headed into the
engine room to make the midnight check. Car 56 had now been
on patrol eight hours. Only two hundred thirty-two hours and two
thousand miles to go.

Kelly looked around at the departing back of the younger trooper.
"I'll bet this is the only car in NorCon that has to stock twenty days
of groceries for a ten-day patrol," she said.

Ben chuckled. "He's still a growing boy."

"Well, if he is, it's all between the ears," the girl replied. "You'd
think that after a year I would have realized that nothing could
penetrate that thick Canuck's skull. He gets me so mad sometimes
that I want to forget I'm a lady." She paused thoughtfully. "Come
to think of it. No one ever accused me of being a lady in the first
place."

"Sounds like love," Ben smiled.

Hunched over on the jump seat with her elbows on her knees
and her chin cupped in both hands, Kelly gave the senior officer
a quizzical sideways look.

Ben was watching his monitors and missed the glance. Kelly
sighed and stared out into the light streaked night of the thruway.
The heavy surge of football traffic had distributed itself into the
general flow on the road and while all lanes were busy, there were no
indications of any over-crowding or jam-ups. Much of the pattern

was shifting from passenger to cargo vehicle as it neared midnight. The football crowds were filtering off at each exchange and exit and the California fans had worked into the blue and yellow—mostly the yellow—for the long trip home. The fewer passenger cars on the thruway and the increase in cargo carriers gave the troopers a breathing spell. The men in the control buckets of the three hundred and four hundred-ton cargo vehicles were the real pro's of the thruways; careful, courteous and fast. The NorCon patrol cars could settle down to watch out for the occasional nuts and drunks that might bring disaster.

Once again, Martin had the patrol car on auto drive in the center of the police lane and he steeled back in his seat. Beside him, Kelly stared moodily into the night.

"How come you've never married, Ben?" she asked. The senior trooper gave her a startled look. "Why, I guess for the same reason you're still a maiden," he answered. "This just doesn't seem to be the right kind of a job for a married man."

Kelly shook her head. "No, it's not the same thing with me," she said. "At least, not entirely the same thing. If I got married, I'd have to quit the Patrol and you wouldn't. And secondly, if you must know the truth, I've never been asked."

Ben looked thoughtfully at the copper-haired Irish-Indian girl. All of a sudden she seemed to have changed in his eyes. He shook his head and turned back to the road monitors.

"I just don't think that a patrol trooper has any business getting married and trying to keep a marriage happy and make a home for a family thirty days out of every three hundred sixty, with an occasional weekend home if you're lucky enough to draw your hometown for a terminal point. This might help the population rate but it sure doesn't do anything for the institution of matrimony."

"I know some troopers that are married," Kelly said.

"But there aren't very many," Ben countered. "Comes the time they pull me off the cars and stick me behind a desk somewhere, then I'll think about it."

"You might be too old by then," Kelly murmured.

Ben grinned. "You sound as though you're worried about it," he said.

"No," Kelly replied softly, "no, I'm not worried about it. Just thinking." She averted her eyes and looked out into the night again. "I wonder what NorCon would do with a husband-wife team?" she murmured, almost to herself.

Ben looked sharply at her and frowned. "Why, they'd probably split them up," he said.

"Split what up?" Clay inquired, standing in the door of the cab.

"Split up all troopers named Clay Ferguson," Kelly said disgustedly, "and use them for firewood—especially the heads. They say that hardwood burns long and leaves a fine ash. And that's what you've been for years."

She sat erect in the jump seat and looked sourly at the young trooper.

Clay shuddered at the pun and squeezed by the girl to get to his seat. "I'll take it now, pop," he said. "Go get your geriatrics treatment."

Ben got out of his seat with a snort. "I'll 'pop' you, skinhead," he snapped. "You may be eight years younger than I am but you only have one third the virility and one tenth the brains. And eight years from now you'll still be in deficit spending on both counts."

"Careful, venerable lord of my destiny," Clay admonished with a grin, "remember how I spent my vacation and remember how you spent yours before you go making unsubstantiated statements about my virility."

Kelly stood up. "If you two will excuse me, I'll go back to the dispensary and take a good jolt of male hormones and then we can come back and finish this man-to-man talk in good locker room company."

"Don't you dare," Ben cried, "I wouldn't let you tamper with one single, tiny one of your feminine traits, princess. I like you just the way you are."

Kelly looked at him with a wide-eyed, cherubic smile. "You really mean that, Ben?"

The older trooper flushed briefly and then turned quickly into the galley. "I'm going to try for some shut-eye. Wake me at two, Clay, if nothing else breaks." He turned to Kelly who still was smiling at him. "And watch out for that lascivious young goat."

"It's all just talk, talk, talk," she said scornful. "You go to bed Ben. I'm going to try something new in psychiatric annals. I'm going to try and psychoanalyze a dummy." She sat back down on the jump seat.

At 2400 hours it was Vincennes Check with the density reports, all down in the past hour. The patrol was settling into what looked like a quiet night routine. Kelly chatted with Ferguson for another half hour and then rose again. "I think I'll try to get some sleep," she said. "I'll put on a fresh pot of coffee for you two before I turn in."

She rattled around in the galley for some time. "Whatcha cooking?" Clay called out. "Making coffee," Kelly replied.

"It take all that time to make coffee?" Clay queried.

"No," she said. "I'm also getting a few things ready so we can have a fast breakfast in case we have to eat on the run. I'm just about through now."

A couple of minutes later she stuck her head into the cab. "Coffee's done. Want some?"

Clay nodded. "Please, princess."

She poured him a cup and set it in the rack beside his seat.

"Thanks," Clay said. "Good night, Hiawatha."

"Good night, Babe," she replied.

"You mean 'Paul Bunyon,' don't you?" Clay asked. "'Babe' was his blue ox."

"I know what I said," Kelly retorted and strolled back to the dispensary. As she passed through the crew cubby, she glanced at Ben sleeping on the bunk recently vacated by Ferguson. She paused and carefully and gently pulled a blanket up over his sleeping form. She smiled down at the trooper and then went softly to her compartment.

In the cab, Clay sipped at his coffee and kept watchful eyes on the video monitors. Beulah was back on auto drive and Clay had dropped her speed to a slow fifty as the traffic thinned.

At 0200 hours he left the cab long enough to go back and shake Ben awake and was himself re-awakened at 0400 to take back control. He let Ben sleep an extra hour before routing him out of the bunk again at 0700. The thin, gray light of the winter morning was just taking hold when Ben came back into the cab. Clay had pulled Beulah off to the service strip and was stopped while he finished transcribing his scribbled notes from the 0700 Washington Criminal Control broadcast.

Ben ran his hand sleepily over his close-cropped head. "Anything exciting?" he asked with a yawn. Clay shook his head. "Same old thing. 'All cars exercise special vigilance over illegal crossovers. Keep all lanes within legal speed limits.' Same old noise."

"Anything new on our hit-runner?"

"Nope."

"Good morning, knights of the open road," Kelly said from the galley door. "Obviously you both went to sleep after I left and allowed our helpless citizens to slaughter each other."

"How do you figure that one?" Ben laughed.

"Oh, it's very simple," she replied. "I managed to get in a full seven hours of sleep. When you sleep, I sleep. I slept. Ergo, you did likewise."

"Nope," Clay said, "for once we had a really quiet night. Let's hope the day is of like disposition."

Kelly began laying out the breakfast things. "You guys want eggs this morning?"

"You gonna cook again today?" Clay inquired.

"Only breakfast," Kelly said. "You have the honors for the rest of the day. The diner is now open and we're taking orders."

"I'll have mine over easy," Ben said. "Make mine sunny-up," Clay called.

Kelly began breaking eggs into the pan, muttering to herself. "Over easy, sunny-up, I like 'em scrambled. Next tour I take I'm going to get on a team where everyone likes scrambled eggs."

A few minutes later, Beulah's crew sat down to breakfast. Ben had just dipped into his egg yolk when the radio blared. "Attention all cars. Special attention Cars 207, 56 and 82."

"Just once," Ben said, "just once, I want to sit down to a meal and get it all down my gullet before that radio gives me indigestion." He laid down his fork and reached for the message pad.

The radio broadcast continued. "A late model, white over green Travelaire, containing two men and believed to be the subjects wanted in earlier broadcast on murder, robbery and hit-run murder, was involved in a service station robbery and murder at Vandalia, Illinois, at approximately 0710 this date. NorCon Criminal Division believes this subject car escaped filter check and left NAT 26-West sometime during the night.

"Owner of this stolen vehicle states it had only half tanks of fuel at the time it was taken. This would indicate wanted subjects stopped for fuel. It is further believed they were recognized by the station attendant from video bulletins sent out by this department last date and that he was shot and killed to prevent giving alarm.

"The shots alerted residents of the area and the subject car was last seen headed south. This vehicle may attempt to regain access to NAT-26-West or it may take another thruway. All units are warned once again to approach this vehicle with extreme caution and only with the assistance of another unit where possible. Acknowledge. Washington Criminal Control out."

Ben looked at the chrono. "They hit Vandalia at 0710, eh. Even in the yellow they couldn't get this far for another half hour. Let's finish breakfast. It may be a long time until lunch."

The crew returned to their meal. While Kelly was cleaning up after breakfast, Clay ran the quick morning engine room check. In the cab, Ben opened the arms rack and brought out two machine pistols and belts. He checked them for loads and laid one on Clay's control seat. He strapped the other around his waist. Then he flipped up a cover in the front panel of the cab. It exposed the breech mechanisms of a pair of twin-mounted 25 mm auto-cannon. The ammunition loads were full. Satisfied, Ben shut the inspection port and climbed into his seat. Clay came forward, saw the machine pistol on his seat and strapped it on without a word. He settled himself in his seat. "Engine room check is all green. Let's go rabbit hunting."

Car 56 moved slowly out into the police lane. Both troopers had their individual sets of video monitors on in front of their seats and were watching them intently. In the growing light of day, a white-topped car was going to be easy to spot.

It had all the earmarks of being another wintery, overcast day. The outside temperature at 0800 was right on the twenty-nine-degree mark and the threat of more snow remained in the air. The 0800 density reports from St. Louis Control were below the 14,000 mark in all lanes in the one-hundred-mile block west of the city. That was to be expected. They listened to the eastbound densities peaking at twenty-six thousand vehicles in the same block, all heading into the metropolis and their jobs. The 0800, 1200 and 1600 hours density reports also carried the weather forecasts for a five-hundred-mile radius from the broadcasting control point. Decreasing temperatures with light to moderate snow was in the works for Car 56 for the first couple of hundred miles west of St. Louis, turning to almost blizzard conditions in central Kansas. Extra units had already been put into service on all thruways through the midwest and snow-burners were waging a losing battle from Wichita west to the Rockies around Alamosa, Colorado.

Outside the temperature was below freezing; inside the patrol car it was a comfortable sixty-eight degrees. Kelly had cleared the galley and taken her place on the jump seat between the two troopers. With all three of them in the cab, Ben cut from the intercom to commercial broadcast to catch the early morning newscasts and some pleasant music. The patrol vehicle glided along at a leisurely sixty miles an hour. An hour out of St. Louis, a big liquid cargo carrier was stopped on the inner edge of the green lane against the divider to the police lane. The trucker had dropped both warning barriers and lights a half mile back. Ben brought Beulah to a halt across the divider from the stopped carrier. "Dropped a track pin," the driver called out to the officers.

Ben backed Beulah across the divider behind the stalled carrier to give them protection while they tried to assist the stalled vehicle.

Donning work helmets to maintain contact with the patrol car, and its remote radio system, the two troopers dismounted and went to see what needed fixing. Kelly drifted back to the dispensary and stretched out on one of the hospital bunks and picked up a new novel.

Beulah's well-equipped machine shop stock room produced a matching pin and it was merely a matter of lifting the stalled carrier and driving it into place in the track assembly. Ben brought the patrol car alongside the carrier and unshipped the crane. Twenty minutes later, Clay and the carrier driver had the new part installed and the tanker was on his way once again.

Clay climbed into the cab and surveyed his grease-stained uniform coveralls and filthy hands. "Your nose is smudged, too, dearie," Martin observed.

Clay grinned, "I'm going to shower and change clothes. Try and see if you can drive this thing until I get back without increasing the pedestrian fatality rate." He ducked back into the crew cubby and stripped his coveralls.

Bored with her book, Kelly wandered back to the cab and took Clay's vacant control seat. The snow had started falling again and in the mid-morning light it tended to soften the harsh, utilitarian landscape of the broad thruway stretching ahead to infinity and spreading out in a mile of speeding traffic on either hand.

"Attention all cars on NAT 26-West and east," Washington Criminal Control radio blared. "Special attention Cars 56 and 82. Suspect vehicle, white over green Travelaire reported re-entered NAT 26-West on St. Louis interchange 179. St. Louis Control reports communications difficulty in delayed report. Vehicle now believed . . ."

"Car 56, Car 56," St. Louis Control broke in. "Our pigeon is in your zone. Commercial carrier reports near miss sideswipe three minutes ago in blue lane approximately three miles west of mile Marker 957.

"Repeating. Car 56, suspect car . . ."

Ben glanced at the radiodometer. It read 969, then clicked to 970.

"This is Five Six, St. Louis," he broke in, "acknowledged. Our position is mile marker 970 . . ."

Kelly had been glued to the video monitors since the first of the bulletin. Suddenly she screamed and banged Ben on the shoulder.

"There they are. There they are," she cried, pointing at the blue lane monitor.

Martin took one look at the white-topped car cutting through traffic in the blue lane and slammed Beulah into high. The safety cocoons slammed shut almost on the first notes of the bull horn. Trapped in the shower, Clay was locked into the stall dripping wet as the water automatically shot off with the movement of the cocoon.

"I have them in sight," Ben reported, as the patrol car lifted on its air pad and leaped forward. "They're in the blue five miles ahead of me and cutting over to the yellow. I estimate their speed at two twenty-five. I am in pursuit."

Traffic gave way as Car 56 hurtled the divider into the blue.

The radio continued to snap orders.

"Cars 112, 206, 76 and 93 establish roadblocks at mile marker crossover 1032. Car 82 divert all blue and yellow to green and white."

Eight Two was one hundred fifty miles ahead but at three-hundred-mile-an-hour speeds, 82's team was very much a part of the operation. This would clear the two high-speed lanes if the suspect car hadn't been caught sooner.

"Cars 414, 227 and 290 in NAT-26-East, move into the yellow to cover in case our pigeon decides to fly the median." The controller continued to move cars into covering positions in the area on all crossovers and turnoffs. The sweating dispatcher looked at his lighted map board and mentally cursed the lack of enough units to cover every exit. State and local authorities already had been notified in the event the fugitives left the thruways and tried to escape on a state freeway.

In Car 56, Ben kept the patrol car roaring down the blue lane through the speeding westbound traffic. The standard emergency signal was doing a partial job of clearing the path, but at those speeds, driver reaction times weren't always fast enough. Ahead, the fleeing suspect car brushed against a light sedan, sending it careening and rocking across the lane. The driver fought for control as it swerved and screeched on its tilting frame. He brought it to a halt amid a haze of blue smoke from burning brakes and bent metal. The white over green Travelaire never slowed, fighting its way out of the blue into the ultra-high yellow and lighter traffic. Ben kept Beulah in bulldog pursuit.

The sideswipe ahead had sent other cars veering in panic and a cluster inadvertently bunched up in the path of the roaring patrol car. Like a flock of hawk-frightened chickens, they tried to scatter as they saw and heard the massive police vehicle bearing down on them. But like chickens, they couldn't decide which way to run. It was a matter of five or six seconds before they parted enough to let the patrol car through. Ben had no choice but to cut the throttle and punch once on the retrojets to brake the hurtling patrol car. The momentary drops in speed unlocked the safety cocoons and in an instant, Clay had leaped from the shower stall and sped to the cab. Hearing, rather than seeing his partner, Martin snapped over his shoulder, "Unrack the rifles. That's the car." Clay reached for the gun rack at the rear of the cab.

Kelly took one look at the young trooper and jumped for the doorway to the galley. A second later she was back. Without a word, she handed the nude Ferguson a dangling pair of uniform coveralls. Clay gasped, dropped the rifles and grabbed the coveralls from her hand and clutched them to his figure. His face was beet-red. Still without speaking, Kelly turned and ran back to her dispensary to be ready for the next acceleration.

Clay was into the coveralls and in his seat almost at the instant Martin whipped the patrol car through the hole in the blue traffic and shoved her into high once more.

There was no question about the fact that the occupants of the fugitive car knew they were being pursued. They shot through the crossover into the yellow lane and now were hurtling down the thruway close to the four-hundred-mile-an-hour mark.

Martin had Beulah riding just under three hundred to make the crossover, still ten miles behind the suspect car and following on video monitor. The air still crackled with commands as St. Louis and Washington Control maneuvered other cars into position as the pursuit went westward past other units blocking exit routes.

Clay read aloud the radiodometer numerals as they clicked off a mile every nine seconds. Car 56 roared into the yellow and the instant Ben had it straightened out, he slammed all finger throttles to full power. Beulah snapped forward and even at three hundred miles an hour, the sudden acceleration pasted the car's crew against the back of their cushioned seats. The patrol car shot forward at more than five hundred miles an hour.

The image of the Travelaire grew on the video monitor and then the two troopers had it in actual sight, a white, racing dot on the broad avenue of the thruway six miles ahead.

Clay triggered the controls for the forward bow cannon and a panel box flashed to "ready fire" signal.

"Negative," Martin ordered. "We're coming up on the road-block. You might miss and hit one of our cars."

"Car 56 to Control," the senior trooper called. "Watch out at the roadblock. He's doing at least five hundred in the yellow and he'll never be able to stop."

Two hundred miles east, the St. Louis controller made a snap decision. "Abandon roadblock. Roadblock cars start west. Maintain two hundred until subject comes into monitor view. Car 56, continue speed estimates of subject car. Maybe we can box him in."

At the roadblock forty-five miles ahead of the speeding fugitives and their relentless pursuer, the four patrol cars pivoted and spread out across the roadway some five hundred feet apart. They lunged forward and lifted up to air-cushion jet drive at just over two hundred miles an hour. Eight pairs of eyes were fixed on video monitors set for the ten-mile block to the rear of the four vehicles.

Beulah's indicated ground speed now edged towards the five hundred fifty mark, close to the maximum speeds the vehicles could attain.

The gap continued to close, but more slowly. "He's firing hotter," Ben called out. "Estimating five thirty on subject vehicle."

Now Car 56 was about three miles astern and still the gap closed. The fugitive car flashed past the site of the abandoned roadblock and fifteen seconds later all four patrol cars racing ahead of the Travelaire broke into almost simultaneous reports of "Here he comes."

A second later, Clay Ferguson yelled out, "There he goes. He's boondocking, he's boondocking."

"He has you spotted," Martin broke in. "He's heading for the median. Cut, cut, cut. Get out in there ahead of him."

The driver of the fugitive car had seen the bulk of the four big patrol cruisers outlined against the slight rise in the thruway almost at the instant he flashed onto their screens ten miles behind them. He broke speed, rocked wildly from side to side, fighting for control and then cut diagonally to the left, heading for the outer edge of the thruway and the unpaved, half-mile-wide strip of landscaped earth that separated the east and westbound segments of NAT-26.

The white and green car was still riding on its airpad when it hit the low, rounded curbing at the edge of the thruway. It hurtled into the air and sailed for a hundred feet across the gently-sloping snow-covered grass, came smashing down in a thick hedgerow of bushes—and kept going.

Car 56 slowed and headed for the curbing. "Watch it, kids," Ben snapped over the intercom, "we may be buying a plot in a second."

Still traveling more than five hundred miles an hour, the huge patrol car hit the curbing and bounced into the air like a rocket boosted elephant. It tilted and smashed its nose in a slanting blow into the snow-covered ground. The sound of smashing and breaking equipment mingled with the roar of the thundering jets, tracks and air drives as the car fought its way back to level travel. It surged forward and smashed through the hedgerow and plunged down the sloping snowbank after the fleeing car.

"Clay," Ben called in a strained voice, "take 'er."

Ferguson's fingers were already in position. "You all right, Ben?" he asked anxiously.

"Think I dislocated a neck vertebra," Ben replied. "I can't move my head. Go get 'em, kid."

"Try not to move your head at all, Ben," Kelly called from her cocoon in the dispensary. "I'll be there the minute we slow down."

A half mile ahead, the fugitive car plowed along the bottom of the gentle draw in a cloud of snow, trying to fight its way up the opposite slope and onto the eastbound thruway.

But the Travelaire was never designed for driving on anything but a modern superhighway. Car 56 slammed through the snow and down to the bottom of the draw. A quarter of a mile ahead of the fugitives, the first of the four roadblock units came plowing over the rise.

The car speed dropped quickly to under a hundred and the cocoons were again retracted. Ben slumped forward in his seat and caught himself. He eased back with a gasp of pain, his head held rigidly straight. Almost the instant he started to straighten up, Kelly flung herself through the cab door. She clasped his forehead and held his head against the back of the control seat.

Suddenly, the fugitive car spun sideways, bogged in the wet snow and muddy ground beneath and stopped. Clay bore down on it and was about two hundred yards away when the canopy of the other vehicle popped open and a sheet of automatic weapons fire raked the patrol car. Only the low angle of the sedan and the nearness of the bulky patrol car saved the troopers. Explosive bullets smashed into the patrol car canopy and sent shards of plastiglass showering down on the trio.

An instant later, the bow cannon on the first of the cut-off patrol units opened fire. An ugly, yellow-red blossom of smoke and fire erupted from the front of the Travelaire and it burst into flames. A second later, the figure of a man staggered out of the burning car, clothes and hair aflame. He took four plunging steps and then fell face down in the snow. The car burned and crackled and a thick funereal pyre of oily, black smoke billowed into the gray sky. It was snowing heavily now, and before the troopers could dismount and plow to the fallen man, a thin layer of snow covered his burned body.

An hour later, Car 56 was again on NAT 26-West, this time heading for Wichita barracks and needed repairs. In the dispensary, Ben Martin was stretched out on a hospital bunk with a traction brace around his neck and a copper-haired medical-surgical patrolwoman fussing over him.

In the cab, Clay peered through the now almost-blinding blizzard that whirled and skirled thick snow across the thruway. Traffic densities were virtually zero despite the efforts of the dragonlike snow-burners trying to keep the roadways clear. The young trooper shivered despite the heavy jacket over his coveralls. Wind whistled through the shell holes in Beulah's canopy and snow sifted and drifted against the back bulkhead.

The cab communications system had been smashed by the gunfire and Clay wore his work helmet both for communications and warmth.

The door to the galley cracked open and Kelly stuck her head in. "How much farther, Clay?" she asked.

"We should be in the barracks in about twenty minutes," the shivering trooper replied.

"I'll fix you a cup of hot coffee," Kelly said. "You look like you need it."

Over the helmet intercom Clay heard her shoving things around in the galley. "My heavens, but this place is a mess," she exclaimed. "I can't even find the coffee bin. That steeplechase driving has got to stop." She paused.

"Clay," she called out, "Have you been drinking in here? It smells like a brewery."

Clay raised mournful eyes to the shattered canopy above him. "My cooking wine" he sighed.

HOW IT WAS WHEN
THE PAST WENT AWAY

Robert Silverberg

The day that an antisocial fiend dumped an amnesifacient drug into the city water supply was one of the finest that San Francisco had had in a long while. The damp cloud that had been hovering over everything for three weeks finally drifted across the bay into Berkeley that Wednesday, and the sun emerged, bright and warm, to give the old town its warmest day so far in 2003. The temperature climbed into the high twenties, and even those oldsters who hadn't managed to learn to convert to the centigrade thermometer knew it was hot. Airconditioners hummed from the Golden Gate to the Embarcadero. Pacific Gas & Electric recorded its highest one-hour load in history between two and three in the afternoon. The parks were crowded. People drank a lot of water, some a good deal more than others. Toward nightfall, the thirstiest ones were already beginning to forget things. By the next morning, everybody in the city was in trouble, with a few exceptions. It had really been an ideal day for committing a monstrous crime.

On the day before the past went away, Paul Mueller had been thinking seriously about leaving the state and claiming refuge in one of the debtor sanctuaries—Reno, maybe, or Caracas. It wasn't altogether his fault, but he was close to a million in the red, and his creditors were getting unruly. It had reached the point where they were sending their robot bill collectors around to harass him in person, just about every three hours.

"Mr. Mueller? I am requested to notify you that the sum of

$8,005.97 is overdue in your account with Modern Age Recreators, Inc. We have applied to your financial representative and have discovered your state of insolvency, and therefore, unless a payment of $395.61 is made by the eleventh of this month, we may find it necessary to begin confiscation procedures against your person. Thus I advise you—"

"—the amount of $11,554.97, payable on the ninth of August, 2002, has not yet been received by Luna Tours, Ltd. Under the credit laws of 1995 we have applied for injunctive relief against you and anticipate receiving a decree of personal service due, if no payment is received by—"

"—interest on the unpaid balance is accruing, as specified in your contract, at a rate of 4 percent per month—"

"—balloon payment now coming due, requiring the immediate payment of—"

Mueller was growing accustomed to the routine. The robots couldn't call him—Pacific Tel & Tel had cut him out of their data net months ago—and so they came around, polite blank-faced machines stenciled with corporate emblems, and in soft purring voices told him precisely how deep in the mire he was at the moment, how fast the penalty charges were piling up, and what they planned to do to him unless he settled his debts instantly. If he tried to duck them, they'd simply track him down in the streets like indefatigable process servers, and announce his shame to the whole city. So he didn't duck them. But fairly soon their threats would begin to materialize.

They could do awful things to him. The decree of personal service, for example, would turn him into a slave; he'd become an employee of his creditor, at a court-stipulated salary, but every cent he earned would be applied against his debt, while the creditor provided him with minimal food, shelter, and clothing. He might find himself compelled to do menial jobs that a robot would spit at, for two or three years, just to clear one debt. Personal confiscation procedures were even worse; under that deal he might well end up as the actual servant of one of the executives of a creditor company, shining shoes and folding shirts. They might also get an open-ended garnishment on him, under which he and his descendants, if any, would pay a stated percentage of their annual income down through the ages until the debt, and the compounding interest thereon, was finally satisfied. There were other techniques for dealing with delinquents, too.

He had no recourse to bankruptcy. The states and the federal government had tossed out the bankruptcy laws in 1995, after the so-called credit epidemic of the 1980s when for a while it was actually fashionable to go irretrievably into debt and throw yourself on the mercy of the courts. The haven of easy bankruptcy was no more; if you became insolvent, your creditors had you in their grip. The only way out was to jump to a debtor sanctuary, a place where local laws barred any extradition for a credit offense. There were about a dozen such sanctuaries, and you could live well there, provided you had some special skill that you could sell at a high price. You needed to make a good living, because in a debtor sanctuary everything was on a strictly cash basis—cash in advance, at that, even for a haircut. Mueller had a skill he thought would see him through: he was an artist, a maker of sonic sculptures, and his work was always in good demand. All he needed was a few thousand dollars to purchase the basic tools of his trade—his last set of sculpting equipment had been repossessed a few weeks ago—and he could set up a studio in one of the sanctuaries, beyond the reach of the robot hounds. He imagined he could still find a friend who would lend him a few thousand dollars. In the name of art, so to speak. In a good cause.

If he stayed within the sanctuary area for ten consecutive years, he would be absolved of his debts and could come forth a free man. There was only one catch, not a small one. Once a man had taken the sanctuary route, he was forever barred from all credit channels when he returned to the outside world. He couldn't even get a post office credit card, let alone a bank loan. Mueller wasn't sure he could live that way, paying cash for everything all the rest of his life. It would be terribly cumbersome and dreary. Worse: it would be barbaric.

He made a note on his memo pad: *Call Freddy Munson in morning and borrow three bigs. Buy ticket to Caracas. Buy sculpting stuff.*

The die was cast—unless he changed his mind in the morning.

He peered moodily out at the row of glistening whitewashed just-post-Earthquake houses descending the steeply inclined street that ran down Telegraph Hill toward Fisherman's Wharf. They sparkled in the unfamiliar sunlight. A beautiful day, Mueller thought. A beautiful day to drown yourself in the bay. Damn. Damn. Damn. He was going to be forty years old soon. He had come into the world on the same bleak day that President John Kennedy had left it. Born in an evil hour, doomed to a dark fate. Mueller scowled. He went to the tap and got a glass of water. It was the only thing he could afford to drink, just now. He asked himself how he ever managed to get into such a mess. Nearly a million in debt!

He lay down dismally to take a nap.

When he woke, toward midnight, he felt better than he had felt for a long time. Some great cloud seemed to have lifted from him, even as it had lifted from the city that day. Mueller was actually in a cheerful mood. He couldn't imagine why.

In an elegant townhouse on Marina Boulevard, the Amazing Montini was rehearsing his act. The Amazing Montini was a professional mnemonist: a small dapper man of sixty, who never forgot a thing. Deeply tanned, his dark hair slicked back at a sharp angle, his small black eyes glistening with confidence, his thin lips fastidiously pursed. He drew a book from a shelf and let it drop open at random. It was an old one-volume edition of Shakespeare, a familiar prop in his nightclub act. He skimmed the page, nodded, looked briefly at another, then another and smiled his inward smile. Life was kind to the Amazing Montini. He earned a comfortable $30,000 a week on tour, having converted a freakish gift into a profitable enterprise. Tomorrow night he'd open for a week at Vegas; then to Manila, Tokyo, Bangkok, Cairo, on around the globe. In twelve weeks he'd earn his year's intake; then he'd relax once more.

It was all so easy. He knew so many good tricks. Let them scream out a twenty-digit number; he'd scream it right back. Let them bombard him with long strings of nonsense syllables; he'd repeat the gibberish flawlessly. Let them draw intricate mathematical formulas on the computer screen; he'd reproduce them down to the last exponent. His memory was perfect, both for visuals and auditories, and for the other registers as well.

The Shakespeare thing, which was one of the simplest routines he had, always awed the impressionable. It seemed so fantastic to most people that a man could memorize the complete works, page by page. He liked to use it as an opener.

He handed the book to Nadia, his assistant. Also his mistress; Montini liked to keep his circle of intimates close. She was twenty years old, taller than he was, with wide frost-gleamed eyes and a torrent of glowing, artificially radiant azure hair: up to the minute in every fashion. She wore a glass bodice, a nice container for the things contained. She was not very bright, but she did the things Montini expected her to do, and did them quite well. She would be replaced, he estimated, in about eighteen more months. He grew bored quickly with his women. His memory was too good.

"Let's start," he said.

She opened the book. "Page 537, left-hand column."

Instantly the page floated before Montini's eyes. "*Henry VI, Part Two*," he said. "*King Henry*: Say, man, were these thy words? *Horner*: An't shall please your majesty, I never said nor thought any such matter: God is my witness, I am falsely accused by the villain. *Peter*: By these ten bones, my lords, he did speak them to me in the garret one night, as we were scouring my Lord of York's armour. *York*: Base dunghill villain, and—"

"Page 778, right-hand column," Nadia said.

"*Romeo and Juliet*. Mercutio is speaking . . . 'an eye would spy out such a quarrel? Thy head is as full of quarrels as an egg is full of meat, and yet thy head hath been beaten as addle as an egg for quarreling. Thou hast quarreled with a man for coughing in the street, because he hath wakened thy dog that hath lain asleep in the sun. Didst thou not—'"

"Page 307, starting fourteen lines down on the right side."

Montini smiled. He liked the passage. A screen would show it to his audience at the performance.

"*Twelfth Night*," he said. "The Duke speaks: 'Too old, by heaven. Let still the woman take an elder than herself, so wears she to him, so sways she level in her husband's heart: For, boy, however we do praise ourselves, our fancies are more giddy and unfirm—"

"Page 495, left-hand column."

"Wait a minute," Montini said. He poured himself a tall glass of water and drank it in three quick gulps. "This work always makes me thirsty."

Taylor Braskett, Lt. Comdr., Ret., U.S. Space Service, strode with springy stride into his Oak Street home, just outside Golden Gate Park. At seventy-one, Commander Braskett still managed to move in a jaunty way, and he was ready to step back into uniform at once if his country needed him. He believed his country did need him, more than ever, now that socialism was running like wildfire through half the nations of Europe. Guard the home front, at least. Protect what's left of traditional American liberty. What we ought to have, Commander Braskett believed, is a network of C-bombs in orbit, ready to rain hellish death on the enemies of democracy. No matter what the treaty says, we must be prepared to defend ourselves.

Commander Braskett's theories were not widely accepted. People respected him for having been one of the first Americans to land on Mars, of course, but he knew that they quietly regarded him as a crank, a crackpot, an antiquated minuteman still fretting about the redcoats. He had enough of a sense of humor to realize that he did cut an absurd figure to these young people. But he was sincere in his determination to help keep America free—to protect the youngsters from the lash of totalitarianism, whether they laughed at him or not. All this glorious sunny day he had been walking through the park, trying to talk to the young ones, attempting to explain his position. He was courteous, attentive, eager to find someone who would ask him questions. The trouble was that no one listened. And the young ones—stripped to the waist in the sunshine, girls as well as boys, taking drugs out in the open, using the foulest obscenities in casual speech—at times, Commander Braskett almost came to think that the battle for America had already been lost. Yet he never gave up all hope.

He had been in the park for hours. Now, at home, he walked past the trophy room, into the kitchen, opened the refrigerator, drew out a bottle of water. Commander Braskett had three bottles of mountain spring water delivered to his home every two days; it was a habit he had begun fifty years ago, when they had first started talking about putting fluorides in the water. He was not unaware of the little smiles they gave him when he admitted that he drank only bottled spring water, but he didn't mind; he had outlived many of the smilers already, and attributed his perfect health to his refusal to touch the polluted, contaminated water that most other people drank. First chlorine, then fluorides. Probably they were putting in some other things by now, Commander Braskett thought.

He drank deeply.

You have no way of telling what sort of dangerous chemicals they might be putting in the municipal water system these days, he told himself. Am I a crank? Then I'm a crank. But a sane man drinks only water he can trust.

Fetally curled, knees pressed almost to chin, trembling, sweating, Nate Haldersen closed his eyes and tried to ease himself of the pain of existence. Another day. A sweet, sunny day. Happy people playing in the park. Fathers and children. He bit his lip, hard, just short of laceration intensity. He was an expert at punishing himself.

Sensors mounted in his bed in the Psychotrauma Ward of Fletcher Memorial Hospital scanned him continuously, sending a constant flow of reports to Dr. Bryce and his team of shrinks. Nate Haldersen knew he was a man without secrets. His hormone count, enzyme ratios, respiration, circulation, even the taste of bile in his mouth—it all became instantaneously known to hospital personnel. When the sensors discovered him slipping below the depression line, ultrasonic snouts came nosing up from the recesses of the mattress, proximity nozzles that sought him out in the bed, found the proper veins, squirted him full of dynajuice to cheer him up. Modern science was wonderful. It could do everything for Haldersen except give him back his family.

The door slid open. Dr. Bryce came in. The head shrink looked his part: tall, solemn yet charming, gray at the temples, clearly a wielder of power and an initiate of mysteries. He sat down beside Haldersen's bed. As usual, he made a big point of not looking at the row of computer outputs next to the bed that gave the latest details of Haldersen's condition.

"Nate?" he said. "How goes?"

"It goes," Haldersen muttered.

"Feel like talking a while?"

"Not specially. Get me a drink of water?"

"Sure," the shrink said. He fetched it and said, "It's a gorgeous day. How about a walk in the park?"

"I haven't left this room in two and a half years, doctor. You know that."

"Always a time to break loose. There's nothing physically wrong with you, you know."

"I just don't feel like seeing people," Haldersen said. He handed back the empty glass. "More?"

"Want something stronger to drink?"

"Water's fine." Haldersen closed his eyes. Unwanted images danced behind the lids: the rocket liner blowing open over the pole, the passengers spilling out like autumn seeds erupting from a pod, Emily tumbling down, down, falling eighty thousand feet, her golden hair swept by the thin cold wind, her short skirt flapping at her hips, her long lovely legs clawing at the sky for a place to stand. And the children falling beside her, angels dropping from heaven, down, down, down, toward the white soothing fleece of the polar ice. They sleep in peace, Haldersen thought, and I missed the plane, and I alone remain. And Job spake, and said, Let the day perish wherein I was born, and the night in which it was said, There is a man child conceived.

"It was eleven years ago," Dr. Bryce told him. "Won't you let go of it?"

"Stupid talk coming from a shrink. Why won't it let go of *me?*"

"You don't want it to. You're too fond of playing your role."

"Today is talking-tough day, eh? Get me some more water."

"Get up and get it yourself," said the shrink.

Haldersen smiled bitterly. He left the bed, crossing the room a little unsteadily, and filled his glass. He had had all sorts of therapy—sympathy therapy, antagonism therapy, drugs, shock, orthodox freuding, the works. They did nothing for him. He was left with the image of an opening pod, and falling figures against the iron-blue sky. The Lord gave, and the Lord hath taken away; blessed be the name of the Lord. My soul is weary of my life. He put the glass to his lips. Eleven years. I missed the plane. I sinned with Marie, and Emily died, and John, and Beth. What did it feel like to fall so far? Was it like flying? Was there ecstasy in it? Haldersen filled the glass again.

"Thirsty today, eh?"

"Yes," Haldersen said.

"Sure you don't want to take a little walk?"

"You know I don't." Haldersen shivered. He turned and caught the psychiatrist by the forearm. "When does it end, Tim? How long do I have to carry this thing around?"

"Until you're willing to put it down."

"How can I make a conscious effort to forget something? Tim, Tim, isn't there some drug I can take, something to wash away a memory that's killing me?"

"Nothing effective."

"You're lying," Haldersen murmured. "I've read about the amnesifacients. The enzymes that eat memory-RNA. The experiments with diisopropyl fluorophosphate. Puromycin. The—"

Dr. Bryce said, "We have no control over their operations. We can't simply go after a single block of traumatic memories while leaving the rest of your mind unharmed. We'd have to bash about at random, hoping we got the trouble spot, but never knowing what else we were blotting out. You'd wake up without your trauma, but maybe without remembering anything else that happened to you between, say, the age of fourteen and forty. Maybe in fifty years we'll know enough to be able to direct the dosage at a specific—"

"I can't wait fifty years."

"I'm sorry, Nate."

"Give me the drug anyway. I'll take my chances on what I lose."

"We'll talk about that some other time, all right? The drugs are experimental. There'd be months of red tape before I could get authorization to try them on a human subject. You have to realize—"

Haldersen turned him off. He saw only with his inner eye, saw the tumbling bodies, reliving his bereavement for the billionth time, slipping easily back into his self-assumed role of Job. I am a brother to dragons, and a companion to owls. My skin is black upon me, and my bones are burned with heat. He hath destroyed me on every side, and I am gone: and mine hope hath he removed like a tree. The shrink continued to speak. Haldersen continued not to listen. He poured himself one more glass of water with a shaky hand.

It was close to midnight on Wednesday before Pierre Gerard, his wife, their two sons and their daughter had a chance to have dinner. They were the proprietors, chefs, and total staff of the Petit Pois restaurant on Sansome Street, and business had been extraordinary, exhaustingly good all evening. Usually they were able to eat about half past five, before the dinner rush began, but today people had begun coming in early—made more expansive by the good weather, no doubt—and there hadn't been a free moment for anybody since the cocktail hour. The Gerards were accustomed to brisk trade, for theirs was perhaps the most popular family-run bistro in the city, with a passionately devoted clientele. Still, a night like this was too much!

They dined modestly on the evening's miscalculations: an overdone rack of lamb, some faintly corky Château Beychevelle '97, a fallen soufflé, and such. They were thrifty people. Their one extravagance was the Evian water that they imported from France. Pierre Gerard had not set foot in his native Lyons for thirty years, but he preserved many of the customs of the motherland, including the traditional attitude toward water. A Frenchman does not drink much water; but what he does drink comes always from the bottle, never from the tap. To do otherwise is to risk a diseased liver. One must guard one's liver.

That night Freddy Munson picked up Helene at her flat on Geary and drove across the bridge to Sausalito for dinner, as usual, at Ondine's. Ondine's was one of only four restaurants, all of them famous old ones, at which Munson ate in fixed rotation. He was a man of firm habits. He awakened religiously at six each morning, and was at his desk in the brokerage house by seven, plugging himself into the data channels to learn what had happened in the European finance markets while he slept. At half past seven local time the New York exchanges opened and the real day's work began. By half past eleven, New York was through for the day, and Munson went around the corner for lunch, always at the Petit Pois, whose proprietor he had helped to make a millionaire by putting him into Consolidated Nucleonics' several components two and a half years before the big merger. At half past one, Munson was back

in the office to transact business for his own account on the Pacific
Coast exchange; three days a week he left at three, but on Tuesdays
and Thursdays he stayed as late as five in order to catch some deals
on the Honolulu and Tokyo exchanges. Afterwards, dinner, a play
or concert, always a handsome female companion. He tried to get
to sleep, or at least to bed, by midnight.

A man in Freddy Munson's position *had* to be orderly. At any
given time, his thefts from his clients ranged from six to nine
million dollars, and he kept all the details of his jugglings in his
head. He couldn't trust putting them on paper because there were
scanner eyes everywhere; and he certainly didn't dare employ the
data net, since it was well know that anything you confided to
one computer was bound to be accessible to some other computer
somewhere, no matter how tight a privacy seal you slapped on it.
So Munson had to remember the intricacies of fifty or more illicit
transactions, a constantly changing chain of embezzlements, and a
man who practices such necessary disciplines of memory soon gets
into the habit of extending discipline to every phase of his life.

Helene snuggled close. Her faintly psychedelic perfume drifted
toward his nostrils. He locked the car into the Sausalito circuit and
leaned back comfortably as the traffic-control computer took over
the steering. Helene said, "At the Bryce place last night I saw two
sculptures by your bankrupt friend."

"Paul Mueller?"

"That's the one. They were very good sculptures. One of them
buzzed at me."

"What were you doing at the Bryce's?"

"I went to college with Lisa Bryce. She invited me over with
Marty."

"I didn't realize you were that old," Munson said.

Helene giggled. "Lisa's a lot younger than her husband, dear.
How much does a Paul Mueller sculpture cost?"

"Fifteen, twenty thousand, generally. More for specials."

"And he's broke, even so?"

"Paul has a rare talent for self-destruction," Munson said. "He
simply doesn't comprehend money. But it's his artistic salvation,
in a way. The more desperately in debt he is, the finer his work
becomes. He creates out of his despair, so to speak. Though he
seems to have overdone the latest crisis. He's stopped working
altogether. It's a sin against humanity when an artist doesn't
work."

"You can be so eloquent, Freddy," Helene said softly.

When the Amazing Montini woke Thursday morning, he did not at once realize that anything had changed. His memory, like a good servant, was always there when he needed to call on it, but the array of perfectly fixed facts he carried in his mind remained submerged until required. A librarian might scan shelves and see books missing; Montini could not detect similar vacancies of his synapses. He had been up for half an hour, had stepped under the molecular bath and had punched for his breakfast and had awakened Nadia to tell her to confirm the pod reservations to Vegas, and finally, like a concert pianist running off a few arpeggios to limber his fingers for the day's chores, Montini reached into his memory bank for a little Shakespeare and no Shakespeare came.

He stood quite still, gripping the astrolabe that ornamented his picture window, and peered out at the bridge in sudden bewilderment. It had never been necessary for him to make a conscious effort to recover data. He merely looked and it was there; but where was Shakespeare? Where was the left hand column of page 136, and the right hand column of page 654, and the right hand column of page 806, sixteen lines down? Gone? He drew blanks. The screen of his mind showed him only empty pages.

Easy. This is unusual, but it isn't catastrophic. You must be tense, for some reason, and you're forcing it, that's all. Relax, pull something else out of storage—

The *New York Times*, Wednesday, October 3, 1973. Yes, there it was, the front page, beautifully clear, the story on the baseball game down in the lower right-hand corner, the headline about the jet accident big and black, even the photo credit visible. Fine. Now let's try—

The *St. Louis Post-Dispatch*, Sunday, April 19, 1987. Montini shivered. He saw the top four inches of the page, nothing else. Wiped clean.

He ran through the files of other newspapers he had memorized for his act. Some were there. Some were not. Some, like the *Post-Dispatch*, were obliterated in part. Color rose to his cheeks. Who had tampered with his memory?

He tried Shakespeare again. Nothing.

He tried the 1997 Chicago data-net directory. It was there.

He tried his third-grade geography textbook. It was there, the big red book with smeary print.

He tried last Friday's five-o'clock xerofax bulletin. Gone.

He stumbled and sank down on the divan he had purchased in Istanbul, he recalled, on the nineteenth of May, 1985, for 4,200 Turkish pounds. "Nadia!" he cried. "Nadia!" His voice was little more than a croak. She came running, her eyes only half frosted, her morning face askew.

"How do I look?" he demanded. "My mouth—is my mouth right? My eyes?"

"Your face is all flushed."

"Aside from that!"

"I don't know," she gasped. "You seem all upset, but—"

"Half my mind is gone," Montini said. "I must have had a stroke. Is there any facial paralysis? That's a symptom. Call my doctor, Nadia! A stroke, a stroke! It's the end for Montini!"

Paul Mueller, awakening at midnight on Wednesday and feeling strangely refreshed, attempted to get his bearings. Why was he fully dressed, and why had he been asleep? A nap, perhaps, that had stretched on too long? He tried to remember what he had been doing earlier in the day, but he was unable to find a clue. He was baffled but not disturbed; mainly he felt a tremendous urge to get to work. The images of five sculptures, fully planned and begging to be constructed, jostled in his mind. Might as well start right now, he thought. Work through till morning. That small twittering silvery one—that's a good one to start with. I'll block out the schematics, maybe even do some of the armature—

"Carole?" he called. "Carole, are you around?"

His voice echoed through the oddly empty apartment.

For the first time Mueller noticed how little furniture there was. A bed—a cot, really, not their double bed—and a table, and a tiny insulator unit for food, and a few dishes. No carpeting. Where were his sculptures, his private collection of his own best work? He walked into his studio and found it bare from wall to wall, all of his tools mysteriously swept away, just a few discarded sketches on the floor. And his wife? "Carole? *Carole?*"

He could not understand any of this. While he dozed, it seemed, someone had cleaned the place out, stolen his furniture, his sculptures, even the carpet. Mueller had heard of such thefts. They came with a van, brazenly, posing as moving men. Perhaps they had given him some sort of drug while they worked. He could not bear the thought that they had taken his sculptures; the rest didn't matter, but he had cherished those dozen pieces dearly. I'd better call the police, he decided, and rushed toward the handset of the data unit, but it wasn't there either. Would burglars take *that* too?

Searching for some answers, he scurried from wall to wall, and saw a note in his own handwriting. *Call Freddy Munson in the morning and borrow three bigs. Buy ticket to Caracas. Buy sculpting stuff.*

Caracas? A vacaction, maybe? And why buy sculpting stuff? Obviously the tools had been gone before he fell asleep, then. Why? And where was his wife? What was going on? He wondered if he ought to call Freddy right now, instead of waiting until morning. Freddy might know. Freddy was always home by midnight, too. He'd have one of his damn girls with him and wouldn't want to be interrupted, but to hell with that; what good was having friends if you couldn't bother them in a time of crisis?

Heading for the nearest public communicator booth, he rushed out of his apartment and nearly collided with a sleek dunning robot in the hallway. The things show no mercy, Mueller thought. They plague you at all hours. No doubt this one was on its way to bother the deadbeat Nicholson family down the hall.

The robot said, "Mr. Paul Mueller? I am a properly qualified representative of International Fabrication Cartel, Amalgamated. I am here to serve notice that there is an unpaid balance in your account to the extent of $9,150.55, which as of 0900 hours tomorrow morning will accrue compounded penalty interest at a rate of 5 percent per month, since you have not responded to our three previous requests for payment. I must further inform you—"

"You're off your neutrinos," Mueller snapped. "I don't owe a dime to I.F.C.! For once in my life I'm in the black, and don't try to make me believe otherwise."

The robot replied patiently, "Shall I give you a printout of the transactions? On the fifth of January, 2003, you ordered the following metal products from us: three 4-meter tubes of antiqued iridium, six 10-centimeter spheres of—"

"The fifth of January, 2003, happens to be three months from now," Mueller said, "and I don't have time to listen to crazy robots. I've got an important call to make. Can I trust you to patch me into the data net without garbling things?"

"I'm not authorized to permit you to make use of my facilities."

"Emergency override," said Mueller. "Human being in trouble. Go argue with that one!"

The robot's conditioning was sound. It yielded at once to his assertion of an emergency and set up a relay to the main communications net. Mueller supplied Freddy Munson's number. "I can provide audio only," the robot said, putting the call through. Nearly a minute passed. Then Freddy Munson's familiar deep voice snarled from the speaker grille in the robot's chest, "Who is it and what do you want?"

"It's Paul. I'm sorry to bust in on you, Freddy, but I'm in big trouble. I think I'm losing my mind, or else everybody else is."

"Maybe everybody else is. What's the problem?"

"All my furniture's gone. A dunning robot is trying to shake me down for nine bigs. I don't know where Carole is. I can't remember what I was doing earlier today. I've got a note here about getting tickets to Caracas that I wrote myself, and I don't know why. And—"

"Skip the rest," Munson said. "I can't do anything for you. I've got problems of my own."

"Can I come over, at least, and talk?"

"Absolutely not!" In a softer voice Munson said, "Listen, Paul, I didn't mean to yell, but something's come up here, something very distressing—"

"You don't need to pretend. You've got Helene with you and you wish I'd leave you alone. Okay."

"No. Honestly," Munson said. "I've got problems, suddenly. I'm in a totally ungood position to give you any help at all. I need help myself."

"What sort? Anything I can do for you?"

"I'm afraid not. And if you'll excuse me, Paul—"

"Just tell me one thing, at least. Where am I likely to find Carole? Do you have any idea?"

"At her husband's place, I'd say."

"*I'm* her husband."

There was a long pause. Munson said finally, "Paul, she divorced you last January and married Pete Castine in April."

"No," Mueller said.

"What, no?"

"No, it isn't possible."

"Have you been popping pills, Paul? Sniffing something? Smoking weed? Look, I'm sorry, but I can't take time now to—"

"At least tell me what day today is."

"Wednesday."

"Which Wednesday?"

"Wednesday the eight of May. Thursday the ninth, actually, by this time of night."

"And the year?"

"For Christ's sake, Paul—"

"The *year?*"

"2003."

Mueller sagged. "Freddy, I've lost half a year somewhere! For me it's last October. 2002. I've some weird kind of amnesia. It's the only explanation."

"Amnesia," Munson said. The edge of tension left his voice. "Is that what you've got? Amnesia? Can there be such a thing as an epidemic of amnesia? Is it contagious? Maybe you better come over here after all. Because's amnesia's my problem too."

Thursday, May 9, promised to be as beautiful as the previous day had been. The sun once again beamed on San Francisco; the sky was clear, the air warm and tender. Commander Braskett awoke early as always, punched for his usual spartan breakfast, studied the morning xerofax news, spent an hour dictating his memoirs, and, about nine, went out for a walk. The streets were strangely crowded, he found, when he got down to the shopping district along Haight Street. People were wandering aimlessly, dazedly, as though they were sleepwalkers. Were they drunk? Drugged? Three times in five minutes Commander Braskett was stopped by young men who wanted to know the date. Not the time, the *date*. He told them, crisply, disdainfully; he tried to be tolerant, but it was difficult for him not to despise people who were so weak that they were unable to refrain from poisoning their minds with stimulants and narcotics and psychedelics and similar trash. At the corner of Haight and Masonic a forlorn-looking pretty girl of about seventeen, with wide blank blue eyes, halted him and said, "Sir, this city is San Francisco, isn't it? I mean, I was supposed to move here from Pittsburgh in May, and if this is May, this is San Francisco, right?" Commander Braskett nodded brusquely and turned away, pained.

He was relieved to see an old friend, Lou Sandler, the manager of the Bank of America office across the way. Sandler was standing outside the bank door. Commander Braskett crossed to him and said, "Isn't it a disgrace, Lou, the way this whole street is filled with addicts this morning? What is it, some historical pageant of the 1960s?" And Sandler gave him an empty smile and said, "Is that my name? Lou? You wouldn't happen to know the last name too, would you? Somehow it's slipped my mind." In that moment Commander Braskett realized that something terrible had happened to his city and perhaps to his country, and that the leftist takeover he had long dreaded must now be at hand, and that it was time for him to don his old uniform again and do what he could to strike back at the enemy.

In joy and in confusion, Nate Haldersen awoke that morning realizing that he had been transformed in some strange and wonderful way. His head was throbbing, but not painfully. It seemed to him that a terrible weight had been lifted from his shoulders, that the fierce dead hand about his throat had at last relinquished its grip.

He sprang from bed, full of questions.

Where am I? What kind of place is this? Why am I not at home? Where are my books? Why do I feel so happy?

This seemed to be a hospital room.

There was a veil across his mind. He pierced its filmy folds and realized that he had committed himself to—to Fletcher Memorial— last August—no, the August before last—suffering with a severe emotional disturbance brought on by—brought on by—

He had never felt happier than this moment.

He saw a mirror. In it was the reflected upper half of Nathaniel Haldersen, Ph.D. Nate Haldersen smiled at himself. Tall, stringy, long-nosed man, absurdly straw-colored hair, absurd blue eyes, thin lips, smiling. Bony body. He undid his pajama top. Pale, hairless chest; bump of bone like an epaulet on each shoulder. I have been sick a long time, Haldersen thought. Now I must get out of here, back to my classroom. End of leave of absence. Where are my clothes?

"Nurse? Doctor?" He pressed his call button three times. "Hello? Anyone here?"

No one came. Odd; they always came. Shrugging, Haldersen moved out into the hall. He saw three orderlies, heads together, buzzing at the far end. They ignored him. A robot servitor carrying breakfast trays glided past. A moment later one of the younger doctors came running through the hall, and would not stop when Haldersen called to him. Annoyed, he went back into his room and looked about for clothing. He found none, only a little stack of magazines on the closet floor. He thumbed the call button three more times. Finally one of the robots entered the room.

"I am sorry," it said, "but the human hospital personnel is busy at present. May I serve you, Dr. Haldersen?"

"I want a suit of clothing. I'm leaving the hospital."

"I am sorry, but there is no record of your discharge. Without authorization from Dr. Bryce, Dr. Reynolds, or Dr. Kamakura, I am not permitted to allow your departure."

Haldersen sighed. He knew better than to argue with a robot. "Where are those three gentlemen right now?"

"They are occupied, sir. As you may know, there is a medical emergency in the city this morning, and Dr. Bryce and Dr. Kamakura are helping to organize the committee of public safety. Dr. Reynolds did not report for duty today and we are unable to trace him. It is believed that he is a victim of the current difficulty."

"*What* current difficulty?"

"Mass loss of memory on the part of the human population," the robot said.

"An epidemic of amnesia?"

"That is one interpretation of the problem."

"How can such a thing—" Haldersen stopped. He understood now the source of his own joy this morning. Only yesterday afternoon he had discussed with Tim Bryce the application of memory-destroying drugs to his own trauma and Bryce had said—

Haldersen no longer knew the nature of his own trauma.

"Wait," he said, as the robot began to leave the room. "I need information. Why have I been under treatment here?"

"You have been suffering from social displacements and dysfunctions whose origin, Dr. Bryce feels, lies in a situation of traumatic personal loss."

"Loss of what?"

"Your family, Dr. Haldersen."

"Yes. That's right. I recall, now—I had a wife and two children. Emily. And a little girl—Margaret, Elizabeth, something like that. And a boy named John. What happened to them?"

"They were passengers aboard Intercontinental Airways Flight 103, Copenhagen to San Francisco, September 5, 1991. The plane underwent explosive decompression over the Arctic Ocean and there were no survivors."

Haldersen absorbed the information as calmly as though he were hearing of the assassination of Julius Caesar.

"Where was I when the accident occurred?"

"In Copenhagen," the robot replied. "You had intended to return to San Francisco with your family on Flight 103; however, according to your data file here, you became involved in an emotional relationship with a woman named Marie Rasmussen, whom you had met in Copenhagen, and failed to return to your hotel in time to go to the airport. Your wife, evidently aware of the situation, chose not to wait for you. Her subsequent death, and that of your children, produced a traumatic guilt reaction in which you came to regard yourself as responsible for their terminations."

"I *would* take that attitude, wouldn't I?" Haldersen said. "Sin and retribution. Mea culpa, mea maxima culpa. I always had a harsh view of sin, even when I was sinning. I should have been an Old Testament prophet."

"Shall I provide more information, sir?"

"Is there more?"

"We have in the files Dr. Bryce's report headed, *The Job Complex: A Study in the Paralysis of Guilt*."

"Spare me that," Haldersen said. "All right, go."

He was alone. The Job Complex, he thought. Not really appropriate, was it? Job was a man without sin, and yet he was punished grievously to satisfy a whim of the Almighty. A little presumptuous, I'd say, to identify myself with him. Cain would have been a better choice. Cain said unto the Lord, My punishment is greater than I can bear. But Cain was a sinner. I was a sinner. I sinned and Emily died for it. When, eleven, eleven-and-a-half years ago? And now I know nothing at all about it except what the machine just told me. Redemption through oblivion, I'd call it. I have expiated my sin and now I'm free. I have no business staying in this hospital any longer. Strait is the gate, and narrow is the way, which leadeth unto life, and few there be that find it. I've got to get out of here. Maybe I can be of some help to others.

He belted his bathrobe, took a drink of water, and went out of the room. No one stopped him. The elevator did not seem to be running, but he found the stairs, and walked down, a little creakily. He had not been this far from his room in more than a year. The lowest floors of the hospital were in chaos—doctors, orderlies, robots, patients, all milling around excitedly. The robots were trying to calm people and get them back to their proper places. "Excuse me," Haldersen said serenely. "Excuse me. Excuse me." He left the hospital, unmolested, by the front door. The air outside was as fresh as young wine; he felt like weeping when it hit his nostrils. He was free. Redemption through oblivion. The disaster high above the Arctic no longer dominated his thoughts. He looked upon it precisely as if it had happened to the family of some other man, long ago. Haldersen began to walk briskly down Van Ness, feeling vigor returning to his legs with every stride. A young woman, sobbing wildly, erupted from a building and collided with him. He caught her, steadied her, was surprised at his own strength as he kept her from toppling. She trembled and pressed her head against his chest. "Can I do anything for you?" he asked. "Can I be of any help?"

Panic had begun to enfold Freddy Munson during dinner at Ondine's Wednesday night. He had begun to be annoyed with

Helene in the midst of the truffled chicken breasts, and so he started to think about the details of business; and to his amazement he did not seem to have the details quite right in his mind; and so he felt the early twinges of terror.

The trouble was that Helene was going on and on about the art of sonic sculpture in general and Paul Mueller in particular. Her interest was enough to arouse faint jealousies in Munson. Was she getting ready to leap from his bed to Paul's? Was she thinking of abandoning the wealthy, glamorous, but essentially prosaic stockbroker for the irresponsible, impecunious, fascinatingly gifted sculptor? Of course, Helene kept company with a number of other men, but Munson knew them and discounted them as rivals; they were nonentities, escorts to fill her idle nights when he was too busy for her. Paul Mueller, however, was another case. Munson could not bear the thought that Helene might leave him for Paul. So he shifted his concentration to the day's maneuvers. He had extracted a thousand shares of the $5.87 convertible preferred of Lunar Transit from the Schaeffer account, pledging it as collateral to cover his shortage in the matter of the Comsat debentures, and then, tapping the Howard account for five thousand Southeast Energy Corporation warrants, he had—or had those warrants come out of the Brewster account? Brewster was big on utilities. So was Howard, but that account was heavy on Mid-Atlantic Power, so would it also be loaded with Southeast Energy? In any case, had he put those warrants up against the Zurich uranium futures, or were they riding as his markers in that Antarctic oil-lease thing? He could not remember.

He could not remember.

He could not remember.

Each transaction had been in its own compartment. The partitions were down, suddenly. Numbers were spilling about in his mind as though his brain were in free fall. All of today's deals were tumbling. It frightened him. He began to gobble his food, wanting now to get out of here, to get rid of Helene, to get home and try to reconstruct his activities of the afternoon. Oddly, he could remember quite clearly all that he had done yesterday—the Xerox switch, the straddle on Steel—but today was washing away minute by minute.

"Are you all right?" Helene asked.

"No, I'm not," he said. "I'm coming down with something."

"The Venus virus. Everybody's getting it."

"Yes, that must be it. The Venus virus. You'd better keep clear of me tonight."

They skipped dessert and cleared out fast. He dropped Helene off at her flat; she hardly seemed disappointed, which bothered him, but not nearly so much as what was happening to his mind. Alone, finally, he tried to jot down an outline of his day, but even more had left him now. In the restaurant he had known which stocks he had handled, though he wasn't sure what he had done with them. Now he couldn't even recall the specific securities. He was out on the limb for millions of dollars of other people's money, and every detail was in his mind, and his mind was falling apart. By the time Paul Mueller called, a little after midnight, Munson was growing desperate. He was relieved, but not exactly cheered, to learn that whatever strange thing had affected his mind had hit Mueller a lot harder. Mueller had forgotten everything since last October.

"You went bankrupt," Munson had to explain to him. "You had this wild scheme for setting up a central clearinghouse for works of art, a kind of stock exchange—the sort of thing only an artist would try to start. You wouldn't let me discourage you. Then you began signing notes, and taking on contingent liabilities, and before the project was six weeks old you were hit with half a dozen lawsuits and it all began to go sour."

"When did this happen, precisely?"

"You conceived the idea at the beginning of November. By Christmas you were in severe trouble. You already had a bunch of personal debts that had gone unpaid from before, and your assets melted away, and you hit a terrible bind in your work and couldn't produce a thing. You really don't remember a thing of this, Paul?"

"Nothing."

"After the first of the year the fastest moving creditors started getting decrees against you. They impounded everything you owned except the furniture, and then they took the furniture. You borrowed from all of your friends, but they couldn't give you enough, because you were borrowing thousands and you owed hundreds of thousands."

"How much did I hit you for?"

"Eleven bigs," Munson said. "But don't worry about that now."

"I'm not. I'm not worrying about a thing. I was in a bind in my work, you say?" Mueller chuckled. "That's all gone. I'm itching to start making things. All I need are the tools—I mean, money to buy the tools."

"What would they cost?"

"Two-and-a-half bigs," Mueller said.

Munson coughed. "All right. I can't transfer the money to your account, because your creditors would lien it right away. I'll get some cash at the bank. You'll have three bigs tomorrow, and welcome to it."

"Bless you, Freddy," Mueller said. "This kind of amnesia is a good thing, eh? I was so worried about money that I couldn't work. Now I'm not worried at all. I guess I'm still in debt, but I'm not fretting. Tell me what happened to my marriage, now."

"Carole got fed up and turned off," said Munson. "She opposed your business venture from the start. When it began to devour you, she did what she could to untangle you from it, but you insisted on trying to patch things together with more loans and she filed for a decree. When she was free, Pete Castine moved in and grabbed her."

"That's the hardest part to believe. That she'd marry an art dealer, a totally noncreative person, a—a parasite, really—"

"They were always good friends," Munson said. "I won't say they were lovers, because I don't know, but they were close. And Pete's not that horrible. He's got taste, intelligence, everything an artist needs except the gift. I think Carole may have been weary of gifted men, anyway."

"How did I take it?" Mueller asked.

"You hardly seemed to notice, Paul. You were so busy with your financial shenanigans."

Mueller nodded. He sauntered to one of his own works, a three-meter-high arrangement of oscillating rods that ran the whole sound spectrum into high kilohertzes, and passed two fingers over the activator eye. The sculpture began to murmur. After a few moments Mueller said, "You sounded awfully upset when I called, Freddy. You say you have some kind of amnesia too?"

Trying to be casual about it, Munson said, "I find I can't remember some important financial transactions I carried out today. Unfortunately, my only record of them is in my head. But maybe the information will come back to me when I've slept on it."

"There's no way I can help you with that."

"No. There isn't."

"Freddy, where is this amnesia coming from?"

Munson shrugged. "Maybe somebody put a drug in the water supply, or spiked the food, or something. These days, you never can tell. Look, I've got to do some work, Paul. If you'd like to sleep here tonight—"

"I'm wide awake, thanks. I'll drop by again in the morning."

When the sculptor was gone, Munson struggled for a feverish hour to reconstruct his data, and failed. Shortly before two he took a four-hour sleep pill. When he awakened, he realized in dismay that he had no memories whatever for the period from April 1

to noon yesterday. During those five weeks he had engaged in
countless securities transactions, using other people's property as
his collateral, and counting on his ability to get each marker in
his game back into its proper place before anyone was likely to go
looking for it. He had always been able to remember everything.
Now he could remember nothing. He reached his office at seven in
the morning, as always, and out of habit plugged himself into the
data channels to study the Zurich and London quotes, but the prices
on the screen were strange to him, and he knew that he was undone.

At that same moment of Thursday morning Dr. Timothy Bryce's
house computer triggered an impulse and the alarm voice in his
pillow said quietly but firmly, "It's time to wake up, Dr. Bryce."
He stirred but lay still. After the prescribed ten-second interval
the voice said, a little more sharply, "It's time to wake up, Dr.
Bryce." Bryce sat up, just in time; the lifting of his head from the
pillow cut off the third, much sterner, repetition which would have
been followed by the opening chords of the *Jupiter* Symphony. The
psychiatrist opened his eyes.

He was surprised to find himself sharing his bed with a strikingly
attractive girl.

She was a honey blonde, deeply tanned, with light-brown eyes,
full pale lips, and a sleek, elegant body. She looked to be fairly
young, a good twenty years younger than he was—perhaps twenty-
five, twenty-eight. She wore nothing, and she was in a deep sleep,
her lower lip sagging in a sort of involuntary pout. Neither her youth
nor her beauty nor her nudity surprised him; he was puzzled simply
because he had no notion who she was or how she had come to be
in bed with him. He felt as though he had never seen her before.
Certainly he didn't know her name. Had he picked her up at some
party last night? He couldn't seem to remember where he had been
last night. Gently he nudged her elbow.

She woke quickly, fluttering her eyelids, shaking her head.

"Oh," she said, as she saw him, and clutched the sheet up to her
throat. Then, smiling, she dropped it again. "That's foolish. No
need to be modest *now*, I guess."

"I guess. Hello."

"Hello," she said. She looked as confused as he was.

"This is going to sound stupid," he said, "but someone must have
slipped me a weird weed last night, because I'm afraid I'm not sure
how I happened to bring you home. Or what your name is."

"Lisa," she said. "Lisa—Falk." She stumbled over the second
name. "And you're—"

"Tim Bryce."

"You don't remember where we met?"

"No," he said.

"Neither do I."

He got out of bed, feeling a little hesitant about his own nakedness, and fighting the inhibition off. "They must have given us both the same thing to smoke, then. You know"—he grinned shyly—"I can't even remember if we had a good time together last night. I hope we did."

"I think we did," she said. "I can't remember it either. But I feel good inside—the way I usually do after I've—" She paused. "We couldn't have met only just last night, Tim."

"How can you tell?"

"I've got the feeling that I've known you longer than that."

Bryce shrugged. "I don't see how. I mean, without being too coarse about it, obviously we were both high last night, really floating, and we met and came here and—"

"No. I feel at home here. As if I moved in with you weeks and weeks ago."

"A lovely idea. But I'm sure you didn't."

"Why do I feel so much at home here, then?"

"In what way?"

"In every way." She walked to the bedroom closet and let her hand rest on the touchplate. The door slid open; evidently he had keyed the house computer to her fingerprints. Had he done that last night too? She reached in. "My clothing," she said. "Look. All these dresses, coats, shoes. A whole wardrobe. There can't be any doubt. We've been living together and don't remember it!"

A chill swept through him. "What have they done to us? Listen, Lisa, let's get dressed and eat and go down to the hospital together for a checkup. We—"

"Hospital?"

"Fletcher Memorial. I'm in the neurological department. Whatever they slipped us last night has hit us both with a lacunary retrograde amnesia—a gap in our memories—and it could be serious. If it's caused brain damage, perhaps it's not irreversible yet, but we can't fool around."

She put her hands to her lips in fear. Bryce felt a sudden warm urge to protect this lovely stranger, to guard and comfort her, and he realized he must be in love with her, even though he couldn't remember who she was. He crossed the room to her and seized her in a brief, tight embrace; she responded eagerly, shivering a little. By a quarter to eight they were out of the house and heading for the hospital through unusually light traffic. Bryce led the girl quickly to the staff lounge. Ted Kamakura was there already, in uniform. The little Japanese psychiatrist nodded curtly and said, "Morning, Tim." Then he blinked. "Good morning, Lisa. How come *you're* here?"

"You know her?" Bryce asked.

"What kind of a question is that?"

"A deadly serious one."

"Of course I know her," Kamakura said, and his smile of greeting abruptly faded. "Why? Is something wrong about that?"

"You may know her, but I don't," said Bryce.

"Oh, God. Not you too!"

"Tell me who she is, Ted."

"She's your wife, Tim. You married her five years ago."

By half past eleven Thursday morning the Gerards had everything set up and going smoothly for the lunch rush at the Petit Pois. The soup caldron was bubbling, the escargot trays were ready to be popped in the oven, the sauces were taking form. Pierre Gerard was a bit surprised when most of the lunchtime regulars failed to show up. Even Mr. Munson, always punctual at half past eleven, did not arrive. Some of these men had not missed weekday lunch at the Petit Pois in fifteen years. Something terrible must have happened on the stock market, Pierre thought, to have kept all these financial men at their desks, and they were too busy to call him and cancel their usual tables. That must be the answer. It was impossible that any of the regulars would forget to call him. The stock market must be exploding. Pierre made a mental note to call his broker after lunch and find out what was going on.

About two Thursday afternoon, Paul Mueller stopped into Metchnikoff's Art Supplies in North Beach to try to get a welding pen, some raw metal, loudspeaker paint, and the rest of the things he needed for the rebirth of his sculpting career. Metchnikoff greeted him sourly with, "No credit at all, Mr. Mueller, not even a nickel!"

"It's all right. I'm a cash customer this time."

The dealer brightened. "In that case it's all right, maybe. You finished with your troubles?"

"I hope so," Mueller said.

He gave the order. It came to about $2,300; when the time came to pay, he explained that he simply had to run down to Montgomery Street to pick up the cash from his friend Freddy Munson, who was holding three bigs for him. Metchnikoff began to glower again.

"Five minutes!" Mueller called. "I'll be back in five minutes!" But when he got to Munson's office, he found the place in confusion, and Munson wasn't there. "Did he leave an envelope for a Mr. Mueller?" he asked a distraught secretary. "I was supposed to pick something important up here this afternoon. Would you please check?" The girl simply ran away from him. So did the next girl. A burly broker told him to get out of the office. "We're closed, fellow," he shouted. Baffled, Mueller left.

Not daring to return to Metchnikoff's with the news that he hadn't been able to raise the cash after all, Mueller simply went home. Three dunning robots were camped outside his door, and each one began to croak its cry of doom as he approached. "Sorry," Mueller said, "I can't remember a thing about any of this stuff," and he went inside and sat down on the bare floor, angry, thinking of the brilliant pieces he could be turning out if he could only get his hands on the tools of his trade. He made sketches instead. At least the ghouls had left him with pencil and paper. Not as efficient as a computer screen and a light-pen, maybe, but Michelangelo and Benvenuto Cellini had managed to make out all right without computer screens and light-pens.

At four o'clock the door bell rang.

"Go *away*, Mueller said through the speaker. "See my accountant! I don't want to hear any more dunnings, and the next time I catch one of you idiot robots by my door I'm going to—"

"It's me, Paul," a nonmechanical voice said.

Carole.

He rushed to the door. There were seven robots out there, surrounding her, and they tried to get in; but he pushed them back so she could enter. A robot didn't dare lay a paw on a human being. He slammed the door in their metal faces and locked it.

Carole looked fine. Her hair was longer than he remembered it, and she had gained about eight pounds in all the right places, and she wore an iridescent peekaboo wrap that he had never seen before, and which was really inappropriate for afternoon wear, but which looked splendid on her. She seemed at least five years younger than she really was; evidently a month and a half of marriage to Pete Castine had done more for her than nine years of marriage to Paul Mueller. She glowed. She also looked strained and tense, but that seemed superficial, the product of some distress of the last few hours.

"I seem to have lost my key," she said.

"What are you doing here?"

"I don't understand you, Paul."

"I mean why'd you come here?"

"I *live* here."

"Do you?" He laughed harshly. "Very funny."

"You always did have a weird sense of humor, Paul." She stepped past him. "Only this isn't any joke. Where *is* everything? The furniture, Paul. My things." Suddenly she was crying. "I must be breaking up. I wake up this morning in a completely strange apartment, all alone, and I spend the whole day wandering in a sort of daze that I don't understand at all, and now I finally come home and I find that you've pawned every damn thing we own, or something and—" She bit her knuckles. "Paul?"

She's got it too, he thought. The amnesia epidemic.

He said quietly, "This is a funny thing to ask, Carole, but will you tell me what today's date is?"

"Why—the fourteenth of September—or is it the fifteenth—"

"2002?"

"What do you think? 1776?"

She's got it worse than I have, Mueller told himself. She's lost a whole extra month. She doesn't remember my business venture. She doesn't remember my losing all the money. *She doesn't remember divorcing me.* She thinks she's still my wife.

"Come in here," he said, and led her to the bedroom. He pointed to the cot that stood where their bed had been. "Sit down, Carole. I'll try to explain. It won't make much sense but I'll try to explain."

Under the circumstances, the concert by the visiting New York Philharmonic for Thursday evening was cancelled. Nevertheless the orchestra assembled for its rehearsal at half past two in the afternoon. The union required so many rehearsals—with pay—a week; therefore the orchestra rehearsed, regardless of external cataclysms. But there were problems. Maestro Alvarez, who used an electronic baton and proudly conducted without a score, thumbed the button for a downbeat and realized abruptly, with a sensation as of dropping through a trapdoor, that the Brahms Fourth was wholly gone from his mind. The orchestra responded raggedly to his faltering leadership. Some of the musicians had no difficulties, but the concertmaster stared in horror at his left hand, wondering how to finger the strings for the notes his violin was supposed to be yielding, and the second oboe could not find the proper keys, and the first bassoon had not yet even managed to remember how to put his instrument together.

By nightfall, Tim Bryce had managed to assemble enough of the story so that he understood what had happened, not only to himself and to Lisa, but to the entire city. A drug, or drugs, almost certainly distributed through the municipal water supply, had leached away nearly everyone's memory. The trouble with modern life, Bryce thought, is that technology gives us the potential for newer and more intricate disasters every year, but it doesn't seem to give us the ability to ward them off. Memory drugs were old stuff, going back thirty, forty years. He had studied several types of them himself. Memory is partly a chemical and partly an electrical process; some drugs went after the electrical end, jamming the synapses over which brain transmissions travel, and some went after the molecular substrata in which longterm memories are locked up. Bryce knew ways of destroying short-term memories by inhibiting synapse transmission, and he knew ways of destroying the deep long-term memories by washing out the complex chains of ribonucleic acid, brain-RNA, by which they are inscribed in the brain. But such drugs were experimental, tricky, unpredictable; he had hesitated to use them on human subjects; he certainly had never imagined that anyone would simply dump them into an aqueduct and give an entire city a simultaneous lobotomy.

His office at Fletcher Memorial had become an improvised center of operations for San Francisco. The mayor was there, pale and shrunken; the chief of police, exhausted and confused, periodically turned his back and popped a pill; a dazed-looking representative of the communications net hovered in a corner, nervously monitoring the hastily rigged system through which the committee of public safety that Bryce had summoned could make its orders known throughout the city.

The mayor was no use at all. He couldn't even remember having run for office. The chief of police was in even worse shape: he had been up all night because he had forgotten, among other things, his home address, and he had been afraid to query a computer about it for fear he'd lose his job for drunkenness. By now the chief of police was aware that he wasn't the only one in the city having memory problems today, and he had looked up his address in the files and even telephoned his wife, but he was close to collapse. Bryce had insisted that both men stay here as symbols of order; he wanted only their faces and their voices, not their fumble-headed official services.

A dozen or so miscellaneous citizens had accumulated in Bryce's office too. At five in the afternoon he had broadcast an all-media appeal, asking anyone whose memory of recent events was unimpaired to come to Fletcher Memorial. "If you haven't had any city water in the past twenty-four hours, you're probably all right. Come down here. We need you." He had drawn a curious assortment. There was a ramrod-straight old space hero, Taylor Braskett, a pure-foods nut who drank only mountain water. There was a family of French restauranteurs, mother, father, three grown children, who preferred mineral water flown in from their native land. There was a computer salesman named McBurney who had been in Los Angeles on business and hadn't had any of the drugged water. There was a retired cop named Adler who lived in Oakland, where there were no memory problems; he had hurried across the bay as soon as he heard that San Francisco was in trouble. That was before all access to the city had been shut off at Bryce's orders. And there were some others, of doubtful value but of definitely intact memory.

The three screens that the communications man had mounted provided a relay of key points in the city. Right now one was monitoring the Fisherman's Wharf district from a camera atop Ghirardelli Square, one was viewing the financial district from a helicopter over the old Ferry Building Museum, and one was relaying a pickup from a mobile truck in Golden Gate Park. The scenes were similar everywhere: people milling about, asking questions, getting no answers. There wasn't any sign of looting yet. There were no fires. The police, those of them able to function, were out in force, and antiriot robots were cruising the bigger streets, just in case they might be needed to squirt their stifling blankets of foam at suddenly panicked mobs.

Bryce said to the mayor. "At half past six I want you to go on all media with an appeal for calm. We'll supply you with everything you have to say."

The mayor moaned.

Bryce said, "Don't worry. I'll feed you the whole speech by bone relay. Just concentrate on speaking clearly and looking straight into the camera. If you come across as a terrified man, it can be the end for all of us. If you look cool, we may be able to pull through."

The mayor put his face in his hands.

Ted Kamakura whispered, "You can't put him on the channels, Tim! He's a wreck, and everyone will see it!"

"The city's mayor has to show himself," Bryce insisted. "Give him a double jolt of bracers. Let him make this one speech and then we can put him to pasture."

"Who'll be the spokesman, then?" Kamakura asked. "You? Me? Police Chief Dennison?"

"I don't know," Bryce muttered. "We need an authority-image to make announcements every half hour or so, and I'm damned if I'll have time. Or you. And Dennison—"

"Gentlemen, may I make a suggestion?" It was the old spaceman, Braskett. "I wish to volunteer as spokesman. You must admit I have a certain look of authority. And I'm accustomed to speaking to the public."

Bryce rejected the idea instantly. That right-wing crackpot, that author of passionate nut letters to every news medium in the state, that latter-day Paul Revere? Him, spokesman for the committee? But in the moment of rejection came acceptance. Nobody really paid attention to far-out political activities like that; probably nine people out of ten in San Francisco thought of Braskett, if at all, simply as the hero of the first Mars expedition. He was a handsome old horse, too, elegantly upright and lean. Deep voice; unwavering eyes. A man of strength and presence.

Bryce said, "Commander Braskett, if we were to make you chairman of the committee of public safety—"

Ted Kamakura gasped.

"—would I have your assurance that such public announcements as you would make would be confined entirely to statements of the policies arrived at by the entire committee?"

Commander Braskett smiled glacially. "You want me to be a figurehead, is that it?"

"To be our spokesman, with the official title of chairman."

"As I said: to be a figurehead. Very well, I accept. I'll mouth my lies like an obedient puppet, and I won't attempt to inject any of my radical, extremist ideas into my statements. Is that what you wish?"

"I think we understand each other perfectly," Bryce said, and smiled, and got a surprisingly warm smile in return.

He jabbed now at his data board. Someone in the path lab eight stories below his office answered, and Bryce said, "Is there an up-to-date analysis yet?"

"I'll switch you to Dr. Madison."

Madison appeared on the screen. He ran the hospital's radio-isotope department, normally: a beefy, red-faced man who looked as though he ought to be a beer salesman. He knew his subject. "It's definitely the water supply, Tim," he said at once. "We tentatively established that an hour and a half ago, of course, but now there's no doubt. I've isolated traces of two different memory-suppressant drugs, and there's the possibility of a third. Whoever it was was taking no chances."

"What are they?" Bryce asked.

"Well, we've got a good jolt of acetylcholine terminase," Madison said, "which will louse up the synapses and interfere with short-term memory fixation. Then there's something else, perhaps a puromycin-derivative protein dissolver, which is going to work on the brain-RNA and smashing up older memories. I suspect also that we've been getting one of the newer experimental amnesifacients, something that I haven't isolated yet, capable of working its way deep and cutting out really basic motor patterns. So they've hit us high, low, and middle."

"That explains a lot. The guys who can't remember what they did yesterday, the guys who've lost a chunk out of their adult memories, and the ones who don't even remember their names—this thing is working on people at all different levels."

"Depending on individual metabolism, age, brain structure, and how much water they had to drink yesterday, yes."

"Is the water supply still tainted?" Bryce asked.

"Tentatively, I'd say no. I've had water samples brought me from the upflow districts, and everything's okay there. The water department has been running its own check; they say the same. Evidently the stuff got into the system early yesterday, came down into the city, and is generally gone by now. Might be some residuals in the pipes; I'd be careful about drinking water even today."

"And what does the pharmacopoeia say about the effectiveness of these drugs?"

Madison shrugged. "Anybody's guess. You'd know that better than I. Do they wear off?"

"Not in the normal sense," said Bryce. "What happens is the brain cuts in a redundancy circuit and gets access to a duplicate set of the affected memories, eventually—shifts to another track, so to speak—provided a duplicate of the sector in question was there in the first place, and provided that the duplicate wasn't blotted out also. Some people are going to get chunks of their memories back, in a few days or a few weeks. Others won't."

"Wonderful," Madison said. "I'll keep you posted, Tim."

Bryce cut off the call and said to the communications man, "You have that bone relay? Get it behind His Honor's ear."

The mayor quivered. The little instrument was fastened in place. Bryce said, "Mr. Mayor, I'm going to dictate a speech, and you're going to broadcast it on all media, and it's the last thing I'm going to ask of you until you've had a chance to pull yourself together. Okay? Listen carefully to what I'm saying, speak slowly, and pretend that tomorrow is election day and your job depends on how well you come across now. You won't be going on live.

There'll be a fifteen-second delay, and we have a wipe circuit so we can correct any stumbles, and there's absolutely no reason to be tense. Are you with me? Will you give it all you've got?"

"My mind is all foggy."

"Simply listen to me and repeat what I say into the camera's eye. Let your political reflexes take over. Here's your chance to make a hero of yourself. We're living history right now, Mr. Mayor. What we do here today will be studied the way the events of the 1906 fire were studied. Let's go, now. Follow me. *People of the wonderful city of San Francisco—*"

The words rolled easily from Bryce's lips, and, wonder of wonders, the mayor caught them and spoke them in a clear, beautifully resonant voice. As he spun out his speech, Bryce felt a surging flow of power going through himself, and he imagined for the moment that he was the elected leader of the city, not merely a self-appointed emergency dictator. It was an interesting, almost ecstatic feeling. Lisa, watching him in action, gave him a loving smile.

He smiled at her. In this moment of glory he was almost able to ignore the ache of knowing that he had lost his entire memory archive of his life with her. Nothing else gone, apparently. But, neatly, with idiot selectivity, the drug in the water supply had sliced away everything pertaining to his five years of marriage. Kamakura had told him, a few hours ago, that it was the happiest marriage of any he knew. Gone. At least Lisa had suffered an identical loss, against all probabilities. Somehow that make it easier to bear; it would have been awful to have one of them remember the good times and the other know nothing. He was almost able to ignore the torment of loss while he kept busy. Almost.

"The mayor's going to be on in a minute," Nadia said. "Will you listen to him? He'll explain what's been going on."

"I don't care," said the Amazing Montini dully.

"It's some kind of epidemic of amnesia. When I was out before, I heard all about it. *Everyone's* got it. It isn't just you! And you thought it was a stroke, but it wasn't. You're all right."

"My mind is a ruin."

"It's only temporary." Her voice was shrill and unconvincing. "It's something in the air, maybe. Some drug they were testing that drifted in. We're all in this together. I can't remember last week at all."

"What do I care," Montini said. "Most of these people, they have no memories even when they are healthy. But me? Me? I am destroyed. Nadia, I should lie down in my grave now. There is no sense in continuing to walk around."

The voice from the loudspeaker said, "Ladies and gentlemen, His Honor Elliot Chase, the Mayor of San Francisco."

"Let's listen," Nadia said.

The mayor appeared on the wallscreen, wearing his solemn face, his we-face-a-grave-challenge-citizens face. Montini glanced at him, shrugged, looked away.

The mayor said, "People of the wonderful city of San Francisco, we have just come through the most difficult day in nearly a century, since the terrible catastrophe of April, 1906. The earth has not quaked today, nor have we been smitten by fire, yet we have been severely tested by sudden calamity.

"As all of you surely know, the people of San Francisco have been afflicted since last night by what can best be termed an epidemic of amnesia. There has been mass loss of memory, ranging from mild cases of forgetfulness to near-total obliteration of identity. Scientists working at Fletcher Memorial Hospital have succeeded in determining the cause of this unique and sudden disaster.

"It appears that criminal saboteurs contaminated the municipal water supply with certain restricted drugs that have the ability to dissolve memory structures. *The effect of these drugs is temporary.* There should be no cause for alarm. Even those who are most severely affected will find their memories gradually beginning to return, and there is every reason to expect full recovery in a matter of hours or days."

"He's lying," said Montini.

"The criminals responsible have not yet been apprehended, but we expect arrests momentarily. The San Francisco area is the only affected region, which means the drugs were introduced into the water system just beyond city limits. Everything is normal in Berkeley, in Oakland, in Marin County, and other outlying areas.

"In the name of public safety I have ordered the bridges to San Francisco closed, as well as the Bay Area Rapid Transit and other means of access to the city. We expect to maintain these restrictions at least until tomorrow morning. The purpose of this is to prevent disorder and to avoid a possible influx of undesirable elements into the city while the trouble persists. We San Franciscans are self-sufficient and can look after our own needs without outside interference. However, I have been in contact with the president and with the governor, and they both have assured me of all possible assistance.

"The water supply is at present free of the drug, and every precaution is being taken to prevent a recurrence of this crime against one million innocent people. However, I am told that some lingering contamination may remain in the pipes for a few hours. I recommend that you keep your consumption of water low until further notice, and that you boil any water you wish to use.

"Lastly. Police Chief Dennison, myself, and your other city officials will be devoting full time to the needs of the city so long as the crisis lasts. Probably we will not have the opportunity to go before the media for further reports. Therefore, I have taken the step of appointing a committee of public safety, consisting of distinguished laymen and scientists of San Francisco, as a coordinating body that will aid in governing the city and reporting to its citizens. The chairman of this committee is the well-known veteran of so many exploits in space, Commander Taylor Braskett. Announcements concerning the developments in the crisis will come from Commander Braskett for the remainder of the evening, and you may consider his words to be those of your city officials. Thank you."

Braskett came on the screen. Montini grunted. "Look at the man they find! A maniac patriot!"

"But the drug will wear off," Nadia said. "Your mind will be all right again."

"I know these drugs. There is no hope. I am destroyed." The Amazing Móntini moved toward the door. "I need fresh air. I will go out. Goodbye, Nadia."

She tried to stop him. He pushed her aside. Entering Marina Park, he made his way to the yacht club; the doorman admitted him, and took no further notice. Montini walked out on the pier. The drug, they say, is temporary. It will wear off. My mind will clear. I doubt this very much. Montini peered at the dark, oily water, glistening with light reflected from the bridge. He explored his damaged mind, scanning for gaps. Whole sections of memory were gone. The walls had crumbled, slabs of plaster falling away to expose bare lath. He could not live this way. Carefully, grunting from the exertion, he lowered himself via a metal ladder into the water, and kicked himself away from the pier. The water was terribly cold. His shoes seemed immensely heavy. He floated toward the island of the old prison, but he doubted that he would remain afloat much longer. As he drifted, he ran through an inventory of his memory, seeing what remained to him and finding less than enough. To test whether even his gift had survived, he attempted to play back a recall of the mayor's speech, and found the words shifting and melting. It is just as well, then, he told himself, and drifted on, and went under.

Carole insisted on spending Thursday night with him.

"We aren't man and wife any more," he had to tell her. "You divorced me."

"Since when are you so conventional? We lived together before we were married, and now we can live together after we were married. Maybe we're inventing a new sin, Paul. Postmarital sex."

"That isn't the point. The point is that you came to hate me because of my financial mess, and you left me. If you try to come back to me now, you'll be going against your own rational and deliberate decision of last January."

"For me last January is still four months away," she said. "I don't hate you. I love you. I always have and always will. I can't imagine how I would ever have come to divorce you, but in any case I don't remember divorcing you, and you don't remember being divorced by me, and so why can't we just keep going from the point where our memories leave off?"

"Among other things, because you happen to be Pete Castine's wife now."

"That sounds completely unreal to me. Something you dreamed."

"Freddy Munson told me, though. It's true."

"If I went back to Pete now," Carole said, "I'd feel sinful. Simply because I supposedly married him, you want me to jump into bed with him? I don't want him. I want you. Can't I stay here?"

"If Pete—"

"If Pete, if Pete, if Pete! In my mind I'm Mrs. Paul Mueller, and in your mind I am too, and to hell with Pete, and with whatever Freddy Munson told you, and everything else. This is a silly argument, Paul. Let's quit it. If you want me to get out, tell me so right now in that many words. Otherwise let me stay."

He couldn't tell her to get out.

He had only the one small cot, but they managed to share it. It was uncomfortable, but in an amusing way. He felt twenty years old again for a while. In the morning they took a long shower together, and then Carole went out to buy some things for breakfast, since his service had been cut off and he couldn't punch for food. A dunning robot outside the door told him, as Carole was leaving, "The decree of personal service due has been requested, Mr. Mueller, and is now pending a court hearing."

"I know you not," Mueller said. "Begone!"

Today, he told himself, he would hunt up Freddy Munson somehow and get that cash from him, and buy the tools he needed, and start working again. Let the world outside go crazy; so long as he was working, all was well. If he couldn't find Freddy, maybe he could swing the purchase on Carole's credit. She was legally divorced from him and none of his credit taint would stain her; as Mrs. Peter Castine she should surely be able to get hold of a couple of bigs to pay Metchnikoff. Possibly the banks were closed on account of the memory crisis today, Mueller considered; but Metchnikoff surely wouldn't demand cash from Carole. He closed his eyes and imagined how good it would feel to be making things once more.

Carole was gone an hour. When she came back, carrying groceries, Pete Castine was with her.

"He followed me," Carole explained. "He wouldn't let me alone."

He was a slim, poised, controlled man, quite athletic, several years older than Mueller—perhaps into his fifties already—but seemingly very young. Calmly he said, "I was sure that Carole had come here. It's perfectly understandable, Paul. She was here all night, I hope?"

"Does it matter?" Mueller asked.

"To some extent. I'd rather have had her spending the night with her former husband than with some third party entirely."

"She was here all night, yes," Mueller said wearily.

"I'd like her to come home with me now. She *is* my wife, after all."

"She has no recollection of that. Neither do I."

"I'm aware of that." Castine nodded amiably. "In my own case, I've forgotten everything that happened to me before the age of twenty-two. I couldn't tell you my father's first name. However, as a matter of objective reality, Carole's my wife, and her parting from you was rather bitter, and I feel she shouldn't stay here any longer."

"Why are you telling all this to me?" Mueller asked. "If you want your wife to go home with you, ask her to go home with you."

"So I did. She says she won't leave unless you direct her to go."

"That's right," Carole said. "I know whose wife I *think* I am. If Paul throws me out I'll go with you. Not otherwise."

Mueller shrugged. "I'd be a fool to throw her out, Pete. I need her and I want her, and whatever breakup she and I had isn't real to us. I know it's tough on you, but I can't help that. I imagine you'll have no trouble getting an annulment once the courts work out some law to cover cases like this."

Castine was silent for a long moment.

At length he said, "How has your work been going, Paul?"

"I gather that I haven't turned out a thing all year."

"That's correct."

"I'm planning to start again. You might say that Carole has inspired me."

"Splendid," said Castine without intonation of any kind. "I trust this little mixup over our—ah—shared wife won't interfere with the harmonious artist-dealer relationship we used to enjoy?"

"Not at all," Mueller said. "You'll still get my whole output. Why the hell should I resent anything you did? Carole was a free agent when you married her. There's only one little trouble."

"Yes?"

"I'm broke. I have no tools, and I can't work without tools, and I have no way of buying tools."

"How much do you need?"

"Two and a half bigs."

Castine said, "Where's your data pickup? I'll make a credit transfer."

"The phone company disconnected it a long time ago."

"Let me give you a check, then. Say, three thousand even? An advance against future sales." Castine fumbled for a while before locating a blank check. "First one of these I've written in five years, maybe. Odd how you get accustomed to spending by telephone. Here you are, and good luck. To both of you." He made a courtly, bitter bow. "I hope you'll be happy together. And call me up when you've finished a few pieces, Paul. I'll send the van. I suppose you'll have a phone again by then." He went out.

"There's a blessing in being able to forget," Nate Haldersen said. "The redemption of oblivion, I call it. What's happened to San Francisco this week isn't necessarily a disaster. For some of us, it's the finest thing in the world."

They were listening to him—at least fifty people, clustering near his feet. He stood on the stage of the bandstand in the park, just across from the De Young Museum. Shadows were gathering. Friday, the second full day of the memory crisis, was ending. Haldersen had slept in the park last night, and he planned to sleep there again tonight; he realized after his escape from the hospital that his apartment had been shut down long ago and his possessions were in storage. It did not matter. He would live off the land and forage for food. The flame of prophecy was aglow in him.

"Let me tell you how it was with me," he cried. "Three days ago I was in a hospital for mental illness. Some of you are smiling, perhaps, telling me I ought to be back there now, but no! You don't understand. I was incapable of facing the world. Wherever I went, I saw happy families, parents and children, and it made me sick with envy and hatred, so that I couldn't function in society. Why? Why? Because my own wife and children were killed in an air disaster in 1991, that's why, and I missed the plane because I was committing sin that day, and for my sin they died, and I lived thereafter in unending torment! But now all that is flushed from my mind. I have sinned, and I have suffered, and now I am redeemed through merciful oblivion!"

A voice in the crowd called, "If you've forgotten all about it, how come you're telling the story to us?"

"A good question! An excellent question!" Haldersen felt sweat bursting from his pores, adrenaline pumping in his veins. "I know the story only because a machine in the hospital told it to me, yesterday morning. But it came to me from the outside, a secondhand tale. The experience of it within me, the scars, all that has been washed away. The pain of it is gone. Oh, yes, I'm sad that my innocent family perished, but a healthy man learns to control his grief after eleven years, he accepts his loss and goes on. I was sick, sick right *here*, and I couldn't live with my grief, but now I can, I look on it objectively, do you see! And that's why I say there's a blessing in being able to forget. What about you, out there? There must be some of you who suffered painful losses too, and now can no longer remember them, now have been redeemed and released from anguish. Are there any? Are there? Raise your hands. Who's been bathed in holy oblivion? Who out there knows that he's been cleansed, even if he can't remember what it is he's been cleansed from?"

Hands were starting to go up.

Freddy Munson had spent Thursday afternoon, Thursday night, and all of Friday holed up in his apartment with every communication link to the outside turned off. He neither took nor made calls, ignored the telescreens, and had switched on the xerofax only three times in the thirty-six hours.

He knew that he was finished, and he was trying to decide how to react to it.

His memory situation seemed to have stabilized. He was still missing only five weeks of market maneuvers. There wasn't any further decay—not that that mattered; he was in trouble enough—and, despite an optimistic statement last night by Mayor Chase, Munson hadn't seen any evidence that memory loss was reversing itself. He was unable to reconstruct any of the vanished details.

There was no immediate peril, he knew. Most of the clients whose accounts he'd been juggling were wealthy old bats who wouldn't worry about their stocks until they got next month's account statements. They had given him discretionary powers, which was how he had been able to tap their resources for his own benefit in the first place. Up to now, Munson had always been able to complete each transaction within a single month, so the account balanced for every statement. He had dealt with the problem of the securities withdrawals that the statements ought to show by gimmicking the house computer to delete all such withdrawals provided there was no net effect from month to month; that way he could borrow 10,000 shares of United Spaceways or Comsat or IBM for two weeks, use the stock as collateral for a deal of his own, and get it back into the proper account in time with no one the wiser. Three weeks from now, though, the end-of-the-month statements were going to go out showing all of his accounts peppered by inexplicable withdrawals, and he was going to catch hell.

The trouble might even start earlier, and come from a different direction. Since the San Francisco trouble had begun, the market had gone down sharply, and he would probably be getting margin calls on Monday. The San Francisco exchange was closed, of course; it hadn't been able to open Thursday morning because so many of the brokers had been hit hard by amnesia. But New York's exchanges were open, and they had reacted badly to the news from San Francisco, probably out of fear that a conspiracy was afoot and the whole country might soon be pushed into chaos. When the local exchange opened again on Monday, if it opened, it would most likely open at the last New York prices, or near them, and keep on going down. Munson would be asked to put up cash or additional securities to cover his loans. He certainly didn't have the cash, and the only way he could get additional securities would be to dip into still more of his accounts, compounding his offense; on the other hand, if he didn't meet the margin calls they'd sell him out and he'd never be able to restore the stock to the proper accounts, even if he succeeded in remembering which shares went where.

He was trapped. He could stick around for a few weeks, waiting for the ax to fall, or he could get out right now. He preferred to get out right now.

And go where?

Caracas? Reno? Sao Paulo? No, debtor sanctuaries wouldn't do him any good, because he wasn't an ordinary debtor. He was a thief, and the sanctuaries didn't protect criminals, only bankrupts. He had to go farther, all the way to Luna Dome. There wasn't any extradition from the moon. There'd be no hope of coming back, either.

Munson got on the phone, hoping to reach his travel agent. Two tickets to Luna, please. One for him, one for Helene; if she didn't feel like coming, he'd go alone. No, not round trip. But the agent didn't answer. Munson tried the number several times. Shrugging, he decided to order direct, and called United Spaceways next. He got a busy signal. "Shall we wait-list your call?" the data net asked. "It will be three days, at the present state of the backlog of calls, before we can put it through."

"Forget it," Munson said.

He had just realized that San Francisco was closed off, anyway. Unless he tried to swim for it, he couldn't get out of the city to go to the spaceport, even if he did manage to buy tickets to Luna. He was caught here until they opened the transit routes again. How long would that be? Monday, Tuesday, next Friday? They couldn't keep the city shut forever—could they?

What it came down to, Munson saw, was a contest of probabilities. Would someone discover the discrepancies in his accounts before he found a way of escaping to Luna, or would his escape access become available too late? Put on those terms, it became an interesting gamble instead of a panic situation. He would spend the weekend trying to find a way out of San Francisco, and if he failed, he would try to be a stoic about facing what was to come.

Calm, now, he remembered that he had promised to lend Paul Mueller a few thousand dollars, to help him equip his studio again. Munson was unhappy over having let that slip his mind. He liked to be helpful. And, even now, what were two or three bigs to him? He had plenty of recoverable assets. Might as well let Paul have a little of the money before the lawyers start grabbing it.

One problem. He had less than a hundred in cash on him—who bothered carrying cash?—and he couldn't telephone a transfer of funds to Mueller's account, because Paul didn't have an account with a data net any more, or even a phone. There wasn't any place to get that much cash, either, at this hour of evening, especially with the city paralyzed. And the weekend was coming. Munson had an idea, though. What if he went shopping with Mueller tomorrow, and simply charged whatever the sculptor needed to his own account? Fine. He reached for the phone to arrange the date, remembered that Mueller could not be called, and decided to tell Paul about it in person. Now. He could use some fresh air, anyway.

He half expected to find robot bailiffs outside, waiting to arrest him. But of course no one was after him yet. He walked to the garage. It was a fine night, cool, starry, with perhaps just a hint of fog in the west. Berkeley's lights glittered through the haze. The streets were quiet. In time of crisis people stay home. He drove quickly to Mueller's place. Four robots were in front of it. Munson eyed them edgily, with the wary look of the man who knows that the sheriff will be after him too, in a little while. But Mueller, when he came to the door, took no notice of the dunners.

Munson said, "I'm sorry I missed connections with you. The money I promised to lend you—"

"It's all right, Freddy. Pete Castine was here this morning and I borrowed the three bigs from him. I've got my studio set up again. Come in and look?"

Munson entered. "Pete Castine?"

"A good investment for him. He makes money if he has work of mine to sell, right? It's in his best interest to help me get started again. Carole and I have been hooking things up all day."

"Carole?" Munson said. Mueller showed him into the studio. The paraphernalia of a sonic sculptor sat on the floor—a welding pen, a vacuum bell, a big texturing vat, some ingots and strands of wire, and such things. Carole was feeding discarded packing cases into the wall disposal unit. Looking up, she smiled uncertainly and ran her hand through her long dark hair.

"Hello, Freddy."

"Everybody good friends again?" he asked, baffled.

"Nobody remembers being enemies," she said. She laughed. "Isn't it wonderful to have your memory blotted out like this?"

"Wonderful," Munson said bleakly.

Commander Braskett said, "Can I offer you people any water?"

Tim Bryce smiled. Lisa Bryce smiled. Ted Kamakura smiled. Even Mayor Chase, that poor empty husk, smiled. Commander Braskett understood those smiles. Even now, after three days of close contact under pressure, they thought he was nuts.

He had had a week's supply of bottled water brought from his home to the command post here at the hospital. Everybody kept telling him that the municipal water was safe to drink now, that the memory drugs were gone from it; but why couldn't they comprehend that his aversion to public water dated back to an era when memory drugs were unknown? There were plenty of other chemicals in the reservoir, after all.

He hoisted his glass in a jaunty toast and winked at them.

Tim Bryce said, "Commander, we'd like you to address the city again at half past ten this morning. Here's your text."

Braskett scanned the sheet. It dealt mostly with the relaxation of the order to boil water before drinking it. "You want me to go on all media," he said, "and tell the people of San Francisco that it's safe for them to drink from the taps, eh? That's a bit awkward for me. Even a figurehead spokesman is entitled to some degree of personal integrity."

Bryce looked briefly puzzled. Then he laughed and took the text back. "You're absolutely right, commander. I can't ask you to make this announcement, in view of—ah—your particular beliefs. Let's change the plan. You open the spot by introducing me, and *I'll* discuss the no-boiling thing. Will that be all right?"

Commander Braskett appreciated the tactful way they deferred to his special obsession. "I'm at your service, doctor," he said gravely.

Bryce finished speaking and the camera lights left him. He said to Lisa, "What about lunch? Or breakfast, or whatever meal it is we're up to now."

"Everything's ready, Tim. Whenever you are."

They ate together in the holograph room, which had become the kitchen of the command post. Massive cameras and tanks of etching fluid surrounded them. The others thoughtfully left them alone. These brief shared meals were the only fragments of privacy he and Lisa had had, in the fifty-two hours since he had awakened to find her sleeping beside him.

He stared across the table in wonder at this delectable blonde girl who they said was his wife. How beautiful her soft brown eyes were against that backdrop of golden hair! How perfect the line of her lips, the curve of her earlobes! Bryce knew that no one would object if he and Lisa went off and locked themselves into one of the private rooms for a few hours. He wasn't that indispensable; and there was so much he had to begin relearning about his wife. But he was unable to leave his post. He hadn't been out of the hospital or even off this floor for the duration of the crisis; he kept himself going by grabbing the sleep wire for half an hour every six hours. Perhaps it was an illusion born of too little sleep and too much data, but he had come to believe that the survival of the city depended on him. He had spent his career trying to heal individual sick minds; now he had a whole city to tend to.

"Tired?" Lisa asked.

"I'm in the tiredness beyond feeling tired. My mind is so clear that my skull wouldn't cast a shadow. I'm nearing nirvana."

"The worst is over, I think. The city's settling down."

"It's still bad, though. Have you seen the suicide figures?"

"Bad?"

"Hideous. The norm in San Francisco is 220 a year. We've had close to five hundred in the last two and a half days. And that's just the reported cases, the bodies discovered, and so on. Probably we can double the figure. Thirty suicides reported Wednesday night, about two hundred on Thursday, the same on Friday, and about fifty so far this morning. At least it seems as if the wave is past its peak."

"But *why*, Tim?"

"Some people react poorly to loss. Especially the loss of a segment of their memories. They're indignant—they're crushed—they're scared—and they reach for the exit pill. Suicide's too easy now, anyway. In the old days you reacted to frustration by smashing the crockery; now you go a deadlier route. Of course, there are special cases. A man named Montini they fished out of the bay—a professional mnemonist, who did a trick act in nightclubs, total recall. I can hardly blame him for caving in. And I suppose there were a lot of others who kept their business in their heads—gamblers, stock-market operators, oral poets, musicians— who might decide to end it all rather than try to pick up the pieces."

"But if the effects of the drug wear off—"

"Do they?" Bryce asked.

"You said so yourself."

"I was making optimistic noises for the benefit of the citizens. We don't have any experimental history for these drugs and human subjects. Hell, Lisa, we don't even know the dosage that was administered; by the time we were able to get water samples most of the system had been flushed clean, and the automatic monitoring devices at the city pumping station were rigged as part of the conspiracy so they didn't show a thing out of the ordinary. I've got no idea at all if there's going to be any measurable memory recovery."

"But there is, Tim. I've already started to get some things back."

"*What?*"

"Don't scream at me like that! You scared me."

He clung to the edge of the table. "Are you really recovering?"

"Around the edges. I remember a few things already. About us."

"Like what?"

"Applying for the marriage license. I'm standing stark naked inside a diagnostat machine and a voice on the loudspeaker is telling me to look straight into the scanners. And I remember the

ceremony, a little. Just a small group of friends, a civil ceremony.
Then we took the pod to Acapulco."

He stared grimly. "When did this start to come back?"

"About seven this morning, I guess."

"Is there more?"

"A bit. Our honeymoon. The robot bellhop who came blundering
in on our wedding night. You don't—"

"Remember it? No. No. Nothing. Blank."

"That's all I remember, this early stuff."

"Yes, of course," he said. "The older memories are always the
first to return in any form of amnesia. The last stuff in is the first
to go." His hands were shaking, not entirely from fatigue. A strange
desolation crept over him. Lisa remembered. He did not. Was it a
function of her youth, or of the chemistry of her brain, or—?

He could not bear the thought that they no longer shared an
oblivion. He didn't want the amnesia to become one-sided for them;
it was humiliating not to remember his own marriage when she did.
You're being irrational, he told himself. Physician, heal thyself!

"Let's go back inside," he said.

"You haven't finished your—"

"Later."

He went into the command room. Kamakura had phones in both
hands and was barking data into a recorder. The screens were alive
with morning scenes, Saturday in the city, crowds in Union Square.
Kamakura hung up both calls and said, "I've got an interesting
report from Dr. Klein at Letterman General. He says they're
getting the first traces of memory recovery this morning. Women
under thirty, only."

"Lisa says she's beginning to remember too," Bryce said.

"Women under thirty," said Kamakura. "Yes. Also the suicide
rate is definitely tapering. We may be starting to come out of it."

"Terrific," Bryce said hollowly.

Haldersen was living in a ten-foot-high bubble that one of his
disciples had blown for him in the middle of Golden Gate Park,
just west of the Arboretum. Fifteen similar bubbles had gone up
around his, giving the region the look of an up-to-date Eskimo
village in plastic igloos. The occupants of the camp, aside from
Haldersen, were men and women who had so little memory left
that they did not know who they were or where they lived. He had
acquired a dozen of these lost ones on Friday, and by late afternoon
on Saturday he had been joined by some forty more. The news
somehow was moving through the city that those without moorings

were welcome to take up temporary residence with the group in the park. It had happened that way during the 1906 disaster, too.

The police had been around a few times to check on them. The first time, a portly lieutenant had tried to persuade the whole group to move to Fletcher Memorial. "That's where most of the victims are getting treatment, you see. The doctors give them something, and then we try to identify them and find their next of kin—"

"Perhaps it's best for these people to remain away from their next of kin for a while," Haldersen suggested. "Some meditation in the park—and exploration of the pleasures of having forgotten—that's all we're doing here." He would not go to Fletcher Memorial himself except under duress. As for the others, he felt he could do more for them in the park than anyone in the hospital could.

The second time the police came, Saturday afternoon when his group was much larger, they brought a mobile communications system. "Dr. Bryce of Fletcher Memorial wants to talk to you," a different lieutenant said.

Haldersen watched the screen come alive. "Hello, doctor. Worried about me?"

"I'm worried about everyone, Nate. What the hell are you doing in the park?"

"Founding a new religion, I think."

"You're a sick man. You ought to come back here."

"No, doctor. I'm not sick any more. I've had my therapy and I'm fine. It was a beautiful treatment: selective obliteration, just as I prayed for. The entire trauma is gone."

Bryce appeared fascinated by that; his frowning expression of offical responsibility vanished a moment, giving place to a look of professional concern. "Interesting," he said. "We've got people who've forgotten only nouns, and people who've forgotten who they married, and people who've forgotten how to play the violin. But you're the first one who's forgotten a trauma. You still ought to come back here, though. You aren't the best judge of your fitness to face the outside environment."

"Oh, but I am," Haldersen said. "I'm doing fine. And my people need me."

"Your people?"

"Waifs. Strays. The total wipeouts."

"We want those people in the hospital, Nate. We want to get them back to their families."

"Is that necessarily a good deed? Maybe some of them can use a spell of isolation from their families. These people look happy, Dr. Bryce. I've heard there are a lot of suicides, but not here. We're practicing mutual supportive therapy. Looking for the joys to be found in oblivion. It seems to work."

Bryce stared silently out of the screen for a long moment. Then he said impatiently, "All right, have it your own way for now. But I wish you'd stop coming on like Jesus and Freud combined, and leave the park. You're still a sick man, Nate, and the people with you are in serious trouble. I'll talk to you later."

The contact broke. The police, stymied, left.

Haldersen spoke briefly to his people at five o'clock. Then he sent them out as missionaries to collect other victims. "Save as many as you can," he said. "Find those who are in complete despair and get them into the park before they can take their own lives. Explain that the loss of one's past is not the loss of all things."

The disciples went forth. And came back leading those less fortunate than themselves. The group grew to more than one hundred by nightfall. Someone found the extruder again and blew twenty more bubbles as shelters for the night. Haldersen preached his sermon of joy, looking out at the blank eyes, the slack faces of those whose identities had washed away on Wednesday. "Why give up?" he asked them. "Now is your chance to create new lives for yourself. The slate is clean! Choose the direction you will take, define your new selves through the exercise of free will—you are reborn in holy oblivion, all of you. Rest, now, those who have just come to us. And you others, go forth again, seek out the wanderers, the drifters, the lost ones hiding in the corners of the city—"

As he finished, he saw a knot of people bustling toward him from the direction of the South Drive. Fearing trouble, Haldersen went out to meet them; but as he drew close he saw half a dozen disciples, clutching a scruffy, unshaven, terrified little man. They hurled him at Haldersen's feet. The man quivered. His eyes glistened; his wedge of a face, sharp-chinned, sharp of cheekbones, was pale.

"It's the one who poisoned the water supply!" someone called. "We found him in a rooming house on Judah Street. With a stack of drugs in his room, and the plans of the water system, and a bunch of computer programs. He admits it. He admits it!"

Haldersen looked down. "Is this true?" he asked. "Are you the one?"

The man nodded.

"What's your name?"

"Won't say. Want a lawyer."

"Kill him now!" a woman shrieked. "Pull his arms and legs off!"

"Kill him!" came an answering cry from the other side of the group. "Kill him!"

The congregation, Haldersen realized, might easily turn into a mob.

He said. "Tell me your name, and I'll protect you. Otherwise I can't be responsible."

"Skinner," the man muttered miserably.

"Skinner. And you contaminated the water supply."

Another nod.

"Why?"

"To get even."

"With whom?"

"Everyone. Everybody."

Classic paranoid. Haldersen felt pity. Not the others; they were calling out for blood.

A tall man bellowed, "Make the bastard drink his own drug!"

"No, kill him! Squash him!"

The voices became more menacing. The angry faces came closer.

"Listen to me," Haldersen called, and his voice cut through the murmurings. "There'll be no killing here tonight."

"What are you going to do, give him to the police?"

"No," said Haldersen. "We'll hold communion together. We'll teach this pitiful man the blessings of oblivion, and then we'll share new joys ourselves. We are human beings. We have the capacity to forgive even the worst of sinners. Where are the memory drugs? Did someone say you had found the memory drugs? Here. Here. Pass it up here. Yes. Brothers, sisters, let us show this dark and twisted soul the nature of redemption. Yes. Yes. Fetch some water, please. Thank you. Here, Skinner. Stand him up, will you? Hold his arms. Keep him from falling down. Wait a second, until I find the proper dose. Yes. Yes. Here, Skinner. Forgiveness. Sweet oblivion."

It was so good to be working again that Mueller didn't want to stop. By early afternoon on Saturday his studio was ready; he had long since worked out the sketches of the first piece; now it was just a matter of time and effort, and he'd have something to show Pete Castine. He worked on far into the evening, setting up his armature and running a few tests of the sound sequences that he proposed to build into the piece. He had some interesting new ideas about the sonic triggers, the devices that would set off the sound effects when the appreciator came within range. Carole had to tell him, finally, that dinner was ready. "I didn't want to interrupt you," she said, "but it looks like I have to, or you won't ever stop."

"Sorry. The creative ecstasy."

"Save some of that energy. There are other ecstasies. The ecstasy of dinner, first."

She had cooked everything herself. Beautiful. He went back to work again afterward, but at half past one in the morning Carole interrupted him. He was willing to stop, now. He had done an honest day's work, and he was sweaty with the noble sweat of a job well done. Two minutes under the molecular cleanser and the sweat was gone, but the good ache of virtuous fatigue remained. He hadn't felt this way in years.

He woke to Sunday thoughts of unpaid debts.

"The robots are still there," he said. "They won't go away, will they? Even thought the whole city's at a standstill, nobody's told the robots to quit."

"Ignore them," Carole said.

"That's what I've been doing. But I can't ignore the debts. Ultimately there'll be a reckoning."

"You're working again, though! You'll have an income coming in."

"Do you know what I owe?" he asked. "Almost a million. If I produced one piece a week for a year, and sold each piece for twenty bigs, I might pay everything off. But I can't work that fast, and the market can't possibly absorb that many Muellers, and Pete certainly can't buy them all for future sale."

He noticed the way Carole's face darkened at the mention of Pete Castine.

He said, "You know what I'll have to do? Go to Caracas, like I was planning before this memory thing started. I can work there, and ship my stuff to Pete. And maybe in two or three years I'll have paid off my debt, a hundred cents on the dollar, and I can start fresh back here. Do you know if that's possible? I mean, if you jump to a debtor sanctuary, are you blackballed for credit forever, even if you pay off what you owe?"

"I don't know," Carole said distantly.

"I'll find that out later. The important thing is that I'm working again, and I've got to go someplace where I can work without being hounded. And then I'll pay everybody off. You'll come with me to Caracas, won't you?"

"Maybe we won't have to go," Carole said.

"But how—"

"You should be working now, shouldn't you?"

He worked, and while he worked he made lists of creditors in his mind, dreaming of the day when every name on every list was crossed off. When he got hungry he emerged from the studio and found Carole sitting gloomily in the living room. Her eyes were red and puffy-lidded.

"What's wrong?" he asked. "You don't want to go to Caracas?"

"Please, Paul—let's not talk about it—"

"I've really got no alternative. I mean, unless we pick one of the other sanctuaries. Sao Paulo? Spalato?"

"It isn't that, Paul."

"What, then?"

"I'm starting to remember again."

The air went out of him. "Oh," he said.

"I remember November, December, January. The crazy things you were doing, the loans, the financial juggling. And the quarrels we had. They were terrible quarrels."

"Oh."

"The divorce. I remember, Paul. It started coming back last night, but you were so happy I didn't want to say anything. And this morning it's much clearer. You still don't remember any of it?"

"Not a thing past last October."

"I do," she said, shakily. "You hit me, do you know that? You cut my lip. You slammed me against the wall, right over there, and then you threw the Chinese vase at me and it broke."

"Oh. Oh."

She went on, "I remember how good Pete was to me, too. I think I can almost remember marrying him, being his wife. Paul, I'm scared. I feel everything fitting into place in my mind, and it's as scary as if my mind was breaking into pieces. It was so good, Paul, these last few days. It was like being a newlywed with you again. But now all the sour parts are coming back, the hate, the ugliness, it's all alive for me again. And I feel so bad about Pete. The two of us, Friday, shutting him out. He was a real gentleman about it. But the fact is that he saved me when I was going under, and I owe him something for that."

"What do you plan to do?" he asked quietly.

"I think I ought to go back to him. I'm his wife. I've got no right to stay here."

"But I'm not the same man you came to hate," Mueller protested. "I'm the old Paul; the one from last year and before. The man you loved. All the hateful stuff is gone from me."

"Not from me, though. Not now."

They were both silent.

"I think I should go back, Paul."

"Whatever you say."

"I think I should. I wish you all kinds of luck, but I can't stay here. Will it hurt your work if I leave again?"

"I won't know until you do."

She told him three or four times that she felt she ought to go back to Castine, and then, politely, he suggested that she should go back right now, if that was how she felt, and she did. He spent half an hour wandering around the apartment, which seemed so awfully empty again. He nearly invited one of the dunning robots in for company. Instead, he went back to work. To his surprise, he worked quite well, and in an hour he had ceased thinking about Carole entirely.

Sunday afternoon, Freddy Munson set up a credit transfer and managed to get most of his liquid assets fed into an old account he kept at the Bank of Luna. Toward evening, he went down to the wharf and boarded a three-man hovercraft owned by a fisherman willing to take his chances with the law. They slipped out into the bay without running lights and crossed the bay on a big diagonal, landing some time later a few miles north of Berkeley. Munson found a cab to take him to the Oakland airport, and caught the midnight shuttle to L.A., where, after a lot of fancy talking, he was able to buy his way aboard the next Luna-bound rocket, lifting off at ten o'clock Monday morning. He spent the night in the spaceport terminal. He had taken with him nothing except the clothes he wore; his fine possessions, his paintings, his suits, his Mueller sculptures, and all the rest remained in his apartment, and ultimately would be sold to satisfy the judgements against him. Too bad. He knew that he wouldn't be coming back to Earth again, either, not with a larceny warrant or worse awaiting him. Also too bad. It had been so nice for so long, here, and who needed a memory drug in the water supply? Munson had only one consolation. It was an article of his philosophy that sooner or later, no matter how neatly you organized your life, fate opened a trapdoor underneath your feet and catapulted you into something unknown and unpleasant. Now he knew that it was true even for him.

Too, too bad. He wondered what his chances were of starting over up there. Did they need stockbrokers on the moon?

Addressing the citizenry on Monday night, Commander Braskett said, "The committee of public safety is pleased to report that we have come through the worst part of the crisis. As many of you have already discovered, memories are beginning to return. The process of recovery will be more swift for some than others, but great progress has been made. Effective at six A.M. tomorrow, access routes to and from San Francisco will reopen. There will be normal mail services and many businesses will return to normal. Fellow citizens, we have demonstrated once again the real fiber of the American spirit. The founding fathers must be smiling down upon us today! How superbly we avoided chaos, and how beautifully we pulled together to help one another in what could have been an hour of turmoil and despair!

"Dr. Bryce requests me to remind you that anyone still suffering severe impairment of memory—especially those experiencing loss of identity, confusion of vital functions, or other disability—should report to the emergency ward at Fletcher Memorial Hospital. Treatment is available there, and computer analysis is at the service of those unable to find their homes and loved ones. I repeat—"

Tim Bryce wished that the good commander hadn't slipped in that plug for the real fiber of the American spirit, especially in view of the necessity to invite the remaining victims to the hospital with his next words. But it would be uncharitable to object. The old spaceman had done a beautiful job all weekend as the Voice of the Crisis, and some patriotic embellishments now were harmless.

The crisis, of course, was nowhere near as close to being over as Commander Braskett's speech had suggested, but public confidence had to be buoyed.

Bryce had the latest figures. Suicides now totaled nine hundred since the start of trouble on Wednesday; Sunday had been an unexpectedly bad day. At least forty thousand people were still unaccounted for, although they were tracing one thousand an hour and getting them back to their families or else into an intensive-care section. Probably seven hundred and fifty thousand more continued to have memory difficulties. Most children had fully recovered, and many of the woman were mending; but older people, and men in general, had experienced scarcely any memory recapture. Even those who were nearly healed had no recall of events of Tuesday and Wednesday, and probably never would; for large numbers of people, though, big blocks of the past would have to be learned from the outside, like history lessons.

Lisa was teaching him their marriage that way.

The trips they had taken—the good times, the bad—the parties, the friends, the shared dreams—she described everything as vividly as she could, and he fastened on each anecdote, trying to make it a part of himself again. He knew it was hopeless, really. He'd know the outlines, never the substance. Yet it was probably the best he could hope for.

He was so horribly tired, suddenly.

He said to Kamakura, "Is there anything new from the park yet? That rumor that Haldersen's actually got a supply of the drug?"

"Seems to be be true, Tim. The word is that he and his friends caught the character who spiked the water supply, and relieved him of a roomful of various amnesifacients."

"We've got to seize them," Bryce said.

Kamakura shook his head. "Not just yet. Police are afraid of any actions in the park. They say it's a volatile situation."

"But if those drugs are loose—"

"Let me worry about it, Tim. Look, why don't you and Lisa go home for a while? You've been here without a break since Thursday."

"So have—"

"No. Everybody else has had a breather. Go on, now. We're over the worst. Relax, get some real sleep, make some love. Get to know that gorgeous wife of yours again a little."

Bryce reddened. "I'd rather stay here until I feel I can afford to leave."

Scowling, Kamakura walked away from him to confer with Commander Braskett. Bryce scanned the screens, trying to figure out what was going on in the park. A moment later, Braskett walked over to him.

"Dr. Bryce?"

"What?"

"You're relieved of duty until sundown Tuesday."

"Wait a second—"

"That's an order, doctor. I'm chairman of the committee of public safety, and I'm telling you to get yourself out of this hospital. You aren't going to disobey an order, are you?"

"Listen, commander—"

"Out. No mutiny, Bryce. Out! Orders."

Bryce tried to protest, but he was too weary to put up much of a fight. By noon, he was on his way home, soupy-headed with fatigue. Lisa drove. He sat quite still, struggling to remember details of marriage. Nothing came.

She put him to bed. He wasn't sure how long he slept; but then he felt her against him; warm, satin-smooth.

"Hello," she said. "Remember me?"

"Yes," he lied gratefully. "Oh, yes, yes, yes!"

Working right through the night, Mueller finished his armature by dawn on Monday. He slept awhile, and in early afternoon began to paint the inner strips of loudspeakers on: a thousand speakers to the inch, no more than a few molecules thick, from which the sounds of his sculpture would issue in resonant fullness. When that was done, he paused to contemplate the needs of his sculpture's superstructure, and by seven that night was ready to move to the next phase. The demons of creativity possessed him; he saw no reason to eat and scarcely any to sleep.

At eight, just as he was getting up momentum for the long night's work, he heard a knock at the door. Carole's signal. He had disconnected the doorbell, and robots didn't have the sense to knock. Uneasily, he went to the door. She was there.

"So?" he said.

"So I came back. So it starts all over."

"What's going on?"

"Can I come in?" she asked.

"I suppose. I'm working, but come in."

She said, "I talked it over with Pete. We both decided I ought to go back to you."

"You aren't much for consistency, are you?"

"I have to take things as they happen. When I lost my memory, I came to you. When I remembered things again, I felt I ought to leave. I didn't *want* to leave. I felt I *ought* to leave. There's a difference."

"Really," he said.

"Really. I went to Pete, but I didn't want to be with him. I wanted to be here."

"I hit you and made your lip bleed. I threw the Ming vase at you."

"It wasn't Ming, it was K'ang-hsi."

"Pardon me. My memory still isn't so good. Anyway, I did terrible things to you, and you hated me enough to want a divorce. So why come back?"

"You were right, yesterday. You aren't the man I came to hate. You're the old Paul."

"And if my memory of the past nine months returns?"

"Even so," she said. "People change. You've been through hell and come out the other side. You're working again. You aren't sullen and nasty and confused. We'll go to Caracas, or wherever you want, and you'll do your work and pay your debts, just as you said yesterday."

"And Pete?"

"He'll arrange an annulment. He's being swell about it."

"Good old Pete," Mueller said. He shook his head. "How long will this neat happy ending last, Carole? If you think there's a chance you'll be bouncing back in the other direction by Wednesday, say so now. I'd rather not get involved again, in that case."

"No chance. None."

"Unless I throw the Chi'ien-lung vase at you."

"K'ang-hsi," she said.

"Yes. K'ang-hsi." He managed to grin. Suddenly he felt the accumulated fatigue of these days register all at once. "I've been working too hard," he said. "An orgy of creativity to make up for lost time. Let's go for a walk."

"Fine," she said.

They went out, just as a dunning robot was arriving. "Top of the evening to you, sir," Mueller said.

"Mr. Mueller, I represent the accounts receivable department of Acme Brass and—"

"See my attorney," he said.

Fog was rolling in off the sea now. There were no stars. The downtown lights were invisible. He and Carole walked west, toward the park. He felt strangely light-headed, not entirely from lack of sleep. Reality and dream had merged; these were unusual days. They entered the park from the Panhandle and strolled toward the museum area, arm in arm, saying nothing much to one another. As they passed the conservatory Mueller became aware of a crowd up ahead, thousands of people staring in the direction of the music shell. "What do you think is going on?" Carole asked. Mueller shrugged. They edged through the crowd.

Ten minutes later they were close enough to see the stage. A tall, thin, wild-looking man with unruly yellow hair was on the stage. Beside him was a small, scrawny man in ragged clothing, and there were a dozen others flanking them, carrying ceramic bowls.

"What's happening?" Mueller asked someone in the crowd.

"Religious ceremony."

"Eh?"

"New religion. Church of Oblivion. That's the head prophet up there. You haven't heard about it yet?"

"Not a thing."

"Started around Friday. You see that ratty-looking character next to the prophet?"

"Yes."

"He's the one that put the stuff in the water supply. He confessed and they made him drink his own drug. Now he doesn't remember a thing, and he's the assistant prophet. Craziest damn stuff!"

"And what are they doing up there?"

"They've got the drug in those bowls. They drink and forget some more. They drink and forget some more."

The gathering fog absorbed the sounds of those on the stage. Mueller strained to listen. He saw the bright eyes of fanaticism; the alleged contaminator of the water looked positively radiant. Words drifted out into the night.

"Brothers and sisters . . . the joy, the sweetness of forgetting . . . come up here with us, take communion with us . . . oblivion . . . redemption . . . even for the most wicked . . . forget . . . forget . . ."

They were passing the bowls around on stage, drinking, smiling. People were going up to receive the communion, taking a bowl, sipping, nodding happily. Toward the rear of the stage the bowls were being refilled by three sober-looking functionaries.

Mueller felt a chill. He suspected that what had been born in this park during this week would endure, somehow, long after the crisis of San Francisco had become part of history; and it seemed to him that something new and frightening had been loosed upon the land.

"Take . . . drink . . . forget . . ." the prophet cried.

And the worshippers cried, "*Take . . . drink . . . forget . . .*"

The bowls were passed.

"What's it all *about?*" Carole whispered.

"Take . . . drink . . . forget . . ."

"*Take . . . drink . . . forget . . .*"

"Blessed is the sweet oblivion."

"*Blessed is the sweet oblivion.*"

"Sweet it is to lay down the burden of one's soul."

"*Sweet it is to lay down the burden of one's soul.*"

"Joyous it is to begin anew."

"*Joyous it is to begin anew.*"

The fog was deepening. Mueller could barely see the aquarium building just across the way. He clasped his hand tightly around Carole's and began to think about getting out of the park.

He had to admit, though, that these people might have hit on something true. Was he not better off for having taken a chemical into his bloodstream, and thereby shedding a portion of his past? Yes, of course. And yet—to mutilate one's mind this way, deliberately, happily, to drink deep of oblivion—

"Blessed are those who are able to forget," the prophet said.

"*Blessed are those who are able to forget,*" the crowd roared in response.

"Blessed are those who are able to forget," Mueller heard his own voice cry. And he began to tremble. And he felt sudden fear: He sensed the power of this strange new movement, the gathering strength of the prophet's appeal to unreason. It was time for a new religion, maybe, a cult that offered emancipation from all inner burdens. They would synthesize this drug and turn it out by the ton, Mueller thought, and repeatedly dose cities with it, so that everyone could be converted, so that everyone might taste the joys of oblivion. No one will be able to stop them. After a while no one will *want* to stop them. And so we'll go on, drinking deep, until we're washed clean of all pain and all sorrow, of all sad recollection, we'll sip a cup of kindness and part with auld lang syne, we'll give up the griefs we carry around, and we'll give up everything else, identity, soul, self, mind. We will drink sweet oblivion. Mueller shivered. Turning suddenly, tugging roughly at Carole's arm, he pushed through the joyful worshipping crowd, and hunted somberly in the fog-wrapped night, trying to find some way out of the park.

THE HIGHEST TREASON

Randall Garrett

The Prisoner

The two rooms were not luxurious, but MacMaine hadn't expected that they would be. The walls were a flat metallic gray, unadorned and windowless. The ceilings and floors were simply continuations of the walls, except for the glow-plates overhead. One room held a small cabinet for his personal possessions, a wide, reasonably soft bed, a small but adequate desk, and, in one corner, a cubicle that contained the necessary sanitary plumbing facilities.

The other room held a couch, two big easy-chairs, a low table, some bookshelves, a squat refrigerator containing food and drink for his occasional snacks—his regular meals were brought in hot from the main kitchen—and a closet that contained his clothing—the insignialess uniforms of a Kerothi officer.

No, thought Sebastian MacMaine, it was not luxurious, but neither did it look like the prison cell it was.

There was comfort here, and even the illusion of privacy, although there were TV pickups in the walls, placed so that no movement in either room would go unnoticed. The switch which cut off the soft white light from the glow plates did not cut off the infrared radiation which enabled his hosts to watch him while he slept. Every sound was heard and recorded.

But none of that bothered MacMaine. On the contrary, he was glad of it. He wanted the Kerothi to know that he had no intention of escaping or hatching any plot against them.

He had long since decided that, if things continued as they had,

Earth would lose the war with Keroth, and Sebastian MacMaine had no desire whatever to be on the losing side of the greatest war ever fought. The problem now was to convince the Kerothi that he fully intended to fight with them, to give them the full benefit of his ability as a military strategist, to do his best to win every battle for Keroth.

And that was going to be the most difficult task of all.

A telltale glow of red blinked rapidly over the door, and a soft chime pinged in time with it.

MacMaine smiled inwardly, although not a trace of it showed on his broad-jawed, blocky face. To give him the illusion that he was a guest rather than a prisoner, the Kerothi had installed an announcer at the door and invariably used it. Not once had any one of them ever simply walked in on him.

"Come in," MacMaine said.

He was seated in one of the easy-chairs in his "living room," smoking a cigarette and reading a book on the history of Keroth, but he put the book down on the low table as a tall Kerothi came in through the doorway.

MacMaine allowed himself a smile of honest pleasure. To most Earthmen, "all the Carrot-skins look alike," and, MacMaine admitted honestly to himself, he hadn't yet trained himself completely to look beyond the strangenesses that made the Kerothi different from Earthmen and see the details that made them different from each other. But this was one Kerothi that MacMaine would never mistake for any other.

"Tallis!" He stood up and extended both hands in the Kerothi fashion. The other did the same, and they clasped hands for a moment. "How are your guts?" he added in Kerothic.

"They function smoothly, my sibling-by-choice," answered Space General Polan Tallis. "And your own?"

"Smoothly, indeed. It's been far too long a time since we have touched."

The Kerothi stepped back a pace and looked the Earthman up and down. "You look healthy enough—for a prisoner. You're treated well, then?"

"Well enough. Sit down, my sibling-by-choice." MacMaine waved toward the couch nearby. The general sat down and looked around the apartment.

"Well, well. You're getting preferential treatment, all right. This is as good as you could expect as a battleship commander. Maybe you're being trained for the job."

MacMaine laughed, allowing the touch of sardonicism that he felt to be heard in the laughter. "I might have hoped so once, Tallis. But I'm afraid I have simply come out even. I have traded nothing for nothing."

General Tallis reached into the pocket of his uniform jacket and took out the thin aluminum case that held the Kerothi equivalent of cigarettes. He took one out, put it between his lips, and lit it with the hotpoint that was built into the case.

MacMaine took an Earth cigarette out of the package on the table and allowed Tallis to light it for him. The pause and the silence, MacMaine knew, were for a purpose. He waited. Tallis had something to say, but he was allowing the Earthman to "adjust to surprise." It was one of the fine points of Kerothi etiquette.

A sudden silence on the part of one participant in a conversation, under these particular circumstances, meant that something unusual was coming up, and the other person was supposed to take the opportunity to brace himself for shock.

It could mean anything. In the Kerothi Space Forces, a superior informed a junior officer of the junior's forthcoming promotion by just such tactics. But the same tactics were used when informing a person of the death of a loved one.

In fact, MacMaine was well aware that such a period of silence was *de rigueur* in a Kerothi court, just before sentence was pronounced, as well as a preliminary to a proposal of marriage by a Kerothi male to the light of his love.

MacMaine could do nothing but wait. It would be indelicate to speak until Tallis felt that he was ready for the surprise.

It was not, however, indelicate to watch Tallis' face closely; it was expected. Theoretically, one was supposed to be able to discern, at least, whether the news was good or bad.

With Tallis, it was impossible to tell, and MacMaine knew it would be useless to read the man's expression. But he watched, nonetheless.

In one way, Tallis' face was typically Kerothi. The orange-pigmented skin and the bright, grass-green eyes were common to all Kerothi. The planet Keroth, like Earth, had evolved several different "races" of humanoid, but, unlike Earth, the distinction was not one of color.

MacMaine took a drag off his cigarette and forced himself to keep his mind off whatever it was that Tallis might be about to say. He was already prepared for a death sentence—even a death sentence by torture. Now, he felt, he could not be shocked. And, rather than build up the tension within himself to an unbearable degree, he thought about Tallis rather than about himself.

Tallis, like the rest of the Kerothi, was unbelievably humanoid. There were internal differences in the placement of organs, and differences in the functions of those organs. For instance, it took two separate organs to perform the same function that the liver performed in Earthmen, and the kidneys were completely absent, that function being performed by special tissues in the lower colon, which meant that the Kerothi were more efficient with water-saving than Earthmen, since the waste products were excreted as relatively dry solids through an all-purpose cloaca.

But, externally, a Kerothi would need only a touch of plastic surgery and some makeup to pass as an Earthman in a stage play. Close up, of course, the job would be much more difficult—as difficult as a Negro trying to disguise himself as a Swede or *vice versa*.

But Tallis was—

"I would have a word," Tallis said, shattering MacMaine's carefully neutral train of thought. It was a standard opening for breaking the pause of adjustment, but it presaged good news rather than bad.

"I await your word," MacMaine said. Even after all this time, he still felt vaguely proud of his ability to handle the subtle idioms of Kerothic.

"I think," Tallis said carefully, "that you may be offered a commission in the Kerothi Space Forces."

Sebastian MacMaine let out his breath slowly, and only then realized that he had been holding it. "I am grateful, my sibling-by-choice," he said.

General Tallis tapped his cigarette ash into a large blue ceramic ashtray. MacMaine could smell the acrid smoke from the alien plant matter that burned in the Kerothi cigarette—a chopped-up inner bark from a Kerothi tree. MacMaine could no more smoke a Kerothi cigarette than Tallis could smoke tobacco, but the two were remarkably similar in their effects.

The "surprise" had been delivered. Now, as was proper, Tallis would move adroitly all around the subject until he was ready to return to it again.

"You have been with us . . . how long, Sepastian?" he asked.

"Two and a third *Kronet*."

Tallis nodded. "Nearly a year of your time."

MacMaine smiled. Tallis was as proud of his knowledge of Earth terminology as MacMaine was proud of his mastery of Kerothic.

"Lacking three weeks," MacMaine said.

"What? Three . . . oh, yes. Well. A long time," said Tallis.

Damn it! MacMaine thought, in a sudden surge of impatience, *get to the point!* His face showed only calm.

"The Board of Strategy asked me to tell you," Tallis continued. "After all, my recommendation was partially responsible for the decision." He paused for a moment, but it was merely a conversational hesitation, not a formal hiatus.

"It was a hard decision, Sepastian—you must realize that. "We have been at war with your race for ten years now. We have taken thousands of Earthmen as prisoners, and many of them have agreed to co-operate with us. But, with one single exception, these prisoners have been the moral dregs of your civilization. They have been men who had no pride of race, no pride of society, no pride of self. They have been weak, self-centered, small-minded, cowards who had no thought for Earth and Earthmen, but only for themselves.

"Not," he said hurriedly, "that all of them are that way—or even the majority. Most of them have the minds of warriors, although, I must say, not *strong* warriors."

That last, MacMaine knew, was a polite concession. The Kerothi had no respect for Earthmen. And MacMaine could hardly blame them. For three long centuries, the people of Earth had had nothing to do but indulge themselves in the pleasures of material wealth. It was a wonder that any of them had any moral fiber left.

"But none of those who had any strength agreed to work with us," Tallis went on. "With one exception. You."

"Am I weak, then?" MacMaine asked.

General Tallis shook his head in a peculiarly humanlike gesture. "No. No, you are not. And that is what has made us pause for three years." His grass-green eyes looked candidly into MacMaine's own. "You aren't the type of person who betrays his own kind. It looks like a trap. After a whole year, the Board of Strategy still isn't sure that there is no trap."

Tallis stopped, leaned forward, and ground out the stub of his cigarette in the blue ashtray. Then his eyes again sought MacMaine's.

"If it were not for what I, personally, know about you, the Board of Strategy would not even consider your proposition."

"I take it, then, that they have considered it?" MacMaine asked with a grin.

"As I said, Sepastian," Tallis said, "you have won your case. After almost a year of your time, your decision has been justified."

MacMaine lost his grin. "I am grateful, Tallis," he said gravely. "I think you must realize that it was a difficult decision to make."

His thoughts went back, across long months of time and longer light-years of space, to the day when that decision had been made.

The Decision

Colonel Sebastian MacMaine didn't feel, that morning, as though this day were different from any other. The sun, faintly veiled by a few wisps of cloud, shone as it always had; the guards at the doors of the Space Force Administration Building saluted him as usual; his brother officers nodded politely, as they always did; his aide greeted him with the usual "Good morning, sir."

The duty list lay on his desk, as it had every morning for years. Sebastian MacMaine felt tense and a little irritated with himself, but he felt nothing that could be called a premonition.

When he read the first item on the duty list, his irritation became a little stronger.

"*Interrogate Kerothi general.*"

The interrogation duty had swung round to him again. He didn't want to talk to General Tallis. There was something about the alien that bothered him, and he couldn't place exactly what it was.

Earth had been lucky to capture the alien officer. In a space war, there's usually very little left to capture after a battle—especially if your side lost the battle.

On the other hand, the Kerothi general wasn't so lucky. The food that had been captured with him would run out in less than six months, and it was doubtful that he would survive on Earth food. It was equally doubtful that any more Kerothi food would be captured.

For two years, Earth had been fighting the Kerothi, and for two years Earth had been winning a few minor skirmishes and losing the major battles. The Kerothi hadn't hit any of the major colonies yet, but they had swallowed up outpost after outpost, and Earth's space fleet was losing ships faster than her factories could turn them out. The hell of it was that nobody on Earth seemed to be very much concerned about it at all.

MacMaine wondered why he let it concern him. If no one else was worried, why did he let it bother him? He pushed the thought from his mind and picked up the questionnaire form that had been made out for that morning's session with the Kerothi general. Might as well get it over with.

He glanced down the list of further duties for the day. It looked as though the routine interrogation of the Kerothi general was likely to provide most of the interest in the day's work at that.

He took the dropchute down to the basement of the building, to the small prison section where the alien officer was being held. The guards saluted nonchalantly as he went in. The routine questioning sessions were nothing new to them.

MacMaine turned the lock on the prisoner's cell door and went in. Then he came to attention and saluted the Kerothi general. He was probably the only officer in the place who did that, he knew; the others treated the alien general as though he were a criminal. Worse, they treated him as though he were a petty thief or a common pickpocket—criminal, yes, but of a definitely inferior type.

General Tallis, as always, stood and returned the salute. "Cut mawnik, Cunnel MacMaine," he said. The Kerothi language lacked many of the voiced consonants of English and Russian, and, as a result, Tallis' use of *B, D, G, J V,* and *Z* made them come out as *P, T, K, CH, F,* and *S.* The English *R,* as it is pronounced in *run* or *rat,* eluded him entirely, and he pronounced it only when he could give it the guttural pronunciation of the German *R.* The terminal *NG* always came out at *NK.* The nasal *M* and *N* were a little more drawn out than in English, but they were easily understandable.

"Good morning, General Tallis," MacMaine said. "Sit down. How do you feel this morning?"

The general sat again on the hard bunk that, aside from the single chair, was the only furniture in the small cell. "Ass well ass coot pe expectet. I ket ferry little exercisse. I . . . how iss it set? . . . I pecome soft? Soft? Iss correct?"

"Correct. You've learned our language very well for so short a time."

The general shrugged off the compliment. "Wen it iss a matteh of learrn in orrter to surfife, one learrnss."

"You think, then, that your survival has depended on your learning our language?"

The general's orange face contrived a wry smile. "Opfiously. Your people fill not learn Kerothic. If I cannot answerr questionss, I am uff no use. Ass lonk ass I am uff use, I will liff. Not?"

MacMaine decided he might as well spring his bomb on the Kerothi officer now as later. "I am not so certain but that you might have stretched out your time longer if you had forced us to learn Kerothic, general," he said in Kerothic. He knew his Kerothic was bad, since it had been learned from the Kerothi spaceman who had been captured with the general, and the man had been badly wounded and had survived only two weeks. But that little bit of basic instruction, plus the work he had done on the books and tapes from the ruined Kerothi ship, had helped him.

"Ah?" The general blinked in surprise. Then he smiled. "Your accent," he said in Kerothic, "is atrocious, but certainly no worse than mine when I speak your *Inklitch*. I suppose you intend to question me in Kerothic now, eh? In the hope that I may reveal more in my own tongue?"

"Possibly you may," MacMaine said with a grin, "but I learned it for my own information."

"For your own what? Oh. I see. Interesting. I know no others of your race who would do such a thing. Anything which is difficult is beneath them."

"Not so, general. I'm not unique. There are many of us who don't think that way."

The general shrugged. "I do not deny it. I merely say that I have met none. Certainly they do not tend to go into military service. Possibly that is because you are not a race of fighters. It takes a fighter to tackle the difficult just because it is difficult."

MacMaine gave him a short, hard laugh. "Don't you think getting information out of *you* is difficult? And yet, we tackle that."

"Not the same thing at all. Routine. You have used no pressure. No threats, no promises, no torture, no stress."

MacMaine wasn't quite sure of his translation of the last two negative phrases. "You mean the application of physical pain? That's barbaric."

"I won't pursue the subject," the general said with sudden irony.

"I can understand that. But you can rest assured that we would never do such a thing. It isn't civilized. Our civil police do use certain drugs to obtain information, but we have so little knowledge of Kerothi body chemistry that we hesitate to use drugs on you."

"The application of stress, you say, is not civilized. Not, perhaps, according to your definition of"—he used the English word—"*cifiliced*. No. Not *cifiliced*—but it works." Again he smiled. "I said that I have become soft since I have been here, but I fear that your civilization is even softer."

"A man can lie, even if his arms are pulled off or his feet crushed," MacMaine said stiffly.

The Kerothi looked startled. When he spoke again, it was in English. "I will say no morr. If you haff questionss to ask, ko ahet. I will not take up time with furtherr talkink."

A little angry with himself and with the general, MacMaine spent the rest of the hour asking routine questions and getting nowhere, filling up the tape in his minicorder with the same old answers that others had gotten.

He left, giving the general a brisk salute and turning before the general had time to return it.

Back in his office, he filed the tape dutifully and started on Item Two of the duty list: *Strategy Analysis of Battle Reports.*

Strategy analysis always irritated and upset him. He knew that if he'd just go about it in the approved way, there would be no irritation—only boredom. But he was constitutionally incapable of working that way. In spite of himself, he always played a little game with himself and with the General Strategy Computer.

The only battle of significance in the past week had been the defense of an Earth outpost called Bennington IV. Theoretically, MacMaine was supposed to check over the entire report, find out where the losing side had erred, and feed correctional information into the Computer. But he couldn't resist stopping after he had read the first section: *Information Known to Earth Commander at Moment of Initial Contact.*

Then he would stop and consider how he, personally, would have handled the situation if he had been the Earth commander. So many ships in such-and-such places. Enemy fleet approaching at such-and-such velocities. Battle array of enemy thus-and-so.

Now what?

MacMaine thought over the information on the defense of Bennington IV and devised a battle plan. There was a weak point in the enemy's attack, but it was rather obvious. MacMaine searched until he found another weak point, much less obvious than the first. He knew it would be there. It was.

Then he proceeded to ignore both weak points and concentrate on what he would do if he were the enemy commander. The weak points were traps; the computer could see them and avoid them. Which was just exactly what was wrong with the computer's logic. In avoiding the traps, it also avoided the best way to hit the enemy. A weak point *is* weak, no matter how well it may be booby-trapped. In baiting a rat trap, you have to use real cheese because an imitation won't work.

Of course, MacMaine thought to himself, *you can always poison the cheese, but let's not carry the analogy too far.*

All right then. How to hit the traps?

It took him half an hour to devise a completely wacky and unorthodox way of hitting the holes in the enemy advance. He checked the time carefully, because there's no point in devising a strategy if the battle is too far gone to use it by the time you've figured it out.

Then he went ahead and read the rest of the report. Earth had lost the outpost. And, worse, MacMaine's strategy would have won the battle if it had been used. He fed it through his small office computer to make sure. The odds were good.

And that was the thing that made MacMaine hate Strategy Analysis. Too often, he won; too often, Earth lost. A computer was fine for working out the logical outcome of a battle if it was given the proper strategy, but it couldn't devise anything new.

Colonel MacMaine had tried to get himself transferred to space duty, but without success. The Commanding Staff didn't want him out there.

The trouble was that they didn't believe MacMaine actually devised his strategy before he read the complete report. How could anyone out-think a computer?

He'd offered to prove it. "Give me a problem," he'd told his immediate superior, General Matsukuo. "Give me the Initial Contact information of a battle I haven't seen before, and I'll show you."

And Matsukuo had said, testily: "Colonel, I will not permit a member of my staff to make a fool of himself in front of the Commanding Staff. Setting yourself up as someone superior to the Strategy Board is the most antisocial type of egocentrism imaginable. You were given the same education at the Academy as every other officer; what makes you think you are better than they? As time goes on, your automatic promotions will put you in a position to vote on such matters—provided you don't prejudice the Promotion Board against you by antisocial behavior. I hold you in the highest regard, colonel, and I will say nothing to the Promotion Board about this, but if you persist I will have to do my duty. Now, I don't want to hear any more about it. Is that clear?"

It was.

All MacMaine had to do was wait, and he'd automatically be promoted to the Commanding Staff, where he would have an equal vote with the others of his rank. One unit vote to begin with and an additional unit for every year thereafter.

It's a great system for running a peacetime social club, maybe, MacMaine thought, *but it's no way to run a fighting force.*

Maybe the Kerothi general was right. Maybe *homo sapiens* just wasn't a race of fighters.

They had been once. Mankind had fought its way to domination of Earth by battling every other form of life on the planet, from the smallest virus to the biggest carnivore. The fight against disease was still going on, as a matter of fact, and Man was still fighting the elemental fury of Earth's climate.

But Man no longer fought with Man. Was that a bad thing? The discovery of atomic energy, two centuries before, had literally made war impossible, if the race was to survive. Small struggles bred bigger struggles—or so the reasoning went. Therefore, the society had unconsciously sought to eliminate the reasons for struggle.

What bred the hatreds and jealousies among men? What caused one group to fight another?

Society had decided that intolerance and hatred were caused by inequality. The jealousy of the inferior toward his superior; the scorn of the superior toward his inferior. The Have-not envies the Have, and the Have looks down upon the Have-not.

Then let us eliminate the Have-not. Let us make sure that everyone is a Have.

Raise the standard of living. Make sure that every human being has the necessities of life—food, clothing, shelter, proper medical care, and proper education. More, give them the luxuries, too—let no man be without anything that is poorer in quality or less in quantity than the possessions of any other. There was no longer any middle class simply because there were no other classes for it to be in the middle of.

"The poor you will have always with you," Jesus of Nazareth had said. But, in a material sense, that was no longer true. The poor were gone—and so were the rich.

But the poor in mind and the poor in spirit were still there—in ever-increasing numbers.

Material wealth could be evenly distributed, but it could not remain that way unless Society made sure that the man who was more clever than the rest could not increase his wealth at the expense of his less fortunate brethren.

Make it a social stigma to show more ability than the average. Be kind to your fellow man; don't show him up as a stupid clod, no matter how cloddish he may be.

All men are created equal, and let's make sure they stay that way!

There could be no such thing as a classless society, of course. That was easily seen. No human being could do everything, learn everything, be everything. There had to be doctors and lawyers and policemen and bartenders and soldiers and machinists and laborers and actors and writers and criminals and bums.

But let's make sure that the differentiation between classes is horizontal, not vertical. As long as a person does his job the best he can, he's as good as anybody else. A doctor is as good as a lawyer, isn't he? Then a garbage collector is just as good as a nuclear physicist, and an astronomer is no better than a street sweeper.

And what of the loafer, the bum, the man who's too lazy or weak-willed to put out any more effort than is absolutely necessary to stay alive? Well, my goodness, the poor chap can't *help* it, can he? It isn't *his* fault, is it? He has to be helped. There is always *something* he is both capable of doing and willing to do. Does he like to sit around all day and do nothing but watch television? Then give him a sheet of paper with all the programs on it and two little boxes marked *Yes* and *No*, and he can put an X in one or the other to indicate whether he likes the program or not. Useful? Certainly. All these sheets can be tallied up in order to find out what sort of program the public likes to see. After all, his vote is just as good as anyone else's, isn't it?

And a Program Analyst is just as good, just as important, and just as well cared-for as anyone else.

And what about the criminal? Well, what *is* a criminal? A person who thinks he's superior to others. A thief steals because he thinks he has more right to something than its real owner. A man kills because he has an idea that he has a better right to live than someone else. In short, a man breaks the law because he feels superior, because he thinks he can outsmart Society and The Law. Or, simply, because he thinks he can outsmart the policeman on the beat.

Obviously, that sort of antisocial behavior can't be allowed. The poor fellow who thinks he's better than anyone else has to be segregated from normal society and treated for his aberrations. But not punished! Heavens no! His erratic behavior isn't *his* fault, is it?

It was axiomatic that there had to be some sort of vertical structure to society, naturally. A child can't do the work of an adult, and a beginner can't be as good as an old hand. Aside from the fact that it was actually impossible to force everyone into a common mold, it was recognized that there had to be some incentive for staying with a job. What to do?

The labor unions had solved that problem two hundred years before. Promotion by seniority. Stick with a job long enough, and you'll automatically rise to the top. That way, everyone had as good a chance as everyone else.

Promotion tables for individual jobs were worked out on the basis of longevity tables, so that by the time a man reached the automatic retirement age he was automatically at the highest position he could hold. No fuss, no bother, no trouble. Just keep your nose clean and live as long as possible.

It eliminated struggle. It eliminated the petty jockeying for position that undermined efficiency in an organization. Everybody deserves an equal chance in life, so make sure everybody gets it.

Colonel Sebastian MacMaine had been born and reared in that society. He could see many of its faults, but he didn't have the orientation to see all of them. As he'd grown older, he'd seen that, regardless of the position a man held according to seniority, a smart man could exercise more power than those above him if he did it carefully.

A man is a slave if he is held rigidly in a pattern and not permitted to step out of that pattern. In ancient times, a slave was born at the bottom of the social ladder, and he remained there all his life. Only rarely did a slave of exceptional merit manage to rise above his assigned position.

But a man who is forced to remain on the bottom step of a stationary stairway is no more a slave than a man who is forced to remain on a given step of an escalator, and no less so.

Slavery, however, has two advantages—one for the individual, and one which, in the long run, can be good for the race. For the individual, it offers security, and that is the goal which by far the greater majority of mankind seeks.

The second advantage is more difficult to see. It operates only in favor of the exceptional individual. There are always individuals who aspire to greater heights than the one they occupy at any given moment, but in a slave society, they are slapped back into place if they act hastily. Just as the one-eyed man in the kingdom of the blind can be king if he taps the ground with a cane, so the gifted individual can gain his ends in a slave society—provided he thinks out the consequences of any act in advance.

The Law of Gravity is a universal edict which enslaves, in a sense, every particle of matter in the cosmos. The man who attempts to defy the "injustice" of that law by ignoring the consequences of its enforcement will find himself punished rather severely. It may be unjust that a bird can fly under its own muscle power, but a man who tries to correct that injustice by leaping out of a skyscraper window and flapping his arms vigorously will find that overt defiance of the Law of Gravity brings very serious penalties indeed. The wise man seeks the loopholes in the law, and loopholes are caused by other laws which counteract—*not defy!*—the given law. A balloon full of hydrogen "falls up" in obedience to the Law of Gravity. A contradiction? A paradox? No. It is the Law of Gravity which causes the density and pressure of a planet's atmosphere to decrease with altitude, and that decrease in pressure forces the balloon upwards until the balance point between atmospheric density and the internal density of the balloon is reached.

The illustration may seem obvious and elementary to the modern man, but it seems so only because he understands, at least to some extent, the laws involved. It was not obvious to even the most learned man of, say, the Thirteenth Century.

Slavery, too, has its laws, and it is as dangerous to defy the laws of a society as it is to defy those of nature, and the only way to escape the punishment resulting from those laws is to find the loopholes. One of the most basic laws of any society is so basic that it is never, *ever* written down.

And that law, like all basic laws, is so simple in expression and so obvious in application that any man above the moron level has an intuitive grasp of it. It is the first law one learns as a child.

Thou shalt not suffer thyself to be caught.

The unthinking man believes that this basic law can be applied by breaking the laws of his society in secret. What he fails to see is that such lawbreaking requires such a fantastic network of lies, subterfuges, evasions, and chicanery that the structure itself eventually breaks down and his guilt is obvious to all. The very steps he has taken to keep from getting caught eventually become signposts that point unerringly at the lawbreaker himself.

Like the loopholes in the law of gravity, the loopholes in the laws of society cannot entail a *defiance* of the law. Only compliance with those laws will be ultimately successful.

The wise man works within the framework of the law—not only the written, but the unwritten law—of his society. In a slave society, any slave who openly rebels will find that he gets squashed pretty quickly. But many a slave-owner has danced willingly to the tune of a slave who was wiser and cleverer than he, without ever knowing that the tune played was not his own.

And that is the second advantage of slavery. It teaches the exceptional individual to think.

When a wise, intelligent individual openly and violently breaks the laws of his society, there are two things which are almost certain: One: he knows that there is no other way to do the thing he feels must be done, and—

Two: he knows that he will pay the penalty for his crime in one way or another.

Sebastian MacMaine knew the operations of those laws. As a member of a self-enslaved society, he knew that to betray any sign of intelligence was dangerous. A slight slip could bring the scorn of the slaves around him; a major offense could mean death. The war with Keroth had thrown him slightly off balance, but after his one experience with General Matsukuo, he had quickly regained his equilibrium.

At the end of his work day, MacMaine closed his desk and left his office precisely on time, as usual. Working overtime, except in the gravest emergencies, was looked upon as antisocialism. The offender was suspected of having Ambition—obviously a Bad Thing.

It was during his meal at the Officers' Mess that Colonel Sebastian MacMaine heard the statement that triggered the decision in his mind.

There were three other officers seated with MacMaine around one of the four-place tables in the big room. MacMaine only paid enough attention to the table conversation to be able to make the appropriate noises at the proper times. He had long since learned to do his thinking under cover of general banalities.

Colonel VanDeusen was a man who would never have made Private First Class in an army that operated on a strict merit system. His thinking was muddy, and his conversation betrayed it. All he felt comfortable in talking about was just exactly what he had been taught. Slogans, banalities, and bromides. He knew his catechism, and he knew it was safe.

"What I mean is, we got nothing to worry about. We all stick together, and we can do anything. As long as we don't rock the boat, we'll come through O.K."

"Sure," said Major Brock, looking up from his plate in blank-faced surprise. "I mean, who says different?"

"Guy on my research team," said VanDeusen, plying his fork industriously. "A wise-guy second looie. One of them."

"Oh," said the major knowingly. "One of them." He went back to his meal.

"What'd he say?" MacMaine asked, just to keep his oar in.

"Ahhh, nothing serious, I guess," said VanDeusen, around a mouthful of steak. "Said we were all clogged up with paper work, makin' reports on tests, things like that. Said, why don't we figure out something to pop those Carrot-skins outa the sky. So I said to him, 'Look, Lootenant,' I said, 'you got your job to do, I got mine. If the paper work's pilin' up,' I said, 'it's because somebody isn't pulling his share. And it better not be you,' I said." He chuckled and speared another cube of steak with his fork. "That settled him down. He's all right, though. Young yet, you know. Soon's he gets the hang of how the Space Force operates, he'll be O.K."

Since VanDeusen was the senior officer at the table, the others listened respectfully as he talked, only inserting a word now and then to show that they were listening.

MacMaine was thinking deeply about something else entirely, but VanDeusen's influence intruded a little. MacMaine was wondering what it was that bothered him about General Tallis, the Kerothi prisoner.

The alien was pleasant enough, in spite of his position. He seemed to accept his imprisonment as one of the fortunes of war. He didn't threaten or bluster, although he tended to maintain an air of superiority that would have been unbearable in an Earthman.

Was that the reason for his uneasiness in the general's presence? No. MacMaine could accept the reason for that attitude; the general's background was different from that of an Earthman, and therefore he could not be judged by Terrestrial standards. Besides, MacMaine could acknowledge to himself that Tallis *was* superior to the norm—not only the norm of Keroth, but that of Earth. MacMaine wasn't sure he could have acknowledged superiority in another Earthman, in spite of the fact that he knew that there must be men who were his superiors in one way or another.

Because of his social background, he knew that he would probably form an intense and instant dislike for any Earthman who talked the way Tallis did, but he found that he actually *liked* the alien officer.

It came as a slight shock when the realization hit MacMaine that his liking for the general was exactly why he was uncomfortable around him. Dammit, a man isn't supposed to like his enemy—and most especially when that enemy does and says things that one would despise in a friend.

Come to think of it, though, did he, MacMaine, actually have any friends? He looked around him, suddenly clearly conscious of the other men in the room. He searched through his memory, thinking of all his acquaintances and relatives.

It was an even greater shock to realize that he would not be more than faintly touched emotionally if any or all of them were to die at that instant. Even his parents, both of whom were now dead, were only dim figures in his memory. He had mourned them when an aircraft accident had taken both of them when he was only eleven, but he found himself wondering if it had been the loss of loved ones that had caused his emotional upset or simply the abrupt vanishing of a kind of security he had taken for granted.

And yet, he felt that the death of General Polan Tallis would leave an empty place in his life.

Colonel VanDeusen was still holding forth.

". . . So I told him. I said, 'Look, Lootenant,' I said, 'don't rock the boat. You're a kid yet, you know,' I said. 'You got equal rights with everybody else,' I said, 'but if you rock the boat, you aren't gonna get along so well.'

" 'You just behave yourself,' I said, 'and pull your share of the load and do your job right and keep your nose clean, and you'll come out all right.

" 'Time I get to be on the General Staff,' I told him, 'why, you'll be takin' over my job, maybe. That's the way it works,' I said.

"He's a good kid. I mean, he's a fresh young punk, that's all. He'll learn, O.K. He'll climb right up, once he's got the right attitude. Why, when I was—"

But MacMaine was no longer listening. It was astonishing to realize that what VanDeusen had said was perfectly true. A blockhead like VanDeusen would simply be lifted to a position of higher authority, only to be replaced by another blockhead. There would be no essential change in the *status quo*.

The Kerothi were winning steadily, and the people of Earth and her colonies were making no changes whatever in their way of living. The majority of people were too blind to be able to see what was happening, and the rest were afraid to admit the danger, even to themselves. It required no great understanding of strategy to see what the inevitable outcome must be.

At some point in the last few centuries, human civilization had taken the wrong path—a path that led only to oblivion.

It was at that moment that Colonel Sebastian MacMaine made his decision.

The Escape

"Are you sure you understand, Tallis?" MacMaine asked in Kerothic.

The alien general nodded emphatically. "Perfectly. Your Kerothic is not so bad that I could misunderstand your instructions. I still don't understand why you are doing this. Oh I know the reasons you've given me, but I don't completely believe them. However, I'll go along with you. The worst that could happen would be for me to be killed, and I would sooner face death in trying to escape than in waiting for your executioners. If this is some sort of trap, some sort of weird way your race's twisted idea of kindness has evolved to dispose of me, then I'll accept your sentence. It's better than starving to death or facing a firing squad."

"Not a firing squad," MacMaine said. "That wouldn't be kind. An odorless, but quite deadly gas would be pumped into this cell while you slept."

"That's worse. When death comes, I want to face it and fight it off as long as possible, not have it sneaking up on me in my sleep. I think I'd rather starve."

"You would," said MacMaine. "The food that was captured with you has nearly run out, and we haven't been able to capture any more. But rather than let you suffer, they would have killed you painlessly." He glanced at the watch on his instrument cuff. "Almost time."

MacMaine looked the alien over once more. Tallis was dressed in the uniform of Earth's Space Force, and the insignia of a full general gleamed on his collar. His face and hands had been sprayed with an opaque, pink-tan film, and his hairless head was covered with a black wig. He wouldn't pass a close inspection, but MacMaine fervently hoped that he wouldn't need to.

Think it out, be sure you're right, then go ahead. Sebastian MacMaine had done just that. For three months, he had worked over the details of his plan, making sure that they were as perfect as he was capable of making them. Even so, there was a great deal of risk involved, and there were too many details that required luck for MacMaine to be perfectly happy about the plan.

But time was running out. As the general's food supply dwindled, his execution date neared, and now it was only two days away. There was no point in waiting until the last minute; it was now or never.

There were no spying TV cameras in the general's cell, no hidden microphones to report and record what went on. No one had ever escaped from the Space Force's prison, therefore, no one ever would.

MacMaine glanced again at his watch. It was time. He reached inside his blouse and took out a fully loaded handgun.

For an instant, the alien officer's eyes widened, and he stiffened as if he were ready to die in an attempt to disarm the Earthman. Then he saw that MacMaine wasn't holding it by the butt; his hand was clasped around the middle of the weapon.

"This is a chance I have to take," MacMaine said evenly. "With this gun, you can shoot me down right here and try to escape alone.

I've told you every detail of our course of action, and, with luck, you might make it alone." He held out his hand, with the weapon resting on his open palm.

General Tallis eyed the Earthman for a long second. Then, without haste, he took the gun and inspected it with a professional eye.

"Do you know how to operate it?" MacMaine asked, forcing calmness into his voice.

"Yes. We've captured plenty of them." Tallis thumbed the stud that allowed the magazine to slide out of the butt and into his hand. Then he checked the mechanism and the power cartridges. Finally, he replaced the magazine and put the weapon into the empty sleeve holster that MacMaine had given him.

MacMaine let his breath out slowly. "All right," he said. "Let's go."

He opened the door of the cell, and both men stepped out into the corridor. At the far end of the corridor, some thirty yards away, stood the two armed guards who kept watch over the prisoner. At that distance, it was impossible to tell that Tallis was not what he appeared to be.

The guard had been changed while MacMaine was in the prisoner's cell, and he was relying on the lax discipline of the soldiers to get him and Tallis out of the cell block. With luck, the guards would have failed to listen too closely to what they had been told by the men they replaced; with even greater luck, the previous guardsmen would have failed to be too explicit about who was in the prisoner's cell. With no luck at all, MacMaine would be forced to shoot to kill.

MacMaine walked casually up to the two men, who came to an easy attention.

"I want you two men to come with me. Something odd has happened, and General Quinby and I want two witnesses as to what went on."

"What happened, sir?" one of them asked.

"Don't know for sure," MacMaine said in a puzzled voice. "The general and I were talking to the prisoner, when all of a sudden he fell over. I think he's dead. I couldn't find a heartbeat. I want you to take a look at him so that you can testify that we didn't shoot him or anything."

Obediently, the two guards headed for the cell, and MacMaine fell in behind them. "You couldn't of shot him, sir," said the second guard confidently. "We would of heard the shot."

"Besides," said the other, "it don't matter much. He was going to be gassed day after tomorrow."

As the trio approached the cell, Tallis pulled the door open a little wider and, in doing so, contrived to put himself behind it so that his face couldn't be seen. The young guards weren't too awed by a full general; after all, they'd be generals themselves someday. They were much more interested in seeing the dead alien.

As the guards reached the cell door, MacMaine unholstered his pistol from his sleeve and brought it down hard on the head of the nearest youth. At the same time, Tallis stepped from behind the door and clouted the other.

Quickly, MacMaine disarmed the fallen men and dragged them into the open cell. He came out again and locked the door securely. Their guns were tossed into an empty cell nearby.

"They won't be missed until the next change of watch, in four hours," MacMaine said. "By then, it won't matter, one way or another."

Getting out of the huge building that housed the administrative offices of the Space Force was relatively easy. A lift chute brought the pair to the main floor, and, this late in the evening, there weren't many people on that floor. The officers and men who had night duty were working on the upper floors. Several times, Tallis had to take a handkerchief from his pocket and pretend to blow his nose in order to conceal his alien features from someone who came too close, but no one appeared to notice anything out of the ordinary.

As they walked out boldly through the main door, fifteen minutes later, the guards merely came to attention and relaxed as a tall colonel and a somewhat shorter general strode out. The general appeared to be having a fit of sneezing, and the colonel was heard to say: "That's quite a cold you've picked up, sir. Better get over to the dispensary and take an anti-coryza shot."

"Mmmf," said the general. "*Ha-CHOO!*"

Getting to the spaceport was no problem at all. MacMaine had an official car waiting, and the two sergeants in the front seat didn't pay any attention to the general getting in the back seat because Colonel MacMaine was talking to them. "We're ready to roll, sergeant," he said to the driver. "General Quinby wants to go straight to the *Manila*, so let's get there as fast as possible. Take-off is scheduled in ten minutes." Then he got into the back seat himself. The one-way glass partition that separated the back seat from the front prevented either of the two men from looking back at their passengers.

Seven minutes later, the staff car was rolling unquestioned through the main gate of Waikiki Spaceport.

It was all so incredibly easy, MacMaine thought. Nobody questioned an official car. Nobody checked anything too closely. Nobody wanted to risk his lifelong security by doing or saying something that might be considered antisocial by a busy general. Besides, it never entered anyone's mind that there could be anything wrong. If there was a war on, apparently no one had been told about it yet.

MacMaine thought, *Was I ever that stubbornly blind? Not quite, I guess, or I'd never have seen what is happening.* But he knew he hadn't been too much more perceptive than those around him. Even to an intelligent man, the mask of stupidity can become a barrier to the outside world as well as a concealment from it.

The Interstellar Ship *Manila* was a small, fast, ten-man blaster-boat, designed to get in to the thick of a battle quickly, strike hard, and get away. Unlike the bigger, more powerful battle cruisers, she could be landed directly on any planet with less than a two-gee pull at the surface. The really big babies had to be parked in an orbit and loaded by shuttle; they'd break up of their own weight if they tried to set down on anything bigger than a good-sized planetoid. As long as their antiacceleration fields were on, they could take unimaginable thrusts along their axes, but the A-A fields were the cause of those thrusts as well as the protection against them. The ships couldn't stand still while they were operating, so they were no protection at all against a planet's gravity. But a blaster-boat was small enough and compact enough to take the strain.

It had taken careful preparation to get the *Manila* ready to go just exactly when MacMaine needed it. Papers had to be forged and put into the chain of command communication at precisely the right times; others had had to be taken out and replaced with harmless near-duplicates so that the Commanding Staff wouldn't discover the deception. He had had to build up the fictional identity of a "General Lucius Quinby" in such a way that it would take a thorough check to discover that the officer who had been put in command of the *Manila* was nonexistent.

It was two minutes until take-off time when the staff car pulled up at the foot of the ramp that led up to the main air lock of the ISS *Manila*. A young-looking captain was standing nervously at the foot of it, obviously afraid that his new commander might be late for the take-off and wondering what sort of decision he would have to make if the general wasn't there at take-off time. MacMaine could imagine his feelings.

"General Quinby" developed another sneezing fit as he stepped out of the car. This was the touchiest part of MacMaine's plan, the weakest link in the whole chain of action. For a space of perhaps a minute, the disguised Kerothi general would have to stand so close to the young captain that the crudity of his make-up job would be detectable. He had to keep that handkerchief over his face, and yet do it in such a way that it would seem natural.

As Tallis climbed out of the car, chuffing windily into the kerchief, MacMaine snapped an order to the sergeant behind the wheel. "That's all. We're taking off almost immediately, so get that car out of here."

Then he walked rapidly over to the captain, who had snapped to attention. There was a definite look of relief on his face, now that he knew his commander was on time.

"All ready for take-off, captain? Everything checked out? Ammunition? Energy packs all filled to capacity? All the crew aboard? Full rations and stores stowed away?"

The captain kept his eyes on MacMaine's face as he answered "Yes, sir; yes, sir; yes, sir," to the rapid fire of questions. He had no time to shift his gaze to the face of his new C.O., who was snuffling his way toward the foot of the landing ramp. MacMaine kept firing questions until Tallis was halfway up the ramp.

Then he said: "Oh, by the way, captain—was the large package containing General Quinby's personal gear brought aboard?"

"The big package? Yes, sir. About fifteen minutes ago."

"Good," said MacMaine. He looked up the ramp. "Are there any special orders at this time, sir?" he asked.

"No," said Tallis, without turning. "Carry on, colonel." He went on up to the air lock. It had taken Tallis hours of practice to say that phrase properly, but the training had been worth it.

After Tallis was well inside the air lock, MacMaine whispered to the young captain, "As you can see, the general has got a rather bad cold. He'll want to remain in his cabin until he's over it. See that anti-coryza shots are sent up from the dispensary as soon as we are out of the Solar System. Now, let's go; we have less than a minute till take-off."

MacMaine went up the ramp with the captain scrambling up behind him.

Tallis was just stepping into the commander's cabin as the two men entered the air lock. MacMaine didn't see him again until the ship was twelve minutes on her way—nearly five billion miles from Earth and still accelerating.

He identified himself at the door and Tallis opened it cautiously.

"I brought your anti-coryza shot, sir," he said. In a small ship like the *Manila*, the captain and the seven crew members could hear any conversation in the companionways. He stepped inside and closed the door. Then he practically collapsed on the nearest chair and had a good case of the shakes.

"So-so f-f-far, s-so good," he said.

General Tallis grasped his shoulder with a firm hand. "Brace up, Sepastian," he said gently in Kerothic. "You've done a beautiful job. I still can't believe it, but I'll have to admit that if this is an act it's a beautiful one." He gestured toward the small desk in one corner of the room and the big package that was sitting on it. "The food is all there. I'll have to eat sparingly, but I can make it. Now, what's the rest of the plan?"

MacMaine took a deep breath, held it, and let it out slowly. His shakes subsided to a faint, almost imperceptible quiver. "The captain doesn't know our destination. He was told that he would receive secret instructions from you." His voice, he noticed thankfully, was almost normal. He reached into his uniform jacket and took out an official-looking sealed envelope. "These are the orders. We are going out to arrange a special truce with the Kerothi."

"*What?*"

"That's what it says here. You'll have to get on the subradio and do some plain and fancy talking. Fortunately, not a man jack aboard this ship knows a word of your language, so they'll think you're arranging truce terms.

"They'll be sitting ducks when your warship pulls up alongside and sends in a boarding party. By the time they realize what has happened, it will be too late."

"You're giving us the ship, too?" Tallis looked at him wonderingly. "And eight prisoners?"

"Nine," said MacMaine. "I'll hand over my sidearm to you just before your men come through the air lock."

General Tallis sat down in the other small chair, his eyes still on the Earthman. "I can't help but feel that this is some sort of trick, but if it is, I can't see through it. Why are you doing this, Sepastian?"

"You may not understand this, Tallis," MacMaine said evenly, "but I am fighting for freedom. The freedom to think."

The Traitor

Convincing the Kerothi that he was in earnest was more difficult than MacMaine had at first supposed. He had done his best, and now, after nearly a year of captivity, Tallis had come to tell him that his offer had been accepted.

General Tallis sat across from Colonel MacMaine, smoking his cigarette absently.

"Just why are they accepting my proposition?" MacMaine asked bluntly.

"Because they can afford to," Tallis said with a smile. "You will be watched, my sibling-by-choice. Watched every moment, for any sign of treason. Your flagship will be a small ten-man blaster-boat—one of our own. You gave us one; we'll give you one. At the worst, we will come out even. At the best, your admittedly brilliant grasp of tactics and strategy will enable us to save thousands of Kerothi lives, to say nothing of the immense savings in time and money."

"All I ask is a chance to prove my ability and my loyalty."

"You've already proven your ability. All of the strategy problems that you have been given over the past year were actual battles that had already been fought. In eighty-seven per cent of the cases, your strategy proved to be superior to our own. In most of the others, it was just as good. In only three cases was the estimate of your losses higher than the actual losses. Actually, we'd be fools to turn you down. We have everything to gain and nothing to lose."

"I felt the same way a year ago," said MacMaine. "Even being watched all the time will allow me more freedom than I had on Earth—if the Board of Strategy is willing to meet my terms."

Tallis chuckled. "They are. You'll be the best-paid officer in the entire fleet; none of the rest of us gets a tenth of what you'll be getting, as far as personal value is concerned. And yet, it costs us practically nothing. You drive an attractive bargain, Sepastian."

"Is that the kind of pay you'd like to get, Tallis?" MacMaine asked with a smile.

"Why not? You'll get your terms: full pay as a Kerothi general, with retirement on full pay after the war is over. The pick of the most beautiful—by your standards—of the Earthwomen we capture. A home on Keroth, built to your specifications, and full citizenship, including the freedom to enter into any business relationships you wish. If you keep your promises, we can keep ours and still come out ahead."

"Good. When do we start?"

"Now," said Tallis rising from his chair. "Put on your dress uniform, and we'll go down to see the High Commander. We've got to give you a set of general's insignia, my sibling-by-choice."

Tallis waited while MacMaine donned the blue trousers and gold-trimmed red uniform of a Kerothi officer. When he was through, MacMaine looked at himself in the mirror. "There's one more thing, Tallis," he said thoughtfully.

"What's that?"

"This hair. I think you'd better arrange to have it permanently removed, according to your custom. I can't do anything about the color of my skin, but there's no point in my looking like one of your wild hill-men."

"You're very gracious," Tallis said. "And very wise. Our officers will certainly come closer to feeling that you are one of us."

"I am one of you from this moment," MacMaine said. "I never intend to see Earth again, except, perhaps, from space—when we fight the final battle of the war."

"That may be a hard battle," Tallis said.

"Maybe," MacMaine said thoughtfully. "On the other hand, if my overall strategy comes out the way I think it will, that battle may never be fought at all. I think that complete and total surrender will end the war before we ever get that close to Earth."

"I hope you're right," Tallis said firmly. "This war is costing far more than we had anticipated, in spite of the weakness of your—that is, of Earth."

"Well," MacMaine said with a slight grin, "at least you've been able to capture enough Earth food to keep me eating well all this time."

Tallis' grin was broad. "You're right. We're not doing too badly at that. Now, let's go; the High Commander is waiting."

MacMaine didn't realize until he walked into the big room that what he was facing was not just a discussion with a high officer, but what amounted to a Court of Inquiry.

The High Commander, a dome-headed, wrinkled, yellow - skinned, hard-eyed old Kerothi, was seated in the center of a long, high desk, flanked on either side by two lower-ranking generals who had the same deadly, hard look. Off to one side, almost like a jury in a jury box, sat twenty or so lesser officers, none of them ranking below the Kerothi equivalent of lieutenant-colonel.

As far as MacMaine could tell, none of the officers wore the insignia of fleet officers, the spaceship-and-comet that showed that the wearer was a fighting man. These were the men of the Permanent Headquarters Staff—the military group that controlled, not only the armed forces of Keroth, but the civil government as well.

"What's this?" MacMaine hissed in a whispered aside, in English.

"Pearr up, my prrotherr," Tallis answered softly, in the same tongue, "all is well."

MacMaine had known, long before he had ever heard of General Polan Tallis, that the Hegemony of Keroth was governed by a military junta, and that all Kerothi were regarded as members of the armed forces. Technically, there were no civilians; they were legally members of the "unorganized reserve," and were under military law. He had known that Kerothi society was, in its own way, as much a slave society as that of Earth, but it had the advantage over Earth in that the system did allow for advance by merit. If a man had the determination to get ahead, and the ability to cut the throat—either literally or figuratively—of the man above him in rank, he could take his place.

On a more strictly legal basis, it was possible for a common trooper to become an officer by going through the schools set up for that purpose, but, in practice, it took both pull and pressure to get into those schools.

In theory, any citizen of the Hegemony could become an officer, and any officer could become a member of the Permanent Headquarters Staff. Actually, a much greater preference was given to the children of officers. Examinations were given periodically for the purpose of recruiting new members for the elite officers' corps, and any citizen could take the examination—once.

But the tests were heavily weighted in favor of those who were already well-versed in matters military, including what might be called the "inside jokes" of the officers' corps. A common trooper had some chance of passing the examination; a civilian had a very minute chance. A noncommissioned officer had the best chance of passing the examination, but there were age limits which usually kept NCO's from getting a commission. By the time a man became a noncommissioned officer, he was too old to be admitted to the officers training schools. There were allowances made for "extraordinary merit," which allowed common troopers or upper-grade NCO's to be commissioned in spite of the general rules, and an astute man could take advantage of those allowances.

Ability could get a man up the ladder, but it had to be a particular kind of ability.

During his sojourn as a "guest" of the Kerothi, MacMaine had
made a point of exploring the history of the race. He knew perfectly
well that the histories he had read were doctored, twisted, and,
in general, totally unreliable in so far as presenting anything that
would be called a history by an unbiased investigator.

But, knowing this, MacMaine had been able to learn a great deal
about the present society. Even if the "history" was worthless as
such, it did tell something about the attitudes of a society that
would make up such a history. And, too, he felt that, in general,
the main events which had been catalogued actully occurred; the
details had been blurred, and the attitudes of the people had been
misrepresented, but the skeleton was essentially factual.

MacMaine felt that he knew what kind of philosophy had
produced the mental attitudes of the Court he now faced, and he
felt he knew how to handle himself before them.

Half a dozen paces in front of the great desk, the color of the floor
tiling was different from that of the rest of the floor. Instead of a
solid blue, it was a dead black. Tallis, who was slightly ahead of
MacMaine, came to a halt as his toes touched the edge of the black
area.

Uh-oh! a balk line, MacMaine thought. He stopped sharply at the
same point. Both of them just stood there for a full minute while
they were carefully inspected by the members of the Court.

Then the High Commander gestured with one hand, and the
officer to his left leaned forward and said: "Why is this one brought
before us in the uniform of an officer, bare of any insignia of rank?"

It could only be a ritual question, MacMaine decided; they must
know why he was there.

"I bring him as a candidate for admission to our Ingroup," Tallis
replied formally, "and ask the indulgence of Your Superiorities
therefor."

"And who are you who ask our indulgence?"

Tallis identified himself at length—name, rank, serial number,
military record, et cetera, et cetera, et cetera.

By the time he had finished, MacMaine was beginning to think
that the recitation would go on forever. The High Commander had
closed his eyes, and he looked as if he had gone to sleep.

There was more formality. Through it all, MacMaine stood at
rigid attention, flexing his calf muscles occasionally to keep the
blood flowing in his legs. He had no desire to disgrace himself by
passing out in front of the Court.

Finally the Kerothi officer stopped asking Tallis questions and
looked at the High Commander. MacMaine got the feeling that

there was about to be a departure from the usual procedure.

Without opening his eyes, the High Commander said, in a brittle, rather harsh voice, "These circumstances are unprecedented." Then he opened his eyes and looked directly at MacMaine. "Never has an animal been proposed for such an honor. In times past, such a proposal would have been mockery of this Court and this Ingroup, and a crime of such monstrous proportions as to merit Excommunication."

MacMaine knew what that meant. The word was used literally; the condemned one was cut off from all communication by having his sensory nerves surgically severed. Madness followed quickly; psychosomatic death followed eventually, as the brain, cut off from any outside stimuli except those which could not be eliminated without death following instantly, finally became incapable of keeping the body alive. Without feedback, control was impossible, and the organism-as-a-whole slowly deteriorated until death was inevitable.

At first, the victim screamed and thrashed his limbs as the brain sent out message after message to the rest of the body, but since the brain had no way of knowing whether the messages had been received or acted upon, the victim soon went into a state comparable to that of catatonia and finally died.

If it was not the ultimate in punishment, it was a damned close approach, MacMaine thought. And he felt that the word "damned" could be used in that sense without fear of exaggeration.

"However," the High Commander went on, gazing at the ceiling, "circumstances change. It would once have been thought vile that a machine should be allowed to do the work of a skilled man, and the thought that a machine might do the work with more precision and greater rapidity would have been almost blasphemous.

"This case must be viewed in the same light. As we are replacing certain of our workers on our outer planets with Earth animals simply because they are capable of doing the work more cheaply, so we must recognize that the same interests of economy govern in this case.

"A computing animal, in that sense, is in the same class as a computing machine. It would be folly to waste their abilities simply because they are not human.

"There also arises the question of command. It has been represented to this court, by certain officers who have been active in investigating the candidate animal, that it would be as degrading to ask a human officer to take orders from an animal as it would be to ask him to take orders from a commoner of the Unorganized Reserve, if not more so. And, I must admit, there is, on the surface of it, some basis for this reasoning.

"But, again, we must not let ourselves be misled. Does not a spaceship pilot, in a sense, take orders from the computer that gives him his orbits and courses? In fact, do not all computers give orders, in one way or another, to those who use them?

"Why, then, should we refuse to take orders from a computing animal?"

He paused and appeared to listen to the silence in the room before going on.

"Stand at ease until the High Commander looks at you again," Tallis said in a low aside.

This was definitely the pause for adjusting to surprise.

It seemed interminable, though it couldn't have been longer than a minute later that the High Commander dropped his gaze from the ceiling to MacMaine. When MacMaine snapped to attention again, the others in the room became suddenly silent.

"We feel," the hard-faced old Kerothi continued, as if there had been no break, "that, in this case, we are justified in employing the animal in question.

"However, we must make certain exceptions to our normal procedure. The candidate is not a machine, and therefore cannot be treated as a machine. Neither is it human, and therefore cannot be treated as human.

"Therefore, this is the judgment of the Court of the Ingroup:

"The animal, having shown itself to be capable of behaving, in some degree, as befits an officer—including, as we have been informed, voluntarily conforming to our custom as regards superfluous hair—it shall henceforth be considered as having the same status as an untaught child or a barbarian, insofar as social conventions are concerned, and shall be entitled to the use of the human pronoun, he.

"Further, he shall be entitled to wear the uniform he now wears, and the insignia of a General of the Fleet. He shall be entitled, as far as personal contact goes, to the privileges of that rank, and shall be addressed as such.

"He will be accorded the right of punishment of an officer of that rank, insofar as disciplining his inferiors is concerned, except that he must first secure the concurrence of his Guardian Officer, as hereinafter provided.

"He shall also be subject to punishment in the same way and for the same offenses as humans of his rank, taking into account physiological differences, except as hereinafter provided.

"His reward for proper service"—The High Commander listed the demands MacMaine had made—"are deemed fitting, and shall be paid, provided his duties in service are carried out as proposed.

"Obviously, however, certain restrictions must be made. General MacMaine, as he is entitled to be called, is employed solely as a Strategy Computer. His ability as such and his knowledge of the psychology of the Earth animals are, as far as we are concerned at this moment, his only useful attributes. Therefore, his command is restricted to that function. He is empowered to act only through the other officers of the Fleet as this Court may appoint; he is not to command directly.

"Further, it is ordered that he shall have a Guardian Officer, who shall accompany him at all times and shall be directly responsible for his actions.

"That officer shall be punished for any deliberate crime committed by the aforesaid General MacMaine as if he had himself committed the crime.

"Until such time as this Court may appoint another officer for the purpose, General Polan Tallis, previously identified in these proceedings, is appointed as Guardian Officer."

The High Commander paused for a moment, then he said: "Proceed with the investment of the insignia."

The Strategy

General Sebastian MacMaine, sometime Colonel of Earth's Space Force, and presently a General of the Kerothi Fleet, looked at the array of stars that appeared to drift by the main viewplate of his flagship, the blaster-boat *Shudos*.

Behind him, General Tallis was saying, "You've done well, Sepastian. Better than anyone could have really expected. Three battles so far, and every one of them won by a margin far greater than anticipated. Any ideas that anyone may have had that you were not wholly working for the Kerothi cause has certainly been dispelled."

"Thanks, Tallis." MacMaine turned to look at the Kerothi officer. "I only hope that I can keep it up. Now that we're ready for the big push, I can't help but wonder what would happen if I were to lose a battle."

"Frankly," Tallis said, "that would depend on several things, the main one being whether or not it appeared that you had deliberately thrown the advantage to the enemy. But nobody expects you, or anyone else, to win every time. Even the most brilliant commander can make an honest mistake, and if it can be shown that it *was* an honest mistake, and one, furthermore, that he could not have been expected to avoid, he wouldn't be punished for it. In your case, I'll admit that the investigation would be a great deal more thorough than normal, and that you wouldn't get as much of the benefit of the doubt as another officer might, but unless there is a deliberate error I doubt that anything serious would happen."

"Do you really believe that, Tallis, or is it just wishful thinking on your part, knowing as you do that your punishment will be the same as mine if I fail?" MacMaine asked flatly.

Tallis didn't hesitate. "If I didn't believe it, I would ask to be relieved as your Guardian. And the moment I did that, you would be removed from command. The moment I feel that you are not acting for the best interests of Keroth, I will act—not only to protect myself, but to protect my people."

"That's fair enough," MacMaine said. "But how about the others?"

"I cannot speak for my fellow officers—only for myself." Then Tallis' voice became cold. "Just keep your hands clean, Sepastian, and all will be well. You will not be punished for mistakes—only for crimes. If you are planning no crimes, this worry of yours is needless."

"I ceased to worry about myself long ago," MacMaine said coolly. "I do not fear personal death, not even by Excommunication. My sole worry is about the ultimate outcome of the war if I should fail. That, and nothing more."

"I believe you," Tallis said. "Let us say no more about it. Your actions are difficult for us to understand, in some ways, that's all. No Kerothi would ever change his allegiance as you have. Nor has any Earth officer that we have captured shown any desire to do so. Oh, some of them have agreed to do almost anything we wanted them to, but these were not the intelligent ones, and even they were only doing it to save their own miserable hides.

"Still, you are an exceptional man, Sepastian, unlike any other of your race, as far as we know. Perhaps it is simply that you are the only one with enough wisdom to seek your intellectual equals rather than remain loyal to a mass of stupid animals who are fit only to be slaves."

"It was because I foresaw their eventual enslavement that I acted as I did," MacMaine admitted. "As I saw it, I had only two choices—to remain as I was and become a slave to the Kerothi or to put myself in your hands willingly and hope for the best. As you—"

He was interrupted by a harsh voice from a nearby speaker.

"Battle stations! Battle stations! Enemy fleet in detector range! Contact in twelve minutes!"

Tallis and MacMaine headed for the Command Room at a fast trot. The three other Kerothi who made up the Strategy Staff came in at almost the same time. There was a flurry of activity as the computers and viewers were readied for action, then the Kerothi looked expectantly at the Earthman.

MacMaine looked at the detector screens. The deployment of the approaching Earth fleet was almost as he had expected it would be. There were slight differences, but they would require only minor changes in the strategy he had mapped out from the information brought in by the Kerothi scout ships.

Undoubtedly, the Kerothi position had been relayed to the Earth commander by their own advance scouts buzzing about in tiny, one-man shells just small enough to be undetectable at normal range.

Watching the positions on the screens carefully, MacMaine called out a series of numbers in an unhurried voice and watched as the orders, relayed by the Kerothi staff, changed the position of parts of the Kerothi fleet. Then, as the computer-led Earth fleet jockeyed to compensate for the change in the Kerothi deployment, MacMaine called out more orders.

The High Commander of Keroth had called MacMaine a "computing animal," but the term was far from accurate. MacMaine couldn't possibly have computed all the variables in that battle, and he didn't try. It was a matter of human intuition against mechanical logic. The advantage lay with MacMaine, for, while the computer could not logically fathom the intuitive processes of its human opponent, MacMaine could and did have an intuitive grasp of the machine's logic. MacMaine didn't need to know every variable in the pattern; he only needed to know the pattern as a whole.

The *Shudos* was well in the rear of the main body of the Kerothi fleet. There was every necessity for keeping MacMaine's flagship out of as much of the fighting as possible.

When the first contact was made, MacMaine was certain of the outcome. His voice became a steady drone as he called out instructions to the staff officers; his mind was so fully occupied with the moving pattern before him that he noticed nothing else in the room around him.

Spaceship against spaceship, the two fleets locked in battle. The warheads of ultralight torpedoes flared their eye-searing explosions soundlessly into the void; ships exploded like overcharged beer bottles as blaster energy caught them and smashed through their screens; men and machines flamed and died, scattering the stripped nuclei of their component atoms through the screaming silence of space.

And through it all, Sebastian MacMaine watched dispassionately, calling out his orders as ten Earthmen died for every Kerothi death.

This was a crucial battle. The big push toward the center of Earth's cluster of worlds had begun. Until now, the Kerothi had been fighting the outposts, the planets on the fringes of Earth's sphere of influence which were only lightly colonized, and therefore relatively easy to take. Earth's strongest fleets were out there, to protect planets that could not protect themselves.

Inside that periphery were the more densely populated planets, the self-sufficient colonies which were more or less able to defend themselves without too much reliance on space fleets as such. But now that the backbone of the Earth's Space Force had been all but broken, it would be a relatively easy matter to mop up planet after planet, since each one could be surrounded separately, pounded into surrender, and secured before going on to the next.

That, at least, had been the original Kerothi intention. But MacMaine had told them that there was another way—a way which, if it succeeded, would save time, lives, and money for the Kerothi. And, if it failed, MacMaine said, they would be no worse off, they would simply have to resume the original plan.

Now, the first of the big colony planets was to be taken. When the protecting Earth fleet was reduced to tatters, the Kerothi would go on to Houston's World as the first step in the big push toward Earth itself.

But MacMaine wasn't thinking of that phase of the war. That was still in the future, while the hellish space battle was still at hand.

He lost track of time as he watched the Kerothi fleet take advantage of their superior tactical position and tear the Earth fleet to bits. Not until he saw the remains of the Earth fleet turn tail and run did he realize that the battle had been won.

The Kerothi fleet consolidated itself. There was no point in pursuing the fleeting Earth ships; that would only break up the solidity of the Kerothi deployment. The losers could afford to scatter; the winners could not. Early in the war, the Kerothi had used that trick against Earth; the Kerothi had broken and fled, and the Earth fleet had split up to chase them down. The scattered Earth ships had suddenly found that they had been led into traps composed of hidden clusters of Kerothi ships. Naturally, the trick had never worked again for either side.

"All right," MacMaine said when it was all over, "let's get on to Houston's World."

The staff men, including Tallis, were already on their feet, congratulating MacMaine and shaking his hands. Even General Hokotan, the Headquarters Staff man, who had been transferred temporarily to the Fleet Force to keep an eye on both MacMaine and Tallis, was enthusiastically pounding MacMaine's shoulder.

No one aboard was supposed to know that Hokotan was a Headquarters officer, but MacMaine had spotted the spy rather easily. There was a difference between the fighters of the Fleet and the politicoes of Headquarters. The politicoes were no harder, perhaps, nor more ruthless, than the fighters, but they were of a different breed. Theirs was the ruthlessness of the bully who steps on those who are weaker rather than the ruthlessness of the man who kills only to win a battle. MacMaine had the feeling that the Headquarters Staff preferred to spend their time browbeating their underlings rather than risk their necks with someone who could fight back, however weakly.

General Hokotan seemed to have more of the fighting quality than most HQ men, but he wasn't a Fleet Officer at heart. He couldn't be compared to Tallis without looking small and mean.

As a matter of cold fact, very few of the officers were in anyway comparable to Tallis—not even the Fleet men. The more MacMaine learned of the Kerothi, the more he realized just how lucky he had been that it had been Tallis, and not some other Kerothi general, who had been captured by the Earth forces. He was not at all sure that his plan would have worked at all with any of the other officers he had met.

Tallis, like MacMaine, was an unusual specimen of his race.

MacMaine took the congratulations of the Kerothi officers with a look of pleasure on his face, and when they had subsided somewhat, he grinned and said:

"Let's get a little work done around here, shall we? We have a planet to reduce yet."

They laughed. Reducing a planet didn't require strategy—only firepower. The planet-based defenses couldn't maneuver, but the energy reserve of a planet is greater than that of any fleet, no matter how large. Each defense point would have to be cut down individually by the massed power of the fleet, cut down one by one until the planet was helpless. The planet as a whole might have more energy reserve than the fleet, but no individual defense point did. The problem was to avoid being hit by the rest of the defense points while one single point was bearing the brunt of the fleet's attack. It wasn't without danger, but it could be done.

And for a job like that, MacMaine's special abilities weren't needed. He could only watch and wait until it was over.

So he watched and waited. Unlike the short-time fury of a space battle, the reduction of a planet took days of steady pounding. When it was over, the blaster-boats of the Kerothi fleet and the shuttles from the great battle cruisers landed on Houston's World and took possession of the planet.

MacMaine was waiting in his cabin when General Hokotan brought the news that the planet was secured.

"They are ours," the HQ spy said with a superior smile. "The sniveling animals didn't even seem to want to defend themselves. They don't even know how to fight a hand-to-hand battle. How could such things have ever evolved intelligence enough to conquer space?" Hokotan enjoyed making such remarks to MacMaine's face, knowing that since MacMaine was technically a Kerothi he couldn't show any emotion when the enemy was insulted.

MacMaine showed none. "Got them all, eh?" he said.

"All but a few who scattered into the hills and forests. But not many of them had the guts to leave the security of their cities, even though we were occupying them."

"How many are left alive?"

"An estimated hundred and fifty million, more or less."

"Good. That should be enough to set an example. I picked Houston's World because we can withdraw from it without weakening our position; its position in space is such that it would constitute no menace to us even if we never reduced it. That way, we can be sure that our little message is received on Earth."

Hokotan's grin was wolfish. "And the whole weak-hearted race will shake with fear, eh?"

"Exactly. Tallis can speak English well enough to be understood. Have him make the announcmeent to them. He can word it however he likes, but the essence is to be this: Houston's World resisted the occupation by Kerothi troops; an example must be made of them to show them what happens to Earthmen who resist."

"That's all?"

"That's enough. Oh, by the way, make sure that there are plenty of their cargo spaceships in good working order; I doubt that we've ruined them all, but if we have, repair some of them.

"And, too, you'd better make sure that you allow some of the merchant spacemen to 'escape,' just in case there are no space pilots among those who took to the hills. We want to make sure that someone can use those ships to take the news back to Earth."

"And the rest?" Hokotan asked, with an expectant look. He knew what was to be done, but he wanted to hear MacMaine say it again.

MacMaine obliged.

"Hang them. Every man, every woman, every child. I want them to be decorating every lamppost and roof-beam on the planet, dangling like overripe fruit when the Earth forces return."

The Results

"I don't understand it," said General Polan Tallis worriedly. "Where are they coming from? How are they doing it? What's happened?"

MacMaine and the four Kerothi officers were sitting in the small dining room that doubled as a recreation room between meals. The nervous strain of the past few months was beginning to tell on all of them.

"Six months ago," Tallis continued jerkily, "we had them beaten. One planet after another was reduced in turn. Then, out of nowhere, comes a fleet of ships we didn't even know existed, and they've smashed us at every turn."

"If they *are* ships," said Loopat, the youngest officer of the *Shudos* staff. "Who ever heard of a battleship that was undetectable at a distance of less than half a million miles? It's impossible!"

"Then we're being torn to pieces by the impossible!" Hokotan snapped. "Before we even know they are anywhere around, they are blasting us with everything they've got! Not even the strategic genius of General MacMaine can help us if we have no time to plot strategy!"

The Kerothi had been avoiding MacMaine's eyes, but now, at the mention of his name, they all looked at him as if their collective gaze had been drawn to him by some unknown attractive force.

"It's like fighting ghosts," MacMaine said in a hushed voice. For the first time, he felt a feeling of awe that was almost akin to fear. What had he done?

In another sense, that same question was in the mind of the Kerothi.

"Have you any notion at all what they are doing or how they are doing it?" asked Tallis gently.

"None," MacMaine answered truthfully. "None at all, I swear to you."

"They don't even behave like Earthmen," said the fourth Kerothi, a thick-necked officer named Ossif. "They not only outfight us, they outthink us at every turn. Is it possible, General MacMaine, that the Earthmen have allies of another race, a race of intelligent beings that we don't know of?" He left unsaid the added implication: "*And that you have neglected to tell us about?*"

"Again," said MacMaine, "I swear to you that I know nothing of any third intelligent race in the galaxy."

"If there were such allies," Tallis said, "isn't it odd that they should wait so long to aid their friends?"

"No odder than that the Earthmen should suddenly develop superweapons that we cannot understand, much less fight against," Hokotan said, with a touch of anger.

"Not 'superweapons'," MacMaine corrected almost absently. "All they have is a method of making their biggest ships indetectable until they're so close that it doesn't matter. When they do register on our detectors, it's too late. But the weapons they strike with are the same type as they've always used, I believe."

"All right, then," Hokotan said, his voice showing more anger. "One weapon or whatever you want to call it. Practical invisibility. But that's enough. An invisible man with a knife is more deadly than a dozen ordinary men with modern armament. Are you sure you know nothing of this, General MacMaine?"

Before MacMaine could answer, Tallis said, "Don't be ridiculous, Hokotan! If he had known that such a weapon existed, would he have been fool enough to leave his people? With that secret, they stand a good chance of beating us in less than half the time it took us to wipe out their fleet—or, rather, to wipe out as much of it as we did."

"They got a new fleet somewhere," said young Loopat, almost to himself.

Tallis ignored him. "If MacMaine deserted his former allegiance, knowing that they had a method of rendering the action of a space drive indetectable, then he was and is a blithering idiot. And we know he isn't."

"All right, all right! I concede that," snapped Hokotan. "He knows nothing. I don't say that I fully trust him, even now, but I'll admit that I cannot see how he is to blame for the reversals of the past few months.

"If the Earthmen had somehow been informed of our activities, or if we had invented a superweapon and they found out about it, I would be inclined to put the blame squarely on MacMaine. But—"

"How would he get such information out?" Tallis cut in sharply. "He has been watched every minute of every day. We know he couldn't send any information to Earth. How could he?"

"Telepathy, for all I know!" Hokotan retorted. "But that's beside the point! I don't trust him any farther than I can see him, and not completely, even then. But I concede that there is no possible connection between this new menace and anything MacMaine might have done.

"This is no time to worry about that sort of thing; we've got to find some way of getting our hands on one of those ghost ships!"

"I do suggest," put in the thick-necked Ossif, "that we keep a closer watch on General MacMaine. Now that the Earth animals are making a comeback, he might decide to turn his coat now, even if he has been innocent of any acts against Keroth so far."

Hokotan's laugh was a short, hard bark. "Oh, we'll watch him, all right, Ossif. But, as Tallis has pointed out, MacMaine is not a fool, and he would certainly be a fool to return to Earth if his leaving it was a genuine act of desertion. The last planet we captured, before this invisibility thing came up to stop us, was plastered all over with notices that the Earth fleet was concentrating on the capture of the arch-traitor MacMaine.

"The price on his head, as a corpse, is enough to allow an Earthman to retire in luxury for life. The man who brings him back alive gets ten times that amount.

"Of course, it's possible that the whole thing is a put-up job—a smoke screen for our benefit. That's why we must and will keep a closer watch. But only a few of the Earth's higher-up would know that it was a smoke screen; the rest believe it, whether it is true or not. MacMaine would have to be very careful not to let the wrong people get their hands on him if he returned."

"It's no smoke screen," MacMaine said in a matter-of-fact tone. "I assure you that I have no intention of returning to Earth. If Keroth loses this war, then I will die—either fighting for the Kerothi or by execution at the hands of Earthmen if I am captured. Or," he added musingly, "perhaps even at the hands of the Kerothi, if someone decides that a scapegoat is needed to atone for the loss of the war."

"If you are guilty of treason," Hokotan barked, "you will die as a traitor! If you are not, there is no need for your death. The Kerothi do not need scapegoats!"

"Talk, talk, talk!" Tallis said with a sudden bellow. "We have agreed that MacMaine has done nothing that could even remotely be regarded as suspicious! He has fought hard and loyally; he has been more ruthless than any of us in destroying the enemy. Very well, we will guard him more closely. We can put him in irons if that's necessary.

"But let's quit yapping and start thinking! We've been acting like frightened children, not knowing what it is we fear, and venting our fear-caused anger on the most handy target!

"Let's act like men—not like children!"

After a moment, Hokotan said: "I agree." His voice was firm, but calm. "Our job will be to get our hands on one of those new Earth ships. Anyone have any suggestions?"

They had all kinds of suggestions, one after another. The detectors, however, worked because they detected the distortion of space which was as necessary for the drive of a ship as the distortion of air was necessary for the movement of a propellor-driven aircraft. None of them could see how a ship could avoid making that distortion, and none of them could figure out how to go about capturing a ship that no one could even detect until it was too late to set a trap.

The discussion went on for days. And it was continued the next day and the next. And the days dragged out into weeks.

Communications with Keroth broke down. The Fleet-to-Head-quarters courier ships, small in size, without armament, and practically solidly packed with drive mechanism, could presumably outrun anything but another unarmed courier. An armed ship of the same size would have to use some of the space for her weapons, which meant that the drive would have to be smaller; if the drive remained the same size, then the armament would make the ship larger. In either case, the speed would be cut down. A smaller ship might outrun a standard courier, but if they got much smaller, there wouldn't be room inside for the pilot.

Nonetheless, courier after courier never arrived at its destination.

And the Kerothi Fleet was being decimated by the hit-and-run tactics of the Earth's ghost ships. And Earth never lost a ship; by the time the Kerothi ships knew their enemy was in the vicinity, the enemy had hit and vanished again. The Kerothi never had a chance to ready their weapons.

In the long run, they never had a chance at all.

MacMaine waited with almost fatalistic complacence for the inevitable to happen. When it did happen, he was ready for it.

The *Shudos*, tiny flagship of what had once been a mighty armada and was now only a tattered remnant, was floating in orbit, along with the other remaining ships of the fleet, around a bloated red-giant sun. With their drives off, there was no way of detecting them at any distance, and the chance of their being found by accident was microscopically small. But they could not wait forever. Water could be recirculated, and energy could be tapped from the nearby sun, but food was gone once it was eaten.

Hokotan's decision was inevitable, and, under the circumstances, the only possible one. He simple told them what they had already known—that he was a Headquarters Staff officer.

"We haven't heard from Headquarters in weeks," he said at last. "The Earth fleet may already be well inside our periphery. We'll have to go home." He produced a document which he had obviously been holding in reserve for another purpose and handed it to Tallis. "Headquarters Staff Orders, Tallis. It empowers me to take command of the Fleet in the event of an emergency, and the decision as to what constitutes an emergency was left up to my discretion. I must admit that this is not the emergency any of us at Headquarters anticipated."

Tallis read through the document. "I see that it isn't," he said dryly. "According to this, MacMaine and I are to be placed under immediate arrest as soon as you find it necessary to act."

"Yes," said Hokotan bitterly. "So you can both consider yourselves under arrest. Don't bother to lock yourselves up—there's no point in it. General MacMaine, I see no reason to inform the rest of the Fleet of this, so we will go on as usual. The orders I have to give are simple: The Fleet will head for home by the most direct possible geodesic. Since we cannot fight, we will simply ignore attacks and keep going as long as we last. We can do nothing else." He paused thoughtfully.

"And, General MacMaine, in case we do not live through this, I would like to extend my apologies. I do not like you; I don't think I could ever learn to like an anim . . . to like a non-Kerothi. But I know when to admit an error in judgment. You have fought bravely and well—better, I know, than I could have done myself. You have shown yourself to be loyal to your adopted planet; you are a Kerothi in every sense of the word except the physical. My apologies for having wronged you."

He extended his hands and MacMaine took them. A choking

sensation constricted the Earthman's throat for a moment, then he got the words out—the words he had to say. "Believe me, General Hokotan, there is no need for an apology. No need whatever."

"Thank you," said Hokotan. Then he turned and left the room.

"All right, Tallis," MacMaine said hurriedly, "let's get moving."

The orders were given to the remnants of the Fleet, and they cut in their drives to head homeward. And the instant they did, there was chaos. Earth's fleet of "ghost ships" had been patrolling the area for weeks, knowing that the Kerothi fleet had last been detected somewhere in the vicinity. As soon as the spatial distortions of the Kerothi drives flashed on the Earth ships' detectors, the Earth fleet, widely scattered over the whole circumambient volume of space, coalesced toward the center of the spatial disturbance like a cloud of bees all heading for the same flower.

Where there had been only the dull red light of the giant star, there suddenly appeared the blinding, blue-white brilliance of disintegrating matter, blossoming like cruel, deadly, beautiful flowers in the midst of the Kerothi ships, then fading slowly as each expanding cloud of plasma cooled.

Sebastian MacMaine might have died with the others except that the *Shudos*, as the flagship, was to trail behind the fleet, so her drive had not yet been activated. The *Shudos* was still in orbit, moving at only a few miles per second when the Earth fleet struck.

Her drive never did go on. A bomb, only a short distance away as the distance from atomic disintegration is measured, sent the *Shudos* spinning away, end over end, like a discarded cigar butt flipped toward a gutter, one side caved in near the rear, as if it had been kicked in by a giant foot.

There was still air in the ship, MacMaine realized groggily as he awoke from the unconsciousness that had been thrust upon him. He tried to stand up, but he found himself staggering toward one crazily-slanted wall. The stagger was partly due to his grogginess, and partly due to the Coriolis forces acting within the spinning ship. The artificial gravity was gone, which meant that the interstellar drive engines had been smashed. He wondered if the emergency rocket drive was still working—not that it would take him anywhere worth going to in less than a few centuries. But, then, Sebastian MacMaine had nowhere to go, anyhow.

Tallis lay against one wall, looking very limp. MacMaine half staggered over to him and knelt down. Tallis was still alive.

The centrifugal force caused by the spinning ship gave an effective pull of less than one Earth gravity, but the weird twists caused by the Coriolis forces made motion and orientation difficult. Besides, the ship was spinning slightly on her long axis as well as turning end-for-end.

MacMaine stood there for a moment, trying to think. He had expected to die. Death was something he had known was inevitable from the moment he made his decision to leave Earth. He had not known how or when it would come, but he had known that it would come soon. He had known that he would never live to collect the reward he had demanded of the Kerothi for "faithful service." Traitor he might be, but he was still honest enough with himself to know that he would never take payment for services he had not rendered.

Now death was very near, and Sebastian MacMaine almost welcomed it. He had no desire to fight it. Tallis might want to stand and fight death to the end, but Tallis was not carrying the monstrous weight of guilt that would stay with Sebastian MacMaine until his death, no matter how much he tried to justify his actions.

On the other hand, if he had to go, he might as well do a good job of it. Since he still had a short time left, he might as well wrap the whole thing up in a neat package. How?

Again, his intuitive ability to see pattern gave him the answer long before he could have reasoned it out.

They will know, he thought, *but they will never be sure they know. I will be immortal. And my name will live forever, although no Earthman will ever again use the surname MacMaine or the given name Sebastian.*

He shook his head to clear it. No use thinking like that now. There were things to be done.

Tallis first. MacMaine made his way over to one of the emergency medical kits that he knew were kept in every compartment of every ship. One of the doors of a wall locker hung open, and the blue-green medical symbol used by the Kerothi showed darkly in the dim light that came from the three unshattered glow plates in the ceiling. He opened the kit, hoping that it contained something equivalent to adhesive tape. He had never inspected a Kerothi medical kit before. Fortunately, he could read Kerothi. If a military government was good for nothing else, at least it was capable of enforcing a simplified phonetic orthography so that words were pronounced as they were spelled. And—

He forced his wandering mind back to his work. The blow on the head, plus the crazy effect the spinning was having on his inner ears, plus the cockeyed gravitational orientation that made his eyes feel as though they were seeing things at two different angles, all combined to make for more than a little mental confusion.

There was adhesive tape, all right. Wound on its little spool, it looked almost homey. He spent several minutes winding the sticky plastic ribbon around Tallis' wrists and ankles.

Then he took the gun from the Kerothi general's sleeve holster—he had never been allowed one of his own—and, holding it firmly in his right hand, he went on a tour of the ship.

It was hard to move around. The centrifugal force varied from point to point throughout the ship, and the corridors were cluttered with debris that seemed to move with a life of its own as each piece shifted slowly under the effects of the various forces working on it. And, as the various masses moved about, the rate of spin of the ship changed as the law of conservation of angular momentum operated. The ship was full of sliding, clattering, jangling noises as the stuff tried to find a final resting place and bring the ship to equilibrium.

He found the door to Ossif's cabin open and the room empty. He found Ossif in Loopat's cabin, trying to get the younger officer to his feet.

Ossif saw MacMaine at the door and said: "You're alive! Good! Help me—" Then he saw the gun in MacMaine's hand and stopped. It was the last thing he saw before MacMaine shot him neatly between the eyes.

Loopat, only half conscious, never even knew he was in danger, and the blast that drilled through his brain prevented him from ever knowing anything again in this life.

Like a man in a dream, MacMaine went on to Hokotan's cabin, his weapon at the ready. He was rather pleased to find that the HQ general was already quite dead, his neck broken as cleanly as if it had been done by a hangman. Hardly an hour before, MacMaine would cheerfully have shot Hokotan where it would hurt the most and watch him die slowly. But the memory of Hokotan's honest apology made the Earth-man very glad that he did not have to shoot the general at all.

There remained only the five-man crew, the NCO technician and his gang, who actually ran the ship. They would be at the tail of the ship, in the engine compartment. To get there, he had to cross the center of spin of the ship, and the change of gravity from one direction to another, decreasing toward zero, passing the null point, and rising again on the other side, made him nauseous. He felt better after his stomach had emptied itself.

Cautiously, he opened the door to the drive compartment and then slammed it hard in sudden fear when he saw what had happened. The shielding had been torn away from one of the energy converters and exposed the room to high-energy radiation. The crewmen were quite dead.

The fear went away as quickly as it had come. So maybe he'd dosed himself with a few hundred Roentgens—so what? A little radiation never hurt a dead man.

But he knew now that there was no possibility of escape. The drive was wrecked, and the only other means of escape, the one-man courier boat that every blaster-boat carried, had been sent out weeks ago and had never returned.

If only the courier boat were still in its cradle—

MacMaine shook his head. No. It was better this way. Much better.

He turned and went back to the dining cabin where Tallis was trussed up. This time, passing the null-gee point didn't bother him much at all.

Tallis was moaning a little and his eyelids were fluttering by the time MacMaine got back. The Earthman opened the medical kit again and looked for some kind of stimulant. He had no knowledge of medical or chemical terms in Kerothic, but there was a box of glass ampoules bearing instructions to "crush and allow patient to inhale fumes." That sounded right.

The stuff smelled like a mixture of spirits of ammonia and butyl mercaptan, but it did the job. Tallis coughed convulsively, turned his head away, coughed again, and opened his eyes. MacMaine tossed the stinking ampoule out into the corridor as Tallis tried to focus his eyes.

"How do you feel?" MacMaine asked. His voice sounded oddly thick in his own ears.

"All right. I'm all right. What happened?" He looked wonderingly around. "Near miss? Must be. Anyone hurt?"

"They're all dead but you and me," MacMaine said.

"Dead? Then we'd better—" He tried to move and then realized that he was bound hand and foot. The sudden realization of his position seemed to clear his brain completely. "Sepastian, what's going on here? Why am I tied up?"

"I had to tie you," MacMaine explained carefully, as though to a child. "There are some things I have to do yet, and I wouldn't want you to stop me. Maybe I should have just shot you while you were unconscious. That would have been kinder to both of us, I think. But . . . but, Tallis, I had to tell somebody. Someone else has to know. Someone else has to judge. Or maybe I just want to unload it on someone else, someone who will carry the burden with me for just a little while. I don't know."

"Sepastian, what are you talking about?" The Kerothi's face shone dully orange in the dim light, his bright green eyes looked steadily at the Earthman, and his voice was oddly gentle.

"I'm talking about treason," said MacMaine. "Do you want to listen?"

"I don't have much choice, do I?" Tallis said. "Tell me one thing first: Are we going to die?"

"You are, Tallis. But I won't. I'm going to be immortal."

Tallis looked at him for a long moment. Then, "All right, Sepastian. I'm no psych man, but I know you're not well. I'll listen to whatever you have to say. But first, untie my hands and feet."

"I can't do that, Tallis. Sorry. But if our positions were reversed, I know what I would do to you when I heard the story. And I can't let you kill me, because there's something more that has to be done."

Tallis knew at that moment that he was looking at the face of Death. And he also knew that there was nothing whatever he could do about it. Except talk. And listen.

"Very well, Sepastian," he said levelly. "Go ahead. Treason, you say? How? Against whom?"

"I'm not quite sure," said Sebastian MacMaine. "I thought maybe you could tell me."

The Reason

"Let me ask you one thing, Tallis," MacMaine said. "Would you do anything in your power to save Keroth from destruction? Anything, no matter how drastic, if you knew that it would save Keroth in the long run?"

"A foolish question. Of course I would. I would give my life."

"Your life? A mere nothing. A pittance. Any man could give his life. Would you consent to live forever for Keroth?"

Tallis shook his head as though he were puzzled. "Live forever? That's twice or three times you've said something about that. I *don't* understand you."

"Would you consent to live forever as a filthy curse on the lips of every Kerothi old enough to speak? Would you consent to be a vile, inhuman monster whose undead spirit would hang over your homeland like an evil miasma for centuries to come, whose very name would touch a flame of hatred in the minds of all who heard it?"

"That's a very melodramatic way of putting it," the Kerothi said, "but I believe I understand what you mean. Yes, I would consent to that if it would be the only salvation of Keroth."

"Would you slaughter helpless millions of your own people so that other billions might survive? Would you ruthlessly smash your system of government and your whole way of life if it were the only way to save the people themselves?"

"I'm beginning to see what you're driving at," Tallis said slowly. "And if it is what I think it is, I think I would like to kill you—very slowly."

"I know, I know. But you haven't answered my question. Would you do those things to save your people?"

"I would," said Tallis coldly. "Don't misunderstand me. I do not loathe you for what you have done to your own people; I hate you for what you have done to mine."

"That's as it should be," said MacMaine. His head was clearing up more now. He realized that he had been talking a little wildly at first. Or was he really insane? Had he been insane from the beginning? No. He knew with absolute clarity that every step he had made had been cold, calculating, and ruthless, but utterly and absolutely sane.

He suddenly wished that he had shot Tallis without wakening him. If his mind hadn't been in such a state of shock, he would have. There was no need to torture the man like this.

"Go on," said Tallis, in a voice that had suddenly become devoid all emotion. "Tell it all."

"Earth was stagnating," MacMaine said, surprised at the sound of his own voice. He hadn't intended to go on. But he couldn't stop now. "You saw how it was. Every standard had become meaningless because no standard was held to be better than any other standard. There was no beauty because beauty was superior to ugliness and we couldn't allow superiority or inferiority. There was no love because in order to love someone or something you must feel that it is in some way superior to that which is not loved. I'm not even sure I know what those terms mean, because I'm not sure I ever thought anything was beautiful, I'm not sure I ever loved anything. I only read about such things in books. But I know I felt the emptiness inside me where those things should have been.

"There was no morality, either. People did not refrain from stealing because it was wrong, but simply because it was pointless to steal what would be given to you if you asked for it. There was no right or wrong.

"We had a form of social contract that we called 'marriage,' but it wasn't the same thing as marriage was in the old days. There was no love. There used to be a crime called 'adultery,' but even the word had gone out of use on the Earth I knew. Instead, it was considered antisocial for a woman to refuse to give herself to other men; to do so might indicate that she thought herself superior or thought her husband to be superior to other men. The same thing applied to men in their relationships with women other than their wives. Marriage was a social contract that could be made or broken at the whim of the individual. It served no purpose because it meant nothing, neither party gained anything by the contract that they couldn't have had without it. But a wedding was an excuse for a gala party at which the couple were the center of attention. So the contract was entered into lightly for the sake of a gay time for a while, then broken again so that the game could be played with someone else—the game of Musical Bedrooms."

He stopped and looked down at the helpless Kerothi. "That doesn't mean much to you, does it? In your society, women are chattel, to be owned, bought, and sold. If you see a woman you want, you offer a price to her father or brother or husband—whoever the owner might be. Then she's yours until you sell her to another. Adultery is a very serious crime on Kerothi, but only because it's an infringement of property rights. There's not much love lost there, either, is there?

"I wonder if either of us knows what love is, Tallis?"

"I love my people," Tallis said grimly.

MacMaine was startled for a moment. He'd never thought about it that way. "You're right, Tallis," he said at last. "You're right. We *do* know. And because I loved the human race, in spite of its stagnation and its spirit of total mediocrity, I did what I had to do."

"You will pardon me," Tallis said, with only the faintest bit of acid in his voice, "if I do not understand exactly what it is that you did." Then his voice grew softer. "Wait. Perhaps I do understand. Yes, of course."

"You think you understand?" MacMaine looked at him narrowly.

"Yes. I said that I am not a psychomedic, and my getting angry with you proves it. You fought hard and well for Keroth, Sepastian, and, in doing so, you had to kill many of your own race. It is not easy for a man to do, no matter how much your reason tells you it *must* be done. And now, in the face of death, remorse has come. I do not completely understand the workings of the Earthman's mind, but I—"

"That's just it; you don't," MacMaine interrupted. "Thanks for trying to find an excuse for me, Tallis, but I'm afraid it isn't so. Listen.

"I had to find out what Earth was up against. I had a pretty good idea already that the Kerothi would win—would wipe us out or enslave us to the last man. And, after I had seen Keroth, I was certain of it. So I sent a message back to Earth, telling them what they were up against, because, up 'til then they hadn't known. As soon as they knew, they reacted as they have always done when they are certain that they face danger. They fought. They unleashed the chained-down intelligence of the few extraordinary Earthmen, and they released the fighting spirit of even the ordinary Earthmen. And they won!"

Tallis shook his head. "You sent no message, Sepastian. You were watched. You know that. You could not have sent a message."

"You saw me send it," MacMaine said. "So did everyone else in the fleet. Hokotan helped me send it—made all the arrangements at my orders. But because you do not understand the workings of the Earthman's mind, you didn't even recognize it as a message.

"Tallis, what would your people have done if an invading force, which had already proven that it could whip Keroth easily, did to one of your planets what we did on Houston's World?"

"If the enemy showed us that they could easily beat us and then hanged the whole population of a planet for resisting? Why, we would be fools to resist. Unless, of course, we had a secret weapon in a hidden pocket, the way Earth had."

"No, Tallis; no. That's where you're making your mistake. Earth didn't have that weapon until *after* the massacre on Houston's World. Let me ask you another thing: Would any Kerothi have ordered that massacre?"

"I doubt it," Tallis said slowly. "Killing that many potential slaves would be wasteful and expensive. We are fighters, not butchers. We kill only when it is necessary to win; the remainder of the enemy is taken care of as the rightful property of the conqueror."

"Exactly. Prisoners were part of the loot, and it's foolish to destroy loot. I noticed that in your history books. I noticed, too, that in such cases, the captives recognized the right of the conqueror to enslave them, and made no trouble. So, after Earth's forces get to Keroth, I don't think we'll have any trouble with you."

"Not if they set us an example like Houston's World," Tallis said, "and can prove that resistance is futile. But I don't understand the message. What was the message and how did you send it?"

"The massacre on Houston's World was the message, Tallis. I even told the Staff, when I suggested it. I said that such an act would strike terror into the minds of Earthmen.

"And it did, Tallis; it did. But that terror was just the goad they needed to make them fight. They had to sit up and take notice. If the Kerothi had gone on the way they were going, taking one planet after another, as they planned, the Kerothi would have won. The people of each planet would think, "It can't happen here." And, since they felt that nothing could be superior to anything else, they were complacently certain that they couldn't be beat. Of course, maybe Earth couldn't beat you, either, but that was all right; it just proved that there was no such thing as superiority.

"But Houston's World jarred them—badly. It had to. 'Hell does more than Heaven can to wake the fear of God in man.' They didn't recognize beauty, but I shoved ugliness down their throats; they didn't know love and friendship, so I gave them hatred and fear.

"The committing of atrocities has been the mistake of aggressors throughout Earth's history. The battle cries of countless wars have called upon the people to remember an atrocity. Nothing else hits an Earthman as hard as a vicious, brutal, unnecessary murder.

"So I gave them the incentive to fight, Tallis. That was my message."

Tallis was staring at him wide eyed. "You *are* insane."

"No. It worked. In six months, they found something that would enable them to blast the devil Kerothi from the skies. I don't know what the society of Earth is like now—and I never will. But at least I know that men are allowed to think again. And I know they'll survive."

He suddenly realized how much time had passed. Had it been too long? No. There would still be Earth ships prowling the vicinity, waiting for any sign of a Kerothi ship that had hidden in the vastness of space by not using its engines.

"I have some things I must do, Tallis," he said, standing up slowly. "Is there anything else you want to know?"

Tallis frowned a little, as though he were trying to think of something, but then he closed his eyes and relaxed. "No, Sepastian. Nothing. Do whatever it is you have to do."

"Tallis," MacMaine said. Tallis didn't open his eyes, and MacMaine was very glad of that. "Tallis, I want you to know that, in all my life, you were the only friend I ever had."

The bright green eyes remained closed. "That may be so. Yes, Sepastian, I honestly think you believe that."

"I do," said MacMaine, and shot him carefully through the head.

The End

—and Epilogue.

"Hold it!" The voice bellowed thunderingly from the loud-speakers of the six Earth ships that had boxed in the derelict. "Hold it! *Don't bomb that ship!* I'll personally have the head of any man who damages that ship!"

In five of the ships, the commanders simply held off the bombardment that would have vaporized the derelict. In the sixth, Major Thornton, the Group Commander, snapped off the microphone. His voice was shaky as he said: "That was close! Another second, and we'd have lost that ship forever."

Captain Verenski's Oriental features had a half-startled, half-puzzled look. "I don't get it. You grabbed that mike control as if you'd been bitten. I know that she's only a derelict. After that burst of fifty-gee acceleration for fifteen minutes, there couldn't be anyone left alive on her. But there must have been a reason for using atomic rockets instead of their antiacceleration fields. What makes you think she's not dangerous?"

"I didn't say she wasn't dangerous," the major snapped. "She may be. Probably is. But we're going to capture her if we can. Look!" He pointed at the image of the ship in the screen.

She wasn't spinning now, or looping end-over-end. After fifteen minutes of high acceleration, her atomic rockets had cut out, and now she moved serenely at constant velocity, looking as dead as a battered tin can.

"I don't see anything," Captain Verenski said.

"The Kerothic symbols on the side. Palatal unvoiced sibilant, rounded—"

"I don't read Kerothic, major," said the captain. "I—" Then he blinked and said, "*Shudos!*"

"That's it. The *Shudos* of Keroth. The flagship of the Kerothi Fleet."

The look in the major's eyes was the same look of hatred that had come into the captain's.

"Even if its armament is still functioning, we have to take the chance," Major Thornton said. "Even if they're all dead, we have to try to get The Butcher's body." He picked up the microphone again.

"Attention, Group. Listen carefully and don't get itchy trigger

fingers. That ship is the *Shudos*. The Butcher's ship. It's a ten-man
ship, and the most she could have aboard would be thirty, even if
they jammed her full to the hull. I don't know of any way that
anyone could be alive on her after fifteen minutes at fifty gees of
atomic drive, but remember that they don't have any idea of how
our counteraction generators damp out spatial distortion either.
Remember what Dr. Pendric said: "No man is superior to any
other in *all* ways. Every man is superior to every other in *some*
way." We may have the counteraction generator, but they may
have something else that we don't know about. So stay alert.

"I am going to take a landing-party aboard. There's a reward
out for The Butcher, and that reward will be split proportionately
among us. It's big enough for us all to enjoy it, and we'll probably
get citations if we bring him in.

"I want ten men from each ship. I'm not asking for volunteers;
I want each ship commander to pick the ten men he thinks will be
least likely to lose their heads in an emergency. I don't want anyone
to panic and shoot when he should be thinking. I don't want anyone
who had any relatives on Houston's World. Sorry, but I can't allow
vengeance yet.

"We're a thousand miles from the *Shudos* now; close in slowly
until we're within a hundred yards. The boarding parties will don
armor and prepare to board while we're closing in. At a hundred
yards, we stop and the boarding parties will land on the hull. I'll
give further orders then.

"One more thing. I don't think her A-A generators could possibly
be functioning, judging from that dent in her hull, but we can't be
sure. If she tries to go into A-A drive, she is to be bombed—no
matter who is aboard. It is better that sixty men die than that The
Butcher escape.

"All right, let's go. Move in."

Half an hour later, Major Thornton stood on the hull of the
Shudos, surrounded by the sixty men of the boarding party.
"Anybody see anything through those windows?" he asked.

Several of the men had peered through the direct-vision ports,
playing spotlight beams through them.

"Nothing alive," said a sergeant, a remark which was followed by
a chorus of agreement.

"Pretty much of a mess in there," said another sergeant. "That
fifty gees mashed everything to the floor. Why'd anyone want to
use acceleration like that?"

"Let's go in and find out," said Major Thornton.

The outer door to the air lock was closed, but not locked. It swung open easily to disclose the room between the outer and inner doors. Ten men went in with the major, the others stayed outside with orders to cut through the hull if anything went wrong.

"If he's still alive," the major said, "we don't want to kill him by blowing the air. Sergeant, start the air-lock cycle."

There was barely room for ten men in the air lock. It had been built big enough for the full crew to use it at one time, but it was only just big enough.

When the inner door opened, they went in cautiously. They spread out and searched cautiously. The caution was unnecessary, as it turned out. There wasn't a living thing aboard.

"Three officers shot through the head, sir," said the sergeant. "One of 'em looks like he died of a broken neck, but it's hard to tell after that fifty gees mashed 'em. Crewmen in the engine room—five of 'em. Mashed up, but I'd say they died of radiation, since the shielding on one of the generators was ruptured by the blast that made that dent in the hull."

"Nine bodies," the major said musingly. "All Kerothi. And all of them probably dead *before* the fifty-gee acceleration. Keep looking, sergeant. We've got to find the tenth man."

Another twenty-minute search gave them all the information they were ever to get.

"No Earth food aboard," said the major. "One spacesuit missing. Handweapons missing. Two emergency survival kits and two medical kits missing. *And*—most important of all—the courier boat is missing." He bit at his lower lip for a moment, then went on. "Outer air lock door left unlocked. Three Kerothi shot—*after* the explosion that ruined the A-A drive, and *before* the fifty-gee acceleration." He looked at the sergeant. "What do you think happened?"

"He got away," the tough-looking noncom said grimly. "Took the courier boat and scooted away from here."

"Why did he set the timer on the drive, then? What was the purpose of that fifty-gee blast?"

"To distract us, I'd say, sir. While we were chasing this thing, he high-tailed it out."

"He might have, at that," the major said musingly. "A one-man courier *could* have gotten away. Our new detection equipment isn't perfect yet. But—"

At that moment, one of the troopers pushed himself down the corridor toward them. "Look, sir! I found this in the pocket of the

Carrot-skin who was taped up in there!" He was holding a piece of
paper.

The major took it, read it, then read it aloud. "Greetings, fellow
Earthmen: When you read this, I will be safe from any power you
may think you have to arrest or punish me. But don't think *you* are
safe from *me*. There are other intelligent races in the galaxy, and I'll
be around for a long time to come. You haven't heard the last of me.
With love—Sebastian MacMaine."

The silence that followed was almost deadly.

"He *did* get away!" snarled the sergeant at last.

"Maybe," said the major. "But it doesn't make sense." He
sounded agitated. "Look. In the first place, how do we know the
courier boat was even aboard? They've been trying frantically to
get word back to Keroth; does it make sense that they'd save this
boat? And why all the fanfare? Suppose he did have a boat? Why
would he attract our attention with that fifty-gee flare? Just so he
could leave us a note?"

"What do you think happened, sir?" the sergeant asked.

"I don't think he had a boat. If he did, he'd want us to think he
was dead, not the other way around. I think he set the drive timer
on this ship, went outside with his supplies, crawled up a drive tube
and waited until that atomic rocket blast blew him into plasma. He
was badly wounded and didn't want us to know that we'd
won. That way, we'd never find him."

There was no belief on the faces of the men around him.

"Why'd he want to do that, sir?" asked the sergeant.

"Because as long as we don't *know*, he'll haunt us. He'll be like
Hitler or Jack the Ripper. He'll be an immortal menace instead of
a dead villain who could be forgotten."

"Maybe so, sir," said the sergeant, but there was an utter lack of
conviction in his voice. "But we'd still better comb this area and
keep our detectors hot. We'll know what he was up to when we
catch him."

"But if we *don't* find him," the major said softly, "we'll *never*
know. That's the beauty of it, sergeant. If we don't find him, then
he's won. In his own fiendish, twisted way, he's won."

"If we don't find him," said the sergeant stolidly, "I think we
better keep a sharp eye out for the next intelligent race we meet.
He might find 'em first."

"Maybe," said the major very softly, "that's just what he wanted.
I wish I knew why."

HAWK AMONG THE SPARROWS

Dean McLaughlin

The map-position scope on the left side of *Pika-Don*'s instrument panel showed where he was, but it didn't show airfields. Right now, Howard Farman needed an airfield. He glanced again at the fuel gauge. Not a chance of making it to Frankfurt, or even into West Germany. Far below, white clouds like a featureless ocean sprawled all the way to the horizon.

Those clouds shouldn't have been there. Less than four hours ago, before he lifted off the *Eagle*, he'd studied a set of weather satellite photos freshly televised down from orbit. Southern France had been almost clear—only a dotting of cottonboll tufts. It should not have been possible for solid overcast to build up so fast. For the dozenth time, he flipped through the meteorological data on his clipboard. No, nothing that could have created such a change.

That made two things he hadn't been able to figure out. The second was even stranger. He'd lifted from the *Eagle*'s deck at midmorning. The French bomb test he'd been snooping had blinded him for a while—how long he didn't know—and *Pika-Don* was thrown out of control. The deadman circuit had cut in; control was re-established. When his sight came back—and it couldn't have been terribly long—the sun had been halfway down in the west.

It wasn't possible. *Pika-Don* didn't carry enough fuel to stay up that long.

Just the same, she had stayed up, and she still had almost half her load. When he couldn't find the *Eagle* near Gibraltar, he'd thought there was enough to take him to the American airbase at

Frankfurt. (And where could the *Eagle* have gone? What could have happened to her radar beacon? Could the French blast have smashed *Pika-Don*'s reception equipment? Everything else seemed to work all right. But he'd made an eyeball search, too. Aircraft tenders didn't just vanish.)

On the map scope, the Rhone valley crawled slowly southward under the north-moving central piplight that marked *Pika-Don*'s inertially computed position. It matched perfectly the radar-scanned terrain displayed on the airspace viewscope on the right-hand side of the instrument panel. Frankfurt was still beyond the horizon, more than four hundred miles off. *Pika-Don* didn't have fuel to cover half that distance.

Well, he wouldn't find an airfield by staying up here, above that carpet of cloud. He eased the throttles back and put *Pika-Don*'s nose down. She'd burn fuel a lot faster down close to the deck, but at Mach 1.5 he could search a lot of ground before the tanks went dry.

Not that he absolutely had to find an airfield. *Pika-Don* could put down almost anywhere if she had to. But an airfield would make it a lot simpler to get a new load of fuel, and it would make less complicated the problems that would come from putting down in a technically still friendly nation.

It was a long way down. He watched the radar-echo altimeter reel downward like a clock thrown into panicked reverse; watched the skin temperature gauge edge up, level out, edge up again as *Pika-Don* descended into thicker air. For the first eighty thousand feet, visibility was perfect, but at twelve thousand feet *Pika-Don* went into the clouds; it was like being swallowed by gray night. Uneasily, Farman watched the radar horizon; these clouds might go down all the way to the ground, and at Mach 1.5 there wouldn't be anything left but a smear if *Pika-Don* hit. She was too sweet an airplane for that. Besides, he was inside.

He broke out into clear air a little under four thousand feet. A small city lay off to his right. He turned toward it. Beaufort, the map scope said. There ought to be some sort of airfield near it. He pulled the throttles back as far as he dared—just enough to maintain airspeed. The Machmeter slipped back to 1.25.

He passed north of the town, scanning the land. No sign of a field. He circled southward, careful to keep his bearing away from the town's center. There'd be trouble enough about his coming down in France—aerial trespass by a nuclear-armed warplane, to start with—without half the townspeople screaming about smashed windows, cracked plaster, and roosters so frightened they stopped laying eggs. The ambassador in Paris was going to earn his paycheck this week.

Still no airfield. He went around again, farther out. Dozens of villages flashed past below. He tore his flight plan, orders, and weather data off their clipboard—crammed the papers into the disposal funnel; wouldn't do to have nosy Frenchmen pawing that stuff, not at all. He substituted the other flight plan—the one they'd given him just in case he had to put down in French or French-friendly territory.

He was starting his third circuit and the fuel gauge was leaning against the red mark when he saw the field. It wasn't much of a place—just a grassy postage stamp with a few old planes in front of three ramshackle sheds and a windsock flopping clumsily over the middle one. He put around, aimed for it, and converted to vertical thrust. Airspeed dropped quickly—there was a momentary surge of wing-surface heating—and then he was hovering only a few miles from the field. He used the deflectors to cover the distance, losing altitude as he went. He jockeyed to a position near the hangars, faced *Pika-Don* into the wind, and let her down.

The engines died—starved of fuel—before he could cut them off.

It took a while to disconnect all the umbilici that linked him into *Pika-Don*'s control and environment systems. Some of the connections were hard to reach. It took a while longer to raise the canopy, climb over the side, and drop to the ground. Two soldiers were waiting for him. They had rifles.

The bigger one—the one with the bushy mustache—spoke dangerously. Farman didn't know French, but their gestures with rifle muzzles were a universal language. He raised his hands. "I'm an American," he said. "I ran out of fuel." He hoped they weren't disciples of the late *grand Charles*. They looked nasty enough.

The two exchanged glances. "*Américain?*" the smaller one asked. He was clean-shaved. His eyes had a deep, hollow look. He didn't sound at all displeased.

Farman nodded vigorously. "Yes. American." He pointed to the fifty-one-star flag on his coverall sleeve. Their faces broke into delighted smiles and they turned their gun muzzles groundward. The small one—he made Farman think of a terrier, and his rifle was absurdly big for him—pointed to a shack beyond the hangars.

At least the natives seemed friendly. Farman went. The area in front of the hangars had been paved—an uneven spread of asphalt. Half a dozen rattletrap airplanes stood in a line, facing out toward the field. Where the pavement met unpaved ground, it was one mud puddle after another. Farman had to be careful where he put his feet;

his flight boots had been clean when he took off this morning. The soldiers didn't seem to mind. They splashed cheerfully through the wet and scuffed their heels on the tufts of grass.

The planes were all the same type—biplanes with open cockpits and two-bladed wooden propellers and radial-type piston engines. The kind of planes, Farman thought, that shouldn't even be flying any more. Nevertheless, they were obviously working airplanes, with oil stains on their cowls and the smell of gasoline and patches glued over holes in the fabric of wings and fuselage. A crop-dusting outfit? Did the French have crop-dusting outfits? Then he realized that those things in front of the cockpits were machine guns. Air-cooled machine guns rigged to shoot through the propeller. And those odd, oval-shaped tail assemblies . . .

Some kind of museum?

"That is strange aeroplane you have," the mustached soldier said. His accent was as thick as the grass on the field. "One like it I have not seen."

Farman hadn't known that either of them spoke English. "I'll need to make some phone calls," he said, thinking of the ambassador in Paris. A mechanic was working on one of the planes they passed; he was standing on a wooden packing crate, tinkering with the engine.

A movie outfit, doing a period flick? But he didn't see any cameras.

Another biplane taxied in from the field—a Nieuport, like the others. Its engine racketed like a lawnmower. It joggled and bounced in the chuckholes. There were a lot of chuckholes in the mud at the pavement's fringe. The plane came up on the pavement and the engine cut out. As the propeller turned around to a spasmodic stop, Farman realized that not just the propeller but the whole engine had been spinning. What kind of crazy way to build airplanes was that?

The Nieuport's pilot climbed up out of the cockpit and dropped to the ground. "Guns jammed again!" he yelled loudly, hellishly mad. He flung a small hammer on the ground at his feet.

Three men came out of the hangar carrying packing crates. They set them down around the Nieuport's nose, got up on them, and started working on the guns. The flier pulled off his scarf and draped it over the cockpit's side. He turned away, spoke a few French words over his shoulder to the mechanics, and walked off.

"Monsieur Blake!" the big soldier hailed. When the flier didn't seem to hear, the soldier ran to him, caught his shoulder. "Monsieur Blake. A countryman." The soldier beside Farman pointed to the flag on Farman's sleeve.

Blake came over, stuffing a goggled cloth helmet into a pocket of his heavy overcoat as he approached. His hand was out in welcome.

"This one has teach all my *Anglais* to me," the big trooper grinned. "Is good, *non?*"

Farman scarcely heard him. All his attention was on this American. "Harry Blake," the man introduced himself. "'Fraid I won't be able to hear you too good for a while." He swung a glance at his Nieuport's motor and raised hands to his ears to signify deafness. He was young—not more than twenty-two or -three—but he had the mature poise of a man much older. "I'm a Lafayette with this outfit. From Springfield, Illinois. You?"

Farman accepted the hand in numb silence. By calling himself a Lafayette, the flier had obliterated Farman's last incredulous doubt. It wasn't possible—not real. Things like this didn't happen.

"Hey, you don't look so good," Blake said, grabbing his arm with a strong hand.

"I'll be all right," Farman said, but he wasn't really sure.

"Come on." Blake steered Farman into the passageway between two of the hangars. "We've got what you need back here."

The troopers came after them. "Monsieur Blake. This man has only now arrived. He has not reported."

Blake waved them away. "I haven't either. We'll report later. Can't you see when a man's breathed too much oil?"

The soldiers turned back. Blake's hand steered Farman onward. Puddles slopped under Blake's boots.

Behind the hangars, the path split in two directions. One way led to a latrine whose door swung loose in the breeze. The other led to a shack huddled up to the back of a hangar. It was hard to guess which path was more frequently used. Blake paused at the parting of the ways. "Think you can make it?"

"I'm all right." He wasn't, really. It takes more than a deep breath and a knuckling of the eyes to adjust a man to having lost six and a half decades. Between books about aerial combat he'd devoured as a kid—two wars and all those brushfire skirmishes—he'd read some Heinlein and Asimov. If it wasn't for that, he'd have had nothing to hang on to. It was like a kick in the belly.

"I'll be all right," he said.

"You're sure? You breathe castor oil a few hours a day and it doesn't do a man's constitution much good. Nothin' to be embarrassed about."

Every now and then, Farman had heard castor oil mentioned, mostly in jokes, but he'd never been sure what it did to a man. Now he remembered it had been used in aircraft engines of this time. Suddenly, he understood all. "That's one problem I don't have."

Blake laughed. "It's a problem we all have." He pushed open the shack's door. Farman went inside at his nod. Blake followed. "Onree!" Blake called out. "Two double brandies."

A round little baldpated Frenchman got up from a stool behind the cloth-draped trestle that served as a bar. He poured two glasses almost full of something dark. Blake picked up one in each hand. "How many for you?"

Whatever it was, it looked evil. "One," Farman said, "for a start." Either this youngster was showing off—which didn't seem likely—or it wasn't as deadly as it looked. "A double, that is."

Blake led the way to a table in the far corner, next to a window. It was a plain wood table, stained and scarred. Farman set his glass down and took a chair before he tried a small taste. It was like a trickle of fire all the way down. He looked at the glass as if it had fangs. "What is this stuff?"

Blake had sampled from each glass on the way to the table, to keep them from spilling. Now he was almost halfway through one of them and the other was close to his hand. "Blackberry brandy," he said with a rueful grin. "It's the only cure we've found. Would you rather have the disease?"

Flight medicine, Farman thought, had a long way to go. He put his glass carefully aside. "My plane doesn't use that kind of oil."

Blake was on him right away. "Something new? I thought they'd tried everything."

"It's a different kind of engine," Farman said. He had to do something with his hands. He took a sip of the brandy, choked, regretted it.

"How long you been flying?" Blake asked.

"Ten, twelve years."

Blake had been about to finish his first glass. He set it down untouched, looked straight at Farman. Slowly, a grin came. "All right. A joke's a joke. You going to be flying with us?"

"Maybe. I don't know," Farman said, holding his brandy glass in both hands, perfectly steady—and all the time, deep inside, the small trapped being that was himself screamed silently, *What's happened to me? What's happened?*

It had been a tricky mission, but he'd flown a lot of tricky ones. Ostensibly, he'd been taking part in a systems-test/training exercise off the northwest coast of Africa. High-altitude Mach 4 aircraft, their internal equipment assisted by the tracking and computer equipment on converted aircraft carriers, were attempting to intercept simulated ballistic warheads making re-entry into the atmosphere. He'd lifted from the deck of the airplane tender *Eagle* in the western Mediterranean. Half an hour later he was circling at Big Ten—one-zero-zero thousand feet—on-station north of the Canary Islands when the signal came that sent him on his true mission.

A guidance system had gone wrong at the Cape, said the talker aboard the *Iwo Jima*, and the range-safety system had failed. The misdirected warhead was arching over the Atlantic, farther and higher than programmed. Instead of splashing in the Atlantic, its projected impact-point was deep in the Sahara. It carried only a concrete block, not thermonuclear weaponry, but diplomatic relations with France—which still maintained military bases in this land it had once governed—were troublesome. Standing orders for such an eventuality were that, as a good-faith demonstration, an attempt should be made to intercept it.

Operation Skeetshoot's master computer said Farman's *Pika-Don* was the only plane able to make the interception. No other plane was in the right position. No other plane had enough altitude or fuel load. No other plane had such an advantageous direction of flight at that moment. Farman sent *Pika-Don* streaking toward interception point at full thrust.

As planned.

Nothing had really gone wrong at the Cape. It was a pretext. Washington knew the French were about to test a new-model nuclear bomb. They would explode it above the atmosphere, in the Van Allen belt; the rocket would be launched from their main testing site, the Saharan oasis of Reggan; they would select the moment of launch to coincide with the arrival of a solar proton storm, when subnuclear particles from the storm would blend with the bomb's fission products, rendering surveillance by other nations more difficult and the findings less certain.

The proton storm had been already on its way when Farman left the *Eagle*'s deck. It was being tracked, not only by American installations around the world, but by French stations also. Code message traffic was high between New Caledonia and Reggan. The time of the storm's arrival was known to within five seconds.

Farman hadn't paid much attention to why Washington wanted to snoop the test; the French were, after all, still allies in spite of the frictions between Paris and Washington. Asking questions like that wasn't Farman's job; he was just the airplane driver. But they'd told him anyway, when they gave him the mission. Something about

Washington wanting to have up-to-date knowledge of France's independent nuclear capability. Such information was needed, they said, for accurate judgment of how dependent France might still be on America's ability to wage modern war. To Farman, the explanation didn't mean much; he didn't understand much about international politics.

But a warhead dropping into the atmosphere, sheathed in the meteor-flame of its fall—*that* he could understand. And a multi-megaton fireball a hundred miles up, blazing like the sun brought suddenly too close—that, too, he could understand. And a Mach 4 airplane riding her shock-wave across the sky, himself inside watching instruments and flight-path guide scopes, and his thumb on the button that would launch the Lance rockets sheathed against her belly. Those were things he understood. They were his job.

Nor did the mission call for him to do more than that. All that was really necessary was to have *Pika-Don* somewhere in the sky above Reggan when the French bomb went off. *Pika-Don* would do everything else, automatically.

All the planes in Operation Skeetshoot were equipped the same as *Pika-Don*. All of them carried elaborate flight recorders; and because they were fitted to intercept thermonuclear warheads, and their own Lance rockets had sub-kiloton fission tips, those recorders included all the instruments needed to monitor a nuclear explosion—even a unit to measure the still not fully understood magnetohydrodynamic disturbances that played inside a nuclear fireball. (And, it was known from previous tests, there was something unusual about the magnetic fields of French bombs.)

Nor would there be much risk if *Pika-Don* were forced down where French nosypokes could get a look at it. All *Pika-Don* carried was standard equipment—equipment the French already knew about, in configurations and for purposes they also understood. There would be nothing the French could find to support a charge of deliberate snooping, no matter how much they might suspect. Not that the possibility was large; the explosion, after all, would be out in space. There'd be no blast effects, certainly, and very little radiation. Enough to tickle the instruments, was all.

And already the hot line between Washington and Paris would be explaining why an American plane was intruding on French-controlled airspace. Everything had been planned.

Farman watched his instruments, his flight-path guide scopes, his radar. *Pika-Don* slashed the thin air so fast she drew blood. She was up to one-three-zero thousand now; rocket launch point lay five thousand higher, two hundred miles ahead. Reggan moved onto the edge of the inertial-guide map-position scope, ahead and off to the south. The projected trajectory of the warhead was a red line striking downward on the foreview guide scope. An X-slash marked Skeetshoot Control's computed interception point.

Something flared on the radar near Reggan. It rose, slowly for a moment, then asymptotically faster and faster, shining on the radar screen like a bright, fierce jewel. The French rocket. Farman's breath caught as he watched it. The thing was going up. The test was on.

It rose, was level with him, then higher. Suddenly, it quivered like a water drop, and suddenly it was gone from the screen in an expanding black blindness like a hole in the universe; and simultaneously the cockpit was full of unendurable white light. The sky was flaming, so bright Farman couldn't look at it, didn't dare. He had just time enough to think, terrified, *Not in the Van Allen belt!* and then *Pika-Don* was spinning, spinning, spinning like a spindle—light flashing into the cockpit, then blackness, brightness, then blackness again, repeating and repeating faster and faster and faster until light and darkness merged to a flickering brilliance that dazzled not only the eyes but the whole brain. Farman battled the controls, but it was like fighting the Almighty's wrath. The flickering blaze went on and on.

And slowed. Stopped, like the last frame of film in a halted movie projector, and it was only daylight again, and *Pika-Don*'s disabled pilot circuit had cut in. She was flying level, northwestward if the compass could be trusted, and if the sun's position could be trusted, the afternoon was more than half gone. Farman was sure that much time had not passed.

The map scope confirmed the compass. So did the airspace radar view. The controls felt all right now, and *Pika-Don* seemed to fly without difficulty. He turned straight north toward the Mediterranean and came out above it not far from Oran. He curved west then, toward the spot where he'd left the *Eagle*. He watched the foreview guide scope for the *Eagle*'s homing beacon. It didn't show up. He spoke on the radio, got no answer. Equipment damage?

He took *Pika-Don* down to fifty thousand. He used the telescope-view scope on the ships his radar picked out. None was the *Eagle*; old freighters, mostly, and two small warships of a type he'd thought wasn't used any more except by the Peruvian Navy.

His orders said, if he couldn't find his base ship, go to Frankfurt. The big base there could take him. He turned *Pika-Don* north-westward. He crossed the French coast. Overcast covered the land.

It shouldn't have been there. Fuel began to run low. It was going into the engines faster than the distance to Frankfurt was narrowing. He tried to cut fuel consumption, but he couldn't cut it enough. He had no choice but to put down in France.

"Look, Mister, either you've got orders to fly with us, or you don't," Blake said. "What outfit are you with?"

It was restricted information, but Farman didn't think it mattered much. "The CIA, I think."

He might as well have said the Seventh Cavalry with General Custer. "Where's your base?" Blake asked.

Farman took another swallow of brandy. He needed it, even if not for the reason Blake thought. It wasn't so bad, this time. He tried to think of a way to explain the thing that had happened to him. "Did you ever read *The Time Machine*?" he asked.

"What's that? A book about clocks?"

"It's a story by H. G. Wells."

"Who's H. G. Wells?"

He wasn't going to make much explanation by invoking H. G. Wells. "It's about a man who . . . who builds a machine that moves through time the way an airplane moves in the air."

"If you're having fun with me, you're doing it good," Blake said.

Farman tried again. "Think of a building—a tall building, with elevators in it. And suppose you don't know about elevators—can't even imagine how they work. And suppose you were on the ground floor, and suppose I came up and told you I was from the twentieth floor."

"I'd say that's doing a lot of supposing," Blake said.

"But you get the idea?"

"Maybe. Maybe not."

"All right. Now imagine that the ground floor is now. Today. And the basement is yesterday. And the second floor is tomorrow, and the third floor is the day after tomorrow, and so on."

"It's a way of thinking about things," Blake said.

Give thanks the elevator had been invented. "Take it one step more, now. Suppose you're on the ground floor, and someone comes down from the twentieth floor."

"He'd of come from somewhere the other side of next week," Blake said.

"That's the idea," Farman said. He took more of the brandy. "What if I told you I . . . just fell down the elevator shaft from sixty-some years up?"

Blake appeared to consider while he started on his second glass. He permitted himself a smile and a chuckle. "I'd say a man's got to be a bit crazy if he wants to fly in this war, and if you want to fight Huns you've come to the right place."

He didn't believe. Well, you couldn't expect him to. "I was born in nineteen fifty-three," Farman told him. "I'm thirty-two years old. My father was born in nineteen twenty. Right now, it's nineteen . . . seventeen?"

"Nineteen *eighteen*," Blake said. "June tenth. Have another brandy."

Farman discovered his glass was empty. He didn't remember emptying it. Shakily, he stood up. "I think I'd better talk to your commanding officer."

Blake waved him back to his chair. "Might as well have another brandy. He hasn't come back yet. My guns jammed and I couldn't get them unjammed, so I came home early. He'll be back when he runs out of bullets or fuel, one or the other."

His back was to the door, so he had to twist around while still talking, to see who came in. The small, razor-mustached man draped his overcoat on a chair and accepted the brandy the barman had poured without having to be asked. "Today, M'sieu Blake, it was a small bit of both." His English had only a flavor of accent. "On coming back, I find I am left with one bullet."

"How was the hunting?"

The Frenchman gave a shrug that was as much a part of France as the Eiffel Tower. "Ah, that man has the lives of a cat, the hide of an old bull elephant, and the skills of a magician."

"Keyserling?" Blake asked.

The newcomer took a chair at the table. "Who else? I have him in my sights. I shoot, and he is gone. It would be a shame to kill this man—he flies superbly!—and I would love to do it very much." He smiled and sipped his brandy.

"This is our CO," Blake said. "Philippe Deveraux. Thirty-three confirmed kills and maybe a dozen not confirmed. The only man on this part of the front with more is Keyserling." He turned to Farman. "I don't think I got your name."

Farman gave it. "He's just over from the States," Blake said. "And he's been funning me with the craziest story you ever heard."

Farman didn't bother to protest. In similar shoes, he'd be just as skeptical. "This Keyserling," he said. "That's Bruno Keyserling?"

He'd read about Keyserling; next to Richthofen, Bruno Keyserling had been the most hated, feared, and respected man in the German air force.

"That's him," Blake said. "There's not a one of us that wouldn't like to get him in our sights." He set his empty glass down hard. "But

420   DEAN McLAUGHLIN

it won't happen that way. He's gotten better men than us. Sooner or later, he'll get us all."

Deveraux had been delicately sipping his drink. Now he set it down. "We shall talk of it later, M'sieu Blake," he said firmly. He addressed Farman. "You have been waiting for me?"

"Yes. I . . ." Suddenly, he realized he didn't know what to say.

"Don't give him the same you gave me," Blake warned. "Now it's business."

"You are a pilot, M'sieu Farman?" Deveraux asked.

Farman nodded. "And I've got a plane that can fly faster and climb higher than anything you've got. I'd like a try at this Keyserling."

"That could possibly be arranged. But I should warn you, M'sieu . . . Farman, did you say?"

"Howard Farman."

"I should warn you, the man is a genius. He has done things his aeroplane should not be possible to do. He has shot down forty-six, perhaps more. Once three in a day. Once two in five minutes. It has been said the man came from nowhere—that he is one of the gods from the *Nibelungenlied*, come to battle for his fatherland. He . . ."

"You might say I'm from nowhere, too," Farman said. "Me and my plane."

When Deveraux had finished his brandy and when Blake had downed his fourth, they went out in front of the hangars again. Farman wanted them to see *Pika-Don*. *Pika-Don* would be at least sixty years ahead of any plane they'd ever seen.

Her skids had cut into the turf like knives. Blake and Deveraux examined her from end to end. They walked around her, their boot tips whipping the grass. "Don't touch anything," Farman told them. "Even a scratch in the wrong place could wreck her." He didn't add that the rockets concealed under her belly could vaporize everything within a hundred yards. The false-skin strips that sealed them from the slipstream were supposed to be tamper-proof, but just to be safe Farman placed himself where they would have to go past him to investigate *Pika-Don*'s underside.

Pika-Don was eighty-nine feet long. Her shark-fin wings spanned less than twenty-five. She was like a needle dart, sleek and shiny and razor-sharp on the leading edge of her wings. Her fuselage was oddly flat-bodied, like a cobra's hood. Her airscoops were like tunnels.

Blake crouched down to examine the gear that retracted the skids. Farman moved close, ready to interrupt if Blake started to fool with the rockets. Instead, Blake discovered the vertical thrust vents and lay down to peer up into them. Deveraux put his head inside one of the tail pipes. It was big enough to crawl into. Slowly, Blake rolled out from under and got to his feet again.

"Do you believe me now?" Farman asked.

"Mister," Blake said, looking at him straight, "I don't know what this thing is, and I don't know how you got it here. But don't try to tell me it flies."

"How do you think I got it here?" Farman demanded. "I'll show you. I'll . . ." He stopped. He'd forgotten he was out of fuel. "Ask your ground crews. They saw me bring her down."

Blake shook his head, fist on hips. "I know an aeroplane when I see one. This thing can't possibly fly."

Deveraux tramped toward them from the tail. "This is indeed the strangest zeppelin I have ever been shown, M'sieu. But obviously, a zeppelin so small—so obviously heavy . . . it can hardly be useful, M'sieu."

"I tell you, this is a *plane*. An *air*plane. It's faster than anything else in the air."

"But it has no wings, M'sieu. No propeller. It does not even have wheels on the undercarriage. How can such a thing as this gain airspeed if it has no wheels?"

Farman was speechless with exasperation. Couldn't they see? Wasn't it obvious?'

"And why does it have so strong the scent of paraffin?" Deveraux asked.

A Nieuport buzzed over the hangars in a sudden burst of sound. It barrel-rolled twice, turned left, then right, then came down onto the grass. Its engine puttered. Its wires sang in the wind. It taxied across the field toward them.

"That'll be Mermier," Blake said. "He got one."

Two more planes followed. They did no acrobatics—merely turned into the wind and set down. They bounced over the turf toward the hangars. One had lost part of its upper wing. Shreds of cloth flickered in the breeze.

Blake and Deveraux still watched the sky beyond the hangars, but no more planes came. Blake's hand clapped Deveraux's shoulder. "Maybe they landed somewhere else."

Deveraux shrugged. "And perhaps they did not live that long. Come. We shall find out."

They walked to the other end of the flight line where the three planes straggled up on the hardstand. Deveraux hurried ahead and Mermier and then the other two pilots climbed out of their cockpits. They talked in French, with many gestures.

Farman recognized a few of the gestures—the universal language of air combat—but others were strange or ambiguous. Abruptly, Deveraux turned away, his face wearing the look of pain nobly borne.

"They won't come back," Blake told Farman quietly. "They were seen going down. Burning." His fist struck the hangar's wall. "Keyserling got Michot. He was the only one of us that had a hope of getting him."

Deveraux came back. His face wore a tight, controlled smile. "M'sieu Farman," he said. "I must ask to be shown the abilities of your machine."

"I'll need five hundred gallons of kerosene," Farman said. That would be enough for a lift-off, a quick crack through the barrier, and a landing. Ten minutes in the air, if he didn't drive her faster than Mach 1.4. Enough to show them something of the things *Pika-Don* could do.

Devereaux frowned, touched his mustache, "Kerosene?"

"Paraffin," Blake said. "Lamp oil." He turned to Farman. "They call it paraffin over here. But five hundred gallons—are you nuts? There isn't an aeroplane flying that needs that much lubricating. Shucks, this whole *escadrille* doesn't use that much *gas* in a week. Besides, it's no good as a lubricant—if it was, you think we'd be using the stuff we do?"

"It's not a lubricant," Farman said. "She burns it. It's fuel. And she burns it fast. She delivers a lot of thrust."

"But . . . five hundred gallons!"

"I'll need that much just for a demonstration flight." He looked straight and firmly into Blake's incredulous eyes and decided not to add that, fully loaded, *Pika-Don* took fifty thousand gallons.

Deveraux smoothed his mustache. "In liters, that is how much?"

"You're going to let him . . .?"

"M'sieu Blake, do you believe this man a fraud?"

Challenged like that, Blake did not back down. "I think he's funning us. He says he'll show us an aeroplane, and he showed us that . . . that thing over there. And when you want to see how it flies, he says it's out of fuel and asks for kerosene—*kerosene* of all things! Enough to go swimming in! Even if that's what she burns, he doesn't need anywhere near that much. And who ever heard of flying an aeroplane with lamp oil?"

Farman took Blake's arm, joggled it, made him turn. "I know," he said. "I'm telling you things it's hard to believe. In your shoes, I wouldn't believe me, either. All right. But let me have a chance to show you. I want to fight the Germans as much as you do." In his thoughts was the picture of a whole *jagdstaffel* of Albatrosses being engulfed by the fireball of one of *Pika-Don*'s rockets. They'd never even see him coming, he'd come at them so fast; even if they saw him, they wouldn't have a chance. Sitting ducks. Fish in a barrel.

"Mister," Blake said, "I don't know what you want all that kerosene for, but I'm sure of one thing—you don't need it to fly. Because if I was ever sure of anything, I know that thing can't fly."

"M'sieu Blake," Deveraux said, moving in front of the American. "This man may perhaps be mistaken, but I do not think he lies. He has a faith in himself. We have need of such men in this war. If he cannot use the paraffin when we have obtained it for him, it will be given to the chef for his stoves. We shall have lost nothing. But we must let him prove his abilities, if he can, for if there is some portion of truth in his claims, why, it is possible that we have before us the man and the machine that shall hurl Bruno Keyserling from the sky."

Blake gave way grudgingly. "If you're funning us, watch out."

"You'll see," Farman promised, grim. And to Deveraux: "Make it a high-grade kerosene. The best you can get." A jet engine could burn kerosene if it had to, but kerosene wasn't a perfect jet fuel any more than wood alcohol could make good martinis. Kerosene was just the nearest thing to jet fuel he could hope to find in 1918. "And we'll have to put it through some kind of filters."

"M'sieu," Deveraux said. "There is only one kind of paraffin. Either it is paraffin, or it is not."

Two days later, while they were waiting for the kerosene to come, Blake took him up in a Caudron two-seater to show him the landmarks. It was a clear day, with only a little dust haze in the direction of the front. Farman didn't think much of learning the landmarks—*Pika-Don*'s map scope was a lot more accurate than any amount of eyeball knowledge. But the scope wouldn't show him the front-line trenches twisting across the landscape, or the location of the German airfields. It might be useful to know such things. Farman borrowed flying clothes, and they were off.

The Caudron looked like nothing so much as a clumsy box kite, or a paleolithic ancestor of the P-38. Its two racketing engines were suspended between the upper and lower wings, one on either side of the passenger nacelle. The tail empennage was joined to the wings by openwork frames of wire-braced wood that extended back from behind the engines. It had a fragile appearance, but it held together sturdily as it lurched across the field like an uncontrolled baby carriage. Finally, after what seemed an interminable length of bumping and bouncing it lofted into the air at a speed that seemed hardly enough to get a feather airborne. A steady windblast tore at Farman's face. Hastily, he slipped the goggles down over his eyes. The climb to six thousand feet seemed to take years.

Blake didn't turn out of their spiral until they reached altitude, then headed east. The air seemed full of crests and hollows, over which the Caudron rode like a boat on a slow-swelled sea. Now and then, woozily, it swayed. A queasy feeling rooted itself in Farman's midsection, as if his stomach was being kneaded and squeezed.

Airsick? No, it couldn't be that. Anything but that. He was an experienced flier with more than ten thousand hours in the air. He couldn't possibly be airsick now. He swallowed hard and firmly held down.

Blake, in the cockpit behind him, yelled and pointed over the side. Farman leaned over. The rush of air almost ripped his goggles off. Far below, small as a diorama, the trench systems snaked across a strip of barren ground—two latticework patterns cut into the earth, roughly parallel to each other, jaggedly angular like toothpick structures that had been crushed. Between them, naked earth as horribly pocked as the surface of the moon.

The Caudron had been following a rivercourse. The trenchlines came down from the hills to the south, crossed the river, and continued northward into the hills on that side. Ahead, over the German trenches, black puffs of antiaircraft fire blossomed in spasmodic, irregular patterns. Blake banked the Caudron and turned south, yelling something over his shoulder about the Swiss border. The antiaircraft barrage slacked off.

Recognizing the front would be no problem, Farman decided. He tried to tell Blake, but the slipstream ripped the words away. He twisted around to say it straight. Something snatched at his sleeve.

He looked. Something had gashed the thick fabric, but there was nothing in sight that could have done it. And for some unaccountable reason Blake was heeling the Caudron over into a dive. The horizon tilted crazily, like water sloshing in a bowl. The Caudron's wire rigging snarled nastily.

"Use the gun!" Blake yelled. He jerked an urgent thumb upward.

There was a machine gun on the upper wing, above and just aft of Farman's cockpit, but for a shocked moment Farman didn't grasp what Blake was talking about. Then a dark airplane shape flashed overhead, so close the buzz of its motor could be heard through the noise of the Caudron's own two engines. The goggled, cruel-mouthed face of its pilot turned to look at them. Blake threw the Caudron into a tight turn that jammed Farman deep in his cockpit. Farman lost sight of the German plane, then found it again. It was coming at them.

It was purple—a dark royal purple—with white trim around the edges of wing and tail, and around the engine cowl. Little flashes of light sparked from its nose, and Farman heard something—it sounded like thick raindrops—spattering the upper wing close to the passenger nacelle. Tracer bullets flashed past like quick fireflies.

"Use the gun!" Blake yelled again. They were climbing now. They leveled off, turned. The German plane came after them. "Use the gun!"

He was being shot at. It was appalling. Things like that didn't happen. In a moment, Farman was too busy to think about it. Somehow he got his seat belt off and stood up in the cockpit, back to the wind. He fumbled with the machine gun's unfamiliar grips. He found the trigger before he knew what it was. The gun chattered and bucked in his grasp. He looked all over the sky for the purple airplane. It was nowhere in sight. Blake hurled the Caudron through another violent maneuver that almost threw Farman overboard, and suddenly there were three German planes behind them, high, the one with the white trim in front and the others trailing. The one with the white trim shifted a little to the left, turned inward again. It nosed down, gun muzzles flickering.

Farman swung the machine gun to bear on the German. He pressed the trigger. The gun stuttered and a spray of tracers streamed aft as it caught in the slipstream. They passed under the German, not even close.

Aerial gunnery wasn't a thing Farman had ever had to learn. Combat was done with guidance systems, computers, and target-seeking missiles, not antique .30 caliber popguns. He raised the gun and fired another burst. Still too low, and passing behind the German, who was boring close in, weaving up, sidewise, and down as he came. The gun didn't have any sights worth mentioning—no target tracking equipment at all. Farman wrestled with the clumsy weapon, trying to keep its muzzle pointed at the German. It should have been easy, but it wasn't. The German kept dodging. Farman emptied the machine gun without once touching the other plane. He spent an eternity dismounting the empty magazine and clipping another into place, all the time holding on one-handed, while

Blake hurled the Caudron through a wild series of gut-wrenching acrobatics.

A section of the cockpit coaming at Farman's knee shattered and disappeared in the wind. He got the gun working again—fired a burst just as the German sidled behind the Caudron's right rudder. Farman's tracers went right through. The rudder exploded in a spray of chips and tatters. The German swung out to the right, gained a few feet altitude, turned in again and down again. His guns hurled blazing streaks. Blake sent the Caudron into a dive, a turn, and a twist that almost somersaulted Farman out of the plane. Abruptly, then, the German was gone. Little scraps were still tearing loose from the rudder, whipped away by the slipstream.

"Where?" Farman shouted, bending down as close to Blake as he could. He meant, where had the German gone, but he wasn't up to asking a question that complicated.

"Skedaddled," Blake yelled up at him. "We've got friends. Look."

Farman looked when Blake aimed his thumb. Five hundred feet above them five Nieuports cruised in neat formation. After a moment, the formation leader waggled his wings and they curved off eastward. Farman looked down and saw they were far behind the French lines, headed northwest. They were flying level and smooth—only the slow, gentle lift and descent of random air currents, like silence at the end of a storm. He sagged down into his cockpit. "You all right?" Blake asked.

"I think so," Farman said. But suddenly, as the Caudron slipped into a downdraft, he wasn't. His stomach wrenched, and he had time enough only to get his head over the cockpit's side before the first gush of vomit came. He was still there, gripping the splintered coaming with both hands, his stomach squeezing itself like a dry sponge, when Blake circled the airfield and slowly brought the Caudron down to a three-point landing. All Farman could think—distantly, with the part of his brain not concerned with his terrible miseries—was how long it had been since anyone, anywhere in the world, had even thought about making a three-point landing.

He wouldn't admit, even to himself, it had been airsickness. But after a while the horizon stopped wheeling around him and he could stand without needing a hand to steady him. He discovered he was very hungry. Blake went down to the mess hall and came back with a half-loaf of black bread and a dented tin of pâté. They went to the shack behind the hangars. Henri gave Blake a bottle of peasant's wine and two glasses. Blake put them down in the middle of the

table and sat down across from Farman. He poured, and they went
to work on the bread and pâté.

"He was trying to kill us," Farman said. It just came out of him.
It had been there ever since the fight. "He was trying to *kill* us."

Blake cut himself another slice of the bread. He gnawed on the
leathery crust. "Sure. And I'd of killed him, given the chance. That's
what we're supposed to do—him and us, both. Nothing personal at
all. I've got to admit I wasn't expecting him, though. They don't
often come this side of the lines. But . . ." He made a rueful grimace.
"He's a tough one to outguess."

"He?"

Blake stopped gnawing, frowned. "You know who it was, don't
you?"

The idea of knowing an enemy's name after such a brief
acquaintance was completely strange to Farman. His mouth made
motions, but no words came out.

"Bruno Keyserling," Blake said. "He's the only man with an
aeroplane painted that way."

"I'm going to get him," Farman said.

"Easier said than done," Blake said. His mouth turned grim.
"You'll have to sharpen up your gunnery quite a bit, if you're going
to make good on that."

"I'm going to get him," Farman repeated, knuckles white on the
table.

The next day it rained. Thick, wet, gray clouds crouched low to
the ground and poured down torrents. All patrols were canceled, and
the fliers sat in the shack behind the hangers, drinking and listening
to the storm as it pelted the shingles. At first light, when he woke
and heard the rain, Farman had borrowed a slicker and gone out to
Pika-Don. She was all right. He'd left her buttoned up tight, and the
rain was doing her no harm.

Blake was still the only man Farman could talk with, except for
Deveraux. None of the other pilots had more than a smattering of
English. When they left the mess hall after a drab lunch, instead of
returning to the drinking shack, Blake led him to one of the hangars.
There, in a back corner, were stacked wooden boxes of ammunition
and others full of the bent-metal sections of disintegrating-link
machine-gun belts. Blake showed Farman how to assemble the
links and how to check both the links and the cartridges for
manufacturing defects. He handed Farman a gauge into which a
properly shaped cartridge should fit perfectly, and they spent the
next several hours inspecting cartridges and assembling belts of

ammunition. It was tedious work. Each cartridge looked just like
the one before it. The imperfections were small.

"Do you always do this yourself?" Farman inspected his grimy
hands, his split cuticles. He wasn't accustomed to this kind of work.
"Every chance I get," Blake said. "There're enough reasons for a gun
to jam without bad ammunition being one of 'em. When you're up
there with Keyserling's circus flying rings around you, all you've got
are your guns and your engine and your wings, and if any of those go,
you go. And it's a long way down."

Farman said nothing for a while. Rain drummed on the roof. Now
and then came the clang of tools being used in another part of the
hangar. "How come you're here?" he asked finally. "What's in it for
you?"

Blake's busy hands paused. He looked at Farman. "Say that again,
slower."

"This here's a French squadron. You're an American. What are
you doing here?"

Blake snorted—not quite a chuckle. "Fighting Germans."

Farman wondered if Blake was making fun of him. He tried again.
"Sure—but why with a bunch of French-men?"

Blake inspected a cartridge, fitted it into the belt. He picked up
another. "Didn't care to transfer," he said. "Could have, when they
started bringing U.S. squadrons over. But I like the plane I've got.
If I transferred, they'd give me a plane the French don't want and
the British don't want, because that's all the American squadrons
are getting. Well, I don't want 'em, either." He dropped a cartridge
in the reject pile.

"I didn't mean that," Farman said. "You joined before America
got into the war—right?"

"Came over in 'sixteen."

"All right. That's what I mean. Why help France?" He couldn't
understand why an American would do anything to help the
personal kingdom of *le grand Charles*. "You weren't involved," he
said. "Why?"

Blake went on inspecting cartridges. "Depends what you mean,
involved. I figure I am. Everyone is. The Germans started this war.
If we can show the world it doesn't pay to start a war, then there won't
be any more. I want that. This is going to be the last war the human
race will ever have."

Farman went back to inspecting cartridges. "Don't get your hopes
too high," he said. It was as near as he could bring himself to telling
Blake how doomed his optimism was. The rain made thunder on the
roof like the march of armies.

Late in the afternoon, two days later, three lorries sputtered into the supply area behind the hangars. They brought fuel for the escadrille, but also, crowded among the drums of gasoline were twenty hundred-liter barrels of kerosene which were carefully put aside and trucked down to the mess hall's kitchen and then—when the error was discovered—had to be reloaded and trucked back up to the hangars again.

Farman had managed to rig a crude filtration system for the kerosene. The stuff they cooked with was full of junk. He'd scrounged sheets of silk, and enlisted a crew of mechanics to scrub empty petrol drums until their innards gleamed like the insides of dairy cans. He even succeeded in testing the rig with a bucket of kerosene cadged from the kitchens. The process was glacially slow, and the end product neither looked nor smelled any different from the stuff he started with. But when he tried it in one of *Pika-Don*'s engines, the engine had started and—at low r.p.m.—had delivered thrust and functioned as it should until the tank was sucked dry. More important, when he inspected, none of the injectors had fouled.

He started the filtering process, and stayed with it through the night and all the next day. He had a mechanic to help him, but he had no confidence in the mechanic's understanding of how vital fuel quality was to an engine. It was not a thing an airplane mechanic of this time could be expected to know. Deveraux came around once, inspected the raw material and sniffed the filtered product, and went away again, having said nothing.

Once, between missions, Blake came and sat to watch. Farman showed him the sludge the filters had taken out of the kerosene. Blake scowled. "It's still kerosene," he said. "You can't fly an aeroplane on kerosene any more than you can feed it birdseed. I don't know what you really want it for, but don't expect me to believe it's for flying."

Farman shrugged. "I'll take *Pika-Don* up tomorrow morning. You can tell me what you think tomorrow afternoon. Fair enough?"

"Maybe," Blake said.

"You think I'm a cushmaker, don't you?"

"Possible. What's a cushmaker?"

Blake hadn't heard the story. Maybe it hadn't been invented yet. Farman explained it—the ultra shaggy joke about the cushmaker who, obliged by an admiral to demonstrate his specialty, after commandeering a battleship and tons of elaborate equipment, and after arduous technological efforts, finally dropped a white-hot sphere of steel amid the ice floes of the Antarctic Ocean, where it went *cussh*.

Blake went away, then. "I'll say this. If you're pulling a deal, you're a cool one." He shook his head. "I just don't know about you."

Morning brought high, ragged clouds. They'd make no trouble for the demonstration flight. Farman waited beside *Pika-Don* while Blake took off and slowly climbed to ten thousand feet, circling over the field the whole time. "I think we are ready, M'sieu," Devereaux said, fingering his trim mustache.

Farman turned to his plane. "Better make everybody stand back," he said. Turbine scream wasn't gentle to unprotected ears. He climbed up on the packing crate—pulled himself up *Pika-Don*'s sloped side and dropped into the cockpit. Looking back, he saw the onlookers had retreated about twenty-five feet. He had quite an audience. He grinned. They'd back off a lot farther when he got the engines going.

He got the cockpit hatch down. He checked the seal; it was tight. He went through the pre-ignition cockpit check. He began the engine start-up cycle, felt the momentary vibration and saw the twitch of instruments coming alive. Engine One caught, ragged for an instant, then steady as the tachometer wound around like a clock gone wild. Its scream of power drilled through the cockpit's insulation. Farman started Engine Two, then Engine Three. He brought them up to standby idle. They burned smooth.

Good enough. He didn't have fuel to waste on all the pre-takeoff operations; some were necessary, some not. He did all the necessary ones, turned the jets into the lift vents, and brought them up to full power. By that time, *Pika-Don* was already off the ground. She bobbled momentarily in the light breeze, and rose like a kite on a string. The sprawling fuselage surface prevented him from looking down at the airfield; it didn't matter. They'd be watching, all right—and probably holding shriek-filled ears. He grinned at the trembling instruments in front of him. He wished he could see their eyes, their open mouths. You'd think they'd never seen a plane fly before.

He took *Pika-Don* up to ten thousand feet. Hovering, he tried to find the image of Blake's Nieuport on the airspace view scope. It didn't show. For a worried moment, Farman wondered if something had gone wrong and Blake had gone down. Then the Nieuport flew past him on the left, a little above. It turned to pass in front of him. He could see Blake's goggled face turned toward him.

Even then, there wasn't an image on the radar. Farman swore. Something was wrong with the equipment.

No time to fiddle with the dials now, though. *Pika-Don* was guzzling the kerosene like a drunk on holiday. He converted to lateral flight. As always, it was like the floor dropping out from under him. He moved all three throttles forward, felt the thrust against his back. For a frightened instant, he saw Blake had turned back—was coming straight at him, head-on. He'd warned Blake not to get ahead of him like that. But *Pika-Don* was dropping fast. At speeds less than Mach 0.5 she had the glide capability of a bowling ball. She slashed underneath the Nieuport with a hundred feet to spare. The altimeter began to unwind, faster and faster. The horizon lifted on the forward view scope like a saucer's rim.

He watched the Machmeter. It was edging up. He could feel the drive of the engines, full thrust now, exciting him like they always did, hurling him across the sky. The altimeter steadied, began to rise again. He tipped *Pika-Don*'s prow upward and cracked the barrier in a rocketing fifty-degree climb. Blake's Nieuport was nowhere in sight.

At forty thousand he cut the engines back, leveled off, and started down. He had to search hard for the airfield; without the map scope he couldn't have found it. It was just another green field in a countryside of green fields. At five thousand feet he converted back to vertical thrust and let *Pika-Don* drop to a landing—quickly for most of the distance to save fuel, with a heavy retarding burst in the last thousand feet. He hovered a moment two hundred feet up, picked out a landing spot, and put down. According to the gauges, less than thirty seconds' fuel was left in the tanks.

He dropped to the ground without waiting for a packing crate to be brought. He stood and looked around in disbelief. There was hardly a man in sight, and none of the escadrille's planes remained on the field. He saw them, finally, small specks flying off eastward. He walked back to the hangars, perplexed. Was that all the impression he'd made? He grabbed the first man he found—a mechanic. "What happened?"

The mechanic grinned and made gestures and gabbled in French. Farman shook him and asked again—or tried to—in pidgin French. All he got was more of the same jabber and some gestures in the general direction of the front lines. "I know they went that way," Farman growled and flung the man away. He stalked back to the shack behind the hangars and asked Henri for a Scotch. He drank it, waited five minutes, and had another. He was deep into his fourth when the men came back.

They trooped into the shack, and Henri set a row of glasses on the counter and went down the line with the brandy bottle. As soon as a glass had been filled, a hand snatched it away. Blake came to Farman's table, a brimful glass in his hand, sat down.

"Howard," he said, "I don't know how that thing of yours works. I don't know even if you can call it an aeroplane. But I've got to admit you got it off the ground, and the only thing I ever saw go past me faster was a bullet. Now, if you'll just tell me one thing . . ."

"Anything you want to know," Farman said, abruptly raised from dejection to smugness.

"How can you fly when you don't have the wind on your face?"

Farman started to laugh, but Blake wasn't even smiling. To him, it wasn't an old joke. He was serious.

With effort, Farman controlled his amusement. "I don't need the wind. In fact, if the window broke, I'd probably be killed. I've got instruments that tell me everything I need to know."

He could see the skeptical expression shaping itself on Blake's face. He started to get up, not quite steady because of the Scotches he'd downed. "Come on. I'll show you the cockpit."

Blake waved him down. "I saw the cockpit. You've got so many things in there you don't have time to look outside. I don't know if I'd call it flying. You might as well be sitting at a desk."

Sometimes, Farman had thought the same thought. But all those instruments were necessary to fly a thing like *Pika-Don*. He wondered if he'd have taken up flying if he'd known it would be like that. "Or maybe a submarine?" he asked, not entirely sarcastic. "The thing is, did I fly circles around you, or didn't I?"

Blake's reply was a rueful shrug. "First, you hung there like a balloon. If I hadn't seen you, I wouldn't believe it. Then all of a sudden you were coming at me like something out of a cannon. I got to admit you had me scared. I never saw anything move like that thing of yours. By the time I got turned around you were out of sight. If we'd been dogfighting, you could of put a string of bullets through me from end to end, and I couldn't of got a shot off."

A shadow intruded onto the table between them. They looked up. "Indeed, M'sieu Farman," Deveraux said, "your machine's speed gives it the ability to attack without the risk of being attacked itself. I will not pretend to understand how it can fly with such small wings, nor how it can rise directly into the air, but I have seen it do these things. That is enough. I must apologize that we could not be here to applaud you when you landed."

So he'd made an impression after all. "Where'd you go? I thought you didn't have any patrols scheduled until this afternoon."

Deveraux pulled out a chair and sat down beside Blake. With delicate care, he placed a half-full wineglass in front of him. "That is true, M'sieu. But we heard the sound of big guns at the front, and our duty is to be in the air at such times, until the matter is clarified, doing such things as will assist our men in the trenches."

"I didn't hear any guns," Farman said. "When I got back here, it was as quiet as a bar mitzvah in Cairo."

He realized almost at once, seeing their faces, that the metaphor had no meaning for them. Well, they hadn't heard of Social Security, either.

"It is curious," Deveraux said. "When we are come to the front, it is as you say—most quiet. The guns have stopped, and we see no aircraft but our own. We search for fifty kilometers along the front. There is no evidence of even small actions. When we come back, I message to commanders at the front, and they tell me there has been no action. Nor have guns in their sectors been made use of—theirs or the Boche—though it is curious . . . some do say that they have heard guns being used in other sectors. And you can see"—he pointed to the window, the clear sky—"it could not have been thunder."

He said it all with the innocent mystification of a small boy, still not sure of all the things in the universe. Farman suddenly laughed and Deveraux blinked, startled.

"Sorry." Farman said. "I just realized. It wasn't guns you heard. It was me."

"You, M'sieu? What jest is this?"

"No joke. What you heard was my plane. It makes a shock wave in the air, just like an explosion's." He looked at their faces. "You don't believe me."

Deveraux's wineglass was empty. Blake stood up, empty brandy glass in hand. He reached for Deveraux's glass, but the Frenchman put his hand in the way. Blake went to the bar with only his own glass. Farman nursed his drink.

"I do not pretend to understand this aeroplane of yours," Deveraux said. "But now that you have shown its abilities . . ."

"Some of them," Farman said. They'd only seen an iceberg tip of what *Pika-Don* could do.

"Yes. But now we have seen," Deveraux said. "I will agree, it is possible your machine could outmatch Bruno Keyserling."

"I know she can," Farman said.

"Perhaps," Deveraux said with a small smile, but very firm. "But I agree—it should be tried. If you will tell us where to mount the guns on your machine . . ."

"I don't need guns," Farman said. "Don't want them."

"But M'sieu, an aeroplane *must* have guns. Without guns, it is like a tiger without teeth and claws."

The thought of machine guns stuck on *Pika-Don*'s prow was a horror. "I've got my own weapons," Farman said. Blake came back, sat down heavily. His glass slopped a little on the table. "Machine guns would . . . they'd destroy her aerodynamic integrity. They'd . . . she probably couldn't even fly with them sticking out in the wind."

"Aerody . . . *what* integrity?" Blake snorted. "What are you talking about?"

Farman leaned forward. "Look. You've seen my plane. All right. Now—you've seen those overlapping strips along her belly, between the ports the skids retract into?"

"I have noticed," Deveraux said.

"There's a rocket under each one of them," Farman said. "Just one of those can wipe out a whole squadron."

"Ah? How many rockets? Eight?"

"Six," Farman said. "How many squadrons have the Germans got in this sector?"

"Two jagdstaffels," Deveraux said. "They are quite enough." He shook his head. "But M'sieu, the men who planned the equipping of your aeroplane did not understand the needs of combat. It is assuming a marksman's skill beyond human abilities to believe that with only six of these rockets you could expect to be effective against enemy aircraft. One must remember, they are not motionless targets, like balloons. It is difficult enough to strike a balloon with rockets—balloons do not move—but to destroy an aeroplane . . . that cannot be done. Often I have expended all my ammunition—hundreds of rounds—without so much as touching my opponent. That you would imagine going into combat with a mere six possibilities of striking your target . . . this is folly. It is not worth the effort."

"They're not just things I shoot off," Farman said. Did he have to explain everything? "In fact, my plane's so fast any weapons system that depends on human senses couldn't possibly work. My rockets find their targets themselves. They are . . ."

He saw the utter disbelief on their faces. "Look," he said, "I've shown you my plane can do everything I told you it could. It flies faster and climbs faster than anything you ever saw. Now, if you'll give me enough fuel to take her up against Keyserling, I'll show you what my rockets can do. They'll wipe him out of the sky like a blob of smoke in a high wind."

"Bruno Keyserling is a very skilled and deadly man," Deveraux said. "A man impossible to kill. We have tried—all of us. He has killed many of our own men, and he will send more of us down in flames before this war ends. I would suggest you be not so confident of yourself and your equipment."

"Just give me enough kerosene for a mission," Farman said. "One mission. Let me worry about the rest of it." He wasn't worried at all. A dogfight between World War I model planes and something from 1985 would be like a wrestling match between a man and a gorilla.

"But M'sieu, you *have* the paraffin," Deveraux said, mildly puzzled. "You have almost two thousand liters."

Farman shook his head. "I burned that. There's just about enough left to fill that glass of yours."

Deveraux looked down at his empty wineglass. "M'sieu, you must be joking."

"No joke," Farman said. "*Pika-Don* flies fast and climbs like a rocket, but you don't get something for nothing—law of conservation of energy, if you know what that is. She drinks fuel like a sewer."

There was a silence—a silence, Farman realized, not only at their own table, but all through the shack. Maybe these fliers understood more English than he thought. Blake downed a large swallow of brandy.

"How much do you need for a mission?" he asked.

"Ten thousand gallons will do for a short one," Farman said. "An hour—hour and a half."

There was another long silence. "M'sieu," Deveraux said at last, "I have wide discretion in the requisition of the usual materials. I am trying to balance in my mind the possible destruction of Bruno Keyserling—which is a thing we all desire—against the difficulty I must expect in explaining my request for so much kitchen fuel. And I remain in doubt you will be able to accomplish as successful as you claim. So I must ask—have I your word of honor as an American that you must have this paraffin to fly your machine?"

"You've got it, on a stack of Bibles."

"The good old USA is alive with con men," Blake said.

"M'sieu Blake," Deveraux said reproachfully, "we must not assume that a man tell lies because he claims ability to do a thing we cannot do ourselves. He is optimistic, yes. But that is a fault of almost all the young men who come to us. If we do not put him to the test, we shall not know if he could do the thing he claims or not."

Blake made a sour twist of his mouth. "All right. But how are you going to explain wanting forty thousand liters of kerosene?"

Deveraux cocked his head to one side, as if listening to a voice no one else could hear. "I think I shall merely tell a part of the truth. That we wish to try a weapon suggested by one of our men, a weapon which makes use of paraffin."

"Such as?" Blake asked.

"If they want details," Farman said, leaning forward, "tell them you're putting it in old winebottles and cramming a rag in the neck. And before you drop the bottle on the Germans you set fire to the rag. The bottle breaks when it hits, and spills burning kerosene over everything."

Blake and Deveraux looked at each other. Delight animated their faces. "Now that's something I think might work," Blake said, rubbing his jaw. "Why didn't somebody think of it before?"

It was the first time Farman had heard him enthusiastic about something. This, at least, was a weapon they could understand. "It might work," he said. "But gasoline does it better. It's called a Molotov cocktail."

"M'sieu Farman," Deveraux said, "I think we shall try that, also." He stood up, wineglass in hand. "Henri!" he called. "More wine!"

Early that afternoon, two men came to the airfield fresh from training school. Boys, really; neither could have been more than seventeen. They were eager to get into the war—looked disconsolate as they came away from reporting to Deveraux. "They'll have to spend a day or two learning their way around," Blake said, a twisty smile curling his mouth. "Some guys just can't wait to get killed."

Their Nieuports were straight from the factory, new as pennies. The smell of dope and varnish surrounded them like an aura. Blake worked his way around them, a point-by-point inspection. The new men would be assigned to his flight. He peered intently at struts and wires and fabric surfaces. "Good aeroplanes," he said finally. Then it was time for him to go out on patrol. Three other men went with him. Farman watched them take off. They disappeared eastward. He went back and saw about readying his jerrybuilt filtration plant for the job of turning ten thousand gallons of cooking oil into aviation fuel.

At first light next morning, the new men stood beside their planes and watched the escadrille fly out on dawn patrol. They looked like children not invited to play. Farman went and checked *Pika-Don*; there was sign of a gummy deposit in her tailpipes, but a close inspection of her compressor blades showed they were clean, and none of the fuel injectors was fouled. He buttoned her up again and headed for the drinking shack. Until he got a shipment of kerosene, he'd have nothing to do.

The escadrille came back three hours later. If there'd been any Germans in the sky that morning, they'd made themselves hard to find. There'd been no action. Six planes refueled at once and went out again. Deveraux took the new men out on an orientation flight. In the afternoon, Blake and another pilot took the new men out for a mock dogfight. When they came back, Farman was waiting at the edge of the field; he had an idea he felt foolish for not having thought of sooner—to make a start on the long kerosene-upgrading job by borrowing a barrel or two of the raw material from the mess hall. He needed Blake to translate and haggle for him.

As Blake taxied up onto the hardstand, Farman saw the tattered fabric fluttering from the right upper wing. He ran over as Blake cut the motor. "Hey! You've been in a fight!"

Blake dropped down from the cockpit. He stripped off helmet and goggles and gloves. Farman repeated his question. Blake grinned and pointed to his ears and shook his head. Farman pointed at the shredded wing.

"Yeah. I've been in a fight," Blake said, his voice loud as if he was trying to talk through the noise his motor had made.

Farman looked out at the other planes taxiing in from the field. "They're all right," Blake said. "We jumped a Brandenburg—what he was doing way off there behind the lines, don't ask me. I got the observer interested in me"—he nodded at the damaged wing—"and Jacques moved in and put a few in the engine. Simple enough."

The other planes of the flight came up on the hard-stand, and the mechanics moved in to turn them around and chock the wheels. The pilots climbed out, and the new men crowded around the other veteran—Jacques, Farman assumed. They pumped his arm and slapped his back and jabbered jubilantly. Jacques managed to break free of them long enough to reach Blake. He grabbed both Blake's arms and spoke with a warm grin. Blake looked a little embarrassed by the attention and managed, finally, to shrug off Jacques' hands without offending. By then the new men had closed in again. A rapid four-way conversation broke out.

Blake got loose again after a minute. "They never saw an aeroplane shot down before." He grinned. "Wasn't much of a shoot-down, really. Jacques put a few in the engine, and it just sort of went into a glide." He nodded at the three men; they were still talking energetically. "I guess they liked the show, even if they don't understand some of it. They're wanting to know why we didn't go on shooting after Jacques got the engine."

It sounded like a reasonable thing to ask. "Well, why didn't you?" He remembered to speak loud.

438 DEAN McLAUGHLIN

Blake shrugged. "Why kill 'em? There's enough people getting killed. They were out of the war as soon as their propeller stopped."

"Well, yes. Sure. But . . ."

"Oh, we made sure they landed close to a convoy on the road, so they'd be captured all right," Blake said. "Didn't want a pair of Huns running loose behind the lines."

"But they were Germans. The enemy."

Blake punched a finger into Farman's ribs. "Once Jacques got their engine, they were just a couple of poor guys in an aeroplane that couldn't fly any more. We got no fight with guys like that. It's the man they worked for we're against. The Kaiser. Besides, that guy in the rear cockpit still had a lot of bullets in his machine gun, and he was sort of mad at us. I figure we were smart to keep our distance."

The new men had a few more training flights the next day, and the day after that they went out with the dawn patrol. The patrol met a flight of German machines led by Keyserling's white-trimmed purple Albatross. It was a fast, cruel scrap. Only one of the new men came back.

"We shouldn't of put 'em on service so quick," Blake said, nodding across the shack toward where the survivor was slowly drinking himself into numbness; he'd been in shock ever since he climbed out of his cockpit. "But we've got to have men. It takes three months to train a man enough so he's got a chance in the air—and Keyserling and his circus kill 'em in five minutes. Like swatting a fly." He picked up his brandy and downed it whole.

Deveraux came and put a hand on Blake's shoulder. "It is true," he said. "One might wish we did not so desperately need men to fight. But we fight a war to preserve civilization, and for that it is necessary that some good men die. And so we have lost one man today. And one other machine is damaged. Do not forget, Keyserling has lost two men in this morning's battle, and three of his aeroplanes will need considerable work before they fly again. We have done well, this day."

"Yeah. Sure. But he was just a kid," Blake said. His open hand banged on the table. Glasses rattled. "A poor, dumb kid. As green as—"

"To keep a civilization is worth a few lives, M'sieu Blake." Deveraux squeezed Blake's shoulder, held the grip a moment, let his hand slip away. He moved off to talk with the men at another table.

"Civilization," Blake muttered.

"Stick around," Farman said. If he lived long enough, Blake would know of Dachau, Bataan, Hiroshima, 'Nam, and the bloody mess France herself would make of her African colonies. And lots more.

"You haven't seen anything yet," Farman said.

The kerosene began to come two days later. It came spas-modically, in odd-sized lots: one day a demijohn arrived; the next, half a lorry load. Kerosene, to these people, was not a strategically vital petrochemical; it was a fluid used in lamps and stoves. It couldn't just be commanded up from the nearest supply dump in anything like the quantities a supersonic jet had to have. Genghis Khan's army might have been similarly inept at meeting a sudden, inexplicable demand for a few thousand pounds of gunpowder.

June became July. The summer sun burned warm. There was talk of heavy fighting to the north, in a place called Bois de Belleau. Farman worked at the makeshift filters day after day. The smell of warm kerosene was a weight in his lungs, an ache in his brain. Some evenings, he was too sickened to eat.

The weeks blended into each other. He didn't have much idle time; there was always more kerosene to be poured into the system, or a filter to be changed and the clogged filter to be scraped and scrubbed and carefully examined for flaws before being used again. After a while, he stopped looking up when he heard the sound of airplane motors.

But in that time he saw airplanes lose power as they left the ground, stall, and nose stiffly into the turf. Their wings snapped like jack-straws. He saw a tattered plane coming back from a dogfight; it fell apart over the field and its pilot died in the wreck. He saw a man bring his plane down, taxi off the field, and die from loss of blood with the engine still puttering. And there were many times when he saw men watch the sky, searching for planes that would not come back, ever.

Some nights, he heard the big guns thunder at the front, like a grumbling storm just beyond the horizon. Muzzle flash and shellburst blazed in the sky.

Several days came when no new loads of kerosene arrived. He used that time to learn what he could about the Germans—their tactics, their formations, the capabilities of their planes. Not much of the information was useful—he'd expected that; matched against *Pika-Don*, they'd be almost motionless targets. But with only ten thousand gallons to fly on, it would be a good idea to know where he'd be most likely to find them. He wouldn't have much more time in the air than just enough to lift off, aim and launch rockets, and return to base. He started planning the mission.

"They stay mostly on their own side of the lines," he said to Deveraux. "All right. When I go up, I don't want you to have any planes on that side. I want to be sure any planes I find over there are theirs, not yours. I'll be going too fast to look at 'em close."

"You ask more than is possible, or even wise," Deveraux said. Breeze ruffled grass on the field. The Frenchman's scarf flapped and fluttered. "It is necessary always to have patrols in all sectors to protect our reconnaissance aeroplanes. If we do not patrol, the reconnaissance aeroplanes would be attacked. They could not do their missions. Perhaps it would be possible to remove patrols from one sector for a few hours—one in which none of our observation missions will be flying. Is not that as much as you shall need?"

"Not quite," Farman said. "I don't think you've thought it all the way through. You cover the front between the Swiss border and the Vosges Mountains. Right?"

"There are several escadrilles with which we share that duty."

"Yeah. Well, that's not important except they'll have to be warned off, too. What I'm asking now is, how many miles of front are you covering? Fifty? Seventy-five?"

"It is fifty kilometers," Deveraux said.

"All right. I'll be flying at about Mac 2. At that speed, I can cover that much distance in three minutes. It takes me twenty miles just to get turned around. I can patrol the whole front, all by myself. You don't need to have anybody else out there."

Deveraux's face wore a scowlish mask. "So fast? I must assume you do not exaggerate, M'sieu."

"At sixty thousand feet, I could do it twice that fast," Farman said. "But I'm going to cruise at forty. Air's too thick for full power flying that low down. I'd burn like a meteor."

"Of course, M'sieu."

Farman couldn't be sure if Deveraux believed him or not.

"But I must say, it would seem you have not considered all the necessities," the Frenchman went on. "Even if you are able to patrol all the sectors, that would be true only should you not find a Boche patrol. Then you would move to attack it, and *voilà*, you would be engaged in combat, M'sieu. You would cease to patrol. And it is not uncommon for the Boche to have four or five flights in the air at one time. Who would be protecting our observation missions while you are fighting?"

"I don't even want any observation flights on that side of the lines while I'm flying," Farman said. "Because I'm going to wipe that sky clean like a blackboard. If you have observation planes over there, they might get it, too. So you don't need to have any patrols out to protect 'em. Anyway, it won't take me more than five minutes from the time I've spotted a flight until I've launched rockets, and then I'll be free to go back on patrol. That's not much more than if I'd took time out for a smoke."

They heard, then, very faint but growing, the sound of aircraft motors. Deveraux turned to search the eastward sky for the approaching planes. "And have you thought, M'sieu, what the Boche would be doing while you are shooting these rockets of yours? Bruno Keyserling and his men are aviators of consummate skill. They would not fly calmly, doing nothing, while you attack them. And even should your rockets each find a target, that would still be only one of their aeroplanes for each rocket. You have, I believe you said, only six."

"They won't even see me coming, I'll jump 'em so fast," Farman said. "They won't have time to do anything but look surprised. And one of my rockets can . . ." He made a wipe-out gesture. "Look. All I'm asking—keep your planes on this side of the lines for a couple of hours. With only ten thousand gallons, I won't be able to stay out even that long. Am I asking too much? Two hours?"

The returning planes were in sight now. There were three of them, strung out, the one in the rear far behind the other two, losing altitude, regaining it, losing it again. Farman didn't know how many had gone out on that particular patrol—he hadn't been paying much attention to such things—but it was rare for a patrol of only three planes to go out. There would be some empty chairs in the mess, this evening.

The first plane came down to land. Its lower wing was shredded close to the fuselage—loose fabric fluttered like torn flags—and the landing gear wheel on that side wobbled oddly. As it touched down, the whole gear collapsed. The wing dipped—caught the ground—and flung the machine into a tangle of broken struts, tail high in the air. Men ran across the field. Farman caught a glimpse of the pilot's arm, waving for help. A thin black thread of smoke began to rise. A moment later it was a fierce inferno. No one could get near it. There wasn't a sign of the man. The second plane landed and taxied across the grass unheeded.

Deveraux turned to Farman again. "No, M'sieu," he said. "You do not ask too much. It is we who ask too much of men."

Farman boosted *Pika-Don* from the field while dawn was still a growing light in the east and all the land was gray. She lifted sluggishly; well, the gunk he was feeding her was a poor substitute for her usual diet. He took her to eight thousand feet before converting to lateral flight. She was down to four before she cracked the barrier and down to three and a half before she bottomed out and started to climb. The Machmeter moved past 1.25. He raised *Pika-Don*'s nose and drove her at the sky.

She broke into sunlight at twenty thousand feet. The sun was gold and the air was as clean as clear ice. Somewhere in the darkness below two armies faced each other as they had faced each other for four years. At forty thousand feet he leveled off and began his loiter pattern—a slim-waisted figure eight course, looping first to the south, then to the north—overflying the German lines from the Swiss border to the Vosges Mountains. He watched the airspace view scope for the pips that would be German aircraft.

Almost always, on good flying days, the Germans sent up patrols a few minutes before sunrise, to intercept the reconnaissance planes the French almost always sent over on good flying days. Bruno Keyserling would be leading one of those patrols. Farman watched particularly the area surrounding the German airfield. The Germans would climb quickly to fighting altitude; as soon as their altitude and motion dissociated them from the ground, *Pika-Don*'s radars would pick them out. He watched the scope, followed his loiter pattern, and waited for the German planes to appear.

Two circuits later, he was still up there. The scope showed the shaded contours of the land, but that was all. Not one German plane—no planes at all, even though the whole escadrille had flown out ahead of him to watch the fight he'd promised. He had fuel enough for six or eight more circuits—it was going faster than he'd counted on—before there'd be only enough to get him back to the field.

And more weeks of filtering kerosene? Not if he could help it. He made two more circuits—still nothing. He put *Pika-Don*'s needle prow downward. If they wouldn't come up and fight, he'd go after them. He checked the German field's position on the map scope. He could fly down straight to the end of its runway, and he had six rockets. One would be enough. Two would destroy it utterly.

He was down below twenty thousand feet when he saw the airplanes. They were flying on a northerly course, as he was, patrolling above the German lines in a Junck's row formation—each plane above, behind, and to the side of the one below it; an upright, diagonal line. A quick glance at the radar scope: not a hint of those planes.

Nuts with the airfield. Not with those planes over there. Flying where they were, using that formation, they had to be Germans. Farman pulled out of this attack dive, immelmanned into a corkscrew turn that would take him back and place him behind their formation. He lost sight of them in that maneuver, but the map scope showed him where they had to be; they didn't have the speed to move far while he was getting into position.

Behind them now, he turned again and drove toward them. Still nothing on the airspace scope, but he knew where they were. He tried the target-tracking radar—the one in the middle of the instrument panel. They didn't show there, either.

But he knew where they were, and in another moment he saw them again. Little black specks, like gnats, only gnats didn't fly in formation. And one rocket anywhere near them . . .

Still they didn't show on the target-tracking scope. It would have to be an eyeball launch, then. He primed the proximity detonators on rockets one and six. There still was no sign that they'd seen him. They didn't even seem to move against the sky.

He launched the rockets at four miles. The distance was a guess—without help from his radars, a guess was all he could do, but the German planes were still only specks. It didn't matter. The rockets were built to heat-seek a target from ten times that distance. He felt the shock as the rockets struck from their sheaths even as he sent *Pika-Don* screaming straight up, engines suddenly at full thrust, and over on her back, and a half-roll, and he was at forty-five thousand feet. Rockets one and six sketched their ionized tracks on the airspace scope, all the way to the edge.

The edge was somewhere beyond the crest of the Vosges Mountains. Farman couldn't understand it. He'd sent those rockets straight as bullets into that formation, proximities primed and warheads armed. They should have climbed right up those Germans' tailpipes and fireballed and wiped those planes from the sky like tinder touched by flame. It hadn't happened.

He brought *Pika-Don* around. On the map scope he found again the position where the German planes had been. They didn't show on the airspace view—what could possibly be wrong with the radar—but they would still be close to where he'd seen them last, and he still had four rockets left. On the airspace scope, the tracks of rockets one and six ended in tiny sparks as their propellants exhausted and their automatic destructs melted them to vapor. He turned *Pika-Don*'s nose down. He armed the warheads, primed the proximities. This time he wouldn't miss.

He saw the German planes from ten miles away. He launched rockets two and five from a distance of five miles. Two seconds later, he launched three and four and turned away in a high-G immelmann. His G-suit seized him like a hand—squeezed, relaxed, and squeezed again as he threw *Pika-Don* into a long, circling curve. The airspace scope flickered, re-oriented itself. His four rockets traced bright streaks across its face.

Explode! he thought. *Explode!*

They didn't. They traced their paths out to the scope's edge. Their destruct mechanisms turned them to vapor. Ahead of him now, again, he could see the disorganized swarm of the jagdstaffel. He hadn't touched one of them. And they still didn't show on the airspace scope.

Farman swore with self-directed disgust. He should have thought of it. Those planes were invisible to radar. They didn't have enough metal among them to make a decent tin can, so his radar equipment rejected the signals they reflected as static. For the same reason, the proximities hadn't worked. The rockets could have passed right through the formation—probably had—without being triggered. As far as the proximities were concerned, they'd flown through empty air. He might as well have tried to shoot down a cloud.

He turned west, back to base. He located the field with the map scope. He had enough fuel to get there, and some to spare. A thought trickled through his mind about the dinosaurs—how their bodies had been perfectly adapted to the world they lived in, and when the world changed their bodies had not been able to adjust to the changes. So they died.

Pika-Don was like that—a flying *Tyrannosaurus rex* whose world now gave it only insects for food.

"Yeah. We saw the whole action," Blake said. He sat with his back against the hangar wall, a wine bottle close to his hand. The sun was bright and the fields were green. A light breeze stirred.

The escadrille had come back a half hour after Farman landed. Farman had hesitated, but then went out to face Deveraux. He was not eager for the confrontation.

Deveraux was philosophically gentle. "You have seen now, M'sieu, the rockets you carried were not an adequate armament for combat situations. Now, if you will show our mechanics where you think it would be best to mount the machine guns they . . ."

"*Pika-Don* flies faster than bullets," Farman said. He kicked at a ridge of dirt between wheel ruts. The dirt was hard, but it broke on the third try. "I even heard of a guy that got ahead of his own bullets and shot himself down. And his plane was a lot slower than mine." He shook his head—looked back toward where *Pika-Don* crouched low to the ground, sleek and sinister-looking, totally useless. "Might as well let her rot there."

He kicked the loosened clod off into the grass.

About eleven o'clock, Blake got a bottle of wine from Henri. It was plain peasant's wine, but that was all right. They sat in the narrow noontide shade of a hangar and worked on it.

"You've got to get in close before you shoot," Blake said. "I don't know where you learned combat, but it didn't look like you learned much. You flew at their formation so fast they wouldn't of seen you until you broke right through'em, but you shot those rockets from a couple of miles away. You can't hit anything at that kind of range."

"I thought I could," Farman said. "And with the kind of warheads they had, it's a good idea to have a few miles distance when they go off."

"You don't think you're funning me with that, do you?" Blake said. He sat up straight—looked at Farman. "Nothing scatters shrapnel that wide."

Farman helped himself from the bottle. "My rockets would have done more than just scatter shrapnel, if they'd gone off."

"Not much good if you've got to shoot 'em from so far off you can't hit the target," Blake said.

It was no use trying again to explain target-seeking missiles. Anyway, they hadn't worked. He'd finally figured that out, too. Their heat-seeking elements had been designed to track on a hot jet's exhaust, or the meteor-flame of a ballistic warhead. All the German planes were putting out was the feeble warmth of a piston engine. That wasn't enough. If he was going to do any good in this war, it wasn't going to be with *Pika-Don*. "Harry, I want you to check me out on your plane."

"Huh?"

"My plane's useless. She hasn't any teeth left," Farman said. "If I'm going to do any more fighting, it's going to be in a plane like yours. I've got more flying hours than all of you put together, but I don't have any cockpit time in your—" He almost called them box kites. "I want you to show me how it flies."

Blake shrugged. "One plane's pretty much like another. They've all got their tricks—like these Nieuports, you don't want to do much diving in them; takes the fabric off the top wings every time. But aside from that the only way you get the feel is by flying 'em."

They walked out to Blake's Nieuport. It looked about as airworthy as a Model T Ford. Farman had a little trouble climbing up until Blake showed him the footholds. It was cramped in the cockpit, and the wicker seat was hard. Blake stood on a packing crate and leaned over the coaming.

Farman put his hand on the stick. That was what it was—an erect rod sticking up between his knees. He'd never seen one like it before. He tried moving it, and it moved with the smoothness of a spoon in a gluepot. "Do you have to fight it like this all the time?" he asked.

"Takes some getting used to," Blake said. "It's easier when she's flying, though."

Farman turned his attention to the instruments. They were a haphazard assortment of circular dials, unevenly distributed, and except for one big dial straight in front of him there was no apparent priority of position given to the more important ones—whichever ones they were. They were all identified, the words lettered across their faces, but the words were French.

"That's the oil pressure," Blake said, tapping the glass in front of a dial. "And that's r.p.m., and that's fuel mixture."

"Oil pressure. Is that important?"

Blake looked at him strangely. "You say you've been flying . . . how long? And you don't know oil pressure?"

"I've never flown a piston engine craft," Farman said. "*Pika-Don* has a different kind. Is it important?"

"Your engine doesn't work too good without it."

"And—fuel mixture, did you say?" Farman asked, putting his finger to the dial Blake had indicated. He was careful not to ask if it was important, though he wasn't sure what difference it made. Mixed with what, he wondered to himself.

"Right," Blake said. "And this here's your compass—don't trust it too far—and that's the altimeter, and here's the gas gauge."

At least those were instruments Farman understood. But he frowned at the altimeter. "Is that the highest this can fly?"

"Those are meters, not feet," Blake said. "This crate can go up as high as I can breathe. Sixteen . . . eighteen thousand feet." He pointed into the cockpit again. "This here's the switch, and that's the throttle, and that's the mixture control."

Farman touched them, one by one, trying to get their feel. His hand encountered a small plumb bob dangling from a cord. "Good-luck charm?" he asked.

Blake laughed. "Yeah, it's good luck all right. Without it I could be flying upside down and not know it."

"Don't you have a turn-and-bank indicator?" Farman wondered.

"Mister, that *is* my turn-and-bank indicator."

"Oh," Farman said, feeling foolish. But how could he have known?

"And these here," Blake went on, unnoticing, "that one tightens the flying wires, and that one the landing wires."

"What kind of wires?"

"Some wires you want tight when you're flying, and some others when you're coming in to land. If you don't, you stand a good chance of coming apart at the wrong time."

"Oh."Flying a Nieuport wasn't going to be as easy as he'd

thought. It would be like trying to ride horseback after driving cars all your life. "My plane doesn't have wires."

"What holds it together?" Blake asked.

Farman ignored him. He was thinking about driving a car, and some of his confidence came back. This Nieuport was a lot different from *Pika-Don*, but her engine wasn't too much different from the one in the BMW he'd had in another place and time—more primitive, maybe, but it worked on the same principles. He could handle a gasoline engine all right.

"Where's the starter?" he asked.

Blake frowned, as if he didn't understand. Then a wry grin cracked his face. He nodded forward—pointed to the propeller's blade. "Right there," he said.

Half a minute later Farman was looking forward through the blur of a spinning propeller. He felt the blast of air on his face, and the stench of exhaust made him want to retch. The oil-pressure gauge worked up. He experimented with throttle settings and fuel-mixture adjustments, trying to learn something about how it handled. It occurred to him that his BMW had two or three times the horsepower this thing had.

Blake handed him a helmet and goggles. Farman put them on. "Taxi her around a bit, until you get the feel," Blake yelled through the engine's blatting. Farman nodded, and Blake bent to pull the chocks from in front of the wheels; one side and then—slipping quickly underneath—the other. The Nieuport lurched forward even before Farman advanced the throttle. It bumped clumsily over the grass.

The thing had no brakes , so when he advanced the throttle again she hurtled forward, bumping and thumping across the field. The airspeed indicator began to show readings. The bumping got worse. He edged the throttle forward a little more. Except for the jouncing and that awful smell, it wasn't much different from driving a car.

The tail came up. It startled him, and it was almost by reflex—seeing the horizon lift in front of him—that Farman pulled the stick back. The bumping stopped as if it were shut off. The engine's sound changed, and air-speed began to slacken. The silly Model T was airborne. He shoved the throttle forward and tried to level out. It shouldn't have been flying at this speed—he'd driven his BMW faster than this, and his BMW was a lot more streamlined.

He was beyond the field's edge now, with a rise of ground ahead of him. He tried to turn, but the Nieuport resisted. He pulled the stick back to clear the hill's crest. The airspeed meter started to unwind. He got over the hill with a few yards to spare, but airspeed was falling back toward zero. He tried to level out again; it wasn't easy to do without an artificial horizon on the instrument panel. The real horizon was rocking back and forth, up and down, and drifting sidewise. He tried turning the other way, and she turned easily but she also nosed down. He hauled back on the stick, swearing loudly. How any man could fly a crazy, contrary thing like this was more than he could understand.

The ground wheeled under him. The engine's sound changed, became a snarl, then a sputter. Wildly, he looked for a place to put down, but there was nothing but orchard under him as far as he could see—which wasn't far because the plane had nosed down again. A queasy, liquid feel began in his stomach, and the stench from the engine didn't help it any.

The engine chose that moment to quit. For a long time—it couldn't really have been more than a few seconds—the only sound was the whisper of air against the wings. Then the Nieuport stalled and plunged down among the trees. Branches snapped and the wings buckled. The Nieuport came to rest midway between the treetops and the ground. It dangled there, swaying a little in the gentle breeze. After a while, Farman thought to turn off the ignition, to reduce the danger of fire. After another while, he began to think about how to climb down.

He met Blake and half a dozen other men before he got out of the orchard. They went back to the Nieuport. Blake looked up at the wreck among the tree branches, made an angry noise that might have been extremely basic English, or it might not, and walked away.

Farman started to go after him but then thought better of it. Another tree branch cracked and the Nieuport sagged a few feet closer to the ground. Farman looked up at the mess one more time, then turned away and followed Blake. It was a long walk back to the field.

Blake was given another Nieuport. The escadrille had several replacements ready—craft that had been sent down from an escadrille in the Somme region that had switched to Spads. The older Nieuports were still good enough for this less active section of the front. Blake spent the rest of the day and all the next with the mechanics, checking it out.

Farman spent the time poking around *Pika-Don*, trying to figure a way she could still be used. There was a space where a Vickers gun could be fitted if he took out the infrared sensor unit, but working out a trigger linkage was beyond him; every cubic inch inside *Pika-Don* was occupied by one or another piece of vital equipment. And at

Mach 2 an orifice the size of a .30-caliber muzzle might be enough to blow the plane apart.

The only other thing he could think of was that the radars were powerful enough to fry a man dead, but it didn't seem likely that Bruno Keyserling would hold still for the hour or two needed for the job.

He gave up. *Pika-Don* was useless. Reluctantly, he resigned himself to asking Deveraux for assignment to a flight school. It would mean swallowing a lot of pride, but if he was going to shoot Keyserling out of the sky, he'd have to learn how to fly a Nieuport.

When the escadrille came back from a patrol, he went out to talk with the Frenchman. Deveraux came toward him, helmet bunched in a still-gloved hand. "I am sorry, M'sieu," he said gravely. He laid his empty hand on Farman's shoulder. "Your friend . . . your country-man . . ."

The patrol had run into a flock of Albatrosses, Keyserling in the lead. No one had seen Blake go down, but several planes had been seen falling, burning like meteors. When the dogfight broke off and the flight had reformed, Blake wasn't with them.

Farman's mind became like cold iron as he heard Deveraux recite the plain, unchangeable facts. It shouldn't have struck him so hard, but Blake was a man he'd known, a man he'd talked with. All the other men here, even Deveraux, were strangers.

"Did anyone see a parachute?"

"M'sieu, such things do not work," Deveraux said. "We do not use them. They catch on the wires. For men in the balloons, perhaps such things can be used, but not for us. Our aeroplane is hit in its vitals, we go down."

"You shouldn't build them with so many wires, then."

Deveraux's reply was a Gallic shrug. "Perhaps not, M'sieu. But they are what hold our aeroplanes together."

"The German planes, too?" Farman asked in a suddenly different voice.

"Of course, M'sieu."

"Get me some kerosene," Farman said.

"Paraffin? Of course, M'sieu. And if you will show the mechanics where to fasten the machine guns they . . ."

Farman shook his head. "I don't need guns. Just get me the kerosene. I'll do the rest. And when I'm done with 'em on this front, I'll go up the line and clean out the rest of 'em.

"Of course, M'sieu," Deveraux said without irony.

Not that Farman cared. This time he'd do what he said he could do. He knew it. "Ten thousand gallons," he said.

Mid-August came, and *Pika-Don* was fueled again. Reports and rumors had been coming down from other sectors of the front that American troops were somewhere in the fighting.

Pika-Don lifted into a sky as clean as polished glass. Later in the day there might be a scatter of cumulus tufts, but it was not yet mid-morning. "It is not good day for fighting," Deveraux had said. "One can make use of the clouds."

It would be a good day for observation planes, though, so the German patrols would be out. And, Farman thought savagely, there'd be fighting enough. He'd see to that.

Once he'd shifted to lateral flight, he didn't try for altitude. *Pika-Don* would guzzle fuel faster at low levels, but he didn't figure the mission to take long. The German field was less than thirty miles away. He fixed its location on the map scope and sent *Pika-Don* toward it at full thrust. *Pika-Don* began to gain altitude, but at ten thousand feet, with the Machmeter moving up past 1.75 he leveled her off and turned her downward along a trajectory that would bring her to ground level just as he reached the German field.

It was almost perfectly calculated. He saw the field ahead of him. It was small—he'd seen pastures that were bigger—and he started to pull out of his descent. He passed over the field with just enough altitude to clear the trees on the far side. It took less than a second—the Machmeter said 2.5, and skin temperature was going up fast. He took *Pika-Don* a few hundred feet up and brought her around—lined her up on the field with the map scope's help—and brought her down again for another pass. This time she flew straight at the open mouth of a hangar in the middle of a row of hangars on the far side of the field.

He brought *Pika-Don* around one more time, but this time he stayed a thousand feet up and kept off to one side of the field. He looked down and felt the satisfaction of a kid who'd just stomped an anthill. Wreckage was still flying through the air. He didn't need rockets. He didn't need machine guns. All he had to have was *Pika-Don* herself.

He turned her south toward the Swiss border. He had seen only a few planes on the ground, which meant that most of them were out on patrol.

Heading south, he took *Pika-Don* up to eighteen thousand feet. On a day like this, with no clouds to hide in, the best altitude for a German patrol would be up close to the operational ceiling. Even if no altitude advantage could be gained, at least the advantage would not be lost to a higher-flying French patrol.

The map scope showed the Swiss border. Farman brought *Pika-*

Don around. The front was not hard to find. It was a sinuous gash across the land, like a bloodless wound. He followed it north, staying to the German side. He watched the sky ahead of him.

He flew the course to the Vosges Mountains at Mach 1.5, partly to save fuel and to minimize the skin-temperature problem; flying this low, the air was a lot thicker than *Pika-Don* was built to fly in. His main reason, though, was that even at Mach 1.5 he was flying through a lot of airspace. With no more sophisticated target-finding equipment than his own bare eyes, he could pass within a mile or less of a German patrol and not see it. Flying as slowly as he could improved his chances.

The mountains rose ahead of him. They weren't very high mountains; their crests lay well below him. He caught sight of the German patrol as he turned *Pika-Don* for another run south.

They were a few hundred yards higher than he was, and so small with distance he'd have thought they were birds except that birds didn't fly this high, nor did birds fly in a neatly stacked Junck's row formation. They hung suspended in the sky, like fleck-marks on a window, and if it hadn't been for their formation he wouldn't have known their direction of flight. They were flying south, as he was now—patrolling the front, as he was.

And they were close—too close. If he turned toward them, they'd be inside the radius of his turn. He'd cross their path in front of them like a black cat, warning them. He mind-fixed their position on the map scope and turned away.

Come at them from eight o'clock, he decided. That would be the best angle. On the outward arc of his circle he took *Pika-Don* up to thirty thousand feet. Then, as *Pika-Don* started to come around for the approach, he started down, full thrust in all three engines. The Mach-meter climbed to 2.0, then 2.5. It edged toward 3.0, trembling. It would mean a heating problem in this soup-thick air, but it wouldn't be for long.

The patrol was almost exactly where he'd seen it before. There hadn't been time for it to move far. With only a small correction *Pika-Don* was driving down toward it like a lance, target-true. The insect-speck planes became recognizable shapes, then rapidly expanded. They ballooned to their full size in a flash and he was almost on top of them.

At the last instant, he moved the controls just enough to avoid collision—passed behind them so close he had a glimpse of round knobs bulging from the cockpits just behind the upper wings—pilots' helmeted heads—and yes! at the bottom of the stack, leading the flight, the purple Albatross of Bruno Keyserling.

Then the whole flight was somewhere behind him. Farman reduced thrust and put *Pika-Don* into a steep climb, over on her back, and down again to level out into the airspace he'd flown through before.

It was all changed. The sky was full of junk, as if someone had emptied a barrel of trash. Fluttering wing sections, bashed fuselages, masses of twisted wreckage without any shape he could recognize. He saw a wingless fuselage falling a-tumble, like a crippled dragonfly. It was all purple, with bits of white on the shattered engine cowl. *Got him!*

And there wasn't a whole plane left in the sky. They hadn't been built to survive the impact of *Pika-Don's* shock wave. Just like the hangars at their field which had exploded when he buzzed them.

He started to curve southward again. He'd tasted blood, wanted more. He'd hardly begun the turn when a whump shook *Pika-Don* and the sky wheeled crazily and the engine function instruments erupted with a Christmas tree of red lights as if engine two had gobbled something that didn't digest too well. (Part of an airplane? Part of a man?) Some of the lights flashed panic, others glared firmly at his eyes. The horizon outside was tipping up on edge, falling over, tipping up again. The controls felt numb in his hands.

Farman knew the drill. When a plane as hot as this one went bad, you got out if you could. At Mach 2 you could hit the ground in less than thirty seconds. He slapped the eject button—felt the rockets blast him upward. A moment later the instrument panel broke away and the seat's firm pressure on his back and thighs were gone. He was tumbling like a wobbling top in midair, suddenly no longer enclosed in several million dollars' worth of airplane. There was the teeth-cracking shock of his chute coming open, and abruptly the confusion of too many things happening too fast stopped. He looked all around for some trace of *Pika-Don*, but there wasn't any.

He tugged at the shrouds to spill air from the chute and drift him westward toward the French lines. The wind was doing some of it, but not enough. A line of planes came toward him. He held his breath, thinking of a school of sharks nosing in toward a man cast overboard. But then he saw the French markings on their wings and sides. They were Nieuports, and the pilot of the leading plane waved. Farman waved back. The flight came on. It circled him once and then curved off. They stayed in sight, though, following him down. When flak bursts started to puff around him, they went down to strafe the German trenches.

He spilled another dollop of air from his chute. He was over the

French lines now. He could see the men in the trenches looking up at him. He floated down toward them, closer and closer. Then, very abruptly, he was down—down among the trenches and barbed wire of the French Seventh Army. He sprawled in the greasy mud of a shell hole. The chute started to drag him, but it caught on a tangle of wire and collapsed.

He got to his hands and knees, fumbling with the parachute harness. A bullet snapped past his ear. He flattened. The Nieuports dived on the German trenches again.

He struggled out of the harness and started to crawl in the direction of the nearest trench. It wasn't far. He scraped the dirt with his belt buckle all the way. Bullets whipped past him like deadly mosquitoes. The soldiers in the trenches reached out to pull him down.

They hugged him. They mobbed around him. There must have been thousands of men in that trench to celebrate the man who'd brought down Bruno Keyserling. Someone pressed a cup of wine into his hands—a soldier in dirty clothes, with mud on his brow and a matted beard. Farman drank gratefully.

After a while, he sat down and just sat there, dead inside. He looked at the dirt wall a few inches from his eyes. The empty cup dangled from his hand. *Pika-Don* was gone, and nothing he could do would rebuild her. Suddenly he was just an ordinary man. He couldn't even fly any more. *Pika-Don* had been the only plane in this age that he knew how to fly, and *Pika-Don* was gone.

He wasn't aware of the passage of time, but only of the heat and dust and the smell of a trench that had been lived in too long by unwashed men. He didn't know what he was going to do. But after a time, the wine began to have its effect. A trickle of life came back into him.

Slowly, he got to his feet. The start of a smile quirked his mouth. On second thought, no, he wasn't just an ordinary man.

The war would be over in a few months. Maybe he didn't know what he'd do, but . . .

The soldier who'd given him the wine was standing a few feet away. Farman held himself crisply erect. It occurred to him the man probably didn't know a word of English.

"How do I get back to America?" he asked, and grinned at the soldier's incomprehension.

A man from the future ought to have *some* advantage over the natives!

THE SUICIDE EXPRESS

Philip José Farmer

1

Before Boarding

"I hate you, Hermann Goering!" The voice sprang out and then flashed away as if it were a gear tooth meshed with the cog of another man's dream and rotated into and then out of his dream.

Riding the crest of the hypnopompic state, Richard Francis Burton knew he was dreaming. But he was helpless to do anything about it. The voice of the intruder had gone.

Now the first dream returned.

He saw the first few moments of his awakening after his death on Earth in 1890 A.D. He had opened his eyes to find himself floating in the air and surrounded by millions, maybe billions, of sleeping men, women and children. He, and he alone, of all the hosts of human beings who had lived since the first apeman spoke and became truly human—he alone had awakened before resurrection.

Why? He had not known then why he had been singled out, and he did not know now. His dream furnished him no clue. What good was a dream without a flash of mantic truth? What was it trying to tell him?

"God alone knows," he said, groaning in his sleep and aware that he was groaning. "God alone knows why I awoke and glimpsed enough of pre-resurrection life—of the limbo between the first death and the second birth—to know that this life is not the result of super-natural powers but is the workings—however mysterious—of beings with a science far beyond that of my time."

Events were fuzzy and encapsulated. A lightning streak of himself in the unmeasurable chamber of floating bodies; another flash of the nameless custodians finding him and putting him back to sleep; then a jerky synopsis of the dream he had had just before the true resurrection on the banks of the river.

God—a beautiful old man in a beard and the clothes of a mid-Victorian gentleman of means and breeding—was poking him in the ribs with an iron cane and telling him that *he owed for his flesh*.

"What? What flesh?" said Burton, dimly aware that he was muttering in his sleep. He could not hear his words in the dream.

"Pay up!" God said. His face melted, then was recast into Burton's own features.

God had not answered in the first dream some five years before. He spoke now: "Make your resurrection worth my while, you fool! I have gone to great expense and even greater pains to give you, and all those other miserable and worthless wretches, a second chance."

"Second chance at what?" Burton replied. He felt frightened at what God might answer. He was much relieved when God the All-Father—only now did Burton see that one eye of Jahweh-Odin was gone; out of the empty socket glared the flames of hell—did not reply. He was gone—no, not gone but metamorphosed into a high gray tower, cylindrical and soaring out of gray mists with the roar of the sea coming up through the mists.

"The Grail!" He saw again the man who had told him of the Big Grail. This man had heard it from another man, who had heard of it from a woman, who had heard it from, and so forth. The Big Grail was one of the legends told by the billions who lived along the river—this river that coiled like a serpent around this planet from pole to pole, issued from the unreachable and plunged into the inaccessible.

A man, some said a subhuman, had managed to climb through the mountains to the North Pole. And he had seen the Big Grail, the Dark Tower, the Misty Castle just before he had stumbled. Some said he was pushed. At any rate, he had fallen headlong and bellowing into the cold seas beneath the mists and died. And then the man, or subhuman, had awakened again along the river. Death was not forever here, although it had lost nothing of its sting.

He had told of his vision. And the story had traveled along the valley of the river faster than a boat could sail, and everybody seemed to have heard of it.

Thus the man now dreaming—Richard Francis Burton, the discover of Lake Tanganyika, the eternal pilgrim and wanderer

—had longed to storm the ramparts of the Big Grail. He would
unveil the secret of resurrection and of this planet, since he was
convinced that the beings who had reshaped this world had also
built that tower.

"Die, Hermann Goering! Die, and leave me in peace!" a man
shouted in German.

Burton opened his eyes. He could see nothing except the pale
sheen of the multitudinous and jampacked stars through the open
window across the room of the hut.

His vision bent to the shape of the black things inside, and he saw
Peter Frigate and Loghu sleeping on their mats by the opposite wall.
He turned his head to see the white, blanket-sized towel under which
Alice Liddell slept. The whiteness of her face was turned towards
him, and the black cloud of her hair spilled out on the ground by
her mat.

That same evening, the single-masted boat on which the four had
been sailing down the river had put into a friendly shore. The little
state of Sevieria was inhabited largely by 16th-century Englishmen,
although its chief was an American who had lived in the late 18th
and early 19th century. John Sevier, founder of the "lost state" of
Franklin, which had later become Tennessee, had welcomed Burton
and his party.

Sevier and his people did not believe in slavery and would not
detain any guest longer than he desired. After permitting them to
charge their grails and so feed themselves, Sevier had invited them
to a party given by the state. It was the celebration of Resurrection
Day; afterwards he had had them conducted to the guest hostelry.

Here Burton and the others had gone to bed. But Burton was
always a light sleeper, and now he was an uneasy one. He had
not been able to fight off wakefulness. The others began breathing
deeply or snoring long before he had succumbed to weariness. And
after an interminable dream, he had wakened on hearing the voice
that had interlocked with his dreams.

Hermann Goering, Burton thought. He had last seen Goering
during the revolt of the Israeli slaves against the German and
his co-chief, Tullios Hostilios, once third king of ancient Rome.
Burton himself had killed Goering, but Goering must be alive again
somewhere along the river. Was the man groaning and shouting in
the neighboring hut one who had also suffered because of Goering,
either on Earth or in the rivervalley?

Burton threw off the black towel and rose swiftly but noiselessly.
He secured a cloth around his loins with magnetic tabs, fastened a

belt of human skin around his waist, and made sure the human-leather scabbard held the flint poignard. Carrying an assegai, a short length of hardwood tipped with a flint point, he left the hut.

The sky was moonless, but it cast a light brighter than the full moon of Earth had ever achieved. It was aflame with huge many-colored stars and pale sheets of cosmic gas, so crowded that it was impossible to determine constellations or sky-marks. The brilliance was strong enough to read by, but on this world of scanty resources and limited technologies, there were no books or newspapers.

The hostelries were set back a mile and a half from the river and placed on one of the second row of hills that edged the river-plain. There were seven of the one-room, leaf-thatch-roofed, bamboo buildings. At a distance, under the enormous branches of the indestructible irontrees or under the giant pines or oaks, were other huts. A half-mile away, on top of a high hill, was a large circular stockade, colloquially termed the "Roundhouse." There the officials of Sevieria and a part of the army slept.

Across the plain, near the river-edge, were the grail-rocks, mushroom-shaped formations of granite. These were spaced every mile on both sides of the river. Three times a day, they discharged the enormous voltages that were converted by the so-called grails into food, liquor, tobacco and narcotics.

There were also high towers of bamboo placed every half-mile along the river shore. Torches flamed all night long on the platforms from which sentinels kept a look-out for invaders.

After scrutinizing the shadows under the trees, Burton walked a few steps to the hut from which the groans and shouts had come.

He pushed the grass curtain aside. The starlight fell through the open window on the face of the sleeper. Burton hissed in surprise. The light revealed the blondish hair and the broad features of a youth he recognized.

Burton moved slowly on bare feet. The sleeper groaned and threw one arm over his face and half-turned. Burton stopped until he was sure that the youth was not faking. Then he resumed his stealthy progress. He placed the assegai on the ground, drew his dagger, and gently thrust the point against the hollow of the throat. The arm flopped over; the eyes opened and stared into Burton's. Burton clamped his hand over the man's open mouth.

"Hermann Goering! Don't move or try to yell! I'll kill you!"

Goering's light-blue eyes looked dark in the shadows, but the paleness of his terror shone out. He quivered and started to sit up, then sank back as the flint dug into his skin.

"How long have you been here?" Burton said. He knew that Goering had not been among the guests at Sevier's party.

"Who . . .?" Goering said in English, then his eyes opened even wider. "Richard Burton? Am I dreaming? Is that you?"

Burton could smell the dreamgum on Goering's breath and the sweat-soaked mat on which he lay. The German was much thinner than the last time he had seen him, when he was gorging himself with the food and liquor from the grails of his prisoners.

Goering said. "I don't know how long I've been here. What time is it?"

"About an hour until dawn, I'd say. It's the day after Resurrection Celebration."

"Then I've been here three days," Goering said. "Could I have a drink of water? My throat's dry as a sarcophagus."

"No wonder. You're a living sarcophagus—if you're addicted to dreamgum."

Burton stood up, gesturing with the assegai at a fired-clay pot on a little bamboo table nearby. "You can drink if you want to. But don't try anything."

Goering rose slowly and staggered to the table. "I'm too weak to give you a fight, even if I wanted to." He drank noisily from the pot and then picked up an apple from the table. Between bites, he said, "What're you doing here? I thought I was rid of you."

"You answer my question first," Burton said, "and be quick about it. You pose a problem that I don't like, you know."

2

Goering started chewing, stopped, stared, then said, "Why should I? I don't have any position of power here, and I couldn't do anything to you if I did. I'm just a guest here. Damned decent people, these; they haven't bothered me at all except to ask if I'm all right now and then. Though I don't know how long they'll let me stay without earning my keep."

"You haven't left the hut?" Burton said. "Then who charged your grail for you? How'd you get so much dreamgum?"

Goering smiled slyly. "I had a big collection from the last place I stayed; somewhere about a thousand miles up the river."

"Doubtless taken forcibly from some poor slaves," Burton said. "But if you were doing so well there, why did you leave?"

Goering began to weep. Tears ran down his face, and over his collarbones—he was naked—and down his chest, and his shoulders shook.

"I . . . I had to get out. I wasn't any good to the others. I was losing my hold over them—spending too much time drinking, smoking marijuana and chewing dreamgum. They said I was too soft on the slaves—and getting too soft myself. They would have killed me or, worse, made me a slave. So I sneaked out one night . . . took the boat, I got away all right and kept going until I put into here. I traded part of my supply to Sevier for two weeks' sanctuary. He agreed to let me alone, let me wrestle with myself until my gum ran out."

Burton stared curiously at Goering. He certainly was not the powerful man that he had known.

"You knew what would happen if you took too much gum," he said. "Nightmares, hallucinations, delusions. Total mental and physical deterioration. You must have seen it happen to others."

"I was a morphine addict on Earth!" Goering cried. "I struggled with it, and I won out for a long time. Then, when things began to go badly for the Third Reich—and even worse for myself—when Hitler began frowning at me, I started taking drugs again!

"But here, when I woke up to a new life, in a young body, when it looked as if I had an eternity of life and youth ahead of me, when there was no stern God in Heaven or Devil in Hell to stop me, I thought I could do exactly as I pleased and get away with it. I would become even greater than the Fuehrer! That little country in which you first found me was to be only the beginning! I could see my empire stretching for thousands of miles up and down the river, on both sides of the valley. I would have been the ruler of ten times the subjects that Hitler ever dreamed of!"

He began weeping again, then paused to take another drink of water, then put a piece of the dreamgum in his mouth. He chewed, his face becoming more relaxed and blissful with each second. Burton hastened to talk to him.

"Why did you take to the gum? Millions use it every day and manage to moderate the habit. But some can't stay away from abuse of it, and you seem to be one of these."

"I kept having nightmares of you plunging the spear into my belly. When I woke up, my belly would hurt as if a genuine flint had gone into my guts, not one of the stuff of dreams. So I'd take gum to remove the hurt and the humiliation suffered by having you kick my ambitions to smithereens. At first, the gum helped. I was great. I was master of the world, Hitler, Napoleon, Julius Caesar, Alexander, Genghis Khan rolled into one. I was even chief again of von Richthofen's Red Death Squadron; those were happy days, the happiest of my life in many ways. But the euphoria soon gave way to hideousness. I plunged into hell; I saw myself accusing myself and behind the accuser a million others. Not myself but the victims of that great and glorious hero, that obscene madman Hitler, whom I worshipped so and in whose names I committed so many crimes."

"You admit you were a criminal?" Burton said. "That's a story different than the one you used to give me. Then you said you were justified in all you did, and you were betrayed by the—"

He stopped, realizing that he had been sidetracked from his original purpose. "That you should be haunted with the specter of a conscience is rather incredible. But perhaps that explains what has puzzled the puritans—why liquor, tobacco, marijuana and dreamgum were offered in the grails along with food. At least, dreamgum seems to be a gift boobytrapped with danger to those who abuse it."

He stepped closer to Goering. The German's eyes were half-closed, and his jaw hung open.

"Earlier, I said you presented a problem. You know my identity. I am traveling under a pseudonym, with good reason. You remember Spruce, one of your slaves? After you were killed, he was revealed, quite by accident, as one of the Ethicals, the people who terraformed this planet into one huge rivervalley and who somehow resurrected all the dead of humanity. Goering, are you listening?"

Goering nodded.

"Spruce killed himself before we could get out of him all we wanted to know. Later, some of his compatriots came to our area and temporarily put everybody to sleep—probably with a gas—intending to take me away to wherever their headquarters are. But they missed me. I was off on a trading trip up the river. When I returned, I realized they were after me, and I've been running ever since. Goering, do you hear me?"

Burton slapped him savagely on his cheek. Goering said, "Ach!" and jumped back and held the side of his face. His eyes were open, and he was grimacing.

"I heard you!" he snarled. "It just didn't seem worthwhile to answer back. Nothing seemed worthwhile, nothing except floating away, far from . . ."

"Shut up and listen!" Burton said. "The Ethicals have men everywhere looking for me. I can't afford to have you alive, do you realize that? I can't trust you. Even if you were a friend, you couldn't be trusted. You're a gummer!"

Goering giggled, stepped up to Burton and tried to put his arms around Burton's neck. Burton pushed him back so hard that he staggered up against the table and only kept from falling by clutching its edges. Again he giggled.

"This is very amusing," he said. "The day I got here, a man asked me if I'd seen you. He described you in detail and gave your name. I told him I knew you well—too well, and that I hoped I'd never see you again, not unless I had you in my power, that is. He said I should notify him if I saw you again. He'd make it worth my while."

Burton wasted no time. He strode up to Goering and seized him with both hands. They were small and delicate for such a powerful man, but they could be like a crab's claws. Goering winced with pain and said, "What're you going to do, kill me again?"

"Not if you tell me the name of the man who asked you about me. Otherwise . . ."

"Go ahead and kill me!" Goering said. "So what? I'll wake up somewhere else, thousands of miles from here, far out of your reach."

Burton pointed at a bamboo box in a corner of the hut. Guessing that it held Goering's supply of gum, he said, "And you'd also wake up without that! Where else could you get so much on such short notice?"

Goering said, "Damn you!" and tried to tear himself loose to get to the box.

"Tell me his name!" Burton said. "Or I'll take the gum and throw it in the river!"

"Agneau. Roger Agneau," Goering said swiftly. "He sleeps in a hut just outside the Roundhouse."

"I'll deal with you later," Burton said, chopped Goering on the side of the neck with the edge of his palm.

He had no sooner let the limp body down than he saw a man crouching outside the entrance to his hut. He withdrew from the curtain, but the stranger must have seen the curtains move out of the corner of his eye. He straightened up and was off like an arrow. Burton ran out after him; in a minute both were in the tall pines and oaks of the hills. His quarry disappeared in the waist-high, tough-fibered grass that grew only on the hills.

Burton slowed to a trot, caught sight of a patch of white—starlight on bare skin—and was off after the fellow. He hoped that the Ethical would not kill himself at once, because he had a plan for extracting information if he could knock him out at once. It involved hypnosis, at which Burton was an adept. But he would have to catch the Ethical first and very quickly. It was possible that the man had some sort of wireless imbedded in his body and was even now in communication with his compatriots—wherever they were. If so, they would come in their flying machines, and he would be lost.

For several minutes he thought he had lost his quarry and that the only thing to do now was to rouse Alice and the others and flee the area. Perhaps this time they should take to the mountains and hide there for a while.

But first he would go to Agneau's hut. There was little chance that Agneau would be there, but it was certainly worth the effort.

3

Burton arrived within sight of the hut just in time to glimpse the back of a man entering it. Burton circled to come up from the side where the darkness of hills and the trees scattered along the plain gave him some concealment. Crouching, he ran until he was at the door to the hut.

He heard a loud cry some distance behind him and whirled to see Goering staggering towards him. He was crying out in German to Agneau, warning him that Burton was just outside. In one hand he held a long spear which he brandished at the Englishman.

Burton turned and hurled himself against the flimsy bamboo-slat door. His shoulder drove into it and broke it from its wooden hinges. The door flew inward and struck Agneau, who had been standing just behind it. Burton, the door and Agneau fell to the floor with Agneau under the door.

Burton rolled off the door, rose, and jumped again with both bare feet on the wood. Agneau screamed and then became silent. Burton heaved the door to one side to find his quarry unconscious and bleeding from the nose. Good! Now if the noise didn't bring the watch and if he could deal quickly enough with Goering, he could carry out his plan.

He looked up just in time to see the starlight on the long black object hurtling at him.

He threw himself to one side, and the spear plunged into the dirt floor with a thump. Its shaft vibrated like a rattlesnake preparing to strike.

Burton stepped into the doorway, estimated Goering's distance and charged his assegai. Its flint plunged into the belly of the German. Goering threw his hands up in the air, screamed, and fell on his side. Burton hoisted Agneau's limp body on his shoulder and carried him out of the hut.

By then there were shouts from the Roundhouse. Torches were flaring up; the sentinel on the nearest watchtower was bellowing. Goering was sitting on the ground, bent over, clutching the shaft close to the wound.

He looked gape-mouthed at Burton and said, "You did it again! You . . ."

He fell over on his face, the death rattle in his throat.

At that moment, Agneau returned to a frenzied consciousness. He twisted himself out of Burton's grip, rolled off his shoulder, fell to the ground. Unlike Goering, he made no noise. He had as much reason to be silent as Burton—more perhaps. Burton was so surprised that he was left standing with the fellow's loin-towel clutched in his hand. Burton went to throw it down but felt something stiff and square within the lining of the towel. He transferred the cloth to his left hand, yanked the assegai from the corpse and ran after Agneau.

The Ethical had launched one of the bamboo canoes beached along the shore. He paddled furiously out into the starlit waters, glancing frequently behind him. Burton raised the assegai behind his shoulder and hurled it. It was a short, thick-shafted weapon, designed for infighting and not as a javelin. But it flew straight and came down at the end of its trajectory in Agneau's back. The Ethical fell forward and at an angle and tipped the narrow craft over. The canoe turned upside down. Agneau did not reappear.

Burton grimaced with disappointment. He had wanted to capture Agneau alive, but he was damned if he would permit the Ethical to escape. There was a chance that Agneau had not contacted other Ethicals yet.

He turned back toward the guest huts. Drums were beating up and down along the shore, and people with burning torches were hastening toward the Roundhouse in answer to the alarm. Burton stopped a woman and asked if he could borrow her torch a moment. She handed it to him but spouted questions at him. He answered that he thought the Choctaws across the river were making a raid. She hurried off towards the assembly before the stockade.

Burton drove the pointed end of the torch into the soft dirt of the bank and examined the towel he had snatched from Agneau. On the inside, just above the hard square in the lining, was a seam sealed with two thin magnetic strips, easily opened. He took the object out of the lining and looked at it by the torchlight.

For a long time he squatted by the shifting light, unable to stop looking or to subdue an almost paralyzing astonishment. A photograph, in this world of no cameras, was unheard-of. But a photograph of *him* was even more incredible, as was the fact that the picture had not been taken on this world! It had to have been made on Earth, that Earth lost now in the welter of stars somewhere in the blazing sky and in God only knew how many thousands of years of time.

Impossibility piled on impossibility! But it was taken at a time and at a place when he knew for certain that no camera had fixed upon him and preserved his image. His mustachioes had been touched away to make him look more like the beardless man he now was. But the retoucher had not bothered to opaque the background nor his clothing. There he was, caught miraculously from the waist up and imprisoned in a flat piece of some material. Flat! When he turned the square, he saw his profile come into view. If he held it almost at right angles to the eye, he could get a three-quarters profile-view of himself.

"1848," he muttered to himself. "When I was a 27 year old subaltern in the East Indian Army. And those are the blue mountains of Goa. This must have been taken when I was convalescing there. But, my God, how? By whom? And how would the Ethicals manage to have it in their possession now?"

Agneau had evidently carried this photo as a mnemonic in his quest for Burton. Probably every one of his hunters had one just like it, concealed in his towel. Up and down the river they were looking for him; there might be thousands, perhaps tens of thousands. Who knew how many agents they had available or how desperately they wanted him or *why* they wanted him?

It had something to do with the fact that he had awakened in that pre-resurrection chamber. They were very much upset by this. Perhaps they were as mystified by him as he was by them. Whatever their reasons, they considered him to be a potential danger. He might find out why if he was taken by them. He also might not like the reason.

Whatever it was, he did not intend to be caught.

After replacing the photo in the towel, he turned to go back to the hut. And at that moment his gaze turned toward the top of the mountains—those unscalable heights that bounded the river valley on both sides.

He saw something flicker against a bright sheet of cosmic gas. It appeared for only the blink of an eye-lid, then was gone.

A few seconds later it came out of nothing, was revealed as a hemispherical and dark object, then disappeared again. This time it was lower, just above the top of the mountain range. If it appeared again, it would be hidden against the dark bulk of the mountains.

But a second flying craft showed itself briefly, reappeared at a lower elevation, and then was gone like the first.

Burton did not wonder about the flying machines. They were bringing the Ethicals. They would take him away, and the people of Sevieria would wonder what had made them fall asleep for an hour or so.

He did not have time to return to the hut and wake the others up. If he waited a moment longer, he would be trapped.

He turned and ran into the river and began swimming toward the other shore, a mile and a half away. But he had gone no more than forty yards when he felt the presence of some huge bulk above. He turned on his back to stare upwards. There was only the soft glare of the stars above. Then, out of the air, fifty feet above him, a disk with a diameter of about sixty feet cut out a section of the sky. It disappeared almost immediately, came into sight again only twenty feet above him.

So they had some means of seeing at a distance in the night and had spotted him in his flight.

"You jackals!" he shouted at them. "You'll not get me anyway!"

He upended and dived and swam straight downwards. The water became colder, and his eardrums began to hurt. Althought his eyes were open, he could see nothing. Suddenly he was pushed by a wall of water, and he knew that the pressure came from displacement by a big object.

The craft had plunged down after him.

There was only one way out. They would have his dead body, but that would be all. He could escape them again, be alive somewhere on the river to outwit them again and strike back at them.

He opened his mouth and breathed in deeply through both his nose and mouth.

The water choked him. Only by a strong effort of will did he keep from closing his lips and trying to fight back against the death around him. He knew with his mind that he would live again, but the cells of his body did not know it. They were striving for life at this second, not in the rationalized future. And they forced from his water-choked throat a cry of despair.

4

The Polar Station

"Yaaaaaaaah!"

The cry raised him off the grass as if he had bounced up off a trampoline. Unlike the first time he had been resurrected, he was not weak and bewildered. He knew what to expect. He would wake on the grassy banks of the river near a grailstone. But he was not prepared for this war of giants in the center of which he found himself.

His first thought was to find a weapon. There was nothing at hand except the grail that always appeared with a resurrectee and the pile of towels of various sizes, colors and thickness. He took one step, seized the handle of the grail and waited. If he had to, he would use the grail as a club. It was light, but it was practically indestructible and very hard.

However, the monsters around him looked as if they could take a grail's battering all day and not feel a thing.

Most of them were at least seven feet tall, some were surely over eight; their massively muscled shoulders were over three feet broad. Their bodies were human, or nearly so, and their white skins were covered with long reddish or brownish hairs. They were not as hairy as a chimpanzee but more so than any man he had ever seen, and he had known some remarkably hirsute human beings.

But the faces gave them an unhuman and frightening aspect, especially since all were snarling with battle-rage. Below a low forehead was a bloom of bone that ran without indentation above the eyes and then continued around to form an O. Though the eyes were as large as his, they looked small compared to the broad face in which they were set. The cheekbones billowed out and then curved sharply inwards. The tremendous nose gave the giants the appearance of a proboscis monkey.

At another time, Burton might have been amused by them. Not now. The roars that tore out of their more-than-gorilla-sized chests were deep as a lion's, and the huge teeth would have made a Kodiak bear think twice before attacking. Their fists, large as his head, held clubs thick and long as wagonpoles or stone axes. They swung their weapons at each other, and when they struck flesh, bones broke with cracks loud as wood splitting. Sometimes the clubs broke, too.

Burton had a moment in which to look around. The light was weak. The sun had only half-risen above the peaks across the river. The air was far colder than any he had felt on this planet except during his defeated attempts to climb to the top of the perpendicular ranges.

Then one of the victors of a combat looked around for another enemy and saw him.

His eyes widened. For a second, he looked as startled as Burton had when he had first opened his eyes. Perhaps he had never seen such a creature as Burton before, any more than Burton had seen one like him. If so, he did not take long to get over his surprise. He bellowed, jumped over the mangled body of his foe and ran toward Burton, raising an axe that could have felled an aurochs.

Burton also ran, his grail in one hand. If he were to lose that, he might as well die anyway. Without it he would either starve or else have to eke out on fish and bamboo sprouts.

He almost made it. An opening appeared before him, and he sped between two titans, their arms around each other and each straining to throw over the other, and another who was backing away before the rain of blows delivered by the club of a fourth. Just as he was almost through, the two wrestlers toppled over on him.

He was going swiftly enough that he was not caught directly under them, but the flailing arm of one struck his left heel. So hard was the blow, it smashed his foot against the ground and stopped him instantly. He fell forward and began to scream. His foot must have been broken, and he had torn the muscles of his thighs.

Nevertheless he tried to rise and to hobble on to the river. Once in it, he could swim away, if he did not faint from the agony. He took two hops on his right foot, only to be seized from behind.

Up into the air he flew, whirling around, and was caught before he began his descent.

The titan was holding him with one hand at arm's length, the enormous and powerful fist clutched around Burton's chest. Burton could hardly breathe, his ribs threatened to cave in.

Despite all this, he had not dropped his grail. Now he raised it against the giant's shoulder.

Lightly, as if brushing off a fly, the giant tapped the metal container with his axe, and the grail was torn from Burton's grip.

The behemoth grinned and bent his arm to bring Burton in closer. Burton weighed one hundred and eighty pounds, but the arm did not quiver under the strain.

For a moment, Burton looked directly into the pale blue eyes sunk in the bony circles. The nose was hairless and lined here and there with many broken veins. The lips protruded because of the bulging prognathous jaws beneath—not, as he had first thought, because the lips were so thick.

Then the titan bellowed and lifted Burton up above his head. Burton hammered the huge arm with his fists, knowing that he made a vain gesture but unwilling to submit like a caught rabbit. Even as he did so, he noted, though not with the full attention of his mind, several things about this scene.

The sun had been just rising above the mountain peaks when he had first awakened. Although the time passed since he had jumped to his feet was only a few minutes, the sun should have cleared the peaks. It had not; it hung at exactly the same height as when he had first seen it.

Moreover, the upward slant of the valley permitted a view for at least four miles. The grailrock by him was the last one. Beyond it was only the plain and the river.

This was the end of the line—or the beginning of the river.

There was no time nor desire for him to appreciate what these meant. He merely noted these during the passage between pain, rage, and terror. Then, as the giant prepared to bring his axe around to splinter Burton's skull, he stiffened and shrieked. It was like being next to a locomotive whistle, deafening. The grip loosened, and Burton fell to the ground. For a moment, he passed out from the pain in his foot.

When he regained consciousness, he had to grind his teeth to keep from yelling again. He groaned and sat up, though not without a race of fire up his leg that made the feeble daylight grow almost black. The battle was roaring all around him, but he was in a little corner of inactivity. By him lay the tree-trunk-thick corpse of the titan who had been about to kill him. The back of his skull, which looked massive enough to resist a battering ram, was caved in.

Around the elephantine corpse crawled another casualty, on all fours. Seeing him, Burton forgot his pain for a moment. The horribly injured man was Hermann Goering.

Both of them had been resurrected at the same spot. Goering had suffered the same fate as he. There was no time to think about the implications of the coincidence. His pain began to come back.

Moreover, Goering started to talk.

Not that he looked as if he had much talk left in him or much time to talk. Blood covered him. His right eye was gone. The corner of his mouth was ripped back to his ear. One of his hands was smashed flat. A rib was sticking through the skin. How he had managed to stay alive, let alone crawl, was beyond Burton's understanding.

"You . . . you!" Goering said hoarsely in German, and he collapsed. A fountain poured out of his mouth and over Burton's legs; his eyes glazed; he was dead.

Burton wondered if he would ever know what he had intended to say. Not that it really mattered. He had more vital things to think about.

About ten yards from him, two titans were standing with their backs to him. Both were breathing hard, apparently resting for a moment before they jumped back into the fight. Then one spoke to the other.

There was no doubt about it. The giant was not just uttering cries. He was using a language.

Burton did not understand it, but he knew it was speech. He did not need the modulated, distinctly syllabic reply of the other to confirm his recognition.

So these were not some type of prehistoric ape but a species of subhuman men. They must have been unknown to the 20th-century science of Earth, since his friend, Frigate, had described to him all the known fossils.

He lay down with his back against the fallen giant's Gothic ribs and brushed some of the long reddish sweaty hairs from his face. He fought nausea and the agony of his foot and the torn muscles of his thighs. If he made too much noise, he might attract those two, and they would finish the job. But what if they did? With his wounds, in a land of such monsters, what chance did he have of surviving?

Worse than his agony of foot, almost, was the thought that on his first trip on the suicide express he had reached his goal.

He had had only an estimated one chance in ten million of arriving at this area, and he might never have made it if he had drowned himself ten thousand times. Yet he had had fantastically good fortune. It might never occur again. And he was to lose it and very soon.

The sun had not risen, but it was moving half-revealed along the tops of the mountains across the river. This was the place that he had speculated would exist; he had come here first shot. Now, as his eyesight failed and the pain lessened, he knew that he was dying. The sickness was born from more than the shattered bones in his foot. He must be bleeding inside.

He tried to rise once more. He would stand, if only on one foot, and shake his fist at the mocking fates and curse them. He would die with a curse on his lips; death might chill him but he would go with the fiery dawn.

5

The Second Station

The red wing of the dawn lightly touching his eyes.

He rose to his feet, knowing that his wounds would be healed and he would be whole again but not quite believing it. Near him was a grail and a pile of six neatly folded towels of various sizes, colors and thicknesses.

Twelve feet away, another man, also naked, was rising from the short bright-green grass that grew everywhere on the river plain. Burton hissed with shock, and his skin grew cold. The blondish hair, broad face and light-blue eyes were those of Hermann Goering.

The German looked as surprised as Burton. He spoke slowly, as if coming out of a deep sleep. "There's something very wrong here."

"Something foul indeed," Burton replied. He knew no more of the pattern of resurrection along the river than any other man. He had never witnessed any, but he had had them described to him by those who had seen them. At dawn, just after the sun topped the unclimbing mountains, a shimmering appeared in the air beside a grailstone. In the flicker of a bird's wing, the distortion solidified, and a naked man or woman or child had appeared from nowhere on the grass by the bank. Always the indispensable grail and the towels were by the "lazarus," having popped out of their own little shimmerings.

Along a conceivably ten to twenty million-mile long rivervalley in which an estimated 35 to 40 billion lived, a million could die per day. It was true that there were no diseases (other than mental) but, though statistics were lacking, a million were probably killed every twenty-four hours by the myriads of wars between the thousand thousand little states, by crimes of passion, by suicides, by executions of criminals and by accidents. There was a steady and numerous traffic of those undergoing the "little resurrection," as it was called. A man died somewhere along the river, and he woke up the next day somewhere else, far from the place of his death.

But never had Burton heard of two dying in the same place and at the same time being resurrected together. The process of selection of area for the new life was random—or so he had always thought.

One such occurrence could conceivably take place, although the probabilities were one in 20 million. But two such, one immediately after the other, was a miracle.

Burton did not believe in miracles. Nothing happened that could not be explained by physical principles—if you knew all the facts.

He did not know them, so he would not worry about the "coincidence" at the moment. The solution to another problem was more demanding. That was, what was he to do about Goering?

The man knew him and could identify him to any Ethicals searching for him.

Burton looked quickly around him and saw a number of men and women approaching (seemingly friendly). There was time for a few words with the German.

"Goering, I can kill you or myself. But I don't want to do either—at the moment, anyway. You know why you're dangerous to me. I shouldn't take a chance with you, you treacherous hyena. But there's something different about you, something I can't put my fingers on. But . . ."

Goering, a fellow notorious for his resilience, seemed to be coming out of his shock. He grinned slyly and said, "I do have you over the barrel, don't I?"

Seeing Burton's snarl, he hastily put up one hand and said, "But I swear to you I won't reveal your identity to anyone! Or do anything to hurt you. Look! Maybe we're not friends, but we at least know each other, and we're in a land of strangers. It's good to have one familiar face by your side. I know. I've suffered too long from loneliness, from desolation of the spirit. I thought I'd go mad. That's partly the reason I took to the dreamgum. Believe me, I won't betray you."

Burton did not believe him. He did think, however, that he could trust him for a while. Goering would want a potential ally, at least until he took the measure of the people in this area and knew what he could or could not do. Besides, Goering might have changed for the better.

No, Burton said to himself. No. There you go again. Verbal cynic though you are, you've always been too forgiving, too ready to overlook injury to yourself and to give your injurer another chance. Don't be a fool again, Burton.

Three days later, he was still uncertain about the man.

Burton had taken the name of Abdul ibn Harun, a 19th-century citizen of Cairo, Egypt. He had several reasons for adopting this guise. One was that he spoke excellent Arabic, knew the Cairo of that period, and had an excuse to cover his head with a towel wrapped as a turban. He hoped this would help disguise his appearance. Goering did not say a word to anybody to contradict the camouflage. Burton was fairly sure of this because he and Goering spent most of their time together. They were quartered in the same hut until they adjusted to the local customs and went through their period of probation. Part of this was intensive military training. Since Burton had been one of the greatest swordsmen of the 19th century and also knew every inflection of fighting with weapons or with hands, he was welcomed as a recruit. In fact, he was promised that he would be an instructor when he learned the language well enough.

Goering got the respect of the locals almost as swiftly. Whatever his other faults, he did not lack courage. He was strong and proficient with arms, jovial, likeable when it suited his purpose, and was not far behind Burton in gaining fluency in the language. He was quick to gain and to use authority, as befitted the ex-Reichmarschal of Hitler's Germany.

This section of the western shore was populated largely by speakers of a language totally unknown even to Burton, a master linguist both on Earth and on the riverplanet. When he had learned enough to ask questions, he deduced that they must have lived somewhere in Central Europe of the Early Bronze Age. They had some curious customs, one of which was public sex. This was interesting enough to Burton, who had co-founded the Royal Anthropological Society in London in 1863 and who had seen some strange things during his explorations in the Old and the New World of Earth. He did not participate but neither was he horrified.

A custom he did adopt joyfully was that of stained whiskers. The males resented the fact that their face hair had been permanently removed by the resurrectors, just as they willynilly had had their prepuces cut off. They could do nothing about the latter outrage, but they could correct the former to a degree. This they did by smearing their upper lips and chins with a dark liquid made from finely ground charcoal, fish glue, oak tannin and several other ingredients. The more dedicated used the dye as a tattoo and underwent a painful and long-drawn-out pricking with a sharp bamboo needle.

Now Burton was doubly disguised; yet he had put himself at the mercy of the man who might betray him at the first opportunity. He had good reason for this in that he wanted to attract an Ethical but did not want the Ethical to be certain of his identity. If the Ethical thought his quarry was trying to disguise himself, he would not smell a trap.

Burton wanted to make sure that he could get away in time before being scooped up in the net. It was a dangerous game, like walking a tightrope over a pit of hungry wolves, but Burton wanted to play it. He would run only when it became absolutely necessary. The rest of the time, he would be the hunted hunting the hunter.

Yet the vision of the Dark Tower, or the Big Grail, was always on the horizon of every thought. Why play cat and mouse when he might be able to storm the very ramparts of the castle within which he presumed the Ethicals had headquarters? Or, if stormed was not the correct description, steal into the tower, effect entrance as a mouse does into a house—or a castle. While the cats were looking elsewhere, the mouse would be sneaking into the Tower, and there the mouse might turn into a tiger.

At this thought, he laughed and earned curious stares from his two hutmates: Goering and the 17th-century Englishman, John Collop. His laugh was half-ridicule of himself at the tiger image. What made him think that he, one man, could do anything to hurt the planet-shapers, resurrectors of billions of dead, feeders and maintainers of those summoned back to life? He twisted his hands and knew that within them, and within the brain that guided them, could be the downfall of the Ethicals. What it was he harbored within himself, he did not know. But they feared him. If he could only find out why . . .

His laugh was only partly self-ridicule. The other half of him believed that he was a tiger among men. *As a man thinks, so is he*, he muttered.

Goering, who had started to wash his face and hands in a clay bowl on the bamboo table, jumped when Burton laughed. He turned and said, "You have a very peculiar laugh, my friend. Somewhat feminine for such a masculine man. It's like . . . like a thrown rock skipping over a lake of ice. Or like a jackal."

"I have something of the jackal and hyena in me." Burton replied. "So my detractors maintained—and they were right. But I am more than that."

He rose from his bed and began to exercise to work the sleep-rust from his muscles. In a few minutes, he would go with the others to a grailstone by the river bank and charge the grails with food and the necessary luxuries so generously provided by the Ethicals.

Afterward there would be an hour of policing the area. Then drill, followed by instruction in the spear, the club, the sling, the obsidian-edged sword, the bow and arrow, the flint axe, and in fighting with bare hands and feet. An hour for rest and talk and lunch. Then an hour in a language class. A two-hour work-stint in helping build the ramparts that marked the boundaries of this little state. A half-hour rest, then the obligatory mile run to build stamina. Dinner from the grails, and the evening off except for those who had guard duty or other tasks.

Such a schedule and such activities were being duplicated in almost every one of the hundreds of thousands of tiny states up and down the river's length. Mankind almost everywhere was at war or preparing for it. The citizens must keep in shape and know how to fight to the best of their ability. The exercises also kept the citizens occupied. No matter how monotonous the martial life, it was better than sitting around wondering what to do for amusement. Freedom from worry about food, rent, bills, and the gnatlike chores and duties that had kept Earthmen busy and fretful was not all a blessing. There was the great battle against ennui, and the leaders of each state were occupied trying to think up ways to keep their people busy.

It should haven been paradise in rivervalley, but it was war, war, war. Other things aside, however, war was, in this place, good. It gave savor to life, erased boredom. Man's greediness and aggressiveness had its worthwhile side.

After dinner, every man and woman was free to do what he wished, as long as he broke no local laws. He could barter the cigarettes and liquor provided by his grail or the fish he'd caught in the river for a better bow and arrows; shields; bowls and cups; tables and chairs; bamboo flutes; clay trumpets; human or fishskin drums; rare stones (which really were rare); necklaces made of the beautifully articulated and colored bones of the deep-river fish, of jade or of carved wood; obsidian mirrors; sandals and shoes; charcoal drawings; the infrequent and expensive bamboo paper; ink and fishbone pens; hats made from the long and tough-fibered hill-grass; bullroarers; little wagons on which to ride down the hillsides; harps made from wood with strings fashioned from the gut of the biggest of the deep-river fish, the "river dragon;" rings of oak for fingers and toes; clay statuettes; and other devices, useful or ornamental, in a number surprising when the poverty of material and technology was considered.

Later, of course, there was the love-making. Burton and his hutmates were denied this for the time being. Only when they had been accepted as full citizens would they be allowed to move into separate houses and live with a woman.

John Collop was a short and slight youth with long yellow hair, a narrow but pleasant face and large blue eyes with very long, upcurving, black eyelashes. In his first conversation with Burton, he had said, after introducing himself, "I was delivered from the darkness of my mother's womb—whose else?—into the light of the God of Earth in 1625. Far too quickly, I descended again into the womb of Mother Nature, confident in the hope of resurrection and not disappointed, as you see. Though I must confess that this afterlife is not that which the parsons led me to expect. But then, how should they know the truth, poor blind devils leading the blind?"

It was not long before Collop told him that he was a member of the Church of the Second Chance.

On hearing this, Burton's eyebrows rose. He had encountered this newreligion at many places along the river. Burton, though a firm infidel, made it his business to investigate thoroughly every religion. Know a man's faith, and you knew at least half the man. Know his wife, and you knew the other half.

The Church had a few simple tenets, some based on fact, most on surmise and hope and wish. In this they differed from no religions born on Earth. But the Second Chancers had one advantage over any Terrestrial religion. They had no difficulty in proving that dead men could be raised—not only once but often.

"And why has mankind been given a Second Chance?" Collop said in his low, earnest voice. "Does he deserve it? No. With few exceptions, men are a mean, miserable, petty, vicious, narrow-minded, exceedingly egotistic, generally disgusting lot. Watching them, the gods – or God – should vomit. But in this divine spew is a clot of compassion, if you will pardon me for using such imagery. Man, however base, has a silver wire of the divine in him. It is no idle phrase that man was made in God's image. There is something worth saving in the worst of us, and out of this something a new man may be fashioned.

"Whoever has given us this new opportunity to save our souls knows this truth. We have been placed here in this rivervalley – on this alien planet under alien skies – to work out our salvation. What our time limit is, I do not know nor do the leaders of my Church even speculate. Perhaps it is forever, or it may be only a hundred years or a thousand. But we must make use of whatever time we do have, my friend."

"You're a lazarus also," Burton said, referring to Collop's translation, which had taken place two weeks before Burton's. "Weren't you sacrificed on the altar of Odin by Norse who clung to the old religion, even if this world isn't the Valhalla they were promised by their priests? Don't you think you wasted your time and breath by preaching to them? They believe n the same old gods, the only difference in their theology now being some adjustments they've made to conditions here. Just as you have clung to your old faith."

"The Norse have no explanations of their new surrounding," Collop said. "But I do. I have a reasonable explanation, one which the Norse will eventually come to accept, to believe in as fervently as I do. They killed me, but some more persuasive member of the Church will come along and talk to them before they stretch him out on the wooden lap of their wooden idol and stab him to the heart. If he does not talk them out of killing him, the next missionary after him will.

"It was true on Earth that the blood of the martyrs is the seed of the church. It is even truer here. For if you kill a man to shut his mouth, he pops up some place elsewhere along the river. And a man who has been martyred a hundred thousand miles away comes along to replace the previous martyr. The Church will win out in the end. Then men will cease these useless, hate-generating wars and begin the real business, the only worthwhile business, that of gaining salvation."

"What you say about the martyrs is true about anyone with an idea," Burton said. "A wicked man who's killed also pops up to commit his evil elsewhere."

"Good will prevail; the truth always wins out," Collop replied.

"I don't know how restricted your mobility was on Earth or how long your life," Burton said, "but both must have been very limited to make you so blind. I know better."

Collop ignored his words. "The Church is not founded on faith alone. It has something very factual, very substantial, on which to base its teachings. Tell me, my friend, Abdul, have you ever heard of anybody being translated dead?"

"A paradox!" Burton cried. "What do you mean – resurrected dead?"

"There are at least three authenticated cases and four more of which the Church has heard but has not been able to validate. These are men and women who were killed at one place on the river and translated to another. Strangely, their bodies were recreated, but they were without the spark of life. Now, why was this?"

"I can't imagine!" Burton said. "You tell me. I listen, for you speak with authority!"

He *could* imagine, since he had heard the same story elsewhere. But he wanted to learn if Collop's story matched the others.

It was the same, even to the names of the dead lazari. The story was that men and women had been identified by those who had known them well on Earth. They were all saintly or near-saintly people; in fact, one of them had been canonized. The theory was that they had attained that state of sanctity which made it no longer necessary to go through the "purgatory' of the riverplanet. Their souls had gone on to . . . someplace . . . and left the excess baggage of their physical bodies behind.

Soon, so the Church said, more would reach this state. And their bodies would be left behind. Eventually, given enough time, the river-valley would become depopulated. All would have shed themselves of their viciousnesses and hates and would have become illuminated with the love of mankind and of God. Even the most depraved, those who seemed to be utterly lost, would be able to abandon their physical beings. All that was needed to attain this grace was love.

Burton sighed, laughed loudly, and said, "Plus ça change, plus c'est la meme. Another fairy tale to give men hope. The old religions have been discredited – alghough some refuse to face even that fact – so new ones must be invented."

"It makes sense," Collop said. "Do you have a better explanation of why we're here?"

"Perhaps. I can make up fairy tales, too."

As a matter of fact, Burton did have an explanation. However, he could not tell it to Collop.

For a while he was silent, thinking of those few and utterly terrifying and bewildering moments, among the few in his life when he had known fear. Unaccountably, he had awakened and had seen the pre-resurrection phase. And after the resurrection on the surface of this planet, he had made friends with a subhuman, Kazz. Because this fellow was able to see a little further into the violet range of the spectrum than Homo Sapiens, he had detected the marks on the foreheads of the risen. Seemingly, these invisible marks were some sort of numbering or cataloging symbols.

It was Kazz who had pointed out to Burton a man who had no such symbol. That had resulted in the questioning of the man, Spruce. Under threat of torture, Spruce had told Burton something of the identity, history and purpose of his group, the Ethicals. Much of what he had said agreed with Collop's theology beliefs.

Spruce could have lied or have given a false picture with half-truths. Moreover, he had killed himself before he had explained about the "soul." Presumably, the "soul" had to be part of the total organization of resurrection. Otherwise, when the body had attained "salvation," and no longer lived, there would be nothing to carry on the essential part of a man. Since the post-Terrestrial life could be explained in physical terms, the "soul" must also be a physical entity, not to be dismissed with the term "supernatural" as it had been on Earth.

There was much that Burton did not know. But he had had a glimpse into the workings of this riverplanet that no other human being possessed.

With the little knowledge he did have, he planned to lever his way into more, to pry open the lid and crawl inside the sanctum. To do so, he would attain the Dark Tower. The only way to get there swiftly was to take what he was already mentally terming The Suicide Express. First he must be discovered by an Ethical. Then he must overpower the Ethical, render him unable to kill himself and somehow extricate more information from him.

Meanwhile, he continued to play the role of Abdul ibn Harun, translated and transplanted Egyptian physician of the 19th century, now a citizen of Bargawhwdzys. As such, he decided to join the Church of the Second Chance. He announced to Collop his disillusionment in Mahomet and his teachings, and so became Collop's first convert in this area.

"Then ye must swear not to take arms against any man nor to defend yourself physically, my dear friend," Collop said.

Burton, outraged, said that he would allow no man to strike at him and go unharmed.

"Tis not unnatural," Collop said gently. "Contrary to habit, yes. But a man may become something other than he has been, something better – if he has the strength of will and the desire."

Burton rapped out a violent no and stalked away. Collop shook his head sadly, but he continued to be as friendly as ever. Not without a sense of humor, he sometimes addressed Burton as his "five-minute convert," not meaning the time it took to bring him into the fold but the time it took Burton to leave the fold.

At this time, Collop got his second convert, Goering. The German who had nothing but sneers and jibes for Collop. Then he began chewing dreamgum, and the night-mares started.

For two nights he kept Collop and Burton awake with his groanings, his tossings, his screams. On the evening of the third day, he asked Collop if he would accept him into the Church. However, he had to make a confession. Collop must understand what sort of person he had been, both on Earth and on this planet.

Collop heard out the mixture of self-abasement and self-aggrandizement. Then he said, "Friend, I care not what ye may have been. Only what you are and what you will be. I listened only because confession is good for the soul. I can see that ye are deeply troubled, that ye have suffered sorrow and grief for what ye have done, yet take some pleasure in what ye once were, a mighty figure among men. Much of what you told me I do not comprehend, because I know not much about your era. Nor does it matter. Only today and tomorrow need be our concern; each day will take care of itself."

It seemed to Burton that Collop did not care what Goering had been but that he did not believe his story of Earthly glory and infamy. There were so many phonies that genuine heroes, or villains, had been depreciated. Too many had taken advantage of the universality of youth, itself a disguise, and the lack of communication, to set themselves up as great ones. Thus, Burton had met three Jesus Christs, two Abrahams, four King Richard the Lion-Hearteds, six Attilas, a dozen Judases (only one of whom could speak Aramic), a George Washington, two Lord Byrons, three Jesse Jameses, any number of Napoleons, a General Custer (who spoke with a heavy Yorkshire accent), a Finn MacCool (who did not know ancient Irish), a Tchaka (who spoke the wrong Zulu dialect) and a number of others who might or might not have been what they claimed to be.

Whatever a man had been on Earth, he had to reestablish himself here. This was not easy, because conditions were radically altered. The greats and the importants of Terra were constantly being humiliated in their claims and denied a chance to prove their identities.

To Collop, the humiliation was a blessing. First, humiliatiion, then humility, he would have said. And then comes humanity as a matter of course.

Goering had been trapped in the Great Design – as Burton termed it – because it was his nature to overindulge, especially with drugs. Knowing that the dreamgum was uprooting the dark things in his personal abyss, was spewing them up into the light, that he was being torn apart, fragmented, he still continued to chew as much as he could. For a while, temporarily made healthful again with a new resurrection, he had been able to deny the call of the drug.

But a few weeks after his arrival in this area he had succumbed, and now the night was ripped apart with his shrieks of "Hermann Goering, I hate you!"

"If this continues," Burton said to Collop, "he will go mad. Or he will kill himself again, or force someone to kill him, so that he can get away from himself. But the suicide will be useless, and it's all to do over again. Tell me truly, now, is this not hell?"

"Purgatory, rather," Collop said. "Purgatory is hell with hope."

8

Two months passed. Burton marked the days off on a pine stick notched with a flint knife. The 14th day of the seventh month of 5 A.R., the fifth year after the resurrection. Burton tried to keep a calendar, for he was, among many other things, a chronicler. But it was difficult. Time did not mean much on the river. The planet had a polar axis that was always at ninety degrees to the ecliptic. There was no change of seasons, and the stars jostled each other and made identification of individual luminaries or of constellations impossible. So many and so bright were they that even the noonday sun at its zenith could not entirely dim the greatest of them. Like ghosts reluctant to retreat before daylight, they hovered in the burning air.

Nevertheless, man needs time as a fish needs water. If he does not have it, he will invent it; so to Burton it was July 13 of 5 A.R.

But Collop, like many, reckoned time as having continued from the year of his Terrestrial death. To him, it was 1667 A.D. He did not believe that his sweet Jesus had been discredited. Rather, this river was the River Jordan; this valley, the vale beyond the shadow of death. He admitted that the afterlife was not that which he had expected. Yet it was, in many respects, a far more glorious place. It was evidence of the all encompassing love of God for his creation. He had given man, altogether undeserving of such a gift, another chance. If this world was not the New Jerusalem, it was a place prepared for its building. Here the bricks, which were the love of God; the mortar, love for man, must be fashioned in this kiln and this mill: the planet of the river of the valley.

Burton poohpoohed the concept, but he could not help loving the little man. Collop was genuine; he was not stoking the furnace of his sweetness with leaves from a book or pages from a theology. He did not operate under forced draft. He burned with a flame that fed on his own being, and this being was love. Love even for the unlovable, the rarest and most difficult species of love.

He told Burton something of his Terrestrial life. He had been a doctor, a farmer, a liberal with unshaken faith in his religion yet full of questions about his faith and the society of his time. He had written a plea for religious tolerance which had aroused both praise and damnation in his time. And he had been a poet, well-known for a short time, then forgotten.

> Lord, let the faithless see
> Miracles ceased, revive in me,
> The leper cleansed, blind heald,
>   dead raised by thee.

"My lines may have died, but their truth has not," he said to Burton. He waved a hand to indicate the hills, the river, the mountains, the people. "As you may see if you open your eyes and do not persist in this stubborn myth of yours that this is the handiwork of men like us."

He continued, "Or grant your premise. It still remains that these Ethicals are but doing the work of their Creator."

"I like better those other lines of yours," Burton said.

> Dull soul aspire;
> Thou art not the earth. Mount higher!
> Heaven gave the spark;
>   to it return the fire.

Collop was pleased, not knowing that Burton was thinking of them in a different sense than that intended by the poet. "Return the fire." That meant somehow finding the Dark Tower, somehow getting into it, discovering the secrets of the Ethicals, and turning their devices against them, if possible. He did not feel gratitude because they had given him a second life. Instead, he was outraged that they should do this without his leave. If they wanted his thanks, why did they not tell him why they had given him another chance? What reason did they have for keeping their motives in the dark? He would find out why. The spark they had restored in him would turn into a raging fire to burn them.

He cursed the fate that had propelled him to a place so near the source of the river, hence so close to the Tower, and in a few minutes had carried him away again, back to some place in the middle of the river, millions of miles away from his goal. Yet, if he had been there once, he could get there again. Not by taking a boat, since the journey would consume at least forty years and probably more. He could count on being captured and enslaved a thousand times over. Escaping from them would add many more years to the trip. And if he were killed along the way, he might find himself raised again far from his goal and have to start all over again.

On the other hand, given the seemingly random selection of resurrection, he could find himself once more near the river's mouth. It was this thought that determined him to board the Suicide Express once more. However, even though he knew that his death would be only temporary, he found it difficult to take the necessary step. His mind told him that death was the only ticket, but his body rebelled. The cells' fierce insistence on survival overcame his will.

For a while he rationalized that he was interested in studying the customs and language of the prehistorics among whom he was living. Then honesty triumphed, and he knew he was only looking for excuses to put off the Grim Moment. Despite this, he did not act.

Burton, Collop and Goering were moved out of their bachelor barracks to take up the normal life of citizens. Each took up residence in a hut, and within a week had found a woman to live with them. Collop's Church did not require celibacy. A member could take an oath of chastity if he wished to. But the Church reasoned that men and women had been resurrected in bodies that retained the full sex of the original. (Or, if lacking on Earth, supplied here.) Women did not bear children any more; something had been subtracted from them or from the men or from both. Nevertheless, it was evident that the makers of resurrection had meant for sex to be used. It was well known, though still denied by some, that sex had other functions than reproduction. So go ahead, youths, and roll in the grass.

Another result of the inexorable logic of the Church (which, by the way, decried reason as being untrustworthy) was that any form of love was allowed, as long as it was voluntary and did not involve cruelty or force. Exploitation of children was forbidden. This was a problem that, given time, would cease to exist. In a few years all children would be adults.

Collop refused to have a hutmate solely to relieve his sexual tensions. He insisted on a woman whom he loved. Burton jibed at him for this, saying that it was a prerequisite easily—therefore cheaply—fulfilled. Collop loved all humanity; hence, he should theoretically take the first woman who would say yes to him.

"As a matter of fact, my friend," Collop said, "that is exactly what happened."

"It's only a coincidence that she's beautiful, passionate and intelligent?" Burton said.

"Though I strive to be more than human, rather, to become a complete human, I am all-too-human," Collop replied. He smiled. "Would you have me deliberately martyr myself by choosing an ugly shrew?"

"I'd think you more of a fool than I do even now," Burton said. "As for me, all I require in a woman is beauty and affection. I don't care a whit about her brains. And I prefer blondes. There's a chord within me that responds to the fingers of a golden-haired woman."

Goering took into his hut a Valkyrie, tall, great-busted, wide-shouldered, an 18th-century Swede. Burton wondered if she was a surrogate for Goering's first wife, the sister-in-law of the Swedish explorer Count von Rosen. Goering admitted that she not only looked like his Karin but even had a voice similar to hers. He seemed to be very happy with her and she with him.

9

Then, one night, during the invariable early-morning rain, Burton was ripped from a deep sleep.

He thought he had heard a scream, but all he could hear now was the explosion of thunder and the crack of nearby lightning. He closed his eyes, only to be jerked upright. A woman had screamed in a nearby hut.

He jumped up, shoved aside the bamboo-slat door, and stuck his head outside. The cold rain hit him in the face. All was dark except for the mountains in the west, lit up by flashes of lightning. Then a bolt struck so close that he was deafened and dazzled. However, he did catch a glimpse of two ghostly white figures just outside Goering's hut. The German had his hands locked around the throat of his mate, who was holding onto his wrists and trying to push him away.

Burton ran out into the rain, slipped on the wet grass and fell. Just as he arose, another flash showed the woman on her knees, bending backward, and Goering's distorted face. At the same time, Collop, wrapping a towel around his waist, came out of his hut. Burton got to his feet and, still silent, ran towards Goering. When he reached the hut, he saw that Goering was gone. He knelt by Karla, felt her heart, and could detect no beat. Another glare of lightning showed him her face, mouth hanging open, eyes bulging.

He rose and shouted, "Goering! Where are you?"

Something struck the back of his head. He fell on his face.

Stunned, he managed to get to his hands and knees, only to be knocked flat again by another heavy blow. Half-conscious, he nevertheless rolled over on his back and raised his legs and hands to defend himself. Lightning revealed Goering standing above him with club in one hand. His face was that of a madman's.

Darkness sliced off the lightning. Something white and blurred leaped upon Goering out of the darkness. The two pale bodies went down onto the grass beside Burton and rolled over and over. They screeched like two tomcats, and another flash showed them clawing at each other like cats. Collop had rescued him.

Burton staggered to his feet and lurched towards them but was knocked down by Collop's body, hurled by Goering. Again Burton got up. Collop bounded to his feet and charged Goering. There was a loud crack, and Collop crumpled. Burton tried to run towards Goering. His legs refused to answer his demands; they took him off at an angle, away from his point of attack. Then another blast of light and noise showed Goering, as if caught in a photograph, suspended in the act of swinging the club at Burton.

Burton felt his arm go numb as it received the impact of the club. Now not only his legs but his left arm disobeyed him. Nevertheless he balled his right hand and tried to swing at Goering. There was another crack; his ribs felt as if they had become unhinged and were driven inwards into his lung. His breath was knocked out of him, and once again he was on the cold wet grass.

Something fell by his side. Despite his agony, he reached out for it. The club was in his hand; Goering must have dropped it. Shuddering with each painful breath, he got to one knee. Where was the madman? Two shadows danced and blurred, merged and half-separated. The hut! His eyes were crossed. He wondered if he had a concussion of the brain, then forgot it as he saw Goering dimly in the illumination of a distant streak of lightning. Two Goerings, rather. One seemed to accompany the other; the one on the left had his feet on the ground; the right one was treading on air.

Both had their hands held high up into the rain, as if they were trying to wash them. And when the two turned and came toward him, he understood that that was what they were trying to do. They were shouting in German (with a single voice), "Take the blood off my hands! Oh, God, wash it off!"

Burton stumbled towards Goering, his club held high. Burton meant to knock him out, but Goering suddenly turned and ran away. Burton followed him as best he could, down the hill, up another one, and then out onto the flat plain. The rains stopped, the thunder and lightning died, and within five minutes the clouds, as always, had cleared away. The stars resumed their interrupted reign; their light gleamed on Goering's white skin.

Like a phantom he flitted ahead of his pursuer, seemingly bent upon getting to the river. Burton kept after him, although he wondered why he was doing so. His legs had regained most of their strength, and his vision was one. Presently, he came upon his quarry.

Goering was squatting by the river and staring intently at the starfractured waves. Burton said, "Are you all right now?"

Goering was startled. He began to rise, then changed his mind. Groaning, he put his head down on his knees.

"I knew what I was doing, but I didn't know why," he said dully. "Karla was telling me she was moving out in the morning, said she couldn't sleep with all the noise I made. Moreover, I was acting strangely. I begged her to stay; I told her I loved her very much, I'd die if she deserted me. She said she was fond of me, had been, rather, but she didn't love me. Suddenly, it seemed that if I wanted to keep her, I'd have to kill her. She ran screaming out of the hut. You know the rest."

"I intended to kill you," Burton said. "But I've cooled off; I can see you're no more responsible than a madman. The people here won't accept that excuse, though. You know what they'll do to you; hang you upside down by your ankles and let you hang until you die."

Goering cried, "I don't understand it! What's happening to me? Those nightmares! Believe me, Burton, if I've sinned, I've paid! But I can't stop paying! My nights are hell, and soon my days will become hell, too! Then I'll have only one way to get peace! I'll kill myself! But it won't do any good! There'll be a few days of rest—then hell again!"

"Stay away from the dreamgum," Burton said. "You'll have to sweat it out. You can do it. You told me you overcame the morphine habit on Earth."

Goering stood up and faced Burton. "That's just it! I haven't touched the gum since I came here!"

Burton was surprised. He said, "What? But I'll swear."

"You assumed I was using the stuff because of the way I was acting! No, I have not had a bit of the gum! But it doesn't make any difference!"

Despite his abhorrence of Goering, Burton felt pity. He said, "You've opened the pandora of yourself, and it looks as if you'll not be able to shut the lid. I don't know how this is going to end, but I wouldn't want to be in your mind. Not that you don't deserve this."

Goering shook himself. It was not fear, however, but the physical manifestation of mental control. In a quiet and determined voice, he said, "I'll defeat them."

"You mean you'll conquer yourself," Burton said. He turned to go but halted for a last word. "What are you going to do?"

Goering gestured at the river. "Drown myself. I'll get a fresh start. Maybe I'll be better equipped the next place. And I certainly don't want to be trussed up like a chicken in a butcher shop window."

"Au revoir. then," Burton said. "And good luck."

"Thank you. You know, you're not a bad sort. Just one word of advice."

"What's that?"

"You'd better stay away from the dreamgum yourself. So far, you've been lucky. But one of these days, it'll take hold of you as it did me. Your devils won't be mine, but they'll be just as monstrous and terrifying."

"Nonsense! I've nothing to hide from myself!" Burton said, and he laughed loudly. "I've chewed enough of the stuff to know."

He walked away, but he was thinking of the warning. He had used the gum only twice in his life on riverplanet; both times had resulted in behavior which had made him swear never to touch the gum again. But then the effects had been externalized; there had been no explosions from the inferno of his unconscious, no hordes of demons galloping out at night to torment him.

On the way back to the hills, he looked behind him once. The dim white figure of Goering was slowly sinking into the black-and-silver waters of the river. Burton saluted, since he was not one to resist the dramatic gesture. Afterward he forgot Goering. The pain in the back of his head, temporarily subdued, came back sharper than before. His knees turned to water, and, only a few yards from his hut, he had to sit down.

He must have become unconscious then, or half-conscious since he had no memory of being dragged along on the grass. When his wits cleared, he found himself lying on a bamboo bed inside a hut.

It was dark with the only illumination the starlight filtering in through tree branches outside the square of window. He turned his head and saw the shadowy and palewhite bulk of a man squatting by him. The features were too indistinct for Burton to distinguish them. Moreover, the man was holding a device before his eyes, the gleaming end of which was pointed at Burton.

10

As soon as Burton turned his head, the man put the device down. He spoke in English. "It's taken me a long time to find you, Richard Burton."

Burton groped around on the floor for a weapon with his left hand, which was hidden from the mans' view. His fingers touched nothing but dirt. He said. "Now you've found me, you damn Ethical, what do you intend doing with me?"

The man shifted slightly and he chuckled. "Nothing." He paused, then said, "I am not one of Them." He laughed again when Burton gasped. "That's not quite true. I am with Them, but I am not of Them."

He picked up the device which he had been aiming at Burton.

"This tells me that you have a fractured skull and a concussion of the brain. You must be very tough, because you should be dead, judging by the extent of the injury. But you may pull out of it, if you take it easy. Unfortunately, you don't have time to convalesce. The others know you're in this area, give or take thirty miles. In a day or so they'll have you pinpointed."

Burton tried to sit up and found that his bones had become soft as taffy in the sun and a bayonet was prying open the back of his skull. Groaning, he lay back down.

"Who are you and what's your business?"

"I can't tell you my name. If—or much more likely when—they catch you, they'll thread out your memory and run it off backwards to the time you woke up in the pre-resurrection bubble. They won't find out what made you wake before your time. But they will know about this conversation. They'll even be able to see me but only as you see me, a pale shadow with no features. They'll hear my voice too, but they won't recognize it. I'm using a transmuter.

"They will, however, be horrified. What they have slowly and reluctantly been suspecting will all of a sudden be revealed as the truth. They have a traitor in their midst."

"I wish I knew what you were talking about," Burton said.

The man said, "I'll tell you this much. You have been told a monstrous lie about the purpose of the resurrection. What Spruce told you, and what that Ethical creation, the Church of the Second Chance, teaches—are lies! All lies! The truth is that you human beings have been given life again only to participate in a scientific experiment. The Ethicals—a misnomer if there ever was one — have reshaped this planet into one rivervalley, built the grailstones, and brought all of you back from the dead for one purpose. To record your history and customs. And, as a secondary matter, to observe your reactions to resurrection and to the mixing of different peoples of different eras. That is all it is: a science project. And when you have served your purpose, back into the dust you go!

"This story about giving all of you another chance at eternal life and salvation because it is their ethical duty—lies! Actually, my people do not believe that you are worth saving. They do not think you have 'souls'!"

Burton was silent for a while. The fellow was certainly sincere. Or, if not sincere, he was very emotionally involved, since he was breathing so heavily.

Finally Burton spoke. "I can't see anybody going to all this expense and labor just to run a scientific experiment or to make historical recordings."

"Time hangs heavy on the hands of immortals. You would be surprised what we do to make eternity interesting. Furthermore, given all time, we can take our time, and we do not let even the most staggering projects dismay us. After the last terrestrial died, the job of setting up the resurrection took several thousands of years, even though the final phase took only one day."

Burton said, "And you? *What are* you doing? And *why* are you doing whatever you're doing?"

"I am the only true Ethical in the whole monstrous race! I do not like toying around with you as if you were puppets, or mere objects to be observed, animals in a laboratory! After all, primitive and vicious though you be, you are sentients! You are, in a sense, as . . . as . . ."

The shadowy speaker waved a shadowy hand as if trying to grasp a word out of the darkness. He continued, "I'll have to use your term for yourselves. You're as *human* as we. Just as the subhumans who first used language were as human as you. And you are our forefathers. For all I know, I may be your direct descendant. My whole people could be descended from you."

"I doubt it," Burton said. "I had no children—that I know of, anyway."

He had many questions, and he began to ask them. But the man was paying no attention. He was holding the device to his forehead. Suddenly, he withdrew it and interrupted Burton in the middle of a sentence. "I've been . . . you don't have a word for it . . . let's say . . . *listening*. They've detected my . . . *wathan* . . . I think you'd call it an aura. They don't know whose *wathan*, just that it's an Ethical's. But they'll be zeroing in within the next five minutes. I have to go."

The pale figure stood up. "You have to go, too."

"Where are you taking me?" Burton said.

"I'm not. You must die; they must find only your corpse. I can't take you with me; it's impossible. But if you die here, they'll lose you again. And we'll meet again. Then . . .!"

"Wait!" Burton said. "I don't understand. Why can't they locate me? They built the resurrection machinery. Don't they know where my particular resurrector is?"

The man chuckled again. "No. Their only recordings of men on Earth were visual, not audible. And the location of the resurrectees in the pre-resurrection bubble was random, since they had planned to scatter you humans along the river in a rough chronological sequence but with a certain amount of mixing. They intend to get down to the individual basis later. Of course, they had no notion then that I would be opposing them. Or that I would select certain of their subjects to aid me in defeating the Plan. So they do not know where you, or the others, will next pop up.

"Now, you may be wondering why I can't set your resurrector so that you'll be translated near your goal, the headwaters. The fact is that I did set yours so that the first time you died, you'd be at the very first grailstone. But you didn't make it; so I presume the Titanthrops killed you. That was unfortunate, since I no longer dare to go near the bubble until I have an excuse. It is forbidden for any but those authorized to enter the pre-resurrection bubble. They're suspicious; they suspect tampering. So it is up to you, and to chance, to get back to the north polar region.

"As for the others, I never had an opportunity to set their resurrectors. They have to go by the laws of probabilities, too. Which, worse luck, are about twenty million to one."

"Others?" Burton said. "Others? But why did you choose us?"

"You have the right aura. So did the others. Believe me, I know what I'm doing; I chose well."

"But you intimated that you woke me up ahead of time . . . in the pre-resurrection bubble, for a purpose. What did it accomplish?"

"It was the only thing that would convince you that the resurrection was not a supernatural event. And it started you on the track of the Ethicals. Am I right? Of course I am. Here!"

He handed Burton a tiny capsule. "Swallow this. You will be dead instantly and out of their reach—for a while. And your brain cells will be so ruptured they'll not be able to read them. Hurry! *I must* go!"

"What if I don't take it?" Burton said. "What if I allow them to capture me now?"

"You don't have the aura for it," the man said.

Almost Burton decided not to take the capsule. Why should he allow this arrogant fellow to order him around?

Then he considered that he should not bite off his nose to spite his face. As it was, he had the choice of playing along with this unknown and somewhat sinister man, or of falling into the hands of the others.

"All right," he said. "But why don't you kill me? Why make me do the job?"

The man laughed and said, "There are certain rules in this game, rules which I don't have time to explain. But you're intelligent, you'll figure out most of them for yourself. One is that we *are* Ethicals. We can give life, but we can't directly take life. It is not unthinkable for us or beyond our ability. Just very difficult."

Abruptly, the man was gone. Burton did not hesitate. He swallowed the capsule. There was a blinding flash . . .

11

The Third Station

And light full in his eyes, from the just risen sun. He had time for one quick look around, saw his grail, his pile of neatly folded towels, a second grail and cubes of towels—and Herman Goering.

Then Burton and the German were seized by small dark men with large heads and bandy legs. These carried spears and flint-headed axes. They wore towels but only as capes secured around their thick short necks. Strips of leather, undoubtedly human skin, ran across their disproportionately large foreheads and around their heads to bind their long, coarse black hair. They looked semi-Mongolian and spoke a tongue unknown to him.

An empty grail was placed upside down over his head; his hands were tied behind him with a leather thong. Blind and helpless, stone-tipped spears digging into his back, he was urged across the plain. Somewhere near, drums thundered, and female voices wailed a chant.

He had walked three hundred paces when he was halted. The drums quit beating, and the women stopped their singsong. He could hear nothing except the blood beating in his ears. What the hell was going on? Was he part of a religious ceremony which required that the victim be blinded? Why not? There had been many cultures on Earth which did not want the ritually slain to view those who shed his blood. The dead man's ghost might want to take revenge on his killers.

But these people must know by now that there were no such things as ghosts. Or did they regard *lazari* as just that, as ghosts that could be dispatched back to their land of origin by simply killing them again?

Goering! He, too, had been translated here. At the same grailstone. The first time could have been coincidence, although the probabilities against it were high. But thrice in succession? No, it was . . .

The first blow drove the side of the grail against his head, made him half-unconscious, sent a vast ringing through him and sparks of light before his eyes, and knocked him to his knees. He never felt the second blow, and so awoke once more in another place—

12

The Fourth Station

And with him was Hermann Goering.

"You and I must be twin souls," Goering said. "We seem to be yoked together by Whoever is responsible for all this."

"The ox and the ass plow together," Burton said, leaving it to the German to decide which he was. Then the two were busy introducing themselves, or attempting to do so, to the people among whom they had arrived. These, as he later found out, were Sumerians of the Old or Classical period; that is, they had lived in Mesopotamia between 2500 and 2300 B.C. The men shaved their heads (no easy custom with flint razors), and the women were bare to the waist. As a group, they had a tendency to short squat bodies, pop-eyes and (to Burton) ugly faces.

But if the index of beauty was not high among them, the pre-Columbian Samoans who made up ten per cent of the population were more than attractive. And, of course, there was the ubiquitous one per cent of people from anywhere and everyplace, 20th-centurions being the most numerous. This was understandable, since the total number of these on Earth had constituted a fourth of humanity. Burton had no scientific statistical data, of course, but his travels had convinced him that the 20th-centurions had been deliberately scattered along the river in a proportion even greater than was to be expected. This was another facet of the riverworld setup which he did not understand. What did the Ethicals intend to gain by this dissemination?

There were too many questions. He needed time to think, and he could not get it if he spent himself with one trip after another on the Suicide Express. This area, unlike most of the others he would visit, offered some peace and quiet for analysis. So he would stay here a while.

And then there was Hermann Goering. Burton wanted to observe his strange form of pilgrim's progress. One of the many things that he had not been able to ask the Mysterious Stranger (Burton tended to think in capitals) was about the dreamgum. Where did it fit into the picture? Another part of the Great Experiment?

Unfortunately Goering did not last long.

The first night he began screaming. He burst out of his hut and ran towards the river, stopping now and then to strike out at the air or to grapple with invisible beings and roll back and forth on the grass. Burton followed him as far as the river's edge. Here Goering prepared to launch himself out into the water, probably to drown himself. But he froze for a moment, began shuddering, and then toppled over, stiff as a statue. His eyes were open, but they saw nothing outside him. All vision was turned inwards. What horrors he was witnessing could not be determined, since he was unable to speak.

His lips writhed soundlessly and did not stop during the ten days that he lived. Efforts to feed him were useless. His jaws were locked tightly. He shrank before Burton's eyes, the flesh evaporating, the skin falling in and the bones beneath resolving into the skeleton. One morning, he went into convulsions, then sat up and screamed. A moment later he was dead.

Curious, Burton did an autopsy on him with the flint knives and obsidian saws available. Goering's distended bladder had burst and poured urine into his body.

Burton proceeded to pull Goering's teeth out before burying him. Teeth were trade items, since they could be strung on a fishgut or a tendon as much-desired necklaces. Goering's scalp also came off.

The Sumerians had picked up the custom of taking scalps from their enemies, the 17th-century Shawnee across the river. They had added the civilized embellishment of sewing scalps together to make capes, skirts, and even curtains. A scalp was not worth as much as teeth in the trade mart, but it was worth something.

It was while digging a grave by a large boulder at the foot of the mountains that Burton had an illuminating flash of memory. He had stopped working to take a drink of water when he happened to look at Goering. The completely stripped head and the features, peaceful now as if sleeping, opened a trapdoor in his mind.

When he had awakened in that colossal chamber and found himself floating in a row of bodies, and had managed to get to the narrow cat-walk between the rows and had prowled around for a while, he had seen this face. It had belonged to the body in the row next to his. Goering, like all the other sleepers, had had his head shaved. Burton had only noted him in passing during the short time before the warders had detected him. Later, after the mass resurrection, when he had met Goering, he had not seen the similarity between the sleeper and this man who had a full head of blondish hair.

But he knew now that this man had occupied the space next to his.

Was it possible that their two resurrectors, so close to each other, had become locked in phase? If so, whenever his death and Goering's took place at the same approximate time, then the two would be raised again by the same grailstone. Goering's jest that they were twin souls might not be so far off the mark.

Burton resumed digging, swearing at the same time because he had so many questions and so few answers. If he had another chance to get his hands on an Ethical, he would drag the answers out of him, no matter what methods he had to use.

The next three months, Burton was busy adjusting himself to the strange society in this area. He found himself fascinated by the new language that was being formed out of the clash between Sumerian and Samoan. Since the former were the most numerous, their tongue dominated. But here, as elsewhere, the major language suffered a Pyrrhic victory. Result of the fusion was a pidgin, a speech with greatly reduced flexion and simplified syntax. Grammatical gender went overboard; words were syncopated; tense and aspect of verbs were cut to a simple present, which was used also for the future. Adverbs of time indicated the past. Subtleties were replaced by expressions that both Sumerian and Samoan could

understand, even if they seemed at first to be awkward and naive.
And many Samoan words, in somewhat changed phonology, drove
out Sumerian words.

This rise of pidgins was taking place everywhere up and down
the rivervalley. Burton reflected that if the Ethicals had intended to
record all human tongues, they had best hurry. The old ones were
dying out, transmuting rather. But for all he knew, they had already
completed the job. Their recorders, so necessary for accomplishing
the physical translation, might also be taking down all speech.

In the meantime, at evenings, when he had a chance to be alone,
he smoked the cigars so generously offered by the grails and tried
to analyze the situation. Whom could he believe, the Ethicals or the
renegade, the Mysterious Stranger? Or were both lying?

Why did the Mysterious Stranger need him to throw a monkey
wrench into their cosmic machinery? What could Burton, a mere
human being, trapped in this valley, so limited by his ignorance, do
to help the Judas?

One thing was certain. If the Stranger did not need him, he would
not have concerned himself with Burton. He wanted to get Burton
into that Tower at the north pole.

Why?

It took Burton two weeks before he thought of the only reason
that could be.

The Stranger had said that he, like the other Ethicals, would not
directly take human life. But he had no scruples about doing so
vicariously, as witness his giving the poison to Burton. So, if he
wanted Burton in the Tower, he needed Burton to kill for him. He
would turn the tiger loose among his own people, open the window
to the hired assassin.

An assassin wants pay. What did the Stranger offer?

Burton sucked the cigar into his lungs, exhaled and then downed
a shot of bourbon. Very well. The Stranger would try to use him.
But let him beware. Burton would also use him.

At the end of three months, Burton decided that he had done
enough drinking. It was time to get out.

He was swimming in the river at the moment and, following the
impulse, he swam to its center. He dived down as far as he could force
himself before the not-to-be-denied will of his body to survive drove
him to claw upwards for the dear air. He did not make it. Afterwards,
he knew that the scavenging fishes would eat his body and his bones
would fall to the mud at the bottom of the reputedly 500-foot deep
river. So much the better. He did not want his body to fall into the

hands of the Ethicals. If what the Stranger had said was true, they might be able to unthread from his mind all he had seen and heard if they got to him before the brain cells were damaged.

He did not think they had succeeded. During the next seven years, as far as he knew, he escaped detection of the Ethicals. If the renegade knew where he was, he did not let Burton know. Burton doubted that anyone did; he himself could not ascertain in what part of the riverplanet he was, how far or how near the Tower headwaters. But he was going, going, going, always on the move. And one day he knew that he must have broken a record of some sort. Death had become second nature to him.

If his count was correct, he had made 777 trips on The Suicide Express.

13

Sometimes Burton thought of himself as a planetary grasshopper, launching himself out into the darkness of death, landing, nibbling a little at the grass, with one eye cocked for the shadow that betrayed the downswoop of the shrike—the Ethicals. In this vast meadow of humanity, he had sampled many blades, tasted briefly, and then had gone on.

Other times he thought of himself as a net scooping up specimens here and there in the huge sea of mankind. He got a few big fish and many sardines, although there was as much, if not more, to be learned from the small as the large fish.

He did not like the metaphor of the net, however, because it reminded him that there was a much larger net out for him.

Whatever metaphors or similes he used, he was a man who got around a lot, to use a 20th-Century Americanism. So much so that he several times came across the leg-end of Burton the Gypsy, or, in one English-speaking area, Richard the Rover, and, in another, the Loping Lazarus. This worried him somewhat, since the Ethicals might get a clue to his method of evasion and be able to take some kind of measures to trap him. Or they might even guess at his basic goal and set up guards near the headwaters.

At the end of the seven years, through much observation of the day-stars and through many conversations, he had formed a picture of the course of the river.

It was not an amphisbaena, a snake with two heads, headwaters at the north pole and mouth at the south pole. It was a Midgard Serpent, with the tail at the north pole, the body coiled around and around the planet and the tail in the serpent's mouth. The river's source stemmed from the north polar sea, zigzagged back and forth across one hemisphere, circled the south pole and then zigzagged across the face of the other hemisphere, back and forth, ever working upward until the mouth opened into the hypothetical polar sea.

Nor was the large body of water so hypothetical. If the story of the Titanthrop, the subhuman who claimed to have seen the Misty Tower, was true, the Tower rose out of the fog-shrouded sea.

Burton had heard the tale only at second-hand. But he had seen the Titanthrops near the beginning of the river on his first "jump," and it seemed reasonable that one might actually have crossed the mountains and gotten close enough to get a glimpse of the polar area. Where one man had gone, another could follow.

And how did the river flow uphill?

Its rate of speed seemed to remain constant even where it should have slowed or refused to go further. From this he postulated localized gravitational fields that urged the mighty stream onwards until it had regained an area where natural gravity would take over. Somewhere, perhaps buried under the river itself, were devices that did this work. Their fields must be very restricted, since the pull of the earth did not vary on human beings in these areas to any detectable degree.

There were too many questions. He must go on until he got to the place or to the beings who could answer them.

And seven years after his first death, he reached the desired area.

It was on his 777th "jump," a number he was convinced was lucky for him. Burton, despite the scoffings of his 20th-century friends, believed steadfastly in most of the superstitions he had nourished on Earth. He often laughed at the superstitions of others, but he knew that some numbers held good fortune for him, that silver placed on his eyes would rejuvenate his body when tired and would help his second sight, the perception that warned him ahead of time of situations evil for him. True, there seemed to be no silver on this mineral-poor world, but if there were, he could use it to advantage.

All that first day, he stayed at the edge of the river. He paid little attention to those who tried to talk to him, giving them a brief smile. Unlike people in most of the areas he had seen, these were not hostile. The sun moved along the eastern peaks, seemingly just clearing their tops. The flaming ball slid across the valley, lower than he had ever seen it before, except when he had landed among the grotesquely nosed Titanthrops. The sun flooded the valley for a while with light and warmth, and then began its circling just above the western mountains. The valley became shadowed, and the air became colder than it had been any other place. Except, of course, on that first jump. The sun continued to circle until it was again at the point where Burton had first seen it on opening his eyes.

Weary from his twenty-four hour vigil, but happy, he turned to look for living quarters. He knew now that he was in the arctic area, but he was not at a point just below the headwaters. This time, he was at the other end, the mouth.

As he turned, he heard a voice, familiar but unidentifiable. (He had heard so many.)

> Dull soul aspire:
> Thou art not the earth. Mount higher!
> Heaven gave the spark;
>   to it return the fire.

"John Collop!"

"Abdul ibn Harun! And they say there are no miracles. What has happened to you since last I saw you?"

"I died the same night you did," Burton said. "And several times since. There are many evil men in this world."

"Tis only natural. There were many on Earth. Yet I dare say their number has been cut down, for the Church has been able to do much good work, praise God. Especially in this area. But come with me, friend. I'll introduce you to my hut-mate. A lovely woman, faithful in a world that still seems to put little value on marital fidelity or, indeed, in virtue of any sort. She was born in the 20th century A.D. and taught English most of her life. Verily, I sometimes think she loves me not so much for myself as for what I can teach her of the speech of my time."

He gave a curious nervous laugh, by which Burton knew that he was joking.

They crossed the plains toward the foothills where fires were burning on small stone platforms before each hut. Most of the men and women had fastened towels around them to form parkas which shielded them from the chill of the shadows.

"A gloomy and shivering place," Burton said. "Why would anybody want to live here?"

"Most of these people be Finns or Swedes of the late 20th century. They are used to the midnight sun. However, ye should be happy you're here. I remember your burning curiosity about the polar regions and your speculations anent. There have been others like you who have gone on down the river to seek their ultima Thule, or if you will pardon me for so terming it, the fool's gold at the end of the rainbow. But all have either failed to return or have come back, daunted by the forbidding obstacles."

"Which are what?" Burton said, grabbing Collop's arm.

"Friend, you're hurting me. Item, the grailrocks cease, so that there is nothing wherewith they may recharge their grails with food. Item, the plains of the valley suddenly terminate, and the river pursues its course between the mountains themselves, through a chasm of icy shadows. Item, what lies beyond, I do not know, for no man has come back to tell me. But I fear they've met the end of all who commit the sin of hubris."

"How far away is this plunge of no return?"

"As the river winds, about 25,000 miles. You may get there with diligent sailing in a year or more. The Almighty Father alone knows how far ye must then go before you arrive at the very end of the river. Belike you'd starve before then, because you'd have to take provisions on your boat after leaving the final grailstoi ?."

"There's one way to find out," Burton said.

"Nothing will stop ye then, Richard Burton?" Collop said. "You will not give up this fruitless chase after the physical when ye should be hot on the track of the metaphysical?"

Burton seized Collop by the arm again. "You said Burton?"

"Yes, I did. Your friend Goering told me some time ago that that was your true name. He also told me other things about you."

"Goering is here?"

Collop nodded and said, "He has been here for about two years now. He lives a mile from here. We can see him tomorrow. You will be pleased at the change in him, I know. He has conquered the dissolution begun by the dreamgum, shaped the fragments of himself into a new, and a far better, man. In fact, he is now the leader of the Church of the Second Chance in this area.

"While you, my friend, have been questing after some irrelevant grail outside you, he has found the holiness inside himself. He almost perished from madness, nearly fell back into the evil ways of his Terrestrial life. But through the grace of God and his true desire to show himself worthy of being given another opportunity at life, he . . . well, you may see for yourself tomorrow. And I pray you will profit from his example."

Collop elaborated. Goering had died almost as many times as Burton, largely by suicide. Unable to stand the nightmares and the day-time self-loathing, he had time and again purchased a brief and useless surcease. Only to be faced with himself the next day. But on arriving at this area, and seeking help from Collop, the man he had once murdered, he had won.

"I am astonished," Burton said. "And I'm happy for Goering. But I have other goals. I would like your promise that you'll tell no one my true identity. Allow me to be Abdul ibn Harun."

Collop said that he would keep silent, although he was disappointed that Burton would not be able to see Goering again and judge for himself what faith and love could do for even the seemingly hopeless and depraved. He then took Burton to his hut and introduced him to his wife, a short, delicately boned brunette. She was very gracious and friendly and insisted on going with the two men while they visited the local boss, the *valkotukkainen*. (This word was regional slang for the white-haired boy or big shot.)

Ville Ahonen was a huge quiet-spoken man who listened patiently. Burton revealed only half of his plan, saying that he wanted to build a boat so he could travel to the end of the river. He did not mention wanting to take it further. But Ahonen had evidently met others like him.

He smiled knowingly and replied that Burton could build a craft. However, the people hereabouts were conservationists. They did not believe in despoiling the land of its trees. Oak and pine were to be left untouched, but bamboo was available. Even this material would have to be purchased with cigarettes and liquor, which would take him some time to accumulate from his grail.

Burton thanked him and left. Later, he slept in a hut near Collop's. He could not get to sleep.

Shortly before the inevitable rains came, he decided to leave the hut. He would go up into the mountains, take refuge under a ledge until the rains ceased, the clouds dissipated, and the eternal (but weak) sun reasserted itself. Now that he was so near to his goal, he did not want to be surprised by them. And it seemed likely that the Ethicals would concentrate agents here. For all he knew, Collop's wife could be one of them.

Before he had walked half a mile, rain struck him and lightning smashed nearby into the ground. By the dazzling flash, he saw something flicker into existence just ahead and about twenty feet above him.

He whirled and ran towards a grove of trees, hoping that they had not seen him and that he could hide there. If he was unobserved, then he could get up into the mountains. And when they had put everybody to sleep here, they would find him gone again . . .

14

The End of the Line

"You gave us a long hard chase, Burton," a man said in English.

Burton opened his eyes. The transition to this place was so unexpected that he was dazed. But only for a second. He was sitting in a chair of some very soft buoyant material. The room was a perfect sphere; the walls were a very pale green and were semitransparent. He could see other spherical chambers on all sides, in front, behind, above and, when he bent over, below. Again he was confused, since the other rooms did not just impinge upon the boundaries of his sphere. They intersected. Sections of the other rooms came into his room, but then became so colorless and clear that he could barely detect them.

On the wall at the opposite end of his room was an oval of darker green. It curved to follow the wall. There was a ghostly forest portrayed in the oval. A phantom fawn trotted across the picture. From it came the odor of pine and dogwood.

Across the bubble from him sat twelve in chairs like his. Six were men; six, women. All were very good-looking. Except for two, all had black or dark brown hair and deeply tanned skins. Three had slight epicanthic folds; one man's hair was so curly it was almost kinky.

The two non-brunettes were a man and a woman. The woman had long wavy yellow hair bound into a psyche knot. The man had red hair, red as the fur of a fox. He was handsome but not as the others. His features were irregular, his nose larger and almost curved, and his eyes were dark green.

All were dressed in silvery or purple blouses with short flaring sleeves and ruffled collars, slender luminescent belts, kilts, and sandals. Both men and women had painted fingernails and toenails, lipstick, earrings and eye makeup.

Above the head of each, almost touching the hair, spun a many-colored globe about a foot across. These whirled and flashed and changed color, running through every hue in the spectrum. From time to time, the globes thrust out long hexagonal arms of green, of blue, of black or of gleaming white. Then the arms would collapse, only to be succeeded by other hexagons.

Burton looked down. He was clad only in a black towel secured at his waist.

"I'll forestall your first question by telling you we won't give you any information on where you are."

The speaker was the red-haired man. He grinned at Burton, showing unhumanly white teeth.

"Very well," Burton said. "What questions will you answer, whoever you are? For instance, how did you find me?"

"My name is Loga," the red-haired man said. "We found you through a combination of detective work and luck. It was a complicated procedure, but I'll simplify it for you. We had a number of agents looking for you, a pitifully small number, considering the 36 billion, six million, nine thousand, six hundred and thirty-seven candidates that live along the river."

Candidates? Burton thought. Candidates for what? For eternal life? Had Spruce told the truth about the purpose behind the resurrection?

Loga said, "We had no idea that you were escaping us by suicide. Even when you were detected in areas so widely separated that you could not possibly have gotten to them except through resurrection, we did not suspect. We thought that you had been killed and thus translated. The years went by. We had no idea where you were. There were other things for us to do, so we pulled all agents from the Burton Case, as we called it, except for some stationed at both ends of the river. Somehow, you had knowledge of the polar tower. Later we found out how. Your friends Goering and Collop were very helpful, although they did not know they were talking to Ethicals, of course."

"Who notified you that I was near the river's end?" Burton said.

Loga smiled and said, "There's no need for you to know. However, we would have caught you anyway. You see, every space in the restoration bubble—the place where you unaccountably awakened during the pre-resurrection phase—has an automatic counter. They were installed for statistical and research purposes. We like to keep records of what's going on. For instance, any candidate who has a higher than average number of deaths sooner or later is a subject for study. Usually later, since we're short-handed.

"It was not until your 777th death that we got around to looking at some of the higher frequency resurrections. Yours had the highest count. You may be congratulated on this, I suppose."

"There are others like myself?"

"They're not being pursued, if that's what you mean. And, relatively speaking, they're not many. We had no idea that it was

you who had racked up this staggering number. Your space in the
PR bubble was empty when we looked at it during our statistical
investigation. Suddenly, we knew the space belonged to you. We
were all aware of the puzzling two technicians who had seen you
identified you by your . . . photograph.

"We set the resurrector so that the next time your body was to
be re-created, an alarm would notify us, and we would bring you
here to this place."

"Suppose I hadn't died again?" Burton said.

"You were destined to die! You planned on trying to enter the
polar sea via the river's mouth, right? That is impossible. The last
hundred miles of the river go through an underground tunnel.
Any boat would be torn to pieces. Like others who have dared
the journey, you would have died."

Burton said, "My photograph—the one I took from Agneau.
That was obviously taken on Earth when I was an officer for John
Company in India. How was that gotten?"

"Research, Mr. Burton," said Loga, still smiling.

Burton wanted to smash the look of superiority on his face. He
did not seem to be restrained by anything; he could, seemingly,
walk over to Loga and strike him. But he knew that the Ethicals
were not likely to sit in the same room with him without safeguards.
They would as soon have given a grizzly bear its freedom.

"Did you ever find out what made me awaken before my time?"
he asked. "Or what made those others gain consciousness, too?"

Loga gave a start. Several of the men and women gasped. All lost
their relaxed appearance.

Loga rallied first. He said, "We've made a thorough examination
of your body. You have no idea how thorough. We have also screened
every component of your . . . psychomorph, I think you could call
it. Or aura, whichever word you prefer." He gestured at the sphere
above his head. "We found no clues whatsoever."

Burton threw his head back and laughed loudly and long.

"So you bastards don't know everything!"

Loga smiled tightly. "No. We never will. Only One is
omnipotent."

He touched his forehead, lips, heart and genitals with the three
longest fingers of his right hand. The others did the same.

"However, I'll tell you that you frightened us—if that'll make you
feel any better. You still do. You see, we're fairly sure that you may
be the one of the men of whom we were warned."

"Warned against? By whom?"

"By a . . . sort of giant computer, a living one. And by its operator." Again he made the curious sign with his fingers. "That's all I care to tell you—even though you won't remember a thing that occurs down here after we send you back to the river-valley."

Burton's mind was clouded with anger, but not so much that he missed the "down here." Did that mean that the resurrection machinery and the hideout of the Ethicals were below the surface of the river-world?

Loga continued, "The data indicates you may be the man who will wreck our plans. Why you should or how you might, we do not know. But we respect our source of information, how highly you can't imagine."

"If you believe that," Burton said, "why don't you just put me in cold storage? Suspend me between those two bars, leave me floating in space, turning around and around like a roast on a spit, until your plans are completed?"

Loga said, "We couldn't do that! That act alone would ruin everything! How would you attain your salvation? Besides, that would mean an unforgivable violence on our part! It's unthinkable!"

"You were being violent when you forced me to run and hide from you," Burton said. "You are being violent now by holding me here against my will. And you will violate me when you destroy my memory of this little tête-à-tête with you."

Loga almost wrung his hands. In a grieved tone, he said, "That is only partly true. We had to take certain measures to protect ourselves. If the man had been anyone but you, we would have left you strictly alone. It's true we violated our own code of ethics by making you flee Theleme and by examining you. That had to be, however. And, believe me, we are paying for this in mental agony."

"You could make up for some of it by telling me why I, why all the human beings that ever lived, have been resurrected. And how you did it."

15

Loga talked, with occasional interruptions from some of the others. The yellow-haired woman broke in most often, and after a while Burton deduced from her attitude and Loga's that she was either his wife or she held a high position.

Another man interrupted at times. When he did, there was a concentration and respect from the others that led Burton to believe he was the head of this group. Once he turned his head so that the light sparkled off one eye. Burton stared, because he had not noticed before that the left eye was a jewel. At least, its hexagonal and slightly protruding and multicolored appearance was that of a jewel. But Burton thought that it probably was a device which gave him a sense, or senses, of perception denied the others. From then on, Burton felt uncomfortable whenever the faceted and gleaming eye was turned on him. What did that many-angled prism see?

At the end of the explanation, Burton, did not know much more than he had before. The Ethicals could see back into the past with a sort of chronoscope; with this they had been able to record whatever physical beings they wished to. Using these records as models, they had then performed the resurrection with energy-matter converters.

"What," Burton said, "would happen if you re-created two bodies of an individual at the same time?"

Loga smiled wryly and said that the experiment had been performed. Only one body had life.

Burton smiled like a cat that has just eaten a mouse. He could almost be seen licking his chops. He said, "I think you're lying to me. Or telling me half-truths. There is a fallacy in all this. If human beings can attain such a rarefiedly high ethical state that they 'go on,' why are you Ethicals, supposedly superior beings, still here? Why haven't you, too, 'gone on'?"

The faces of all but Loga and the jewel-eyed man became rigid. Loga laughed and said, "Very shrewd. An excellent point. I can only answer that some of us do go on. But we have higher qualifications than you candidates. More is demanded of us, ethically speaking."

"I still think you're lying," Burton said. "However, there's nothing I can do about it." He grinned and said, "Not just now, anyway."

"If you persist in that attitude, you will never go on," Loga said. "But we felt that we owed it to you to explain what we are doing—as best we could. When we catch those others who have been tampered with, we'll do the same for them."

"There's a Judas among you," Burton said, enjoying the effect of his words on his captors.

But the jewel-eyed man said, "Why don't you tell him the truth, Loga? It'll wipe off that sickening smirk and put him in his proper place."

Loga hesitated, then said, "Very well, Thanabur. Burton, you will have to be very careful from now on. No more suicides, and you must fight as hard to stay alive as you did on Earth, when you thought you had only one life. There is a limit to the number of times a man may be resurrected. After a certain amount—it varies and there's no way to predict the individual allotment—the psychomorph seems unable to reattach itself to the body. Every death weakens the 'attraction' between body and psychomorph. Eventually, the psychomorph comes to the point of no return. It becomes a—well, to use an unscientific term—a 'lost soul.' It wanders bodiless through the universe; we can detect these unattached psychomorphs with our instruments, unlike those of the—how shall I put it?—the 'saved,' which disappear entirely from our ken.

"So you see, you must give up this form of travel by death. This is why continued suicide by those poor unfortunates who cannot face life is, if not the unforgivable sin, the irrevocable."

The jewel-eyed man said. "The traitor, the filthy unknown who claims to be aiding you—was actually using you for his own purposes. He did not tell you that you were expending your chance for eternal life by carrying out his—and your—designs. He, or she, whoever the traitor is, is evil. Evil, evil!

"Therefore, you must be careful from now on. You may have a residue of a dozen or slightly more deaths left to you. Or your next death may be your last!"

Burton stood up and shouted, "You don't want me to reach the river's end? Why? Why?"

Loga said, "Au revoir. Forgive us for this violence."

Burton did not see any of the twelve persons point an instrument at him. But consciousness sprang from him as swiftly as an arrow from the bow, and he awoke . . .

16

At the Point of Departure—Theleme

There the first person to greet him was his 20th-century Yankee friend, Peter Frigate. Frigate lost his customary reserve on seeing him, and wept. Burton cried a little himself and had difficulty for a while in answering Frigate's many piled-one-on-the-other questions. First, Burton had to find out what Frigate, Loghu and Alice had done after he had disappeared. Frigate replied that the three had looked for him, then had sailed back up the river to Theleme.

"Where have you been?" Frigate said.

"From going to and fro in the earth, and from walking up and down in it," Burton said. "However, unlike Satan, I found at least several perfect and upright men, fearing God and eschewing evil. Damn few, though. Most men and women are still the selfish, ignorant, superstitious, self-blinding, hypocritical, cowardly wretches they were on Earth. And in most the old red-eyed killer ape struggles with its keeper, society, and would break out and bloody its hands."

Frigate chattered away as the two walked towards the huge stockade a mile away, the council building which housed the administration of the state of Theleme. Burton half-listened. He was shaking and his heart was beating hard, but not because of his home-coming.

He remembered!

Contrary to what Loga had promised, he remembered both his wakening in the pre-resurrection bubble, so many years ago, and the inquisition with the twelve Ethicals.

There was only one explanation. One of the twelve must have tampered with him and had somehow prevented the blocking of his memory and done so without the others knowing of it.

One of the twelve was the Mysterious Stranger, the renegade.

Which one? At present, there was no way of determining. But some day he would find out. Meanwhile, he had a friend in court, a man who might be using Burton for his own ends. And the time would come when Burton would use him.

There were the other human beings with whom the Stranger had also tampered. Perhaps he would find them; together they would assault the Tower.

Odysseus had his Athena. Usually Odysseus had had to get out of perilous situations through his own wits and courage. But every now and then, when the goddess had been able, she had given Odysseus a helping hand.

Odysseus had his Athena; Burton, his Mysterious Stranger.

Frigate said, "What do you plan on doing, Dick?"

"I'm going to build a boat and sail up the river. All the way! Want to come along?"